Collected Fiction: 1896–1910

ARTHUR MACHEN

Collected Fiction

Volume 2: 1896–1910

Edited by S. T. Joshi

Hippocampus Press

New York

Published by Hippocampus Press
P.O. Box 641, New York, NY 10156.
www.hippocampuspress.com

Cover illustration © 2019 by Matthew Jaffe, MatthewRJaffe.com.
Frontispiece photograph by E. O. Hoppé, provided by Mark Valentine.
Cover design by Daniel V. Sauer, DanSauerDesign.com
Hippocampus Press logo designed by Anastasia Damianakos.

First edition, 2019
1 3 5 7 9 8 6 4 2

ISBN 978-1-61498-285-2 three-volume set
ISBN 978-1-61498-249-4 volume 2
ISBN 978-1-61498-253-1 e-book

Contents

Introduction

As he noted in his poignant 1923 introduction to *The Hill of Dreams,* after the completion of *The Three Impostors* in 1895 Arthur Machen spent the next year and a half working on his signature novel, seeking to weed out the Stevensonian flourishes in his prose and to write with simplicity and sincerity. The result is a novel that is likely to endure as one of the pinnacles of his literary expression.

In 1897 Machen wrote the series of ten prose poems later collected as *Ornaments in Jade* (1924). Some of the individual pieces appeared in magazines, although even these were published a full decade after their composition. They appeared in such journals as the *Neolith* (an exquisite small-press periodical edited by E. Nesbit and containing the work of Lord Dunsany and other notable writers) and the *Academy* (a leading intellectual journal of the period, to which Machen extensively contributed all manner of work).

"The White People," which H. P. Lovecraft believed to be the second-greatest weird tale ever written (after Algernon Blackwood's "The Willows"), was written in 1899 and first published in *Horlick's Magazine* in 1904. *Horlick's* was edited by Machen's friend and colleague A. E. Waite, a mystic and occultist with whom Machen collaborated on various projects. *Horlick's* also serialised the novella "A Fragment of Life" (written in 1899–1904) and *The Hill of Dreams,* the latter appearing in 1904 as "The Garden of Avallaunius."

As mentioned in the introduction to Volume 1, the inheritance Machen received in 1887 upon the death of his father allowed him to write without thought of monetary worries until 1901. He was then forced to work, initially acting with the Benson Shakespeare Repertory Company and others, and also beginning his extensive work as a journalist. In 1902 he published his idiosyncratic treatise on aesthetics, *Hieroglyphics: A Note upon Ecstasy in Literature.* In 1906 appeared *The*

House of Souls, a landmark volume of his weird tales (the British edition also included the entire text of the episodic novel *The Three Impostors*). The next year he wrote his second novel, *The Secret Glory.*

The publication history of that work is highly complicated. The novel is a pungent condemnation of the British school system and also a portrayal of the increasingly mystical outlook of its protagonist, Ambrose Meyrick. Many sections of it appeared in the *Academy* and other periodicals, mostly in 1907–08, as self-standing stories, articles, or sketches; some of these were subsequently reprinted in various books of Machen's work, as late as *The Cosy Room and Other Stories* (1936). *The Secret Glory* was published as a book in 1922, but it lacked the final two chapters that Machen had written; perhaps his publisher felt that the book was already quite lengthy. At any rate, Machen acceded to his publisher's request and wrote a brief epilogue (printed here in the Appendix) to summarise in a highly condensed (and, frankly, unsatisfying) manner the substance of those final two chapters.

I was the first scholar to obtain the manuscript of these chapters from the Beinecke Rare Book and Manuscript Library of Yale University, and I subsequently sent copies to Machen scholars in England; the result was the publication of these chapters as a separate booklet in 1992; the novel itself, with the two chapters added, appeared in 1999. However, the transcription of those two chapters in these editions is at times erroneous, and the text as presented here constitutes the first appearance of a corrected version.

A few words can be devoted to the textual history of the works in this volume. I have used the Martin Secker (1922) edition of *The Hill of Dreams* as the foundation of my text, as there appear to be minimal revisions by Machen from the 1907 edition. I have taken the text of the prose poems from *Ornaments in Jade* (Knopf, 1924), although these were also subsequently reprinted in *Holy Terrors* (1946). For "The White People" and "A Fragment of Life" I have used the texts as printed in *The House of Souls* (1906). For *The Secret Glory* I have used the first edition for the first four chapters and my transcription of the manuscript for the final two.

—S. T. JOSHI

The Hill of Dreams

I

There was a glow in the sky as if great furnace doors were opened.

But all the afternoon his eyes had looked on glamour; he had strayed in fairyland. The holidays were nearly done, and Lucian Taylor had gone out resolved to lose himself, to discover strange hills and prospects that he had never seen before. The air was still, breathless, exhausted after heavy rain, and the clouds looked as if they had been moulded of lead. No breeze blew upon the hill, and down in the well of the valley not a dry leaf stirred, not a bough shook in all the dark January woods.

About a mile from the rectory he had diverged from the main road by an opening that promised mystery and adventure. It was an old neglected lane, little more than a ditch, worn ten feet deep by its winter waters, and shadowed by great untrimmed hedges, densely woven together. On each side were turbid streams, and here and there a torrent of water gushed down the banks, flooding the lane. It was so deep and dark that he could not get a glimpse of the country through which he was passing, but the way went down and down to some unconjectured hollow.

Perhaps he walked two miles between the high walls of the lane before its descent ceased, but he thrilled with the sense of having journeyed very far, all the long way from the known to the unknown. He had come as it were into the bottom of a bowl amongst the hills, and black woods shut out the world. From the road behind him, from the road before him, from the unseen wells beneath the trees, rivulets of waters swelled and streamed down towards the centre, to the brook that crossed the lane. Amid the dead and wearied silence of the air, beneath leaden and motionless clouds, it was strange to hear such a tumult of gurgling and rushing water, and he stood for a while on the quivering footbridge and watched the rush of dead wood and torn branches and wisps of straw all hurrying madly past him, to plunge into the heaped spume, the barmy froth that had gathered against a fallen tree.

Then he climbed again, and went up between limestone rocks, higher and higher, till the noise of waters became indistinct, a faint humming of swarming hives in summer. He walked some distance on level ground, till there was a break in the banks and a stile on which he could lean and look out. He found himself, as he had hoped, afar and forlorn; he had strayed into outland and occult territory. From the eminence of the lane, skirting the brow of a hill, he looked down into deep valleys and dingles, and beyond, across the trees, to remoter country, wild bare hills and dark wooded lands meeting the grey still sky. Immediately beneath his feet the ground sloped steep down to the valley, a hillside of close grass patched with dead bracken, and dotted here and there with stunted thorns, and below there were deep oakwoods, all still and silent, and lonely as if no one ever passed that way. The grass and bracken and thorns and woods, all were brown and grey beneath the leaden sky; and as Lucian looked he was amazed, as though he were reading a wonderful story, the meaning of which was a little greater than his understanding. Then, like the hero of a fairy-book, he went on and on, catching now and again glimpses of the amazing country into which he had penetrated, and perceiving rather than seeing that as the day waned everything grew more grey and sombre. As he advanced he heard the evening sounds of the farms, the low of the cattle, and the barking of the sheepdogs; a faint thin noise from far away. It was growing late, and as the shadows blackened he walked faster, till once more the lane began to descend, there was a sharp turn, and he found himself, with a good deal of relief, and a little disappointment, on familiar ground. He had nearly described a circle, and knew this end of the lane very well; it was not much more than a mile from home. He walked smartly down the hill; the air was all glimmering and indistinct, transmuting trees and hedges into ghostly shapes, and the walls of the White House Farm flickered on the hillside, as if they were moving towards him. Then a change came. First, a little breath of wind brushed with a dry whispering sound through the hedges, the few leaves left on the boughs began to stir, and one or two danced madly, and as the wind freshened and came up from a new quarter, the sapless branches above rattled against one another like bones. The growing breeze seemed to clear the air and lighten it. He was passing the stile where a path led to old Mrs. Gibbon's desolate little cottage, in the middle of the fields, at some distance even from the lane, and he saw the light blue smoke of her chimney rise distinct above the gaunt green-gage trees, against a pale band that was broadening along the horizon. As he passed the stile with his head bent, and his eyes on the ground, something white started out from the black shadow of the hedge, and in the strange twilight, now tinged with a flush from the west, a figure seemed to swim past him and disappear. For a moment he wondered who it could be, the light was so flickering and unsteady, so unlike the real atmosphere of the day, when he recollected it was only Annie Morgan, old Morgan's daughter at the White House. She was three years older than he, and it annoyed him to find that though she was only fifteen, there had been a dreadful increase in her height since the summer holidays. He had got to the bottom of the hill, and lifting up his eyes, saw the strange changes of the sky. The pale band had broadened into a clear vast space of light, and above, the heavy leaden clouds were breaking apart and driving across the heaven before the wind. He stopped to watch, and looked up at the great mound that jutted out from the hills into mid-valley. It was a natural formation, and always it must have had something of the form of a fort, but its steepness had been increased by Roman art, and there were high banks on the summit which Lucian's father had told him were the *vallum* of the camp, and a deep ditch had been dug to the north to sever it from the hillside. On this summit oaks had grown, queer stunted-looking trees with twisted and contorted trunks, and writhing branches; and these now stood out black against the lighted sky. And then the air changed once more; the flush increased, and a spot like blood appeared in the pond by the gate, and all the clouds were touched with fiery spots and dapples of flame; here and there it looked as if awful furnace doors were being opened.

The wind blew wildly, and it came up through the woods with a noise like a scream, and a great oak by the roadside ground its boughs together with a dismal grating jar. As the red gained in the sky, the earth and all upon it glowed, even the grey winter fields and the bare hillsides crimsoned, the waterpools were cisterns of molten brass, and the very road glittered. He was wonder-struck, almost aghast, before the scarlet magic of the afterglow. The old Roman fort was invested with fire; flames from heaven were smitten about its walls, and above there was a dark floating cloud, like fume of smoke, and every haggard writhing tree shewed as black as midnight against the black of the furnace.

When he got home he heard his mother's voice calling: "Here's Lucian at last. Mary, Master Lucian has come, you can get the tea ready." He told a long tale of his adventures, and felt somewhat mortified when his father seemed perfectly acquainted with the whole course of the lane, and knew the names of the wild woods through which he had passed in awe.

"You must have gone by the Darren, I suppose"—that was all he said. "Yes, I noticed the sunset; we shall have some stormy weather. I don't expect to see many in church to-morrow."

There was buttered toast for tea "because it was holidays". The red curtains were drawn, and a bright fire was burning, and there was the old familiar furniture, a little shabby, but charming from association. It was much pleasanter than the cold and squalid schoolroom; and much better to be reading *Chambers's Journal* than learning Euclid; and better to talk to his father and mother than to be answering such remarks as: "I say, Taylor, I've torn my trousers; how much to do you charge for mending?" "Lucy, dear, come quick and sew this button on my shirt."

That night the storm woke him, and he groped with his hands amongst the bedclothes, and sat up, shuddering, not knowing where he was. He had seen himself, in a dream, within the Roman fort, working some dark horror, and the furnace doors were opened and a blast of flame from heaven was smitten upon him.

Lucian went slowly, but not discreditably, up the school, gaining prizes now and again, and falling in love more and more with useless reading and unlikely knowledge. He did his elegiacs and iambics well enough, but he preferred exercising himself in the rhymed Latin of the Middle Ages. He liked history, but he loved to meditate on a land laid waste, Britain deserted by the legions, the rare pavements riven by frost, Celtic magic still brooding on the wild hills and in the black depths of the forest, the rosy marbles stained with rain, and the walls growing grey. The masters did not encourage these researches; a pure enthusiasm, they felt, should be for cricket and football, the *dilettanti* might even play fives and read Shakespeare without blame, but healthy English boys should have nothing to do with decadent periods. He was once found guilty of recommending Villon to a school-fellow named Barnes. Barnes tried to extract unpleasantness from the text during preparation, and rioted in his place, owing to his incapacity for the language. The matter was a serious one; the headmaster had never heard of Villon, and the culprit gave up the name of his literary admirer without remorse. Hence, sorrow for Lucian, and complete immunity for the miserable illiterate Barnes, who resolved to confine his researches to the Old Testament, a book which the headmaster knew well. As for Lucian, he plodded on, learning his work decently, and sometimes doing very creditable Latin and Greek prose. His school-fellows thought him quite mad, and tolerated him, and indeed were very kind to him in their barbarous manner. He often remembered in after life acts of generosity and good nature done by wretches like Barnes, who had no care for old French nor for curious metres, and such recollections always moved him to emotion. Travellers tell such tales; cast upon cruel shores amongst savage races, they have found no little kindness and warmth of hospitality.

He looked forward to the holidays as joyfully as the rest of them. Barnes and his friend Duscot used to tell him their plans and anticipations; they were going home to brothers and sisters, and to cricket, more cricket, or to football, more football, and in the winter there were parties and jollities of all sorts. In return he would announce his intention of studying the Hebrew language, or perhaps Provençal, with a walk up a bare and desolate mountain by way of open-air amusement, and on a rainy day for choice. Whereupon Barnes would impart to Duscot his confident belief that old Taylor was quite cracked. It was a queer, funny life that of school, so very unlike anything in *Tom Brown*. He once saw the headmaster patting the head of the bishop's little boy, while he called him "my little man", and smiled hideously. He told the tale grotesquely in the lower fifth room the same day, and earned much applause, but forfeited all liking directly by proposing a voluntary course of scholastic logic. One barbarian threw him to the ground and another jumped on him, but it was done very pleasantly. There were, indeed, some few of a worse class in the school, solemn sycophants, prigs perfected from tender years, who thought life already "serious", and yet, as the headmaster said, were "joyous, manly young fellows". Some of these dressed for dinner at home, and talked of dances when they came back in January. But this virulent sort was comparatively infrequent, and achieved great success in after life. Taking his school days as a whole, he always spoke up for the system, and years afterwards he described with enthusiasm the strong beer at a roadside tavern, some way out of the town. But he always maintained that the taste for tobacco, acquired in early life, was the great note of the English Public School.

Three years after Lucian's discovery of the narrow lane and the vision of the flaming fort, the August holidays brought him home at a time of great heat. It was one of those memorable years of English weather, when some Provençal spell seems wreathed round the island in the northern sea, and the grasshoppers chirp loudly as the cicadas, the hills smell of rosemary, and white walls of the old farmhouses blaze in the sunlight as if they stood in Arles or Avignon or famed Tarascon by Rhone.

Lucian's father was late at the station, and consequently Lucian bought the *Confessions of an English Opium Eater* which he saw on the bookstall. When his father did drive up, Lucian noticed that the old trap had had a new coat of dark paint, and that the pony looked advanced in years.

"I was afraid that I should be late, Lucian," said his father, "though I made old Polly go like anything. I was just going to tell George to put her into the trap when young Philip Harris came to me in a terrible state. He said his father fell down 'all of a sudden like' in the middle of the field, and they couldn't make him speak, and would I please to come and see him. So I had to go, though I couldn't do anything for the poor fellow. They had sent for Dr. Burrows, and I am afraid he will find it a bad case of sunstroke. The old people say they never remember such a heat before."

The pony jogged steadily along the burning turnpike road, taking revenge for the hurrying on the way to the station. The hedges were white with the limestone dust, and the vapour of heat palpitated over the fields. Lucian shewed his *Confessions* to his father, and began to talk of the beautiful bits he had already found. Mr. Taylor knew the book well—had read it many years before. Indeed he was almost as difficult to surprise as that character in Daudet, who had one formula for all the chances of life, and when he saw the drowned Academician dragged out of the river, merely observed *"J'ai vu tout ça."* Mr. Taylor the parson, as his parishioners called him, had read the fine books and loved the hills and woods, and now knew no more of pleasant or sensational surprises. Indeed the living was much depreciated in value, and his own private means were reduced almost to vanishing point, and under such circumstances the great style loses many of its finer savours. He was very fond of Lucian, and cheered by his return, but in the evening he would be a sad man again, with his head resting on one hand, and eyes reproaching sorry fortune.

Nobody called out "Here's your master with Master Lucian; you can get tea ready", when the pony jogged up to the front door. His mother had been dead a year, and a cousin kept house. She was a respectable person called Deacon, of middle age, and ordinary standards; and, consequently, there was cold mutton on the table. There was a cake, but nothing of flour, baked in ovens, would rise at Miss Deacon's evocation. Still, the meal was laid in the beloved "parlour", with the view of hills and valleys and climbing woods from the open window, and the old furniture was still pleasant to see, and the old books in the shelves had many memories. One of the most respected of the arm-chairs had become weak in the castors and had to be artfully propped up, but Lucian found it very comfortable after the hard forms. When tea was over he went out and strolled in the garden and orchards, and looked over the stile down into the brake, where foxgloves and bracken and broom mingled with the hazel undergrowth, where he knew of secret glades and untracked recesses, deep in the woven green, the cabinets for many years of his lonely meditations. Every path about his home, every field and hedgerow had dear and friendly memories for him; and the odour of the meadowsweet was better than the incense steaming in the sunshine. He loitered, and hung over the stile till the far-off woods began to turn purple, till the white mists were wreathing in the valley.

Day after day, through all that August, morning and evening were wrapped in haze; day after day the earth shimmered in the heat, and the air was strange, unfamiliar. As he wandered in the lanes and saun-tered by the cool sweet verge of the woods, he saw and felt that noth-ing was common or accustomed, for the sunlight transfigured the meadows and changed all the form of the earth. Under the violent Provençal sun, the elms and beeches looked exotic trees, and in the early morning when the mists were thick the hills had put on an un-earthly shape.

The one adventure of the holidays was the visit to the Roman fort, to that fantastic hill about whose steep bastions and haggard oaks he had seen the flames of sunset writhing nearly three years before. Ever since that Saturday evening in January, the lonely valley had been a de-sirable place to him; he had watched the green battlements in summer and winter weather, had seen the heaped mounds rising dimly amidst the drifting rain, had marked the violent height swim up from the ice-white mists of summer evenings, had watched the fairy bulwarks glimmer and vanish in hovering April twilight. In the hedge of the lane there was a gate on which he used to lean and look down south to where the hill surged up so suddenly, its summit defined on summer evenings not only by the rounded ramparts but by the ring of dense green foliage that marked the circle of oak trees. Higher up the lane, on the way he had come that Saturday afternoon, one could see the white walls of Morgan's farm on the hillside to the north, and on the south there was the stile with the view of old Mrs. Gibbon's cottage smoke; but down in the hollow, looking over the gate, there was no hint of human work, except those green and antique battlements, on which the oaks stood in circle, guarding the inner wood.

The ring of the fort drew him with stronger fascination during that hot August weather. Standing, or as his headmaster would have said, "mooning" by the gate, and looking into that enclosed and secret valley, it seemed to his fancy as if there were a halo about the hill, an aureole that played like flame around it. One afternoon as he gazed from his station by the gate the sheer sides and the swelling bulwarks were more than ever things of enchantment; the green oak ring stood out against the sky as still and bright as in a picture, and Lucian, in spite of his re-spect for the law of trespass, slid over the gate. The farmers and their men were busy on the uplands with the harvest, and the adventure was irresistible. At first he stole along by the brook in the shadow of the alders, where the grass and the flowers of wet meadows grew richly; but as he drew nearer to the fort, and its height now rose sheer above him, he left all shelter, and began desperately to mount. There was not a breath of wind; the sunlight shone down on the bare hillside; the loud chirp of the grasshoppers was the only sound. It was a steep ascent and grew steeper as the valley sank away. He turned for a moment, and looked down towards the stream which now seemed to wind remote between the alders; above the valley there were small dark figures moving in the cornfield, and now and again there came the faint echo of a high-pitched voice singing through the air as on a wire. He was wet with heat; the sweat streamed off his face, and he could feel it trickling all over his body. But above him the green bastions rose defiant, and the dark ring of oaks promised coolness. He pressed on, and higher, and at last began to crawl up the *vallum*, on hands and knees, grasping the turf and here and there the roots that had burst through the red earth. And then he lay, panting with deep breaths, on the summit.

Within the fort it was all dusky and cool and hollow; it was as if one stood at the bottom of a great cup. Within, the wall seemed higher than without, and the ring of oaks curved up like a dark green vault. There were nettles growing thick and rank in the foss; they looked different from the common nettles in the lanes, and Lucian, letting his hand touch a leaf by accident, felt the sting burn like fire. Beyond the ditch there was an undergrowth, a dense thicket of trees, stunted and old, crooked and withered by the winds into awkward and ugly forms; beech and oak and hazel and ash and yew twisted and so shortened and deformed that each seemed, like the nettle, of no common kind. He began to fight his way through the ugly growth, stumbling and getting hard knocks from the rebound of the twisted boughs. His foot struck once or twice against something harder than wood, and looking down he saw stones white with the leprosy of age, but still shewing the work of the axe. And farther, the roots of the stunted trees gripped the foot-high relics of a wall; and a round heap of fallen stones nourished rank, unknown herbs, that smelt poisonous. The earth was black and unctuous, and bubbling under the feet, left no track behind. From it, in the darkest places where the shadow was thickest, swelled the growth of an abominable fungus, making the still air sick with its corrupt odour, and he shuddered as he felt the horrible thing pulped beneath his feet. Then there was a gleam of sunlight, and as he thrust the last boughs apart, he stumbled into the open space in the heart of the camp. It was a lawn of sweet close turf in the centre of the matted brake, of clean firm earth from which no shameful growth sprouted, and near the middle of the glade was a stump of a felled yew-tree, left untrimmed by the woodman. Lucian thought it must have been made for a seat; a crooked bough through which a little sap still ran was a support for the back, and he sat down and rested after his toil. It was not really so comfortable a seat as one of the school forms, but the satisfaction was to find anything at all that would serve for a chair. He sat there, still panting after the climb and his struggle through the dank and jungle-like thicket, and he felt as if he were growing hotter and hotter; the sting of the nettle was burning his hand, and the tingling fire seemed to spread all over his body.

Suddenly, he knew that he was alone. Not merely solitary; that he had often been amongst the woods and deep in the lanes; but now it was a wholly different and a very strange sensation. He thought of the valley winding far below him, all its fields by the brook green and peaceful and still, without path or track. Then he had climbed the abrupt surge of the hill, and passing the green and swelling battlements, the ring of oaks, and the matted thicket, had come to the central space. And behind there were, he knew, many desolate fields, wild as common, untrodden, unvisited. He was utterly alone. He still grew hotter as he sat on the stump, and at last lay down at full length on the soft grass, and more at his ease felt the waves of heat pass over his body.

And then he began to dream, to let his fancies stray over half-imagined, delicious things, indulging a virgin mind in its wanderings. The hot air seemed to beat upon him in palpable waves, and the nettle sting tingled and itched intolerably; and he was alone upon the fairy hill, within the great mounds, within the ring of oaks, deep in the heart of the matted thicket. Slowly and timidly he began to untie his boots, fumbling with the laces, and glancing all the while on every side at the ugly misshapen trees that hedged the lawn. Not a branch was straight, not one was free, but all were interlaced and grew one about another; and just above ground, where the cankered stems joined the protuberant roots, there were forms that imitated the human shape, and faces and twining limbs that amazed him. Green mosses were hair, and tresses were stark in grey lichen; a twisted root swelled into a limb; in the hollows of the rotted bark he saw the masks of men. His eyes were fixed and fascinated by the simulacra of the wood, and could not see his hands, and so at last, and suddenly, it seemed, he lay in the sunlight, beautiful with his olive skin, dark haired, dark eyed, the gleaming bodily vision of a strayed faun.

Quick flames now quivered in the substance of his nerves, hints of mysteries, secrets of life passed trembling through his brain, unknown desires stung him. As he gazed across the turf and into the thicket, the sunshine seemed really to become green, and the contrast between the bright glow poured on the lawn and the black shadow of the brake made an odd flickering light, in which all the grotesque postures of stem and root began to stir; the wood was alive. The turf beneath him heaved and sank as with the deep swell of the sea. He fell asleep, and lay still on the grass, in the midst of the thicket.

He found out afterwards that he must have slept for nearly an hour. The shadows had changed when he awoke; his senses came to him with a sudden shock, and he sat up and stared at his bare limbs in stupid amazement. He huddled on his clothes and laced his boots, wondering what folly had beset him. Then, while he stood indecisive, hesitating, his brain a whirl of puzzled thought, his body trembling, his hands shaking; as with electric heat, sudden remembrance possessed him. A flaming blush shone red on his cheeks, and glowed and thrilled through his limbs. As he awoke, a brief and slight breeze had stirred in a nook of the matted boughs, and there was a glinting that might have been the flash of sudden sunlight across shadow, and the branches rustled and murmured for a moment, perhaps at the wind's passage.

He stretched out his hands, and cried to his visitant to return; he entreated the dark eyes that had shone over him, and the scarlet lips that had kissed him. And then panic fear rushed into his heart, and he ran blindly, dashing through the wood. He climbed the *vallum,* and looked out, crouching, lest anybody should see him. Only the shadows were changed, and a breath of cooler air mounted from the brook; the fields were still and peaceful, the black figures moved, far away, amidst the corn, and the faint echo of the high-pitched voices sang thin and distant on the evening wind. Across the stream, in the cleft on the hill, opposite to the fort, the blue wood smoke stole up a spiral pillar from the chimney of old Mrs. Gibbon's cottage. He began to run full tilt down the steep surge of the hill, and never stopped till he was over the gate and in the lane again. As he looked back, down the valley to the south, and saw the violent ascent, the green swelling bulwarks, and the dark ring of oaks; the sunlight seemed to play about the fort with an aureole of flame.

"Where on earth have you been all this time, Lucian?" said his cousin when he got home. "Why, you look quite ill. It is really madness of you to go walking in such weather as this. I wonder you haven't got a sunstroke. And the tea must be nearly cold. I couldn't keep your father waiting, you know."

He muttered something about being rather tired, and sat down to his tea. It was not cold, for the "cosy" had been put over the pot, but it was black and bitter strong, as his cousin expressed it. The draught was unpalatable, but it did him good, and the thought came with great consolation that he had only been asleep and dreaming queer, nightmarish dreams. He shook off all his fancies with resolution, and thought the loneliness of the camp, and the burning sunlight, and possibly the nettle sting, which still tingled most abominably, must have been the only factors in his farrago of impossible recollections. He remembered that when he had felt the sting, he had seized a nettle with thick folds of his handkerchief, and having twisted off a good length, had put it in his pocket to shew his father. Mr. Taylor was almost interested when he came in from his evening stroll about the garden and saw the specimen.

"Where did you manage to come across that, Lucian?" he said. "You haven't been to Caermaen, have you?"

"No. I got it in the Roman fort by the common."

"Oh, the twyn. You must have been trespassing then. Do you know what it is?"

"No. I thought it looked different from the common nettles."

"Yes; it's a Roman nettle—*arctic pilulifera*. It's a rare plant. Burrows says it's to be found at Caermaen, but I was never able to come across it. I must add it to the *flora* of the parish."

Mr. Taylor had begun to compile a *flora* accompanied by a *hortus siccus*, but both stayed on high shelves dusty and fragmentary. He put the specimen on his desk, intending to fasten it in the book, but the maid swept it away, dry and withered, in a day or two.

Lucian tossed and cried out in his sleep that night, and the awakening in the morning was, in a measure, a renewal of the awakening in the fort. But the impression was not so strong, and in a plain room it seemed all delirium, a phantasmagoria. He had to go down to Caermaen in the afternoon, for Mrs. Dixon, the vicar's wife, had "commanded" his presence at tea. Mr. Dixon, though fat and short and clean shaven, ruddy of face, was a safe man, with no extreme views on anything. He "deplored" all extreme party convictions, and thought the great needs of our beloved Church were conciliation, moderation, and above all "amolgamation"—so he pronounced the word. Mrs. Dixon was tall, imposing, splendid, well fitted for the episcopal order, with gifts that would have shone at the palace. There were daughters, who studied German Literature, and thought Miss Frances Ridley Havergal wrote poetry, but Lucian had no fear of them; he dreaded the boys. Everybody said they were such fine, manly fellows, such gentlemanly boys, with such a good manner, sure to get on in the world. Lucian had said "Bother!" in a very violent manner when the gracious invitation was conveyed to him, but there was no getting out of it. Miss Deacon did her best to make him look smart; his ties were all so disgraceful that she had to supply the want with a narrow ribbon of a sky-blue tint; and she brushed him so long and so violently that he quite understood why a horse sometimes bites and sometimes kicks the groom. He set out between two and three in a gloomy frame of mind; he knew too well what spending the afternoon with honest manly boys meant. He found the reality more lurid than his anticipation. The boys were in the field, and the first remark he heard when he got in sight of the group was:

"Hullo, Lucian, how much for the tie?" "Fine tie," another, a stranger, observed. "You bagged it from the kitten, didn't you?"

Then they made up a game of cricket, and he was put in first. He was l.b.w. in his second over, so they all said, and had to field for the rest of the afternoon. Arthur Dixon, who was about his own age, forgetting all the laws of hospitality, told him he was a beastly muff when he missed a catch, rather a difficult catch. He missed several catches, and it seemed as if he were always panting after balls, which, as Edward Dixon said, any fool, even a baby, could have stopped. At last the game broke up, solely from Lucian's lack of skill, as everybody declared. Edward Dixon, who was thirteen, and had a swollen red face and a projecting eye, wanted to fight him for spoiling the game, and the others agreed that he funked the fight in a rather dirty manner. The strange boy, who was called De Carti, and was understood to be faintly related to Lord De Carti of M'Carthytown, said openly that the fellows at his place wouldn't stand such a sneak for five minutes. So the afternoon passed off very pleasantly indeed, till it was time to go into the vicarage for weak tea, home-made cake, and unripe plums. He got away at last. As he went out at the gate, he heard De Carti's final observation:

"We like to dress well at our place. His governor must be beastly poor to let him go about like that. D'y' see his trousers are all ragged at heel? Is old Taylor a gentleman?"

It had been a very gentlemanly afternoon, but there was a certain relief when the vicarage was far behind, and the evening smoke of the little town, once the glorious capital of Siluria, hung haze-like over the ragged roofs and mingled with the river mist. He looked down from the height of the road on the huddled houses, saw the points of light start out suddenly from the cottages on the hillside beyond, and gazed at the long lovely valley fading in the twilight, till the darkness came and all that remained was the sombre ridge of the forest. The way was pleasant through the solemn scented lane, with glimpses of dim country, the vague mystery of night overshadowing the woods and meadows. A warm wind blew gusts of odour from the meadowsweet by the brook, now and then bee and beetle span homeward through the air, booming a deep note as from a great organ far away, and from the verge of the wood came the "who-oo, who-oo, who-oo" of the owls, a wild strange sound that mingled with the whirr and rattle of the nightjar, deep in the bracken. The moon swam up through the films of misty cloud, and hung, a golden glorious lantern, in mid-air; and, set in the dusky hedge, the little green fires of the glowworms appeared. He sauntered slowly up the lane, drinking in the religion of the scene, and thinking the country by night as mystic and wonderful as a dimly-lit cathedral. He had quite forgotten the "manly young fellows" and their sports, and only wished as the land began to shimmer and gleam in the moonlight that he knew by some medium of words or colour how to represent the loveliness about his way.

"Had a pleasant evening, Lucian?" said his father when he came in.

"Yes, I had a nice walk home. Oh, in the afternoon we played cricket. I didn't care for it much. There was a boy named De Carti there; he is staying with the Dixons. Mrs. Dixon whispered to me when we were going in to tea, 'He's a second cousin of Lord De Carti's,' and she looked quite grave as if she were in church."

The parson grinned grimly and lit his old pipe.

"Baron De Carti's great-grandfather was a Dublin attorney," he remarked. "Which his name was Jeremiah M'Carthy. His prejudiced fellow-citizens called him the Unjust Steward, also the Bloody Attorney, and I believe that 'to hell with M'Carthy' was quite a popular cry about the time of the Union."

Mr. Taylor was a man of very wide and irregular reading and a tenacious memory; he often used to wonder why he had not risen in the Church. He had once told Mr. Dixon a singular and *drolatique* anecdote concerning the bishop's college days, and he never discovered why the prelate did not bow according to his custom when the name of Taylor was called at the next visitation. Some people said the reason was lighted candles, but that was impossible, as the Reverend and Honourable Smallwood Stafford, Lord Beamys's son, who had a cure of souls in the cathedral city, was well known to burn no end of candles, and with him the bishop was on the best of terms. Indeed the bishop often stayed at Coplesey (pronounced "Copsey") Hall, Lord Beamys's place in the west.

Lucian had mentioned the name of De Carti with intention, and had perhaps exaggerated a little Mrs. Dixon's respectful manner. He knew such incidents cheered his father, who could never look at these subjects from a proper point of view, and, as people said, sometimes made the strangest remarks for a clergyman. This irreverent way of treating serious things was one of the great bonds between father and son, but it tended to increase their isolation. People said they would often have liked to asked Mr. Taylor to garden-parties, and tea-parties, and other cheap entertainments, if only he had not been such an *extreme* man and so *queer.* Indeed, a year before, Mr. Taylor had gone to a garden-party at the Castle, Caermaen, and had made such fun of the

bishop's recent address on missions to the Portuguese, that the
Gervases and Dixons and all who heard him were quite shocked and
annoyed. And, as Mrs. Meyrick of Lanyravon observed, his black coat
was perfectly *green* with age; so on the whole the Gervases did not like
to invite Mr. Taylor again. As for the son, nobody cared to have him;
Mrs. Dixon, as she said to her husband, really asked him out of charity.

"I am afraid he seldom gets a real meal at home," she remarked,
"so I thought he would enjoy a good wholesome tea for once in a way.
But he is such an *unsatisfactory* boy, he would only have one slice of that
nice plain cake, and I couldn't get him to take more than two plums.
They were really quite ripe too, and boys are usually so fond of fruit."

Thus Lucian was forced to spend his holidays chiefly in his own
company, and make the best he could of the ripe peaches on the south
wall of the rectory garden. There was a certain corner where the heat
of that hot August seemed concentrated, reverberated from one wall
to the other, and here he liked to linger of mornings, when the mists
were still thick in the valleys, "mooning", meditating, extending his
walk from the quince to the medlar and back again, beside the
mouldering walls of mellowed brick. He was full of a certain wonder
and awe, not unmixed with a swell of strange exultation, and wished
more and more to be alone, to think over that wonderful afternoon
within the fort. In spite of himself the impression was fading; he could
not understand that feeling of mad panic terror that drove him
through the thicket and down the steep hillside; yet, he had experienced so clearly the physical shame and reluctance of the flesh; he recollected that for a few seconds after his awakening the sight of his own
body had made him shudder and writhe as if it had suffered some pro-
foundest degradation. He saw before him a vision of two forms; a faun
with tingling and prickling flesh lay expectant in the sunlight, and there
was also the likeness of a miserable shamed boy, standing with trembling body and shaking, unsteady hands. It was all confused, a procession of blurred images, now of rapture and ecstasy, and now of terror
and shame, floating in a light that was altogether phantasmal and unreal.
He dared not approach the fort again; he lingered in the road to Caermaen that passed behind it, but a mile away, and separated by the wild
land and a strip of wood from the towering battlements. Here he was
looking over a gate one day, doubtful and wondering, when he heard a

heavy step behind him, and glancing round quickly saw it was old Morgan of the White House.

"Good afternoon, Master Lucian," he began. "Mr. Taylor pretty well, I suppose? I be goin' to the house a minute; the men in the fields are wantin' some more cider. Would you come and taste a drop of cider, Master Lucian? It's very good, sir, indeed."

Lucian did not want any cider, but he thought it would please old Morgan if he took some, so he said he should like to taste the cider very much indeed. Morgan was a sturdy, thick-set old man of the ancient stock; a stiff churchman, who breakfasted regularly on fat broth and Caerphilly cheese in the fashion of his ancestors; hot, spiced elder wine was for winter nights, and gin for festal seasons. The farm had always been the freehold of the family, and when Lucian, in the wake of the yeoman, passed through the deep porch by the oaken door, down into the long dark kitchen, he felt as though the seventeenth century still lingered on. One mullioned window, set deep in the sloping wall, gave all the light there was through quarries of thick glass in which there were whorls and circles, so that the lapping rose-branch and the garden and the fields beyond were distorted to the sight. Two heavy beams, oaken but whitewashed, ran across the ceiling; a little glow of fire sparkled in the great fireplace, and a curl of blue smoke fled up the cavern of the chimney. Here was the genuine chimney-corner of our fathers; there were seats on each side of the fireplace where one could sit snug and sheltered on December nights, warm and merry in the blazing light, and listen to the battle of the storm, and hear the flame spit and hiss at the falling snowflakes. At the back of the fire were great blackened tiles with raised initials and a date.—I.M., 1684.

"Sit down, Master Lucian, sit down, sir," said Morgan.

"Annie," he called through one of the numerous doors, "here's Master Lucian, the parson, would like a drop of cider. Fetch a jug, will you, directly?"

"Very well, father," came the voice from the dairy, and presently the girl entered, wiping the jug she held. In his boyish way Lucian had been a good deal disturbed by Annie Morgan; he could see her on Sundays from his seat in church, and her skin, curiously pale, her lips that seemed as though they were stained with some brilliant pigment, her black hair, and the quivering black eyes, gave him odd fancies which he had hardly shaped to himself. Annie had grown into a woman in three years, and he was still a boy. She came into the kitchen, curtsying and smiling.

"Good-day, Master Lucian, and how is Mr. Taylor, sir?"

"Pretty well, thank you. I hope you are well."

"Nicely, sir, thank you. How nice your voice do sound in church, Master Lucian, to be sure. I was telling father about it last Sunday."

Lucian grinned and felt uncomfortable, and the girl set down the jug on the round table and brought a glass from the dresser. She bent close over him as she poured out the green oily cider, fragrant of the orchard; her hand touched his shoulder for a moment, and she said, "I beg your pardon, sir," very prettily. He looked up eagerly at her face; the black eyes, a little oval in shape, were shining, and the lips smiled. Annie wore a plain dress of some black stuff, open at the throat; her skin was beautiful. For a moment the ghost of a fancy hovered unsubstantial in his mind; and then Annie curtsied as she handed him the cider, and replied to his thanks with, "And welcome kindly, sir."

The drink was really good; not thin, nor sweet, but round and full and generous, with a fine yellow flame twinkling through the green when one held it up to the light. It was like a stray sunbeam hovering on the grass in a deep orchard, and he swallowed the glassful with relish, and had some more, warmly commending it. Mr. Morgan was touched.

"I see you do know a good thing, sir," he said. "Iss, indeed, now, it's good stuff, though it's my own makin'. My old grandfather he planted the trees in the time of the wars, and he was a very good judge of an apple in his day and generation. And a famous grafter he was, to be sure. You will never see no swelling in the trees he grafted at all whatever. Now there's James Morris, Penyrhaul, he's a famous grafter, too, and yet them Redstreaks he grafted for me five year ago, they be all swollen-like below the graft already. Would you like to taste a Blemmin pippin, now, Master Lucian? there be a few left in the loft, I believe."

Lucian said he should like an apple very much, and the farmer went out by another door, and Annie stayed in the kitchen talking. She said Mrs. Trevor, her married sister, was coming to them soon to spend a few days.

"She's got such a beautiful baby," said Annie, "and he's quite sensible-like already, though he's only nine months old. Mary would like to see you, sir, if you would be so kind as to step in; that is, if it's not troubling you at all, Master Lucian. I suppose you must be getting a fine scholar now, sir?"

"I am doing pretty well, thank you," said the boy. "I was first in my form last term."

"Fancy! To think of that! D'you hear, father, what a scholar Master Lucian be getting?"

"He be a rare grammarian, I'm sure," said the farmer. "You do take after your father, sir; I always do say that nobody have got such a good deliverance in the pulpit."

Lucian did not find the Blenheim Orange as good as the cider, but he ate it with all the appearance of relish, and put another, with thanks, in his pocket. He thanked the farmer again when he got up to go; and Annie curtsied and smiled, and wished him good-day, and welcome, kindly.

Lucian heard her saying to her father as he went out what a nice-mannered young gentleman he was getting, to be sure; and he went on his way, thinking that Annie was really very pretty, and speculating as to whether he would have the courage to kiss her, if they met in a dark lane. He was quite sure she would only laugh, and say, "Oh, Master Lucian!"

For many months he had occasional fits of recollection, both cold and hot; but the bridge of time, gradually lengthening, made those dreadful and delicious images grow more and more indistinct, till at last they all passed into that wonderland which a youth looks back upon in amazement, not knowing why this used to be a symbol of terror or that of joy. At the end of each term he would come home and find his father a little more despondent, and harder to cheer even for a moment; and the wall paper and the furniture grew more and more dingy and shabby. The two cats, loved and ancient beasts, that he remembered when he was quite a little boy, before he went to school, died miserably, one after the other. Old Polly, the pony, at last fell down in the stable from the weakness of old age, and had to be killed there; the battered old trap ran no longer along the well-remembered lanes. There was long meadow grass on the lawn, and the trained fruit trees on the wall had got quite out of hand. At last, when Lucian was seventeen, his father was obliged to take him from school; he could no longer afford the fees. This was the sorry ending of many hopes, and dreams of a double-first, a fellowship, distinction and glory that the poor parson had long entertained for his son, and the two moped together, in the shabby room, one on each side of the sulky fire, thinking of dead days and finished plans, and seeing a grey future in the years that advanced towards them. At one time there seemed some chance of a distant relative coming forward to Lucian's assistance; and indeed it was quite settled that he should go up to London with certain definite aims. Mr. Taylor told the good news to his acquaintances—his coat was too green now for any pretence of friendship; and Lucian himself spoke of his plans to Burrows the doctor and Mr. Dixon, and one or two others. Then the whole scheme fell through, and the parson and his son suffered much sympathy. People, of course, had to say they were sorry, but in reality the news was received with high spirits, with the joy with which one sees a stone, as it rolls down a steep place, give yet another bounding leap towards the pool beneath. Mrs. Dixon heard the pleasant tidings from Mrs. Colley, who came in to talk about the Mothers' Meeting and the Band of Hope. Mrs. Dixon was nursing little Æthelwig, or some such name, at the time, and made many affecting observations on the general righteousness with which the world was governed. Indeed, poor Lucian's disappointment seemed distinctly to increase her faith in the Divine Order, as if it had been some example in Butler's *Analogy*.

"Aren't Mr. Taylor's views very *extreme?*" she said to her husband the same evening.

"I am afraid they are," he replied. "I was quite *grieved* at the last Diocesan Conference at the way in which he spoke. The dear old bishop had given an address on Auricular Confession; he was *forced* to do so, you know, after what had happened, and I must say that I never felt prouder of our beloved Church."

Mr. Dixon told all the Homeric story of the conference, reciting the achievements of the champions, "deploring" this and applauding that. It seemed that Mr. Taylor had had the audacity to quote authorities which the bishop could not very well repudiate, though they were directly opposed to the "safe" episcopal pronouncement.

Mrs. Dixon of course was grieved; it was "sad" to think of a clergyman behaving so shamefully.

"But you know, dear," she proceeded, "I have been thinking about that unfortunate Taylor boy and his disappointments, and after what you've just told me, I am sure it's some kind of judgment on them both. Has Mr. Taylor forgotten the vows he took at his ordination? But don't you think, dear, I am right, and that he has been punished: 'The sins of the fathers'?"

Somehow or other Lucian divined the atmosphere of threatenings and judgments, and shrank more and more from the small society of the countryside. For his part, when he was not "mooning" in the beloved fields and woods of happy memory, he shut himself up with books, reading whatever could be found on the shelves, and amassing a store of incongruous and obsolete knowledge. Long did he linger with the men of the seventeenth century; delaying the gay sunlit streets with Pepys, and listening to the charmed sound of the Restoration Revel; roaming by peaceful streams with Izaak Walton, and the great Catholic divines; enchanted with the portrait of Herbert the loving ascetic; awed by the mystic breath of Crashaw. Then the cavalier poets sang their gallant songs; and Herrick made Dean Prior magic ground by the holy incantation of a verse. And in the old proverbs and homely sayings of the time he found the good and beautiful English life, a time full of grace and dignity and rich merriment. He dived deeper and deeper into his books; he had taken all obsolescence to be his province; in his disgust at the stupid usual questions, "Will it pay?" "What good is it?" and so forth, he would only read what was uncouth and useless. The strange pomp and symbolism of the Cabala, with its hint of more terrible things; the Rosicrucian mysteries of Fludd, the enigmas of Vaughan, dreams of alchemists—all these were his delight. Such were his companions, with the hills and hanging woods, the brooks and lonely waterpools; books, the thoughts of books, the stirrings of imagination, all fused into one phantasy by the magic of the outland country. He held himself aloof from the walls of the fort; he was content to see the heaped mounds, the violent height with faery bulwarks, from the gate in the lane, and to leave all within the ring of oaks in the mystery of his boyhood's vision. He professed to laugh at himself and at his fancies of that hot August afternoon, when sleep came to him within the thicket, but in his heart of hearts there was something that never faded—something that glowed like the red glint of a gypsy's fire seen from afar across the hills and mists of the night, and known to be burning in a wild land. Sometimes, when he was sunken in his books, the flame of delight shot up, and shewed him a whole province and continent of his nature, all shining and aglow; and in the midst of the exultation and triumph he would draw back, a little afraid. He had become ascetic in his studious and melancholy isolation, and the vision of such ecstasies frightened him. He began to write a little; at first very tentatively and feebly, and then with more confidence. He shewed some of his verses to his father, who told him with a sigh that he had once hoped to write—in the old days at Oxford, he added.

"They are very nicely done," said the parson; "but I'm afraid you won't find anybody to print them, my boy."

So he pottered on; reading everything, imitating what struck his fancy, attempting the effect of the classic metres in English verse, trying his hand at a masque, a Restoration comedy, forming impossible plans for books which rarely got beyond half a dozen lines on a sheet of paper; beset with splendid fancies which refused to abide before the pen. But the vain joy of conception was not altogether vain, for it gave him some armour about his heart.

The months went by, monotonous, and sometimes blotted with despair. He wrote and planned and filled the waste-paper basket with hopeless efforts. Now and then he sent verses or prose articles to magazines, in pathetic ignorance of the trade. He felt the immense difficulty of the career of literature without clearly understanding it; the battle was happily in a mist, so that the host of the enemy, terribly arrayed, was to some extent hidden. Yet there was enough of difficulty to appal; from following the intricate course of little nameless brooks, from hushed twilight woods, from the vision of the mountains, and the breath of the great wind, passing from deep to deep, he would come home filled with thoughts and emotions, mystic fancies which he yearned to translate into the written word. And the result of the effort seemed always to be bathos! Wooden sentences, a portentous stilted style, obscurity, and awkwardness clogged the pen; it seemed impossible to win the great secret of language; the stars glittered only in the darkness, and vanished away in clearer light. The periods of despair were often long and heavy, the victories very few and trifling; night after night he sat writing after his father had knocked out his last pipe, filling a page with difficulty in an hour, and usually forced to thrust the stuff away in despair, and go unhappily to bed, conscious that after all his labour he had done nothing. And these were moments when the accustomed vision of the land alarmed him, and the wild domed hills and darkling woods seemed symbols of some terrible secret in the inner life of that stranger—himself. Sometimes when he was deep in his books and papers, sometimes on a lonely walk, sometimes amidst the tiresome chatter of Caermaen "society", he would thrill with a sudden sense of awful hidden things, and there ran that quivering flame through his nerves that brought back the recollection of the matted thicket, and that earlier appearance of the bare black boughs enwrapped with flames. Indeed, though he avoided the solitary lane, and the sight of the sheer height, with its ring of oaks and moulded mounds, the image of it grew more intense as the symbol of certain hints and suggestions. The exultant and insurgent flesh seemed to have its temple and castle within those olden walls, and he longed with all his heart to escape, to set himself free in the wilderness of London, and to be secure amidst the murmur of modern streets.

II

Lucian was growing really anxious about his manuscript. He had gained enough experience at twenty-three to know that editors and publishers must not be hurried; but his book had been lying at Messrs. Beit's office for more than three months. For six weeks he had not dared to expect an answer, but afterwards life had become agonising. Every morning, at post-time, the poor wretch nearly choked with anxiety to know whether his sentence had arrived, and the rest of the day was racked with alternate pangs of hope and despair. Now and then he was almost assured of success; conning over these painful and eager pages in memory, he found parts that were admirable, while again, his inexperience reproached him, and he feared he had written a raw and awkward book, wholly unfit for print. Then he would compare what he remembered of it with notable magazine articles and books praised by reviewers, and fancy that after all there might be good points in the thing; he could not help liking the first chapter for instance. Perhaps the letter might come to-morrow. So it went on; week after week of sick torture made more exquisite by such gleams of hope; it was as if he were stretched in anguish on the rack, and the pain relaxed and kind words spoken now and again by the tormentors, and then once more the grinding pang and burning agony. At last he could bear suspense no longer, and he wrote to Messrs. Beit, enquiring in a humble manner whether the manuscript had arrived in safety. The firm replied in a very polite letter, expressing regret that their reader had been suffering from a cold in the head, and had therefore been unable to send in his report. A final decision was promised in a week's time, and the letter ended with apologies for the delay and a hope that he had suffered no inconvenience. Of course the "final decision" did not come at the end of the week, but the book was returned at the end of three weeks, with a circular thanking the author for his kindness in submitting the manuscript, and regretting that the firm did not see their way to producing it. He felt relieved; the operation that he had dreaded and deprecated for so long was at last over, and he would no longer grow sick of mornings when the letters were brought in. He took his parcel to the sunny corner of the garden, where the old wooden seat stood sheltered from the biting March winds. Messrs. Beit had put in with the circular one of their short lists, a neat booklet, headed: *Messrs. Beit & Co.'s Recent Publications.*

He settled himself comfortably on the seat, lit his pipe, and began to read: "*A Bad Un to Beat:* a Novel of Sporting Life, by the Honourable Mrs. Scudamore Runnymede, author of *Yoicks, With the Mudshire Pack, The Sportleigh Stables,* etc., etc., 3 vols. At all Libraries." The *Press,* it seemed, pronounced this to be a "charming book. Mrs. Runnymede has wit and humour enough to furnish forth half-a-dozen ordinary sporting novels." "Told with the sparkle and vivacity of a past-mistress in the art of novel writing," said the *Review;* while Miranda, of *Smart Society,* positively bubbled with enthusiasm. "You must forgive me, Aminta," wrote this young person, "if I have not sent the description I promised of Madame Lulu's new creations and others of that ilk. I must a tale unfold; Tom came in yesterday and began to rave about the Honourable Mrs. Scudamore Runnymede's last novel, *A Bad Un to*

Beat. He says all the Smart Set are talking of it, and it seems the police have to regulate the crowd at Mudie's. You know I read everything Mrs. Runnymede writes, so I set out Miggs directly to beg, borrow or steal a copy, and I confess I burnt the midnight oil before I laid it down. Now, mind you get it, you will find it so awfully *chic.*" Nearly all the novelists on Messrs. Beit's list were ladies, their works all ran to three volumes, and all of them pleased the *Press,* the *Review,* and Miranda of *Smart Society.* One of these books, *Millicent's Marriage,* by Sarah Pocklington Sanders, was pronounced fit to lie on the schoolroom table, on the drawing-room bookshelf, or beneath the pillow of the most gently nurtured of our daughters. "This," the reviewer went on, "is high praise, especially in these days when we are deafened by the loud-voiced clamour of self-styled 'artists'. We would warn the young men who prate so persistently of style and literature, construction and prose harmonies, that we believe the English reading public will have none of them. Harmless amusement, a gentle flow of domestic interest, a faithful reproduction of the open and manly life of the hunting field, pictures of innocent and healthy English girlhood such as Miss Sanders here affords us; these are the topics that will always find a welcome in our homes, which remain bolted and barred against the abandoned artist and the scrofulous stylist."

He turned over the pages of the little book and chuckled in high relish; he discovered an honest enthusiasm, a determination to strike a blow for the good and true that refreshed and exhilarated. A beaming face, spectacled and whiskered probably, an expansive waistcoat, and a tender heart, seemed to shine through the words which Messrs. Beit had quoted; and the alliteration of the final sentence; that was good too; there was style for you if you wanted it. The champion of the blushing cheek and the gushing eye shewed that he too could handle the weapons of the enemy if he cared to trouble himself with such things. Lucian leant back and roared with indecent laughter till the tabby tom-cat who had succeeded to the poor dead beasts looked up reproachfully from his sunny corner, with a face like the reviewer's, innocent and round and whiskered. At last he turned to his parcel and drew out some half-dozen sheets of manuscript, and began to read in a rather desponding spirit; it was pretty obvious, he thought, that the stuff was poor and beneath the standard of publication. The book had

taken a year and a half in the making; it was a pious attempt to translate into English prose the form and mystery of the domed hills, the
magic of occult valleys, the sound of the red swollen brook swirling
through leafless woods. Day-dreams and toil at nights had gone into
the eager pages, he had laboured hard to do his very best, writing and
rewriting, weighing his cadences, beginning over and over again,
grudging no patience, no trouble if only it might be pretty good; good
enough to print and sell to a reading public which had become critical.
He glanced through the manuscript in his hand, and to his astonishment, he could not help thinking that in its measure it was decent
work. After three months his prose seemed fresh and strange as if it
had been wrought by another man, and in spite of himself he found
charming things, and impressions that were not commonplace. He
knew how weak it all was compared with his own conceptions; he had
seen an enchanted city, awful, glorious, with flame smitten about its
battlements, like the cities of the Sangraal, and he had moulded his
copy in such poor clay as came to his hand; yet, in spite of the gulf that
yawned between the idea and the work, he knew as he read that the
thing accomplished was very far from a failure. He put back the leaves
carefully, and glanced again at Messrs. Beit's list. It had escaped his notice that *A Bad Un to Beat* was in its third three-volume edition. It was a
great thing, at all events, to know in what direction to aim, if he wished
to succeed. If he worked hard, he thought, he might some day win the
approval of the coy and retiring Miranda of *Smart Society;* that modest
maiden might in his praise interrupt her task of disinterested advertisement, her philanthropic counsels to "go to Jumper's, and mind you
ask for Mr. C. Jumper, who will shew you the lovely blue paper with
the yellow spots at ten shillings the piece". He put down the pamphlet,
and laughed again at the books and the reviewers: so that he might not
weep. This then was English fiction, this was English criticism, and
farce, after all, was but an ill-played tragedy.

The rejected manuscript was hidden away, and his father quoted
Horace's maxim as to the benefit of keeping literary works for some
time "in the wood". There was nothing to grumble at, though Lucian
was inclined to think the duration of the reader's catarrh a little exaggerated. But this was a trifle; he did not arrogate to himself the position of a small commercial traveller, who expects prompt civility as a

matter of course, and not at all as a favour. He simply forgot his old book, and resolved that he would make a better one if he could. With the hot fit of resolution, the determination not to be snuffed out by one refusal upon him, he began to beat about in his mind for some new scheme. At first it seemed that he had hit upon a promising subject; he began to plot out chapters and scribble hints for the curious story that had entered his mind, arranging his circumstances and noting the effects to be produced with all the enthusiasm of the artist. But after the first breath the aspect of the work changed; page after page was tossed aside as hopeless, the beautiful sentences he had dreamed of refused to be written, and his puppets remained stiff and wooden, devoid of life or motion. Then all the old despairs came back, the agonies of the artificer who strives and perseveres in vain; the scheme that seemed of amorous fire turned to cold hard ice in his hands. He let the pen drop from his fingers, and wondered how he could have ever dreamed of writing books. Again, the thought occurred that he might do something if he could only get away, and join the sad procession in the murmuring London streets, far from the shadow of those awful hills. But it was quite impossible; the relative who had once promised assistance was appealed to, and wrote expressing his regret that Lucian had turned out a "loafer", wasting his time in scribbling, instead of trying to earn his living. Lucian felt rather hurt at this letter, but the parson only grinned grimly as usual. He was thinking of how he signed a cheque many years before, in the days of his prosperity, and the check was payable to this didactic relative, then in but a poor way, and of a thankful turn of mind.

The old rejected manuscript had almost passed out of his recollection. It was recalled oddly enough. He was looking over the *Reader,* and enjoying the admirable literary criticisms, some three months after the return of his book, when his eye was attracted by a quoted passage in one of the notices. The thought and style both wakened memory, the cadences were familiar and beloved. He read through the review from the beginning; it was a very favourable one, and pronounced the volume an immense advance on Mr. Ritson's previous work. "Here, undoubtedly, the author has discovered a vein of pure metal," the reviewer added, "and we predict that he will go far." Lucian had not yet reached his father's stage, he was unable to grin in the manner of that irreverent parson. The passage selected for high praise was taken almost word for word from the manuscript now resting in his room, the work that had not reached the high standard of Messrs. Beit & Co., who, curiously enough, were the publishers of the book reviewed in the *Reader.* He had a few shillings in his possession, and wrote at once to a bookseller in London for a copy of *The Chorus in Green,* as the author had oddly named the book. He wrote on June 21st, and thought he might fairly expect to receive the interesting volume by the 24th; but the postman, true to his tradition, brought nothing for him, and in the afternoon he resolved to walk down to Caermaen, in case it might have come by a second post; or it might have been mislaid at the office; they forgot parcels sometimes, especially when the bag was heavy and the weather hot. This 24th was a sultry and oppressive day; a grey veil of cloud obscured the sky, and a vaporous mist hung heavily over the land, and fumed up from the valleys. But at five o'clock, when he started, the clouds began to break, and the sunlight suddenly streamed down through the misty air, making ways and channels of rich glory, and bright islands in the gloom. It was a pleasant and shining evening when, passing by devious back streets to avoid the barbarians (as he very rudely called the respectable inhabitants of the town), he reached the post-office; which was also the general shop.

"Yes, Mr. Taylor, there is something for you, sir," said the man. "Williams the postman forgot to take it up this morning," and he handed over the packet. Lucian took it under his arm and went slowly through the ragged winding lanes till he came into the country. He got over the first stile on the road, and sitting down in the shelter of a hedge, cut the strings and opened the parcel. *The Chorus in Green* was got up in what reviewers call a dainty manner: a bronze-green cloth, well-cut gold lettering, wide margins and black "old-face" type, all witnessed to the good taste of Messrs. Beit & Co. He cut the pages hastily and began to read. He soon found that he had wronged Mr. Ritson— that old literary hand had by no means stolen his book wholesale, as he had expected. There were about two hundred pages in the pretty little volume, and of these about ninety were Lucian's, dovetailed into a rather different scheme with skill that was nothing short of exquisite. And Mr. Ritson's own work was often very good; spoilt here and there for some tastes by the "cataloguing" method, a somewhat materialistic way of taking an inventory of the holy country things; but, for that very reason, contrasting to a great advantage with Lucian's hints and dreams and note of haunting. And here and there Mr. Ritson had made little alterations in the style of the passages he had conveyed, and most of these alterations were amendments, as Lucian was obliged to confess, though he would have liked to argue one or two points with his collaborator and corrector. He lit his pipe and leant back comfortably in the hedge, thinking things over, weighing very coolly his experience of humanity, his contact with the "society" of the countryside, the affair of *The Chorus in Green,* and even some little incidents that had struck him as he was walking through the streets of Caermaen that evening. At the post-office, when he was enquiring for his parcel, he had heard two old women grumbling in the street; it seemed, so far as he could make out, that both had been disappointed in much the same way. Each had applied for an alms at the vicarage; they were probably shiftless old wretches who liked beer for supper all their lives, and had forgotten the duties of economy and "laying up treasure upon earth". One was a Roman Catholic, hardened, and beyond the reach of conversion; she had been advised to ask alms of the priests, "who are always creeping and crawling about". The other old sinner was a dissenter, and "Mr. Dixon has quite enough to do to relieve good Church people." Mrs. Dixon, assisted by Henrietta, was, it seemed, the lady high almoner, who dispensed these charities. As she said to Mrs. Colley, they would end by keeping all the beggars in the county, and they really couldn't afford it. A large family was an expensive thing, and the girls *must* have new frocks. "Mr. Dixon is always telling me and the girls that we must not *demoralise* the people by indiscriminate charity." Lucian had heard of these sage counsels, and thought of them as he listened to the bitter complaints of the gaunt, hungry old women. In the back street by which he passed out of the town he saw a large "healthy" boy kicking a sick cat; the poor creature had just strength enough to crawl under an outhouse door; probably to die in torments. He did not find much satisfaction in thrashing the boy, but he did it with hearty good will. Further on, at the corner where the turnpike used to be, was a big notice, announcing a meeting at the schoolroom in aid of the missions to the Portuguese. "Under the Patronage of the Lord Bishop of the Diocese", was the imposing headline; the Rever-

end Merivale Dixon, vicar of Caermaen, was to be in the chair, supported by Stanley Gervase, Esq., J.P., and by many of the clergy and
gentry of the neighbourhood. Senhor Diabo, "formerly a Romanist
priest, now an evangelist in Lisbon", would address the meeting.
"Funds are urgently needed to carry on this good work," concluded
the notice. So he lay well back in the shade of the hedge, and thought
whether some sort of an article could not be made by vindicating the
terrible Yahoos; one might point out that they were in many respects a
simple and unsophisticated race, whose faults were the result of their
enslaved position, while such virtues as they had were all their own.
They might be compared, he thought, much to their advantage, with
more complex civilisations. There was no hint of anything like the Beit
system of publishing in existence amongst them, the great Yahoo nation would surely never feed and encourage a scabby Houyhnhnm, ex-
pelled for his foulness from the horse-community, and the witty dean,
in all his minuteness, had said nothing of "safe" Yahoos. On reflection, however, he did not feel quite secure of this part of his defence;
he remembered that the leading brutes had favourites, who were employed in certain simple domestic offices about their masters, and it
seemed doubtful whether the contemplated vindication would not
break down on this point. He smiled queerly to himself as he thought
of these comparisons, but his heart burnt with a dull fury. Throwing
back his unhappy memory, he recalled all the contempt and scorn he
had suffered; as a boy he had heard the masters murmuring their dis-
dain of him and of his desire to learn other than ordinary school work.
As a young man he had suffered the insolence of these wretched people about him; their cackling laughter at his poverty jarred and grated
in his ears, he saw the acrid grin of some miserable idiot woman, some
creature beneath the swine in intelligence and manners, merciless, as
he went by with his eyes on the dust, in his ragged clothes. He and his
father seemed to pass down an avenue of jeers and contempt, and contempt from such animals as these! This putrid filth, moulded into human shape, made only to fawn on the rich and beslaver them, thinking
no foulness too foul if it were done in honour of those in power and
authority; and no refined cruelty of contempt too cruel if it were contempt of the poor and humble and oppressed; it was to this obscene
and ghastly throng that he was something to be pointed at. And these

men and women spoke of sacred things, and knelt before the awful altar of God, before the altar of tremendous fire, surrounded as they professed by Angels and Archangels and all the Company of Heaven; and in their very church they had one aisle for the rich and another for the poor. And the species was not peculiar to Caermaen; the rich business men in London and the successful brother author were probably amusing themselves at the expense of the poor struggling creature they had injured and wounded; just as the "healthy" boy had burst into a great laugh when the miserable sick cat cried out in bitter agony, and trailed its limbs slowly, as it crept away to die. Lucian looked into his own life and his own will; he saw that in spite of his follies, and his want of success, he had not been consciously malignant, he had never deliberately aided in oppression, or looked on it with enjoyment and approval, and he felt that when he lay dead beneath the earth, eaten by swarming worms, he would be in a purer company than now, when he lived amongst human creatures. And he was to call this loathsome beast, all sting and filth, brother! "I had rather call the devils my brothers," he said in his heart, "I would fare better in hell." Blood was in his eyes, and as he looked up the sky seemed of blood, and the earth burnt with fire.

The sun was sinking low on the mountain when he set out on the way again. Burrows, the doctor, coming home in his trap, met him a little lower on the road, and gave him a friendly good-night.

"A long way round on this road, isn't it?" said the doctor. "As you have come so far, why don't you try the short cut across the fields? You will find it easily enough; second stile on the left hand, and then go straight ahead."

He thanked Dr. Burrows and said he would try the short cut, and Burrows span on homeward. He was a gruff and honest bachelor, and often felt very sorry for the lad, and wished he could help him. As he drove on, it suddenly occurred to him that Lucian had an awful look on his face, and he was sorry he had not asked him to jump in, and to come to supper. A hearty slice of beef, with strong ale, whisky and soda afterwards, a good pipe, and certain Rabelaisian tales which the doctor had treasured for many years, would have done the poor fellow a lot of good, he was certain. He half turned round on his seat, and looked to see if Lucian were still in sight, but he had passed the corner, and the doctor drove on, shivering a little; the mists were beginning to rise from the wet banks of the river.

Lucian trailed slowly along the road, keeping a look-out for the stile the doctor had mentioned. It would be a little of an adventure, he thought, to find his way by an unknown track; he knew the direction in which his home lay, and he imagined he would not have much difficulty in crossing from one stile to another. The path led him up a steep bare field, and when he was at the top, the town and the valley winding up to the north stretched before him. The river was stilled at the flood, and the yellow water, reflecting the sunset, glowed in its deep pools like dull brass. These burning pools, the level meadows fringed with shuddering reeds, the long dark sweep of the forest on the hill, were all clear and distinct, yet the light seemed to have clothed them with a new garment, even as voices from the streets of Caermaen sounded strangely, mounting up thin with the smoke. There beneath him lay the huddled cluster of Caermaen, the ragged and uneven roofs that marked the winding and sordid streets, here and there a pointed gable rising above its meaner fellows; beyond he recognised the piled mounds that marked the circle of the amphitheatre, and the dark edge of trees that grew where the Roman wall whitened and waxed old beneath the frosts and rains of eighteen hundred years. Thin and strange, mingled together, the voices came up to him on the hill; it was as if an outland race inhabited the ruined city and talked in a strange language of strange and terrible things. The sun had slid down the sky, and hung quivering over the huge dark dome of the mountain like a burnt sacrifice, and then suddenly vanished. In the afterglow the clouds began to writhe and turn scarlet, and shone so strangely reflected in the pools of the snake-like river, that one would have said the still waters stirred, the fleeting and changing of the clouds seeming to quicken the stream, as if it bubbled and sent up gouts of blood. But already about the town the darkness was forming; fast, fast the shadows crept upon it from the forest, and from all sides banks and wreaths of curling mist were gathering, as if a ghostly leaguer were being built up against the city, and the strange race who lived in its streets. Suddenly there burst out from the stillness the clear and piercing music of the *réveillé*, calling, recalling, iterated, reiterated, and ending with one long high fierce shrill note with which the steep hills rang. Perhaps a boy in the school band was practising on his bugle, but for Lucian it was magic. For him it was the note of the Roman trumpet, *tuba mirum spargens sonum,* filling all the hollow valley with its command, reverberated in dark places in the far forest, and resonant in the old graveyards without the walls. In his imagination he saw the earthen gates of the tombs broken open, and the serried legion swarming to the eagles. Century by century they passed by; they rose, dripping, from the river bed, they rose from the level, their armour shone in the quiet orchard, they gathered in ranks and companies from the cemetery, and as the trumpet sounded, the hill fort above the town gave up its dead. By hundreds and thousands the ghostly battle surged about the standard, behind the quaking mist, ready to march against the mouldering walls they had built so many years before.

He turned sharply; it was growing very dark, and he was afraid of missing his way. At first the path led him by the verge of a wood; there was a noise of rustling and murmuring from the trees as if they were taking evil counsel together. A high hedge shut out the sight of the darkening valley, and he stumbled on mechanically, without taking much note of the turnings of the track, and when he came out from the wood shadow to the open country, he stood for a moment quite bewildered and uncertain. A dark wild twilight country lay before him, confused dim shapes of trees near at hand, and a hollow below his feet, and the further hills and woods were dimmer, and all the air was very still. He gazed about him, scanning the dusty earth, and trying to make out some familiar shape, some well-known form of hill or wood. Suddenly the darkness about him glowed; a furnace fire had shot up on the mountain, and for a moment the little world of the woodside and the steep hill shone in a pale light, and he thought he saw his path beaten out in the turf before him. The great flame sank down to a red glint of fire, and it led him on down the ragged slope, his feet striking against ridges of ground, and falling from beneath him at a sudden dip. The bramble bushes shot out long prickly vines, amongst which he was entangled, and lower he was held back by wet bubbling earth. He had descended into a dark and shady valley, beset and tapestried with gloomy thickets; the weird wood noises were the only sounds, strange, unutterable mutterings, dismal, inarticulate. He pushed on in what he hoped was the right direction, stumbling from stile to gate, peering through mist and shadow, and still vainly seeking for any known landmark. Presently another sound broke upon the grim air, the murmur of water poured over stones, gurgling against the old misshapen roots of trees, and running clear in a deep channel. He passed into the chill breath of the brook, and almost fancied he heard two voices speaking in its murmur; there seemed a ceaseless utterance of words, an endless argument. With a mood of horror pressing on him, he listened to the noise of waters, and the wild fancy seized him that he was not deceived, that two unknown beings stood together there in the darkness and tried the balances of his life, and spoke his doom. The hour in the matted thicket rushed over the great bridge of years to his thought; he had sinned against the earth, and the earth trembled and shook for vengeance. He stayed still for a moment, quivering with fear, and at last went on blindly, no longer caring for the path, if only he might escape from the toils of that dismal shuddering hollow. As he plunged through the hedges the bristling thorns tore his face and hands; he fell amongst stinging-nettles and was pricked as he beat out his way amidst the gorse. He raced headlong, his head over his shoulder, through a windy wood, bare of undergrowth; there lay about the ground mouldering stumps, the relics of trees that had thundered to their fall, crashing and tearing to earth, long ago; and from these remains there flowed out a pale thin radiance, filling the spaces of the sounding wood with a dream of light. He had lost all count of the track; he felt he had fled for hours, climbing and descending, and yet not advancing; it was as if he stood still and the shadows of the land went by, in a vision. But at last a hedge, high and straggling, rose before him, and as he broke through it, his feet slipped, and he fell headlong down a steep bank into a lane. He lay still, half-stunned, for a moment, and then rising unsteadily, he looked desperately into the darkness before him, uncertain and bewildered. In front it was black as a midnight cellar, and he turned about, and saw a glint in the distance, as if a candle were flickering in a farmhouse window. He began to walk with trembling feet towards the light, when suddenly something pale started out from the shadows before him, and seemed to swim and float down the air. He was going down hill, and he hastened onwards, and he could see the bars of a stile framed dimly against the sky, and the figure still advanced with that gliding motion. Then, as the road declined to the valley, the landmark he had been seeking appeared. To his right there surged up in the darkness the dark-er summit of the Roman fort, and the streaming fire of the great full moon glowed through the bars of the wizard oaks, and made a halo shine about the hill. He was now quite close to the white appearance, and saw that it was only a woman walking swiftly down the lane; the floating movement was an effect due to the sombre air and the moon's glamour. At the gate, where he had spent so many hours gazing at the fort, they walked foot to foot, and he saw it was Annie Morgan.

"Good evening, Master Lucian," said the girl, "it's very dark, sir, indeed."

"Good evening, Annie," he answered, calling her by her name for the first time, and he saw that she smiled with pleasure. "You are out late, aren't you?"

"Yes, sir; but I've been taking a bit of supper to old Mrs. Gibbon. She's been very poorly the last few days, and there's nobody to do any-thing for her."

Then there were really people who helped one another; kindness and pity were not mere myths, fictions of "society", as useful as Doe and Roe, and as non-existent. The thought struck Lucian with a shock; the evening's passion and delirium, the wild walk and physical fatigue had almost shattered him in body and mind. He was "degenerate", *dec-adent,* and the rough rains and blustering winds of life, which a stronger man would have laughed at and enjoyed, were to him "hail-storms and fire-showers". After all, Messrs. Beit, the publishers, were only sharp men of business, and these terrible Dixons and Gervases and Colleys merely the ordinary limited clergy and gentry of a quiet country town; sturdier sense would have dismissed Dixon as an old humbug, Stanley Gervase, Esquire, J.P., as a "bit of a bounder", and the ladies as "rather a shoddy lot". But he was walking slowly now in painful silence, his heavy, lagging feet striking against the loose stones. He was not think-ing of the girl beside him; only something seemed to swell and grow and swell within his heart; it was all the torture of his days, weary hopes and weary disappointment, scorn rankling and throbbing, and the thought "I had rather call the devils my brothers and live with them in hell." He choked and gasped for breath, and felt involuntary muscles working in his face, and the impulses of a madman stirring him; he himself was in truth the realisation of the vision of Caermaen that night, a city with moldering walls beset by the ghostly legion. Life and the world and the laws of the sunlight had passed away, and the resurrection and kingdom of the dead began. The Celt assailed him, becoming from the weird wood he called the world, and his far-off ancestors, the "little people" crept out of their caves, muttering charms and incantations in hissing inhuman speech; he was beleaguered by desires that had slept in his race for ages.

"I am afraid you are very tired, Master Lucian. Would you like me to give you my hand over this rough bit?"

He had stumbled against a great round stone and had nearly fallen. The woman's hand sought his in the darkness; as he felt the touch of the soft warm flesh he moaned, and a pang shot through his arm to his heart. He looked up and found he had only walked a few paces since Annie had spoken; he had thought they had wandered for hours together. The moon was just mounting above the oaks, and the halo round the dark hill brightened. He stopped short, and keeping his hold of Annie's hand, looked into her face. A hazy glory of moonlight shone around them and lit up their eyes. He had not greatly altered since his boyhood; his face was pale olive in colour, thin and oval; marks of pain had gathered about the eyes, and his black hair was already stricken with grey. But the eager, curious gaze still remained, and what he saw before him lit up his sadness with a new fire. She stopped too, and did not offer to draw away, but looked back with all her heart. They were alike in many ways; her skin was also of that olive colour, but her face was sweet as a beautiful summer night, and her black eyes shewed no dimness, and the smile on the scarlet lips was like a flame when it brightens a dark and lonely land.

"You are sorely tired, Master Lucian, let us sit down here by the gate."

It was Lucian who spoke next: "My dear, my dear." And their lips were together again, and their arms locked together, each holding the other fast. And then the poor lad let his head sink down on his sweetheart's breast, and burst into a passion of weeping. The tears streamed down his face, and he shook with sobbing, in the happiest moment that he had ever lived. The woman bent over him and tried to comfort him, but his tears were his consolation and his triumph. Annie was whispering to him, her hand laid on his heart; she was whispering beautiful, wonderful words, that soothed him as a song. He did not know what they meant.

"Annie, dear, dear Annie, what are you saying to me? I have never heard such beautiful words. Tell me, Annie, what do they mean?"

She laughed, and said it was only nonsense that the nurses sang to the children.

"No, no, you are not to call me Master Lucian any more," he said, when they parted, "you must call me Lucian; and I, I worship you, my dear Annie."

He fell down before her, embracing her knees, and adored, and she allowed him, and confirmed his worship. He followed slowly after her, passing the path which led to her home with a longing glance. Nobody saw any difference in Lucian when he reached the rectory. He came in with his usual dreamy indifference, and told how he had lost his way by trying the short cut. He said he had met Dr. Burrows on the road, and that he had recommended the path by the fields. Then, as dully as if he had been reading some story out of a newspaper, he gave his father the outlines of the Beit case, producing the pretty little book called *The Chorus in Green*. The parson listened in amazement.

"You mean to tell me that *you* wrote this book?" he said. He was quite roused.

"No; not all of it. Look; that bit is mine, and that; and the beginning of this chapter. Nearly the whole of the third chapter is by me."

He closed the book without interest, and indeed he felt astonished at his father's excitement. The incident seemed to him unimportant.

"And you say that eighty or ninety pages of this book are yours, and these scoundrels have stolen your work?"

"Well, I suppose they have. I'll fetch the manuscript, if you would like to look at it."

The manuscript was duly produced, wrapped in brown paper, with Messrs. Beit's address label on it, and the post-office dated stamps.

"And the other book has been out a month." The parson, forgetting the sacerdotal office, and his good habit of grinning, swore at Messrs. Beit and Mr. Ritson, calling them damned thieves, and then began to read the manuscript, and to compare it with the printed book.

"Why, it's splendid work. My poor fellow," he said after a while, "I had no notion you could write so well. I used to think of such things in the old days at Oxford; 'old Bill', the tutor, used to praise my essays, but I never wrote anything like this. And this infernal ruffian of a Ritson has taken all your best things and mixed them up with his own rot to make it go down. Of course you'll expose the gang?"

Lucian was mildly amused; he couldn't enter into his father's feelings at all. He sat smoking in one of the old easy chairs, taking the rare relish of a hot grog with his pipe, and gazing out of his dreamy eyes at the violent old parson. He was pleased that his father liked his book, because he knew him to be a deep and sober scholar and a cool judge of good letters; but he laughed to himself when he saw the magic of print. The parson had expressed no wish to read the manuscript when it came back in disgrace; he had merely grinned, said something about boomerangs, and quoted Horace with relish. Whereas now, before the book in its neat case, lettered with another man's name, his approbation of the writing and his disapproval of the "scoundrels", as he called them, were loudly expressed, and, though a good smoker, he blew and puffed vehemently at his pipe.

"You'll expose the rascals, of course, won't you?" he said again.

"Oh no, I think not. It really doesn't matter much, does it? After all, there are some very weak things in the book; doesn't it strike you as 'young'? I have been thinking of another plan, but I haven't done much with it lately. But I believe I've got hold of a really good idea this time, and if I can manage to see the heart of it I hope to turn out a manuscript worth stealing. But it's so hard to get at the core of an idea—the heart, as I call it," he went on after a pause. "It's like having a box you can't open, though you know there's something wonderful inside. But I do believe I've a fine thing in my hands, and I mean to try my best to work it."

Lucian talked with enthusiasm now, but his father, on his side, could not share these ardours. It was his part to be astonished at excitement over a book that was not even begun, the mere ghost of a book flitting elusive in the world of unborn masterpieces and failures. He had loved good letters, but he shared unconsciously in the general belief that literary attempt is always pitiful, though he did not subscribe to the other half of the popular faith—that literary success is a matter of very little importance. He thought well of books, but only of printed books; in manuscripts he put no faith, and the *paulo-post-futurum* tense he could not in any manner conjugate. He returned once more to the topic of palpable interest.

"But about this dirty trick these fellows have played on you. You won't sit quietly and bear it, surely? It's only a question of writing to the papers."

"They wouldn't put the letter in. And if they did, I should only get laughed at. Some time ago a man wrote to the *Reader,* complaining of his play being stolen. He said that he had sent a little one-act comedy to Burleigh, the great dramatist, asking for his advice. Burleigh gave his advice and took the idea for his own very successful play. So the man said, and I daresay it was true enough. But the victim got nothing by his complaint. 'A pretty state of things,' everybody said. 'Here's a Mr. Tomson, that no one has ever heard of, bothers Burleigh with his rubbish, and then accuses him of petty larceny. Is it likely that a man of Burleigh's position, a playwright who can make his five thousand a year easily, would borrow from an unknown Tomson?' I should think it very likely, indeed," Lucian went on, chuckling, "but that was their verdict. No; I don't think I'll write to the papers."

"Well, well, my boy, I suppose you know your own business best. I think you are mistaken, but you must do as you like."

"It's all so unimportant," said Lucian, and he really thought so. He had sweeter things to dream of, and desired no communion of feeling with that madman who had left Caermaen some few hours before. He felt he had made a fool of himself, he was ashamed to think of the fatuity of which he had been guilty; such boiling hatred was not only wicked, but absurd. A man could do no good who put himself into a position of such violent antagonism against his fellow-creatures; so Lucian rebuked his heart, saying that he was old enough to know better. But he remembered that he had sweeter things to dream of; there was a secret ecstasy that he treasured and locked tight away, as a joy too exquisite even for thought till he was quite alone; and then there was that scheme for a new book that he had laid down hopelessly some time ago; it seemed to have arisen into life again within the last hour; he understood that he had started on a false tack, he had taken the wrong aspect of his idea. Of course the thing couldn't be written in that way; it was like trying to read a page turned upside down; and he saw those characters he had vainly sought suddenly disambushed, and a splendid inevitable sequence of events unrolled before him.

It was a true resurrection; the dry plot he had constructed revealed itself as a living thing, stirring and mysterious, and warm as life itself. The parson was smoking stolidly to all appearance, but in reality he was full of amazement at his own son, and now and again he slipped sly furtive glances towards the tranquil young man in the arm-chair by the empty hearth. In the first place, Mr. Taylor was genuinely impressed by what he had read of Lucian's work; he had so long been accustomed to look upon all effort as futile, that success amazed him. In the abstract, of course, he was prepared to admit that some people did write well and got published and made money, just as other persons successfully backed an outsider at heavy odds; but it had seemed as improbable that Lucian should shew even the beginnings of achievement in one direction as in the other. Then the boy evidently cared so little about it; he did not appear to be proud of being worth robbing, nor was he angry with the robbers.

He sat back luxuriously in the disreputable old chair, drawing long slow wreaths of smoke, tasting his whisky from time to time, and evidently well at ease with himself. The father saw him smile, and it suddenly dawned upon him that his son was very handsome; he had such kind gentle eyes and a kind mouth, and his pale cheeks were flushed like a girl's. Mr. Taylor felt moved. What a harmless young fellow Lucian had been; no doubt a little queer and different from others, but wholly inoffensive and patient under disappointment and Miss Deacon. Her contribution to the evening's discussion had been characteristic; she had remarked, firstly, that writing was a very unsettling occupation, and secondly, that it was extremely foolish to entrust one's property to people of whom one knew nothing. Father and son had smiled together at these observations, which were probably true enough. Mr. Taylor at last left Lucian alone; he shook hands with a good deal of respect, and said, almost deferentially:

"You mustn't work too hard, old fellow. I wouldn't stay up too late, if I were you, after that long walk. You must have gone miles out of your way."

"I'm not tired now, though. I feel as if I could write my new book on the spot"; and the young man laughed a gay sweet laugh that struck the father as a new note in his son's life.

He sat still a moment after his father had left the room. He cherished his chief treasure of thought in its secret place; he would not enjoy it yet. He drew up a chair to the table at which he wrote or tried to write, and began taking pens and paper from the drawer. There was a great pile of ruled paper there; all of it used, on one side, and signifying many hours of desperate scribbling, of heart-searching and rack of his brain; an array of poor, eager lines written by a waning fire with waning hope; all useless and abandoned. He took up the sheets cheerfully, and began in delicious idleness to look over these fruitless efforts. A page caught his attention; he remembered how he wrote it while a November storm was dashing against the panes; and there was another, with a queer blot in one corner; he had got up from his chair and looked out, and all the earth was white fairyland, and the snowflakes whirled round and round in the wind. Then he saw the chapter begun of a night in March: a great gale blew that night and rooted up one of the ancient yews in the churchyard. He had heard the trees shrieking in the woods, and the long wail of the wind, and across the heaven a white moon fled awfully before the streaming clouds. And all these poor abandoned pages now seemed sweet, and past unhappiness was transmuted into happiness, and the nights of toil were holy. He turned over half a dozen leaves and began to sketch out the outlines of the new book on the unused pages; running out a skeleton plan on one page, and dotting fancies, suggestions, hints on others. He wrote rapidly, overjoyed to find that loving phrases grew under his pen; a particular scene he had imagined filled him with desire; he gave his hand free course, and saw the written work glowing; and action and all the heat of existence quickened and beat on the wet page. Happy fancies took shape in happier words, and when at last he leant back in his chair he felt the stir and rush of the story as if it had been some portion of his own life. He read over what he had done with a renewed pleasure in the nimble and flowing workmanship, and as he put the little pile of manuscript tenderly in the drawer he paused to enjoy the anticipation of to-morrow's labour.

And then—but the rest of the night was given to tender and delicious things, and when he went up to bed a scarlet dawn was streaming from the east.

III

For days Lucian lay in a swoon of pleasure, smiling when he was addressed, sauntering happily in the sunlight, hugging recollection warm to his heart. Annie had told him that she was going on a visit to her married sister, and said, with a caress, that he must be patient. He protested against her absence, but she fondled him, whispering her charms in his ear till he gave in and then they said good-bye, Lucian adoring on his knees. The parting was as strange as the meeting, and that night when he laid his work aside, and let himself sink deep into the joys of memory, all the encounter seemed as wonderful and impossible as magic.

"And you really don't mean to do anything about those rascals?" said his father.

"Rascals? Which rascals? Oh, you mean Beit. I had forgotten all about it. No; I don't think I shall trouble. They're not worth powder and shot."

And he returned to his dream, pacing slowly from the medlar to the quince and back again. It seemed trivial to be interrupted by such questions; he had not even time to think of the book he had recommenced so eagerly, much less of this labour of long ago. He recollected without interest that it cost him many pains, that it was pretty good here and there, and that it had been stolen, and it seemed that there was nothing more to be said on the matter. He wished to think of the darkness in the lane, of the kind voice that spoke to him, of the kind hand that sought his own, as he stumbled on the rough way. So far, it was wonderful. Since he had left school and lost the company of the worthy barbarians who had befriended him there, he had almost lost the sense of kinship with humanity; he had come to dread the human form as men dread the hood of the cobra. To Lucian a man or a woman meant something that stung, that spoke words that rankled, and poisoned his life with scorn. At first such malignity shocked him: he would ponder over words and glances and wonder if he were not mistaken, and he still sought now and then for sympathy. The poor boy had romantic ideas about women; he believed they were merciful and pitiful, very kind to the unlucky and helpless. Men perhaps had to be different; after all, the duty of a man was to get on in the world, or, in plain language, to make money, to be successful; to cheat rather than to be cheated, but always to be successful; and he could understand that one who fell below this high standard must expect to be severely judged by his fellows. For example, there was young Bennett, Miss Spurry's nephew. Lucian had met him once or twice when he was spending his holidays with Miss Spurry, and the two young fellows compared literary notes together. Bennett shewed some beautiful things he had written, over which Lucian had grown both sad and enthusiastic. It was such exquisite magic verse, and so much better than anything he ever hoped to write, that there was a touch of anguish in his congratulations. But when Bennett, after many vain prayers to his aunt, threw up a safe position in the bank, and betook himself to a London garret, Lucian was not surprised at the general verdict.

Mr. Dixon, as a clergyman, viewed the question from a high standpoint and found it all deplorable, but the general opinion was that Bennett was a hopeless young lunatic. Old Mr. Gervase went purple when his name was mentioned, and the young Dixons sneered very merrily over the adventure.

"I always thought he was a beastly young ass," said Edward Dixon, "but I didn't think he'd chuck away his chances like that. Said he couldn't stand a bank! I hope he'll be able to stand bread and water. That's all those littery fellows get, I believe, except Tennyson and Mark Twain and those sort of people."

Lucian of course sympathised with the unfortunate Bennett, but such judgments were after all only natural. The young man might have stayed in the bank and succeeded to his aunt's thousand a year, and everybody would have called him a very nice young fellow—"clever, too." But he had deliberately chosen, as Edward Dixon had said, to chuck his chances away for the sake of literature; piety and a sense of the main chance had alike pointed the way to a delicate course of wheedling, to a little harmless practising on Miss Spurry's infirmities, to frequent compliances of a soothing nature, and the "young ass" had been blind to the direction of one and the other. It seemed almost right that the vicar should moralise, that Edward Dixon should sneer, and that Mr. Gervase should grow purple with contempt. Men, Lucian thought, were like judges, who may pity the criminal in their hearts, but are forced to vindicate the outraged majesty of the law by a severe sentence. He felt the same considerations applied to his own case; he knew that his father should have had more money, that his clothes should be newer and of a better cut, that he should have gone to the university and made good friends. If such had been his fortune he could have looked his fellow-men proudly in the face, upright and unashamed. Having put on the whole armour of a first-rate West End tailor, with money in his purse, having taken anxious thought for the morrow, and having some useful friends and good prospects; in such a case he might have held his head high in a gentlemanly and Christian community. As it was he had usually avoided the reproachful glance of his fellows, feeling that he deserved their condemnation. But he had cherished for a long time his romantic sentimentalities about women; literary conventions borrowed from the minor poets and pseudo-mediævalists, or so he thought afterwards. But, fresh from school, wearied a little with the perpetual society of barbarian though worthy boys, he had in his soul a charming image of womanhood, before which he worshipped with mingled passion and devotion. It was a nude figure, perhaps, but the shining arms were to be wound about the neck of a vanquished knight, there was rest for the head of a wounded lover; the hands were stretched forth to do works of pity, and the smiling lips were to murmur not love alone, but consolation in defeat. Here was the refuge for a broken heart; here the scorn of men would but make tenderness increase; here was all pity and all charity with loving-kindness. It was a delightful picture, conceived in the "come rest on this bosom", and "a ministering angel thou" manner, with touches of allurement that made devotion all the sweeter. He soon found that he had idealised a little; in the affair of young Bennett, while the men were contemptuous the women were virulent. He had been rather fond of Agatha Gervase, and she, so other ladies said, had "set her cap" at him. Now, when he rebelled, and lost the goodwill of his aunt, dear Miss Spurry, Agatha insulted him with all conceivable rapidity. "After all, Mr. Bennett," she said, "you will be nothing better than a beggar; now will you? You mustn't think me cruel, but I can't help speaking the truth. *Write books!*" Her expression filled up the incomplete sentence; she waggled with indignant emotion. These passages came to Lucian's ears, and indeed the Gervases boasted of "how well poor Agatha had behaved".

"Never mind, Gathy," old Gervase had observed. "If the impudent young puppy comes here again, we'll see what Thomas can do with the horse-whip."

"Poor dear child," Mrs. Gervase added in telling the tale, "and she was so fond of him too. But of course it couldn't go on after his shameful behaviour."

But Lucian was troubled; he sought vainly for the ideal womanly, the tender note of "come rest on this bosom". Ministering angels, he felt convinced, do not rub red pepper and sulphuric acid into the wounds of suffering mortals.

Then there was the case of Mr. Vaughan, a squire in the neighbourhood, at whose board all the aristocracy of Caermaen had feasted for years. Mr. Vaughan had a first-rate cook, and his cellar was rare, and he was never so happy as when he shared his good things with his friends. His mother kept his house, and they delighted all the girls with frequent dances, while the men sighed over the amazing champagne. Investments proved disastrous, and Mr. Vaughan had to sell the grey manor-house by the river. He and his mother took a little modern stucco villa in Caermaen, wishing to be near their dear friends. But the men were "very sorry; rough on you, Vaughan. Always thought those Patagonians were risky, but you wouldn't hear of it. Hope we shall see you before very long; you and Mrs. Vaughan must come to tea some day after Christmas."

"Of course we are all very sorry for them," said Henrietta Dixon. "No, we haven't called on Mrs. Vaughan yet. They have no regular servant, you know; only a woman in the morning. I hear old mother Vaughan, as Edward will call her, does nearly everything. And their house is absurdly small; it's little more than a cottage. One really can't call it a gentleman's house."

Then Mr. Vaughan, his heart in the dust, went to the Gervases and tried to borrow five pounds of Mr. Gervase. He had to be ordered out of the house, and, as Edith Gervase said, it was all very painful; "he went out in such a funny way," she added, "just like the dog when he's had a whipping. Of course it's sad, even if it is all his own fault, as everybody says, but he looked so ridiculous as he was going down the steps that I couldn't help laughing." Mr. Vaughan heard the ringing, youthful laughter as he crossed the lawn.

Young girls like Henrietta Dixon and Edith Gervase naturally viewed the Vaughans' comical position with all the high spirits of their age, but the elder ladies could not look at matters in this frivolous light.

"Hush, dear, hush," said Mrs. Gervase, "it's all too shocking to be a laughing matter. Don't you agree with me, Mrs. Dixon? The sinful extravagance that went on at Pentre always *frightened* me. You remember that ball they gave last year? Mr. Gervase assured me that the champagne must have cost *at least* a hundred and fifty shillings the dozen."

"It's dreadful, isn't it," said Mrs. Dixon, "when one thinks of how many poor people there are who would be thankful for a crust of bread?"

"Yes, Mrs. Dixon," Agatha joined in, "and you know how absurdly the Vaughans spoilt the cottagers. Oh, it was really wicked; one would think Mr. Vaughan wished to make them above their station. Edith and I went for a walk one day nearly as far as Pentre, and we begged a glass of water of old Mrs. Jones who lives in that pretty cottage near the brook. She began praising the Vaughans in the most fulsome manner, and shewed us some flannel things they had given her at Christmas. I assure you, my dear Mrs. Dixon, the flannel was the very best quality; no lady could wish for better. It couldn't have cost less than half-a-crown a yard."

"I know, my dear, I know. Mr. Dixon always said it couldn't last. How often I have heard him say that the Vaughans were pauperising all the common people about Pentre, and putting every one else in a most unpleasant position. Even from a worldly point of view it was very poor taste on their part. So different from the *true* charity that Paul speaks of."

"I only wish they had given away nothing worse than flannel," said Miss Colley, a young lady of very strict views. "But I assure you there was a perfect orgy, I can call it nothing else, every Christmas. Great joints of prime beef, and barrels of strong beer, and snuff and tobacco distributed wholesale; as if the poor wanted to be encouraged in their disgusting habits. It was really impossible to go through the village for weeks after; the whole place was poisoned with the fumes of horrid tobacco pipes."

"Well, we see how that sort of thing ends," said Mrs. Dixon, summing up judicially. "We had intended to call, but I really think it would be impossible after what Mrs. Gervase has told us. The idea of Mr. Vaughan trying to sponge on poor Mr. Gervase in that shabby way! I think meanness of that kind is so hateful."

It was the practical side of all this that astonished Lucian. He saw that in reality there was no high-flown quixotism in a woman's nature; the smooth arms, made he had thought for caressing, seemed muscular; the hands meant for the doing of works of pity in his system, appeared dexterous in the giving of "stingers", as Barnes might say, and the smiling lips could sneer with great ease. Nor was he more fortunate in his personal experiences. As has been told, Mrs. Dixon spoke of him in connection with "judgments", and the younger ladies did not exactly cultivate his acquaintance. Theoretically they "adored" books and thought poetry "too sweet", but in practice they preferred talking about mares and fox-terriers and their neighbours.

They were nice girls enough, very like other young ladies in other country towns, content with the teaching of their parents, reading the Bible every morning in their bedrooms, and sitting every Sunday in church amongst the well-dressed "sheep" on the right hand. It was not their fault if they failed to satisfy the ideal of an enthusiastic dreamy boy, and indeed, they would have thought his feigned woman immodest, absurdly sentimental, a fright ("never wears stays, my dear") and *horrid*.

At first he was a good deal grieved at the loss of that charming tender woman, the work of his brain. When the Miss Dixons went haughtily by with a scornful waggle, when the Miss Gervases passed in the wagonette laughing as the mud splashed him, the poor fellow would look up with a face of grief that must have been very comic; "like a dying duck", as Edith Gervase said. Edith was really very pretty, and he would have liked to talk to her, even about fox-terriers, if she would have listened. One afternoon at the Dixons' he really forced himself upon her, and with all the obtuseness of an enthusiastic boy tried to discuss the *Lotus Eaters* of Tennyson. It was too absurd. Captain Kempton was making signals to Edith all the time, and Lieutenant Gatwick had gone off in disgust, and he had promised to bring her a puppy "by Vick out of Wasp". At last the poor girl could bear it no longer:

"Yes, it's very sweet," she said at last. "When did you say you were going to London, Mr. Taylor?"

It was about the time that his disappointment became known to everybody, and the shot told. He gave her a piteous look and slunk off, "just like the dog when he's had a whipping", to use Edith's own expression. Two or three lessons of this description produced their due effect; and when he saw a male Dixon or Gervase approaching him he bit his lip and summoned up his courage. But when he descried a "ministering angel" he made haste and hid behind a hedge or took to the woods. In course of time the desire to escape became an instinct, to be followed as a matter of course; in the same way he avoided the adders on the mountain. His old ideals were almost if not quite forgotten; he knew that the female of the *bête humaine,* like the adder, would in all probability sting, and he therefore shrank from its trail, but without any feeling of special resentment. The one had a poisoned tongue as the other had a poisoned fang, and it was well to leave them both alone. Then had come that sudden fury of rage against all humanity, as he went out of Caermaen carrying the book that had been stolen from him by the enterprising Beit. He shuddered as he thought of how nearly he had approached the verge of madness, when his eyes filled with blood and the earth seemed to burn with fire. He remembered how he had looked up to the horizon and the sky was blotched with scarlet; and the earth was deep red, with red woods and red fields. There was something of horror in the memory, and in the vision of that wild night walk through dim country, when every shadow seemed a symbol of some terrible impending doom. The murmur of the brook, the wind shrilling through the wood, the pale light flowing from the mouldered trunks, and the picture of his own figure fleeing and fleeting through the shades; all these seemed unhappy things that told a story in fatal hieroglyphics. And then the life and laws of the sunlight had passed away, and the resurrection and kingdom of the dead began. Though his limbs were weary, he had felt his muscles grow strong as steel; a woman, one of the hated race, was beside him in the darkness, and the wild beast woke within him, ravening for blood and brutal lust; all the raging desires of the dim race from which he came assailed his heart. The ghosts issued out from the weird wood and from the caves in the hills, besieging him, as he had imagined the spiritual legion besieging

Caermaen, beckoning him to a hideous battle and a victory that he had never imagined in his wildest dreams. And then out of the darkness the kind voice spoke again, and the kind hand was stretched out to draw him up from the pit. It was sweet to think of that which he had found at last; the boy's picture incarnate, all the passion and compassion of his longing, all the pity and love and consolation. She, that beautiful passionate woman offering up her beauty in sacrifice to him, she was worthy indeed of his worship. He remembered how his tears had fallen upon her breast, and how tenderly she had soothed him, whispering those wonderful unknown words that sang to his heart. And she had made herself defenceless before him, caressing and fondling the body that had been so despised. He exulted in the happy thought that he had knelt down on the ground before her, and had embraced her knees and worshipped. The woman's body had become his religion; he lay awake at night looking into the darkness with hungry eyes, wishing for a miracle, that the appearance of the so-desired form might be shaped before him. And when he was alone in quiet places in the wood, he fell down again on his knees, and even on his face, stretching out vain hands in the air, as if they would feel her flesh. His father noticed in those days that the inner pocket of his coat was stuffed with papers; he would see Lucian walking up and down in a secret shady place at the bottom of the orchard, reading from his sheaf of manuscript, replacing the leaves, and again drawing them out. He would walk a few quick steps, and pause as if enraptured, gazing in the air as if he looked through the shadows of the world into some sphere of glory, feigned by his thought. Mr. Taylor was almost alarmed at the sight; he concluded of course that Lucian was writing a book. In the first place, there seemed something immodest in seeing the operation performed under one's eyes; it was as if the "make-up" of a beautiful actress were done on the stage, in full audience; as if one saw the rounded calves fixed in position, the fleshings drawn on, the voluptuous outlines of the figure produced by means purely mechanical, blushes mantling from the paint-pot, and the golden tresses well secured by the wigmaker. Books, Mr. Taylor thought, should swim into one's ken mysteriously; they should appear all printed and bound, without apparent genesis; just as children are suddenly told that they have a little sister, found by mamma in the garden. But Lucian was not only engaged in composition; he was plainly rapturous, enthusiastic; Mr. Taylor saw him throw up his hands, and bow his head with strange gesture. The parson began to fear that his son was like some of those mad Frenchmen of whom he had read, young fellows who had a sort of fury of literature, and gave their whole lives to it, spending days over a page, and years over a book, pursuing art as Englishmen pursue money, building up a romance as if it were a business. Now Mr. Taylor held firmly by the "walking-stick" theory; he believed that a man of letters should have a real profession, some solid employment in life. "Get something to do," he would have liked to say, "and then you can write as much as you please. Look at Scott, look at Dickens and Trollope." And then there was the social point of view; it might be right, or it might be wrong, but there could be no doubt that the literary man, as such, was not thought much of in English society. Mr. Taylor knew his Thackeray, and he remembered that old Major Pendennis, society personified, did not exactly boast of his nephew's occupation. Even Warrington was rather ashamed to own his connection with journalism, and Pendennis himself laughed openly at his novel-writing as an agreeable way of making money, a useful appendage to the cultivation of dukes, his true business in life. This was the plain English view, and Mr. Taylor was no doubt right enough in thinking it good, practical common sense. Therefore when he saw Lucian loitering and sauntering, musing amorously over his manuscript, exhibiting manifest signs of that fine fury which Britons have ever found absurd, he felt grieved at heart, and more than ever sorry that he had not been able to send the boy to Oxford.

"B.N.C. would have knocked all this nonsense out of him," he thought. "He would have taken a double First like my poor father and made something of a figure in the world. However, it can't be helped." The poor man sighed, and lit his pipe, and walked in another part of the garden.

But he was mistaken in his diagnosis of the symptoms. The book that Lucian had begun lay unheeded in the drawer; it was a secret work that he was engaged on, and the manuscripts that he took out of that inner pocket never left him day or night. He slept with them next to his heart, and he would kiss them when he was quite alone, and pay them such devotion as he would have paid to her whom they symbolised. He wrote on these leaves a wonderful ritual of praise and devotion; it was the liturgy of his religion. Again and again he copied and recopied this madness of a lover; dallying all days over the choice of a word, searching for more exquisite phrases. No common words, no such phrases as he might use in a tale would suffice; the sentences of worship must stir and be quickened, they must glow and burn, and be decked out as with rare work of jewellery. Every part of that holy and beautiful body must be adored; he sought for terms of extravagant praise, he bent his soul and mind low before her, licking the dust under her feet, abased and yet rejoicing as a Templar before the image of Baphomet. He exulted more especially in the knowledge that there was nothing of the conventional or common in his ecstasy; he was not the fervent, adoring lover of Tennyson's poems, who loves with passion and yet with a proud respect, with the love always of a gentleman for a lady. Annie was not a lady; the Morgans had farmed their land for hundreds of years; they were what Miss Gervase and Miss Colley and the rest of them called common people. Tennyson's noble gentleman thought of their ladies with something of reticence: they imagined them dressed in flowing and courtly robes, walking with slow dignity; they dreamed of them as always stately, the future mistresses of their houses, mothers of their heirs. Such lovers bowed, but not too low, remembering their own honour, before those who were to be equal companions and friends as well as wives. It was not such conceptions as these that he embodied in the amazing emblems of his ritual; he was not, he told himself, a young officer, "something in the city", or a rising barrister engaged to a Miss Dixon or a Miss Gervase. He had not thought of looking out for a nice little house in a good residential suburb where they would have pleasant society; there were to be no consultations about wall papers, or jocose whispers from friends as to the necessity of having a room that would do for a nursery. No glad young thing had leant on his arm while they chose the suite in white enamel, and china for "our bedroom", the modest salesman doing his best to spare their blushes. When Edith Gervase married she would get mamma to look out for two really good servants, "as we must begin quietly", and mamma would make sure that the drains and everything were right. Then her "girl friends" would come on a certain solemn day to see all her "lovely things". "Two dozen of everything!" "Look,

Ethel, did you ever see such ducky frills?" "And that insertion, isn't it quite too sweet?" "My dear Edith, you are a lucky girl." "All the under-linen specially made by Madame Lulu!" "What delicious things!" "I hope he knows what a prize he is winning." "Oh! do look at those lovely ribbon-bows!" "You darling, how happy you must be." "Real Valenciennes!" Then a whisper in the lady's ear, and her reply, "Oh, *don't,* Nelly!" So they would chirp over their treasures, as in Rabelais they chirped over their cups: and every thing would be done in due order till the wedding-day, when mamma, who had strained her sinews and the commandments to bring the match about, would weep and look indig-nantly at the unhappy bridegroom. "I *hope* you'll be kind to her, Robert." Then in a rapid whisper to the bride: "Mind, you *insist* on Wyman's flushing the drains when you come back; servants are so careless and dirty too. Don't let him go about by himself in Paris. Men are so *queer;* one never knows. You *have* got the pills?" And aloud, after these *secreta,* "God bless you, my dear; good-bye! *cluck, cluck,* good-bye!"

There were stranger things written in the manuscript pages that Lucian cherished, sentences that burnt and glowed like "coals of fire which hath a most vehement flame". There were phrases that stung and tingled as he wrote them, and sonorous words poured out in ec-stasy and rapture, as in some of the old litanies. He hugged the thought that a great part of what he had invented was in the true sense of the word occult: page after page might have been read aloud to the uniniti-ated without betraying the inner meaning. He dreamed night and day over these symbols, he copied and re-copied the manuscript nine times before he wrote it out fairly in a little book which he made himself of a skin of creamy vellum. In his mania for acquirements that should be entirely useless he had gained some skill in illumination, or limning as he preferred to call it, always choosing the obscurer word as the ob-scurer arts. First he set himself to the severe practice of the text; he spent many hours and days of toil in struggling to fashion the serried columns of black letter, writing and re-writing till he could shape the massive character with firm true hand. He cut his quills with the pa-tience of a monk in the scriptorium, shaving and altering the nib, light-ening and increasing the pressure and flexibility of the points, till the pen satisfied him, and gave a stroke both broad and even. Then he made experiments in inks, searching for some medium that would rival the glossy black letter of the old manuscripts; and not till he could produce a fair page of text did he turn to the more entrancing labour of the capitals and borders and ornaments. He mused long over the Lombardic letters, as glorious in their way as a cathedral, and trained his hand to execute the bold and flowing lines; and then there was the art of the border, blossoming in fretted splendour all about the page. His cousin, Miss Deacon, called it all a great waste of time, and his father thought he would have done much better in trying to improve his ordinary handwriting, which was both ugly and illegible. Indeed, there seemed but a poor demand for the limner's art. He sent some specimens of his skill to an "artistic firm" in London; a verse of the "Maud", curiously emblazoned, and a Latin hymn with the notes priced on a red stave. The firm wrote civilly, telling him that his work, though good, was not what they wanted, and enclosing an illuminated text. "We have great demand for this sort of thing," they concluded, "and if you care to attempt something in this style we should be pleased to look at it." The said text was "Thou, God, seest me." The letter was of a degraded form, bearing much the same relation to the true character as a "churchwarden gothic" building does to Canterbury Cathedral; the colours were varied. The initial was pale gold, the *h* pink, the *o* black, the *u* blue, and the first letter was somehow connected with a bird's nest containing the young of the pigeon, who were waited on by the female bird.

"What a pretty text," said Miss Deacon. "I should like to nail it up in my room. Why don't you try to do something like that, Lucian? You might make something by it."

"I sent them these," said Lucian, "but they don't like them much."

"My dear boy! I should think not! Like them! What were you thinking of to draw those queer stiff flowers all round the border? Roses? They don't look like roses at all events. Where do you get such ideas from?"

"But the design is appropriate; look at the words."

"My dear Lucian, I can't read the words; it's such a queer old-fashioned writing. Look how plain that text is; one can see what it's about. And this other one; I can't make it out at all."

"It's a Latin hymn."

"A Latin hymn? Is it a Protestant hymn? I may be old-fashioned,

but *Hymns Ancient and Modern* is quite good enough for me. This is the
music, I suppose? But, my dear boy, there are only four lines, and who
ever heard of notes shaped like that: you have made some square and
some diamond-shape? Why didn't you look in your poor mother's old
music? It's in the ottoman in the drawing-room. I could have shewn you
how to make the notes; there are crotchets, you know, and quavers."

Miss Deacon laid down the illuminated *Urbs Beata* in despair; she
felt convinced that her cousin was "next door to an idiot".

And he went out into the garden and raged behind a hedge. He
broke two flower-pots and hit an apple-tree very hard with his stick,
and then, feeling more calm, wondered what was the use in trying to
do anything. He would not have put the thought into words, but in his
heart he was aggrieved that his cousin liked the pigeons and the text,
and did not like his emblematical roses and the Latin hymn. He knew
he had taken great pains over the work, and that it was well done, and
being still a young man he expected praise. He found that in this hard
world there was a lack of appreciation; a critical spirit seemed abroad.
If he could have been scientifically observed as he writhed and smarted
under the strictures of "the old fool", as he rudely called his cousin,
the spectacle would have been extremely diverting. Little boys sometimes enjoy a very similar entertainment; either with their tiny fingers
or with mamma's nail scissors they gradually deprive a fly of its wings
and legs. The odd gyrations and queer thin buzzings of the creature as
it spins comically round and round never fail to provide a fund of
harmless amusement. Lucian, indeed, fancied himself a very ill-used
individual; but he should have tried to imitate the nervous organisation
of the flies, which, as mamma says, "can't really feel".

But now, as he prepared the vellum leaves, he remembered his art
with joy; he had not laboured to do beautiful work in vain. He read
over his manuscript once more, and thought of the designing of the
pages. He made sketches on furtive sheets of paper, and hunted up
books in his father's library for suggestions. There were books about
architecture, and mediæval iron work, and brasses which contributed
hints for adornment; and not content with mere pictures he sought in
the woods and hedges, scanning the strange forms of trees, and the
poisonous growth of great water-plants, and the parasite twining of
honeysuckle and briony. In one of these rambles he discovered a red

earth which he made into a pigment, and he found in the unctuous juice of a certain fern an ingredient which he thought made his black ink still more glossy. His book was written all in symbols, and in the same spirit of symbolism he decorated it, causing wonderful foliage to creep about the text, and shewing the blossom of certain mystical flowers, with emblems of strange creatures, caught and bound in rose thickets. All was dedicated to love and a lover's madness, and there were songs in it which haunted him with their lilt and refrain. When the book was finished it replaced the loose leaves as his constant companion by day and night. Three times a day he repeated his ritual to himself, seeking out the loneliest places in the woods, or going up to his room; and from the fixed intentness and rapture of his gaze, the father thought him still severely employed in the questionable process of composition. At night he contrived to wake for his strange courtship; and he had a peculiar ceremony when he got up in the dark and lit his candle. From a steep and wild hillside, not far from the house, he had cut from time to time five large boughs of spiked and prickly gorse. He had brought them into the house, one by one, and had hidden them in the big box that stood beside his bed. Often he woke up weeping and murmuring to himself the words of one of his songs, and then when he had lit the candle, he would draw out the gorse-boughs, and place them on the floor, and taking off his nightgown, gently lay himself down on the bed of thorns and spines. Lying on his face, with the candle and the book before him, he would softly and tenderly repeat the praises of his dear, dear Annie, and as he turned over page after page, and saw the raised gold of the majuscules glow and flame in the candle-light, he pressed the thorns into his flesh. At such moments he tasted in all its acute savour the joy of physical pain; and after two or three experiences of such delights he altered his book, making a curious sign in vermilion on the margin of the passages where he was to inflict on himself this sweet torture. Never did he fail to wake at the appointed hour, a strong effort of will broke through all the heaviness of sleep, and he would rise up, joyful though weeping, and reverently set his thorny bed upon the floor, offering his pain with his praise. When he had whispered the last word, and had risen from the ground, his body would be all freckled with drops of blood; he used to view the marks with pride. Here and there a spine would be left deep in the flesh, and he would pull these out roughly, tearing through the skin. On some nights when he had pressed with more fervour on the thorns his thighs would stream with blood, red beads standing out on the flesh, and trickling down to his feet. He had some difficulty in washing away the bloodstains so as not to leave any traces to attract the attention of the servant; and after a time he returned no more to his bed when his duty had been accomplished. For a coverlet he had a dark rug, a good deal worn, and in this he would wrap his naked bleeding body, and lie down on the hard floor, well content to add an aching rest to the account of his pleasures. He was covered with scars, and those that healed during the day were torn open afresh at night; the pale olive skin was red with the angry marks of blood, and the graceful form of the young man appeared like the body of a tortured martyr. He grew thinner and thinner every day, for he ate but little; the skin was stretched on the bones of his face, and the black eyes burnt in dark purple hollows. His relations noticed that he was not looking well.

"Now, Lucian, it's perfect madness of you to go on like this," said Miss Deacon, one morning at breakfast. "Look how your hand shakes; some people would say that you have been taking brandy. And all that you want is a little medicine, and yet you won't be advised. You know it's not my fault; I have asked you to try Dr. Jelly's Cooling Powders again and again."

He remembered the forcible exhibition of the powders when he was a boy, and felt thankful that those days were over. He only grinned at his cousin and swallowed a great cup of strong tea to steady his nerves, which were shaky enough. Mrs. Dixon saw him one day in Caermaen; it was very hot, and he had been walking rather fast. The scars on his body burnt and tingled, and he tottered as he raised his hat to the vicar's wife. She decided without further investigation that he must have been drinking in public-houses.

"It seems a mercy that poor Mrs. Taylor was taken," she said to her husband. "She has certainly been spared a great deal. That wretched young man passed me this afternoon; he was quite intoxicated."

"How very sad," said Mr. Dixon. "A little port, my dear?"

"Thank you, Merivale, I will have another glass of sherry. Dr. Burrows is always scolding me and saying I *must* take something to keep up my energy, and this sherry is so weak."

The Dixons were not teetotalers. They regretted it deeply, and blamed the doctor, who "insisted on some stimulant". However, there was some consolation in trying to convert the parish to total abstinence, or, as they curiously called it, temperance. Old women were warned of the sin of taking a glass of beer for supper; aged labourers were urged to try Cork-ho, the new temperance drink; an uncouth beverage, styled coffee, was dispensed at the reading-room. Mr. Dixon preached an eloquent "temperance" sermon, soon after the above conversation, taking as his text: *Beware of the leaven of the Pharisees.* In his discourse he shewed that fermented liquor and leaven had much in common, that beer was at the present day "put away" during Passover by the strict Jews; and in a moving peroration he urged his dear brethren, "and more especially those amongst us who are poor in this world's goods", to beware indeed of that evil leaven which was sapping the manhood of our nation. Mrs. Dixon cried after church:

"Oh, Merivale, what a beautiful sermon! How earnest you were. I hope it will do good."

Mr. Dixon swallowed his port with great decorum, but his wife fuddled herself every evening with cheap sherry. She was quite unaware of the fact, and sometimes wondered in a dim way why she always had to scold the children after dinner. And so strange things sometimes happened in the nursery, and now and then the children looked queerly at one another after a red-faced woman had gone out, panting.

Lucian knew nothing of his accuser's trials, but he was not long in hearing of his own intoxication. The next time he went down to Caermaen he was hailed by the doctor.

"Been drinking again to-day?"

"No," said Lucian in a puzzled voice. "What do you mean?"

"Oh, well, if you haven't, that's all right, as you'll be able to take a drop with me. Come along in?"

Over the whisky and pipes Lucian heard of the evil rumours affecting his character.

"Mrs. Dixon assured me you were staggering from one side of the street to the other. You quite frightened her, she said. Then she asked me if I recommended her to take one or two ounces of spirit at bedtime for the palpitation; and of course I told her two would be better. I have my living to make here, you know. And upon my word, I think she wants it; she's always gurgling inside like a waterworks. I wonder how old Dixon can stand it."

"I like 'ounces of spirit'," said Lucian. "That's taking it medicinally, I suppose. I've often heard of ladies who have to 'take it medicinally'; and that's how it's done?"

"That's it. 'Dr. Burrows won't *listen* to me': 'I tell him how I dislike the taste of spirits, but he says they are absolutely *necessary* for my constitution': 'my medical man *insists* on something at bedtime'; that's the style."

Lucian laughed gently; all these people had become indifferent to him; he could no longer feel savage indignation at their little hypocrisies and malignancies. Their voices uttering calumny, and morality, and futility had become like the thin shrill angry note of a gnat on a summer evening; he had his own thoughts and his own life, and he passed on without heeding.

"You come down to Caermaen pretty often, don't you?" said the doctor. "I've seen you two or three times in the last fortnight."

"Yes, I enjoy the walk."

"Well, look me up whenever you like, you know. I am often in just at this time, and a chat with a human being isn't bad, now and then. It's a change for me: I'm often afraid I shall lose my patients."

The doctor had the weakness of these terrible puns, dragged headlong into the conversation. He sometimes exhibited them before Mrs. Gervase, who would smile in a faint and dignified manner, and say:

"Ah, I see. Very amusing indeed. We had an old coachmen once who was very clever, I believe, at that sort of thing, but Mr. Gervase was obliged to send him away, the laughter of the other domestics was so very boisterous."

Lucian laughed, not boisterously, but good-humouredly, at the doctor's joke. He liked Burrows, feeling that he was a man and not an automatic gabbling machine.

"You look a little pulled down," said the doctor, when Lucian rose to go. "No, you don't want my medicine. Plenty of beef and beer will do you more good than drugs. I daresay it's the hot weather that has thinned you a bit. Oh, you'll be all right again in a month."

As Lucian strolled out of the town on his way home, he passed a

small crowd of urchins assembled at the corner of an orchard. They
were enjoying themselves immensely. The "healthy" boy, the same
whom he had seen some weeks ago operating on a cat, seemed to have
recognised his selfishness in keeping his amusements to himself. He
had found a poor lost puppy, a little creature with bright pitiful eyes,
almost human in their fond friendly gaze. It was not a well-bred little
dog; it was certainly not that famous puppy "by Vick out of Wasp"; it
had rough hair and a foolish long tail which it wagged beseechingly, at
once deprecating severity and asking kindness. The poor animal had
evidently been used to gentle treatment; it would look up in a boy's
face, and give a leap, fawning on him, and then bark in a small doubtful voice, and cower a moment on the ground, astonished perhaps at
the strangeness, the bustle and animation. The boys were beside themselves with eagerness; there was quite a babble of voices, arguing, discussing, suggesting. Each one had a plan of his own which he brought
before the leader, a stout and sturdy youth.

"Drown him! What be you thinkin' of, mun?" he was saying.
"'Tain't no sport at all. You shut your mouth, gwaes. Be you goin' to
ask your mother for the boiling water? Iss, Bob Williams, I do know all
that: but where be you a-going to get the fire from? Be quiet, mun,
can't you? Thomas Trevor, be this dog yourn or mine? Now, look you,
if you don't all of you shut your bloody mouths, I'll take the dog 'ome
and keep him. There now!"

He was a born leader of men. A singular depression and lowness
of spirit shewed itself on the boys' faces. They recognised that the
threat might very possibly be executed, and their countenances were at
once composed to humble attention. The puppy was still cowering on
the ground in the midst of them: one or two tried to relieve the tension
of their feelings by kicking him in the belly with their hobnail boots. It
cried out with the pain and writhed a little, but the poor little beast did
not attempt to bite or even snarl. It looked up with those beseeching
friendly eyes at its persecutors, and fawned on them again, and tried to
wag its tail and be merry, pretending to play with a straw on the road,
hoping perhaps to win a little favour in that way.

The leader saw the moment for his master-stroke. He slowly drew
a piece of rope from his pocket.

"What do you say to that, mun? Now, Thomas Trevor! We'll hang him over that there bough. Will that suit you, Bobby Williams?"

There was a great shriek of approval and delight. All was again bustle and animation. "I'll tie it round his neck?" "Get out, mun, you don't know how it be done." "Iss, I do, Charley." "Now, let me, gwaes, now do let me." "You be sure he won't bite?" "He bain't mad, be he?" "Suppose we were to tie up his mouth first?"

The puppy still fawned and curried favour, and wagged that sorry tail, and lay down crouching on one side on the ground, sad and sorry in his heart, but still with a little gleam of hope; for now and again he tried to play, and put up his face, praying with those fond, friendly eyes. And then at last his gambols and poor efforts for mercy ceased, and he lifted up his wretched voice in one long dismal whine of despair. But he licked the hand of the boy that tied the noose.

He was slowly and gently swung into the air as Lucian went by unheeded; he struggled, and his legs twisted and writhed. The "healthy" boy pulled the rope, and his friends danced and shouted with glee. As Lucian turned the corner, the poor dangling body was swinging to and fro, the puppy was dying, but he still kicked a little.

Lucian went on his way hastily, and shuddering with disgust. The young of the human creature were really too horrible; they defiled the earth, and made existence unpleasant, as the pulpy growth of a noxious and obscene fungus spoils an agreeable walk. The sight of those malignant little animals with mouths that uttered cruelty and filth, with hands dexterous in torture, and feet swift to run all evil errands, had given him a shock and broken up the world of strange thoughts in which he had been dwelling. Yet it was no good being angry with them: it was their nature to be very loathsome. Only he wished they would go about their hideous amusements in their own back gardens where nobody could see them at work; it was too bad that he should be interrupted and offended in a quiet country road. He tried to put the incident out of his mind, as if the whole thing had been a disagreeable story, and the visions amongst which he wished to move were beginning to return, when he was again rudely disturbed. A little girl, a pretty child of eight or nine, was coming along the lane to meet him. She was crying bitterly and looking to left and right, and calling out some word all the time.

"Jack, Jack, Jack! Little Jackie! Jack!"

Then she burst into tears afresh, and peered into the hedge, and tried to peep through a gate into a field.

"Jackie, Jackie, Jackie!"

She came up to Lucian, sobbing as if her heart would break, and dropped him an old-fashioned curtsy.

"Oh, please sir, have you seen my little Jackie?"

"What do you mean?" said Lucian. "What is it you've lost?"

"A little dog, please sir. A little tarrier dog with white hair. Father gave me him a month ago, and said I might keep him. Some one did leave the garden gate open this afternoon, and he must 'a got away, sir, and I was so fond of him sir, he was so playful and loving, and I be afraid he be lost."

She began to call again, without waiting for an answer.

"Jack, Jack, Jack!"

"I'm afraid some boys have got your little dog," said Lucian. "They've killed him. You'd better go back home."

He went on, walking as fast as he could in his endeavour to get beyond the noise of the child's crying. It distressed him, and he wished to think of other things. He stamped his foot angrily on the ground as he recalled the annoyances of the afternoon, and longed for some hermitage on the mountains, far above the stench and the sound of humanity.

A little farther, and he came to Croeswen, where the road branched off to right and left. There was a triangular plot of grass between the two roads; there the cross had once stood, "the goodly and famous roode" of the old local chronicle. The words echoed in Lucian's ears as he went by on the right hand. "There were five steps that did go up to the first pace, and seven steps to the second pace, all of clene hewn ashler. And all above it was most curiously and gloriously wrought with thorowgh carved work; in the highest place was the Holy Roode with Christ upon the Cross having Marie on the one syde and John on the other. And below were six splendent and glisteringe archaungels tha bore up the roode, and beneath them in their stories were the most fair and noble images of the xij Apostles and of divers other Saints and Martirs. And in the lowest storie there was a marvellous imagerie of divers Beasts, such as oxen and horses and swine, and little dogs and peacocks, all done in the finest and most curious wise, so that they all seemed as they were caught in a Wood of Thorns, the which is their torment of this life. And here once in the year was a marvellous solemn service, when the parson of Caermaen came out with the singers and all the people, singing the psalm *Benedicite omnia opera* as they passed along the road in their procession. And when they stood at the roode the priest did there his service, making certain prayers for the beasts, and then he went up to the first pace and preached a sermon to the people, shewing them that as our lord Jhu dyed upon the Tree of his deare mercy for us, so we too owe mercy to the beasts his Creatures, for that they are all his poor lieges and silly servants. And that like as the Holy Aungells do their suit to him on high, and the Blessed xij Apostles and the Martirs, and all the Blissful Saints served him aforetime on earth and now praise him in heaven, so also do the beasts serve him, though they be in torment of life and below men. For their spirit goeth downward, as Holy Writ teacheth us."

It was a quaint old record, a curious relic of what the modern inhabitants of Caermaen called the Dark Ages. A few of the stones that had formed the base of the cross still remained in position, grey with age, blotched with black lichen and green moss. The remainder of the famous rood had been used to mend the roads, to build pigsties and domestic offices; it had turned Protestant, in fact. Indeed, if it had remained, the parson of Caermaen would have had no time for the service; the coffee-stall, the Portuguese Missions, the Society for the Conversion of the Jews, and important social duties took up all his leisure. Besides, he thought the whole ceremony unscriptural.

Lucian passed on his way, wondering at the strange contrasts of the Middle Ages. How was it that people who could devise so beautiful a service believed in witchcraft, demoniacal possession and obsession, in the incubus and succubus, and in the Sabbath and in many other horrible absurdities? It seemed astonishing that anybody could even pretend to credit such monstrous tales, but there could be no doubt that the dread of old women who rode on broomsticks and liked black cats was once a very genuine terror.

A cold wind blew up from the river at sunset, and the scars on his body began to burn and tingle. The pain recalled his ritual to him, and he began to recite it as he walked along. He had cut a branch of thorn from the hedge and placed it next to his skin, pressing the spikes into the flesh with his hand till the warm blood ran down. He felt it was an exquisite and sweet observance for her sake; and then he thought of the secret golden palace he was building for her, the rare and wonderful city rising in his imagination. As the solemn night began to close about the earth, and the last glimmer of the sun faded from the hills, he gave himself anew to the woman, his body and his mind, all that he was, and all that he had.

IV

In the course of the week Lucian again visited Caermaen. He wished to view the amphitheatre more precisely, to note the exact position of the ancient walls, to gaze up the valley from certain points within the town, to imprint minutely and clearly on his mind the surge of the hills about the city, and the dark tapestry of the hanging woods. And he lingered in the museum where the relics of the Roman occupation had been stored; he was interested in the fragments of tessellated floors, in the glowing gold of drinking cups, the curious beads of fused and coloured glass, the carved amber-work, the scent-flagons that still retained the memory of unctuous odours, the necklaces, brooches, hair-pins of gold and silver, and other intimate objects which had once belonged to Roman ladies. One of the glass flagons, buried in damp earth for many hundred years, had gathered in its dark grave all the splendours of the light, and now shone like an opal with a moonlight glamour and gleams of gold and pale sunset green, and imperial purple. Then there were the wine jars of red earthenware, the memorial stones from graves, and the heads of broken gods, with fragments of occult things used in the secret rites of Mithras. Lucian read on the labels where all these objects were found: in the churchyard, beneath the turf of the meadow, and in the old cemetery near the forest; and whenever it was possible he would make his way to the spot of discovery, and imagine the long darkness that had hidden gold and stone and amber. All these investigations were necessary for the scheme he had in view, so he became for some time quite a familiar figure in the dusty deserted streets and in the meadows by the river. His continual visits to Caermaen were a tortuous puzzle to the inhabitants, who flew to their windows at the sound of a step on the uneven pavements. They were at a loss in their conjectures; his motive for coming down three times a week must of course be bad, but it seemed undiscoverable. And Lucian on his side was at first a good deal put out by occasional encounters with members of the Gervase or Dixon or Colley tribes; he had often to stop and exchange a few conventional expressions, and such meetings, casual as they were, annoyed and distracted him. He was no longer infuriated or wounded by sneers of contempt or by the cackling laughter of the young people when they passed him on the road (his hat was a shocking one and his untidiness terrible), but such incidents were unpleasant just as the smell of a drain was unpleasant, and threw the strange mechanism of his thoughts out of gear for the time. Then he had been disgusted by the affair of the boys and the little dog; the loathsomeness of it had quite broken up his fancies. He had read books of modern occultism, and remembered some of the experiments described. The adept, it was alleged, could transfer the sense of consciousness from his brain to the foot or hand, he could annihilate the world around him and pass into another sphere. Lucian wondered whether he could not perform some such operation for his own benefit. Human beings were constantly annoying him and getting in his way; was it not possible to annihilate the race, or at all events to reduce them to wholly insignificant forms? A certain process suggested itself to his mind, a work partly mental and partly physical, and after two or three experiments he found to his astonishment and delight that it was successful. Here, he thought, he had discovered one of the secrets of true magic; this was the key to the symbolic transmutations of the eastern tales. The adept could, in truth, change those who were obnoxious to him into harmless and unimportant shapes, not as in the letter of the old stories, by transforming the enemy, but by transforming himself. The magician puts men below him by going up higher, as one looks down on a mountain city from a loftier crag. The stones on the road and such petty obstacles do not trouble the wise man on the great journey, and so Lucian, when obliged to stop and converse with his fellow-creatures, to listen to their poor pretences and inanities, was no more inconvenienced than when he had to climb an awkward stile in the course of a walk. As for the more unpleasant manifestations of humanity: after all they no longer concerned him. Men intent on the great purpose did not suffer the current of their thoughts to be broken by the buzzing of a fly caught in a spider's web, so why should he be perturbed by the misery of a puppy in the hands of village boys? The fly, no doubt, endured its tortures; lying helpless and bound in those slimy bands, it cried out in its thin voice when the claws of the horrible monster fastened on it; but its dying agonies had never vexed the reverie of a lover. Lucian saw no reason why the boys should offend him more than the spider, or why he should pity the dog more than he pitied the fly. The talk of the men and women might be wearisome and inept and often malignant; but he could not imagine an alchemist at the moment of success, a general in the hour of victory, or a financier with a gigantic scheme of swindling well on the market being annoyed by the buzz of insects. The spider is, no doubt, a very terrible brute with a hideous mouth and hairy tiger-like claws when seen through the microscope; but Lucian had taken away the microscope from his eyes. He could now walk the streets of Caermaen confident and secure, without any dread of interruption, for at a moment's notice the transformation could be effected. Once Dr. Burrows caught him and made him promise to attend a bazaar that was to be held in aid of the Hungarian Protestants; Lucian assented the more willingly as he wished to pay a visit to certain curious mounds on a hill a little way out of the town, and he calculated on slinking off from the bazaar early in the afternoon. Lord Beamys was visiting Sir Vivian Ponsonby, a local magnate, and had kindly promised to drive over and declare the bazaar open. It was a solemn moment when the carriage drew up and the great man alighted. He was rather an evil-looking old nobleman, but the clergy and gentry, their wives and sons and daughters welcomed him with great and unctuous joy. Conversations were broken off in mid-sentence, slow people gaped, not realising why their friends had so suddenly left them, the Meyricks came up hot and perspiring in fear lest they should be too late, Miss Colley, a yellow virgin of austere regard, smiled largely, Mrs. Dixon beckoned wildly with her parasol to the "girls" who were idly strolling in a distant part of the field, and the archdeacon ran at full speed. The air grew dark with bows, and resonant with the genial laugh of the archdeacon, the cackle of the younger ladies, and the shrill parrot-like voices of the matrons; those smiled who had never smiled before, and on some maiden faces there hovered that look of adoring ecstasy with which the old masters graced their angels. Then, when all the due rites had been performed, the company turned and began to walk towards the booths of their small Vanity Fair. Lord Beamys led the way with Mrs. Gervase, Mrs. Dixon followed with Sir Vivian Ponsonby, and the multitudes that followed cried, saying, "What a dear old man!"—"Isn't it *kind* of him to come all this way?"—"What a sweet expression, isn't it?"—"I think he's an old love"—"One of the good old sort"—"Real English nobleman"—"Oh most correct, I assure you; if a girl gets into trouble, notice to quit at once"—"Always stands by the Church"—"Twenty livings in his gift"—"Voted for the Public Worship Regulation Act"—"Ten thousand acres strictly preserved." The old lord was leering pleasantly and muttering to himself: "Some fine gals here. Like the looks of that filly with the pink hat. Ought to see more of her. She'd give Lotty points."

The pomp swept slowly across the grass: the archdeacon had got hold of Mr. Dixon, and they were discussing the misdeeds of some clergyman in the rural deanery.

"I can scarce credit it," said Mr. Dixon.

"Oh, I assure you, there can be no doubt. We have witnesses. There can be no question that there was a procession at Llanfihangel on the Sunday before Easter; the choir and minister went round the church, carrying palm branches in their hands."

"Very shocking."

"It has distressed the bishop. Martin is a hard-working man enough, and all that, but those sort of things can't be tolerated. The bishop told me that he had set his face against processions."

"Quite right: the bishop is perfectly right. Processions are unscriptural."

"It's the thin end of the wedge, you know, Dixon."

"Exactly. I have always resisted anything of the kind here."

"Right. *Principiis obsta,* you know. Martin is so *imprudent.* There's a *way* of doing things."

The "scriptural" procession led by Lord Beamys broke up when the stalls were reached, and gathered round the nobleman as he declared the bazaar open.

Lucian was sitting on a garden-seat, a little distance off, looking dreamily before him. And all that he saw was a swarm of flies clustering and buzzing about a lump of tainted meat that lay on the grass.

The spectacle in no way interrupted the harmony of his thoughts, and soon after the opening of the bazaar he went quietly away, walking across the fields in the direction of the ancient mounds he desired to inspect.

All these journeys of his to Caermaen and its neighbourhood had a peculiar object; he was gradually levelling to the dust the squalid kraals of modern times, and rebuilding the splendid and golden city of Siluria. All this mystic town was for the delight of his sweetheart and himself; for her the wonderful villas, the shady courts, the magic of tessellated pavements, and the hangings of rich stuffs with their intricate and glowing patterns. Lucian wandered all day through the shining streets, taking shelter sometimes in the gardens beneath the dense and gloomy ilex trees, and listening to the plash and trickle of the fountains. Sometimes he would look out of a window and watch the crowd and colour of the market-place, and now and again a ship came up the river bringing exquisite silks and the merchandise of unknown lands in the Far East. He had made a curious and accurate map of the town he proposed to inhabit, in which every villa was set down and named. He drew his lines to scale with the gravity of a surveyor, and studied the plan till he was able to find his way from house to house on the darkest summer night. On the southern slopes about the town there were vineyards, always under a glowing sun, and sometimes he ventured to the furthest ridge of the forest, where the wild people still lingered, that he might catch the golden gleam of the city far away, as the light quivered and scintillated on the glittering tiles. And there were gardens outside the city gates where strange and brilliant flowers grew, filling the hot air with their odour, and scenting the breeze that blew along the streets. The dull modern life was far away, and people who saw him at this period wondered what was amiss; the abstraction of his glance was obvious, even to eyes not over-sharp. But men and women had lost all their power of annoyance and vexation; they could no longer even interrupt his thought for a moment. He could listen to Mr. Dixon with apparent attention, while he was in reality enraptured by the entreating music of the double flute, played by a girl in the garden of Avallaunius, for that was the name he had taken. Mr. Dixon was innocently discoursing archæology, giving a brief *résumé* of the view expressed by Mr. Wyndham at the last meeting of the antiquarian society.

"There can be no doubt that the temple of Diana stood there in pagan times," he concluded, and Lucian assented to the opinion, and asked a few questions which seemed pertinent enough. But all the time the flute notes were sounding in his ears, and the ilex threw a purple shadow on the white pavement before his villa. A boy came forward from the garden; he had been walking amongst the vines and plucking the ripe grapes, and the juice had trickled down over his breast. Standing beside the girl, unashamed in the sunlight, he began to sing one of Sappho's love songs. His voice was as full and rich as a woman's, but purged of all emotion; he was an instrument of music in the flesh. Lucian looked at him steadily; the white perfect body shone against the roses and the blue of the sky, clear and gleaming as marble in the glare of the sun. The words he sang burned and flamed with passion, and he was as unconscious of their meaning as the twin pipes of the flute. And the girl was smiling. The vicar shook hands and went on, well pleased with his remarks on the temple of Diana and also with Lucian's polite interest.

"He is by no means wanting in intelligence," he said to his family. "A little curious in manner, perhaps, but not stupid."

"Oh, papa," said Henrietta, "don't you think he is rather silly? He can't talk about anything—anything interesting, I mean. And he pretends to know a lot about books, but I heard him say the other day he had never read *The Prince of the House of David* or *Ben-Hur.* Fancy!"

The vicar had not interrupted Lucian. The sun still beat upon the roses, and a little breeze bore the scent of them to his nostrils together with the smell of grapes and vine-leaves. He had become curious in sensation, and as he leant back upon the cushions covered with glistening yellow silk, he was trying to analyse a strange ingredient in the perfume of the air. He had penetrated far beyond the crude distinctions of modern times, beyond the rough: "there's a smell of roses", "there must be sweetbriar somewhere". Modern perceptions of odour were, he knew, far below those of the savage in delicacy. The degraded black fellow of Australia could distinguish odours in a way that made the consumer of "damper" stare in amazement, but the savage's sensations were all strictly utilitarian. To Lucian as he sat in the cool porch, his feet on the marble, the air came laden with scents as subtly and wonderfully interwoven and contrasted as the harmonica of a great master.

The stained marble of the pavement gave a cool reminiscence of the Italian mountain, the blood-red roses palpitating in the sunlight sent out an odour mystical as passion itself, and there was the hint of inebriation in the perfume of the trellised vines. Besides these, the girl's desire and the unripe innocence of the boy were as distinct as benzoin and myrrh, both delicious and exquisite, and exhaled as freely as the scent of the roses. But there was another element that puzzled him, an aromatic suggestion of the forest. He understood it at last; it was the vapour of the great red pines that grew beyond the garden; their spicy needles were burning in the sun, and the smell was as fragrant as the fume of incense blown from far. The soft entreaty of the flute and the swelling rapture of the boy's voice beat on the air together, and Lucian wondered whether there were in the nature of things any true distinction between the impressions of sound and scent and colour. The violent blue of the sky, the song, and the odours seemed rather varied symbols of one mystery than distinct entities. He could almost imagine that the boy's innocence was indeed a perfume, and that the palpitating roses had become a sonorous chant.

In the curious silence which followed the last notes, when the boy and girl had passed under the purple ilex shadow, he fell into a reverie. The fancy that sensations are symbols and not realities hovered in his mind, and led him to speculate as to whether they could not actually be transmuted one into another. It was possible, he thought, that a whole continent of knowledge had been undiscovered; the energies of men having been expended in unimportant and foolish directions. Modern ingenuity had been employed on such trifles as locomotive engines, electric cables, and cantilever bridges; on elaborate devices for bringing uninteresting people nearer together; the ancients had been almost as foolish, because they had mistaken the symbol for the thing signified. It was not the material banquet which really mattered, but the thought of it; it was almost as futile to eat and take emetics and eat again as to invent telephones and high-pressure boilers. As for some other ancient methods of enjoying life, one might as well set oneself to improve calico printing at once.

"Only in the garden of Avallaunius," said Lucian to himself, "is the true and exquisite science to be found."

He could imagine a man who was able to live in one sense while he pleased; to whom, for example, every impression of touch, taste, hearing, or seeing should be translated into odour; who at the desired kiss should be ravished with the scent of dark violets, to whom music should be the perfume of a rose-garden at dawn.

When, now and again, he voluntarily resumed the experience of common life, it was that he might return with greater delight to the garden in the city of refuge. In the actual world the talk was of Nonconformists, the lodger franchise, and the Stock Exchange; people were constantly reading newspapers, drinking Australian Burgundy, and doing other things equally absurd. They either looked shocked when the fine art of pleasure was mentioned, or confused it with going to musical comedies, drinking bad whisky, and keeping late hours in disreputable and vulgar company. He found to his amusement that the profligate were by many degrees duller than the pious, but that the most tedious of all were the persons who preached promiscuity, and called their system of "pigging" the "New Morality".

He went back to the city lovingly, because it was built and adorned for his love. As the metaphysicians insist on the consciousness of the ego as the implied basis of all thought, so he knew that it was she in whom he had found himself, and through whom and for whom all the true life existed. He felt that Annie had taught him the rare magic which had created the garden of Avallaunius. It was for her that he sought strange secrets and tried to penetrate the mysteries of sensation, for he could only give her wonderful thoughts and a wonderful life, and a poor body stained with the scars of his worship.

It was with this object, that of making the offering of himself a worthy one, that he continually searched for new and exquisite experiences. He made lovers come before him and confess their secrets; he pried into the inmost mysteries of innocence and shame, noting how passion and reluctance strive together for the mastery. In the amphitheatre he sometimes witnessed strange entertainments in which such tales as *Daphnis and Chloe* and *The Golden Ass* were performed before him. These shows were always given at night-time; a circle of torch-bearers surrounded the stage in the centre, and above, all the tiers of seats were dark. He would look up at the soft blue of the summer sky, and at the vast dim mountain hovering like a cloud in the west, and then at the scene illumined by a flaring light, and contrasted with violent shadows. The subdued mutter of conversation in a strange language rising from bench after bench, swift hissing whispers of explanation, now and then a shout or a cry as the interest deepened, the restless tossing of the people as the end drew near, an arm lifted, a cloak thrown back, the sudden blaze of a torch lighting up purple or white or the gleam of gold in the black serried ranks; these were impressions that seemed always amazing. And above, the dusky light of the stars, around, the sweet-scented meadows, and the twinkle of lamps from the still city, the cry of the sentries about the walls, the wash of the tide filling the river, and the salt savour of the sea. With such a scenic ornament he saw the tale of Apuleius represented, heard the names of Fotis and Byrrhaena and Lucius proclaimed, and the deep intonation of such sentences as *Ecce Veneris hortator et armiger Liber advenit ultro.* The tale went on through all its marvellous adventures, and Lucian left the amphitheatre and walked beside the river where he could hear indistinctly the noise of voices and the singing Latin, and note how the rumour of the stage mingled with the murmur of the shuddering reeds and the cool lapping of the tide. Then came the farewell of the cantor, the thunder of applause, the crash of cymbals, the calling of the flutes, and the surge of the wind in the great dark wood.

At other times it was his chief pleasure to spend a whole day in a vineyard planted on the steep slope beyond the bridge. A grey stone seat had been placed beneath a shady laurel, and here he often sat without motion or gesture for many hours. Below him the tawny river swept round the town in a half circle; he could see the swirl of the yellow water, its eddies and miniature whirlpools, as the tide poured up from the south. And beyond the river the strong circuit of the walls, and within, the city glittered like a charming piece of mosaic. He freed himself from the obtuse modern view of towns as places where human beings live and make money and rejoice or suffer, for from the standpoint of the moment such facts were wholly impertinent. He knew perfectly well that for his present purpose the tawny sheen and shimmer of the tide was the only fact of importance about the river, and so he regarded the city as a curious work in jewellery. Its radiant marble porticoes, the white walls of the villas, a dome of burning copper, the flash and scintillation of tiled roofs, the quiet red of brickwork, dark groves of ilex, and cypress, and laurel, glowing rose-gardens, and here and there the silver of a fountain, seemed arranged and contrasted with a wonderful art, and the town appeared a delicious ornament, every cube of colour owing its place to the thought and inspiration of the artificer. Lucian, as he gazed from his arbour amongst the trellised vines, lost none of the subtle pleasures of the sight; noting every *nuance* of colour, he let his eyes dwell for a moment on the scarlet flash of poppies, and then on a glazed roof which in the glance of the sun seemed to spout white fire. A square of vines was like some rare green stone; the grapes were massed so richly amongst the vivid leaves, that even from far off there was a sense of irregular flecks and stains of purple running through the green. The laurel garths were like cool jade; the gardens, where red, yellow, blue and white gleamed together in a mist of heat, had the radiance of opal; the river was a band of dull gold. On every side, as if to enhance the preciousness of the city, the woods hung dark on the hills; above, the sky was violet, specked with minute feathery clouds, white as snowflakes. It reminded him of a beautiful bowl in his villa; the ground was of that same brilliant blue, and the artist had fused into the work when it was hot particles of pure white glass.

For Lucian this was a spectacle that enchanted many hours; leaning on one hand, he would gaze at the city glowing in the sunlight till the purple shadows grew down the slopes and the long melodious trumpet sounded for the evening watch. Then, as he strolled beneath the trellises, he would see all the radiant facets glimmering out, and the city faded into haze, a white wall shining here and there, and the gardens veiled in a dim glow of colour. On such an evening he would go home with the sense that he had truly lived a day, having received for many hours the most acute impressions of beautiful colour.

Often he spent the night in the cool court of his villa, lying amidst soft cushions heaped upon the marble bench. A lamp stood on the table at his elbow, its light making the water in the cistern twinkle. There was no sound in the court except the soft continual plashing of the fountain. Throughout these still hours he would meditate, and he became more than ever convinced that man could, if he pleased, become lord of his own sensations. This, surely, was the true meaning concealed under the beautiful symbolism of alchemy. Some years before he had read many of the wonderful alchemical books of the later Middle Ages, and had suspected that something other than the turning of lead into gold was intended. This impression was deepened when he looked into *Lumen de Lumine* by Vaughan, the brother of the Silurist, and he had long puzzled himself in the endeavour to find a reasonable interpretation of the hermetic mystery, and of the red powder, "glistening and glorious in the sun". And the solution shone out at last, bright and amazing, as he lay quiet in the court of Avallaunius.

He knew that he himself had solved the riddle, that he held in his hand the powder of projection, the philosopher's stone transmuting all it touched to fine gold; the gold of exquisite impressions. He understood now something of the alchemical symbolism; the crucible and the furnace, the "Green Dragon", and the "Son Blessed of the Fire" had, he saw, a peculiar meaning. He understood too why the uninitiated were warned of the terror and danger through which they must pass; and the vehemence with which the adepts disclaimed all desire for material riches no longer struck him as singular. The wise man does not endure the torture of the furnace in order that he may be able to compete with operators in pork and company promoters; neither a steam yacht, nor a grouse-moor, nor three liveried footmen would add at all to his gratifications. Again Lucian said to himself:

"Only in the court of Avallaunius is the true science of the exquisite to be found."

He saw the true gold into which the beggarly matter of existence may be transmuted by spagyric art; a succession of delicious moments, all the rare flavours of life concentrated, purged of their lees, and preserved in a beautiful vessel. The moonlight fell green on the fountain and on the curious pavements, and in the long sweet silence of the night he lay still and felt that thought itself was an acute pleasure, to be expressed perhaps in terms of odour or colour by the true artist.

And he gave himself other and even stranger gratifications. Outside the city walls, between the baths and the amphitheatre, was a tavern, a place where wonderful people met to drink wonderful wine. There he saw priests of Mithras and Isis and of more occult rites from the East, men who wore robes of bright colours, and grotesque ornaments, symbolising secret things. They spoke amongst themselves in a rich jargon of coloured words, full of hidden meanings and the sense of matters unintelligible to the uninitiated, alluding to what was concealed beneath roses, and calling each other by strange names. And there were actors who gave the shows in the amphitheatre, officers of the legion who had served in wild places, singers, and dancing girls, and heroes of strange adventure.

The walls of the tavern were covered with pictures painted in violent hues; blues and reds and greens jarring against one another and lighting up the gloom of the place. The stone benches were always crowded, the sunlight came in through the door in a long bright beam, casting a dancing shadow of vine leaves on the further wall. There a painter had made a joyous figure of the young Bacchus driving the leopards before him with his ivy-staff, and the quivering shadow seemed a part of the picture. The room was cool and dark and cavernous, but the scent and heat of the summer gushed in through the open door. There was ever a full sound, with noise and vehemence, there, and the rolling music of the Latin tongue never ceased.

"The wine of the siege, the wine that we saved," cried one.

"Look for the jar marked *Faunus;* you will be glad."

"Bring me the wine of the Owl's Face."

"Let us have the wine of Saturn's Bridge."

The boys who served brought the wine in dull red jars that struck a charming note against their white robes. They poured out the violet and purple and golden wine with calm sweet faces as if they were assisting in the mysteries, without any sign that they heard the strange words that flashed from side to side. The cups were all of glass: some were of deep green, of the colour of the sea near the land, flawed and specked with the bubbles of the furnace. Others were of brilliant scarlet, streaked with irregular bands of white, and having the appearance of white globules in the moulded stem. There were cups of dark glowing blue, deeper and more shining than the blue of the sky, and running through the substance of the glass were veins of rich gamboge yellow, twining from the brim to the foot. Some cups were of a troubled and clotted red, with alternating blotches of dark and light, some were variegated with white and yellow stains, some wore a film of rainbow colours, some glittered, shot with gold threads through the clear crystal, some were as if sapphires hung suspended in running water, some sparkled with the glint of stars, some were black and golden like tortoiseshell.

A strange feature was the constant and fluttering motion of hands and arms. Gesture made a constant commentary on speech; white fingers, whiter arms, and sleeves of all colours, hovered restlessly, appeared and disappeared with an effect of threads crossing and recrossing on the loom. And the odour of the place was both curious and memorable; something of the damp cold breath of the cave meeting the hot blast of summer, the strangely mingled aromas of rare wines as they fell plashing and ringing into the cups, the drugged vapour of the East that the priests of Mithras and Isis bore from their steaming temples; these were always strong and dominant. And the women were scented, sometimes with unctuous and overpowering perfumes, and to the artist the experiences of those present were hinted in subtle and delicate *nuances* of odour.

They drank their wine and caressed all day in the tavern. The women threw their round white arms about their lovers' necks, they intoxicated them with the scent of their hair, the priests muttered their fantastic jargon of Theurgy. And through the sonorous clash of voices there always seemed the ring of the cry:

"Look for the jar marked *Faunus;* you will be glad."

Outside, the vine tendrils shook on the white walls glaring in the sunshine; the breeze swept up from the yellow river, pungent with the salt sea savour.

These tavern scenes were often the subject of Lucian's meditation as he sat amongst the cushions on the marble seat. The rich sound of the voices impressed him above all things, and he saw that words have a far higher reason than the utilitarian office of imparting a man's thought. The common notion that language and linked words are important only as a means of expression he found a little ridiculous; as if electricity were to be studied solely with the view of "wiring" to people, and all its other properties left unexplored, neglected. Language, he understood, was chiefly important for the beauty of its sounds, by its possession of words resonant, glorious to the ear, by its capacity, when exquisitely arranged, of suggesting wonderful and indefinable impressions, perhaps more ravishing and farther removed from the domain of strict thought than the impressions excited by music itself. Here lay hidden the secret of the sensuous art of literature, it was the secret of suggestion, the art of causing delicious sensation by the use of words. In a way, therefore, literature was independent of thought; the mere English listener, if he had an ear attuned, could recognise the beauty of a splendid Latin phrase.

Here was the explanation of the magic of *Lycidas*. From the standpoint of the formal understanding it was an affected lament over some wholly uninteresting and unimportant Mr. King; it was full of nonsense about "shepherds" and "flocks" and "muses" and such stale stock of poetry; the introduction of St. Peter on a stage thronged with nymphs and river gods was blasphemous, absurd, and, in the worst taste; there were touches of greasy Puritanism, the twang of the conventicle was only too apparent. And *Lycidas* was probably the most perfect piece of pure literature in existence; because every word and phrase and line were sonorous, ringing and echoing with music.

"Literature," he re-enunciated in his mind, "is the sensuous art of causing exquisite impressions by means of words."

And yet there was something more; besides the logical thought, which was often a hindrance, a troublesome though inseparable accident, besides the sensation, always a pleasure and a delight, besides these there were the indefinable inexpressible images which all fine literature summons to the mind. As the chemist in his experiments is sometimes astonished to find unknown, unexpected elements in the crucible or the receiver, as the world of material things is considered by some a thin veil of the immaterial universe, so he who reads wonderful prose or verse is conscious of suggestions that cannot be put into words, which do not rise from the logical sense, which are rather parallel to than connected with the sensuous delight. The world so disclosed is rather the world of dreams, rather the world in which children sometimes live, instantly appearing, and instantly vanishing away, a world beyond all expression or analysis, neither of the intellect nor of the senses. He called these fancies of his "Meditations of a Tavern", and was amused to think that a theory of letters should have risen from the eloquent noise that rang all day about the violet and golden wine.

"Let us seek for more exquisite things," said Lucian to himself. He could almost imagine the magic transmutation of the senses accomplished, the strong sunlight was an odour in his nostrils; it poured down on the white marble and the palpitating roses like a flood. The sky was a glorious blue, making the heart joyous, and the eyes could rest in the dark green leaves and purple shadow of the ilex. The earth seemed to burn and leap beneath the sun, he fancied he could see the vine tendrils stir and quiver in the heat, and the faint fume of the scorching pine needles was blown across the gleaming garden to the seat beneath the porch. Wine was before him in a cup of carved amber; a wine of the colour of a dark rose, with a glint as of a star or of a jet of flame deep beneath the brim; and the cup was twined about with a delicate wreath of ivy. He was often loath to turn away from the still contemplation of such things, from the mere joy of the violent sun, and the responsive earth. He loved his garden and the view of the tessellated city from the vineyard on the hill, the strange clamour of the tavern, and white Fotis appearing on the torch-lit stage. And there were shops in the town in which he delighted, the shops of the perfume makers, and jewellers, and dealers in curious ware. He loved to see all things made for ladies' use, to touch the gossamer silks that were to touch their bodies, to finger the beads of amber and the gold chains which would stir above their hearts, to handle the carved hairpins and brooches, to smell odours which were already dedicated to love.

But though these were sweet and delicious gratifications, he knew that there were more exquisite things of which he might be a spectator. He had seen the folly of regarding fine literature from the standpoint of the logical intellect, and he now began to question the wisdom of looking at life as if it were a moral representation. Literature, he knew, could not exist without some meaning, and considerations of right and wrong were to a certain extent inseparable from the conception of life, but to insist on ethics as the chief interest of the human pageant was surely absurd. One might as well read *Lycidas* for the sake of its denunciation of "our corrupted Clergy", or Homer for "manners and customs". An artist entranced by a beautiful landscape did not greatly concern himself with the geological formation of the hills, nor did the lover of a wild sea inquire as to the chemical analysis of the water. Lucian saw a coloured and complex life displayed before him, and he sat enraptured at the spectacle, not concerned to know whether actions were good or bad, but content if they were curious.

In this spirit he made a singular study of corruption. Beneath his feet, as he sat in the garden porch, was a block of marble through which there ran a scarlet stain. It began with a faint line, thin as a hair, and grew as it advanced, sending out offshoots to right and left, and broadening to a pool of brilliant red. There were strange lives into which he looked that were like the block of marble; women with grave sweet faces told him the astounding tale of their adventures, and how, they said, they had met the faun when they were little children. They told him how they had played and watched by the vines and the fountains, and dallied with the nymphs, and gazed at images reflected in the water pools, till the authentic face appeared from the wood. He heard others tell how they had loved the satyrs for many years before they knew their race; and there were strange stories of those who had longed to speak but knew not the word of the enigma, and searched in all strange paths and ways before they found it.

He heard the history of the woman who fell in love with her slave-boy, and tempted him for three years in vain. He heard the tale from the woman's full red lips, and watched her face, full of the ineffable sadness of lust, as she described her curious stratagems in mellow phrases. She was drinking a sweet yellow wine from a gold cup as she spoke, and the odour in her hair and the aroma of the precious wine seemed to mingle with the soft strange words that flowed like an unguent from a carven jar. She told how she bought the boy in the market of an Asian city, and had him carried to her house in the grove of fig-trees. "Then," she went on, "he was led into my presence as I sat between the columns of my court. A blue veil was spread above to shut out the heat of the sun, and rather twilight than light shone on the painted walls, and the wonderful colours of the pavement, and the images of Love and the Mother of Love. The men who brought the boy gave him over to my girls, who undressed him before me, one drawing gently away his robe, another stroking his brown and flowing hair, another praising the whiteness of his limbs, and another caressing him, and speaking loving words in his ear. But the boy looked sullenly at them all, striking away their hands, and pouting with his lovely and splendid lips, and I saw a blush, like the rosy veil of dawn, reddening his body and his cheeks. Then I made them bathe him, and anoint him with scented oils from head to foot, till his limbs shone and glistened with the gentle and mellow glow of an ivory statue. Then I said: 'You are bashful, because you shine alone amongst us all; see, we too will be your fellows.' The girls began first of all, fondling and kissing one another, and doing for each other the offices of waiting-maids. They drew out the pins and loosened the bands of their hair, and I never knew before that they were so lovely. The soft and shining tresses flowed down, rippling like sea-waves; some had hair golden and radiant as this wine in my cup, the faces of others appeared amidst the blackness of ebony; there were locks that seemed of burnished and scintillating copper, some glowed with hair of tawny splendour, and others were crowned with the brightness of the sardonyx. Then, laughing, and without the appearance of shame, they unfastened the brooches and bands which sustained their robes, and so allowed silk and linen to flow swiftly to the stained floor, so that one would have said there was a sudden apparition of the fairest nymphs. With many festive and jocose words they began to incite each other to mirth, praising the beauties that shone on every side, and calling the boy by a girl's name, they invited him to be their playmate. But he refused, shaking his head, and still standing dumbfounded and abashed, as if he saw a forbidden and terrible spectacle. Then I ordered the women to undo my hair and my clothes, making them caress me with the tenderness of the fondest lover, but without avail, for the foolish boy still scowled and pouted out his lips, stained with an imperial and glorious scarlet."

She poured out more of the topaz-coloured wine in her cup, and Lucian saw it glitter as it rose to the brim and mirrored the gleam of the lamps. The tale went on, recounting a hundred strange devices. The woman told how she had tempted the boy by idleness and ease, giving him long hours of sleep, and allowing him to recline all day on soft cushions, that swelled about him, enclosing his body. She tried the experiment of curious odours: causing him to smell always about him the oil of roses, and burning in his presence rare gums from the East. He was allured by soft dresses, being clothed in silks that caressed the skin with the sense of a fondling touch. Three times a day they spread before him a delicious banquet, full of savour and odour and colour; three times a day they endeavoured to intoxicate him with delicate wine.

"And so," the lady continued, "I spared nothing to catch him in the glistening nets of love; taking only sour and contemptuous glances in return. And at last in an incredible shape I won the victory, and then, having gained a green crown fighting in agony against his green and crude immaturity, I devoted him to the theatre, where he amused the people by the splendour of his death."

On another evening he heard the history of the man who dwelt alone, refusing all allurements, and was at last discovered to be the lover of a black statue. And there were tales of strange cruelties, of men taken by mountain robbers, and curiously maimed and disfigured, so that when they escaped and returned to the town, they were thought to be monsters and killed at their own doors. Lucian left no dark or secret nook of life unvisited; he sat down, as he said, at the banquet resolved to taste all the savours, and to leave no flagon unvisited.

His relations grew seriously alarmed about him at this period. While he heard with some inner ear the suave and eloquent phrases of singular tales, and watched the lamp-light in amber and purple wine, his father saw a lean pale boy, with black eyes that burnt in hollows, and sad and sunken cheeks.

"You ought to try and eat more, Lucian," said the parson; "and why don't you have some beer?"

He was looking feebly at the roast mutton and sipping a little water; but he would not have eaten or drunk with more relish if the choicest meat and drink had been before him.

His bones seemed, as Miss Deacon said, to be growing through his skin; he had all the appearance of an ascetic whose body has been reduced to misery by long and grievous penance. People who chanced to see him could not help saying to one another: "How ill and wretched that Lucian Taylor looks!" They were of course quite unaware of the joy and luxury in which his real life was spent, and some of them began to pity him, and to speak to him kindly.

It was too late for that. The friendly words had as much lost their meaning as the words of contempt. Edward Dixon hailed him cheerfully in the street one day:

"Come in to my den, won't you, old fellow?" he said. "You won't see the pater. I've managed to bag a bottle of his old port. I know you smoke like a furnace, and I've got some ripping cigars. You will come, won't you! I can tell you the pater's booze is first rate."

He gently declined and went on. Kindness and unkindness, pity and contempt had become for him mere phrases; he could not have distinguished one from the other. Hebrew and Chinese, Hungarian and Pushtu would be pretty much alike to an agricultural labourer; if he cared to listen he might detect some general differences in sound, but all four tongues would be equally devoid of significance.

To Lucian, entranced in the garden of Avallaunius, it seemed very strange that he had once been so ignorant of all the exquisite meanings of life. Now, beneath the violet sky, looking through the brilliant trellis of the vines, he saw the picture; before, he had gazed in sad astonishment at the squalid rag which was wrapped about it.

V

And he was at last in the city of the unending murmuring streets, a part of the stirring shadow, of the amber-lighted gloom.

It seemed a long time since he had knelt before his sweetheart in the lane, the moon-fire streaming upon them from the dark circle of the fort, the air and the light and his soul full of haunting, the touch of the unimaginable thrilling his heart; and now he sat in a terrible "bed-sitting-room" in a western suburb, confronted by a heap and litter of papers on the desk of a battered old bureau.

He had put his breakfast-tray out on the landing, and was thinking of the morning's work, and of some very dubious pages that he had blackened the night before. But when he had lit his disreputable briar, he remembered there was an unopened letter waiting for him on the table; he had recognised the vague, staggering script of Miss Deacon, his cousin. There was not much news; his father was "just the same as usual", there had been a good deal of rain, the farmers expected to make a lot of cider, and so forth. But at the close of the letter Miss Deacon became useful for reproof and admonition.

"I was at Caermaen on Tuesday," she said, "and called on the Gervases and the Dixons. Mr. Gervase smiled when I told him you were a literary man, living in London, and said he was afraid you wouldn't find it a very practical career. Mrs. Gervase was very proud of Henry's success; he passed fifth for some examination, and will begin with nearly four hundred a year. I don't wonder the Gervases are delighted. Then I went to the Dixons, and had tea. Mrs. Dixon wanted to know if you had published anything yet, and I said I thought not. She shewed me a book everybody is talking about, called the *Dog and the Doctor*. She says it's selling by thousands, and that one can't take up a paper without seeing the author's name. She told me to tell you that you ought to try to write something like it. Then Mr. Dixon came in from the study, and your name was mentioned again. He said he was afraid you had made rather a mistake in trying to take up literature as if it were a profession, and seemed to think that a place in a house of business would be more *suitable* and more practical. He pointed out that you had not had the advantages of a university training, and said that you would find men who had made good friends, and had the *tone* of the university, would be before you at every step. He said Edward was doing very well at Oxford. He writes to them that he knows several noblemen, and that young Philip Bullingham (son of Sir John Bulling-ham) is his most intimate friend; of course this is *very* satisfactory for the Dixons. I am afraid, my dear Lucian, you have rather overrated your powers. Wouldn't it be better, even now, to look out for some *real work* to do, instead of wasting your time over those silly old books? I know quite well how the Gervases and the Dixons feel; they think idleness so injurious for a young man, and likely to lead to *bad habits*. You know, my dear Lucian, I am only writing like this because of my affection for you, so I am sure, my dear boy, you won't be offended."

Lucian pigeon-holed the letter solemnly in the receptacle lettered "Barbarians". He felt that he ought to ask himself some serious questions: "Why haven't I passed fifth? why isn't Philip (son of Sir John) my most intimate friend? why am I an idler, liable to fall into bad habits?" but he was eager to get to his work, a curious and intricate piece of analysis. So the battered bureau, the litter of papers, and the thick fume of his pipe, engulfed him and absorbed him for the rest of the morning. Outside were the dim October mists, the dreary and languid life of a side street, and beyond, on the main road, the hum and jangle of the gliding trains. But he heard none of the uneasy noises of the quarter, not even the shriek of the garden gates nor the yelp of the butcher on his rounds, for delight in his great task made him unconscious of the world outside.

He had come by curious paths to this calm hermitage between Shepherd's Bush and Acton Vale. The golden weeks of the summer passed on in their enchanted procession, and Annie had not returned, neither had she written. Lucian, on his side, sat apart, wondering why his longing for her were not sharper. As he thought of his raptures he would smile faintly to himself, and wonder whether he had not lost the world and Annie with it. In the garden of Avallaunius his sense of external things had grown dim and indistinct; the actual, material life seemed every day to become a show, a fleeting of shadows across a great white light. At last the news came that Annie Morgan had been married from her sister's house to a young farmer, to whom, it appeared, she had been long engaged, and Lucian was ashamed to find himself only conscious of amusement, mingled with gratitude. She had been the key that opened the shut palace, and he was now secure on the throne of ivory and gold. A few days after he had heard the news he repeated the adventure of his boyhood; for the second time he scaled the steep hillside, and penetrated the matted brake. He expected violent disillusion, but his feeling was rather astonishment at the activity of boyish imagination. There was no terror nor amazement now in the green bulwarks, and the stunted undergrowth did not seem in any way extraordinary. Yet he did not laugh at the memory of his sensations, he was not angry at the cheat. Certainly it had been all illusion, all the heats and chills of boyhood, its thoughts of terror were without significance. But he recognised that the illusions of the child only differed from those of the man in that they were more picturesque; belief in fairies and belief in the Stock Exchange as bestowers of happiness were equally vain, but the latter form of faith was ugly as well as inept. It was better, he knew, and wiser, to wish for a fairy coach than to cherish longings for a well-appointed brougham and liveried servants.

He turned his back on the green walls and the dark oaks without any feeling of regret or resentment. After a little while he began to think of his adventures with pleasure; the ladder by which he had mounted had disappeared, but he was safe on the height. By the chance fancy of a beautiful girl he had been redeemed from a world of misery and torture, the world of external things into which he had come a stranger, by which he had been tormented. He looked back at a kind of vision of himself seen as he was a year before, a pitiable creature burning and twisting on the hot coals of the pit, crying lamentably to the laughing bystanders for but one drop of cold water wherewith to cool his tongue. He confessed to himself, with some contempt, that he had been a social being, depending for his happiness on the goodwill of others; he had tried hard to write, chiefly, it was true, from love of the art, but a little from a social motive. He had imagined that a written book and the praise of responsible journals would ensure him the respect of the county people. It was a quaint idea, and he saw the lamentable fallacies naked; in the first place, a painstaking artist in words was not respected by the respectable; secondly, books should not be written with the object of gaining the goodwill of the landed and commercial interests; thirdly and chiefly, no man should in any way depend on another.

From this utter darkness, from danger of madness, the ever dear and sweet Annie had rescued him. Very beautifully and fitly, as Lucian thought, she had done her work without any desire to benefit him, she had simply willed to gratify her own passion, and in doing this had handed to him the priceless secret. And he, on his side, had reversed the process; merely to make himself a splendid offering for the acceptance of his sweetheart, he had cast aside the vain world, and had found the truth, which now remained with him, precious and enduring.

And since the news of the marriage he found that his worship of her had by no means vanished; rather in his heart was the eternal treasure of a happy love, untarnished and spotless; it would be like a mirror of gold without alloy, bright and lustrous for ever. For Lucian, it was no defect in the woman that she was desirous and faithless; he had not conceived an affection for certain moral or intellectual accidents, but for the very woman. Guided by the self-evident axiom that humanity is to be judged by literature, and not literature by humanity, he detected the analogy between *Lycidas* and Annie. Only the dullard would object to the nauseous cant of the one, or to the indiscretions of the other. A sober critic might say that the man who could generalise Herbert and Laud, Donne and Herrick, Sanderson and Juxon, Hammond and Lancelot Andrewes into "our corrupted Clergy" must be either an imbecile or a scoundrel, or probably both. The judgment would be perfectly true, but as a criticism of *Lycidas* it would be a piece of folly. In the case of the woman one could imagine the attitude of the conventional lover; of the chevalier who, with his tongue in his cheek, "reverences and respects" all women, and coming home early in the morning writes a leading article on St. English Girl. Lucian, on the other hand, felt profoundly grateful to the delicious Annie, because she had at precisely the right moment voluntarily removed her image from his way. He confessed to himself that, latterly, he had a little dreaded her return as an interruption; he had shivered at the thought that their relations would become what was so terribly called an "intrigue" or "affair". There would be all the threadbare and common stratagems, the vulgarity of secret assignations, and an atmosphere suggesting the period of Mr. Thomas Moore and Lord Byron and "segars". Lucian had been afraid of all this; he had feared lest love itself should destroy love.

He considered that now, freed from the torment of the body, leaving untasted the green water that makes thirst more burning, he was perfectly initiated in the true knowledge of the splendid and glorious love. There seemed to him a monstrous paradox in the assertion that there could be no true love without a corporal presence of the beloved; even the popular sayings of "Absence makes the heart grow fonder," and "familiarity breeds contempt", witnessed to the contrary. He thought, sighing, and with compassion, of the manner in which men are continually led astray by the cheat of the senses. In order that the unborn might still be added to the born, nature had inspired men with the wild delusion that the bodily companionship of the lover and the beloved was desirable above all things, and so, by the false show of pleasure, the human race was chained to vanity, and doomed to an eternal thirst for the non-existent.

Again and again he gave thanks for his own escape; he had been set free from a life of vice and sin and folly, from all the dangers and illusions that are most dreaded by the wise. He laughed as he remembered what would be the common view of the situation. An ordinary lover would suffer all the sting of sorrow and contempt; there would be grief for a lost mistress, and rage at her faithlessness, and hate in the heart; one foolish passion driving on another, and driving the man to ruin. For what would be commonly called the real woman he now cared nothing; if he had heard that she had died in her farm in Utter Gwent, he would have experienced only a passing sorrow, such as he might feel at the death of any one he had once known. But he did not think of the young farmer's wife as the real Annie; he did not think of the frost-bitten leaves in winter as the real rose. Indeed, the life of many reminded him of the flowers; perhaps more especially of those flowers which to all appearance are for many years but dull and dusty clumps of green, and suddenly, in one night, burst into the flame of blossom, and fill all the misty lawns with odour: till the morning. It was in that night that the flower lived, not through the long unprofitable years; and, in like manner, many human lives, he thought, were born in the evening and dead before the coming of day. But he had preserved the precious flower in all its glory, not suffering it to wither in the hard light, but keeping it in a secret place, where it could never be destroyed. Truly now, and for the first time, he possessed Annie, as a man possesses the gold which he has dug from the rock and purged of its baseness.

He was musing over these things when a piece of news, very strange and unexpected, arrived at the rectory. A distant, almost a mythical relative, known from childhood as "Cousin Edward in the Isle of Wight", had died, and by some strange freak had left Lucian two thousand pounds. It was a pleasure to give his father five hundred pounds, and the rector on his side forgot for a couple of days to lean his head on his hand. From the rest of the capital, which was well invested, Lucian found he would derive something between sixty and seventy pounds a year, and his old desires for literature and a refuge in the murmuring streets returned to him. He longed to be free from the incantations that surrounded him in the country, to work and live in a new atmosphere; and so, with many good wishes from his father, he came to the retreat in the waste places of London.

He was in high spirits when he found the square, clean room, horribly furnished, in the by-street that branched from the main road, and advanced in an unlovely sweep to the mud pits and the desolation that was neither town nor country. On every side monotonous grey streets, each house the replica of its neighbour, to the east an unexplored wilderness, north and west and south the brickfields and market-gardens, everywhere the ruins of the country, the tracks where sweet lanes had been, gangrened stumps of trees, the relics of hedges, here and there an oak stripped of its bark, white and haggard and leprous, like a corpse. And the air seemed always grey, and the smoke from the brickfields was grey.

At first he scarcely realised the quarter into which chance had led him. His only thought was of the great adventure of letters in which he proposed to engage, and his first glance round his "bed-sitting-room" shewed him that there was no piece of furniture suitable for his purpose. The table, like the rest of the suite, was of bird's-eye maple; but the maker seemed to have penetrated the druidic secret of the rocking-stone, the thing was in a state of unstable equilibrium perpetually. For some days he wandered through the streets, inspecting the second-hand furniture shops, and at last, in a forlorn byway, found an old Japanese bureau, dishonoured and forlorn, standing amongst rusty bed-steads, sorry china, and all the refuse of homes dead and desolate. The bureau pleased him in spite of its grime and grease and dirt. Inlaid mother-of-pearl, the gleam of lacquer dragons in red gold, and hits of curious design shone through the film of neglect and ill-usage, and when the woman of the shop shewed him the drawers and well and pigeon-holes, he saw that it would be an apt instrument for his studies.

The bureau was carried to his room and replaced the "bird's-eye" table under the gas-jet. As Lucian arranged what papers he had accu-mulated: the sketches of hopeless experiments, shreds and tatters of stories begun but never completed, outlines of plots, two or three note-books scribbled through and through with impressions of the abandoned hills, he felt a thrill of exaltation at the prospect of work to be accomplished, of a new world all open before him.

He set out on the adventure with a fury of enthusiasm; his last thought at night when all the maze of streets was empty and silent was of the problem, and his dreams ran on phrases, and when he awoke in the morning he was eager to get back to his desk. He immersed him-self in a minute, almost a microscopic analysis of fine literature. It was no longer enough, as in the old days, to feel the charm and incantation of a line or a word; he wished to penetrate the secret, to understand something of the wonderful suggestion, all apart from the sense, that seemed to him the *differentia* of literature, as distinguished from the long follies of "character-drawing", "psychological analysis", and all the stuff that went to make the three-volume novel of commerce.

He found himself curiously strengthened by the change from the hills to the streets. There could be no doubt, he thought, that living a lonely life, interested only in himself and his own thoughts, he had be-come in a measure inhuman. The form of external things, black depths in woods, pools in lonely places, those still valleys curtained by hills on every side, sounding always with the ripple of their brooks, had be-come to him an influence like that of a drug, giving a certain peculiar colour and outline to his thoughts. And from early boyhood there had been another strange flavour in his life, the dream of the old Roman world, those curious impressions that he had gathered from the white walls of Caermaen, and from the looming bastions of the fort. It was in reality the subconscious fancies of many years that had rebuilt the golden city, and had shewn him the vine-trellis and the marbles and the sunlight in the garden of Avallaunius. And the rapture of love had made it all so vivid and warm with life, that even now, when he let his pen drop, the rich noise of the tavern and the chant of the theatre sounded above the murmur of the streets. Looking back, it was as much a part of his life as his schooldays, and the tessellated pavements were as real as the square of faded carpet beneath his feet.

But he felt that he had escaped. He could now survey those splendid and lovely visions from without, as if he read of opium dreams, and he no longer dreaded a weird suggestion that had once beset him, that his very soul was being moulded into the hills, and passing into the black mirror of still waterpools. He had taken refuge in the streets, in the harbour of a modern suburb, from the vague, dreaded magic that had charmed his life. Whenever he felt inclined to listen to the old wood-whisper or to the singing of the fauns he bent more earnestly to his work, turning a deaf ear to the incantations.

In the curious labour of the bureau he found refreshment that was continually renewed. He experienced again, and with a far more violent impulse, the enthusiasm that had attended the writing of his book a year or two before, and so, perhaps, passed from one drug to another. It was, indeed, with something of rapture that he imagined the great procession of years all to be devoted to the intimate analysis of words, to the construction of the sentence, as if it were a piece of jewellery or mosaic.

Sometimes, in the pauses of the work, he would pace up and down his cell, looking out of the window now and again and gazing for an instant into the melancholy street. As the year advanced the days grew more and more misty, and he found himself the inhabitant of a little island wreathed about with the waves of a white and solemn sea. In the afternoon the fog would grow denser, shutting out not only sight but sound; the shriek of the garden gates, the jangling of the tram-bell echoed as if from far away. Then there were days of heavy incessant rain; he could see a grey drifting sky and the drops plashing in the street, and the houses all dripping and saddened with wet.

He cured himself of one great aversion. He was no longer nauseated at the sight of a story begun and left unfinished. Formerly, even when an idea rose in his mind bright and wonderful, he had always approached the paper with a feeling of sickness and dislike, remembering all the hopeless beginnings he had made. But now he understood that to begin a romance was almost a separate and special art, a thing apart from the story, to be practised with sedulous care. Whenever an opening scene occurred to him he noted it roughly in a book, and he devoted many long winter evenings to the elaboration of these beginnings. Sometimes the first impression would yield only a paragraph or a sentence, and once or twice but a splendid and sonorous word, which seemed to Lucian all dim and rich with unsurmised adventure. But often he was able to write three or four vivid pages, studying above all things the hint and significance of the words and actions, striving to work into the lines the atmosphere of expectation and promise, and the murmur of wonderful events to come.

In this one department of his task the labour seemed almost endless. He would finish a few pages and then rewrite them, using the same incident and nearly the same words, but altering that indefinite something which is scarcely so much style as manner, or atmosphere. He was astonished at the enormous change that was thus effected, and often, though he himself had done the work, he could scarcely describe in words how it was done. But it was clear that in this art of manner, or suggestion, lay all the chief secrets of literature, that by it all the great miracles were performed. Clearly it was not style, for style in itself was untranslatable, but it was that high theurgic magic that made the English *Don Quixote,* roughly traduced by some Jervas, perhaps the best of all English books. And it was the same element that made the journey of Roderick Random to London, so ostensibly a narrative of coarse jokes and common experiences and burlesque manners, told in no very choice diction, essentially a wonderful vision of the eighteenth century, carrying to one's very nostrils the aroma of the Great North Road, iron-bound under black frost, darkened beneath shuddering woods, haunted by highwaymen, with an adventure waiting beyond every turn, and great old echoing inns in the midst of lonely winter lands.

It was this magic that Lucian sought for his opening chapters; he tried to find that quality that gives to words something beyond their sound and beyond their meaning, that in the first lines of a book should whisper things unintelligible but all significant. Often he worked for many hours without success, and the grim wet dawn once found him still searching for hieroglyphic sentences, for words mystical, symbolic. On the shelves, in the upper part of his bureau, he had placed the books which, however various as to matter, seemed to have a part in this curious quality of suggestion, and in that sphere which might almost be called supernatural. To these books he often had recourse, when further effort appeared altogether hopeless, and certain pages in Coleridge and Edgar Allan Poe had the power of holding him in a trance of delight, subject to emotions and impressions which he knew to transcend altogether the realm of the formal understanding. Such lines as:

> Bottomless vales and boundless floods,
> And chasms, and caves, and Titan woods,
> With forms that no man can discover
> For the dews that drip all over;

had for Lucian more than the potency of a drug, lulling him into a splendid waking-sleep, every word being a supreme incantation. And it was not only his mind that was charmed by such passages, for he felt at the same time a strange and delicious bodily languor that held him motionless, without the desire or power to stir from his seat. And there were certain phrases in *Kubla Khan* that had such a magic that he would sometimes wake up, as it were, to the consciousness that he had been lying on the bed or sitting in the chair by the bureau, repeating a single line over and over again for two or three hours. Yet he knew perfectly well that he had not been really asleep; a little effort recalled a constant impression of the wall paper, with its pink flowers on a buff ground, and of the muslin-curtained window, letting in the grey winter light. He had been some seven months in London when this odd experience first occurred to him. The day opened dreary and cold and clear, with a gusty and restless wind whirling round the corner of the street, and lifting the dead leaves and scraps of paper that littered the roadway into eddying mounting circles, as if a storm of black rain were to come. Lucian had sat late the night before, and rose in the morning feeling weary and listless and heavy-headed. While he dressed, his legs dragged him as with weights, and he staggered and nearly fell in bending down to the mat outside for his tea-tray. He lit the spirit lamp on the hearth with shaking, unsteady hands, and could scarcely pour out the tea when it was ready. A delicate cup of tea was one of his few luxuries; he was fond of the strange flavour of the green leaf, and this morning he drank the straw-coloured liquid eagerly, hoping it would disperse the cloud of languor. He tried his best to coerce himself into the sense of vigour and enjoyment with which he usually began the day, walking briskly up and down and arranging his papers in order. But he could not free himself from depression; even as he opened the dear bureau a wave of melancholy came upon him, and he began to ask himself whether he were not pursuing a vain dream, searching for treasures that had no existence. He drew out his cousin's letter and read it again, sadly enough. After all there was a good deal of truth in what she said; he had "overrated" his powers, he had no friends, no real education. He began to count up the months since he had come to London; he had received his two thousand pounds in March, and in May he had said good-bye to the woods and to the dear and friendly paths. May, June, July, August, September, October, November, and half of December had gone by; and what had he to shew? Nothing but the experiment, the attempt, futile scribblings which had no end nor shining purpose. There was nothing in his desk that he could produce as evidence of his capacity, no fragment even of accomplishment. It was a thought of intense bitterness, but it seemed as if the barbarians were in the right—a place in a house of business would have been more suitable. He leaned his head on his desk overwhelmed with the severity of his own judgment. He tried to comfort himself again by the thought of all the hours of happy enthusiasm he had spent amongst his papers, working for a great idea with infinite patience. He recalled to mind something that he had always tried to keep in the background of his hopes, the foundation stone of his life, which he had hidden out of sight. Deep in his heart was the hope that he might one day write a valiant book; he scarcely dared to entertain the aspiration, he felt his incapacity too deeply, but yet this longing was the foundation of all his painful and patient effort. This he had proposed in secret to himself, that if he laboured without ceasing, without tiring, he might produce something which would at all events be art, which would stand wholly apart from the objects shaped like books, printed with printers' ink, and called by the name of books that he had read. Giotto, he knew, was a painter, and the man who imitated walnut-wood on the deal doors opposite was a painter, and he had wished to be a very humble pupil in the class of the former. It was better, he thought, to fail in attempting exquisite things than to succeed in the department of the utterly contemptible; he had vowed he would be the dunce of Cervantes's school rather than top-boy in the academy of *A Bad Un to Beat* and *Millicent's Marriage*. And with this purpose he had devoted himself to laborious and joyous years, so that however mean his capacity, the pains should not be wanting. He tried now to rouse himself from a growing misery by the recollection of this high aim, but it all seemed hopeless vanity. He looked out into the grey street, and it stood a symbol of his life, chill and dreary and grey and vexed with a horrible wind. There were the dull inhabitants of the quarter going about their common business; a man was crying "mackerel" in a doleful voice, slowly passing up the street, and staring into the white-curtained "parlours", searching for the face of a purchaser behind the India-rubble plants, stuffed birds, and piles of gaudy gilt books that adorned the windows. One of the blistered doors over the way banged, and a woman came scurrying out on some errand, and the garden gate shrieked two melancholy notes as she opened it and let it swing back after her. The little patches called gardens were mostly untilled, uncared for, squares of slimy moss, dotted with clumps of coarse ugly grass, but here and there were the blackened and rotting remains of sunflowers and marigolds. And beyond, he knew, stretched the labyrinth of streets more or less squalid, but all grey and dull, and behind were the mud pits and the steaming heaps of yellowish bricks, and to the north was a great wide cold waste, treeless, desolate, swept by bitter wind. It was all like his own life, he said again to himself, a maze of unprofitable dreariness and desolation, and his mind grew as black and hopeless as the winter sky. The morning went thus dismally till twelve o'clock, and he put on his hat and great-coat. He always went out for an hour every day between twelve and one; the exercise was a necessity, and the landlady made his bed in the interval. The wind blew the smoke from the chimneys into his face as he shut the door, and with the acrid smoke came the prevailing odour of the street, a blend of cabbage-water and burnt bones and the faint sickly vapour from the brickfields. Lucian walked mechanically for the hour, going eastward, along the main road. The wind pierced him, and the dust was blinding, and the dreariness of the street increased his misery. The row of common shops, full of common things, the blatant public-houses, the Independent chapel, a horrible stucco parody of a Greek temple with a façade of hideous columns that was a nightmare, villas like smug Pharisees, shops again, a church in cheap Gothic, an old garden blasted and riven by the builder, these were the pictures of the way. When he got home again he flung himself on the bed, and lay there stupidly till sheer hunger roused him. He ate a hunch of bread and drank some water, and began to pace up and down the room, wondering whether there were no escape from despair. Writing seemed quite impossible, and hardly knowing what he did he opened his bureau and took out a book from the shelves. As his eyes fell on the page the air grew dark and heavy as night, and the wind wailed suddenly, loudly, terribly.

"By woman wailing for her Demon lover." The words were on his lips when he raised his eyes again. A broad band of pale clear light was shining into the room, and when he looked out of the window he saw the road all brightened by glittering pools of water, and as the last drops of the rain-storm starred these mirrors the sun sank into the wrack. Lucian gazed about him, perplexed, till his eyes fell on the clock above his empty hearth. He had been sitting, motionless, for nearly two hours without any sense of the passage of time, and without ceasing he had murmured those words as he dreamed an endless wonderful story. He experienced somewhat the sensations of Coleridge himself; strange, amazing, ineffable things seemed to have been presented to him, not in the form of the idea, but actually and materially, but he was less fortunate than Coleridge in that he could not, even vaguely, image to himself what he had seen. Yet when he searched his mind he knew that the consciousness of the room in which he sat had never left him; he had seen the thick darkness gather, and had heard the whirl of rain hissing through the air. Windows had been shut down with a crash, he had noted the pattering footsteps of people running to shelter, the landlady's voice crying to some one to look at the rain

coming in under the door. It was like peering into some old bitumi-
nous picture, one could see at last that the mere blackness resolved itself into the likeness of trees and rocks and travellers. And against this
background of his room, and the storm, and the noises of the street,
his vision stood out illuminated, he felt he had descended to the very
depths, into the caverns that are hollowed beneath the soul. He tried
vainly to record the history of his impressions; the symbols remained
in his memory, but the meaning was all conjecture.

The next morning, when he awoke, he could scarcely understand
or realise the bitter depression of the preceding day. He found it had
all vanished away and had been succeeded by an intense exaltation. Afterwards, when at rare intervals he experienced the same strange possession of the consciousness, he found this to be the invariable result,
the hour of vision was always succeeded by a feeling of delight, by sensations of brightened and intensified powers. On that bright December
day after the storm he rose joyously, and set about the labour of the
bureau with the assurance of success, almost with the hope of formi-
dable difficulties to be overcome. He had long busied himself with
those curious researches which Poe had indicated in the *Philosophy of
Composition,* and many hours had been spent in analysing the singular
effects which may be produced by the sound and resonance of words.
But he had been struck by the thought that in the finest literature there
were more subtle tones than the loud and insistent music of "never
more", and he endeavoured to find the secret of those pages and sentences which spoke, less directly, and less obviously, to the soul rather
than to the ear, being filled with a certain grave melody and the sensation of singing voices. It was admirable, no doubt, to write phrases that
shewed at a glance their designed rhythm, and rang with sonorous
words, but he dreamed of a prose in which the music should be less
explicit, of neumes rather than notes. He was astonished that morning
at his own fortune and facility; he succeeded in covering a page of
ruled paper wholly to his satisfaction, and the sentences, when he read
them out, appeared to suggest a weird elusive chanting, exquisite but
almost imperceptible, like the echo of the plainsong reverberated from
the vault of a monastic church.

He thought that such happy mornings well repaid him for the anguish of depression which he sometimes had to suffer, and for the

strange experience of "possession" recurring at rare intervals, and usually after many weeks of severe diet. His income, he found, amounted to sixty-five pounds a year, and he lived for weeks at a time on fifteen shillings a week. During these austere periods his only food was bread, at the rate of a loaf a day; but he drank huge draughts of green tea, and smoked a black tobacco, which seemed to him a more potent mother of thought than any drug from the scented East. "I hope you go to some nice place for dinner," wrote his cousin; "there used to be some excellent eating-houses in London where one could get a good cut from the joint, *with plenty of gravy,* and a boiled potato, for a shilling. Aunt Mary writes that you should try Mr. Jones's in Water Street, Islington, whose father came from near Caermaen, and was always most comfortable in her day. I daresay the walk there would do you good. It is such a pity you smoke that horrid tobacco. I had a letter from Mrs. Dolly (Jane Diggs, who married your cousin John Dolly) the other day, and she said they would have been delighted to take you for only twenty-five shillings a week for the sake of the family if you had not been a smoker. She told me to ask you if you had ever seen a horse or a dog smoking tobacco. They are such nice, comfortable people, and the children would have been company for you. Johnnie, who used to be such a dear little fellow, has just gone into an office in the City, and seems to have excellent prospects. How I wish, my dear Lucian, that you could do something in the same way. Don't forget Mr. Jones's in Water Street, and you might mention your name to him."

Lucian never troubled Mr. Jones; but these letters of his cousin's always refreshed him by the force of contrast. He tried to imagine himself a part of the Dolly family, going dutifully every morning to the City on the 'bus, and returning in the evening for high tea. He could conceive the fine odour of hot roast beef hanging about the decorous house on Sunday afternoons, papa asleep in the dining-room, mamma lying down, and the children quite good and happy with their "Sundays books". In the evening, after supper, one read the *Quiver* till bedtime. Such pictures as these were to Lucian a comfort and a help, a remedy against despair. Often when he felt overwhelmed by the difficulty of the work he had undertaken, he thought of the alternative career, and was strengthened.

He returned again and again to that desire of a prose which should sound faintly, not so much with an audible music, but with the memory and echo of it. In the night, when the last tram had gone jangling by, and he had looked out and seen the street all wrapped about in heavy folds of the mist, he conducted some of his most delicate experiments. In that white and solitary midnight of the suburban street he experienced the curious sense of being on a tower, remote and apart and high above all the troubles of the earth. The gas lamp, which was nearly opposite, shone in a pale halo of light, and the houses themselves were merely indistinct marks and shadows amidst that palpable whiteness, shutting out the world and its noises. The knowledge of the swarming life that was so still, though it surrounded him, made the silence seem deeper than that of the mountains before the dawn; it was as if he alone stirred and looked out amidst a host sleeping at his feet. The fog came in by the open window in freezing puffs, and as Lucian watched he noticed that it shook and wavered like the sea, tossing up wreaths and drifts across the pale halo of the lamp, and, these vanishing, others succeeded. It was as if the mist passed by from the river to the north, as if it still passed by in the silence.

He would shut his window gently, and sit down in his lighted room with all the consciousness of the white advancing shroud upon him. It was then that he found himself in the mood for curious labours, and able to handle with some touch of confidence the more exquisite instruments of the craft. He sought for that magic by which all the glory and glamour of mystic chivalry were made to shine through the burlesque and gross adventures of Don Quixote, by which Hawthorne had lit his infernal Sabbath fires, and fashioned a burning aureole about the village tragedy of the *Scarlet Letter*. In Hawthorne the story and the suggestion, though quite distinct and of different worlds, were rather parallel than opposed to one another; but Cervantes had done a stranger thing. One read of Don Quixote, beaten, dirty, and ridiculous, mistaking windmills for giants, sheep for an army; but the impression was of the enchanted forest, of Avalon, of the San Graal, "far in the spiritual city". And Rabelais shewed him, beneath the letter, the Tourainian sun shining on the hot rock above Chinon, on the maze of narrow, climbing streets, on the high-pitched, gabled roofs, on the grey-blue *tourelles*, pricking upward from the fantastic labyrinth of walls. He heard the sound of sonorous plainsong from the monastic

choir, of gross exuberant gaiety from the rich vineyards; he listened to
the eternal mystic mirth of those that halted in the purple shadow of
the *sorbier* by the white, steep road. The gracious and ornate *châteaux* on
the Loire and the Vienne rose fair and shining to confront the incredible secrets of vast, dim, far-lifted Gothic naves, that seemed ready to
take the great deep, and float away from the mist and dust of earthly
streets to anchor in the haven of the clear city that hath foundations.
The rank tale of the *garde-robe,* of the farm-kitchen, mingled with the
reasoned, endless legend of the schools, with luminous Platonic argument; the old pomp of the Middle Ages put on the robe of a fresh life.
There was a smell of wine and of incense, of June meadows and of ancient books, and through it all he hearkened, intent, to the exultation
of chiming bells ringing for a new feast in a new land. He would cover
pages with the analysis of these marvels, tracking the suggestion concealed beneath the words, and yet glowing like the golden threads in a
robe of samite, or like that device of the old binders by which a vivid
picture appeared on the shut edges of a book. He tried to imitate this
art, to summon even the faint shadow of the great effect, rewriting a
page of Hawthorne, experimenting and changing an epithet here and
there, noting how sometimes the alteration of a trifling word would
plunge a whole scene into darkness, as if one of those blood-red fires
had instantly been extinguished. Sometimes, for severe practice, he attempted to construct short tales in the manner of this or that master.
He sighed over these desperate attempts, over the clattering pieces of
mechanism which would not even simulate life; but he urged himself
to an infinite perseverance. Through the white hours he worked on
amidst the heap and litter of papers; books and manuscripts over-
flowed from the bureau to the floor; and if he looked out he saw the
mist still pass by, still passing from the river to the north.

It was not till the winter was well advanced that he began at all to
explore the region in which he lived. Soon after his arrival in the grey
street he had taken one or two vague walks, hardly noticing where he
went or what he saw; but for all the summer he had shut himself in his
room, beholding nothing but the form and colour of words. For his
morning walk he almost invariably chose the one direction, going
along the Uxbridge Road towards Notting Hill, and returning by the
same monotonous thoroughfare. Now, however, when the new year

was beginning its dull days, he began to diverge occasionally to right and left, sometimes eating his luncheon in odd corners, in the bulging parlours of eighteenth-century taverns, that still fronted the surging sea of modern streets, or perhaps in brand new "publics" on the broken borders of the brickfields, smelling of the clay from which they had swollen. He found waste by-places behind railway embankments where he could smoke his pipe sheltered from the wind; sometimes there was a wooden fence by an old pear-orchard where he sat and gazed at the wet desolation of the market-gardens, munching a few currant biscuits by way of dinner. As he went farther afield a sense of immensity slowly grew upon him; it was as if, from the little island of his room, that one friendly place, he pushed out into the grey unknown, into a city that for him was uninhabited as the desert.

He came back to his cell after these purposeless wanderings always with a sense of relief, with the thought of taking refuge from grey. As he lit the gas and opened the desk of his bureau and saw the pile of papers awaiting him, it was as if he had passed from the black skies and the stinging wind and the dull maze of the suburb into all the warmth and sunlight and violent colour of the south.

VI

It was in this winter after his coming to the grey street that Lucian first experienced the pains of desolation. He had all his life known the delights of solitude, and had acquired that habit of mind which makes a man find rich company on the bare hillside and leads him into the heart of the wood to meditate by the dark waterpools. But now in the blank interval when he was forced to shut up his desk, the sense of loneliness overwhelmed him and filled him with unutterable melancholy. On such days he carried about with him an unceasing gnawing torment in his breast; the anguish of the empty page awaiting him in his bureau, and the knowledge that it was worse than useless to attempt the work. He had fallen into the habit of always using this phrase "the work" to denote the adventure of literature; it had grown in his mind to all the austere and grave significance of "the great work" on the lips of the alchemists; it included every trifling and laborious page and the vague magnificent fancies that sometimes hovered below him. All else had become mere by-play, unimportant, trivial; the work was the end, and the means and the food of his life—it raised him up in the morning to renew the struggle, it was the symbol which charmed him as he lay down at night. All through the hours of toil at the bureau he was enchanted, and when he went out and explored the unknown coasts, the one thought allured him, and was the coloured glass between his eyes and the world. Then as he drew nearer home his steps would quicken, and the more weary and grey the walk, the more he rejoiced as he thought of his hermitage and of the curious difficulties that awaited him there. But when, suddenly and without warning, the faculty disappeared, when his mind seemed a hopeless waste from which nothing could arise, then he became subject to a misery so piteous that the barbarians themselves would have been sorry for him. He had known some foretaste of these bitter and inexpressible griefs in the old country days, but then he had immediately taken refuge in the hills, he had rushed to the dark woods as to an anodyne, letting his heart drink in all the wonder and magic of the wild land. Now in these days of January, in the suburban street, there was no such refuge.

He had been working steadily for some weeks, well enough satisfied on the whole with the daily progress, glad to awake in the morning, and to read over what he had written on the night before. The new year opened with faint and heavy weather and a breathless silence in the air, but in a few days the great frost set in. Soon the streets began to suggest the appearance of a beleaguered city, the silence that had preceded the frost deepened, and the mist hung over the earth like a dense white smoke. Night after night the cold increased, and people seemed unwilling to go abroad, till even the main thoroughfares were empty and deserted, as if the inhabitants were lying close in hiding. It was at this dismal time that Lucian found himself reduced to impotence. There was a sudden break in his thought, and when he wrote on valiantly, hoping against hope, he only grew more aghast on the discovery of the imbecilities he had committed to paper. He ground his teeth together and persevered, sick at heart, feeling as if all the world were fallen from under his feet, driving his pen on mechanically, till he was overwhelmed. He saw the stuff he had done without veil or possible concealment, a lamentable and wretched sheaf of verbiage, worse, it seemed, than the efforts of his boyhood. He was not longer tautological, he avoided tautology with the infernal art of a leader-writer, filling his wind bags and mincing words as if he had been a trained journalist on the staff of the *Daily Post*. There seemed all the matter of an insufferable tragedy in these thoughts; that his patient and enduring toil was in vain, that practice went for nothing, and that he had wasted the labour of Milton to accomplish the tenth-rate. Unhappily he could not "give in"; the longing, the fury for the work burnt within him like a burning fire; he lifted up his eyes in despair.

It was then, while he knew that no one could help him, that he languished for help, and then, though he was aware that no comfort was possible, he fervently wished to be comforted. The only friend he had was his father, and he knew that his father would not even understand his distress. For him, always, the printed book was the beginning and end of literature; the agony of the maker, his despair and sickness, were as accursed as the pains of labour. He was ready to read and admire the work of the great Smith, but he did not wish to hear of the period when the great Smith had writhed and twisted like a scotched worm, only hoping to be put out of his misery, to go mad or die, to escape somehow from the bitter pains. And Lucian knew no one else. Now and then he read in the paper the fame of the great *littérateurs;* the Gypsies were entertaining the Prince of Wales, the Jolly Beggars were dining with the Lord Mayor, the Old Mumpers were mingling amicably and gorgeously with the leading members of the Stock Exchange. He was so unfortunate as to know none of these gentlemen, but it hardly seemed likely that they could have done much for him in any case. Indeed, in his heart, he was certain that help and comfort from without were in the nature of things utterly impossible, his ruin and grief were within, and only his own assistance could avail. He tried to reassure himself, to believe that his torments were a proof of his vocation, that the facility of the novelist who stood six years deep in contracts to produce romances was a thing wholly undesirable, but all the while he longed for but a drop of that inexhaustible fluency which he professed to despise.

He drove himself out from that dreary contemplation of the white paper and the idle pen. He went into the frozen and deserted streets, hoping that he might pluck the burning coal from his heart, but the fire was not quenched. As he walked furiously along the grim iron roads he fancied that those persons who passed him cheerfully on their way to friends and friendly hearths shrank from him into the mists as they went by. Lucian imagined that the fire of his torment and anguish must in some way glow visibly about him; he moved, perhaps, in a nimbus that proclaimed the blackness and the flames within. He knew, of course, that in misery he had grown delirious, that the well-coated, smooth-hatted personages who loomed out of the fog upon him were in reality shuddering only with cold, but in spite of common sense he still conceived that he saw on their faces an evident horror and disgust, and something of the repugnance that one feels at the sight of a venomous snake, half-killed, trailing its bleeding vileness out of sight. By design Lucian tried to make for remote and desolate places, and yet when he had succeeded in touching on the open country, and knew that the icy shadow hovering through the mist was a field, he longed for some sound and murmur of life, and turned again to roads where pale lamps were glimmering, and the dancing flame of firelight shone across the frozen shrubs. And the sight of these homely fires, the thought of affection and consolation waiting by them, stung him the more sharply perhaps because of the contrast with his own chills and weariness and helpless sickness, and chiefly because he knew that he had long closed an everlasting door between his heart and such felicities. If those within had come out and had called him by his name to enter and be comforted, it would have been quite unavailing, since between them and him there was a great gulf fixed. Perhaps for the first time he realised that he had lost the art of humanity for ever. He had thought when he closed his ears to the wood whisper and changed the fauns' singing for the murmur of the streets, the black pools for the shadows and amber light of London, that he had put off the old life, and had turned his soul to healthy activities, but the truth was that he had merely exchanged one drug for another. He could not be human, and he wondered whether there were some drop of the fairy blood in his body that made him foreign and a stranger in the world.

He did not surrender to desolation without repeated struggles. He strove to allure himself to his desk by the promise of some easy task; he would not attempt invention, but he had memoranda and rough jottings of ideas in his note-books, and he would merely amplify the suggestions ready to his hand. But it was hopeless, again and again it was hopeless. As he read over his notes, trusting that he would find some hint that might light up the dead fires, and kindle again that pure flame of enthusiasm, he found how desperately his fortune had fallen. He could see no light, no colour in the lines he had scribbled with eager trembling fingers; he remembered how splendid all these things had been when he wrote them down, but now they were meaningless, faded into grey. The few words he had dashed on to the paper, enraptured at the thought of the happy hours they promised, had become mere jargon, and when he understood the idea it seemed foolish, dull, unoriginal. He discovered something at last that appeared to have a grain of promise, and determined to do his best to put it into shape, but the first paragraph appalled him; it might have been written by an unintelligent schoolboy. He tore the paper in pieces, and shut and locked his desk, heavy despair sinking like lead into his heart. For the rest of that day he lay motionless on the bed, smoking pipe after pipe in the hope of stupefying himself with tobacco fumes. The air in the room became blue and thick with smoke; it was bitterly cold, and he wrapped himself up in his great-coat and drew the counterpane over him. The night came on and the window darkened, and at last he fell asleep.

He renewed the effort at intervals, only to plunge deeper into misery. He felt the approaches of madness, and knew that his only hope was to walk till he was physically exhausted, so that he might come home almost fainting with fatigue, but ready to fall asleep the moment he got into bed. He passed the mornings in a kind of torpor, endeavouring to avoid thought, to occupy his mind with the pattern of the paper, with the advertisements at the end of a book, with the curious greyness of the light that glimmered through the mist into his room, with the muffled voices that rumbled now and then from the street. He tried to make out the design that had once coloured the faded carpet on the floor, and wondered about the dead artist in Japan, the adorner of his bureau. He speculated as to what his thoughts had been as he inserted the rainbow mother-of-pearl and made that great flight of shining birds, dipping their wings as they rose from the reeds, or how he had conceived the lacquer dragons in red gold, and the fantastic houses in the garden of peach-trees. But sooner or later the oppression of his grief returned, the loud shriek and clang of the garden-gate, the warning bell of some passing bicyclist steering through the fog, the noise of his pipe falling to the floor, would suddenly awaken him to the sense of misery. He knew that it was time to go out; he could not bear to sit still and suffer. Sometimes he cut a slice of bread and put it in his pocket, sometimes he trusted to the chance of finding a public-house, where he could have a sandwich and a glass of beer. He turned always from the main streets and lost himself in the intricate suburban byways, willing to be engulfed in the infinite whiteness of the mist.

The roads had stiffened into iron ridges, the fences and trees were glittering with frost crystals, everything was of strange and altered aspect. Lucian walked on and on through the maze, now in a circle of shadowy villas, awful as the buried streets of Herculaneum, now in lanes dipping onto open country, that led him past great elm-trees whose white boughs were all still, and past the bitter lonely fields where the mist seemed to fade away into grey darkness. As he wandered along these unfamiliar and ghastly paths he became the more convinced of his utter remoteness from all humanity, he allowed that grotesque suggestion of there being something visibly amiss in his outward appearance to grow upon him, and often he looked with a horrible expectation into the faces of those who passed by, afraid lest his own senses gave him false intelligence, and that he had really assumed some frightful and revolting shape. It was curious that, partly by his own fault, and largely, no doubt, through the operation of mere coincidence, he was once or twice strongly confirmed in this fantastic delusion. He came one day into a lonely and unfrequented byway, a country lane falling into ruin, but still fringed with elms that had formed an avenue leading to the old manor-house. It was now the road of communication between two far outlying suburbs, and on these winter nights lay as black, dreary, and desolate as a mountain track. Soon after the frost began, a gentleman had been set upon in this lane as he picked his way between the corner where the 'bus had set him down, and his home where the fire was blazing, and his wife watched the clock. He was stumbling uncertainly through the gloom, growing a little nervous because the walk seemed so long, and peering anxiously for the lamp at the end of his street, when the two footpads rushed at him out of the fog. One caught him from behind, the other struck him with a heavy bludgeon, and as he lay senseless they robbed him of his watch and money, and vanished across the fields. The next morning all the suburb rang with the story; the unfortunate merchant had been grievously hurt, and wives watched their husbands go out in the morning with sickening apprehension, not knowing what might happen at night. Lucian of course was ignorant of all these rumours, and struck into the gloomy by-road without caring where he was or whither the way would lead him.

He had been driven out that day as with whips, another hopeless attempt to return to the work had agonised him, and existence seemed an intolerable pain. As he entered the deeper gloom, where the fog hung heavily, he began, half consciously, to gesticulate; he felt convulsed with torment and shame, and it was a sorry relief to clench his nails into his palm and strike the air as he stumbled heavily along, bruising his feet against the frozen ruts and ridges. His impotence was hideous, he said to himself, and he cursed himself and his life, breaking out into a loud oath, and stamping on the ground. Suddenly he was shocked at a scream of terror, it seemed in his very ear, and looking up he saw for a moment a woman gazing at him out of the mist, her features distorted and stiff with fear. A momentary convulsion twitched her arms into the ugly mimicry of a beckoning gesture, and she turned and ran for dear life, howling like a beast.

Lucian stood still in the road while the woman's cries grew faint and died away. His heart was chilled within him as the significance of this strange incident became clear. He remembered nothing of his violent gestures; he had not known at the time that he had sworn out loud, or that he was grinding his teeth with impotent rage. He only thought of that ringing scream, of the horrible fear on the white face that had looked upon him, of the woman's headlong flight from his presence. He stood trembling and shuddering, and in a little while he was feeling his face, searching for some loathsome mark, for the stigmata of evil branding his forehead. He staggered homewards like a drunken man, and when he came into the Uxbridge Road some children saw him and called after him as he swayed and caught at the lamp-post. When he got to his room he sat down at first in the dark. He did not dare to light the gas. Everything in the room was indistinct, but he shut his eyes as he passed the dressing-table, and sat in a corner, his face turned to the wall. And when at last he gathered courage and the flame leapt hissing from the jet, he crept piteously towards the glass, and ducked his head, crouching miserably, and struggling with his terrors before he could look at his own image.

To the best of his power he tried to deliver himself from these more grotesque fantasies; he assured himself that there was nothing terrific in his countenance but sadness, that his face was like the face of other men. Yet he could not forget that reflection he had seen in the woman's eyes, how the surest mirrors had shewn him a horrible dread, her soul itself quailing and shuddering at an awful sight. Her scream rang and rang in his ears; she had fled away from him as if he offered some fate darker than death.

He looked again and again into the glass, tortured by a hideous uncertainty. His senses told him there was nothing amiss, yet he had had a proof, and yet, as he peered most earnestly, there was, it seemed, something strange and not altogether usual in the expression of the eyes. Perhaps it might be the unsteady flare of the gas, or perhaps a flaw in the cheap looking-glass, that gave some slight distortion to the image. He walked briskly up and down the room and tried to gaze steadily, indifferently, into his own face. He would not allow himself to be misguided by a word. When he had pronounced himself incapable of humanity, he had only meant that he could not enjoy the simple things of common life. A man was not necessarily monstrous, merely because he did not appreciate high tea, a quiet chat about the neighbours, and a happy noisy evening with the children. But with what message, then, did he appear charged that the woman's mouth grew so stark? Her hands had jerked up as if they had been pulled with frantic wires; she seemed for the instant like a horrible puppet. Her scream was a thing from the nocturnal Sabbath.

He lit a candle and held it close up to the glass so that his own face glared white at him, and the reflection of the room became an indistinct darkness. He saw nothing but the candle flame and his own shining eyes, and surely they were not as the eyes of common men. As he put down the light, a sudden suggestion entered his mind, and he drew a quick breath, amazed at the thought. He hardly knew whether to rejoice or to shudder. For the thought he conceived was this: that he had mistaken all the circumstances of the adventure, and had perhaps repulsed a sister who would have welcomed him to the Sabbath.

He lay awake all night, turning from one dreary and frightful

thought to the other, scarcely dozing for a few hours when the dawn
came. He tried for a moment to argue with himself when he got up;
knowing that his true life was locked up in the bureau, he made a desperate attempt to drive the phantoms and hideous shapes from his
mind. He was assured that his salvation was in the work, and he drew
the key from his pocket, and made as if he would have opened the
desk. But the nausea, the remembrances of repeated and utter failure,
were too powerful. For many days he hung about the Manor Lane, half
dreading, half desiring another meeting, and he swore he would not
again mistake the cry of rapture, nor repulse the arms extended in a
frenzy of delight. In those days he dreamed of some dark place where
they might celebrate and make the marriage of the Sabbath, with such
rites as he had dared to imagine.

It was perhaps only the shock of a letter from his father that rescued him from these evident approaches to madness. Mr. Taylor wrote
how they had missed him at Christmas, how the farmers had enquired
after him, of the homely familiar things that recalled his boyhood, his
mother's voice, the friendly fireside, and the good old fashions that
had nurtured him. He remembered that he had once been a boy, loving the cake and puddings and the radiant holly, and all the seventeenth-century mirth that lingered on in the ancient farmhouses. And
there came to him the more holy memory of Mass on Christmas
morning. How sweet the dark and frosty earth had smelt as he walked
beside his mother down the winding lane, and from the stile near the
church they had seen the world glimmering to the dawn, and the wandering lanthorns advancing across the fields. Then he had come into
the church and seen it shining with candles and holly, and his father in
pure vestments of white linen sang the longing music of the liturgy at
the altar, and the people answered him, till the sun rose with the grave
notes of the Paternoster, and a red beam stole through the chancel
window.

The worst horror left him as he recalled the memory of these dear
and holy things. He cast away the frightful fancy that the scream he
had heard was a shriek of joy, that the arms, rigidly jerked out, invited
him to an embrace. Indeed, the thought that he had longed for such an
obscene illusion, that he had gloated over the recollection of that stark
mouth, filled him with disgust. He resolved that his senses were de-

ceived, that he had neither seen nor heard, but had for a moment externalised his own slumbering and morbid dreams. It was perhaps necessary that he should be wretched, that his efforts should be discouraged, but he would not yield utterly to madness.

Yet when he went abroad with such good resolutions, it was hard to resist an influence that seemed to come from without and within. He did not know it, but people were everywhere talking of the great frost, of the fog that lay heavy on London, making the streets dark and terrible, of strange birds that came fluttering about the windows in the silent squares. The Thames rolled out duskily, bearing down the jarring ice-blocks, and as one looked on the black water from the bridges it was like a river in a northern tale. To Lucian it all seemed mythical, of the same substance as his own fantastic thoughts. He rarely saw a newspaper, and did not follow from day to day the systematic readings of the thermometer, the reports of ice-fairs, of coaches driven across the river at Hampton, of the skating on the fens; and hence the iron roads, the beleaguered silence and the heavy folds of mist appeared as amazing as a picture, significant, appalling. He could not look out and see a common suburban street foggy and dull, nor think of the inhabitants as at work or sitting cheerfully eating nuts about their fires; he saw a vision of a grey road vanishing, of dim houses all empty and deserted, and the silence seemed eternal. And when he went out and passed through street after street, all void, by the vague shapes of houses that appeared for a moment and were then instantly swallowed up, it seemed to him as if he had strayed into a city that had suffered some inconceivable doom, that he alone wandered where myriads had once dwelt. It was a town as great as Babylon, terrible as Rome, marvellous as Lost Atlantis, set in the midst of a white wilderness surrounded by waste places. It was impossible to escape from it; if he skulked between hedges, and crept away beyond the frozen pools, presently the serried stony lines confronted him like an army, and far and far they swept away into the night, as some fabled wall that guards an empire in the vast dim east. Or in that distorting medium of the mist, changing all things, he imagined that he trod an infinite desolate plain, abandoned from ages, but circled and encircled with dolmen and menhir that loomed out at him, gigantic, terrible. All London was one grey temple of an awful rite, ring within ring of wizard stones circled about some central place, every circle was an initiation, every initiation eternal loss. Or perhaps he was astray for ever in a land of grey rocks. He had seen the light of home, the flicker of the fire on the walls; close at hand, it seemed, was the open door, and he had heard dear voices calling to him across the gloom, but he had just missed the path. The lamps vanished, the voices sounded thin and died away, and yet he knew that those within were waiting, that they could not bear to close the door, but waited, calling his name, while he had missed the way, and wandered in the pathless desert of the grey rocks. Fantastic, hideous, they beset him wherever he turned, piled up into strange shapes, pricked with sharp peaks, assuming the appearance of goblin towers, swelling into a vague dome like a fairy rath, huge and terrible. And as one dream faded into another, so these last fancies were perhaps the most tormenting and persistent; the rocky avenues became the camp and fortalice of some half-human, malignant race who swarmed in hiding, ready to bear him away into the heart of their horrible hills. It was awful to think that all his goings were surrounded, that in the darkness he was watched and surveyed, that every step but led him deeper and deeper into the labyrinth.

When, of an evening, he was secure in his room, the blind drawn down and the gas flaring, he made vigorous efforts toward sanity. It was not of his free will that he allowed terror to overmaster him, and he desired nothing better than a placid and harmless life, full of work and clear thinking. He knew that he deluded himself with imagination, that he had been walking through London suburbs and not through Pandemonium, and that if he could but unlock his bureau all those ugly forms would be resolved into the mist. But it was hard to say if he consoled himself effectually with such reflections, for the return to common sense meant also the return to the sharp pangs of defeat. It recalled him to the bitter theme of his own inefficiency, to the thought that he only desired one thing of life, and that this was denied him. He was willing to endure the austerities of a monk in a severe cloister, to suffer cold, to be hungry, to be lonely and friendless, to forbear all the consolation of friendly speech, and to be glad of all these things, if only he might be allowed to illuminate the manuscript in quietness. It seemed a hideous insufferable cruelty, that he should so fervently desire that which he could never gain.

He was led back to the old conclusion; he had lost the sense of humanity, he was wretched because he was an alien and a stranger amongst citizens. It seemed probable that the enthusiasm of literature, as he understood it, the fervent desire for the fine art, had in it something of the inhuman, and dissevered the enthusiast from his fellow-creatures. It was possible that the barbarian suspected as much, that by some slow process of rumination he had arrived at his fixed and inveterate hatred of all artists. It was no doubt a dim unconscious impression, by no means a clear reasoned conviction; the average Philistine, if pressed for the reasons of his dislike, would either become inarticulate, ejaculating "faugh" and "pah" like an old-fashioned Scots Magazine, or else he would give some imaginary and absurd reason, alleging that all "littery men" were poor, that composers never cut their hair, that painters were rarely public-school men, that sculptors couldn't ride straight to hounds to save their lives, but clearly these imbecilities were mere afterthoughts; the average man hated the artist from a deep instinctive dread of all that was strange, uncanny, alien to his nature; he gibbered, uttered his harsh, semi-bestial "faugh", and dismissed Keats to his gallipots from much the same motives as usually impelled the black savages to dismiss the white man on an even longer journey.

Lucian was not especially interested in this hatred of the barbarian for the maker, except from this point, that it confirmed him in his belief that the love of art dissociated the man from the race. One touch of art made the whole world alien, but surely miseries of the civilised man cast amongst savages were not so much caused by dread of their ferocity as by the terror of his loneliness. He feared their spears less than his own thoughts; he would perhaps in his last despair leave his retreat and go forth to perish at their hands, so that he might at least die in company, and hear the sound of speech before death. And Lucian felt most keenly that in his case there was a double curse; he was as isolated as Keats, and as inarticulate as his reviewers. The consolation of the work had failed him, and he was suspended in the void between two worlds.

It was no doubt the composite effect of his failures, his loneliness of soul, and solitude of life, that had made him invest those common streets with such grim and persistent terrors. He had perhaps yielded to a temptation without knowing that he had been tempted, and, in the

manner of De Quincey, had chosen the subtle in exchange for the
more tangible pains. Unconsciously, but still of free will, he had preferred the splendour and the gloom of a malignant vision before his
corporal pains, before the hard reality of his own impotence. It was
better to dwell in vague melancholy, to stray in the forsaken streets of
a city doomed from ages, to wander amidst forlorn and desperate
rocks than to awake to a gnawing and ignoble torment, to confess that
a house of business would have been more suitable and more practical,
that he had promised what he could never perform. Even as he struggled to beat back the phantasmagoria of the mist, and resolved that he
would no longer make all the streets a stage of apparitions, he hardly
realised what he had done, or that the ghosts he had called might de-
part and return again.

He continued his long walks, always with the object of producing a
physical weariness and exhaustion that would enable him to sleep of
nights. But even when he saw the foggy and deserted avenues in their
proper shape, and allowed his eyes to catch the pale glimmer of the
lamps, and the dancing flame of the firelight, he could not rid himself
of the impression that he stood afar off, that between those hearths
and himself there was a great gulf fixed. As he paced down the foot-
path he could often see plainly across the frozen shrubs into the
homely and cheerful rooms. Sometimes, late in the evening, he caught
a passing glimpse of the family at tea, father, mother, and children
laughing and talking together, well pleased with each other's company.
Sometimes a wife or a child was standing by the garden gate peering
anxiously through the fog, and the sight of it all, all the little details, the
hideous but comfortable arm-chairs turned ready to the fire, maroon-
red curtains being drawn close to shut out the ugly night, the sudden
blaze and illumination as the fire was poked up so that it might be
cheerful for father; these trivial and common things were acutely significant. They brought back to him the image of a dead boy—himself.
They recalled the shabby old "parlour" in the country, with its shabby
old furniture and fading carpet, and renewed a whole atmosphere of
affection and homely comfort. His mother would walk to the end of
the drive and look out for him when he was late (wandering then
about the dark woodlands); on winter evenings she would make the
fire blaze, and have his slippers warming by the hearth, and there was

probably buttered toast "as a treat". He dwelt on all these insignificant petty circumstances, on the genial glow and light after the muddy winter lanes, on the relish of the buttered toast and the smell of the hot tea, on the two old cats curled fast asleep before the fender, and made them instruments of exquisite pain and regret. Each of these strange houses that he passed was identified in his mind with his own vanished home; all was prepared and ready as in the old days, but he was shut out, judged and condemned to wander in the frozen mist, with weary feet, anguished and forlorn, and they that would pass from within to help him could not, neither could he pass to them. Again, for the hundredth time, he came back to the sentence, he could not gain the art of letters and he had lost the art of humanity. He saw the vanity of all his thoughts; he was an ascetic caring nothing for warmth and cheerfulness and the small comforts of life, and yet he allowed his mind to dwell on such things. If one of those passers-by, who walked briskly, eager for home, should have pitied him by some miracle and asked him to come in, it would have been worse than useless, yet he longed for pleasures that he could not have enjoyed. It was as if he were come to a place of torment, where they who could not drink longed for water, where they who could feel no warmth shuddered in the eternal cold. He was oppressed by the grim conceit that he himself still slept within the matted thicket, imprisoned by the green bastions of the Roman fort. He had never come out, but a changeling had gone down the hill, and now stirred about the earth.

Beset by such ingenious terrors, it was not wonderful that outward events and common incidents should abet his fancies. He had succeeded one day in escaping from the mesh of the streets, and fell on a rough and narrow lane that stole into a little valley. For the moment he was in a somewhat happier mood; the afternoon sun glowed through the rolling mist, and the air grew clearer. He saw quiet and peaceful fields, and a wood descending in a gentle slope from an old farmstead of warm red brick. The farmer was driving the slow cattle home from the hill, and his loud halloo to his dog came across the land a cheerful mellow note. From another side a cart was approaching the clustered barns, hesitating, pausing while the great horses rested, and then starting again into lazy motion. In the well of the valley a wandering line of bushes shewed where a brook crept in and out amongst the meadows, and, as Lucian stood, lingering, on the bridge, a soft and idle breath ruffled through the boughs of a great elm. He felt soothed, as by calm music, and wondered whether it would not be better for him to live in some such quiet place, within reach of the streets and yet remote from them. It seemed a refuge for still thoughts; he could imagine himself sitting at rest beneath the black yew tree in the farm garden, at the close of a summer day. He had almost determined that he would knock at the door and ask if they would take him as a lodger, when he saw a child running towards him down the lane. It was a little girl, with bright curls tossing about her head, and, as she came on, the sunlight glowed upon her, illuminating her brick-red frock and the yellow king-cups in her hat. She had run with her eyes on the ground, chirping and laughing to herself, and did not see Lucian till she was quite near him. She started and glanced into his eyes for a moment, and began to cry; he stretched out his hand, and she ran from him screaming, frightened no doubt by what was to her a sudden and strange apparition. He turned back towards London, and the mist folded him in its thick darkness, for on that evening it was tinged with black.

It was only by the intensest strain of resolution that he did not yield utterly to the poisonous anodyne which was always at hand. It had been a difficult struggle to escape from the mesh of the hills, from the music of the fauns, and even now he was drawn by the memory of these old allurements. But he felt that here, in his loneliness, he was in greater danger, and beset by a blacker magic. Horrible fancies rushed wantonly into his mind; he was not only ready to believe that something in his soul sent a shudder through all that was simple and inno-cent, but he came trembling home one Saturday night, believing, or half-believing, that he was in communion with evil. He had passed through the clamorous and blatant crowd of the "high street", where, as one climbed the hill, the shops seemed all aflame, and the black night air glowed with the flaring gas-jets and the naphtha lamps, hiss-ing and wavering before the February wind. Voices, raucous, clamant, abominable, were belched out of the blazing public-houses as the doors swung to and fro, and above these doors were hideous brassy lamps, very slowly swinging in a violent blast of air, so that they might have been infernal thuribles, censing the people. Some man was calling his wares in one long continuous shriek that never stopped or paused, and, as a respond, a deeper, louder voice roared to him from across the road. An Italian whirled the handle of his piano-organ in a fury, and a ring of imps danced mad figures around him, danced and flung up their legs till the rags dropped from some of them, and they still danced on. A flare of naphtha, burning with a rushing noise, threw a light on one point of the circle, and Lucian watched a lank girl of fifteen as she came round and round to the flash. She was quite drunk, and had kicked her petticoats away, and the crowd howled laughter and applause at her. Her black hair poured down and leapt on her scarlet bodice; she sprang and leapt round the ring, laughing in Bacchic frenzy, and led the orgy to triumph. People were crossing to and fro, jostling against each other, swarming about certain shops and stalls in a dense dark mass that quivered and sent out feelers as if it were one writhing organism. A little farther a group of young men, arm in arm, were marching down the roadway chanting some music-hall verse in full chorus, so that it sounded like plainsong. An impossible hubbub, a hum of voices angry as swarming bees, the squeals of five or six girls who ran in and out, and dived up dark passages and darted back into the crowd; all these mingled together till his ears quivered. A young fellow was playing the concertina, and he touched the keys with such slow fingers that the tune wailed solemn into a dirge; but there was nothing so strange as the burst of sound that swelled out when the public-house doors were opened.

He walked amongst these people, looked at their faces, and looked at the children amongst them. He had come out thinking that he would see the English working class, "the best-behaved and the best-tempered crowd in the world", enjoying the simple pleasure of the Saturday night's shopping. Mother bought the joint for Sunday's dinner, and perhaps a pair of boots for father; father had an honest glass of beer, and the children were given bags of sweets, and then all these worthy people went decently home to their well-earned rest. De Quincey had enjoyed the sight in his day, and had studied the rise and fall of onions and potatoes. Lucian, indeed, had desired to take these simple emotions as an opiate, to forget the fine fret and fantastic trouble of his own existence in plain things and the palpable joy of rest after labour. He was only afraid lest he should be too sharply reproached by the sight of these men who fought bravely year after year against starvation, who knew nothing of intricate and imagined grief, but only the weariness of relentless labour, of the long battle for their wives and children. It would be pathetic, he thought, to see them content with so little, brightened by the expectation of a day's rest and a good dinner, forced, even then, to reckon every penny, and to make their children laugh with halfpence. Either he would be ashamed before so much content, or else he would be again touched by the sense of his inhumanity which could take no interest in the common things of life. But still he went to be at least taken out of himself, to be forced to look at another side of the world, so that he might perhaps forget a little while his own sorrows.

He was fascinated by what he saw and heard. He wondered whether De Quincey also had seen the same spectacle, and had concealed his impressions out of reverence for the average reader. Here there were no simple joys of honest toilers, but wonderful orgies, that drew out his heart to horrible music. At first the violence of sound and sight had overwhelmed him; the lights flaring in the night wind, the array of naphtha lamps, the black shadows, the roar of voices. The dance about the piano-organ had been the first sign of an inner meaning, and the face of the dark girl as she came round and round to the flame had been amazing in its utter furious abandon. And what songs they were singing all around him, and what terrible words rang out, only to excite peals of laughter. In the public-houses the workmen's wives, the wives of small tradesmen, decently dressed in black, were drinking their faces to a flaming red, and urging their husbands to drink more. Beautiful young women, flushed and laughing, put their arms round the men's necks and kissed them, and then held up the glass to their lips. In the dark corners, at the openings of side streets, the children were talking together, instructing each other, whispering what they had seen; a boy of fifteen was plying a girl of twelve with whisky, and presently they crept away. Lucian passed them as they turned to go, and both looked at him. The boy laughed, and the girl smiled quietly. It was above all in the faces around him that he saw the most astounding things, the Bacchic fury unveiled and unashamed. To his eyes it seemed as if these revellers recognised him as a fellow, and smiled up in his face, aware that he was in the secret. Every instinct of religion, of civilisation even, was swept away; they gazed at one another and at him absolved of all scruples, children of the earth and nothing more. Now and then a couple detached themselves from the swarm, and went away into the darkness, answering the jeers and laughter of their friends as they vanished.

On the edge of the pavement, not far from where he was standing, Lucian noticed a tall and lovely young woman who seemed to be alone. She was in the full light of a naphtha flame, and her bronze hair and flushed cheeks shone illuminate as she viewed the orgy. She had dark brown eyes, and a strange look as of an old picture in her face; and her eyes brightened with an urgent gleam. He saw the revellers nudging each other and glancing at her, and two or three young men went up and asked her to come for a walk. She shook her head and said "No thank you" again and again, and seemed as if she were looking for somebody in the crowd.

"I'm expecting a friend," she said at last to a man who proposed a drink and a walk afterwards; and Lucian wondered what kind of friend would ultimately appear. Suddenly she turned to him as he was about to pass on, and said in a low voice:

"I'll go for a walk with you if you like; you just go on, and I'll follow in a minute."

For a moment he looked steadily at her. He saw that the first glance had misled him; her face was not flushed with drink as he had supposed, but it was radiant with the most exquisite colour, a red flame glowed and died on her cheek, and seemed to palpitate as she spoke. The head was set on the neck nobly, as in a statue, and about the ears the bronze hair strayed into little curls. She was smiling and waiting for his answer.

He muttered something about being very sorry, and fled down the hill out of the orgy, from the noise of roaring voices and the glitter of the great lamps very slowly swinging in the blast of wind. He knew that he had touched the brink of utter desolation; there was death in the woman's face, and she had indeed summoned him to the Sabbath. Somehow he had been able to refuse on the instant, but if he had delayed he knew he would have abandoned himself to her body and soul. He locked himself in his room and lay trembling on the bed, wondering if some subtle sympathy had shewn the woman her perfect companion. He looked in the glass, not expecting now to see certain visible and outward signs, but searching for the meaning of that strange glance that lit up his eyes. He had grown even thinner than before in the last few months, and his cheeks were wasted with hunger and sorrow, but there were still about his features the suggestion of a curious classic grace, and the look as of a faun who has strayed from the vineyards and olive gardens. He had broken away, but now he felt the mesh of her net about him, a desire for her that was a madness, as if she held every nerve in his body and drew him to her, to her mystic world, to the rosebush where every flower was a flame.

He dreamed all night of the perilous things he had refused, and it was loss to awake in the morning, pain to return to the world. The frost had broken and the fog had rolled away, and the grey street was filled with a clear grey light. Again he looked out on the long dull sweep of the monotonous houses, hidden for the past weeks by a curtain of mist. Heavy rain had fallen in the night, and the garden rails were still dripping, the roofs still dark with wet, all down the line the dingy white blinds were drawn in the upper windows. Not a soul walked the street; every one was asleep after the exertions of the night before; even on the main road it was only at intervals that some straggler paddled by. Presently a woman in a brown ulster shuffled off on some errand, then a man in shirt-sleeves poked out his head, holding the door half-open, and stared up at a window opposite. After a few minutes he slunk in again, and three loafers came slouching down the street, eager for mischief or beastliness of some sort. They chose a house that seemed rather smarter than the rest, and, irritated by the neat curtains, the little grass plot with its dwarf shrub, one of the ruffians drew out a piece of chalk and wrote some words on the front door. His friends kept watch for him, and the adventure achieved, all three bolted, bellowing yahoo laughter. Then a bell began, tang, tang, tang, and here and there children appeared on their way to Sunday-school, and the chapel "teachers" went by with verjuice eyes and lips, scowling at the little boy who cried "Piper, piper!" On the main road many respectable people, the men shining and ill-fitted, the women hideously bedizened, passed in the direction of the Independent nightmare, the stuccoed thing with Doric columns, but on the whole life was stagnant. Presently Lucian smelt the horrid fumes of roast beef and cabbage; the early risers were preparing the one-o'clock meal, but many lay in bed and put off dinner till three, with the effect of prolonging the cabbage atmosphere into the late afternoon. A drizzly rain began as the people were coming out of church, and the mothers of little boys in velvet and little girls in foolishness of every kind were impelled to slap their offspring, and to threaten them with father. Then the torpor of beef and beer and cabbage settled down on the street; in some houses they snorted and read the Parish Magazine, in some they snored and read the murders and collected filth of the week; but the only movement of the afternoon was a second procession of children, now bloated and distended with food, again answering the summons of tang, tang, tang. On the main road the trams, laden with impossible people, went humming to and fro, and young men who wore bright blue ties cheerfully haw-hawed and smoked penny cigars. They annoyed the shiny and respectable and verjuice-lipped, not by the frightful stench of the cigars, but because they were cheerful on Sunday. By and by the children, having heard about Moses in the Bulrushes and Daniel in the Lion's Den, came straggling home in an evil humour. And all the day it was as if on a grey sheet grey shadows flickered, passing by.

And in the rose-garden every flower was a flame! He thought in symbols, using the Persian imagery of a dusky court, surrounded by white cloisters, gilded by gates of bronze. The stars came out, the sky glowed a darker violet, but the cloistered wall, the fantastic trellises in stone, shone whiter. It was like a hedge of may-blossom, like a lily within a cup of lapis-lazuli, like sea-foam tossed on the heaving sea at dawn. Always those white cloisters trembled with the lute music, always the garden sang with the clear fountain, rising and falling in the mysterious dusk. And there was a singing voice stealing through the white lattices and the bronze gates, a soft voice chanting of the Lover and the Beloved, of the Vineyard, of the Gate and the Way. Oh! the language was unknown; but the music of the refrain returned again and again, swelling and trembling through the white nets of the latticed cloisters. And every rose in the dusky air was a flame.

He had seen the life which he expressed by these symbols offered to him, and he had refused it; and he was alone in the grey street, with its lamps just twinkling through the dreary twilight, the blast of a ribald chorus sounding from the main road, a doggerel hymn whining from some parlour, to the accompaniment of the harmonium. He wondered why he had turned away from that woman who knew all secrets, in whose eyes were all the mysteries. He opened the desk of his bureau, and was confronted by the heap and litter of papers, lying in confusion as he had left them. He knew that there was the motive of his refusal; he had been unwilling to abandon all hope of the work. The glory and the torment of his ambition glowed upon him as he looked at the manuscript; it seemed so pitiful that such a single desire should be thwarted. He was aware that if he chose to sit down now before the desk he could, in a manner, write easily enough—he could produce a tale which would be formally well constructed and certain of favourable reception. And it would not be the utterly commonplace, entirely hopeless favourite of the circulating library; it would stand in those ranks where the real thing is skilfully counterfeited, amongst the books which give the reader his orgy of emotions, and yet contrive to be superior, and "art", in his opinion. Lucian had often observed this species of triumph, and had noted the acclamation that never failed the clever sham. *Romola,* for example, had made the great host of the serious, the portentous, shout for joy, while the real book, *The Cloister and the Hearth,* was a comparative failure.

He knew that he could write a *Romola;* but he thought the art of counterfeiting half-crowns less detestable than this shabby trick of imitating literature. He had refused definitely to enter the atelier of the gentleman who pleased his clients by ingeniously simulating the grain of walnut; and though he had seen the old oaken aumbry kicked out contemptuously into the farmyard, serving perhaps the necessities of hens or pigs, he would not apprentice himself to the masters of veneer. He paced up and down the room, glancing now and again at his papers, and wondering if there were not hope for him. A great thing he could never do, but he had longed to do a true thing, to imagine sincere and genuine pages.

He was stirred again to this fury for the work by the event of the evening before, by all that had passed through his mind since the melancholy dawn. The lurid picture of that fiery street, the flaming shops and flaming glances, all its wonders and horrors, lit by the naphtha flares and by the burning souls, had possessed him; and the noises, the shriek and the whisper, the jangling rattle of the piano-organ, the long-continued scream of the butcher as he dabbled in the blood, the lewd litany of the singers, these seemed to be resolved into an infernal overture, loud with the expectation of lust and death. And how the spectacle was set in the cloud of dark night, a phantom play acted on that fiery stage, beneath those hideous brassy lamps, very slowly swinging in a violent blast. As all the medley of outrageous sights and sounds now fused themselves within his brain into one clear impression, it seemed that he had indeed witnessed and acted in a drama, that all the scene had been prepared and vested for him, and that the choric songs he had heard were but preludes to a greater act. For in that woman was the consummation and catastrophe of it all, and the whole stage waited for their meeting. He fancied that after this the voices and the lights died away, that the crowd sank swiftly into the darkness, and that the street was at once denuded of the great lamps and of all its awful scenic apparatus.

Again, he thought, the same mystery would be represented before him; suddenly on some dark and gloomy night, as he wandered lonely on a deserted road, the wind hurrying before him, suddenly a turn would bring him again upon the fiery stage, and the antique drama would be re-enacted. He would be drawn to the same place, to find that woman still standing there; again he would watch the rose radiant and palpitating upon her cheek, the argent gleam in her brown eyes, the bronze curls gilding the white splendour of her neck. And for the second time she would freely offer herself. He could hear the wail of the singers swelling to a shriek, and see the dusky dancers whirling round in a faster frenzy, and the naphtha flares tinged with red, as the woman and he went away into the dark, into the cloistered court where every flower was a flame, whence he would never come out.

His only escape was in the desk; he might find salvation if he could again hide his heart in the heap and litter of papers, and again be rapt by the cadence of a phrase. He threw open his window and looked out on the dim world and the glimmering amber lights. He resolved that he would rise early in the morning, and seek once more for his true life in the work.

But there was a strange thing. There was a little bottle on the mantelpiece, a bottle of dark blue glass, and he trembled and shuddered before it, as if it were a fetish.

VII

It was very dark in the room. He seemed by slow degrees to awake from a long and heavy torpor, from an utter forgetfulness, and as he raised his eyes he could scarcely discern the pale whiteness of the paper on the desk before him. He remembered something of a gloomy winter afternoon, of driving rain, of gusty wind: he had fallen asleep over his work, no doubt, and the night had come down.

He lay back in his chair, wondering whether it were late; his eyes were half closed, and he did not make the effort and rouse himself. He could hear the stormy noise of the wind, and the sound reminded him of the half-forgotten days. He thought of his boyhood, and the old rectory, and the great elms that surrounded it. There was something pleasant in the consciousness that he was still half dreaming; he knew he could wake up whenever he pleased, but for the moment he amused himself by the pretence that he was a little boy again, tired with his rambles and the keen air of the hills. He remembered how he would sometimes wake up in the dark at midnight, and listen sleepily for a moment to the rush of the wind straining and crying amongst the trees, and hear it beat upon the walls, and then he would fall to dreams again, happy in his warm, snug bed.

The wind grew louder, and the windows rattled. He half opened his eyes and shut them again, determined to cherish that sensation of long ago. He felt tired and heavy with sleep; he imagined that he was exhausted by some effort; he had, perhaps, been writing furiously, without rest. He could not recollect at the instant what the work had been; it would be delightful to read the pages when he had made up his mind to bestir himself.

Surely that was the noise of boughs, swaying and grinding in the wind. He remembered one night at home when such a sound had roused him suddenly from a deep sweet sleep. There was a rushing and beating as of wings upon the air, and a heavy dreary noise, like thunder far away upon the mountain. He had got out of bed and looked from behind the blind to see what was abroad. He remembered the strange sight he had seen, and he pretended it would be just the same if he cared to look out now. There were clouds flying awfully from before the moon, and a pale light that made the familiar land look strange and terrible. The blast of wind came with a great shriek, and the trees tossed and bowed and quivered; the wood was scourged and horrible, and the night air was ghastly with a confused tumult, and voices as of a host. A huge black cloud rolled across the heaven from the west and covered up the moon, and there came a torrent of bitter hissing rain.

It was all a vivid picture to him as he sat in his chair, unwilling to wake. Even as he let his mind stray back to that night of the past years, the rain beat sharply on the window-panes, and though there were no trees in the grey suburban street, he heard distinctly the crash of boughs. He wandered vaguely from thought to thought, groping indistinctly amongst memories, like a man trying to cross from door to door in a darkened unfamiliar room. But, no doubt, if he were to look out, by some magic the whole scene would be displayed before him. He would not see the curve of monotonous two-storied houses, with here and there a white blind, a patch of light, and shadows appearing and vanishing, not the rain plashing in the muddy road, not the amber of the gas-lamp opposite, but the wild moonlight poured on the dearly loved country; far away the dim circle of the hills and woods, and beneath him the tossing trees about the lawn, and the wood heaving under the fury of the wind.

He smiled to himself, amidst his lazy meditations, to think how real it seemed, and yet it was all far away, the scenery of an old play long ended and forgotten. It was strange that after all these years of trouble and work and change he should be in any sense the same person as that little boy peeping out, half frightened, from the rectory window. It was as if looking in the glass one should see a stranger, and yet know that the image was a true reflection.

The memory of the old home recalled his father and mother to him, and he wondered whether his mother would come if he were to cry out suddenly. One night, on just such a night as this, when a great storm blew from the mountain, a tree had fallen with a crash and a bough had struck the roof, and he awoke in a fright, calling for his mother. She had come and had comforted him, soothing him to sleep, and now he shut his eyes, seeing her face shining in the uncertain flickering candle light, as she bent over his bed. He could not think she had died; the memory was but a part of the evil dreams that had come afterwards.

He said to himself that he had fallen asleep and dreamed sorrow and agony, and he wished to forget all the things of trouble. He would return to happy days, to the beloved land, to the dear and friendly paths across the fields. There was the paper, white before him, and when he chose to stir, he would have the pleasure of reading his work. He could not quite recollect what he had been about, but he was somehow conscious that he had been successful and had brought some long labour to a worthy ending. Presently he would light the gas, and enjoy the satisfaction that only the work could give him, but for the time he preferred to linger in the darkness, and to think of himself as straying from stile to stile through the scented meadows, and listening to the bright brook that sang to the alders.

It was winter now, for he heard the rain and the wind, and the swaying of the trees, but in those old days how sweet the summer had been. The great hawthorn bush in blossom, like a white cloud upon the earth, had appeared to him in twilight, he had lingered in the enclosed valley to hear the nightingale, a voice swelling out from the rich gloom, from the trees that grew around the well. The scent of the meadowsweet was blown to him across the bridge of years, and with it came the dream and the hope and the longing, and the afterglow red in the sky, and the marvel of the earth. There was a quiet walk that he knew so well; one went up from a little green by-road, following an unnamed brooklet scarce a foot wide, but yet wandering like a river, gurgling over its pebbles, with its dwarf bushes shading the pouring water. One went through the meadow grass, and came to the larch wood that grew from hill to hill across the stream, and shone a brilliant tender green, and sent vague sweet spires to the flushing sky. Through the wood the path wound, turning and dipping, and beneath, the brown fallen needles of last year were soft and thick, and the resinous cones gave out their odour as the warm night advanced, and the shadows darkened. It was quite still; but he stayed, and the faint song of the brooklet sounded like the echo of a river beyond the mountains. How strange it was to look into the wood, to see the tall straight stems rising, pillar-like, and then the dusk, uncertain, and then the blackness. So he came out from the larch wood, from the green cloud and the vague shadow, into the dearest of all hollows, shut in on one side by the larches and before him by high violent walls of turf, like the slopes of a fort, with a clear line dark against the twilight sky, and a weird thorn bush that grew large, mysterious, on the summit, beneath the gleam of the evening star.

And he retraced his wanderings in those deep old lanes that began from the common road and went away towards the unknown, climbing steep hills, and piercing the woods of shadows, and dipping down into valleys that seemed virgin, unexplored, secret for the foot of man. He entered such a lane not knowing where it might bring him, hoping he had found the way to fairyland, to the woods beyond the world, to that vague territory that haunts all the dreams of a boy. He could not tell where he might be, for the high banks rose steep, and the great hedges made a green vault above. Marvellous ferns grew rich and thick in the dark red earth, fastening their roots about the roots of hazel and beech and maple, clustering like the carven capitals of a cathedral pillar. Down, like a dark shaft, the lane dipped to the well of the hills, and came amongst the limestone rocks. He climbed the bank at last, and looked out into a country that seemed for a moment the land he sought, a mysterious realm with unfamiliar hills and valleys and fair plains all golden, and white houses radiant in the sunset light.

And he thought of the steep hillsides where the bracken was like a wood, and of bare places where the west wind sang over the golden gorse, of still circles in mid-lake, of the poisonous yew-tree in the middle of the wood, shedding its crimson cups on the dank earth. How he lingered by certain black waterpools hedged on every side by drooping wych-elms and black-stemmed alders, watching the faint waves widening to the banks as a leaf or a twig dropped from the trees.

And the whole air and wonder of the ancient forest came back to him. He had found his way to the river valley, to the long lovely hollow between the hills, and went up and up beneath the leaves in the warm hush of midsummer, glancing back now and again through the green alleys, to the river winding in mystic esses beneath, passing hidden glens receiving the streams that rushed down the hillside, ice-cold from the rock, passing the immemorial tumulus, the graves where the legionaries waited for the trumpet, the grey farmhouses sending the blue wreaths of wood smoke into the still air. He went higher and higher, till at last he entered the long passage of the Roman road, and from this, the ridge and summit of the wood, he saw the waves of green swell and dip and sink towards the marshy level and the gleaming yellow sea. He looked on the surging forest, and thought of the strange deserted city mouldering into a petty village on its verge, of its encircling walls melting into the turf, of vestiges of an older temple which the earth had buried utterly.

It was winter now, for he heard the wail of the wind, and a sudden gust drove the rain against the panes, but he thought of the bee's song in the clover, of the foxgloves in full blossom, of the wild roses, delicate, enchanting, swaying on a long stem above the hedge. He had been in strange places, he had known sorrow and desolation, and had grown grey and weary in the work of letters, but he lived again in the sweetness, in the clear bright air of early morning, when the sky was blue in June, and the mist rolled like a white sea in the valley. He laughed when he recollected that he had sometimes fancied himself unhappy in those days; in those days when he could be glad because the sun shone, because the wind blew fresh on the mountain. On those bright days he had been glad, looking at the fleeting and passing of the clouds upon the hills, and had gone up higher to the broad dome of the mountain, feeling that joy went up before him.

He remembered how, a boy, he had dreamed of love of an adorable and ineffable mystery which transcended all longing and desire. The time had come when all the wonder of the earth seemed to prefigure this alone, when he found the symbol of the Beloved in hill and wood and stream, and every flower and every dark pool discoursed a pure ecstasy. It was the longing for longing, the love of love, that had come to him when he awoke one morning just before the dawn, and for the first time felt the sharp thrill of passion.

He tried in vain to express to himself the exquisite joys of innocent desire. Even now, after troubled years, in spite of some dark cloud that overshadowed the background of his thought, the sweetness of the boy's imagined pleasure came like a perfume into his reverie. It was no love of a woman but the desire of womanhood, the Eros of the Unknown, that made the heart tremble. He hardly dreamed that such a love could ever be satisfied, that the thirst of beauty could be slaked. He shrank from all contact of actuality, not venturing so much as to imagine the inner place and sanctuary of the mysteries. It was enough for him to adore in the outer court, to know that within, in the sweet gloom, were the vision and the rapture, the altar and the sacrifice.

He remembered, dimly, the passage of many heavy years since that time of hope and passion, but, perhaps, the vague shadow would pass away, and he could renew the boy's thoughts, the unformed fancies that were part of the bright day, of the wild roses in the hedgerow. All other things should be laid aside, he would let them trouble him no more after this winter night. He saw now that from the first he had allowed his imagination to bewilder him, to create a fantastic world in which he suffered, moulding innocent forms into terror and dismay. Vividly, he saw again the black circle of oaks, growing in a haggard ring upon the bastions of the Roman fort. The noise of the storm without grew louder, and he thought how the wind had come up the valley with the sound of a scream, how a great tree had ground its boughs together, shuddering before the violent blast. Clear and distinct, as if he were standing now in the lane, he saw the steep slopes surging from the valley, and the black crown of the oaks set against the flaming sky, against a blaze and glow of light as if great furnace doors were opened. He saw the fire as it were smitten about the bastions, about the heaped mounds that guarded the fort, and the crooked evil boughs seemed to writhe in the blast of flame that beat from heaven. Strangely with the sight of the burning fort mingled the impression of a dim white shape floating up the dusk of the lane towards him, and he saw across the valley of years a girl's face, a momentary apparition that shone and vanished away.

Then there was a memory of another day, of violent summer, of white farmhouse walls blazing in the sun, and a far call from the reapers in the cornfields. He had climbed the steep slope and penetrated the matted thicket and lay in the heat alone on the soft short grass that grew within the fort. There was a cloud of madness, and confusion of broken dreams that had no meaning or clue but only an indefinable horror and defilement. He had fallen asleep as he gazed at the knotted fantastic boughs of the stunted brake about him, and when he woke he was ashamed, and fled away fearing that "they" would pursue him. He did not know who "they" were, but it seemed as if a woman's face watched him from between the matted boughs, and that she summoned to her side awful companions who had never grown old through all the ages.

He looked up, it seemed, at a smiling face that bent over him, as he sat in the cool dark kitchen of the old farmhouse, and wondered why the sweetness of those red lips and the kindness of the eyes mingled with the nightmare in the fort, with the horrible Sabbath he had imagined as he lay sleeping on the hot soft turf. He had allowed these disturbed fancies, all this mad wrack of terror and shame that he had gathered to his mind, to trouble him for too long a time; presently he would light up the room, and leave all the old darkness of his life behind him, and from henceforth he would walk in the day.

He could still distinguish, though very vaguely, the pile of papers beside him, and he remembered, now, that he had finished a long task that afternoon, before he fell asleep. He could not trouble himself to recollect the exact nature of the work, but he was sure that he had done well; in a few minutes, perhaps, he would strike a match, and read the title, and amuse himself with his own forgetfulness. But the sight of the papers lying there in order made him think of his beginnings, of those first unhappy efforts which were so impossible and so hopeless. He saw himself bending over the table in the old familiar room, desperately scribbling, and then laying down his pen dismayed at the sad results on the page. It was late at night, his father had been long in bed, and the house was still. The fire was almost out, with only a dim glow here and there amongst the cinders, and the room was growing chilly. He rose at last from his work and looked out on a dim earth and a dark and cloudy sky.

Night after night he had laboured on, persevering in his effort, even through the cold sickness of despair, when every line was doomed as it was made. Now, with the consciousness that he knew at least the conditions of literature, and that many years of thought and practice had given him some sense of language, he found these early struggles both pathetic and astonishing. He could not understand how he had persevered so stubbornly, how he had had the heart to begin a fresh page when so many folios of blotted, painful effort lay torn, derided, impossible in their utter failure. It seemed to him that it must have been a miracle or an infernal possession, a species of madness, that had driven him on, every day disappointed, and every day hopeful.

And yet there was a joyous side to the illusion. In these dry days that he lived in, when he had bought, by a long experience and by countless hours of misery, a knowledge of his limitations, of the vast gulf that yawned between the conception and the work, it was pleasant to think of a time when all things were possible, when the most splendid design seemed an affair of a few weeks. Now he had come to a frank acknowledgment; so far as he was concerned, he judged every book wholly impossible till the last line of it was written, and he had learnt patience, the art of sighing and putting the fine scheme away in the pigeon-hole of what could never be. But to think of those days! Then one could plot out a book that should be more curious than Rabelais, and jot down the outlines of a romance to surpass Cervantes, and design renaissance tragedies and volumes of *contes,* and comedies of the Restoration; everything was to be done, and the masterpiece was always the rainbow cup, a little way before him.

He touched the manuscript on the desk, and the feeling of the pages seemed to restore all the papers that had been torn so long ago. It was the atmosphere of the silent room that returned, the light of the shaded candle falling on the abandoned leaves. This had been painfully excogitated while the snowstorm whirled about the lawn and filled the lanes, this was of the summer night, this of the harvest moon rising like a fire from the tithebarn on the hill. How well he remembered those half-dozen pages of which he had once been so proud; he had thought out the sentences one evening, while he leaned on the foot-bridge and watched the brook swim across the road. Every word smelt of the meadowsweet that grew thick upon the banks; now, as he recalled the cadence and the phrase that had seemed so charming, he saw again the ferns beneath the vaulted roots of the beech, and the green light of the glowworm in the hedge.

And in the west the mountains swelled to a great dome, and on the dome was a mound, the memorial of some forgotten race, that grew dark and large against the red sky, when the sun set. He had lingered below it in the solitude, amongst the winds, at evening, far away from home; and oh, the labour and the vain efforts to make the form of it and the awe of it in prose, to write the hush of the vast hill, and the sadness of the world below sinking into the night, and the mystery, the suggestion of the rounded hillock, huge against the magic sky.

He had tried to sing in words the music that the brook sang, and the sound of the October wind rustling through the brown bracken on the hill. How many pages he had covered in the effort to shew a white winter world, a sun without warmth in a grey-blue sky, all the fields, all the land white and shining, and one high summit where the dark pines towered, still in the still afternoon, in the pale violet air.

To win the secret of words, to make a phrase that would murmur of summer and the bee, to summon the wind into a sentence, to conjure the odour of the night into the surge and fall and harmony of a line; this was the tale of the long evenings, of the candle flame white upon the paper and the eager pen.

He remembered that in some fantastic book he had seen a bar or two of music, and, beneath, the inscription that here was the musical expression of Westminster Abbey. His boyish effort seemed hardly less ambitious, and he no longer believed that language could present the melody and the awe and the loveliness of the earth. He had long known that he, at all events, would have to be content with a far approach, with a few broken notes that might suggest, perhaps, the magistral everlasting song of the hill and the streams.

But in those far days the impossible was but a part of the wonderland that lay before him, of the world beyond the wood and the mountain. All was to be conquered, all was to be achieved; he had but to make the journey and he would find the golden world and the golden word, and hear those songs that the sirens sang. He touched the manuscript; whatever it was, it was the result of painful labour and disappointment, not of the old flush of hope, but it came of weary days, of correction and re-correction. It might be good in its measure; but afterwards he would write no more for a time. He would go back again to the happy world of masterpieces, to the dreams of great and perfect books, written in an ecstasy.

Like a dark cloud from the sea came the memory of the attempt he had made, of the poor piteous history that had once embittered his life. He sighed and said alas, thinking of his folly, of the hours when he was shaken with futile, miserable rage. Some silly person in London had made his manuscript more saleable and had sold it without rendering an account of the profits, and for that he had been ready to curse humanity. Black, horrible, as the memory of a stormy day, the rage of his heart returned to his mind, and he covered his eyes, endeavouring to darken the picture of terror and hate that shone before him. He tried to drive it all out of his thought, it vexed him to remember these foolish trifles; the trick of a publisher, the small pomposities and malignancies of the country folk, the cruelty of a village boy, had inflamed him almost to the pitch of madness. His heart had burnt with fury, and when he looked up the sky was blotched, and scarlet as if it rained blood.

Indeed he had almost believed that blood had rained upon him, and cold blood from a sacrifice in heaven; his face was wet and chill and dripping, and he had passed his hand across his forehead and looked at it. A red cloud had seemed to swell over the hill, and grow great, and come near to him; he was but an ace removed from raging madness.

It had almost come to that; the drift and the breath of the scarlet cloud had well-nigh touched him. It was strange that he had been so deeply troubled by such little things, and strange how after all the years he could still recall the anguish and rage and hate that shook his soul as with a spiritual tempest.

The memory of all that evening was wild and troubled; he resolved that it should vex him no more, that now, for the last time, he would let himself be tormented by the past. In a few minutes he would rise to a new life, and forget all the storms that had gone over him.

Curiously, every detail was distinct and clear in his brain. The figure of the doctor driving home, and the sound of the few words he had spoken came to him in the darkness, through the noise of the storm and the pattering of the rain. Then he stood upon the ridge of the hill and saw the smoke drifting up from the ragged roofs of Caermaen, in the evening calm; he listened to the voices mounting thin and clear, in a weird tone, as if some outland folk were speaking in an unknown tongue of awful things.

He saw the gathering darkness, the mystery of twilight changing the huddled squalid village into an unearthly city, into some dreadful Atlantis, inhabited by a ruined race. The mist falling fast, the gloom that seemed to issue from the black depths of the forest, to advance palpably towards the walls, were shaped before him; and beneath, the river wound, snake-like, about the town, swimming to the flood and glowing in its still pools like molten brass. And as the water mirrored the afterglow and sent ripples and gouts of blood against the shuddering reeds, there came suddenly the piercing trumpet-call, the loud reiterated summons that rose and fell, that called and recalled, echoing through all the valley, crying to the dead as the last note rang. It summoned the

legion from the river and the graves and the battlefield, the host floated up from the sea, the centuries swarmed about the eagles, the array
was set for the last great battle, behind the leaguer of the mist.

He could imagine himself still wandering through the dim, unknown, terrible country, gazing affrighted at hills and woods that
seemed to have put on an unearthly shape, stumbling amongst the bri-
ars that caught his feet. He lost his way in a wild country, and the red
light that blazed up from the furnace on the mountains only shewed
him a mysterious land, in which he strayed aghast, with the sense of
doom weighing upon him. The dry mutter of the trees, the sound of
an unseen brook, made him afraid as if the earth spoke of his sin, and
presently he was fleeing through a desolate shadowy wood, where a
pale light flowed from the mouldering stumps, a dream of light that
shed a ghostly radiance.

And then again the dark summit of the Roman fort, the black
sheer height rising above the valley, and the moonfire streaming
around the ring of oaks, glowing about the green bastions that guarded
the thicket and the inner place.

The room in which he sat appeared the vision, the trouble of the
wind and rain without was but illusion, the noise of the waves in the
seashell. Passion and tears and adoration and the glories of the summer night returned, and the calm sweet face of the woman appeared,
and he thrilled at the soft touch of her hand on his flesh.

She shone as if she had floated down into the lane from the moon
that swam between films of cloud above the black circle of the oaks.
She led him away from all terror and despair and hate, and gave herself
to him with rapture, shewing him love, kissing his tears away, pillowing
his cheek upon her breast.

His lips dwelt on her lips, his mouth upon the breath of her
mouth, her arms were strained about him, and oh! she charmed him
with her voice, with sweet kind words, as she offered her sacrifice.
How her scented hair fell down, and floated over his eyes, and there
was a marvellous fire called the moon, and her lips were aflame, and
her eyes shone like a light on the hills.

All beautiful womanhood had come to him in the lane. Love had
touched him in the dusk and had flown away, but he had seen the
splendor and the glory, and his eyes had seen the enchanted light.

AVE ATQUE VALE

The old words sounded in his ears like the ending of a chant, and he heard the music's close. Once only in his weary hapless life, once the world had passed away, and he had known her, the dear, dear Annie, the symbol of all mystic womanhood.

The heaviness of languor still oppressed him, holding him back amongst these old memories, so that he could not stir from his place. Oddly, there seemed something unaccustomed about the darkness of the room, as if the shadows he had summoned had changed the aspect of the walls. He was conscious that on this night he was not altogether himself; fatigue and the weariness of sleep, and the waking vision had perplexed him. He remembered how once or twice when he was a little boy he had opened his eyes on the midnight darkness startled by an uneasy dream, and had stared with a frightened gaze into nothingness, not knowing where he was, all trembling, and breathing quick, till he touched the rail of his bed, and the familiar outlines of the looking-glass and the chiffonier began to glimmer out of the gloom. So now he touched the pile of manuscript and the desk at which he had worked so many hours, and felt reassured, though he smiled at himself, and he felt the old childish dread, the longing to cry out for some one to bring a candle, and shew him that he really was in his own room. He glanced up for an instant, expecting to see perhaps the glitter of the brass gas-jet that was fixed on the wall, just beside his bureau, but it was too dark, and he could not rouse himself and make the effort that would drive the cloud and the muttering thoughts away.

He leant back again, picturing the wet street without, the rain driving like fountain spray about the gas-lamp, the shrilling of the wind on those waste places to the north. It was strange how in the brick and stucco desert where no trees were, he all the time imagined the noise of tossing boughs, the grinding of the boughs together. There was a great storm and tumult in this wilderness of London, and for the sound of the rain and the wind he could not hear the hum and jangle of the trams, and the jar and shriek of the garden gates as they opened and shut. But he could imagine his street, the rain-swept desolate curve of it, as it turned northward, and beyond the empty suburban roads, the twinkling villa windows, the ruined field, the broken lane, and then yet another suburb rising, a solitary gas-lamp glimmering at a corner, and the plane tree lashing its boughs, and driving great showers against the glass.

It was wonderful to think of. For when these remote roads were ended one dipped down the hill into the open country, into the dim world beyond the glint of friendly fires. To-night, how waste they were, these wet roads, edged with the red-brick houses, with shrubs whipped by the wind against one another, against the paling and the wall. There the wind swayed the great elms scattered on the sidewalk, the remnants of the old stately fields, and beneath each tree was a pool of wet, and a torment of raindrops fell with every gust. And one passed through the red avenues, perhaps by a little settlement of flickering shops, and passed the last sentinel wavering lamp, and the road became a ragged lane, and the storm screamed from hedge to hedge across the open fields. And then, beyond, one touched again upon a still remoter avant-garde of London, an island amidst the darkness, surrounded by its pale of twinkling, starry lights.

He remembered his wanderings amongst these outposts of the town, and thought how desolate all their ways must be to-night. They were solitary in wet and wind, and only at long intervals some one pattered and hurried along them, bending his eyes down to escape the drift of rain. Within the villas, behind the close-drawn curtains, they drew about the fire, and wondered at the violence of the storm, listening for each great gust as it gathered far away, and rocked the trees, and at last rushed with a huge shock against their walls as if it were the coming of the sea. He thought of himself walking, as he had often walked, from lamp to lamp on such a night, treasuring his lonely thoughts, and weighing the hard task awaiting him in his room. Often in the evening, after a long day's labour, he had thrown down his pen in utter listlessness, feeling that he could struggle no more with ideas and words, and he had gone out into driving rain and darkness, seeking the word of the enigma as he tramped on and on beneath these outer battlements of London.

Or on some grey afternoon in March or November he had sickened of the dull monotony and the stagnant life that he saw from his window, and had taken his design with him to the lonely places, halting now and again by a gate, and pausing in the shelter of a hedge through which the austere wind shivered, while, perhaps, he dreamed of Sicily, or of sunlight on the Provençal olives. Often as he strayed solitary from street to field, and passed the Syrian fig tree imprisoned in Britain, nailed to an ungenial wall, the solution of the puzzle became evident, and he laughed and hurried home eager to make the page speak, to note the song he had heard on his way.

Sometimes he had spent many hours treading this edge and brim of London, now lost amidst the dun fields, watching the bushes shaken by the wind, and now looking down from a height whence he could see the dim waves of the town, and a barbaric water tower rising from a hill, and the snuff-coloured cloud of smoke that seemed blown up from the streets into the sky.

There were certain ways and places that he had cherished; he loved a great old common that stood on high ground, curtained about with ancient spacious houses of red brick, and their cedarn gardens. And there was on the road that led to this common a space of ragged uneven ground with a pool and a twisted oak, and here he had often stayed in autumn and looked across the mist and the valley at the great theatre of the sunset, where a red cloud like a charging knight shone and conquered a purple dragon shape, and golden lances glittered in a field of faery green.

Or sometimes, when the unending prospect of trim, monotonous, modern streets had wearied him, he had found an immense refreshment in the discovery of a forgotten hamlet, left in a hollow, while all new London pressed and surged on every side, threatening the rest of the red roofs with its vulgar growth. These little peaceful houses, huddled together beneath the shelter of trees, with their bulging leaded windows and uneven roofs, somehow brought back to him the sense of the country, and soothed him with the thought of the old farmhouses, white or grey, the homes of quiet lives, harbours where, perhaps, no tormenting thoughts ever broke in.

For he had instinctively determined that there was neither rest nor health in all the arid waste of streets about him. It seemed as if in those dull rows of dwellings, in the prim new villas red and white and staring, there must be a leaven working which transformed all to base vulgarity. Beneath the dull sad slates, behind the blistered doors, love turned to squalid intrigue, mirth to drunken clamour, and the mystery of life became a common thing; religion was sought for in the greasy piety and flatulent oratory of the Independent chapel, the stuccoed nightmare of the Doric columns. Nothing fine, nothing rare, nothing exquisite, it seemed, could exist in the weltering suburban sea, in the habitations which had risen from the stench and slime of the brickfields. It was as if the sickening fumes that steamed from the burning bricks had been sublimed into the shape of houses, and those who lived in these grey places could also claim kinship with the putrid mud.

Hence he had delighted in the few remains of the past that he could find still surviving on the suburb's edge, in the grave old houses that stood apart from the road, in the mouldering taverns of the eighteenth century, in the huddled hamlets that had preserved only the glow and the sunlight of all the years that had passed over them. It appeared to him that vulgarity and greasiness and squalor had come with a flood, that not only the good but also the evil in man's heart had been made common and ugly, that a sordid scum was mingled with all the springs, of death as of life. It would be alike futile to search amongst these mean two-storied houses for a splendid sinner as for a splendid saint; the very vices of these people smelt of cabbage water and a pothouse vomit.

And so he had often fled away from the serried maze that encircled him, seeking for the old and worn and significant as an antiquary looks for the fragments of the Roman temple amidst the modern shops. In some way the gusts of wind and the beating rain of the night reminded him of an old house that had often attracted him with a strange indefinable curiosity. He had found it on a grim grey day in March, when he had gone out under a leaden-moulded sky, cowering from a dry freezing wind that brought with it the gloom and the doom of far unhappy Siberian plains. More than ever that day the suburb had oppressed him; insignificant, detestable, repulsive to body and mind, it was the only hell that a vulgar age could conceive or make, an inferno created not by Dante but by the jerry-builder. He had gone out to the north, and when he lifted up his eyes again he found that he had chanced to turn up by one of the little lanes that still strayed across the broken fields. He had never chosen this path before because the lane at its outlet was so wholly degraded and offensive, littered with rusty tins and broken crockery, and hedged in with a paling fashioned out of scraps of wire, rotting timber, and bending worn-out rails. But on this day, by happy chance, he had fled from the high road by the first

opening that offered, and he no longer groped his way amongst obscene refuse, sickened by the bloated bodies of dead dogs, and fetid
odours from unclean decay, but the malpassage had become a peaceful
winding lane, with warm shelter beneath its banks from the dismal
wind. For a mile he had walked on quietly, and then a turn in the road
shewed him a little glen or hollow, watered by such a tiny rushing
brooklet as his own woods knew, and beyond, alas, the glaring fore-
guard of a "new neighbourhood"; raw red villas, semi-detached, and
then a row of lamentable shops.

But as he was about to turn back, in the hope of finding some other outlet, his attention was charmed by a small house that stood back a
little from the road on his right hand. There had been a white gate, but
the paint had long faded to grey and black, and the wood crumbled
under the touch, and only moss marked out the lines of the drive. The
iron railing round the lawn had fallen, and the poor flower-beds were
choked with grass and a faded growth of weeds. But here and there a
rosebush lingered amidst suckers that had sprung grossly from the
root, and on each side of the hall door were box trees, untrimmed,
ragged, but still green. The slate roof was all stained and livid, blotched
with the drippings of a great elm that stood at one corner of the neglected lawn, and marks of damp and decay were thick on the uneven walls,
which had been washed yellow many years before. There was a porch of
trellis work before the door, and Lucian had seen it rock in the wind,
swaying as if every gust must drive it down. There were two windows
on the ground floor, one on each side of the door, and two above,
with a blind space where a central window had been blocked up.

This poor and desolate house had fascinated him. Ancient and
poor and fallen, disfigured by the slate roof and the yellow wash that
had replaced the old mellow dipping tiles and the warm red walls, and
disfigured again by spots and patches of decay; it seemed as if its happy days were for ever ended. To Lucian it appealed with a sense of
doom and horror; the black streaks that crept upon the walls, and the
green drift upon the roof, appeared not so much the work of foul
weather and dripping boughs, as the outward signs of evil working and
creeping in the lives of those within.

The stage seemed to him decked for doom, painted with the symbols of tragedy; and he wondered as he looked whether any one were

so unhappy as to live there still. There were torn blinds in the windows, but he had asked himself, who could be so brave as to sit in that room, darkened by the dreary box, and listen of winter nights to the rain upon the window, and the moaning of wind amongst the tossing boughs that beat against the roof.

He could not imagine that any chamber in such a house was habitable. Here the dead had lain, through the white blind the thin light had filtered on the rigid mouth, and still the floor must be wet with tears and still that great rocking elm echoed the groaning and the sobs of those who watched. No doubt, the damp was rising, and the odour of the earth filled the house, and made such as entered draw back, foreseeing the hour of death.

Often the thought of this strange old house had haunted him; he had imagined the empty rooms where a heavy paper peeled from the walls and hung in dark strips; and he could not believe that a light ever shone from those windows that stared black and glittering on the neglected lawn. But to-night the wet and the storm seemed curiously to bring the image of the place before him, and as the wind sounded he thought how unhappy those must be, if any there were, who sat in the musty chambers by a flickering light, and listened to the elm-tree moaning and beating and weeping on the walls.

And to-night was Saturday night; and there was about that phrase something that muttered of the condemned cell, of the agony of a doomed man. Ghastly to his eyes was the conception of any one sitting in that room to the right of the door behind the larger box tree, where the wall was cracked above the window and smeared with a black stain in an ugly shape.

He knew how foolish it had been in the first place to trouble his mind with such conceits of a dreary cottage on the outskirts of London. And it was more foolish now to meditate these things, fantasies, feigned forms, the issue of a sad mood and a bleak day of spring. For soon, in a few moments, he was to rise to a new life. He was but reckoning up the account of his past, and when the light came he was to think no more of sorrow and heaviness, of real or imagined terrors. He had stayed too long in London, and he would once more taste the breath of the hills, and see the river winding in the long lovely valley; ah! he would go home.

Something like a thrill, the thrill of fear, passed over him as he remembered that there was no home. It was in the winter, a year and a half after his arrival in town, that he had suffered the loss of his father. He lay for many days prostrate, overwhelmed with sorrow and with the thought that now indeed he was utterly alone in the world. Miss Deacon was to live with another cousin in Yorkshire; the old home was at last ended and done. He felt sorry that he had not written more frequently to his father: there were things in his cousin's letters that had made his heart sore. "Your poor father was always looking for your letters," she wrote, "they used to cheer him so much. He nearly broke down when you sent him that money last Christmas; he got it into his head that you were starving yourself to send it him. He was hoping so much that you would have come down this Christmas, and kept asking me about the plum-puddings months ago."

It was not only his father that had died, but with him the last strong link was broken, and the past life, the days of his boyhood, grew faint as a dream. With his father his mother died again, and the long years died, the time of his innocence, the memory of affection. He was sorry that his letters had gone home so rarely; it hurt him to imagine his father looking out when the post came in the morning, and forced to be sad because there was nothing. But he had never thought that his father valued the few lines that he wrote, and indeed it was often difficult to know what to say. It would have been useless to write of those agonising nights when the pen seemed an awkward and outlandish instrument, when every effort ended in shameful defeat, or of the happier hours when at last wonder appeared and the line glowed, crowned and exalted. To poor Mr. Taylor such tales would have seemed but trivial histories of some Oriental game, like an odd story from a land where men have time for the infinitely little, and can seriously make a science of arranging blossoms in a jar, and discuss perfumes instead of politics. It would have been useless to write to the rectory of his only interest, and so he wrote seldom.

And then he had been sorry because he could never write again and never see his home. He had wondered whether he would have gone down to the old place at Christmas, if his father had lived. It was curious how common things evoked the bitterest griefs, but his father's anxiety that the plum-pudding should be good, and ready for him, had brought the tears into his eyes. He could hear him saying in a nervous voice that attempted to be cheerful: "I suppose you will be thinking of the Christmas puddings soon, Jane; you remember how fond Lucian used to be of plum-pudding. I hope we shall see him this December." No doubt poor Miss Deacon paled with rage at the suggestion that she should make Christmas pudding in July; and returned a sharp answer; but it was pathetic. The wind wailed, and the rain dashed and beat again and again upon the window. He imagined that all his thoughts of home, of the old rectory amongst the elms, had conjured into his mind the sound of the storm upon the trees, for, to-night, very clearly he heard the creaking of the boughs, the noise of boughs moaning and beating and weeping on the walls, and even a pattering of wet, on wet earth, as if there were a shrub near the window that shook off the raindrops, before the gust.

That thrill, as it were a shudder of fear, passed over him again, and he knew not what had made him afraid. There were some dark shadow on his mind that saddened him, it seemed as if a vague memory of terrible days hung like a cloud over his thought, but it was all indefinite, perhaps the last grim and ragged edge of the melancholy wrack that had swelled over his life and the bygone years. He shivered and tried to rouse himself and drive away the sense of dread and shame that seemed so real and so awful, and yet he could not grasp it. But the torpor of sleep, the burden of the work that he had ended a few hours before still weighed down his limbs and bound his thoughts. He could scarcely believe that he had been busy at his desk a little while ago, and that just before the winter day closed in and the rain began to fall he had laid down the pen with a sigh of relief, and had slept in his chair. It was rather as if he had slumbered deeply through a long and weary night, as if an awful vision of flame and darkness and the worm that dieth not had come to him sleeping. But he would dwell no more on the darkness; he went back to the early days in London when he had said farewell to the hills and to the waterpools, and had set to work in this little room in the dingy street.

How he had toiled and laboured at the desk before him! He had put away the old wild hopes of the masterpiece and executed in a fury of inspiration, wrought out in one white heat of creative joy; it was enough if by dint of long perseverance and singleness of desire he could at last, in pain and agony and despair, after failure and disappointment and effort constantly renewed, fashion something of which he need not be ashamed. He had put himself to school again, and had, with what patience he could command, ground his teeth into the rudiments, resolved that at last he would test out the heart of the mystery. They were good nights to remember, these; he was glad to think of the little ugly room, with its silly wall paper and its "bird's-eye" furniture, lighted up, while he sat at the bureau and wrote on into the cold stillness of the London morning, when the flickering lamplight and the daystar shone together. It was an interminable labour, and he had always known it to be as hopeless as alchemy. The gold, the great and glowing masterpiece, would never shine amongst the dead ashes and smoking efforts of the crucible, but in the course of the life, in the interval between the failures, he might possibly discover curious things.

These were the good nights that he could look back on without any fear or shame, when he had been happy and content on a diet of bread and tea and tobacco, and could hear of some imbecility passing into its hundredth thousand, and laugh cheerfully—if only that last page had been imagined aright, if the phrases noted in the still hours rang out their music when he read them in the morning. He remembered the drolleries and fantasies that the worthy Miss Deacon used to write to him, and how he had grinned at her words of reproof, admonition, and advice. She had once instigated Dolly *fils* to pay him a visit, and that young prop of respectability had talked about the extraordinary running of Bolter at the Scurragh meeting in Ireland; and then, glancing at Lucian's books, had enquired whether any of them had "warm bits". He had been kind though patronising, and seemed to have moved freely in the most brilliant society of Stoke Newington. He had not been able to give any information as to the present condition of Edgar Allan Poe's old school. It appeared eventually that his report at home had not been a very favourable one, for no invitation to high tea had followed, as Miss Deacon had hoped. The Dollys knew many nice people, who were well off, and Lucian's cousin, as she afterwards said, had done *her* best to introduce him to the *beau monde* of those northern suburbs.

But after the visit of the young Dolly, with what joy he had returned to the treasures which he had concealed from profane eyes. He had looked out and seen his visitor on board the tram at the street corner, and he laughed out loud, and locked his door. There had been moments when he was lonely, and wished to hear again the sound of friendly speech; but after such an irruption of suburban futility, it was a keen delight to feel that he was secure on his tower, that he could absorb himself in his wonderful task as safe and silent as if he were in mid-desert.

But there was one period that he dared not revive; he could not bear to think of those weeks of desolation and terror in the winter after his coming to London. His mind was sluggish, and he could not quite remember how many years had passed since that dismal experience; it sounded all an old story, but yet it was still vivid, a flaming scroll of terror from which he turned his eyes away. One awful scene glowed into his memory, and he could not shut out the sight of an orgy, of dusky figures whirling in a ring, of lurid naphtha flares blazing in the darkness, of great glittering lamps, like infernal thuribles, very slowly swaying in a violent blast of air. And there was something else, something which he could not remember, but it filled him with terror, but it slunk in the dark places of his soul, as a wild beast crouches in the depths of a cave.

Again, and without reason, he began to image to himself that old mouldering house in the field. With what a loud incessant noise the wind must be clamouring about on this fearful night, how the great elm swayed and cried in the storm, and the rain dashed and pattered on the windows, and dripped on the sodden earth from the shaking shrubs beside the door. He moved uneasily on his chair, and struggled to put the picture out of his thoughts; but in spite of himself he saw the stained uneven walls, that ugly blot of mildew above the window, and perhaps a feeble gleam of light filtered through the blind, and some one, unhappy above all and for ever lost, sat within the dismal room. Or rather, every window was black, without a glimmer of hope, and he who was shut in thick darkness heard the wind and the rain, and the noise of the elm-tree moaning and beating and weeping on the walls.

For all his effort the impression would not leave him, and as he sat before his desk looking into the vague darkness he could almost see that chamber which he had so often imagined; the low whitewashed ceiling held up by a heavy beam, the smears of smoke and long usage, the cracks and fissures of the plaster. Old furniture, shabby, deplorable, battered, stood about the room; there was a horsehair sofa worn and tottering, and a dismal paper, patterned in a livid red, blackened and mouldered near the floor, and peeled off and hung in strips from the dank walls. And there was that odour of decay, of the rank soil steaming, of rotting wood, a vapour that choked the breath and made the heart full of fear and heaviness.

Lucian again shivered with a thrill of dread; he was afraid that he had overworked himself and that he was suffering from the first symptoms of grave illness. His mind dwelt on confused and terrible recollections, and with a mad ingenuity gave form and substance to phantoms; and even now he drew a long breath, almost imagining that the air in his room was heavy and noisome, that it entered his nostrils with some taint of the crypt. And his body was still languid, and though he made a half motion to rise he could not find enough energy for the effort, and he sank again into the chair. At all events, he would think no more of that sad house in the field; he would return to those long struggles with letters, to the happy nights when he had gained victories.

He remembered something of his escape from the desolation and the worse than desolation that had obsessed him during that first winter in London. He had gone free one bleak morning in February, and after those dreary terrible weeks the desk and the heap and litter of papers had once more engulfed and absorbed him. And in the succeeding summer, of a night when he lay awake and listened to the birds, shining images came wantonly to him. For an hour, while the dawn brightened, he had felt the presence of an age, the resurrection of the life that the green fields had hidden, and his heart stirred for joy when he knew that he held and possessed all the loveliness that had so long mouldered. He could scarcely fall asleep for eager and leaping thoughts, and as soon as his breakfast was over he went out and bought paper and pens of a certain celestial stationer in Notting Hill. The street was not changed as he passed to and fro on his errand. The rattling wagons jostled by at intervals, a rare hansom came spinning down from London, there sounded the same hum and jangle of the gliding trams. The languid life of the pavement was unaltered; a few people, unclassed, without salience or possible description, lounged and walked from east to west, and from west to east, or slowly dropped into the byways to wander in the black waste to the north, or perhaps go astray in the systems that stretched towards the river. He glanced down these by-roads as he passed, and was astonished, as always, at their mysterious and desert aspect. Some were utterly empty; lines of neat, appalling residences, trim and garnished as if for occupation, edging the white glaring road; and not a soul was abroad, and not a sound broke their stillness. It was a picture of the desolation of midnight lighted up, but empty and waste as the most profound and solemn hours before the day. Other of these byroads, of older settlement, were furnished with more important houses, standing far back from the pavement, each in a little wood of greenery, and thus one might look down as through a forest vista, and see a way smooth and guarded with low walls and yet untrodden, and all a leafy silence. Here and there in some of these echoing roads a figure seemed lazily advancing in the distance, hesitating and delaying, as if lost in the labyrinth. It was difficult to say which were the more dismal, these deserted streets that wandered away to right and left, or the great main thoroughfare with its narcotic and shadowy life. For the latter appeared vast, interminable, grey, and those who travelled by it were scarcely real, the bodies of the living, but rather the uncertain and misty shapes that come and go across the desert in an Eastern tale, when men look up from the sand and see a caravan pass them, all in silence, without a cry or a greeting. So they passed and repassed each other on those pavements, appearing and vanishing, each intent on his own secret, and wrapped in obscurity. One might have sworn that not a man saw his neighbour who met him or jostled him, that here every one was a phantom for the other, though the lines of their paths crossed and recrossed, and their eyes stared like the eyes of live men. When two went by together, they mumbled and cast distrustful glances behind them as though afraid all the world was an enemy, and the pattering of feet was like the noise of a shower of rain. Curious appearances and simulations of life gathered at points in the road, for at intervals the villas ended and shops began in a dismal row, and looked so hopeless that one wondered who could buy. There were women fluttering uneasily about the greengrocers, and shabby things in rusty black touched and retouched the red lumps that an unshaven butcher offered, and already in the corner public there was a confused noise, with a tossing of voices that rose and fell like a Jewish chant, with the senseless stir of marionettes jerked into an imitation of gaiety. Then, in crossing a side street that seemed like grey mid-winter in stone, he trespassed from one world to another, for an old decayed house amidst its garden held the opposite corner. The laurels had grown into black skeletons, patched with green drift, the ilex gloomed over the porch, the deodar had blighted the flower-beds. Dark ivies swarmed over an elm-tree, and a brown clustering fungus sprang in gross masses on the lawn, shewing where the roots of dead trees mouldered. The blue verandah, the blue balcony over the door, had faded to grey, and the stucco was blotched with ugly marks of weather, and a dank smell of decay, that vapour of black rotten earth in old town gardens, hung heavy about the gates. And then a row of musty villas had pushed out in shops to the pavement, and the things in faded black buzzed and stirred about the limp cabbages, and the red lumps of meat.

It was the same terrible street, whose pavements he had trodden so often, where sunshine seemed but a gaudy light, where the fume of burning bricks always drifted. On black winter nights he had seen the sparse lights glimmering through the rain and drawing close together, as the dreary road vanished in long perspective. Perhaps this was its most appropriate moment, when nothing of its smug villas and skeleton shops remained but the bright patches of their windows, when the old house amongst its mouldering shrubs was but a dark cloud, and the streets to the north and south seemed like starry wastes, beyond them the blackness of infinity. Always in the daylight it had been to him abhorred and abominable, and its grey houses and purlieus had been fungus-like sproutings, an efflorescence of horrible decay.

But on that bright morning neither the dreadful street nor those who moved about it appalled him. He returned joyously to his den, and reverently laid out the paper on his desk. The world about him was but a grey shadow hovering on a shining wall; its noises were faint as the rustling of trees in a distant wood. The lovely and exquisite forms of those who served the Amber Venus were his distinct, clear, and manifest visions, and for one amongst them who came to him in a fire of bronze hair his heart stirred with the adoration of love. She it was who stood forth from all the rest and fell down prostrate before the radiant form in amber, drawing out her pins in curious gold, her glowing brooches of enamel, and pouring from a silver box all her treasures of jewels and precious stones, chrysoberyl and sardonyx, opal and diamond, topaz and pearl. And then she stripped from her body her precious robes and stood before the goddess in the glowing mist of her hair, praying that to her who had given all and came naked to the shrine, love might be given, and the grace of Venus. And when at last, after strange adventures, her prayer was granted, then when the sweet light came from the sea, and her lover turned at dawn to that bronze glory, he saw beside him a little statuette of amber. And in the shrine, far in Britain where the black rains stained the marble, they found the splendid and sumptuous statue of the Golden Venus, the last fine robe of silk that the lady had dedicated falling from her fingers, and the jewels lying at her feet. And her face was like the lady's face when the sun had brightened it on that day of her devotion.

The bronze mist glimmered before Lucian's eyes; he felt as though the soft floating hair touched his forehead and his lips and his hands. The fume of burning bricks, the reek of cabbage water, never reached his nostrils that were filled with the perfume of rare unguents, with the breath of the violet sea in Italy. His pleasure was an inebriation, an ecstasy of joy that destroyed all the vile Hottentot kraals and mud avenues as with one white lightning flash, and through the hours of that day he sat enthralled, not contriving a story with patient art, but rapt into another time, and entranced by the urgent gleam in the lady's eyes.

The little tale of *The Amber Statuette* had at last issued from a humble office in the spring after his father's death. The author was utterly unknown; the author's Murray was a wholesale stationer and printer in process of development, so that Lucian was astonished when the book became a moderate success. The reviewers had been sadly irritated, and even now he recollected with cheerfulness an article in an influential daily paper, an article pleasantly headed: "Where are the disinfectants?"

And then—but all the months afterwards seemed doubtful, there were only broken revelations of the laborious hours renewed, and the white nights when he had seen the moonlight fade and the gaslight grow wan at the approach of dawn.

He listened. Surely that was the sound of rain falling on sodden ground, the heavy sound of great swollen drops driven down from wet leaves by the gust of wind, and then again the strain of boughs sang above the tumult of the air, there was a doleful noise as if the storm shook the masts of a ship. He had only to get up and look out of the window and he would see the treeless empty street, and the rain starring the puddles under the gas-lamp, but he would wait a little while.

He tried to think why, in spite of all his resolutions, a dark horror seemed to brood more and more over all his mind. How often he had sat and worked on just such nights as this, contented if the words were in accord though the wind might wail, though the air were black with rain. Even about the little book that he had made there seemed some taint, some shuddering memory that came to him across the gulf of forgetfulness. Somehow the remembrance of the offering to Venus, of the phrases that he had so lovingly invented, brought back again the dusky figures that danced in the orgy, beneath the brassy glittering lamps; and again the naphtha flares shewed the way to the sad house in the fields, and the red glare lit up the mildewed walls and the black hopeless windows. He gasped for breath, he seemed to inhale a heavy air that reeked of decay and rottenness, and the odour of the clay was in his nostrils.

That unknown cloud that had darkened his thoughts grew blacker and engulfed him, despair was heavy upon him, his heart fainted with a horrible dread. In a moment, it seemed, a veil would be drawn away and certain awful things would appear.

He strove to rise from his chair, to cry out, but he could not. Deep, deep the darkness closed upon him, and the storm sounded far away. The Roman fort surged up, terrific, and he saw the writhing boughs in a ring, and behind them a glow and heat of fire. There were hideous shapes that swarmed in the thicket of the oaks; they called and beckoned to him, and rose into the air, into the flame that was smitten from heaven about the walls. And amongst them was the form of the beloved, but jets of flame issued from her breasts, and beside her was a horrible old woman, naked; and they, too, summoned him to mount the hill.

He heard Dr. Burrows whispering of the strange things that had been found in old Mrs. Gibbon's cottage, obscene figures, and unknown contrivances. She was a witch, he said, and the mistress of witches.

He fought against the nightmare, against the illusion that bewildered him. All his life, he thought, had been an evil dream, and for the common world he had fashioned an unreal red garment, that burned in his eyes. Truth and the dream were so mingled that now he could not divide one from the other. He had let Annie drink his soul beneath the hill, on the night when the moonfire shone, but he had not surely seen her exalted in the flame, the Queen of the Sabbath. Dimly he remembered Dr. Burrows coming to see him in London, but had he not imagined all the rest?

Again he found himself in the dusky lane, and Annie floated down to him from the moon above the hill. His head sank upon her breast again, but, alas, it was aflame. And he looked down, and he saw that his own flesh was aflame, and he knew that the fire could never be quenched.

There was a heavy weight upon his head, his feet were nailed to the floor, and his arms bound tight beside him. He seemed to himself to rage and struggle with the strength of a madman; but his hand only stirred and quivered a little as it lay upon the desk.

Again he was astray in the mist; wandering through the waste avenues of a city that had been ruined from ages. It had been splendid as Rome, terrible as Babylon, and for ever the darkness had covered it, and it lay desolate for ever in the accursed plain. And far and far the grey passages stretched into the night, into the icy fields, into the place of eternal gloom.

Ring within ring the awful temple closed around him; unending circles of vast stones, circle within circle, and every circle loss throughout all ages. In the centre was the sanctuary of the infernal rite, and he was borne thither as in the eddies of a whirlpool, to consummate his ruin, to celebrate the wedding of the Sabbath. He flung up his arms and beat the air, resisting with all his strength, with muscles that could throw down mountains; and this time his little finger stirred for an instant, and his foot twitched upon the floor.

Then suddenly a flaring street shone before him. There was darkness round about him, but it flamed with hissing jets of light and naphtha fires, and great glittering lamps swayed very slowly in a violent blast of air. A horrible music, and the exultation of discordant voices, swelled in his ears, and he saw an uncertain tossing crowd of dusky figures that circled and leapt before him. There was a noise like the chant of the lost, and then there appeared in the midst of the orgy, beneath a red flame, the figure of a woman. Her bronze hair and flushed cheeks were illuminate, and an argent light shone from her eyes, and with a smile that froze his heart her lips opened to speak to him. The tossing crowd faded away, falling into a gulf of darkness, and then she drew out from her hair pins of curious gold, and glowing brooches in enamel, and poured out jewels before him from a silver box, and then she stripped from her body her precious robes, and stood in the glowing mist of her hair, and held out her arms to him. But he raised his eyes and saw the mould and decay gaining on the walls of a dismal room, and a gloomy paper was dropping to the rotting floor. A vapour of the grave entered his nostrils, and he cried out with a loud scream; but there was only an indistinct guttural murmur in his throat.

And presently the woman fled away from him, and he pursued her. She fled away before him through midnight country, and he followed after her, chasing her from thicket to thicket, from valley to valley. And at last he captured her and won her with horrible caresses, and they went up to celebrate and make the marriage of the Sabbath. They were within the matted thicket, and they writhed in the flames, insatiable, for ever. They were tortured, and tortured one another, in the sight of thousands who gathered thick about them; and their desire rose up like a black smoke.

Without, the storm swelled to the roaring of an awful sea, the wind grew to a shrill long scream, the elm-tree was riven and split with the crash of a thunderclap. To Lucian the tumult and the shock came as a gentle murmur, as if a brake stirred before a sudden breeze in summer. And then a vast silence overwhelmed him.

A few minutes later there was a shuffling of feet in the passage, and the door was softly opened. A woman came in, holding a light, and she peered curiously at the figure sitting quite still in the chair before the desk. The woman was half dressed, and she had let her splendid bronze hair flow down, her cheeks were flushed, and as she advanced into the shabby room, the lamp she carried cast quaking shadows on the mouldering paper, patched with marks of rising damp, and hanging in strips from the wet, dripping wall. The blind had not been drawn, but no light nor glimmer of light filtered through the window, for a great straggling box tree that beat the rain upon the panes shut out even the night. The woman came softly, and as she bent down over Lucian an argent gleam shone from her brown eyes, and the little curls upon her neck were like golden work upon marble. She put her hand to his heart, and looked up, and beckoned to some one who was waiting by the door.

"Come in, Joe," she said. "It's just as I thought it would be: 'Death by misadventure'"; and she held up a little empty bottle of dark blue glass that was standing on the desk. "He would take it, and I always knew he would take a drop too much one of these days."

"What's all those papers that he's got there?"

"Didn't I tell you? It was crool to see him. He got it into 'is 'ead he could write a book; he's been at it for the last six months. Look 'ere."

She spread the neat pile of manuscript broadcast over the desk, and took a sheet at haphazard. It was all covered with illegible hopeless scribblings; only here and there it was possible to recognise a word.

"Why, nobody could read it, if they wanted to."

"It's all like that. He thought it was beautiful. I used to 'ear him jabbering to himself about it, dreadful nonsense it was he used to talk. I did my best to tongue him out of it, but it wasn't any good."

"He must have been a bit dotty. He's left you everything?"

"Yes."

"You'll have to see about the funeral."

"There'll be the inquest and all that first."

"You've got evidence to shew he took the stuff."

"Yes, to be sure I have. The doctor told him he would be certain to do for himself, and he was found two or three times quite silly in the streets. They had to drag him away from a house in Halden Road. He was carrying on dreadful, shaking at the gaite, and calling out it was 'is 'ome and they wouldn't let him in. I heard Dr. Manning myself tell 'im in this very room that he'd kill 'imself one of these days. Joe! Aren't you ashamed of yourself. I declare you're quite rude, and it's almost Sunday too. Bring the light over here, can't you?"

The man took up the blazing paraffin lamp, and set it on the desk, beside the scattered heap of that terrible manuscript. The flaring light shone through the dead eyes into the dying brain, and there was a glow within, as if great furnace doors were opened.

Ornaments in Jade

The Rose Garden

And afterwards she went very softly, and opened the window and looked out. Behind her, the room was in a mystical semi-darkness; chairs and tables were hovering, ill-defined shapes; there was but the faintest illusory glitter from the talc moons in the rich Indian curtain which she had drawn across the door. The yellow silk draperies of the bed were but suggestions of colour, and the pillow and the white sheets glimmered as a white cloud in a far sky at twilight.

She turned from the dusky room, and with dewy tender eyes gazed out across the garden towards the lake. She could not rest nor lay herself down to sleep; though it was late, and half the night had passed, she could not rest. A sickle moon was slowly drawing upwards through certain filmy clouds that stretched in a long band from east to west, and a pallid light began to flow from the dark water, as if there also some vague planet were rising. She looked with eyes insatiable for wonder; and she found a strange eastern effect in the bordering of reeds, in their spear-like shapes, in the liquid ebony that they shadowed, in the fine inlay of pearl and silver as the moon shone free; a bright symbol in the steadfast calm of the sky.

There were faint stirring sounds heard from the fringe of reeds, and now and then the drowsy, broken cry of the waterfowl, for they knew that the dawn was not far off. In the centre of the lake was a carved white pedestal, and on it shone a white boy, holding the double flute to his lips.

Beyond the lake the park began, and sloped gently to the verge of the wood, now but a dark cloud beneath the sickle moon. And then beyond, and farther still, undiscovered hills, grey bands of cloud, and the steep pale height of the heaven. She gazed on with her tender eyes, bathing herself, as it were, in the deep rest of the night, veiling her soul with the half-light and the half-shadow, stretching out her delicate hands into the coolness of the misty silvered air, wondering at her hands.

And then she turned from the window, and made herself a divan of cushions on the Persian carpet, and half sat, half lay there, as motionless, as ecstatic as a poet dreaming under roses, far in Ispahan. She had gazed out, after all, to assure herself that sight and the eyes shewed nothing but a glimmering veil, a gauze of curious lights and figures: that in it there was no reality nor substance. He had always told her that there was only one existence, one science, one religion, that the external world was but a variegated shadow which might either conceal or reveal the truth; and now she believed.

He had shewn her that bodily rapture might be the ritual and expression of the ineffable mysteries, of the world beyond sense, that must be entered by the way of sense; and now she believed. She had never much doubted any of his words, from the moment of their meeting a month before. She had looked up as she sat in the arbour, and her father was walking down through the avenue of roses, bringing to her the stranger, thin and dark, with a pointed beard and melancholy eyes. He murmured something to himself as they shook hands; she heard the rich, unknown words that sounded as the echo of far music. Afterwards he had told her what those words signified:

> "How say ye that I was lost? I wandered among roses.
> Can he go astray that enters the rose garden?
> The Lover in the house of the Beloved is not forlorn.
> I wandered among roses. How say ye that I was lost?"

His voice, murmuring the strange words, had persuaded her, and now she had the rapture of the perfect knowledge. She had looked out into the silvery uncertain night in order that she might experience the sense that for her these things no longer existed. She was not any more a part of the garden, or of the lake, or of the wood, or of the life that she had led hitherto. Another line that he had quoted came to her:

> "The kingdom of I and We forsake and your home in annihilation make."

It had seemed at first almost nonsense—if it had been possible for him to talk nonsense; but now she was filled and thrilled with the meaning of it. Herself was annihilated; at his bidding she had destroyed all her old feelings and emotions, her likes and dislikes, all the inherited loves and hates that her father and mother had given her; the old life had been thrown utterly away.

It grew light, and when the dawn burned she fell asleep, murmuring: "How say ye that I was lost?"

THE TURANIANS

The smoke of the tinkers' camp rose a thin pale blue from the heart of the wood.

Mary had left her mother at work on "things", and had gone out with a pale and languid face into the hot afternoon. She had talked of walking across the fields to the Green, and of having a chat with the doctor's daughter, but she had taken the other path that crept down towards the hollow and the dark thickets of the wood.

After all, she had felt too lazy to rouse herself, to make the effort of conversation, and the sunlight scorched the path that was ruled straight from stile to stile across the brown August fields, and she could see, even from far away, how the white dust clouds were smoking on the road by the Green. She hesitated, and at last went down under the far-spreading oak-trees, by a winding way of grass that cooled her feet.

Her mother, who was very kind and good, used to talk to her sometimes on the evils of "exaggeration", on the necessity of avoiding phrases violently expressed, words of too fierce an energy. She remembered how she had run into the house a few days before and had called her mother to look at a rose in the garden that "burnt like a flame". Her mother had said the rose was very pretty, and a little later had hinted her doubts as to the wisdom of "such very strong expressions".

"I know, my dear Mary," she had said, "that in your case it isn't affectation. You really *feel* what you say, don't you? Yes; but is it nice to feel like that? Do you think that it's quite *right*, even?"

The mother had looked at the girl with a curious wistfulness, almost as if she would say something more, and sought for the fit words, but could not find them. And then she merely remarked:

"You haven't seen Alfred Moorhouse since the tennis party, have you? I must ask him to come next Tuesday; you like him?"

The daughter could not quite see the link between her fault of "exaggeration" and the charming young barrister, but her mother's warning recurred to her as she strayed down the shadowed path, and felt the long dark grass cool and refreshing about her feet. She would not have put this sensation into words, but she thought it was as though her ankles were gently, sweetly kissed as the rich grass touched them, and her mother would have said it was not right to think such things.

And what a delight there was in the colours all about her! It was as though she walked in a green cloud; the strong sunlight was filtered through the leaves, reflected from the grass, and made all visible things, the tree-stems, the flowers, and her own hands seem new, transformed into another likeness. She had walked by the wood-path over and over again, but to-day it had become full of mystery and hinting, and every turn brought a surprise.

To-day the mere sense of being alone under the trees was an acute secret joy, and as she went down deeper and the wood grew dark about her, she loosened her brown hair, and when the sun shone over the fallen tree she saw her hair was not brown but bronze and golden, glowing on her pure white dress.

She stayed by the well in the rock, and dared to make the dark water her mirror, looking to right and left with shy glances and listening for the rustle of parted boughs, before she would match her gold with luminous ivory. She saw wonders in a glass as she leaned over the shadowed mysterious pool, and smiled at the smiling nymph, whose lips parted as if to whisper secrets.

As she went on her way, the thin blue smoke rose from a gap in the trees, and she remembered her childish dread of "the gypsies". She walked a little farther, and laid herself to rest on a smooth patch of turf, and listened to the strange intonations that sounded from the camp. "Those horrible people" she had heard the yellow folk called, but she found now a pleasure in voices that sang and, indistinctly heard, were almost chanting, with a rise and fall of notes and a wild wail, and the solemnity of unknown speech. It seemed a fit music for the unknown woodland, in harmony with the drip of the well, and the birds' sharp notes, and the rustle and hurry of the wood creatures.

She rose again and went on till she could see the red fire between the boughs; and the voices thrilled into an incantation. She longed to summon up courage, and talk to these strange wood-folk, but she was afraid to burst into the camp. So she sat down under a tree and waited, hoping that one of them might happen to come her way.

There were six or seven men, as many women, and a swarm of fantastic children, lolling and squatting about the fire, gabbling to one another in their singsong speech. They were people of curious aspect, short and squat, high-cheekboned, with dingy yellow skin and long almond eyes; only in one or two of the younger men there was a suggestion of a wild, almost faun-like grace, as of creatures who always moved between the red fire and the green leaf. Though everybody called them gypsies, they were in reality Turanian metal-workers, degenerated into wandering tinkers; their ancestors had fashioned the bronze battle-axes, and they mended pots and kettles. Mary waited under the tree, sure that she had nothing to fear, and resolved not to run away if one of them appeared.

The sun sank into a mass of clouds and the air grew close and heavy; a mist steamed up about the trees, a blue mist like the smoke of a wood-fire. A strange smiling face peered out from between the leaves, and the girl knew that her heart leapt as the young man walked towards her.

The Turanians moved their camp that night. There was a red glint, like fire, in the vast shadowy west, and then a burning paten floated up from a wild hill. A procession of weird bowed figures passed across the crimson disk, one stumbling after another in long single file, each bending down beneath his huge shapeless pack, and the children crawled last, goblin-like, fantastic.

The girl was lying in her white room, caressing a small green stone, a curious thing cut with strange devices, awful with age. She held it close to the luminous ivory, and the gold poured upon it.

She laughed for joy, and murmured and whispered to herself, asking herself questions in the bewilderment of her delight. She was afraid to say anything to her mother.

THE IDEALIST

"Did you notice Symonds while Beever was telling that story just now?" said one clerk to the other.

"No. Why? Didn't he like it?"

The second clerk had been putting away his papers and closing his desk in a grave and business-like manner, but when Beever's story was recalled to him he began to bubble anew, tasting the relish of the tale for a second time.

"He's a fair scorcher, old Beever," he remarked between little gasps of mirth. "But didn't Symonds like it?"

"Like it? He looked disgusted, I can tell you. Made a face, something in this style:" and the man drew his features into a design of sour disapproval, as he gave his hat the last polish with his coatsleeve.

"Well, I'm off now," he said. "I want to get home early, as there's tart for tea," and he fashioned another grimace, an imitation of his favourite actor's favourite contortion.

"Well, good-bye," said his friend. "You are a hot 'un, you are. You're worse than Beever. See you on Monday. What will Symonds say?" and he shouted after him as the door swung to and fro.

Charles Symonds, who had failed to see the humour of Mr. Beever's tale, had left the office a few minutes earlier and was now pacing slowly westward, mounting Fleet Street. His fellow clerk had not been much amiss in his observation. Symonds had heard the last phrases of Beever's story, and unconsciously had looked half round towards the group, angry and disgusted at their gross and stupid merriment. Beever and his friends seemed to him guilty of sacrilege; he likened them to plough-boys pawing and deriding an exquisite painted panel, blaring out their contempt and brutal ignorance. He could not control his features; in spite of himself he looked loathing at the three yahoos. He would have given anything if he could have found words and told them what he thought, but even to look displeasure was difficult. His shyness was a perpetual amusement to the other clerks, who often did little things to annoy him, and enjoyed the spectacle of Symonds inwardly raging and burning like Etna, but too hopelessly diffident to say a word. He would turn dead man's white, and grind his teeth at an insult, and pretend to join in the laugh, and pass it off as a joke. When he was a boy his mother was puzzled by him, not knowing whether he were sullen or insensible, or perhaps very good-tempered.

He climbed Fleet Street, still raw with irritation, partly from a real disgust at the profane coarseness of the clerks, and partly from a feeling that they talked so because they knew he hated such gross farces and novels. It was hideous to live and work with such foul creatures, and he glanced back fury at the City, the place of the stupid, the blatant, the intolerable.

He passed into the rush and flood of the Strand, into the full tide of a Saturday afternoon, still meditating the outrage, and constructing a cutting sentence for future use, heaping up words which should make Beever tremble. He was quite aware that he would never utter one of those biting phrases, but the pretence soothed him, and he began to remember other things. It was in late November and the clouds were already gathering for the bright solemnity of the sunset, flying to their places before the wind. They curled into fantastic shapes, high up there in the wind's whirlpool, and Symonds, looking towards the sky, was attracted by two grey writhing clouds that drew together in the west, in the far perspective of the Strand. He saw them as if they had been living creatures, noting every change and movement and transformation, till the shaking winds made them one and drove a vague form away to the south.

The curious interest he had taken in the cloud shapes had driven away the thought of the office, of the fetid talk which he so often heard. Beever and his friends ceased to exist, and Symonds escaped to his occult and private world which no one had ever divined. He lived far away down in Fulham, but he let the buses rock past him, and walked slowly, endeavouring to prolong the joys of anticipation. Almost with a visible gesture he drew himself apart, and went solitary, his eyes downcast, and gazing not on the pavement but on certain clear imagined pictures.

He quickened his steps as he passed along the northern pavement of Leicester Square, hurrying to escape the sight of the enamelled strange spectra who were already beginning to walk and stir abroad, issuing from their caves and waiting for the gas-light. He scowled as he looked up and chanced to see on a hoarding an icon with raddled cheeks and grinning teeth, at which some young men were leering; and one was recalling this creature's great song:

"And that's the way they do it.
How d'ye fink it's done?
Oh, *that's* the way they do it.
Doesn't it taike the bun?"

Symonds scowled at the picture of her, remembering how Beever had voted her "good goods", how the boys bellowed the chorus under his windows of Saturday nights. Once he had opened the window as they passed by, and had sworn at them and cursed them, in a whisper, lest he should be overheard.

He peered curiously at the books in a Piccadilly shop; now and then when he could save a few pounds he had made purchases there, but the wares which the bookseller dealt in were expensive, and he was obliged to be rather neatly dressed at the office, and he had other esoteric expenses. He had made up his mind to learn Persian and he hesitated as to whether he should turn back now, and see if he could pick up a grammar in Great Russell Street at a reasonable price. But it was growing dark, and the mists and shadows that he loved were gathering and inviting him onwards to those silent streets near the river.

When he at last diverged from the main road he made his way by a devious and eccentric track, threading an intricate maze of streets which to most people would have been dull and gloomy and devoid of interest. But to Symonds these backwaters of London were as bizarre and glowing as a cabinet of Japanese curios; he found here his delicately chased bronzes, work in jade, the flush and flame of extraordinary colours. He delayed at a corner, watching a shadow on a lighted blind, watching it fade and blacken and fade, conjecturing its secrets, inventing dialogue for this drama in *Ombres Chinoises*. He glanced up at another window, and saw a room vivid, in a hard yellow light of flaming gas, and lurked in the shelter of an old elm till he was perceived and the curtains were drawn hastily. On the way he had chosen, it was his fortune to pass many well-ordered decent streets, by villas detached and semi-detached, half hidden behind flowering-shrubs and evergreens. At this hour, on a Saturday in November, few were abroad, and Symonds was often able, crouching down by the fence, to peer into a lighted room, to watch persons who thought themselves utterly unobserved. As he came near to his home he went through meaner streets, and he stopped at a corner, observing two children at play, regarding them with the minute scrutiny of an entomologist at the microscope. A woman who had been out shopping crossed the road and drove the children home, and Symonds moved on, hastily, but with a long sigh of enjoyment.

His breath came quick, in gusts, as he drew out his latch-key. He lived in an old Georgian house, and he raced up the stairs, and locked the door of the great lofty room in which he lived. The evening was damp and chilly, but the sweat streamed down his face. He struck a match, and there was a strange momentary vision of the vast room, almost empty of furniture, a hollow space bordered by grave walls and the white glimmer of the corniced ceiling.

He lit a candle, opened a large box that stood in a corner, and set to work. He seemed to be fitting together some sort of lay figure; a vague hint of the human shape increased under his hands. The candle sparkled at the other end of the room, and Symonds was sweating over his task in a cavern of dark shadow. His nervous shaking fingers fumbled over that uncertain figure, and then he began to draw out incongruous monstrous things. In the dusk, white silk shimmered, laces and delicate frills hovered for a moment, as he bungled over the tying of knots, the fastening of bands. The old room grew rich, heavy, vaporous with subtle scents; the garments that were passing through his hands had been drenched with fragrance. Passion had contorted his face; he grinned stark in the candle-light.

When he had finished the work he drew it with him to the window, and lighted three more candles. In his excitement, for that night he forgot the effect of *Ombres Chinoises,* and those who passed and happened to look up at the white staring blind found singular matter for speculation.

WITCHCRAFT

"Rather left the others behind, haven't we, Miss Custance?" said the captain, looking back to the gate and the larchwood.

"I'm afraid we have, Captain Knight. I hope you don't mind very much, do you?"

"Mind? Delighted, you know. Sure this damp air isn't bad for you, Miss Custance?"

"Oh, d'you think it's damp? I like it. Ever since I can remember I've enjoyed these quiet autumn days. I won't hear of father's going anywhere else."

"Charmin' place, the Grange. Don't wonder you like comin' down here."

Captain Knight glanced back again and suddenly chuckled.

"I say, Miss Custance," he said, "I believe the whole lot's lost their way. Don't see a sign of them. Didn't we pass another path on the left?"

"Yes, and don't you remember you wanted to turn off?"

"Yes, of course. I thought it looked more possible, don't you know. That's where they must have gone. Where does it lead?"

"Oh, nowhere exactly. It dwindles and twists about a lot, and I'm afraid the ground is rather marshy."

"You don't say so?" The captain laughed out loud. "How awfully sick Ferris will be. He hates crossing Piccadilly if there's a bit of mud about."

"Poor Mr. Ferris!" And the two went on, picking their way on the rough path, till they came in sight of a little old cottage sunken alone in a hollow amongst the woods.

"Oh, you must come and see Mrs. Wise," said Miss Custance. "She's such a dear old thing, I'm sure you'd fall in love with her. And she'd never forgive me if she heard afterwards that we'd passed so close without coming in. Only for five minutes, you know."

"Certainly, Miss Custance. Is that the old lady there at the door?"

"Yes. She's always been so good to us children, and I know she'll talk of our coming to see her for months. You don't mind, do you?"

"I shall be charmed, I'm sure," and he looked back once more to see if there were any appearance of Ferris and his party.

"Sit down, Miss Ethel, sit down, please, miss," said the old woman when they went in. "And please to sit down here, sir, will you be so kind?"

She dusted the chairs, and Miss Custance enquired after the rheumatism and the bronchitis, and promised to send something from the Grange. The old woman had good country manners, and spoke well, and now and then politely tried to include Captain Knight in the conversation. But all the time she was quietly looking at him.

"Yes, sir, I be a bit lonely at times," she said when her visitors rose. "I do miss Nathan sorely; you can hardly remember my husband, can you, Miss Ethel? But I have the Book, sir, and good friends too."

A couple of days later Miss Custance came alone to the cottage. Her hand trembled as she knocked at the door.

"Is it done?" she asked, when the old woman appeared.

"Come in, miss," said Mrs. Wise, and she shut the door, and put up the wooden bolt. Then she crept to the hearth, and drew out something from a hiding-place in the stones.

"Look at that," she said, shewing it to the young lady. "Isn't it a picture?"

Miss Custance took the object into her fine delicate hands, and glanced at it, and then flushed scarlet.

"How horrible!" she exclaimed. "What did you do that for? You never told me."

"It's the only way, miss, to get what you want."

"It's a loathsome thing. I wonder you're not ashamed of yourself."

"I be as much ashamed as you be, I think," said Mrs. Wise, and she leered at the pretty, shy-faced girl. Their eyes met and their eyes laughed at one another.

"Cover it up, please, Mrs. Wise; I needn't look at it now, at all events. But are you sure?"

"There's never been a mishap since old Mrs. Cradoc taught me, and she's been dead for sixty year and more. She used to tell of her grandmother's days when there were meetings in the wood over there."

"And you're quite sure?"

"You do as I tell you. You must take it like this"; and the old woman whispered her instructions, and would have put out a hand in illustration, but the girl pushed it away.

"I understand now, Mrs. Wise. No, don't do that. I quite see what you mean. Here's the money."

"And whatever you do, don't you forget the ointment as I told you," said Mrs. Wise.

*   *   *

"I've been to read to poor old Mrs. Wise," Ethel said that evening to Captain Knight. "She's over eighty and her eyesight is getting very bad."

"Very good of you, Miss Custance, I'm sure," said Captain Knight, and he moved away to the other end of the drawing-room, and began to talk to a girl in yellow, with whom he had been exchanging smiles at a distance, ever since the men came in from the dining-room.

That night, when she was alone in her room, Ethel followed Mrs. Wise's instructions. She had hidden the object in a drawer, and as she drew it out, she looked about her, though the curtains were drawn close.

She forgot nothing, and when it was done she listened.

THE CEREMONY

From her childhood, from those early and misty days which began to seem unreal, she recollected the grey stone in the wood.

It was something between the pillar and the pyramid in shape, and its grey solemnity amidst the leaves and the grass shone and shone from those early years, always with some hint of wonder. She remembered how, when she was quite a little girl, she had strayed one day, on a hot afternoon, from her nurse's side, and only a little way in the wood the grey stone rose from the grass, and she cried out and ran back in panic terror.

"What a silly little girl," the nurse had said. "It's only the . . . stone." She had quite forgotten the name that the servant had given, and she was always ashamed to ask as she grew older.

But always that hot day, that burning afternoon of her childhood when she had first looked consciously on the grey image in the wood, remained not a memory but a sensation. The wide wood swelling like the sea, the tossing of the bright boughs in the sunshine, the sweet smell of the grass and flowers, the beating of the summer wind upon her cheek, the gloom of the underglade rich, indistinct, gorgeous, significant as old tapestry; she could feel it and see it all, and the scent of it was in her nostrils. And in the midst of the picture, where the strange plants grew gross in shadow, was the old grey shape of the stone.

But there were in her mind broken remnants of another and far earlier impression. It was all uncertain, the shadow of a shadow, so vague that it might well have been a dream that had mingled with the confused waking thoughts of a little child. She did not know that she remembered, she rather remembered the memory. But again it was a summer day, and a woman, perhaps the same nurse, held her in her arms, and went through the wood. The woman carried bright flowers in one hand; the dream had in it a glow of bright red, and the perfume of cottage roses. Then she saw herself put down for moment on the grass, and the red colour stained the grim stone, and there was nothing else—except that one night she woke up and heard the nurse sobbing.

She often used to think of the strangeness of very early life; one came, it seemed, from a dark cloud, there was a glow of light, but for a moment, and afterwards the night. It was as if one gazed at a velvet curtain, heavy, mysterious, impenetrable blackness, and then, for the twinkling of an eye, one spied through a pin-hole a storied town that flamed, with fire about its walls and pinnacles. And then again the folding darkness, so that sight became illusion, almost in the seeing. So to her was that earliest, doubtful vision of the grey stone, of the red colour spilled upon it, with the incongruous episode of the nursemaid, who wept at night.

But the later memory was clear; she could feel, even now, the inconsequent terror that sent her away shrieking, running to the nurse's skirts. Afterwards, through the days of girlhood, the stone had taken its place amongst the vast array of unintelligible things which haunt every child's imagination. It was part of life, to be accepted and not questioned; her elders spoke of many things which she could not understand, she opened books and was dimly amazed, and in the Bible there were many phrases which seemed strange. Indeed, she was often puzzled by her parents' conduct, by their looks at one another, by their half-words, and amongst all these problems which she hardly recognised as problems was the grey ancient figure rising from dark grass.

Some semi-conscious impulse made her haunt the wood where shadow enshrined the stone. One thing was noticeable; that all through the summer months the passers-by dropped flowers there. Withered blossoms were always on the ground, amongst the grass, and on the stone fresh blooms constantly appeared. From the daffodil to the

Michaelmas daisy there was marked the calendar of the cottage gardens, and in the winter she had seen sprays of juniper and box, mistletoe and holly. Once she had been drawn through the bushes by a red glow, as if there had been a fire in the wood, and when she came to the place, all the stone shone and all the ground about it was bright with roses.

In her eighteenth year she went one day into the wood, carrying with her a book that she was reading. She hid herself in a nook of hazel, and her soul was full of poetry, when there was a rustling, the rapping of parted boughs returning to their place. Her concealment was but a little way from the stone, and she peered through the net of boughs, and saw a girl timidly approaching. She knew her quite well; it was Annie Dolben, the daughter of a labourer, lately a promising pupil at Sunday-school. Annie was a nice-mannered girl, never failing in her curtsy, wonderful for her knowledge of the Jewish Kings. Her face had taken an expression that whispered, that hinted strange things; there was a light and a glow behind the veil of flesh. And in her hand she bore lilies.

The lady hidden in hazels watched Annie come close to the grey image; for a moment her whole body palpitated with expectation, almost the sense of what was to happen dawned upon her. She watched Annie crown the stone with flowers, she watched the amazing ceremony that followed.

And yet, in spite of all her blushing shame, she herself bore blossoms to the wood a few months later. She laid white hothouse lilies upon the stone, and orchids of dying purple, and crimson exotic flowers. Having kissed the grey image with devout passion, she performed there all the antique immemorial rite.

PSYCHOLOGY

Mr. Dale, who had quiet rooms in a western part of London, was very busily occupied one day with a pencil and little scraps of paper. He would stop in the middle of his writing, of his monotonous tramp from door to window, jot down a line of hieroglyphics, and turn again to his work. At lunch he kept his instruments on the table beside him, and a little note-book accompanied him on his evening walk about the

Green. Sometimes he seemed to experience a certain difficulty in the act of writing, as if the heat of shame or even incredulous surprise held his hand, but one by one the fragments of paper fell into the drawer, and a full feast awaited him at the day's close.

As he lit his pipe at dusk, he was standing by the window and looking out into the street. In the distance cab-lights flashed to and fro, up and down the hill, on the main road. Across the way he saw the long line of sober grey houses, cheerfully lit up for the most part, displaying against the night the dining-room and the evening meal. In one house, just opposite, there was brighter illumination, and the open windows shewed a modest dinner-party in progress, and here and there a drawing-room on the first floor glowed ruddy, as the tall shaded lamp was lit. Everywhere Dale saw a quiet and comfortable respectability; if there were no gaiety there was no riot, and he thought himself fortunate to have got "rooms" in so sane and meritorious a street.

The pavement was almost deserted. Now and again a servant would dart out from a side door and scurry off in the direction of the shops, returning in a few minutes in equal haste. But foot passengers were rare, and only at long intervals a stranger would drift from the highway and wander with slow speculation down Abingdon Road, as if he had passed its entrance a thousand times and had at last been piqued with curiosity and the desire of exploring the unknown. All the inhabitants of the quarter prided themselves on their quiet and seclusion, and many of them did not so much as dream that if one went far enough the road degenerated and became abominable, the home of the hideous, the mouth of a black purlieu. Indeed stories, ill and malodorous, were told of the streets parallel, to east and west, which perhaps communicated with the terrible sink beyond, but those who lived at the good end of Abingdon Road knew nothing of their neighbours.

Dale leant far out of his window. The pale London sky deepened to violet as the lamps were lit, and in the twilight the little gardens before the houses shone, seemed as if they grew more clear. The golden laburnum but reflected the last bright yellow veil that had fallen over the sky after sunset, the white hawthorn was a gleaming splendour, the red may a flameless fire in the dusk. From the open window, Dale could note the increasing cheerfulness of the diners opposite, as the moderate cups were filled and emptied; blinds in the higher stories brightened up and down the street when the nurses came up with the children. A gentle breeze that smelt of grass and woods and flowers fanned away the day's heat from the pavement stones, rustled through the blossoming boughs, and sank again, leaving the road to calm.

All the scene breathed the gentle domestic peace of the stories; there were regular lives, dull duties done, sober and common thoughts on every side. He felt that he needed not to listen at the windows, for he could divine all the talk, and guess the placid and usual channels in which the conversation flowed. Here there were no spasms, nor raptures, nor the red storms of romance, but a safe rest; marriage and birth and begetting were no more here than breakfast and lunch and afternoon tea.

And then he turned away from the placid transparency of the street, and sat down before his lamp and the papers he had so studiously noted. A friend of his, an "impossible" man named Jenyns, had been to see him the night before, and they had talked about the psychology of the novelists, discussing their insight, and the depth of their probe.

"It is all very well as far as it goes," said Jenyns. "Yes, it is perfectly accurate. Guardsmen do like chorus-girls, the doctor's daughter is fond of the curate, the grocer's assistant of the Baptist persuasion has sometimes religious difficulties, 'smart' people no doubt think a great deal about social events and complications: the Tragic Comedians felt and wrote all that stuff, I dare say. But do you think that is all? Do you call a description of the gilt tools on the morocco here an exhaustive essay on Shakespeare?"

"But what more is there?" said Dale. "Don't you think, then, that human nature has been fairly laid open? What more?"

"Songs of the frantic lupanar; delirium of the madhouse. Not extreme wickedness, but the insensate, the unintelligible, the lunatic passion and idea, the desire that must come from some other sphere that we cannot even faintly imagine. Look for yourself; it is easy."

Dale looked now at the ends and scraps of paper. On them he had carefully registered all the secret thoughts of the day, the crazy lusts, the senseless furies, the foul monsters that his heart had borne, the maniac phantasies that he had harboured. In every note he found a rampant madness, the equivalents in thought of mathematical absurdity, of two-sided triangles, of parallel straight lines which met.

"And we talk of absurd dreams," he said to himself. "And these are wilder than the wildest visions. And our sins; but these are the sins of nightmare.

"And every day," he went on, "we lead two lives, and the half of our soul is madness, and half heaven is lit by a black sun. I say I am a man, but who is the other that hides in me?"

TORTURE

"I really do not know what to do with him," said the father. "He seems absolutely stupid."

"Poor boy!" said his mother, "I am afraid he is not well. He doesn't look in good health."

"But what's the matter with him? He eats well enough; he had two helpings of meat, and two of pudding to-day at dinner, and a quarter of an hour afterwards he was munching some sweet stuff. His appetite's all right, you see, anyhow."

"But he's very pale. He makes me feel anxious."

"And he makes me feel anxious. Look at this letter from Wells, the headmaster. Here you see he says: 'It seems almost impossible to get him to play games; he has had two or three thrashings, as I hear, for shirking cricket. And his form master gives me a very bad account of his work during the term, so that I fear the school is doing him little if any good.' And you see, Mary, it isn't as if he were a little boy; he was fifteen last April. It's getting serious, you know."

"What d'you think we had better do?"

"I wish I knew. Look at him here. He's only been home for a week, and you'd think he'd be in the best of spirits, enjoying himself with the squire's boys, and singing and racketing about all over the place. And you know the way he has been going on, almost from the day he came back; lounging and crawling from the house to the garden and back again, staying in bed half the day, and coming down with his eyes half open. I must insist on that being put a stop to, at all events. I shall trust to you to get him up at a proper time."

"Very well, dear. I thought he looked so tired."

"But he does nothing to make him tired! I wouldn't mind so much if the fellow were bookish, but you see what Wells says on that score. Why, I can't even get him to read a story-book. I declare his face is enough to make one angry. One can see he's totally devoid of any interest in anything."

"I am afraid he's unhappy, Robert."

"Unhappy! A schoolboy unhappy! Well, I wish you'd see what you can do. I find it perfectly useless to talk to him myself."

It was curious, but the father was quite right in laughing at the notion of his son's unhappiness. Harry was, in his quiet way, in the best of spirits. It was perfectly true that he hated cricket, and, the headmaster might have added, he hated other boys. He cared nothing for printed matter of any kind, whether fact or fiction, and he found *Treasure Island* as dull as Cicero. But all through the past term he had been pondering an idea; it had been with him in the early mornings in the dormitory, in schooltime and in playtime, and he watched with it at night, long after the other boys had gone to sleep. Before the coming of the idea he had found his existence unhappy enough. He had a puffy, unwholesome face and sandy hair, and his great wide mouth was made the subject of many jests. He was unpopular because he did not like games, and because he would not bathe unless he were flung into the water, and he was always in trouble over his lessons, which he could not understand. He burst out crying one night in the middle of preparation, and of course he would not say what was the matter. The fact was that he had been trying to extract the meaning from some weary nonsense about triangles, known by the absurd name of Euclid, and he had found it utterly impossible to learn the rabid stuff by heart. The impossibility of it, and the hopeless cloud in his mind, and the terror of the thrashing he would get in the morning, broke him down; the "blubbering idiot", as they said.

Those were unhappy times, but that very night his idea came to him, and the holidays became indeed desirable, and ten times desirable. Every day and all the day he elaborated and re-elaborated his great thought, and though he was as stupid, unpopular, and unprofitable as ever, he was no longer wretched.

When he got home at the end of term he lost no time in setting about his task. It was true that he was sleepy and heavy in the mornings, but that was because he worked till late at night. He found it impossible to do much in the day-time; his parents spied out his ways, and he knew that he was much too dull to invent lies and explanations. The day after his return his father had come across him as he slunk into a dark corner of the shrubbery with something hidden under his coat. He could only stand and look hopeless, idiotic, when an empty beer bottle was drawn forth; he could not say what he was doing or what he wanted with a green glass bottle. His father had left him, telling him not to play the fool, and he felt that he was always watched. When he took the cord from the back-kitchen one of the maids was peering after him down the passage, and his mother found him trying to bind a large log of wood to the trunk of one of the trees. She wanted to know what he was doing, and whether he could not find some more sensible amusement, and he stared at her with his heavy white face. He knew that he was under observation, and so he worked at night. The two servant girls who slept in the next room often awoke, fancying they heard a queer sort of noise, a "chink-chink", as one of them described the sensation, but they could not make out what it was.

And at last he was ready. He was "loafing about" one afternoon, and he happened to meet Charlotte Emery, a little girl of twelve, the daughter of a neighbour. Harry flushed to a dull burning red.

"Come for a walk with me to the Beeches?" he said. "I wish you would."

"Oh, I mustn't, Harry. Mother wouldn't like it."

"Do come. I've got a new game; grand fun."

"Is it really? What sort of game is it?"

"I can't shew you here. Just walk on towards the Beeches, and I'll follow you directly. I knew you would."

Harry ran full tilt to the hiding-place where he had bestowed his apparatus. He soon overtook Charlotte, and the two went off together towards the Beeches, a lonely wooded hill a mile away. The boy's father would have been astonished if he could have seen him; Harry was glowing and burning with that dull red colour, but he laughed as he walked beside Charlotte.

When they were alone together in the wood, Charlotte said:

"Now you must shew me the game. You promised."

"I know. But you must do just as I tell you."

"Yes, I will."

"Even if it hurts?"

"Yes. But you wouldn't hurt me, Harry. I like you."

The boy stared at her, gazed with his dull, fishy, light blue eyes; his white, unwholesome face glared at her almost in terror. She was a dark girl, olive-skinned, with black eyes and black hair, and the scent of her hair had already half intoxicated him, as they walked close together.

"You like me," he said at last, stuttering.

"Yes, I like you very much. I love you, Harry dear. Won't you give me a kiss?" And she put her arm round his neck, round the neck of the ugly, pasty schoolboy. The leaden marks under his eyes seemed to grow darker.

He dropped the parcel that he held under one arm. It broke open and the contents fell to the ground. There were three or four fantastic instruments, ugly little knives made of green bottle-glass, clumsily set into wooden handles. He had stolen a broom for this purpose. And there were some lengths of rope, fitted with running nooses. It was the idea that he had so long cherished.

But he threw himself full length upon the grass, and burst into tears—the "blubbering idiot".

MIDSUMMER

The old farmhouse on the hill flushed rose in the afterglow, and then, as the dusk began to mount from the brook, faded and yet grew brighter, its whitewashed walls gleaming as though light flowed from them, as the moon gleams when the red clouds turn to grey.

The ancient hawthorn tree at the barn-end became a tall black stem and its leaves and boughs a black mass against the pale uncertain blue of the twilight sky. Leonard looked up with a great sigh of relief. He was perched on the stile by the bridge, and as the wind fell, the ripple of the water swelled into a sweeter song, and there was no other sound to be heard. His pipe was finished, and though he knew that his rooms up at the farm looked out on the red rose and the white, he could not make up his mind to leave the view of the shimmering unearthly walls, and the melody of clear running water.

The contrast of it all with London was almost too immense, hardly realised or credible. A few hours before, and his ears seemed bursting with the terrible battle of the streets, with the clangour and jangle of great waggons thundering over the stones, with the sharp rattle of hansoms, the heavy rumble of swaying omnibuses. And during the journey his eyes still saw the thronging crowds, the turbid, furious streams of men that pushed eastward and westward, hurrying and jostling one another, wearying the brain with their constant movement, the everlasting flux and reflux of white faces. And the air, a hot smoke, a faint sick breath as though from a fever-stricken city; the sky, all grey heat that beat upon weary men, as they looked up through the cloud of dust that went before and followed them.

And now he was soothed in the deep silence and soothed by the chanting water, his eyes saw the valley melting into soft shadow, and in his nostrils was the ineffable incense of a summer night, that as a medicine allayed all the trouble and pain of body and mind. He wet his hands in the dew of the long grass and bathed his forehead, as if all the defilement and anguish of the streets should thus be washed utterly away.

He tried to analyse the scent of the night. The green leaves that overshadowed the brook and made the water dark at noon, gave out their odour, and the deep meadow grass was fragrant, a gale of scent breathed from the huge elder-bush that lit up the vague hillside, hanging above the well. But the meadow-sweet was bursting into blossom at his feet, and ah! the wild red roses drooped down from dreamland.

At last he began to climb the hillside towards those white magic walls that had charmed him. His two rooms were at the end of the long low farmhouse, and though there was a passage leading to the big kitchen, Leonard's sitting-room opened immediately on the garden, on the crimson roses. He could go and come as he pleased without disturbing the household, or as the pleasant farmer had expressed it, he had a home of his own. He entered and locked the door, and lit the two candles that stood in bright brass candlesticks on the mantelpiece. The room had a low ceiling crossed by a whitewashed beam, the walls were bulging and uneven, decked with samplers, with faded prints, and in a corner stood a glass cupboard, displaying quaint flowery china of some forgotten local pattern.

The room was as quiet, as full of peace, as the air and the night, and Leonard knew that here, at the old bureau, he would find the treasure he had been long vainly seeking. He was tired, but he did not feel inclined to go to bed. He lit his pipe again, and began to arrange his papers, and idly sat down at the bureau, thinking of the task, or rather of the delight, before him. An idea flashed suddenly into his mind, and he began to write hurriedly, in an ecstasy, afraid lest he should lose what he had so happily found.

At midnight his window was still bright on the hill, and he laid down his pen with a sigh of pleasure at the accomplished work. And now he could not go to bed; he felt he must wander into the night, and summon sleep from the velvet air, from the scent of darkness, from the dew. He gently unlocked and locked the door, and walked slowly between the Persian roses, and climbed the stone stile in the garden wall. The moon was mounting to a throne, in full splendour; below, at a little distance, there seemed the painted scene of a village, and higher, beyond the farmhouse, a great wood began. And as he thought of the green retreats he had glanced at in the sunlit evening, he was filled with a longing for the wood-world at night, with a desire for its darkness, for the mystery of it beneath the moon. He followed the path he had noted, till on the wood's verge he looked back and found that the shape of the farmhouse had fallen into the night and vanished.

He entered the shadow, treading softly, and let the track lead him away from the world. The night became full of whisperings, of dry murmuring noises; it seemed soon as if a stealthy host were beneath the trees, every man tracking another. Leonard quite forgot his work, and its triumph, and felt as though his soul were astray in a new dark sphere that dreams had foretold. He had come to a place remote, without form or colour, made alone of shadow and overhanging gloom. Unconsciously he wandered from the path, and for a time he fought his way through the undergrowth, struggling with interlacing boughs and brambles that dragged back his feet.

At last he got free, and found that he had penetrated into a broad avenue, piercing, it seemed, through the heart of the wood. The moon shone bright from above the tree-tops, and gave a faint green colour to the track which ascended to an open glade; a great amphitheatre amidst the trees. He was tired, and lay down in the darkness beside the turfy road, and wondered whether he had lit on some forgotten way, on some great path that the legions had trodden. And as he lay there watching, gazing at the pale moonlight, he saw a shadow advancing on the grass before him.

"A breath of wind must be stirring some bough behind me," he thought, but in the instant a woman went by, and then the shadows and white women followed thick.

Leonard gripped hard at a stick he was carrying, and drove his nails into the flesh. He saw the farmer's daughter, the girl who had waited on him a few hours before, and behind her came girls with like faces, no doubt the quiet modest girls of the English village, of the English farmhouse.

For a moment they fronted him, shameless, unabashed before one another, and then they had passed.

He had seen their smiles, he had seen their gestures, and things that he had thought the world had long forgotten.

The white writhing figures passed up towards the glade, and the boughs hid them, but he never doubted as to what he had seen.

NATURE

"And there was a broad level by the river," Julian went on, telling the story of his holiday. "A broad level of misty meadows, divided by low banks, between the hills and the river. They say the Roman world is lost beneath the turf, that a whole city sleeps there, gold and marble and amber all buried for ever."

"You did not see anything?"

"No, I suppose not. I used to get up early, and go out, and leave the little modern village behind me, hidden in the hot haze. And then I would stand in the misty meadows, and watch the green turf shimmer and lighten, as the grey halo rolled away. Oh! the silence. There was no sound except the lapping of the river, the wash of the water on the reeds.

"The banks are yellow mud," he went on, "but in the early morning, as the sun began to shine in the mist, they pearled and grew like silver. There was a low mound that hid something, and on it an old thorn tree bent towards the east; it was a little way from the tide's brim. I stood there and saw the woods swell out of the haze in the early morning, and that white sun seemed to encompass the town with gleaming walls. If I had stayed still, I think I should have seen the glittering legion and the eagles, I should have heard the sonorous trumpets pealing from the walls."

"I expect you have seen and heard more than that," said his friend. "I always told you that the earth too, and the hills, and even the old walls are a language, hard to translate."

"And I came upon a place that made me think of that," said Julian. "It was far from the town; I lost my way amongst those rolling hills, and strayed by footpaths from field to wood, and all that I saw of man was here and there a blue smoke that crawled up from the earth, from the tree, it might be, or the brook, for I could see no house. I went on, always with the sense that I was following an unknown object, and, suddenly, a shape rose from forgotten dreams. An old farmhouse, built of grey, silvering stones; a long barn wavering and dipping down to a black pool, pine trees overhanging the roof. It was all dim, as if it had been seen reflected in water. I went a little nearer, and I found that I was lifted free of the maze of hills. I fronted the mountain, looking across a deep broad valley, and all the year the mountain winds must blow upon the porch; they look from their deep windows and see the fleeting of the clouds and the sun, on that vast green hillside. Yellow flowers were shaking in the garden, for even on that still day the mountain wind swept across the valley. But those grey glistening walls! A light flowed from them, and they spoke of something beyond thought.

"I visited, too, the river valley, passing out to the north. The town was soon hidden behind trees, behind a curtain of Lombardy poplars, whispering of Italy, of the vine, the olive garden. The curving lane led me beneath orchards, their under-boughs dark-green, almost black, in the shadow, and the road winding between orchard and river led me into the long valley, where the forest is as a cloud upon the hill. I watched the yellow tide cease, and the water flow clear, and the breath of the wind was unearthly. It was there that I saw the burning pools."

"You stayed for the sunset?"

"Yes, I stayed all day within the valley. The sky was grey, but not cloudy; rather it was a glowing of silver light that made the earth seem dim and yet shining. Indeed, I say that though the sun was hidden, you would have dreamed that white moons were floating through the air, for now and again I saw the misty hillside pale and lighten, and a tree would appear suddenly in mid-forest, and glitter as if it blossomed. Yes, and in the calm meadows by the riverside there were little points of brightness, as if tongues of white fire sparkled in the grey grass."

"And the river itself?"

"It was all the day a hieroglyphic, winding in esses beneath those haunting banks, colourless, and yet alight like all the world around. At last, in the evening, I sat down beneath a wych-elm on the slope, where I breathed the scent and knew the heavy stillness of the wood. Then a strong wind blew, high up in heaven, and the grey veil vanished. The sky was clear pale blue; in the west there was exhibited an opal burning green, and beneath a purple wall. Then, in the middle of the purple, a rent opened; there was a red glint, and red momentary rays, as if rose-hot metal were beaten and dinted on the anvil, and the sparks fled abroad. So the sun sank.

"I thought I would wait and see all the valley, the river, and the level, and the woods sink into twilight, become sombre, formless. The light went out from the river, the water paled as it flowed between the sad reeds and grasses. I heard a harsh melancholy cry, and above, in the dusky air, a flight of great birds passed seaward in changing, hieroglyphic order. The keen line of the hills by sunset home seemed to melt away, to become vague.

"Then I saw the sky was blossoming in the north. Rose gardens appeared there, with golden hedges, and bronze gates, and the great purple wall caught fire as it grew leaden. The earth was lit again, but with unnatural jewelled colours; the palest light was sardonyx, the darkness was amethyst. And then the valley was aflame. Fire in the wood, the fire of a sacrifice beneath the oaks. Fire in the level fields, a great burning in the north, and vehement flame to the south, above the town. And in the still river the very splendour of fire, yes, as if all precious things were cast into its furnace pools, as if gold and roses and jewels became flame."

"And then?"

"Then, the shining of the evening star."

"And you," said his friend, "perhaps without knowing, have told me the story of a wonderful and incredible passion."

Julian stared at him, in amazement.

"You are quite right," he said at length.

THE HOLY THINGS

The sky was blue above Holborn, and only one little cloud, half white, half golden, floated on the wind's way from west to east. The long aisle of the street was splendid in the full light of the summer, and away in the west, where the houses seemed to meet and join, it was as a rich tabernacle, mysterious, the carven house of holy things.

A man came into the great highway from a quiet court. He had been sitting under plane-tree shade for an hour or more, his mind racked with perplexities and doubts, with the sense that all was without meaning or purpose, a tangle of senseless joys and empty sorrows. He had stirred in it and fought and striven, and now disappointment and success were alike tasteless. To struggle was weariness, to attain was weariness, to do nothing was weariness. He had felt, a little while before, that from the highest to the lowest things of life there was no choice, there was not one thing that was better than another: the savour of the cinders was no sweeter than the savour of the ashes. He had done work which some men liked and others disliked, and liking and disliking were equally tiresome to him. His poetry or his pictures or whatever it was that he worked at had utterly ceased to interest him, and he had tried to be idle, and found idleness as impossible as work. He had lost the faculty for making and he had lost the power of resting; he dozed in the day-time and started up and cried at night. Even that morning he had doubted and hesitated, wondering whether to stay indoors or to go out, sure that in either plan there was an infinite weariness and disgust.

When he at last went abroad he let the crowd push him into the quiet court, and at the same time cursed them in a low voice for doing so; he tried to persuade himself that he had meant to go somewhere else. When he sat down he desperately endeavoured to rouse himself, and as he knew that all the strong interests are egotistic, he made an effort to grow warm over the work he had done, to find a glow of satisfaction in the thought that he had accomplished something. It was nonsense; he had found out a clever trick and had made the most of it, and it was over. Besides, how would it interest him if afterwards he was praised when he was dead? And what was the use of trying to invent some new tricks? It was folly; and he ground his teeth as a new idea came into his mind and was rejected. To get drunk always made him so horribly ill, and other things were more foolish and tiresome than poesy or painting, whichever it was.

He could not even rest on the uncomfortable bench, beneath the dank, stinking plane tree. A young man and a girl came up and sat next to him, and the girl said, "Oh, isn't it beautiful to-day?" and then they began to jabber to one another—the blasted fools! He flung himself from the seat and went out into Holborn.

As far as one could see, there were two processions of omnibuses, cabs, and vans that went east and west and west and east. Now the long line would move on briskly, now it stopped. The horses' feet rattled and pattered on the asphalt, the wheels ground and jarred, a bicyclist wavered in and out between the serried ranks, jangling his bell. The foot passengers went to and fro on the pavement, with an endless change of unknown faces; there was an incessant hum and murmur of voices. In the safety of a blind passage an Italian whirled round the handle of his piano-organ; the sound of it swelled and sank as the traffic surged and paused, and now and then one heard the shrill voices of the children who danced and shrieked in time to the music. Close to the pavement a coster pushed his barrow and proclaimed flowers in an odd intonation, reminding one of the Gregorian chant. The cyclist went by again with his jangling insistent bell, and a man who stood by the lamp-post set fire to his pastille ribbon, and let the faint blue smoke rise into the sun. Away in the west, where the houses seemed to meet, the play of sunlight on the haze made, as it were, golden mighty shapes that paused and advanced, and paused again.

He had viewed the scene hundreds of times, and for a long while had found it a nuisance and a weariness. But now as he walked stupidly, slowly, along the southern side of Holborn, a change fell. He did not in the least know what it was, but there seemed to be a strange air, and a new charm that soothed his mind.

When the traffic was stopped, to his soul there was a solemn hush that summoned remnants of a far-off memory. The voices of the passengers sank away, the street was endued with a grave and reverent expectation. A shop that he passed had a row of electric lamps burning above the door, and the golden glow of them in the sunlight was, he felt, significant. The grind and jar of the wheels, as the procession moved on again, gave out a chord of music, the opening of some high service that was to be done, and now, in an ecstasy, he was sure that he heard the roll and swell and triumph of the organ, and shrill sweet choristers began to sing. So the music sank and swelled and echoed in the vast aisle—in Holborn.

What could these lamps mean, burning in the bright sunlight? The music was hushed in a grave close, and in the rattle of traffic he heard the last deep sonorous notes shake against the choir walls—he had passed beyond the range of the Italian's instrument. But then a rich voice began alone, rising and falling in monotonous but awful modulations, singing a longing triumphant song, bidding the faithful lift up their hearts, be joined in heart with the Angels and Archangels, with the Thrones and Dominations. He could see no longer, he could not see the man who passed close beside him, pushing his barrow, and calling flowers.

Ah! He could not be mistaken, he was sure now. The air was blue with incense, he smelt the adorable fragrance. The time had almost come. And then the silvery, reiterated, instant summons of a bell; and again, and again.

The tears fell from his eyes, in his weeping the tears poured a rain upon his cheeks. But he saw in the distance, in the far distance, the carven tabernacle, golden mighty figures moving slowly, imploring arms stretched forth.

There was a noise of a great shout; the choir sang in the tongue of his boyhood that he had forgotten:

SANT. . . SANT. . . SANT

Then the silvery bell tinkled anew; and again, and again. He looked and saw the Holy, White, and Shining Mysteries exhibited—in Holborn.

The White People

PROLOGUE

Sorcery and sanctity," said Ambrose, "these are the only realities. Each is an ecstasy, a withdrawal from the common life."

Cotgrave listened, interested. He had been brought by a friend to this mouldering house in a northern suburb, through an old garden to the room where Ambrose the recluse dozed and dreamed over his books.

"Yes," he went on, "magic is justified of her children. There are many, I think, who eat dry crusts and drink water, with a joy infinitely sharper than anything within the experience of the 'practical' epicure."

"You are speaking of the saints?"

"Yes, and of the sinners, too. I think you are falling into the very general error of confining the spiritual world to the supremely good; but the supremely wicked, necessarily, have their portion in it. The merely carnal, sensual man can no more be a great sinner than he can be a great saint. Most of us are just indifferent, mixed-up creatures; we muddle through the world without realising the meaning and the inner sense of things, and, consequently, our wickedness and our goodness are alike second-rate, unimportant."

"And you think the great sinner, then, will be an ascetic, as well as the great saint?"

"Great people of all kinds forsake the imperfect copies and go to the perfect originals. I have no doubt but that many of the very highest among the saints have never done a 'good action' (using the words in their ordinary sense). And, on the other hand, there have been those who have sounded the very depths of sin, who all their lives have never done an 'ill deed.'"

He went out of the room for a moment, and Cotgrave, in high delight, turned to his friend and thanked him for the introduction.

"He's grand," he said. "I never saw that kind of lunatic before."

Ambrose returned with more whisky and helped the two men in a liberal manner. He abused the teetotal sect with ferocity, as he handed the seltzer, and pouring out a glass of water for himself, was about to resume his monologue, when Cotgrave broke in—

"I can't stand it, you know," he said, "your paradoxes are too monstrous. A man may be a great sinner and yet never do anything sinful! Come!"

"You're quite wrong," said Ambrose. "I never make paradoxes; I wish I could. I merely said that a man may have an exquisite taste in Romanée Conti, and yet never have even smelt four ale. That's all, and it's more like a truism than a paradox, isn't it? Your surprise at my remark is due to the fact that you haven't realised what sin is. Oh, yes, there is a sort of connection between Sin with the capital letter, and actions which are commonly called sinful: with murder, theft, adultery, and so forth. Much the same connection that there is between the A, B, C and fine literature. But I believe that the misconception—it is all but universal—arises in great measure from our looking at the matter through social spectacles. We think that a man who does evil to us and to his neighbours must be very evil. So he is, from a social standpoint; but can't you realise that Evil in its essence is a lonely thing, a passion of the solitary, individual soul? Really, the average murderer, quâ murderer, is not by any means a sinner in the true sense of the word. He is simply a wild beast that we have to get rid of to save our own necks from his knife. I should class him rather with tigers than with sinners."

"It seems a little strange."

"I think not. The murderer murders not from positive qualities, but from negative ones; he lacks something which non-murderers possess. Evil, of course, is wholly positive—only it is on the wrong side. You may believe me that sin in its proper sense is very rare; it is probable that there have been far fewer sinners than saints. Yes, your standpoint is all very well for practical, social purposes; we are naturally inclined to think that a person who is very disagreeable to us must be a very great sinner! It is very disagreeable to have one's pocket picked, and we pronounce the thief to be a very great sinner. In truth, he is merely an undeveloped man. He cannot be a saint, of course; but he may be, and often is, an infinitely better creature than thousands who have never broken a single commandment. He is a great nuisance to *us,* I admit, and we very properly lock him up if we catch him; but between his troublesome and unsocial action and evil— Oh, the connection is of the weakest."

It was getting very late. The man who had brought Cotgrave had probably heard all this before, since he assisted with a bland and judicious smile, but Cotgrave began to think that his "lunatic" was turning into a sage.

"Do you know," he said, "you interest me immensely? You think, then, that we do not understand the real nature of evil?"

"No, I don't think we do. We over-estimate it and we under-estimate it. We take the very numerous infractions of our social 'bye-laws'—the very necessary and very proper regulations which keep the human company together—and we get frightened at the prevalence of 'sin' and 'evil'. But this is really nonsense. Take theft, for example. Have you any *horror* at the thought of Robin Hood, of the Highland caterans of the seventeenth century, of the moss-troopers, of the company promoters of our day?

"Then, on the other hand, we underrate evil. We attach such an enormous importance to the 'sin' of meddling with our pockets (and our wives) that we have quite forgotten the awfulness of real sin."

"And what is sin?" said Cotgrave.

"I think I must reply to your question by another. What would your feelings be, seriously, if your cat or your dog began to talk to you, and to dispute with you in human accents? You would be overwhelmed with horror. I am sure of it. And if the roses in your garden sang a weird song, you would go mad. And suppose the stones in the road began to swell and grow before your eyes, and if the pebble that you noticed at night had shot out stony blossoms in the morning?

"Well, these examples may give you some notion of what sin really is."

"Look here," said the third man, hitherto placid, "you two seem pretty well wound up. But I'm going home. I've missed my tram, and I shall have to walk."

Ambrose and Cotgrave seemed to settle down more profoundly when the other had gone out into the early misty morning and the pale light of the lamps.

"You astonish me," said Cotgrave. "I had never thought of that. If that is really so, one must turn everything upside down. Then the essence of sin really is—"

"In the taking of heaven by storm, it seems to me," said Ambrose. "It appears to me that it is simply an attempt to penetrate into another and higher sphere in a forbidden manner. You can understand why it is so rare. There are few, indeed, who wish to penetrate into other spheres, higher or lower, in ways allowed or forbidden. Men, in the mass, are amply content with life as they find it. Therefore there are few saints, and sinners (in the proper sense) are fewer still, and men of genius, who partake sometimes of each character, are rare also. Yes; on the whole, it is, perhaps, harder to be a great sinner than a great saint."

"There is something profoundly unnatural about sin? Is that what you mean?"

"Exactly. Holiness requires as great, or almost as great, an effort; but holiness works on lines that *were* natural once; it is an effort to recover the ecstasy that was before the Fall. But sin is an effort to gain the ecstasy and the knowledge that pertain alone to angels, and in making this effort man becomes a demon. I told you that the mere murderer is not *therefore* a sinner; that is true, but the sinner is sometimes a murderer. Gilles de Raiz is an instance. So you see that while the good and the evil are to man as he now is—to man the social, civilised being—evil is unnatural in a much deeper sense than good. The saint endeavours to recover a gift which he has lost; the sinner tries to obtain something which was never his. In brief, he repeats the Fall."

"But are you a Catholic?" said Cotgrave.

"Yes; I am a member of the persecuted Anglican Church."

"Then, how about those texts which seem to reckon as sin that which you would set down as a mere trivial dereliction?"

"Yes; but in one place the word 'sorcerers' comes in the same sentence, doesn't it? That seems to me to give the key-note. Consider: can you imagine for a moment that a false statement which saves an innocent man's life is a sin? No; very good, then, it is not the mere liar who is excluded by those words; it is, above all, the 'sorcerers' who use the material life, who use the failings incidental to material life as instruments to obtain their infinitely wicked ends. And let me tell you this: our higher senses are so blunted, we are so drenched with materialism, that we should probably fail to recognise real wickedness if we encountered it."

"But shouldn't we experience a certain horror—a terror such as you hinted we would experience if a rose tree sang—in the mere presence of an evil man?"

"We should if we were natural: children and women feel this horror you speak of, even animals experience it. But with most of us convention and civilisation and education have blinded and deafened and obscured the natural reason. No, sometimes we may recognise evil by its hatred of the good—one doesn't need much penetration to guess at the influence which dictated, quite unconsciously, the 'Blackwood' review of Keats—but this is purely incidental; and, as a rule, I suspect that the Hierarchs of Tophet pass quite unnoticed, or, perhaps, in certain cases, as good but mistaken men."

"But you used the word 'unconscious' just now, of Keats' reviewers. Is wickedness ever unconscious?"

"Always. It must be so. It is like holiness and genius in this as in other points; it is a certain rapture or ecstasy of the soul; a transcendent effort to surpass the ordinary bounds. So, surpassing these, it surpasses also the understanding, the faculty that takes note of that which comes before it. No, a man may be infinitely and horribly wicked and never suspect it. But I tell you, evil in this, its certain and true sense, is rare, and I think it is growing rarer."

"I am trying to get hold of it all," said Cotgrave. "From what you say, I gather that the true evil differs generically from that which we call evil?"

"Quite so. There is, no doubt, an analogy between the two; a resemblance such as enables us to use, quite legitimately, such terms as the 'foot of the mountain' and the 'leg of the table'. And, sometimes, of course, the two speak, as it were, in the same language. The rough miner, or 'puddler', the untrained, undeveloped 'tiger-man', heated by a quart or two above his usual measure, comes home and kicks his irritating and injudicious wife to death. He is a murderer. And Gilles de Raiz was a murderer. But you see the gulf that separates the two? The 'word', if I may so speak, is accidentally the same in each case, but the 'meaning' is utterly different. It is flagrant 'Hobson Jobson' to confuse the two, or rather, it is as if one supposed that Juggernaut and the Argonauts had something to do etymologically with one another. And no doubt the same weak likeness, or analogy, runs between all the 'social' sins and the real spiritual sins, and in some cases, perhaps, the lesser may be 'schoolmasters' to lead one on to the greater—from the shadow to the reality. If you are anything of a theologian, you will see the importance of all this."

"I am sorry to say," remarked Cotgrave, "that I have devoted very little of my time to theology. Indeed, I have often wondered on what grounds theologians have claimed the title of Science of Sciences for their favourite study; since the 'theological' books I have looked into have always seemed to me to be concerned with feeble and obvious pieties, or with the kings of Israel and Judah. I do not care to hear about those kings."

Ambrose grinned.

"We must try to avoid theological discussion," he said. "I perceive that you would be a bitter disputant. But perhaps the 'dates of the kings' have as much to do with theology as the hobnails of the murderous puddler with evil."

"Then, to return to our main subject, you think that sin is an esoteric, occult thing?"

"Yes. It is the infernal miracle as holiness is the supernal. Now and then it is raised to such a pitch that we entirely fail to suspect its existence; it is like the note of the great pedal pipes of the organ, which is so deep that we cannot hear it. In other cases it may lead to the lunatic asylum, or to still stranger issues. But you must never confuse it with mere social misdoing. Remember how the Apostle, speaking of the 'other side', distinguishes between 'charitable' actions and charity. And as one may give all one's goods to the poor, and yet lack charity; so, remember, one may avoid every crime and yet be a sinner."

"Your psychology is very strange to me," said Cotgrave, "but I confess I like it, and I suppose that one might fairly deduce from your premises the conclusion that the real sinner might very possibly strike the observer as a harmless personage enough?"

"Certainly; because the true evil has nothing to do with social life or social laws, or if it has, only incidentally and accidentally. It is a lonely passion of the soul—or a passion of the lonely soul—whichever you like. If, by chance, we understand it, and grasp its full significance, then, indeed, it will fill us with horror and with awe. But this emotion is widely distinguished from the fear and the disgust with which we regard the ordinary criminal, since this latter is largely or entirely founded on the regard which we have for our own skins or purses. We hate a murderer, because we know that we should hate to be murdered, or to have any one that we like murdered. So, on the 'other side', we venerate the saints, but we don't 'like' them as we like our friends. Can you persuade yourself that you would have 'enjoyed' St. Paul's company? Do you think that you and I would have 'got on' with Sir Galahad?

"So with the sinners, as with the saints. If you met a very evil man, and recognised his evil; he would, no doubt, fill you with horror and awe; but there is no reason why you should 'dislike' him. On the contrary, it is quite possible that if you could succeed in putting the sin out of your mind you might find the sinner capital company, and in a little while you might have to reason yourself back into horror. Still, how awful it is. If the roses and the lilies suddenly sang on this coming morning; if the furniture began to move in procession, as in De Maupassant's tale!"

"I am glad you have come back to that comparison," said Cotgrave, "because I wanted to ask you what it is that corresponds in humanity to these imaginary feats of inanimate things. In a word—what is sin? You have given me, I know, an abstract definition, but I should like a concrete example."

"I told you it was very rare," said Ambrose, who appeared willing to avoid the giving of a direct answer. "The materialism of the age, which has done a good deal to suppress sanctity, has done perhaps more to suppress evil. We find the earth so very comfortable that we have no inclination either for ascents or descents. It would seem as if the scholar who decided to 'specialise' in Tophet, would be reduced to purely antiquarian researches. No palæontologist could shew you a *live* pterodactyl."

"And yet you, I think, have 'specialised', and I believe that your researches have descended to our modern times."

"You are really interested, I see. Well, I confess that I have dabbled a little, and if you like I can shew you something that bears on the very curious subject we have been discussing."

Ambrose took a candle and went away to a far, dim corner of the room. Cotgrave saw him open a venerable bureau that stood there, and from some secret recess he drew out a parcel, and came back to the window where they had been sitting.

Ambrose undid a wrapping of paper, and produced a green pocket-book.

"You will take care of it?" he said. "Don't leave it lying about. It is one of the choicer pieces in my collection, and I should be very sorry if it were lost."

He fondled the faded binding.

"I knew the girl who wrote this," he said. "When you read it, you will see how it illustrates the talk we have had to-night. There is a sequel, too, but I won't talk of that."

"There was an odd article in one of the reviews some months ago," he began again, with the air of a man who changes the subject. "It was written by a doctor—Dr. Coryn, I think, was the name. He says that a lady, watching her little girl playing at the drawing-room window, suddenly saw the heavy sash give way and fall on the child's fingers. The lady fainted, I think, but at any rate the doctor was summoned, and when he had dressed the child's wounded and maimed fingers he was summoned to the mother. She was groaning with pain, and it was found that three fingers of her hand, corresponding with those that had been injured on the child's hand, were swollen and inflamed, and later, in the doctor's language, purulent sloughing set in."

Ambrose still handled delicately the green volume.

"Well, here it is," he said at last, parting with difficulty, it seemed, from his treasure.

"You will bring it back as soon as you have read it," he said, as they went out into the hall, into the old garden, faint with the odour of white lilies.

There was a broad red band in the east as Cotgrave turned to go, and from the high ground where he stood he saw that awful spectacle of London in a dream.

THE GREEN BOOK

The morocco binding of the book was faded, and the colour had grown faint, but there were no stains nor bruises nor marks of usage. The book looked as if it had been bought "on a visit to London" some seventy or eighty years ago, and had somehow been forgotten and suffered to lie away out of sight. There was an old, delicate, lingering odour about it, such an odour as sometimes haunts an ancient piece of furniture for a century or more. The end-papers, inside the binding, were oddly decorated with coloured patterns and faded gold. It looked small, but the paper was fine, and there were many leaves, closely covered with minute, painfully formed characters.

I found this book (the manuscript began) in a drawer in the old bureau that stands on the landing. It was a very rainy day and I could not go out, so in the afternoon I got a candle and rummaged in the bureau. Nearly all the drawers were full of old dresses, but one of the small ones looked empty, and I found this book hidden right at the back. I wanted a book like this, so I took it to write in. It is full of secrets. I have a great many other books of secrets I have written, hidden in a safe place, and I am going to write here many of the old secrets and some new ones; but there are some I shall not put down at all. I must not write down the real names of the days and months which I found out a year ago, nor the way to make the Aklo letters, or the Chian language, or the great beautiful Circles, nor the Mao Games, nor the chief songs. I may write something about all these things but not the way to do them, for peculiar reasons. And I must not say who the Nymphs are, or the Dôls, or Jeelo, or what voolas mean. All these are most secret secrets, and I am glad when I remember what they are, and how many wonderful languages I know, but there are some things that I call the secrets of the secrets of the secrets that I dare not think of unless I am quite alone, and then I shut my eyes, and put my hands over them and whisper the word, and the Alala comes. I only do this at night in my room or in certain woods that I know, but I must not describe them, as they are secret woods. Then there are the Ceremonies, which are all of them important, but some are more delightful than others—there are the White Ceremonies, and the Green Ceremonies, and the Scarlet Ceremonies. The Scarlet Ceremonies are the best, but there is only one place where they can be performed properly, though there is a very nice imitation which I have done in other places. Besides these, I have the dances, and the Comedy, and I have done the Comedy sometimes when the others were looking, and they didn't understand anything about it. I was very little when I first knew about these things.

When I was very small, and mother was alive, I can remember remembering things before that, only it has all got confused. But I remember when I was five or six I heard them talking about me when they thought I was not noticing. They were saying how queer I was a year or two before, and how nurse had called my mother to come and listen to me talking all to myself, and I was saying words that nobody could understand. I was speaking the Xu language, but I only remember a very few of the words, as it was about the little white faces that used to look at me when I was lying in my cradle. They used to talk to me, and I learnt their language and talked to them in it about some great white place where they lived, where the trees and the grass were all white, and there were white hills as high up as the moon, and a cold wind. I have often dreamed of it afterwards, but the faces went away when I was very little. But a wonderful thing happened when I was about five. My nurse was carrying me on her shoulder; there was a field of yellow corn, and we went through it, it was very hot. Then we came to a path through a wood, and a tall man came after us, and went with us till we came to a place where there was a deep pool, and it was very dark and shady. Nurse put me down on the soft moss under a tree, and she said: "She can't get to the pond now." So they left me there, and I sat quite still and watched, and out of the water and out of the wood came two wonderful white people, and they began to play and dance and sing. They were a kind of creamy white like the old ivory figure in the drawing-room; one was a beautiful lady with kind dark eyes, and a grave face, and long black hair, and she smiled such a strange sad smile at the other, who laughed and came to her. They played together, and danced round and round the pool, and they sang a song till I fell asleep. Nurse woke me up when she came back, and she was looking something like the lady had looked, so I told her all about it, and asked her why she looked like that. At first she cried, and then she looked very frightened, and turned quite pale. She put me down on the grass and stared at me, and I could see she was shaking all over. Then she said I had been dreaming, but I knew I hadn't. Then she made me promise not to say a word about it to anybody, and if I did I should be thrown into the black pit. I was not frightened at all, though nurse was, and I never forgot about it, because when I shut my eyes and it was quite quiet, and I was all alone, I could see them again, very faint and far away, but very splendid; and little bits of the song they sang came into my head, but I couldn't sing it.

I was thirteen, nearly fourteen, when I had a very singular adventure, so strange that the day on which it happened is always called the White Day. My mother had been dead for more than a year, and in the morning I had lessons, but they let me go out for walks in the afternoon. And this afternoon I walked a new way, and a little brook led me into a new country, but I tore my frock getting through many bushes, and beneath the low branches of trees, and up thorny thickets on the hills, and by dark woods full of creeping thorns. And it was a long, long way. It seemed as if I was going on for ever and ever, and I had to creep by a place like a tunnel where a brook must have been, but all the water had dried up, and the floor was rocky, and the bushes had grown overhead till they met, so that it was quite dark. And I went on and on through that dark place; it was a long, long way. And I came to a hill that I never saw before. I was in a dismal thicket full of black twisted boughs that tore me as I went through them, and I cried out because I was smarting all over, and then I found that I was climbing, and I went up and up a long way, till at last the thicket stopped and I came out crying just under the top of a big bare place, where there were ugly grey stones lying all about on the grass, and here and there a little twisted, stunted tree came out from under a stone, like a snake. And I went up, right to the top, a long way. I never saw such big ugly stones before; they came out of the earth some of them, and some looked as if they had been rolled to where they were, and they went on and on as far as I could see, a long, long way. I looked out from them and saw the country, but it was strange. It was winter time, and there were black terrible woods hanging from the hills all round; it was like seeing a large room hung with black curtains, and the shape of the trees seemed quite different from any I had ever seen before. I was afraid. Then beyond the woods there were other hills round in a great ring, but I had never seen any of them; it all looked black, and everything had a voor over it. It was all so still and silent, and the sky was heavy and grey and sad, like a wicked voorish dome in Deep Dendo. I went on into the dreadful rocks. There were hundreds and hundreds of them. Some were like horrid-grinning men; I could see their faces as if they would jump at me out of the stone, and catch hold of me, and drag me with them back into the rock, so that I should always be there. And there were other rocks that were like animals, creeping, horrible animals, putting out their tongues, and others were like words that I could not say, and others like dead people lying on the grass. I went on among them, though they frightened me, and my heart was full of wicked songs that they put into it; and I wanted to make faces and twist myself about in the way they did, and I went on and on a long way till at last I liked the rocks, and they didn't frighten me any more. I sang the songs I thought of; songs full of words that must not be spoken or written down. Then I made faces like the faces on the rocks, and I twisted myself about like the twisted ones, and I lay down flat on the ground like the dead ones, and I went up to one that was grinning, and put my arms round him and hugged him. And so I went on and on through the rocks till I came to a round mound in the middle of them. It was higher than a mound, it was nearly as high as our house, and it was like a great basin turned upside down, all smooth and round and green, with one stone, like a post, sticking up at the top. I climbed up the sides, but they were so steep I had to stop or I should have rolled all the way down again, and I should have knocked against the stones at the bottom, and perhaps been killed. But I wanted to get up to the very top of the big round mound, so I lay down flat on my face, and took hold of the grass with my hands and drew myself up, bit by bit, till I was at the top. Then I sat down on the stone in the middle, and looked all round about. I felt I had come such a long, long way, just as if I were a hundred miles from home, or in some other country, or in one of the strange places I had read about in the "Tales of the Genie" and the "Arabian Nights", or as if I had gone across the sea, far away, for years and I had found another world that nobody had ever seen or heard of before, or as if I had somehow flown through the sky and fallen on one of the stars I had read about where everything is dead and cold and grey, and there is no air, and the wind doesn't blow. I sat on the stone and looked all round and down and round about me. It was just as if I was sitting on a tower in the middle of a great empty town, because I could see nothing all around but the grey rocks on the ground. I couldn't make out their shapes any more, but I could see them on and on for a long way, and I looked at them, and they seemed as if they had been arranged into patterns, and shapes, and figures. I knew they couldn't be, because I had seen a lot of them coming right out of the earth, joined to the deep rocks below, so I looked again, but still I saw nothing but circles, and small circles inside big ones, and pyramids, and domes, and spires, and they seemed all to go round and round the place where I was sitting, and the more I looked, the more I saw great big rings of rocks, getting bigger and bigger, and I stared so long that it felt as if they were all moving and turning, like a great wheel, and I was turning, too, in the middle. I got quite dizzy and queer in the head, and everything began to be hazy and not clear, and I saw little sparks of blue light, and the stones looked as if they were springing and dancing and twisting as they went round and round and round. I was frightened again, and I cried out loud, and jumped up from the stone I was sitting on, and fell down. When I got up I was so glad they all looked still, and I sat down on the top and slid down the mound, and went on again. I danced as I went in the peculiar way the rocks had danced when I got giddy, and I was so glad I could do it quite well, and I danced and danced along, and sang extraordinary songs that came into my head. At last I came to the edge of that great flat hill, and there were no more rocks, and the way went again through a dark thicket in a hollow. It was just as bad as the other one I went through climbing up, but I didn't mind this one, because I was so glad I had seen those singular dances and could imitate them. I went down, creeping through the bushes, and a tall nettle stung me on my leg, and made me burn, but I didn't mind it, and I tingled with the boughs and the thorns, but I only laughed and sang. Then I got out of the thicket into a close valley, a little secret place like a dark passage that nobody ever knows of, because it was so narrow and deep and the woods were so thick round it. There is a steep bank with trees hanging over it, and there the ferns keep green all through the winter, when they are dead and brown upon the hill, and the ferns there have a sweet, rich smell like what oozes out of fir trees. There was a little stream of water running down this valley, so small that I could easily step across it. I drank the water with my hand, and it tasted like bright, yellow wine, and it sparkled and bubbled as it ran down over beautiful red and yellow stones, so that it seemed alive and all colours at once. I drank it, and I drank more with my hand, but I couldn't drink enough, so I lay down and bent my head and sucked the water up with my lips. It tasted much better, drinking it that way, and a ripple would come up to my mouth and give me a kiss, and I laughed, and drank again, and pretended there was a nymph, like the one in the old picture at home, who lived in the water and was kissing me. So I bent low down to the water, and put my lips softly to it, and whispered to the nymph that I would come again. I felt sure it would not be common water, I was so glad when I got up and went on; and I danced again and went up and up the valley, under hanging hills. And when I came to the top, the ground rose up in front of me, tall and steep as a wall, and there was nothing but the green wall and the sky. I thought of "for ever and for ever, world without end, Amen"; and I thought I must have really found the end of the world, because it was like the end of everything, as if there could be nothing at all beyond, except the kingdom of Voor, where the light goes when it is put out, and the water goes when the sun takes it away. I began to think of all the long, long way I had journeyed, how I had found a brook and followed it, and followed it on, and gone through bushes and thorny thickets, and dark woods full of creeping thorns. Then I had crept up a tunnel under trees, and climbed a thicket, and seen all the grey rocks, and sat in the middle of them when they turned round, and then I had gone on through the grey rocks and come down the hill through the stinging thicket and up the dark valley, all a long, long way. I wondered how I should get home again, if I could ever find the way, and if my home was there any more, or if it were turned and everybody in it into grey rocks, as in the "Arabian Nights". So I sat down on the grass and thought what I should do next. I was tired, and my feet were hot with walking, and as I looked about I saw there was a wonderful well just under the high, steep wall of grass. All the ground round it was covered with bright, green, dripping moss; there was every kind of moss there, moss like beautiful little ferns, and like palms and fir trees, and it was all green as jewellery, and drops of water hung on it like diamonds. And in the middle was the great well, deep and shining and beautiful, so clear it looked as if I could touch the red sand at the bottom, but it was far below. I stood by it and looked in, as if I were looking in a glass. At the bottom of the well, in the middle of it, the red grains of sand were moving and stirring all the time, and I saw how the water bubbled up, but at the top it was quite smooth, and full and brimming. It was a great well, large like a bath, and with the shining, glittering green moss about it, it looked like a great white jewel, with green jewels all round. My feet were so hot and tired that I took off my boots and stockings, and let my feet down into the water, and the water was soft and cold, and when I got up I wasn't tired any more, and I felt I must go on, farther and farther, and see what was on the other side of the wall. I climbed up it very slowly, going sideways all the time, and when I got to the top and looked over, I was in the queerest country I had seen, stranger even than the hill of the grey rocks. It looked as if earth-children had been playing there with their spades, as it was all hills and hollows, and castles and walls made of earth and covered with grass. There were two mounds like big beehives, round and great and solemn, and then hollow basins, and then a steep mounting wall like the ones I saw once by the seaside where the big guns and the soldiers were. I nearly fell into one of the round hollows, it went away from under my feet so suddenly, and I ran fast down the side and stood at the bottom and looked up. It was strange and solemn to look up. There was nothing but the grey, heavy sky and the sides of the hollow; everything else had gone away, and the hollow was the whole world, and I thought that at night it must be full of ghosts and moving shadows and pale things when the moon shone down to the bottom at the dead of the night, and the wind wailed up above. It was so strange and solemn and lonely, like a hollow temple of dead heathen gods. It reminded me of a tale my nurse had told me when I was quite little; it was the same nurse that took me into the wood where I saw the beautiful white people. And I remembered how nurse had told me the story one winter night, when the wind was beating the trees against the wall, and crying and moaning in the nursery chimney. She said there was, somewhere or other, a hollow pit, just like the one I was standing in, everybody was afraid to go into it or near it, it was such a bad place. But once upon a time there was a poor girl who said she would go into the hollow pit, and everybody tried to stop her, but she would go. And she went down into the pit and came back laughing, and said there was nothing there at all, except green grass and red stones, and white stones and yellow flowers. And soon after people saw she had most beautiful emerald earrings, and they asked how she got them, as she and her mother were quite poor. But she laughed, and said her earrings were not made of emeralds at all, but only of green grass. Then, one day, she wore on her breast the reddest ruby that any one had ever seen, and it was as big as a hen's egg, and glowed and sparkled like a hot burning coal of fire. And they asked how she got it, as she and her mother were quite poor. But she laughed, and said it was not a ruby at all, but only a red stone. Then one day she wore round her neck the loveliest necklace that any one had ever seen, much finer than the queen's finest, and it was made of great bright diamonds, hundreds of them, and they shone like all the stars on a night in June. So they asked her how she got it, as she and her mother were quite poor. But she laughed, and said they were not diamonds at all, but only white stones. And one day she went to the Court, and she wore on her head a crown of pure angel-gold, so nurse said, and it shone like the sun, and it was much more splendid than the crown the king was wearing himself, and in her ears she wore the emeralds, and the big ruby was the brooch on her breast, and the great diamond necklace was sparkling on her neck. And the king and queen thought she was some great princess from a long way off, and got down from their thrones and went to meet her, but somebody told the king and queen who she was, and that she was quite poor. So the king asked why she wore a gold crown, and how she got it, as she and her mother were so poor. And she laughed, and said it wasn't a gold crown at all, but only some yellow flowers she had put in her hair. And the king thought it was very strange, and said she should stay at the Court, and they would see what would happen next. And she was so lovely that everybody said that her eyes were greener than the emeralds, that her lips were redder than the ruby, that her skin was whiter than the diamonds, and that her hair was brighter than the golden crown. So the king's son said he would marry her, and the king said he might. And the bishop married them, and there was a great supper, and afterwards the king's son went to his wife's room. But just when he had his hand on the door, he saw a tall, black man, with a dreadful face, standing in front of the door, and a voice said—

> Venture not upon your life,
> This is mine own wedded wife.

Then the king's son fell down on the ground in a fit. And they came and tried to get into the room, but they couldn't, and they hacked at the door with hatchets, but the wood had turned hard as iron, and at last everybody ran away, they were so frightened at the screaming and laughing and shrieking and crying that came out of the room. But next day they went in, and found there was nothing in the room but thick black smoke, because the black man had come and taken her away. And on the bed there were two knots of faded grass and a red stone, and some white stones, and some faded yellow flowers. I remembered this tale of nurse's while I was standing at the bottom of the deep hollow; it was so strange and solitary there, and I felt afraid. I could not see any stones or flowers, but I was afraid of bringing them away without knowing, and I thought I would do a charm that came into my head to keep the black man away. So I stood right in the very middle of the hollow, and I made sure that I had none of those things on me, and then I walked round the place, and touched my eyes, and my lips, and my hair in a peculiar manner, and whispered some queer words that nurse taught me to keep bad things away. Then I felt safe and climbed up out of the hollow, and went on through all those mounds and hollows and walls, till I came to the end, which was high above all the rest, and I could see that all the different shapes of the earth were arranged in patterns, something like the grey rocks, only the pattern was different. It was getting late, and the air was indistinct, but it looked from where I was standing something like two great figures of people lying on the grass. And I went on, and at last I found a certain wood, which is too secret to be described, and nobody knows of the passage into it, which I found out in a very curious manner, by seeing some little animal run into the wood through it. So I went in after the animal by a very narrow dark way, under thorns and bushes, and it was almost dark when I came to a kind of open place in the middle. And there I saw the most wonderful sight I have ever seen, but it was only for a minute, as I ran away directly, and crept out of the wood by the passage I had come by, and ran and ran as fast as ever I could, because I was afraid, what I had seen was so wonderful and so strange and beautiful. But I wanted to get home and think of it, and I did not know what might not happen if I stayed by the wood. I was hot all over and trembling, and my heart was beating, and strange cries that I could not help came from me as I ran from the wood. I was glad that a great white moon came up from over a round hill and shewed me the way, so I went back through the mounds and hollows and down the close valley, and up through the thicket over the place of the grey rocks, and

so at last I got home again. My father was busy in his study, and the
servants had not told about my not coming home, though they were
frightened, and wondered what they ought to do, so I told them I had
lost my way, but I did not let them find out the real way I had been. I
went to bed and lay awake all through the night, thinking of what I had
seen. When I came out of the narrow way, and it looked all shining,
though the air was dark, it seemed so certain, and all the way home I
was quite sure that I had seen it, and I wanted to be alone in my room,
and be glad over it all to myself, and shut my eyes and pretend it was
there, and do all the things I would have done if I had not been so
afraid. But when I shut my eyes the sight would not come, and I began
to think about my adventures all over again, and I remembered how
dusky and queer it was at the end, and I was afraid it must be all a mistake, because it seemed impossible it could happen. It seemed like one
of nurse's tales, which I didn't really believe in, though I was frightened at the bottom of the hollow; and the stories she told me when I
was little came back into my head, and I wondered whether it was really there what I thought I had seen, or whether any of her tales could
have happened a long time ago. It was so queer; I lay awake there in
my room at the back of the house, and the moon was shining on the
other side towards the river, so the bright light did not fall upon the
wall. And the house was quite still. I had heard my father come upstairs, and just after the clock struck twelve, and after the house was
still and empty, as if there was nobody alive in it. And though it was all
dark and indistinct in my room, a pale glimmering kind of light shone
in through the white blind, and once I got up and looked out, and
there was a great black shadow of the house covering the garden, looking like a prison where men are hanged; and then beyond it was all
white; and the wood shone white with black gulfs between the trees. It
was still and clear, and there were no clouds in the sky. I wanted to
think of what I had seen but I couldn't, and I began to think of all the
tales that nurse had told me so long ago that I thought I had forgotten,
but they all came back, and mixed up with the thickets and the grey
rocks and the hollows in the earth and the secret wood, till I hardly
knew what was new and what was old, or whether it was not all dreaming. And then I remembered that hot summer afternoon, so long ago,
when nurse left me by myself in the shade, and the white people came

out of the water and out of the wood, and played, and danced, and sang, and I began to fancy that nurse told me about something like it before I saw them, only I couldn't recollect exactly what she told me. Then I wondered whether she had been the white lady, as I remembered she was just as white and beautiful, and had the same dark eyes and black hair; and sometimes she smiled and looked like the lady had looked, when she was telling me some of her stories, beginning with "Once on a time", or "In the time of the fairies". But I thought she couldn't be the lady, as she seemed to have gone a different way into the wood, and I didn't think the man who came after us could be the other, or I couldn't have seen that wonderful secret in the secret wood. I thought of the moon: but it was afterwards when I was in the middle of the wild land, where the earth was made into the shape of great figures, and it was all walls, and mysterious hollows, and smooth round mounds, that I saw the great white moon come up over a round hill. I was wondering about all these things, till at last I got quite frightened, because I was afraid something had happened to me, and I remembered nurse's tale of the poor girl who went into the hollow pit, and was carried away at last by the black man. I knew I had gone into a hollow pit too, and perhaps it was the same, and I had done something dreadful. So I did the charm over again, and touched my eyes and my lips and my hair in a peculiar manner, and said the old words from the fairy language, so that I might be sure I had not been carried away. I tried again to see the secret wood, and to creep up the passage and see what I had seen there, but somehow I couldn't, and I kept on thinking of nurse's stories. There was one I remembered about a young man who once upon a time went hunting, and all the day he and his hounds hunted everywhere, and they crossed the rivers and went into all the woods, and went round the marshes, but they couldn't find anything at all, and they hunted all day till the sun sank down and began to set behind the mountain. And the young man was angry because he couldn't find anything, and he was going to turn back, when just as the sun touched the mountain, he saw come out of a brake in front of him a beautiful white stag. And he cheered to his hounds, but they whined and would not follow, and he cheered to his horse, but it shivered and stood stock still, and the young man jumped off the horse and left the hounds and began to follow the white stag all alone. And soon it was quite dark, and the sky was black, without a single star shining in it, and the stag went away into the darkness. And though the man had brought his gun with him he never shot at the stag, because he wanted to catch it, and he was afraid he would lose it in the night. But he never lost it once, though the sky was so black and the air was so dark, and the stag went on and on till the young man didn't know a bit where he was. And they went through enormous woods where the air was full of whispers and a pale, dead light came out from the rotten trunks that were lying on the ground, and just as the man thought he had lost the stag, he would see it all white and shining in front of him, and he would run fast to catch it, but the stag always ran faster, so he did not catch it. And they went through the enormous woods, and they swam across rivers, and they waded through black marshes where the ground bubbled, and the air was full of will-o'-the-wisps, and the stag fled away down into rocky narrow valleys, where the air was like the smell of a vault, and the man went after it. And they went over the great mountains, and the man heard the wind come down from the sky, and the stag went on and the man went after. At last the sun rose and the young man found he was in a country that he had never seen before; it was a beautiful valley with a bright stream running through it, and a great, big round hill in the middle. And the stag went down the valley, towards the hill, and it seemed to be getting tired and went slower and slower, and though the man was tired, too, he began to run faster, and he was sure he would catch the stag at last. But just as they got to the bottom of the hill, and the man stretched out his hand to catch the stag, it vanished into the earth, and the man began to cry; he was so sorry that he had lost it after all his long hunting. But as he was crying he saw there was a door in the hill, just in front of him, and he went in, and it was quite dark, but he went on, as he thought he would find the white stag. And all of a sudden it got light, and there was the sky, and the sun shining, and birds singing in the trees, and there was a beautiful fountain. And by the fountain a lovely lady was sitting, who was the queen of the fairies, and she told the man that she had changed herself into a stag to bring him there because she loved him so much. Then she brought out a great gold cup, covered with jewels, from her fairy palace, and she offered him wine in the cup to drink. And he drank, and the more he drank the more he longed to drink, because the wine was enchanted. So he kissed the lovely lady, and she became his wife, and he stayed all that day and all that night in the hill where she lived, and when he woke he found he was lying on the ground, close to where he had seen the stag first, and his horse was there and his hounds were there waiting, and he looked up, and the sun sank behind the mountain. And he went home and lived a long time, but he would never kiss any other lady because he had kissed the queen of the fairies, and he would never drink common wine any more, because he had drunk enchanted wine. And sometimes nurse told me tales that she had heard from her great-grandmother, who was very old, and lived in a cottage on the mountain all alone, and most of these tales were about a hill where people used to meet at night long ago, and they used to play all sorts of strange games and do queer things that nurse told me of, but I couldn't understand, and now, she said, everybody but her great-grandmother had forgotten all about it, and nobody knew where the hill was, not even her great-grandmother. But she told me one very strange story about the hill, and I trembled when I remembered it. She said that people always went there in summer, when it was very hot, and they had to dance a good deal. It would be all dark at first, and there were trees there, which made it much darker, and people would come, one by one, from all directions, by a secret path which nobody else knew, and two persons would keep the gate, and every one as they came up had to give a very curious sign, which nurse shewed me as well as she could, but she said she couldn't shew me properly. And all kinds of people would come; there would be gentle folks and village folks, and some old people and boys and girls, and quite small children, who sat and watched. And it would all be dark as they came in, except in one corner where some one was burning something that smelt strong and sweet, and made them laugh, and there one would see a glaring of coals, and the smoke mounting up red. So they would all come in, and when the last had come there was no door any more, so that no one else could get in, even if they knew there was anything beyond. And once a gentleman who was a stranger and had ridden a long way, lost his path at night, and his horse took him into the very middle of the wild country, where everything was upside down, and there were dreadful marshes and great stones everywhere, and holes underfoot, and the trees looked like gibbet-posts, because they had great black arms that stretched out across the way. And this strange gentleman was very frightened, and his horse began to shiver all over, and at last it stopped and wouldn't go any far-ther, and the gentleman got down and tried to lead the horse, but it wouldn't move, and it was all covered with a sweat, like death. So the gentleman went on all alone, going farther and farther into the wild country, till at last he came to a dark place, where he heard shouting and singing and crying, like nothing he had ever heard before. It all sounded quite close to him, but he couldn't get in, and so he began to call, and while he was calling, something came behind him, and in a minute his mouth and arms and legs were all bound up, and he fell in-to a swoon. And when he came to himself, he was lying by the road-side, just where he had first lost his way, under a blasted oak with a black trunk, and his horse was tied beside him. So he rode on to the town and told the people there what had happened, and some of them were amazed; but others knew. So when once everybody had come, there was no door at all for anybody else to pass in by. And when they were all inside, round in a ring, touching each other, some one began to sing in the darkness, and some one else would make a noise like thunder with a thing they had on purpose, and on still nights people would hear the thundering noise far, far away beyond the wild land, and some of them, who thought they knew what it was, used to make a sign on their breasts when they woke up in their beds at dead of night and heard that terrible deep noise, like thunder on the moun-tains. And the noise and the singing would go on and on for a long time, and the people who were in a ring swayed a little to and fro; and the song was in an old, old language that nobody knows now, and the tune was queer. Nurse said her great-grandmother had known some one who remembered a little of it, when she was quite a little girl, and nurse tried to sing some of it to me, and it was so strange a tune that I turned all cold and my flesh crept as if I had put my hand on some-thing dead. Sometimes it was a man that sang and sometimes it was a woman, and sometimes the one who sang it did it so well that two or three of the people who were there fell to the ground shrieking and tearing with their hands. The singing went on, and the people in the ring kept swaying to and fro for a long time, and at last the moon would rise over a place they called the Tole Deol, and came up and shewed them swinging and swaying from side to side, with the sweet thick smoke curling up from the burning coals, and floating in circles all around them. Then they had their supper. A boy and a girl brought it to them; the boy carried a great cup of wine, and the girl carried a cake of bread, and they passed the bread and the wine round and round, but they tasted quite different from common bread and common wine, and changed everybody that tasted them. Then they all rose up and danced, and secret things were brought out of some hiding place, and they played extraordinary games, and danced round and round and round in the moonlight, and sometimes people would suddenly disappear and never be heard of afterwards, and nobody knew what had happened to them. And they drank more of that curious wine, and they made images and worshipped them, and nurse shewed me how the images were made one day when we were out for a walk, and we passed by a place where there was a lot of wet clay. So nurse asked me if I would I like to know what those things were like that they made on the hill, and I said yes. Then she asked me if I would promise never to tell a living soul a word about it, and if I did I was to be thrown into the black pit with the dead people, and I said I wouldn't tell anybody, and she said the same thing again and again, and I promised. So she took my wooden spade and dug a big lump of clay and put it in my tin bucket, and told me to say if any one met us that I was going to make pies when I went home. Then we went on a little way till we came to a little brake growing right down into the road, and nurse stopped, and looked up the road and down it, and then peeped through the hedge into the field on the other side, and then she said, "Quick!" and we ran into the brake, and crept in and out among the bushes till we had gone a good way from the road. Then we sat down under a bush, and I wanted so much to know what nurse was going to make with the clay, but before she would begin she made me promise again not to say a word about it, and she went again and peeped through the bushes on every side, though the lane was so small and deep that hardly anybody ever went there. So we sat down, and nurse took the clay out of the bucket, and began to knead it with her hands, and do queer things with it, and turn it about. And she hid it under a big dock-leaf for a minute or two and then she brought it out again, and then she stood up and sat down and walked round the clay in a peculiar manner, and all the time she was softly singing a sort of rhyme, and her face got very red. Then she sat down again, and took the clay in her hands and began to shape it into a doll, but not like the dolls I have at home, and she made the queerest doll I had ever seen, all out of the wet clay, and hid it under a bush to get dry and hard, and all the time she was making it she was singing these rhymes to herself, and her face got redder and redder. So we left the doll there, hidden away in the bushes where nobody would ever find it. And a few days later we went the same walk, and when we came to that narrow, dark part of the lane where the brake runs down to the bank, nurse made me promise all over again, and she looked about, just as she had done before, and we crept into the bushes till we got to the green place where the little clay man was hidden. I remember it all so well, though I was only eight, and it is eight years ago now as I am writing it down, but the sky was a deep violet blue, and in the middle of the brake where we were sitting there was a great elder tree covered with blossoms, and on the other side there was a clump of meadowsweet, and when I think of that day the smell of the meadowsweet and elder blossom seems to fill the room, and if I shut my eyes I can see the glaring blue sky, with little clouds very white floating across it, and nurse who went away long ago sitting opposite me and looking like the beautiful white lady in the wood. So we sat down and nurse took out the clay doll from the secret place where she had hidden it, and she said we must "pay our respects", and she would shew me what to do, and I must watch her all the time. So she did all sorts of queer things with the little clay man, and I noticed she was all streaming with perspiration, though we had walked so slowly, and then she told me to "pay my respects", and I did everything she did, because I liked her, and it was such an odd game. And she said that if one loved very much, the clay man was very good, if one did certain things with it, and if one hated very much, it was just as good, only one had to do different things, and we played with it a long time, and pretended all sorts of things. Nurse said her great-grandmother had told her all about these images, but what we did was no harm at all, only a game. But she told me a story about these images that frightened me very much, and that was what I remembered that night when I was lying awake in my room in the pale, empty darkness, thinking of what I had seen and the secret wood. Nurse said there was once a young lady of the high gentry, who lived in a great castle. And she was so beautiful that all the gentlemen wanted to marry her, because she was the loveliest lady that anybody had ever seen, and she was kind to everybody, and everybody thought she was very good. But though she was polite to all the gentlemen who wished to marry her, she put them off, and said she couldn't make up her mind, and she wasn't sure she wanted to marry anybody at all. And her father, who was a very great lord, was angry, though he was so fond of her, and he asked her why she wouldn't choose a bachelor out of all the handsome young men who came to the castle. But she only said she didn't love any of them very much, and she must wait, and if they pestered her, she said she would go and be a nun in a nunnery. So all the gentlemen said they would go away and wait for a year and a day, and when a year and a day were gone, they would come back again and ask her to say which one she would marry. So the day was appointed and they all went away; and the lady had promised that in a year and a day it would be her wedding day with one of them. But the truth was, that she was the queen of the people who danced on the hill on summer nights, and on the proper nights she would lock the door of her room, and she and her maid would steal out of the castle by a secret passage that only they knew of, and go away up to the hill in the wild land. And she knew more of the secret things than any one else, and more than any one knew before or after, because she would not tell anybody the most secret secrets. She knew how to do all the awful things, how to destroy young men, and how to put a curse on people, and other things that I could not understand. And her real name was the Lady Avelin, but the dancing people called her Cassap, which meant somebody very wise, in the old language. And she was whiter than any of them and taller, and her eyes shone in the dark like burning rubies; and she could sing songs that none of the others could sing, and when she sang they all fell down on their faces and worshipped her. And she could do what they called the shib-show, which was a very wonderful enchantment. She would tell the great lord, her father, that she wanted to go into the woods to gather flowers, so he let her go, and she and her maid went into the woods where nobody came, and the maid would keep watch. Then the lady would lie down under the trees and begin to sing a particular song, and she stretched out her arms, and from every part of the wood great serpents would come, hissing and gliding in and out among the trees, and shooting out their forked tongues as they crawled up to the lady. And they all came to her, and twisted round her, round her body, and her arms, and her neck, till she was covered with writhing serpents, and there was only her head to be seen. And she whispered to them, and she sang to them, and they writhed round and round, faster and faster, till she told them to go. And they all went away directly, back to their holes, and on the lady's breast there would be a most curious, beautiful stone, shaped something like an egg, and coloured dark blue and yellow, and red, and green, marked like a serpent's scales. It was called a glame stone, and with it one could do all sorts of wonderful things, and nurse said her great-grandmother had seen a glame stone with her own eyes, and it was for all the world shiny and scaly like a snake. And the lady could do a lot of other things as well, but she was quite fixed that she would not be married. And there were a great many gentlemen who wanted to marry her, but there were five of them who were chief, and their names were Sir Simon, Sir John, Sir Oliver, Sir Richard, and Sir Rowland. All the others believed she spoke the truth, and that she would choose one of them to be her man when a year and a day was done; it was only Sir Simon, who was very crafty, who thought she was deceiving them all, and he vowed he would watch and try if he could find out anything. And though he was very wise he was very young, and he had a smooth, soft face like a girl's, and he pretended, as the rest did, that he would not come to the castle for a year and a day, and he said he was going away beyond the sea to foreign parts. But he really only went a very little way, and came back dressed like a servant girl, and so he got a place in the castle to wash the dishes. And he waited and watched, and he listened and said nothing, and he hid in dark places, and woke up at night and looked out, and he heard things and he saw things that he thought were very strange. And he was so sly that he told the girl that waited on the lady that he was really a young man, and that he had dressed up as a girl because he loved her so very much and wanted to be in the same house with her, and the girl was so pleased that she told him many things, and he was more than ever certain that the Lady Avelin was deceiving him and the others. And he was so clever, and told the servant so many lies, that one night he managed to hide in the Lady Avelin's room behind the curtains. And he stayed quite still and never moved, and at last the lady came. And she bent down under the bed, and raised up a stone, and there was a hollow place underneath, and out of it she took a waxen image, just like the clay one that I and nurse had made in the brake. And all the time her eyes were burning like rubies. And she took the little wax doll up in her arms and held it to her breast, and she whispered and she murmured, and she took it up and she laid it down again, and she held it high, and she held it low, and she laid it down again. And she said, "Happy is he that begat the bishop, that ordered the clerk, that married the man, that had the wife, that fashioned the hive, that harboured the bee, that gathered the wax that my own true love was made of." And she brought out of an aumbry a great golden bowl, and she brought out of a closet a great jar of wine, and she poured some of the wine into the bowl, and she laid her mannikin very gently in the wine, and washed it in the wine all over. Then she went to a cupboard and took a small round cake and laid it on the image's mouth, and then she bore it softly and covered it up. And Sir Simon, who was watching all the time, though he was terribly frightened, saw the lady bend down and stretch out her arms and whisper and sing, and then Sir Simon saw beside her a handsome young man, who kissed her on the lips. And they drank wine out of the golden bowl together, and they ate the cake together. But when the sun rose there was only the little wax doll, and the lady hid it again under the bed in the hollow place. So Sir Simon knew quite well what the lady was, and he waited and he watched, till the time she had said was nearly over, and in a week the year and a day would be done. And one night, when he was watching behind the curtains in her room, he saw her making more wax dolls. And she made five, and hid them away. And the next night she took one out, and held it up, and filled the golden bowl with water, and took the doll by the neck and held it under the water. Then she said—

> Sir Dickon, Sir Dickon, your day is done,
> You shall be drowned in the water wan.

And the next day news came to the castle that Sir Richard had been drowned at the ford. And at night she took another doll and tied a violet cord round its neck and hung it up on a nail. Then she said—

> Sir Rowland, your life has ended its span,
> High on a tree I see you hang.

And the next day news came to the castle that Sir Rowland had been hanged by robbers in the wood. And at night she took another doll, and drove her bodkin right into its heart. Then she said—

> Sir Noll, Sir Noll, so cease your life,
> Your heart piercèd with the knife.

And the next day news came to the castle that Sir Oliver had fought in a tavern, and a stranger had stabbed him to the heart. And at night she took another doll, and held it to a fire of charcoal till it was melted. Then she said—

> Sir John, return, and turn to clay,
> In fire of fever you waste away.

And the next day news came to the castle that Sir John had died in a burning fever. So then Sir Simon went out of the castle and mounted his horse and rode away to the bishop and told him everything. And the bishop sent his men, and they took the Lady Avelin, and everything she had done was found out. So on the day after the year and a day, when she was to have been married, they carried her through the town in her smock, and they tied her to a great stake in the marketplace, and burned her alive before the bishop with her wax image hung round her neck. And people said the wax man screamed in the burning of the flames. And I thought of this story again and again as I was lying awake in my bed, and I seemed to see the Lady Avelin in the marketplace, with the yellow flames eating up her beautiful white body. And I thought of it so much that I seemed to get into the story myself, and I fancied I was the lady, and that they were coming to take me to be burnt with fire, with all the people in the town looking at me. And I wondered whether she cared, after all the strange things she had done, and whether it hurt very much to be burned at the stake. I tried again and again to forget nurse's stories, and to remember the secret I had seen that afternoon, and what was in the secret wood, but I could only see the dark and a glimmering in the dark, and then it went away, and I only saw myself running, and then a great moon came up white over a dark round hill. Then all the old stories came back again, and the queer rhymes that nurse used to sing to me; and there was one beginning "Halsy cumsy Helen musty", that she used to sing very softly when she wanted me to go to sleep. And I began to sing it to myself inside of my head, and I went to sleep.

The next morning I was very tired and sleepy, and could hardly do my lessons, and I was very glad when they were over and I had had my dinner, as I wanted to go out and be alone. It was a warm day, and I went to a nice turfy hill by the river, and sat down on my mother's old shawl that I had brought with me on purpose. The sky was grey, like the day before, but there was a kind of white gleam behind it, and from where I was sitting I could look down on the town, and it was all still and quiet and white, like a picture. I remembered that it was on that hill that nurse taught me to play an old game called "Troy Town", in which one had to dance, and wind in and out on a pattern in the grass, and then when one had danced and turned long enough the other person asks you questions, and you can't help answering whether you want to or not, and whatever you are told to do you feel you have to do it. Nurse said there used to be a lot of games like that that some people knew of, and there was one by which people could be turned into anything you liked, and an old man her great-grandmother had seen had known a girl who had been turned into a large snake. And there was another very ancient game of dancing and winding and turning, by which you could take a person out of himself and hide him away as long as you liked, and his body went walking about quite empty, without any sense in it. But I came to that hill because I wanted to think of what had happened the day before, and of the secret of the wood. From the place where I was sitting I could see beyond the town, into the opening I had found, where a little brook had led me into an unknown country. And I pretended I was following the brook over again, and I went all the way in my mind, and at last I found the wood, and crept into it under the bushes, and then in the dusk I saw something that made me feel as if I were filled with fire, as if I wanted to dance and sing and fly up into the air, because I was changed and wonderful. But what I saw was not changed at all, and had not grown old, and I wondered again and again how such things could happen, and whether nurse's stories were really true, because in the daytime in the open air everything seemed quite different from what it was at night, when I was frightened, and thought I was to be burned alive. I once told my father one of her little tales, which was about a ghost, and asked him if it was true, and he told me it was not true at all, and that only common, ignorant people believed in such rubbish. He was very angry with nurse for telling me the story, and scolded her, and after that I promised her I would never whisper a word of what she told me, and if I did I should be bitten by the great black snake that lived in the pool in the wood. And all alone on the hill I wondered what was true. I had seen something very amazing and very lovely, and I knew a story, and if I had really seen it, and not made it up out of the dark, and the black bough, and the bright shining that was mounting up to the sky from over the great round hill, but had really seen it in truth, then there were all kinds of wonderful and lovely and terrible things to think of, so I longed and trembled, and I burned and got cold. And I looked down on the town, so quiet and still, like a little white picture, and I thought over and over if it could be true. I was a long time before I could make up my mind to anything; there was such a strange fluttering at my heart that seemed to whisper to me all the time that I had not made it up out of my head, and yet it seemed quite impossible, and I knew my father and everybody would say it was dreadful rubbish. I never dreamed of telling him or anybody else a word about it, because I knew it would be of no use, and I should only get laughed at or scolded, so for a long time I was very quiet, and went about thinking and wondering; and at night I used to dream of amazing things, and sometimes I woke up in the early morning and held out my arms with a cry. And I was frightened, too, because there were dangers, and some awful thing would happen to me, unless I took great care, if the story were true. These old tales were always in my head, night and morning, and I went over them and told them to myself over and over again, and went for walks in the places where nurse had told them to me; and when I sat in the nursery by the fire in the evenings I used to fancy nurse was sitting in the other chair, and telling me some wonderful story in a low voice, for fear anybody should be listening. But she used to like best to tell me about things when we were right out in the country, far from the house, because she said she was telling me such secrets, and walls have ears. And if it was something more than ever secret, we had to hide in brakes or woods; and I used to think it was such fun creeping along a hedge, and going very softly, and then we would get behind the bushes or run into the wood all of a sudden, when we were sure that none was watching us; so we knew that we had our secrets quite all to ourselves, and nobody else at all knew anything about them. Now and then, when we had hidden ourselves as I have described, she used to shew me all sorts of odd things. One day, I remember, we were in a hazel brake, overlooking the brook, and we were so snug and warm, as though it was April; the sun was quite hot, and the leaves were just coming out. Nurse said she would shew me something funny that would make me laugh, and then she shewed me, as she said, how one could turn a whole house upside down, without anybody being able to find out, and the pots and pans would jump about, and the china would be broken, and the chairs would tumble over of themselves. I tried it one day in the kitchen, and I found I could do it quite well, and a whole row of plates on the dresser fell off it, and cook's little work-table tilted up and turned right over "before her eyes", as she said, but she was so frightened and turned so white that I didn't do it again, as I liked her. And afterwards, in the hazel copse, when she had shewn me how to make things tumble about, she shewed me how to make rapping noises, and I learnt how to do that, too. Then she taught me rhymes to say on certain occasions, and peculiar marks to make on other occasions, and other things that her great-grandmother had taught her when she was a little girl herself. And these were all the things I was thinking about in those days after the strange walk when I thought I had seen a great secret, and I wished nurse were there for me to ask her about it, but she had gone away more than two years before, and nobody seemed to know what had become of her, or where she had gone. But I shall always remember those days if I live to be quite old, because all the time I felt so strange, wondering and doubting, and feeling quite sure at one time, and making up my mind, and then I would feel quite sure that such things couldn't happen really, and it began all over again. But I took great care not to do certain things that might be very dangerous. So I waited and wondered for a long time, and though I was not sure at all, I never dared to try to find out. But one day I became sure that all that nurse said was quite true, and I was all alone when I found it out. I trembled all over with joy and terror, and as fast as I could I ran into one of the old brakes where we used to go—it was the one by the lane, where nurse made the little clay man—and I ran into it, and I crept into it; and when I came to the place where the elder was, I covered up my face with my hands and lay down flat on the grass, and I stayed there for two hours without moving, whispering to myself delicious, terrible things, and saying some words over and over again. It was all true and wonderful and splendid, and when I remembered the story I knew and thought of what I had really seen, I got hot and I got cold, and the air seemed full of scent, and flowers, and singing. And first I wanted to make a little clay man, like the one nurse had made so long ago, and I had to invent plans and stratagems, and to look about, and to think of things beforehand, because nobody must dream of anything that I was doing or going to do, and I was too old to carry clay about in a tin bucket. At last I thought of a plan, and I brought the wet clay to the brake, and did everything that nurse had done, only I made a much finer image than the one she had made; and when it was finished I did everything that I could imagine and much more than she did, because it was the likeness of something far better. And a few days later, when I had done my lessons early, I went for the second time by the way of the little brook that had led me into a strange country. And I followed the brook, and went through the bushes, and beneath the low branches of trees, and up thorny thickets on the hill, and by dark woods full of creeping thorns, a long, long way. Then I crept through the dark tunnel where the brook had been and the ground was stony, till at last I came to the thicket that climbed up the hill, and though the leaves were coming out upon the trees, everything looked almost as black as it was on the first day that I went there. And the thicket was just the same, and I went up slowly till I came out on the big bare hill, and began to walk among the wonderful rocks. I saw the terrible voor again on everything, for though the sky was brighter, the ring of wild hills all around was still dark, and the hanging woods looked dark and dreadful, and the strange rocks were as grey as ever; and when I looked down on them from the great mound, sitting on the stone, I saw all their amazing circles and rounds within rounds, and I had to sit quite still and watch them as they began to turn about me, and each stone danced in its place, and they seemed to go round and round in a great

whirl, as if one were in the middle of all the stars and heard them rushing through the air. So I went down among the rocks to dance with
them and to sing extraordinary songs; and I went down through the
other thicket, and drank from the bright stream in the close and secret
valley, putting my lips down to the bubbling water; and then I went on
till I came to the deep, brimming well among the glittering moss, and I
sat down. I looked before me into the secret darkness of the valley,
and behind me was the great high wall of grass, and all around me
there were the hanging woods that made the valley such a secret place.
I knew there was nobody here at all besides myself, and that no one
could see me. So I took off my boots and stockings, and let my feet
down into the water, saying the words that I knew. And it was not cold
at all, as I expected, but warm and very pleasant, and when my feet
were in it I felt as if they were in silk, or as if the nymph were kissing
them. So when I had done, I said the other words and made the signs,
and then I dried my feet with a towel I had brought on purpose, and
put on my stockings and boots. Then I climbed up the steep wall, and
went into the place where there are the hollows, and the two beautiful
mounds, and the round ridges of land, and all the strange shapes. I did
not go down into the hollow this time, but I turned at the end, and
made out the figures quite plainly, as it was lighter, and I had remembered the story I had quite forgotten before, and in the story the two
figures are called Adam and Eve, and only those who know the story
understand what they mean. So I went on and on till I came to the secret wood which must not be described, and I crept into it by the way
I had found. And when I had gone about halfway I stopped, and
turned round, and got ready, and I bound the handkerchief tightly
round my eyes, and made quite sure that I could not see at all, not a
twig, nor the end of a leaf, nor the light of the sky, as it was an old red
silk handkerchief with large yellow spots, that went round twice and
covered my eyes, so that I could see nothing. Then I began to go on,
step by step, very slowly. My heart beat faster and faster, and something rose in my throat that choked me and made me want to cry out,
but I shut my lips, and went on. Boughs caught in my hair as I went,
and great thorns tore me; but I went on to the end of the path. Then I
stopped, and held out my arms and bowed, and I went round the first
time, feeling with my hands, and there was nothing. I went round the

second time, feeling with my hands, and there was nothing. Then I went round the third time, feeling with my hands, and the story was all true, and I wished that the years were gone by, and that I had not so long a time to wait before I was happy for ever and ever.

Nurse must have been a prophet like those we read of in the Bible. Everything that she said began to come true, and since then other things that she told me of have happened. That was how I came to know that her stories were true and that I had not made up the secret myself out of my own head. But there was another thing that happened that day. I went a second time to the secret place. It was at the deep brimming well, and when I was standing on the moss I bent over and looked in, and then I knew who the white lady was that I had seen come out of the water in the wood long ago when I was quite little. And I trembled all over, because that told me other things. Then I remembered how sometime after I had seen the white people in the wood, nurse asked me more about them, and I told her all over again, and she listened, and said nothing for a long, long time, and at last she said, "You will see her again." So I understood what had happened and what was to happen. And I understood about the nymphs; how I might meet them in all kinds of places, and they would always help me, and I must always look for them, and find them in all sorts of strange shapes and appearances. And without the nymphs I could never have found the secret, and without them none of the other things could happen. Nurse had told me all about them long ago, but she called them by another name, and I did not know what she meant, or what her tales of them were about, only that they were very queer. And there were two kinds, the bright and the dark, and both were very lovely and very wonderful, and some people saw only one kind, and some only the other, but some saw them both. But usually the dark appeared first, and the bright ones came afterwards, and there were extraordinary tales about them. It was a day or two after I had come home from the secret place that I first really knew the nymphs. Nurse had shewn me how to call them, and I had tried, but I did not know what she meant, and so I thought it was all nonsense. But I made up my mind I would try again, so I went to the wood where the pool was, where I saw the white people, and I tried again. The dark nymph, Alanna, came, and she turned the pool of water into a pool of fire. . . .

EPILOGUE

"That's a very queer story," said Cotgrave, handing back the green book to the recluse, Ambrose. "I see the drift of a good deal, but there are many things that I do not grasp at all. On the last page, for example, what does she mean by 'nymphs'?"

"Well, I think there are references throughout the manuscript to certain 'processes' which have been handed down by tradition from age to age. Some of these processes are just beginning to come within the purview of science, which has arrived at them—or rather at the steps which lead to them—by quite different paths. I have interpreted the reference to 'nymphs' as a reference to one of these processes."

"And you believe that there are such things?"

"Oh, I think so. Yes, I believe I could give you convincing evidence on that point. I am afraid you have neglected the study of alchemy? It is a pity, for the symbolism, at all events, is very beautiful, and moreover if you were acquainted with certain books on the subject, I could recall to your mind phrases which might explain a good deal in the manuscript that you have been reading."

"Yes; but I want to know whether you seriously think that there is any foundation of fact beneath these fancies. Is it not all a department of poetry; a curious dream which man has indulged himself?"

"I can only say that it is no doubt better for the great mass of people to dismiss it all as a dream. But if you ask my veritable belief—that goes quite the other way. No; I should not say belief, but rather knowledge. I may tell you that I have known cases in which men have stumbled quite by accident on certain of these 'processes', and have been astonished by wholly unexpected results. In the cases I am thinking of there could have been no possibility of 'suggestion' or subconscious action of any kind. One might as well suppose a schoolboy 'suggesting' the existence of Æschylus to himself, while he plods mechanically through the declensions.

"But you have noticed the obscurity," Ambrose went on, "and in this particular case it must have been dictated by instinct, since the writer never thought that her manuscripts would fall into other hands. But the practice is universal, and for most excellent reasons. Powerful and sovereign medicines, which are, of necessity, virulent poisons also, are kept in a locked cabinet. The child may find the key by chance, and drink herself dead; but in most cases the search is educational, and the phials contain precious elixirs for him who has patiently fashioned the key for himself."

"You do not care to go into details?"

"No, frankly, I do not. No, you must remain unconvinced. But you saw how the manuscript illustrates the talk we had last week?"

"Is this girl still alive?"

"No. I was one of those who found her. I knew the father well; he was a lawyer, and had always left her very much to herself. He thought of nothing but deeds and leases, and the news came to him as an awful surprise. She was missing one morning; I suppose it was about a year after she had written what you have read. The servants were called, and they told things, and put the only natural interpretation on them— a perfectly erroneous one.

"They discovered that green book somewhere in her room, and I found her in the place that she described with so much dread, lying on the ground before the image."

"It was an image?"

"Yes, it was hidden by the thorns and the thick undergrowth that had surrounded it. It was a wild, lonely country; but you know what it was like by her description, though of course you will understand that the colours have been heightened. A child's imagination always makes the heights higher and the depths deeper than they really are; and she had, unfortunately for herself, something more than imagination. One might say, perhaps, that the picture in her mind which she succeeded in a measure in putting into words, was the scene as it would have appeared to an imaginative artist. But it is a strange, desolate land."

"And she was dead?"

"Yes. She had poisoned herself—in time. No; there was not a word to be said against her in the ordinary sense. You may recollect a story I told you the other night about a lady who saw her child's fingers crushed by a window?"

"And what was this statue?"

"Well, it was of Roman workmanship, of a stone that with the centuries had not blackened, but had become white and luminous. The thicket had grown up about it and concealed it, and in the Middle Ages the followers of a very old tradition had known how to use it for their own purposes. In fact it had been incorporated into the monstrous mythology of the Sabbath. You will have noted that those to whom a sight of that shining whiteness had been vouchsafed by chance, or rather, perhaps, by apparent chance, were required to blindfold themselves on their second approach. That is very significant."

"And is it there still?"

"I sent for tools, and we hammered it into dust and fragments."

"The persistence of tradition never surprises me," Ambrose went on after a pause. "I could name many an English parish where such traditions as that girl had listened to in her childhood are still existent in occult but unabated vigour. No, for me, it is the 'story', not the 'sequel', which is strange and awful, for I have always believed that wonder is of the soul."

A Fragment of Life

I

Edward Darnell awoke from a dream of an ancient wood, and of a clear well rising into grey film and vapour beneath a misty, glimmering heat; and as his eyes opened he saw the sunlight bright in the room, sparkling on the varnish of the new furniture. He turned and found his wife's place vacant, and with some confusion and wonder of the dream still lingering in his mind, he rose also, and began hurriedly to set about his dressing, for he had overslept a little, and the 'bus passed the corner at 9.15. He was a tall, thin man, dark-haired and dark-eyed, and in spite of the routine of the City, the counting of coupons, and all the mechanical drudgery that had lasted for ten years, there still remained about him the curious hint of a wild grace, as if he had been born a creature of the antique wood, and had seen the fountain rising from the green moss and the grey rocks.

The breakfast was laid in the room on the ground floor, the back room with the French windows looking on the garden, and before he sat down to his fried bacon he kissed his wife seriously and dutifully. She had brown hair and brown eyes, and though her lovely face was grave and quiet, one would have said that she might have awaited her husband under the old trees, and bathed in the pool hollowed out of the rocks.

They had a good deal to talk over while the coffee was poured out and the bacon eaten, and Darnell's egg brought in by the stupid, staring servant-girl of the dusty face. They had been married for a year, and they had got on excellently, rarely sitting silent for more than an hour, but for the past few weeks Aunt Marian's present had afforded a subject for conversation which seemed inexhaustible. Mrs. Darnell had been Miss Mary Reynolds, the daughter of an auctioneer and estate

agent in Notting Hill, and Aunt Marian was her mother's sister, who
was supposed rather to have lowered herself by marrying a coal merchant, in a small way, at Turnham Green. Marian had felt the family
attitude a good deal, and the Reynoldses were sorry for many things
that had been said, when the coal merchant saved money and took up
land on building leases in the neighbourhood of Crouch End, greatly
to his advantage, as it appeared. Nobody had thought that Nixon
could ever do very much; but he and his wife had been living for years
in a beautiful house at Barnet, with bow-windows, shrubs, and a pad-
dock, and the two families saw but little of each other, for Mr. Reynolds was not very prosperous. Of course, Aunt Marian and her
husband had been asked to Mary's wedding, but they had sent excuses
with a nice little set of silver apostle spoons, and it was feared that
nothing more was to be looked for. However, on Mary's birthday her
aunt had written a most affectionate letter, enclosing a cheque for a
hundred pounds from "Robert" and herself, and ever since the receipt
of the money the Darnells had discussed the question of its judicious
disposal. Mrs. Darnell had wished to invest the whole sum in Government securities, but Mr. Darnell had pointed out that the rate of interest was absurdly low, and after a good deal of talk he had persuaded
his wife to put ninety pounds of the money in a safe mine, which was
paying five per cent. This was very well, but the remaining ten pounds,
which Mrs. Darnell had insisted on reserving, gave rise to legends and
discourses as interminable as the disputes of the schools.

At first Mr. Darnell had proposed that they should furnish the
"spare" room. There were four bedrooms in the house: their own
room, the small one for the servant, and two others overlooking the
garden, one of which had been used for storing boxes, ends of rope,
and odd numbers of "Quiet Days" and "Sunday Evenings", besides
some worn suits belonging to Mr. Darnell which had been carefully
wrapped up and laid by, as he scarcely knew what to do with them.
The other room was frankly waste and vacant, and one Saturday afternoon, as he was coming home in the 'bus, and while he revolved that
difficult question of the ten pounds, the unseemly emptiness of the
spare room suddenly came into his mind, and he glowed with the idea
that now, thanks to Aunt Marian, it could be furnished. He was busied
with this delightful thought all the way home, but when he let himself

in, he said nothing to his wife, since he felt that his idea must be matured. He told Mrs. Darnell that, having important business, he was obliged to go out again directly, but that he should be back without fail for tea at half-past six; and Mary, on her side, was not sorry to be alone, as she was a little behind-hand with the household books. The fact was, that Darnell, full of the design of furnishing the spare bedroom, wished to consult his friend Wilson, who lived at Fulham, and had often given him judicious advice as to the laying out of money to the very best advantage. Wilson was connected with the Bordeaux wine trade, and Darnell's only anxiety was lest he should not be at home.

However, it was all right; Darnell took a tram along the Goldhawk Road, and walked the rest of the way, and was delighted to see Wilson in the front garden of his house, busy amongst his flower-beds.

"Haven't seen you for an age," he said cheerily, when he heard Darnell's hand on the gate; "come in. Oh, I forgot," he added, as Darnell still fumbled with the handle, and vainly attempted to enter. "Of course you can't get in; I haven't shewn it you."

It was a hot day in June, and Wilson appeared in a costume which he had put on in haste as soon as he arrived from the City. He wore a straw hat with a neat pugaree protecting the back of his neck, and his dress was a Norfolk jacket and knickers in heather mixture.

"See," he said, as he let Darnell in; "see the dodge. You don't *turn* the handle at all. First of all push hard, and then pull. It's a trick of my own, and I shall have it patented. You see, it keeps undesirable characters at a distance—such a great thing in the suburbs. I feel I can leave Mrs. Wilson alone now; and, formerly, you have no idea how she used to be pestered."

"But how about visitors?" said Darnell. "How do they get in?"

"Oh, we put them up to it. Besides," he said vaguely, "there is sure to be somebody looking out. Mrs. Wilson is nearly always at the window. She's out now; gone to call on some friends. The Bennetts' At Home day, I think it is. This is the first Saturday, isn't it? You know J. W. Bennett, don't you? Ah, he's in the House; doing very well, I believe. He put me on to a very good thing the other day."

"But, I say," said Wilson, as they turned and strolled towards the front door, "what do you wear those black things for? You look hot. Look at me. Well, I've been gardening, you know, but I feel as cool as a cucumber. I dare say you don't know where to get these things? Very few men do. Where do you suppose I got 'em?"

"In the West End, I suppose," said Darnell, wishing to be polite.

"Yes, that's what everybody says. And it is a good cut. Well, I'll tell you, but you needn't pass it on to everybody. I got the tip from Jameson—you know him, 'Jim-Jams', in the China trade, 39 Eastbrook—and he said he didn't want everybody in the City to know about it. But just go to Jennings, in Old Wall, and mention my name, and you'll be all right. And what d'you think they cost?"

"I haven't a notion," said Darnell, who had never bought such a suit in his life.

"Well, have a guess."

Darnell regarded Wilson gravely.

The jacket hung about his body like a sack, the knickerbockers drooped lamentably over his calves, and in prominent positions the bloom of the heather seemed about to fade and disappear.

"Three pounds, I suppose, at least," he said at length.

"Well, I asked Dench, in our place, the other day, and he guessed four ten, and his father's got something to do with a big business in Conduit Street. But I only gave thirty-five and six. To measure? Of course; look at the cut, man."

Darnell was astonished at so low a price.

"And, by the way," Wilson went on, pointing to his new brown boots, "you know where to go for shoe-leather? Oh, I thought everybody was up to that! There's only one place. 'Mr. Bill', in Gunning Street,—nine and six."

They were walking round and round the garden, and Wilson pointed out the flowers in the beds and borders. There were hardly any blossoms, but everything was neatly arranged.

"Here are the tuberous-rooted Glasgownias," he said, shewing a rigid row of stunted plants; "those are Squintaceæ; this is a new introduction, Moldavia Semperflorida Andersonii; and this is Prattsia."

"When do they come out?" said Darnell.

"Most of them in the end of August or beginning of September," said Wilson briefly. He was slightly annoyed with himself for having talked so much about his plants, since he saw that Darnell cared nothing for flowers; and, indeed, the visitor could hardly dissemble vague recollections that came to him; thoughts of an old, wild garden, full of odours, beneath grey walls, of the fragrance of the meadowsweet beside the brook.

"I wanted to consult you about some furniture," Darnell said at last. "You know we've got a spare room, and I'm thinking of putting a few things into it. I haven't exactly made up my mind, but I thought you might advise me."

"Come into my den," said Wilson. "No; this way, by the back"; and he shewed Darnell another ingenious arrangement at the side door whereby a violent high-toned bell was set pealing in the house if one did but touch the latch. Indeed, Wilson handled it so briskly that the bell rang a wild alarm, and the servant, who was trying on her mistress's things in the bedroom, jumped madly to the window and then danced a hysteric dance. There was plaster found on the drawing-room table on Sunday afternoon, and Wilson wrote a letter to the *Fulham Chronicle,* ascribing the phenomenon "to some disturbance of a seismic nature."

For the moment he knew nothing of the great results of his contrivance, and solemnly led the way towards the back of the house. Here there was a patch of turf, beginning to look a little brown, with a background of shrubs. In the middle of the turf, a boy of nine or ten was standing all alone, with something of an air.

"The eldest," said Wilson. "Havelock. Well, Lockie, what are ye doing now? And where are your brother and sister?"

The boy was not at all shy. Indeed, he seemed eager to explain the course of events.

"I'm playing at being Gawd," he said, with an engaging frankness. "And I've sent Fergus and Janet to the bad place. That's in the shrubbery. And they're never to come out any more. And they're burning for ever and ever."

"What d'you think of that?" said Wilson admiringly. "Not bad for a youngster of nine, is it? They think a lot of him at the Sunday-school. But come into my den."

The den was an apartment projecting from the back of the house. It had been designed as a back kitchen and washhouse, but Wilson had draped the "copper" in art muslin and had boarded over the sink, so that it served as a workman's bench.

"Snug, isn't it?" he said, as he pushed forward one of the two wicker chairs. "I think out things here, you know; it's quiet. And what about this furnishing? Do you want to do the thing on a grand scale?"

"Oh, not at all. Quite the reverse. In fact, I don't know whether the sum at our disposal will be sufficient. You see the spare room is ten feet by twelve, with a western exposure, and I thought if we *could* manage it, that it would seem more cheerful furnished. Besides, it's pleasant to be able to ask a visitor; our aunt, Mrs. Nixon, for example. But she is accustomed to have everything very nice."

"And how much do you want to spend?"

"Well, I hardly think we should be justified in going much beyond ten pounds. That isn't enough, eh?"

Wilson got up and shut the door of the back kitchen impressively.

"Look here," he said, "I'm glad you came to me in the first place. Now you'll just tell me where you thought of going yourself."

"Well, I had thought of the Hampstead Road," said Darnell in a hesitating manner.

"I just thought you'd say that. But I'll ask you, what is the good of going to those expensive shops in the West End? You don't get a better article for your money. You're merely paying for fashion."

"I've seen some nice things in Samuel's, though. They get a brilliant polish on their goods in those superior shops. We went there when we were married."

"Exactly, and paid ten per cent more than you need have paid. It's throwing money away. And how much did you say you had to spend? Ten pounds. Well, I can tell you where to get a beautiful bedroom suite, in the very highest finish, for six pound ten. What d'you think of that? China included, mind you; and a square of carpet, brilliant colours, will only cost you fifteen and six. Look here, go any Saturday afternoon to Dick's, in the Seven Sisters Road, mention my name, and ask for Mr. Johnston. The suite's in ash, 'Elizabethan' they call it. Six pound ten, including the china, with one of their 'Orient' carpets, nine by nine, for fifteen and six. Dick's."

Wilson spoke with some eloquence on the subject of furnishing. He pointed out that the times were changed, and that the old heavy style was quite out of date.

"You know," he said, "it isn't like it was in the old days, when people used to buy things to last hundreds of years. Why, just before the wife and I were married, an uncle of mine died up in the North and left me his furniture. I was thinking of furnishing at the time, and I thought the things might come in handy; but I assure you there wasn't a single article that I cared to give house-room to. All dingy, old mahogany; big bookcases and bureaus, and claw-legged chairs and tables. As I said to the wife (as she was soon afterwards), 'We don't exactly want to set up a chamber of horrors, do we?' So I sold off the lot for what I could get. I must confess I like a cheerful room."

Darnell said he had heard that artists liked the old-fashioned furniture.

"Oh, I dare say. The 'unclean cult of the sunflower', eh? You saw that piece in the *Daily Post?* I hate all that rot myself. It isn't healthy, you know, and I don't believe the English people will stand it. But talking of curiosities, I've got something here that's worth a bit of money."

He dived into some dusty receptacle in a corner of the room, and shewed Darnell a small, worm-eaten Bible, wanting the first five chapters of Genesis and the last leaf of the Apocalypse. It bore the date of 1753.

"It's my belief that's worth a lot," said Wilson. "Look at the worm-holes. And you see it's 'imperfect', as they call it. You've noticed that some of the most valuable books are 'imperfect' at the sales?"

The interview came to an end soon after, and Darnell went home to his tea. He thought seriously of taking Wilson's advice, and after tea he told Mary of his idea and of what Wilson had said about Dick's.

Mary was a good deal taken by the plan when she had heard all the details. The prices struck her as very moderate. They were sitting one on each side of the grate (which was concealed by a pretty cardboard screen, painted with landscapes), and she rested her cheek on her hand, and her beautiful dark eyes seemed to dream and behold strange visions. In reality she was thinking of Darnell's plan.

"It would be very nice in some ways," she said at last. "But we must talk it over. What I am afraid of is that it will come to much more than ten pounds in the long run. There are so many things to be considered. There's the bed. It would look shabby if we got a common bed without brass mounts. Then the bedding, the mattress, and blankets, and sheets, and counterpane would all cost something."

She dreamed again, calculating the cost of all the necessaries, and Darnell stared anxiously; reckoning with her, and wondering what her conclusion would be. For a moment the delicate colouring of her face, the grace of her form, and the brown hair, drooping over her ears and clustering in little curls about her neck, seemed to hint at a language which he had not yet learned; but she spoke again.

"The bedding would come to a great deal, I am afraid. Even if Dick's are considerably cheaper than Boon's or Samuel's. And, my dear, we must have some ornaments on the mantelpiece. I saw some very nice vases at eleven-three the other day at Wilkin and Dodd's. We should want six at least, and there ought to be a centre-piece. You see how it mounts up."

Darnell was silent. He saw that his wife was summing up against his scheme, and though he had set his heart on it, he could not resist her arguments.

"It would be nearer twelve pounds, than ten," she said.

"The floor would have to be stained round the carpet (nine by nine, you said?), and we should want a piece of linoleum to go under the washstand. And the walls would look very bare without any pictures."

"I thought about the pictures," said Darnell; and he spoke quite eagerly. He felt that here, at least, he was unassailable. "You know there's the 'Derby Day' and the 'Railway Station', ready framed, standing in the corner of the box-room already. They're a bit old-fashioned, perhaps, but that doesn't matter in a bedroom. And couldn't we use some photographs? I saw a very neat frame in natural oak in the City, to hold half a dozen, for one and six. We might put in your father, and your brother James, and Aunt Marian, and your grandmother, in her widow's cap—and any of the others in the album. And then there's that old family picture in the hair-trunk—that might do over the mantelpiece."

"You mean your great-grandfather in the gilt frame? But that's *very* old-fashioned, isn't it? He looks so queer in his wig. I don't think it would quite go with the room, somehow."

Darnell thought a moment. The portrait was a "kitcat" of a young gentleman, bravely dressed in the fashion of 1750, and he very faintly remembered some old tales that his father had told him about this ancestor—tales of the woods and fields, of the deep sunken lanes, and the forgotten country in the west.

"No," he said, "I suppose it is rather out of date. But I saw some very nice prints in the City, framed and quite cheap."

"Yes, but everything counts. Well, we will talk it over, as you say. You know we must be careful."

The servant came in with the supper, a tin of biscuits, a glass of milk for the mistress, and a modest pint of beer for the master, with a little cheese and butter. Afterwards Edward smoked two pipes of honeydew, and they went quietly to bed; Mary going first, and her husband following a quarter of an hour later, according to the ritual established from the first days of their marriage. Front and back doors were locked, the gas was turned off at the meter, and when Darnell got upstairs he found his wife already in bed, her face turned round on the pillow.

She spoke softly to him as he came into the room.

"It would be impossible to buy a presentable bed at anything under one pound eleven, and good sheets are dear, anywhere."

He slipped off his clothes and slid gently into bed, putting out the candle on the table. The blinds were all evenly and duly drawn, but it was a June night, and beyond the walls, beyond that desolate world and wilderness of grey Shepherd's Bush, a great golden moon had floated up through magic films of cloud, above the hill, and the earth was filled with a wonderful light between red sunset lingering over the mountain and that marvellous glory that shone into the woods from the summit of the hill. Darnell seemed to see some reflection of that wizard brightness in the room; the pale walls and the white bed and his wife's face lying amidst brown hair upon the pillow were illuminated, and listening he could almost hear the corncrake in the fields, the fern-owl sounding his strange note from the quiet of the rugged place where the bracken grew, and, like the echo of a magic song, the melody of the nightingale that sang all night in the alder by the little brook. There was nothing that he could say, but he slowly stole his arm under his wife's neck, and played with the ringlets of brown hair. She never moved, she lay there gently breathing, looking up to the blank ceiling of the room with her beautiful eyes, thinking also, no doubt, thoughts that she could not utter, kissing her husband obediently when he asked her to do so, and he stammered and hesitated as he spoke.

They were nearly asleep, indeed Darnell was on the very eve of dreaming, when she said very softly—

"I am afraid, darling, that we could never afford it." And he heard her words through the murmur of the water, dripping from the grey rock, and falling into the clear pool beneath.

Sunday morning was always an occasion of idleness. Indeed, they would never have got breakfast if Mrs. Darnell, who had the instincts of the housewife, had not awoke and seen the bright sunshine, and felt that the house was too still. She lay quiet for five minutes, while her husband slept beside her, and listened intently, waiting for the sound of Alice stirring down below. A golden tube of sunlight shone through some opening in the Venetian blinds, and it shone on the brown hair that lay about her head on the pillow, and she looked steadily into the room at the "duchesse" toilet-table, the coloured ware of the wash-stand, and the two photogravures in oak frames, "The Meeting" and "The Parting", that hung upon the wall. She was half dreaming as she listened for the servant's footsteps, and the faint shadow of a shade of a thought came over her, and she imagined dimly, for the quick moment of a dream, another world where rapture was wine, where one wandered in a deep and happy valley, and the moon was always rising red above the trees. She was thinking of Hampstead, which represented to her the vision of the world beyond the walls, and the thought of the heath led her away to Bank Holidays, and then to Alice. There was not a sound in the house; it might have been midnight for the stillness if the drawling cry of the Sunday paper had not suddenly echoed round the corner of Edna Road, and with it came the warning clank and shriek of the milkman with his pails.

Mrs. Darnell sat up, and wide awake, listened more intently. The girl was evidently fast asleep, and must be roused, or all the work of the day would be out of joint, and she remembered how Edward hated any fuss or discussion about household matters, more especially on a Sunday, after his long week's work in the City. She gave her husband an affectionate glance as he slept on, for she was very fond of him, and so she gently rose from the bed and went in her nightgown to call the maid.

The servant's room was small and stuffy, the night had been very hot, and Mrs. Darnell paused for a moment at the door, wondering whether the girl on the bed was really the dusty-faced servant who bustled day by day about the house, or even the strangely bedizened creature, dressed in purple, with a shiny face, who would appear on the Sunday afternoon, bringing in an early tea, because it was her "evening out". Alice's hair was black and her skin was pale, almost of the olive tinge, and she lay asleep, her head resting on one arm, reminding Mrs. Darnell of a queer print of a "Tired Bacchante" that she had seen long ago in a shop window in Upper Street, Islington. And a cracked bell was ringing; that meant five minutes to eight, and nothing done.

She touched the girl gently on the shoulder, and only smiled when her eyes opened, and waking with a start, she got up in sudden confusion. Mrs. Darnell went back to her room and dressed slowly while her husband still slept, and it was only at the last moment, as she fastened her cherry-coloured bodice, that she roused him, telling him that the bacon would be overdone unless he hurried over his dressing.

Over the breakfast they discussed the question of the spare room all over again. Mrs. Darnell still admitted that the plan of furnishing it attracted her, but she could not see how it could be done for the ten pounds, and as they were prudent people they did not care to encroach on their savings. Edward was highly paid, having (with allowances for extra work in busy weeks) a hundred and forty pounds a year, and Mary had inherited from an old uncle, her godfather, three hundred pounds, which had been judiciously laid out in mortgage at 4½ per cent. Their total income, then, counting in Aunt Marian's present, was a hundred and fifty-eight pounds a year, and they were clear of debt, since Darnell had bought the furniture for the house out of money which he had saved for five or six years before. In the first few years of his life in the City his income had, of course, been smaller, and at first he had lived very freely, without a thought of laying by. The theatres and music-halls had attracted him, and scarcely a week passed without his going (in the pit) to one or the other; and he had occasionally bought photographs of actresses who pleased him. These he had solemnly burnt when he became engaged to Mary; he remembered the evening well; his heart had been so full of joy and wonder, and the landlady had complained bitterly of the mess in the grate when he came home from the City the next night. Still, the money was lost, as far as he could recollect, ten or twelve shillings; and it annoyed him all the more to reflect that if he had put it by, it would have gone far towards the purchase of an "Orient" carpet in brilliant colours. Then there had been other expenses of his youth: he had purchased three-penny and even fourpenny cigars, the latter rarely, but the former frequently, sometimes singly, and sometimes in bundles of twelve for half-a-crown. Once a meerschaum pipe had haunted him for six weeks; the tobacconist had drawn it out of a drawer with some air of secrecy as he was buying a packet of "Lone Star". Here was another useless expense, these American-manufactured tobaccos; his "Lone Star", "Long Judge", "Old Hank", "Sultry Clime", and the rest of them cost from a shilling to one and six the two-ounce packet; whereas now he got excellent loose honeydew for threepence halfpenny an ounce. But the crafty tradesman, who had marked him down as a buyer of expensive fancy goods, nodded with his air of mystery, and, snapping open the case, displayed the meerschaum before the dazzled eyes of Darnell. The bowl was carved in the likeness of a female figure, shewing the head and *torso,* and the mouthpiece was of the very best amber—only twelve and six, the man said, and the amber alone, he declared, was worth more than that. He explained that he felt some delicacy about shewing the pipe to any but a regular customer, and was willing to take a little under cost price and "cut the loss". Darnell resisted for the time, but the pipe troubled him, and at last he bought it. He was pleased to shew it to the younger men in the office for a while, but it never smoked very well, and he gave it away just before his marriage, as from the nature of the carving it would have been impossible to use it in his wife's presence. Once, while he was taking his holidays at Hastings, he had purchased a malacca cane—a useless thing that had cost seven shillings—and he reflected with sorrow on the innumerable evenings on which he had rejected his landlady's plain fried chop, and had gone out to *flâner* among the Italian restaurants in Upper Street, Islington (he lodged in Holloway), pampering himself with expensive delicacies: cutlets and green peas, braised beef with tomato sauce, fillet steak and chipped potatoes, ending the banquet very often with a small wedge of Gruyère, which cost twopence. One night, after receiving a rise in his salary, he had actually drunk a quarter-flask of Chianti and had added the enormities of Benedictine, coffee, and cigarettes to an expenditure already disgraceful, and sixpence to the waiter made the bill amount to four shillings instead of the shilling that would have provided him with a wholesome and sufficient repast at home. Oh, there were many other items in this account of extravagance, and Darnell had often regretted his way of life, thinking that if he had been more careful, five or six pounds a year might have been added to their income.

And the question of the spare room brought back these regrets in an exaggerated degree. He persuaded himself that the extra five pounds would have given a sufficient margin for the outlay that he desired to make; though this was, no doubt, a mistake on his part. But he saw quite clearly that, under the present conditions, there must be no levies made on the very small sum of money that they had saved. The rent of the house was thirty-five, and rates and taxes added another ten pounds—nearly a quarter of their income for house-room. Mary kept down the housekeeping bills to the very best of her ability, but meat was always dear, and she suspected the maid of cutting surreptitious slices from the joint and eating them in her bedroom with bread and treacle in the dead of night, for the girl had disordered and eccentric appetites. Mr. Darnell thought no more of restaurants, cheap or dear; he took his lunch with him to the City, and joined his wife in the evening at high tea—chops, a bit of steak, or cold meat from the Sunday's dinner. Mrs. Darnell ate bread and jam and drank a little milk in the middle of the day; but, with the utmost economy, the effort to live within their means and to save for future contingencies was a very hard one. They had determined to do without change of air for at least three years, as the honeymoon at Walton-on-the-Naze had cost a good deal; and it was on this ground that they had, somewhat illogically, reserved the ten pounds, declaring that as they were not to have any holiday they would spend the money on something useful.

And it was this consideration of utility that was finally fatal to Darnell's scheme. They had calculated and recalculated the expense of the bed and bedding, the linoleum, and the ornaments, and by a great deal of exertion the total expenditure had been made to assume the shape of "something very little over ten pounds", when Mary said quite suddenly—

"But, after all, Edward, we don't really *want* to furnish the room at all. I mean it isn't necessary. And if we did so it might lead to no end of expense. People would hear of it and be sure to fish for invitations. You know we have relatives in the country, and they would be almost certain, the Mallings, at any rate, to give hints."

Darnell saw the force of the argument and gave way. But he was bitterly disappointed.

"It would have been very nice, wouldn't it?" he said with a sigh.

"Never mind, dear," said Mary, who saw that he was a good deal cast down. "We must think of some other plan that will be nice and useful too."

She often spoke to him in that tone of a kind mother, though she was by three years the younger.

"And now," she said, "I must get ready for church. Are you coming?"

Darnell said that he thought not. He usually accompanied his wife to morning service, but that day he felt some bitterness in his heart, and preferred to lounge under the shade of the big mulberry tree that stood in the middle of their patch of garden—relic of the spacious lawns that had once lain smooth and green and sweet, where the dismal streets now swarmed in a hopeless labyrinth.

So Mary went quietly and alone to church. St. Paul's stood in a neighbouring street, and its Gothic design would have interested a curious enquirer into the history of a strange revival. Obviously, mechanically, there was nothing amiss. The style chosen was "geometrical decorated", and the tracery of the windows seemed correct. The nave, the aisles, the spacious chancel, were reasonably proportioned; and, to be quite serious, the only feature obviously wrong was the substitution of a low "chancel wall" with iron gates for the rood screen with the loft and rood. But this, it might plausibly be contended, was merely an adaptation of the old idea to modern requirements, and it would have been quite difficult to explain why the whole building, from the mere mortar setting between the stones to the Gothic gas standards, was a mysterious and elaborate blasphemy. The canticles were sung to Joll in B flat, the chants were "Anglican", and the sermon was the gospel for the day, amplified and rendered into the more modern and graceful English of the preacher. And Mary came away.

After their dinner (an excellent piece of Australian mutton, bought in the "World Wide" Stores, in Hammersmith), they sat for some time in the garden, partly sheltered by the big mulberry tree from the observation of their neighbours. Edward smoked his honeydew, and Mary looked at him with placid affection.

"You never tell me about the men in your office," she said at length. "Some of them are nice fellows, aren't they?"

"Oh, yes, they're very decent. I must bring some of them round, one of these days."

He remembered with a pang that it would be necessary to provide whisky. One couldn't ask the guest to drink table beer at tenpence the gallon.

"Who are they, though?" said Mary. "I think they might have given you a wedding present."

"Well, I don't know. We never have gone in for that sort of thing. But they're very decent chaps. Well, there's Harvey; 'Sauce' they call him behind his back. He's mad on bicycling. He went in last year for the Two Miles Amateur Record. He'd have made it, too, if he could have got into better training.

"Then there's James, a sporting man. You wouldn't care for him. I always think he smells of the stable."

"How horrid!" said Mrs. Darnell, finding her husband a little frank, lowering her eyes as she spoke.

"Dickenson might amuse you," Darnell went on. "He's always got a joke. A terrible liar, though. When he tells a tale we never know how much to believe. He swore the other day he'd seen one of the governors buying cockles off a barrow near London Bridge, and Jones, who's just come, believed every word of it."

Darnell laughed at the humorous recollection of the jest.

"And that wasn't a bad yarn about Salter's wife," he went on. "Salter is the manager, you know. Dickenson lives close by, in Notting Hill, and he said one morning that he had seen Mrs. Salter, in the Portobello Road, in red stockings, dancing to a piano organ."

"He's a little coarse, isn't he?" said Mrs. Darnell. "I don't see much fun in that."

"Well, you know, amongst men it's different. You might like Wallis; he's a tremendous photographer. He often shews us photos he's taken of his children—one, a little girl of three, in her bath. I asked him how he thought she'd like it when she was twenty-three."

Mrs. Darnell looked down and made no answer.

There was silence for some minutes while Darnell smoked his pipe. "I say, Mary," he said at length, "what do you say to our taking a paying guest?"

"A paying guest! I never thought of it. Where should we put him?"

"Why, I was thinking of the spare room. The plan would obviate your objection, wouldn't it? Lots of men in the City take them, and make money of it too. I dare say it would add ten pounds a year to our income. Redgrave, the cashier, finds it worth his while to take a large house on purpose. They have a regular lawn for tennis and a billiard-room."

Mary considered gravely, always with the dream in her eyes. "I don't think we could manage it, Edward," she said; "it would be inconvenient in many ways." She hesitated for a moment. "And I don't think I should care to have a young man in the house. It is so very small, and our accommodation, as you know, is so limited."

She blushed slightly, and Edward, a little disappointed as he was, looked at her with a singular longing, as if he were a scholar confronted with a doubtful hieroglyph, either wholly wonderful or altogether commonplace. Next door children were playing in the garden, playing shrilly, laughing, crying, quarrelling, racing to and fro. Suddenly a clear, pleasant voice sounded from an upper window.

"Enid! Charles! Come up to my room at once!"

There was an instant sudden hush. The children's voices died away.

"Mrs. Parker is supposed to keep her children in great order," said Mary. "Alice was telling me about it the other day. She had been talking to Mrs. Parker's servant. I listened to her without any remark, as I don't think it right to encourage servants' gossip; they always exaggerate everything. And I dare say children often require to be corrected."

The children were struck silent as if some ghastly terror had seized them.

Darnell fancied that he heard a queer sort of cry from the house, but could not be quite sure. He turned to the other side, where an elderly, ordinary man with a grey moustache was strolling up and down on the further side of his garden. He caught Darnell's eye, and Mrs. Darnell looking towards him at the same moment, he very politely raised his tweed cap. Darnell was surprised to see his wife blushing fiercely.

"Sayce and I often go into the City by the same 'bus," he said, "and as it happens we've sat next to each other two or three times lately. I believe he's a traveller for a leather firm in Bermondsey. He struck me as a pleasant man. Haven't they got rather a good-looking servant?"

"Alice has spoken to me about her—and the Sayces," said Mrs. Darnell. "I understand that they are not very well thought of in the neighbourhood. But I must go in and see whether the tea is ready. Alice will be wanting to go out directly."

Darnell looked after his wife as she walked quickly away. He only dimly understood, but he could see the charm of her figure, the delight of the brown curls clustering about her neck, and he again felt that sense of the scholar confronted by the hieroglyphic. He could not have expressed his emotion, but he wondered whether he would ever find the key, and something told him that before she could speak to him his own lips must be unclosed. She had gone into the house by the back kitchen door, leaving it open, and he heard her speaking to the girl about the water being "really boiling". He was amazed, almost indignant with himself; but the sound of the words came to his ears as strange, heart-piercing music, tones from another, wonderful sphere. And yet he was her husband, and they had been married nearly a year; and yet, whenever she spoke, he had to listen to the sense of what she said, constraining himself, lest he should believe she was a magic creature, knowing the secrets of immeasurable delight.

He looked out through the leaves of the mulberry tree. Mr. Sayce had disappeared from his view, but he saw the light-blue fume of the cigar that he was smoking floating slowly across the shadowed air. He was wondering at his wife's manner when Sayce's name was mentioned, puzzling his head as to what could be amiss in the household of a most respectable personage, when his wife appeared at the dining-room window and called him in to tea. She smiled as he looked up, and he rose hastily and walked in, wondering whether he were not a little "queer", so strange were the dim emotions and the dimmer impulses that rose within him.

Alice was all shining purple and strong scent, as she brought in the teapot and the jug of hot water. It seemed that a visit to the kitchen had inspired Mrs. Darnell in her turn with a novel plan for disposing of the famous ten pounds. The range had always been a trouble to her, and when sometimes she went into the kitchen, and found, as she said, the fire "roaring halfway up the chimney", it was in vain that she reproved the maid on the ground of extravagance and waste of coal. Alice was ready to admit the absurdity of making up such an enormous fire merely to bake (they called it "roast") a bit of beef or mutton, and to boil the potatoes and the cabbage; but she was able to shew Mrs. Darnell that the fault lay in the defective contrivance of the range, in an oven which "would not get hot". Even with a chop or a steak it was

almost as bad; the heat seemed to escape up the chimney or into the
room, and Mary had spoken several times to her husband on the
shocking waste of coal, and the cheapest coal procurable was never
less than eighteen shillings the ton. Mr. Darnell had written to the
landlord, a builder, who had replied in an illiterate but offensive communication, maintaining the excellence of the stove and charging all
the faults to the account of "your good lady", which really implied that
the Darnells kept no servant, and that Mrs. Darnell did everything. The
range, then, remained, a standing annoyance and expense. Every
morning, Alice said, she had the greatest difficulty in getting the fire to
light at all, and once lighted it "seemed as if it fled right up the chimney". Only a few nights before Mrs. Darnell had spoken seriously to
her husband about it; she had got Alice to weigh the coals expended in
cooking a cottage pie, the dish of the evening, and deducting what remained in the scuttle after the pie was done, it appeared that the
wretched thing had consumed nearly twice the proper quantity of fuel.

"You remember what I said the other night about the range?" said
Mrs. Darnell, as she poured out the tea and watered the leaves. She
thought the introduction a good one, for though her husband was a
most amiable man, she guessed that he had been just a little hurt by
her decision against his furnishing scheme.

"The range?" said Darnell. He paused as he helped himself to the
marmalade and considered for a moment. "No, I don't recollect. What
night was it?"

"Tuesday. Don't you remember? You had 'overtime', and didn't
get home till quite late."

She paused for a moment, blushing slightly; and then began to re-
capitulate the misdeeds of the range, and the outrageous outlay of coal
in the preparation of the cottage pie.

"Oh, I recollect now. That was the night I thought I heard the
nightingale (people say there are nightingales in Bedford Park), and the
sky was such a wonderful deep blue."

He remembered how he had walked from Uxbridge Road Station,
where the green 'bus stopped, and in spite of the fuming kilns under
Acton, a delicate odour of the woods and summer fields was mysteriously in the air, and he had fancied that he smelt the red wild roses,
drooping from the hedge. As he came to his gate he saw his wife

standing in the doorway, with a light in her hand, and he threw his arms violently about her as she welcomed him, and whispered something in her ear, kissing her scented hair. He had felt quite abashed a moment afterwards, and he was afraid that he had frightened her by his nonsense; she seemed trembling and confused. And then she had told him how they had weighed the coal.

"Yes, I remember now," he said. "It is a great nuisance, isn't it? I hate to throw away money like that."

"Well, what do you think? Suppose we bought a really good range with aunt's money? It would save us a lot, and I expect the things would taste much nicer."

Darnell passed the marmalade, and confessed that the idea was brilliant.

"It's much better than mine, Mary," he said quite frankly. "I am so glad you thought of it. But we must talk it over; it doesn't do to buy in a hurry. There are so many makes."

Each had seen ranges which looked miraculous inventions; he in the neighbourhood of the City; she in Oxford Street and Regent Street, on visits to the dentist. They discussed the matter at tea, and afterwards they discussed it walking round and round the garden, in the sweet cool of the evening.

"They say the 'Newcastle' will burn anything, coke even," said Mary.

"But the 'Glow' got the gold medal at the Paris Exhibition," said Edward.

"But what about the 'Eutopia' Kitchener? Have you seen it at work in Oxford Street?" said Mary. "They say their plan of ventilating the oven is quite unique."

"I was in Fleet Street the other day," answered Edward, "and I was looking at the 'Bliss' Patent Stoves. They burn less fuel than any in the market—so the makers declare."

He put his arm gently round her waist. She did not repel him; she whispered quite softly—

"I think Mrs. Parker is at her window," and he drew his arm back slowly.

"But we will talk it over," he said. "There is no hurry. I might call at some of the places near the City, and you might do the same thing in Oxford Street and Regent Street and Piccadilly, and we could compare notes."

Mary was quite pleased with her husband's good temper. It was so nice of him not to find fault with her plan; "He's so good to me," she thought, and that was what she often said to her brother, who did not care much for Darnell. They sat down on the seat under the mulberry, close together, and she let Darnell take her hand, and as she felt his shy, hesitating fingers touch her in the shadow, she pressed them ever so softly, and as he fondled her hand, his breath was on her neck, and she heard his passionate, hesitating voice whisper, "My dear, my dear," as his lips touched her cheek. She trembled a little, and waited. Darnell kissed her gently on the cheek and drew away his hand, and when he spoke he was almost breathless.

"We had better go in now," he said. "There is a heavy dew, and you might catch cold."

A warm, scented gale came to them from beyond the walls. He longed to ask her to stay out with him all night beneath the tree, that they might whisper to one another, that the scent of her hair might inebriate him, that he might feel her dress still brushing against his ankles. But he could not find the words, and it was absurd, and she was so gentle that she would do whatever he asked, however foolish it might be, just because he asked her. He was not worthy to kiss her lips; he bent down and kissed her silk bodice, and again he felt that she trembled, and he was ashamed, fearing that he had frightened her.

They went slowly into the house, side by side, and Darnell lit the gas in the drawing-room, where they always sat on Sunday evenings. Mrs. Darnell felt a little tired and lay down on the sofa, and Darnell took the arm-chair opposite. For a while they were silent, and then Darnell said suddenly—

"What's wrong with the Sayces? You seemed to think there was something a little strange about them. Their maid looks quite quiet."

"Oh, I don't know that one ought to pay any attention to servants' gossip. They're not always very truthful."

"It was Alice told you, wasn't it?"

"Yes. She was speaking to me the other day, when I was in the kitchen in the afternoon."

"But what was it?"

"Oh, I'd rather not tell you, Edward. It's not pleasant. I scolded Alice for repeating it to me."

Darnell got up and took a small, frail chair near the sofa.

"Tell me," he said again, with an odd perversity. He did not really care to hear about the household next door, but he remembered how his wife's cheeks flushed in the afternoon, and now he was looking at her eyes.

"Oh, I really couldn't tell you, dear. I should feel ashamed."

"But you're my wife."

"Yes, but it doesn't make any difference. A woman doesn't like to talk about such things."

Darnell bent his head down. His heart was beating; he put his ear to her mouth and said, "Whisper."

Mary drew his head down still lower with her gentle hand, and her cheeks burned as she whispered—

"Alice says that—upstairs—they have only—one room furnished. The maid told her—herself."

With an unconscious gesture she pressed his head to her breast, and he in turn was bending her red lips to his own, when a violent jangle clamoured through the silent house. They sat up, and Mrs. Darnell went hurriedly to the door.

"That's Alice," she said. "She is always in in time. It has only just struck ten."

Darnell shivered with annoyance. His lips, he knew, had almost been opened. Mary's pretty handkerchief, delicately scented from a little flagon that a school friend had given her, lay on the floor, and he picked it up, and kissed it, and hid it away.

The question of the range occupied them all through June and far into July. Mrs. Darnell took every opportunity of going to the West End and investigating the capacity of the latest makes, gravely viewing the new improvements and hearing what the shopmen had to say; while Darnell, as he said, "kept his eyes open" about the City. They accumulated quite a literature of the subject, bringing away illustrated pamphlets, and in the evenings it was an amusement to look at the pictures. They viewed with reverence and interest the drawings of great ranges for hotels and public institutions, mighty contrivances furnished with a series of ovens each for a different use, with wonderful apparatus for grilling, with batteries of accessories which seemed to invest the cook almost with the dignity of a chief engineer. But when, in one of the lists, they encountered the images of little toy "cottage" ranges, for four pounds, and even for three pounds ten, they grew scornful, on the strength of the eight or ten pound article which they meant to purchase—when the merits of the divers patents had been thoroughly thrashed out.

The "Raven" was for a long time Mary's favourite. It promised the utmost economy with the highest efficiency, and many times they were on the point of giving the order. But the "Glow" seemed equally seductive, and it was only £8. 5s. as compared with £9. 7s. 6d., and though the "Raven" was supplied to the Royal Kitchen, the "Glow" could shew more fervent testimonials from continental potentates.

It seemed a debate without end, and it endured day after day till that morning, when Darnell woke from the dream of the ancient wood, of the fountains rising into grey vapour beneath the heat of the sun. As he dressed, an idea struck him, and he brought it as a shock to the hurried breakfast, disturbed by the thought of the City 'bus which passed the corner of the street at 9.15.

"I've got an improvement on your plan, Mary," he said, with triumph. "Look at that," and he flung a little book on the table.

He laughed. "It beats your notion all to fits. After all, the great expense is the coal. It's not the stove—at least that's not the real mischief. It's the coal is so dear. And here you are. Look at those oil stoves. They don't burn any coal, but the cheapest fuel in the world—oil; and for two pounds ten you can get a range that will do everything you want."

"Give me the book," said Mary, "and we will talk it over in the evening, when you come home. Must you be going?"

Darnell cast an anxious glance at the clock.

"Good-bye," and they kissed each other seriously and dutifully, and Mary's eyes made Darnell think of those lonely waterpools, hidden in the shadow of the ancient woods.

So, day after day, he lived in the grey phantasmal world, akin to death, that has, somehow, with most of us, made good its claim to be called life. To Darnell the true life would have seemed madness, and when, now and again, the shadows and vague images reflected from its splendour fell across his path, he was afraid, and took refuge in what he would have called the sane "reality" of common and usual incidents and interests. His absurdity was, perhaps, the more evident, inasmuch as "reality" for him was a matter of kitchen ranges, of saving a few shillings; but in truth the folly would have been greater if it had been concerned with racing stables, steam yachts, and the spending of many thousand pounds.

But so went forth Darnell, day by day, strangely mistaking death for life, madness for sanity, and purposeless and wandering phantoms for true beings. He was sincerely of opinion that he was a City clerk, living in Shepherd's Bush—having forgotten the mysteries and the far-shining glories of the kingdom which was his by legitimate inheritance.

II

All day long a fierce and heavy heat had brooded over the City, and as Darnell neared home he saw the mist lying on all the damp lowlands, wreathed in coils about Bedford Park to the south, and mounting to the west, so that the tower of Acton Church loomed out of a grey lake. The grass in the squares and on the lawns which he overlooked as the 'bus lumbered wearily along was burnt to the colour of dust. Shepherd's Bush Green was a wretched desert, trampled brown, bordered with monotonous poplars, whose leaves hung motionless in air that was still, hot smoke. The foot passengers struggled wearily along the pavements, and the reek of the summer's end mingled with the breath of the brickfields made Darnell gasp, as if he were inhaling the poison of some foul sick-room.

He made but a slight inroad into the cold mutton that adorned the tea-table, and confessed that he felt rather "done up" by the weather and the day's work.

"I have had a trying day, too," said Mary. "Alice has been very queer and troublesome all day, and I have had to speak to her quite seriously. You know I think her Sunday evenings out have a rather unsettling influence on the girl. But what is one to do?"

"Has she got a young man?"

"Of course: a grocer's assistant from the Goldhawk Road—Wilkin's, you know. I tried them when we settled here, but they were not very satisfactory."

"What do they do with themselves all the evening? They have from five to ten, haven't they?"

"Yes; five, or sometimes half-past, when the water won't boil. Well, I believe they go for walks usually. Once or twice he has taken her to the City Temple, and the Sunday before last they walked up and down Oxford Street, and then sat in the Park. But it seems that last Sunday they went to tea with his mother at Putney. I should like to tell the old woman what I really think of her."

"Why? What happened? Was she nasty to the girl?"

"No; that's just it. Before this, she has been very unpleasant on several occasions. When the young man first took Alice to see her—that was in March—the girl came away crying; she told me so herself. Indeed, she said she never wanted to see old Mrs. Murry again; and I told Alice that, if she had not exaggerated things, I could hardly blame her for feeling like that."

"Why? What did she cry for?"

"Well, it seems that the old lady—she lives in quite a small cottage in some Putney back street—was so stately that she would hardly speak. She had borrowed a little girl from some neighbour's family, and had managed to dress her up to imitate a servant, and Alice said nothing could be sillier than to see that mite opening the door, with her black dress and her white cap and apron, and she hardly able to turn the handle, as Alice said. George (that's the young man's name) had told Alice that it was a little bit of a house; but he said the kitchen was comfortable, though very plain and old-fashioned. But, instead of going straight to the back, and sitting by a big fire on the old settle that they had brought up from the country, that child asked for their names (did you ever hear such nonsense?) and shewed them into a little poky parlour, where old Mrs. Murry was sitting 'like a duchess', by a fire-place full of coloured paper, and the room as cold as ice. And she was so grand that she would hardly speak to Alice."

"That must have been very unpleasant."

"Oh, the poor girl had a dreadful time. She began with: 'Very pleased to make your acquaintance, Miss Dill. I know so very few persons in service.' Alice imitates her mincing way of talking, but I can't do it. And then she went on to talk about her family, how they had farmed their own land for five hundred years—such stuff! George had told Alice all about it: they had had an old cottage with a good strip of garden and two fields somewhere in Essex, and that old woman talked almost as if they had been country gentry, and boasted about the Rector, Dr. Somebody, coming to see them so often, and of Squire Somebody Else always looking them up, as if they didn't visit them out of kindness. Alice told me it was as much as she could do to keep from laughing in Mrs. Murry's face, her young man having told her all about the place, and how small it was, and how the Squire had been so kind about buying it when old Murry died and George was a little boy, and his mother not able to keep things going. However, that silly old woman 'laid it on thick', as you say, and the young man got more and more uncomfortable, especially when she went on to speak about marrying in one's own class, and how unhappy she had known young men to be who had married beneath them, giving some very pointed looks at Alice as she talked. And then such an amusing thing happened: Alice had noticed George looking about him in a puzzled sort of way, as if he couldn't make out something or other, and at last he burst out and asked his mother if she had been buying up the neighbours' ornaments, as he remembered the two green cut-glass vases on the mantelpiece at Mrs. Ellis's, and the wax flowers at Miss Turvey's. He was going on, but his mother scowled at him, and upset some books, which he had to pick up; but Alice quite understood she had been borrowing things from her neighbours, just as she had borrowed the little girl, so as to look grander. And then they had tea—water bewitched, Alice calls it—and very thin bread and butter, and rubbishy foreign pastry from the Swiss shop in the High Street—all sour froth and rancid fat, Alice declares. And then Mrs. Murry began boasting again about her family, and snubbing Alice and talking at her, till the girl came away quite furious, and very unhappy, too. I don't wonder at it, do you?"

"It doesn't sound very enjoyable, certainly," said Darnell, looking dreamily at his wife. He had not been attending very carefully to the subject-matter of her story, but he loved to hear a voice that was incantation in his ears, tones that summoned before him the vision of a magic world.

"And has the young man's mother always been like this?" he said after a long pause, desiring that the music should continue.

"Always, till quite lately, till last Sunday in fact. Of course Alice spoke to George Murry at once, and said, like a sensible girl, that she didn't think it ever answered for a married couple to live with the man's mother, 'especially,' she went on, 'as I can see your mother hasn't taken much of a fancy to me.' He told her, in the usual style, it was only his mother's way, that she didn't really mean anything, and so on; but Alice kept away for a long time, and rather hinted, I think, that it might come to having to choose between her and his mother. And so affairs went on all through the spring and summer, and then, just before the August Bank Holiday, George spoke to Alice again about it, and told her how sorry the thought of any unpleasantness made him, and how he wanted his mother and her to get on with each other, and how she was only a bit old-fashioned and queer in her ways, and had spoken very nicely to him about her when there was nobody by. So the long and the short of it was that Alice said she might come with them on the Monday, when they had settled to go to Hampton Court—the girl was always talking about Hampton Court, and wanting to see it. You remember what a beautiful day it was, don't you?"

"Let me see," said Darnell dreamily. "Oh yes, of course—I sat out under the mulberry tree all day, and we had our meals there: it was quite a picnic. The caterpillars were a nuisance, but I enjoyed the day very much." His ears were charmed, ravished with the grave, supernal melody, as of antique song, rather of the first made world in which all speech was descant, and all words were sacraments of might, speaking not to the mind but to the soul. He lay back in his chair, and said—

"Well, what happened to them?"

"My dear, would you believe it; but that wretched old woman behaved worse than ever. They met as had been arranged, at Kew Bridge, and got places, with a good deal of difficulty, in one of those char-à-banc things, and Alice thought she was going to enjoy herself tremendously. Nothing of the kind. They had hardly said 'Good morning,' when old Mrs. Murry began to talk about Kew Gardens, and how beautiful it must be there, and how much more convenient it was than Hampton, and no expense at all; just the trouble of walking over the bridge. Then she went on to say, as they were waiting for the char-à-banc, that she had always heard there was nothing to see at Hampton, except a lot of nasty, grimy old pictures, and some of them not fit for any decent woman, let alone girl, to look at, and she wondered why the

Queen allowed such things to be shewn, putting all kinds of notions into girls' heads that were light enough already; and as she said that she looked at Alice so nastily—horrid old thing—that, as she told me afterwards, Alice would have slapped her face if she hadn't been an elderly woman, and George's mother. Then she talked about Kew again, saying how wonderful the hot-houses were, with palms and all sorts of wonderful things, and a lily as big as a parlour table, and the view over the river. George was very good, Alice told me. He was quite taken aback at first, as the old woman had promised faithfully to be as nice as ever she could be; but then he said, gently but firmly, 'Well, mother, we must go to Kew some other day, as Alice has set her heart on Hampton for to-day, and I want to see it myself!' All Mrs. Murry did was to snort, and look at the girl like vinegar, and just then the char-à-banc came up, and they had to scramble for their seats. Mrs. Murry grumbled to herself in an indistinct sort of voice all the way to Hampton Court. Alice couldn't very well make out what she said, but now and then she seemed to hear bits of sentences, like: *Pity to grow old, if sons grow bold;* and *Honour thy father and mother;* and *Lie on the shelf, said the housewife to the old shoe, and the wicked son to his mother;* and *I gave you milk and you give me the go-by.* Alice thought they must be proverbs (except the Commandment, of course), as George was always saying how old-fashioned his mother is; but she says there were so many of them, and all pointed at her and George, that she thinks now Mrs. Murry must have made them up as they drove along. She says it would be just like her to do it, being old-fashioned, and ill-natured too, and fuller of talk than a butcher on Saturday night. Well, they got to Hampton at last, and Alice thought the place would please her, perhaps, and they might have some enjoyment. But she did nothing but grumble, and out loud too, so that people looked at them, and a woman said, so that they could hear, 'Ah well, they'll be old themselves some day,' which made Alice very angry, for, as she said, they weren't doing anything. When they shewed her the chestnut avenue in Bushey Park, she said it was so long and straight that it made her quite dull to look at it, and she thought the deer (you know how pretty they are, really) looked thin and miserable, as if they would be all the better for a good feed of hog-wash, with plenty of meal in it. She said she knew they weren't happy by the look in their eyes, which seemed to tell her that their keepers beat them. It was the same with everything; she said she remembered market-gardens in Hammersmith and Gunnersbury that had a better show of flowers, and when they took her to the place where the water is, under the trees, she burst out with its being rather hard to tramp her off her legs to shew her a common canal, with not so much as a barge on it to liven up a bit. She went on like that the whole day, and Alice told me she was only too thankful to get home and get rid of her. Wasn't it wretched for the girl?"

"It must have been, indeed. But what happened last Sunday?"

"That's the most extraordinary thing of all. I noticed that Alice was rather queer in her manner this morning; she was a longer time washing up the breakfast things, and she answered me quite sharply when I called to her to ask when she would be ready to help me with the wash; and when I went into the kitchen to see about something, I noticed that she was going about her work in a sulky sort of way. So I asked her what was the matter, and then it all came out. I could scarcely believe my own ears when she mumbled out something about Mrs. Murry thinking she could do very much better for herself; but I asked her one question after another till I had it all out of her. It just shews one how foolish and empty-headed these girls are. I told her she was no better than a weather-cock. If you will believe me, that horrid old woman was quite another person when Alice went to see her the other night. Why, I can't think, but so she was. She told the girl how pretty she was; what a neat figure she had; how well she walked; and how she'd known many a girl not half so clever or well-looking earning her twenty-five or thirty pounds a year, and with good families. She seems to have gone into all sorts of details, and made elaborate calculations as to what she would be able to save, 'with decent folks, who don't screw, and pinch, and lock up everything in the house', and then she went off into a lot of hypocritical nonsense about how fond she was of Alice, and how she could go to her grave in peace, knowing how happy her dear George would be with such a good wife, and about her savings from good wages helping to set up a little home, ending up with 'And, if you take an old woman's advice, deary, it won't be long before you hear the marriage bells.'"

"I see," said Darnell; "and the upshot of it all is, I suppose, that the girl is thoroughly dissatisfied?"

"Yes, she is so young and silly. I talked to her, and reminded her of how nasty old Mrs. Murry had been, and told her that she might change her place and change for the worse. I think I have persuaded her to think it over quietly, at all events. Do you know what it is, Edward? I have an idea. I believe that wicked old woman is trying to get Alice to leave us, that she may tell her son how changeable she is; and I suppose she would make up some of her stupid old proverbs: 'A changeable wife, a troublesome life,' or some nonsense of the kind. Horrid old thing!"

"Well, well," said Darnell, "I hope she won't go, for your sake. It would be such a bother for you, hunting for a fresh servant."

He refilled his pipe and smoked placidly, refreshed somewhat after the emptiness and the burden of the day. The French window was wide open, and now at last there came a breath of quickening air, distilled by the night from such trees as still wore green in that arid valley. The song to which Darnell had listened in rapture, and now the breeze, which even in that dry, grim suburb still bore the word of the woodland, had summoned the dream to his eyes, and he meditated over matters that his lips could not express.

"She must, indeed, be a villainous old woman," he said at length.

"Old Mrs. Murry? Of course she is; the mischievous old thing! Trying to take the girl from a comfortable place where she is happy."

"Yes; and not to like Hampton Court! That shews how bad she must be, more than anything."

"It is beautiful, isn't it?"

"I shall never forget the first time I saw it. It was soon after I went into the City; the first year. I had my holidays in July, and I was getting such a small salary that I couldn't think of going away to the seaside, or anything like that. I remember one of the other men wanted me to come with him on a walking tour in Kent. I should have liked that, but the money wouldn't run to it. And do you know what I did? I lived in Great College Street then, and the first day I was off, I stayed in bed till past dinner-time, and lounged about in an arm-chair with a pipe all the afternoon. I had got a new kind of tobacco—one and four for the two-ounce packet—much dearer than I could afford to smoke, and I was enjoying it immensely. It was awfully hot, and when I shut the window and drew down the red blind it grew hotter; at five o'clock the

room was like an oven. But I was so pleased at not having to go into
the City, that I didn't mind anything, and now and again I read bits
from a queer old book that had belonged to my poor dad. I couldn't
make out what a lot of it meant, but it fitted in somehow, and I read
and smoked till tea-time. Then I went out for a walk, thinking I should
be better for a little fresh air before I went to bed; and I went wandering away, not much noticing where I was going, turning here and there
as the fancy took me. I must have gone miles and miles, and a good
many of them round and round, as they say they do in Australia if they
lose their way in the bush; and I am sure I couldn't have gone exactly
the same way all over again for any money. Anyhow, I was still in the
streets when the twilight came on, and the lamp-lighters were trotting
round from one lamp to another. It was a wonderful night: I wish you
had been there, my dear."

"I was quite a little girl then."

"Yes, I suppose you were. Well, it was a wonderful night. I remember, I was walking in a little street of little grey houses all alike,
with stucco copings and stucco door-posts; there were brass plates on
a lot of the doors, and one had 'Maker of Shell Boxes' on it, and I was
quite pleased, as I had often wondered where those boxes and things
that you buy at the seaside came from. A few children were playing
about in the road with some rubbish or other, and men were singing in
a small public-house at the corner, and I happened to look up, and I
noticed what a wonderful colour the sky had turned. I have seen it
since, but I don't think it has ever been quite what it was that night, a
dark blue, glowing like a violet, just as they say the sky looks in foreign
countries. I don't know why, but the sky or something made me feel
quite queer; everything seemed changed in a way I couldn't understand. I remember, I told an old gentleman I knew then—a friend of
my poor father's, he's been dead for five years, if not more—about
how I felt, and he looked at me and said something about fairyland; I
don't know what he meant, and I dare say I didn't explain myself
properly. But, do you know, for a moment or two I felt as if that little
back street was beautiful, and the noise of the children and the men in
the public-house seemed to fit in with the sky and become part of it.
You know that old saying about 'treading on air' when one is glad!
Well, I really felt like that as I walked, not exactly like air, you know,

but as if the pavement was velvet or some very soft carpet. And then—I suppose it was all my fancy—the air seemed to smell sweet, like the incense in Catholic churches, and my breath came queer and catchy, as it does when one gets very excited about anything. I felt altogether stranger than I've ever felt before or since."

Darnell stopped suddenly and looked up at his wife. She was watching him with parted lips, with eager, wondering eyes.

"I hope I'm not tiring you, dear, with all this story about nothing. You have had a worrying day with that stupid girl; hadn't you better go to bed?"

"Oh, no, please, Edward. I'm not a bit tired now. I love to hear you talk like that. Please go on."

"Well, after I had walked a bit further, that queer sort of feeling seemed to fade away. I said a bit further, and I really thought I had been walking about five minutes, but I had looked at my watch just before I got into that little street, and when I looked at it again it was eleven o'clock. I must have done about eight miles. I could scarcely believe my own eyes, and I thought my watch must have gone mad; but I found out afterwards it was perfectly right. I couldn't make it out, and I can't now; I assure you the time passed as if I walked up one side of Edna Road and down the other. But there I was, right in the open country, with a cool wind blowing on me from a wood, and the air full of soft rustling sounds, and notes of birds from the bushes, and the singing noise of a little brook that ran under the road. I was standing on the bridge when I took out my watch and struck a wax light to see the time; and it came upon me suddenly what a strange evening it had been. It was all so different, you see, to what I had been doing all my life, particularly for the year before, and it almost seemed as if I couldn't be the man who had been going into the City every day in the morning and coming back from it every evening after writing a lot of uninteresting letters. It was like being pitched all of a sudden from one world into another. Well, I found my way back somehow or other, and as I went along I made up my mind how I'd spend my holiday. I said to myself, 'I'll have a walking tour as well as Ferrars, only mine is to be a tour of London and its environs,' and I had got it all settled when I let myself into the house about four o'clock in the morning, and the sun was shining, and the street almost as still as the wood at midnight!"

"I think that was a capital idea of yours. Did you have your tour? Did you buy a map of London?"

"I had the tour all right. I didn't buy a map; that would have spoilt it, somehow; to see everything plotted out, and named, and measured. What I wanted was to feel that I was going where nobody had been before. That's nonsense, isn't it? as if there could be any such places in London, or England either, for the matter of that."

"I know what you mean; you wanted to feel as if you were going on a sort of voyage of discovery. Isn't that it?"

"Exactly, that's what I was trying to tell you. Besides, I didn't want to buy a map. I made a map."

"How do you mean? Did you make a map out of your head?"

"I'll tell you about it afterwards. But do you really want to hear about my grand tour?"

"Of course I do; it must have been delightful. I call it a most original idea."

"Well, I was quite full of it, and what you said just now about a voyage of discovery reminds me of how I felt then. When I was a boy I was awfully fond of reading of great travellers—I suppose all boys are—and of sailors who were driven out of their course and found themselves in latitudes where no ship had ever sailed before, and of people who discovered wonderful cities in strange countries; and all the second day of my holidays I was feeling just as I used to when I read these books. I didn't get up till pretty late. I was tired to death after all those miles I had walked; but when I had finished my breakfast and filled my pipe, I had a grand time of it. It was such nonsense, you know; as if there could be anything strange or wonderful in London."

"Why shouldn't there be?"

"Well, I don't know; but I have thought afterwards what a silly lad I must have been. Anyhow, I had a great day of it, planning what I would do, half making-believe—just like a kid—that I didn't know where I might find myself, or what might happen to me. And I was enormously pleased to think it was all my secret, that nobody else knew anything about it, and that, whatever I might see, I would keep to myself. I had always felt like that about the books. Of course, I loved reading them, but it seemed to me that, if I had been a discoverer, I would have kept my discoveries a secret. If I had been Columbus, and, if it could possibly have been managed, I would have found America all by myself, and never have said a word about it to anybody. Fancy! how beautiful it would be to be walking about in one's own town, and talking to people, and all the while to have the thought that one knew of a great world beyond the seas, that nobody else dreamed of. I should have loved that!

"And that is exactly what I felt about the tour I was going to make. I made up my mind that nobody should know; and so, from that day to this, nobody has heard a word of it."

"But you are going to tell me?"

"You are different. But I don't think even you will hear everything; not because I won't, but because I can't tell many of the things I saw."

"Things you saw? Then you really did see wonderful, strange things in London?"

"Well, I did and I didn't. Everything, or pretty nearly everything, that I saw is standing still, and hundreds of thousands of people have looked at the same sights—there were many places that the fellows in the office knew quite well, I found out afterwards. And then I read a book called 'London and its Surroundings'. But (I don't know how it is) neither the men at the office nor the writers of the book seem to have seen the things that I did. That's why I stopped reading the book; it seemed to take the life, the real heart, out of everything, making it as dry and stupid as the stuffed birds in a museum.

"I thought about what I was going to do all that day, and went to bed early, so as to be fresh. I knew wonderfully little about London, really; though, except for an odd week now and then, I had spent all my life in town. Of course I knew the main streets—the Strand, Regent Street, Oxford Street, and so on—and I knew the way to the school I used to go to when I was a boy, and the way into the City. But I had just kept to a few tracks, as they say the sheep do on the mountains; and that made it all the easier for me to imagine that I was going to discover a new world."

Darnell paused in the stream of his talk. He looked keenly at his wife to see if he were wearying her, but her eyes gazed at him with unabated interest—one would have almost said that they were the eyes of one who longed and half expected to be initiated into the mysteries, who knew not what great wonder was to be revealed. She sat with her back to the open window, framed in the sweet dusk of the night, as if a painter had made a curtain of heavy velvet behind her; and the work that she had been doing had fallen to the floor. She supported her head with her two hands placed on each side of her brow, and her eyes were as the wells in the wood of which Darnell dreamed in the night-time and in the day.

"And all the strange tales I had ever heard were in my head that morning," he went on, as if continuing the thoughts that had filled his mind while his lips were silent. "I had gone to bed early, as I told you, to get a thorough rest, and I had set my alarum clock to wake me at three, so that I might set out at an hour that was quite strange for the beginning of a journey. There was a hush in the world when I awoke, before the clock had rung to arouse me, and then a bird began to sing and twitter in the elm-tree that grew in the next garden, and I looked out of the window, and everything was still, and the morning air breathed in pure and sweet, as I had never known it before. My room was at the back of the house, and most of the gardens had trees in them, and beyond these trees I could see the backs of the houses of the next street rising like the wall of an old city; and as I looked the sun rose, and the great light came in at my window, and the day began.

"And I found that when I was once out of the streets just about me that I knew, some of the queer feeling that had come to me two days before came back again. It was not nearly so strong, the streets no longer smelt of incense, but still there was enough of it to shew me what a strange world I passed by. There were things that one may see again and again in many London streets: a vine or a fig tree on a wall, a lark singing in a cage, a curious shrub blossoming in a garden, an odd shape of a roof, or a balcony with an uncommon-looking trellis-work in iron. There's scarcely a street, perhaps, where you won't see one or other of such things as these; but that morning they rose to my eyes in a new light, as if I had on the magic spectacles in the fairy tale, and just like the man in the fairy tale, I went on and on in the new light. I remember going through wild land on a high place; there were pools of water shining in the sun, and great white houses in the middle of dark, rocking pines, and then on the turn of the height I came to a little lane that went aside from the main road, a lane that led to a wood, and in the lane was a little old shadowed house, with a bell turret in the roof, and a porch of trellis-work all dim and faded into the colour of the sea; and in the garden there were growing tall, white lilies, just as we saw them that day we went to look at the old pictures; they were shining like silver, and they filled the air with their sweet scent. It was from near that house I saw the valley and high places far away in the sun. So, as I say, I went 'on and on', by woods and fields, till I came to a little town on the top of a hill, a town full of old houses bowing to the ground beneath their ears, and the morning was so still that the blue smoke rose up straight into the sky from all the roof-tops, so still that I heard far down in the valley the song of a boy who was singing an old song through the streets as he went to school, and as I passed through the awakening town, beneath the old, grave houses, the church bells began to ring.

"It was soon after I had left this town behind me that I found the Strange Road. I saw it branching off from the dusty high road, and it looked so green that I turned aside into it, and soon I felt as if I had really come into a new country. I don't know whether it was one of the roads the old Romans made that my father used to tell me about; but it was covered with deep, soft turf, and the great tall hedges on each side looked as if they had not been touched for a hundred years; they had grown so broad and high and wild that they met overhead, and I could only get glimpses here and there of the country through which I was passing, as one passes in a dream. The Strange Road led me on and on, up and down hill; sometimes the rose bushes had grown so thick that I could scarcely make my way between them, and sometimes the road broadened out into a green, and in one valley a brook, spanned by an old wooden bridge, ran across it. I was tired, and I found a soft and shady place beneath an ash tree, where I must have slept for many hours, for when I woke up it was late in the afternoon. So I went on again, and at last the green road came out into the highway, and I looked up and saw another town on a high place with a great church in the middle of it, and when I went up to it there was a great organ sounding from within, and the choir was singing."

There was a rapture in Darnell's voice as he spoke, that made his story well-nigh swell into a song, and he drew a long breath as the words ended, filled with the thought of that far-off summer day, when some enchantment had informed all common things, transmuting them into a great sacrament, causing earthly works to glow with the fire and the glory of the everlasting light.

And some splendour of that light shone on the face of Mary as she sat still against the sweet gloom of the night, her dark hair making her face more radiant. She was silent for a little while, and then she spoke—

"Oh, my dear, why have you waited so long to tell me these wonderful things? I think it is beautiful. Please go on."

"I have always been afraid it was all nonsense," said Darnell. "And I don't know how to explain what I feel. I didn't think I could say so much as I have to-night."

"And did you find it the same day after day?"

"All through the tour? Yes, I think every journey was a success. Of course, I didn't go so far afield every day; I was too tired. Often I rested all day long, and went out in the evening, after the lamps were lit, and then only for a mile or two. I would roam about old, dim squares, and hear the wind from the hills whispering in the trees; and when I knew I was within call of some great glittering street, I was sunk in the silence of ways where I was almost the only passenger, and the lamps were so few and faint that they seemed to give out shadows instead of light. And I would walk slowly, to and fro, perhaps for an hour at a time, in such dark streets, and all the time I felt what I told you about its being my secret—that the shadow, and the dim lights, and the cool of the evening, and trees that were like dark low clouds were all mine, and mine alone, that I was living in a world that nobody else knew of, into which no one could enter.

"I remembered one night I had gone farther. It was somewhere in the far west, where there are orchards and gardens, and great broad lawns that slope down to trees by the river. A great red moon rose that night through mists of sunset, and thin, filmy clouds, and I wandered by a road that passed through the orchards, till I came to a little hill, with the moon shewing above it glowing like a great rose. Then I saw figures pass between me and the moon, one by one, in a long line, each bent double, with great packs upon their shoulders. One of them was singing, and then in the middle of the song I heard a horrible shrill laugh, in the thin cracked voice of a very old woman, and they disappeared into the shadow of the trees. I suppose they were people going to work, or coming from work in the gardens; but how like it was to a nightmare!

"I can't tell you about Hampton; I should never finish talking. I was there one evening, not long before they closed the gates, and there were very few people about. But the grey-red, silent, echoing courts, and the flowers falling into dreamland as the night came on, and the dark yews and shadowy-looking statues, and the far, still stretches of water beneath the avenues; and all melting into a blue mist, all being hidden from one's eyes, slowly, surely, as if veils were dropped, one by one, on a great ceremony! Oh! my dear, what could it mean? Far away, across the river, I heard a soft bell ring three times, and three times, and again three times, and I turned away, and my eyes were full of tears.

"I didn't know what it was when I came to it; I only found out afterwards that it must have been Hampton Court. One of the men in the office told me he had taken an A. B. C. girl there, and they had great fun. They got into the maze and couldn't get out again, and then they went on the river and were nearly drowned. He told me there were some spicy pictures in the galleries; his girl shrieked with laughter, so he said."

Mary quite disregarded this interlude.

"But you told me you had made a map. What was it like?"

"I'll shew it you some day, if you want to see it. I marked down all the places I had gone to, and made signs—things like queer letters—to remind me of what I had seen. Nobody but myself could understand it. I wanted to draw pictures, but I never learnt how to draw, so when I tried nothing was like what I wanted it to be. I tried to draw a picture of that town on the hill that I came to on the evening of the first day; I wanted to make a steep hill with houses on top, and in the middle, but high above them, the great church, all spires and pinnacles, and above it, in the air, a cup with rays coming from it. But it wasn't a success. I made a very strange sign for Hampton Court, and gave it a name that I made up out of my head."

The Darnells avoided one another's eyes as they sat at breakfast the next morning. The air had lightened in the night, for rain had fallen at dawn; and there was a bright blue sky, with vast white clouds rolling across it from the south-west, and a fresh and joyous wind blew in at the open window; the mists had vanished. And with the mists there seemed to have vanished also the sense of strange things that had possessed Mary and her husband the night before; and as they looked out into the clear light they could scarcely believe that the one had spoken and the other had listened a few hours before to histories very far removed from the usual current of their thoughts and of their lives. They glanced shyly at one another, and spoke of common things, of the question whether Alice would be corrupted by the insidious Mrs. Murry, or whether Mrs. Darnell would be able to persuade the girl that the old woman must be actuated by the worst motives.

"And I think, if I were you," said Darnell, as he went out, "I should step over to the stores and complain of their meat. That last piece of beef was very far from being up to the mark—full of sinew."

III

It might have been different in the evening, and Darnell had matured a plan by which he hoped to gain much. He intended to ask his wife if she would mind having only one gas, and that a good deal lowered, on the pretext that his eyes were tired with work; he thought many things might happen if the room were dimly lit, and the window opened, so that they could sit and watch the night, and listen to the rustling murmur of the tree on the lawn. But his plans were made in vain, for when he got to the garden gate his wife, in tears, came forth to meet him.

"Oh, Edward," she began, "such a dreadful thing has happened! I never liked him much, but I didn't think he would ever do such awful things."

"What do you mean? Who are you talking about? What has happened? Is it Alice's young man?"

"No, no. But come in, dear. I can see that woman opposite watching us: she's always on the look out."

"Now, what is it?" said Darnell, as they sat down to tea. "Tell me, quick! you've quite frightened me."

"I don't know how to begin, or where to start. Aunt Marian has thought that there was something queer for weeks. And then she found—oh, well, the long and short of it is that Uncle Robert has been carrying on dreadfully with some horrid girl, and aunt has found out everything!"

"Lord! you don't say so! The old rascal! Why, he must be nearer seventy than sixty!"

"He's just sixty-five; and the money he has given her—"

The first shock of surprise over, Darnell turned resolutely to his mince.

"We'll have it all out after tea," he said; "I am not going to have my meals spoilt by that old fool of a Nixon. Fill up my cup, will you, dear?"

"Excellent mince this," he went on, calmly. "A little lemon juice and a bit of ham in it? I thought there was something extra. Alice all right to-day? That's good. I expect she's getting over all that nonsense."

He went on calmly chattering in a manner that astonished Mrs. Darnell, who felt that by the fall of Uncle Robert the natural order had been inverted, and had scarcely touched food since the intelligence had arrived by the second post. She had started out to keep the appointment her aunt had made early in the morning, and had spent most of the day in a first-class waiting-room at Victoria Station, where she had heard all the story.

"Now," said Darnell, when the table had been cleared, "tell us all about it. How long has it been going on?"

"Aunt thinks now, from little things she remembers, that it must have been going on for a year at least. She says there has been a horrid kind of mystery about uncle's behaviour for a long time, and her nerves were quite shaken, as she thought he must be involved with Anarchists, or something dreadful of the sort."

"What on earth made her think that?"

"Well, you see, once or twice when she was out walking with her husband, she has been startled by whistles, which seemed to follow them everywhere. You know there are some nice country walks at Barnet, and one in particular, in the fields near Totteridge, that uncle and aunt rather made a point of going to on fine Sunday evenings. Of course, this was not the first thing she noticed, but, at the time, it made a great impression on her mind; she could hardly get a wink of sleep for weeks and weeks."

"Whistling?" said Darnell. "I don't quite understand. Why should she be frightened by whistling?"

"I'll tell you. The first time it happened was one Sunday in last May. Aunt had a fancy they were being followed a Sunday or two before, but she didn't see or hear anything, except a sort of crackling noise in the hedge. But this particular Sunday they had hardly got through the stile into the fields, when she heard a peculiar kind of low whistle. She took no notice, thinking it was no concern of hers or her husband's, but as they went on she heard it again, and then again, and it followed them the whole walk, and it made her so uncomfortable, because she didn't know where it was coming from or who was doing it, or why. Then, just as they got out of the fields into the lane, uncle said he felt quite faint, and he thought he would try a little brandy at the 'Turpin's Head', a small public-house there is there. And she looked at him and saw his face was quite purple—more like apoplexy, as she says, than fainting fits, which make people look a sort of greenish-white. But she said nothing, and thought perhaps uncle had a peculiar way of fainting of his own, as he always was a man to have his own way of doing everything. So she just waited in the road, and he went ahead and slipped into the public, and aunt says she thought she saw a little figure rise out of the dusk and slip in after him, but she couldn't be sure. And when uncle came out he looked red instead of purple, and said he felt much better; and so they went home quietly together, and nothing more was said. You see, uncle had said nothing about the whistling, and aunt had been so frightened that she didn't dare speak, for fear they might be both shot.

"She wasn't thinking anything more about it, when two Sundays afterwards the very same thing happened just as it had before. This time aunt plucked up a spirit, and asked uncle what it could be. And what do you think he said? 'Birds, my dear, birds.' Of course aunt said to him that no bird that ever flew with wings made a noise like that: sly, and low, with pauses in between; and then he said that many rare sorts of birds lived in North Middlesex and Hertfordshire. 'Nonsense, Robert,' said aunt, 'how can you talk so, considering it has followed us all the way, for a mile or more?' And then uncle told her that some birds were so attached to man that they would follow one about for miles sometimes; he said he had just been reading about a bird like that in a book of travels. And do you know that when they got home he actually shewed her a piece in the *Hertfordshire Naturalist* which they took in to oblige a friend of theirs, all about rare birds found in the neighbourhood, all the most outlandish names, aunt says, that she had never heard or thought of, and uncle had the impudence to say that it must have been a Purple Sandpiper, which, the paper said, had 'a low shrill note, constantly repeated'. And then he took down a book of Siberian Travels from the bookcase and shewed her a page which told how a man was followed by a bird all day long through a forest. And that's what Aunt Marian says vexes her more than anything almost; to think that he should be so artful and ready with those books, twisting them to his own wicked ends. But, at the time, when she was out walking, she simply couldn't make out what he meant by talking about birds in that random, silly sort of way, so unlike him, and they went on, that horrible whistling following them, she looking straight ahead and walking fast, really feeling more huffy and put out than frightened. And when they got to the next stile, she got over and turned round, and 'lo and behold,' as she says, there was no Uncle Robert to be seen! She felt herself go quite white with alarm, thinking of that whistle, and making sure he'd been spirited away or snatched in some way or another, and she had just screamed out 'Robert' like a mad woman, when he came quite slowly round the corner, as cool as a cucumber, holding something in his hand. He said there were some flowers he could never pass, and when aunt saw that he had got a dandelion torn up by the roots, she felt as if her head were going round."

Mary's story was suddenly interrupted. For ten minutes Darnell had been writhing in his chair, suffering tortures in his anxiety to avoid wounding his wife's feelings, but the episode of the dandelion was too much for him, and he burst into a long, wild shriek of laughter, aggravated by suppression into the semblance of a Red Indian's war-whoop. Alice, who was washing-up in the scullery, dropped some three shillings' worth of china, and the neighbours ran out into their gardens wondering if it were murder. Mary gazed reproachfully at her husband.

"How can you be so unfeeling, Edward?" she said, at length, when Darnell had passed into the feebleness of exhaustion. "If you had seen the tears rolling down poor Aunt Marian's cheeks as she told me, I don't think you would have laughed. I didn't think you were so hard-hearted."

"My dear Mary," said Darnell, faintly, through sobs and catching of the breath, "I am awfully sorry. I know it's very sad, really, and I'm not unfeeling; but it is such an odd tale, now, isn't it? The Sandpiper, you know, and then the dandelion!"

His face twitched and he ground his teeth together. Mary looked gravely at him for a moment, and then she put her hands to her face, and Darnell could see that she also shook with merriment.

"I am as bad as you," she said, at last. "I never thought of it in that way. I'm glad I didn't, or I should have laughed in Aunt Marian's face, and I wouldn't have done that for the world. Poor old thing; she cried as if her heart would break. I met her at Victoria, as she asked me, and we had some soup at a confectioner's. I could scarcely touch it; her tears kept dropping into the plate all the time; and then we went to the waiting-room at the station, and she cried there terribly."

"Well," said Darnell, "what happened next? I won't laugh any more."

"No, we mustn't; it's much too horrible for a joke. Well, of course aunt went home and wondered and wondered what could be the matter, and tried to think it out, but, as she says, she could make nothing of it. She began to be afraid that uncle's brain was giving way through overwork, as he had stopped in the City (as he said) up to all hours lately, and he had to go Yorkshire (wicked old story-teller!), about some very tiresome business connected with his leases. But then she reflected that however queer he might be getting, even his queerness couldn't make whistles in the air, though, as she said, he was always a wonderful man. So she had to give that up; and then she wondered if there were anything the matter with her, as she had read about people who heard noises when there was really nothing at all. But that wouldn't do either, because though it might account for the whistling, it wouldn't account for the dandelion or the Sandpiper, or for fainting fits that turned purple, or any of uncle's queerness. So aunt said she could think of nothing but to read the Bible every day from the beginning, and by the time she got into Chronicles she felt rather better, especially as nothing had happened for three or four Sundays. She noticed uncle seemed absent-minded, and not as nice to her as he might be, but she put that down to too much work, as he never came home before the last train, and had a hansom twice all the way, getting there between three and four in the morning. Still, she felt it was no good bothering her head over what couldn't be made out or explained anyway, and she was just settling down, when one Sunday evening it began all over again, and worse things happened. The whistling followed them just as it did before, and poor aunt set her teeth and said nothing to uncle, as she knew he would only tell her stories, and they were walking on, not saying a word, when something made her look back, and there was a horrible boy with red hair, peeping through the hedge just behind, and grinning. She said it was a dreadful face, with something unnatural about it, as if it had been a dwarf, and before she had time to have a good look, it popped back like lightning, and aunt all but fainted away."

"A red-headed *boy?*" said Darnell. "I thought— What an extraordinary story this is. I've never heard of anything so queer. Who was the boy?"

"You will know in good time," said Mrs. Darnell. "It *is* very strange, isn't it?"

"Strange!" Darnell ruminated for a while.

"I know what I think, Mary," he said at length. "I don't believe a word of it. I believe your aunt is going mad, or has gone mad, and that she has delusions. The whole thing sounds to me like the invention of a lunatic."

"You are quite wrong. Every word is true, and if you will let me go on, you will understand how it all happened."

"Very good, go ahead."

"Let me see, where was I? Oh, I know, aunt saw the boy grinning in the hedge. Yes, well, she was dreadfully frightened for a minute or two; there was something so queer about the face, but then she plucked up a spirit and said to herself, 'After all, better a boy with red hair than a big man with a gun,' and she made up her mind to watch Uncle Robert closely, as she could see by his look he knew all about it; he seemed as if he were thinking hard and puzzling over something, as if he didn't know what to do next, and his mouth kept opening and shutting, like a fish's. So she kept her face straight, and didn't say a word, and when he said something to her about the fine sunset, she took no notice. 'Don't you hear what I say, Marian?' he said, speaking quite crossly, and bellowing as if it were to somebody in the next field. So aunt said she was very sorry, but her cold made her so deaf, she couldn't hear much. She noticed uncle looked quite pleased, and relieved too, and she knew he thought she hadn't heard the whistling.

Suddenly uncle pretended to see a beautiful spray of honeysuckle high up in the hedge, and he said he must get it for aunt, only she must go on ahead, as it made him nervous to be watched. She said she would, but she just stepped aside behind a bush where there was a sort of cover in the hedge, and found she could see him quite well, though she scratched her face terribly with poking it into a rose bush. And in a minute or two out came the boy from behind the hedge, and she saw uncle and him talking, and she knew it was the same boy, as it wasn't dark enough to hide his flaming red head. And uncle put out his hand as if to catch him, but he just darted into the bushes and vanished. Aunt never said a word at the time, but that night when they got home she charged uncle with what she'd seen and asked him what it all meant. He was quite taken aback at first, and stammered and stuttered and said a spy wasn't his notion of a good wife, but at last he made her swear secrecy, and told her that he was a very high Freemason, and that the boy was an emissary of the order, who brought him messages of the greatest importance. But aunt didn't believe a word of it, as an uncle of hers was a mason, and he never behaved like that. It was then she began to be afraid that it was really Anarchists, or something of the kind, and every time the bell rang she thought that uncle had been found out, and the police had come for him."

"What nonsense! As if a man with house property would be an Anarchist."

"Well, she could see there must be some horrible secret, and she didn't know what else to think. And then she began to have the things through the post."

"Things through the post! What do you mean by that?"

"All sorts of things; bits of broken bottle-glass, packed carefully as if it were jewellery; parcels that unrolled and unrolled worse than Chinese boxes, and then had 'cat' in large letters when you came to the middle; old artificial teeth, a cake of red paint, and at last cockroaches."

"Cockroaches by post! Stuff and nonsense; your aunt's mad."

"Edward, she shewed me the box; it was made to hold cigarettes, and there were three dead cockroaches inside. And when she found a box of exactly the same kind, half-full of cigarettes, in uncle's greatcoat pocket, then her head began to turn again."

Darnell groaned, and stirred uneasily in his chair, feeling that the tale of Aunt Marian's domestic troubles was putting on the semblance of an evil dream.

"Anything else?" he asked.

"My dear, I haven't repeated half the things poor aunt told me this afternoon. There was the night she thought she saw a ghost in the shrubbery. She was anxious about some chickens that were just due to hatch out, so she went out after dark with some egg and bread-crumbs, in case they might be out. And just before her she saw a figure gliding by the rhododendrons. It looked like a short, slim man dressed as they used to be hundreds of years ago; she saw the sword by his side, and the feather in his cap. She thought she should have died, she said, and though it was gone in a minute, and she tried to make out it was all her fancy, she fainted when she got into the house. Uncle was at home that night, and when she came to and told him he ran out, and stayed out for half-an-hour or more, and then came in and said he could find nothing; and the next minute aunt heard that low whistle just outside the window, and uncle ran out again."

"My dear Mary, do let us come to the point. What on earth does it all lead to?"

"Haven't you guessed? Why, of course it was that girl all the time."

"Girl? I thought you said it was a boy with a red head?"

"Don't you see? She's an actress, and she dressed up. She won't leave uncle alone. It wasn't enough that he was with her nearly every evening in the week, but she must be after him on Sundays too. Aunt found a letter the horrid thing had written, and so it has all come out. Enid Vivian she calls herself, though I don't suppose she has any right to one name or the other. And the question is, what is to be done?"

"Let us talk of that again. I'll have a pipe, and then we'll go to bed."

They were almost asleep when Mary said suddenly—

"Doesn't it seem queer, Edward? Last night you were telling me such beautiful things, and to-night I have been talking about that disgraceful old man and his goings on."

"I don't know," answered Darnell, dreamily. "On the walls of that great church upon the hill I saw all kinds of strange grinning monsters, carved in stone."

The misdemeanours of Mr. Robert Nixon brought in their train consequences strange beyond imagination. It was not that they continued to develop on the somewhat fantastic lines of these first adventures which Mrs. Darnell had related; indeed, when "Aunt Marian" came over to Shepherd's Bush, one Sunday afternoon, Darnell wondered how he had had the heart to laugh at the misfortunes of a broken-hearted woman.

He had never seen his wife's aunt before, and he was strangely surprised when Alice shewed her into the garden where they were sitting on the warm and misty Sunday in September. To him, save during these latter days, she had always been associated with ideas of splendour and success: his wife had always mentioned the Nixons with a tinge of reverence; he had heard, many times, the epic of Mr. Nixon's struggles and of his slow but triumphant rise. Mary had told the story as she had received it from her parents, beginning with the flight to London from some small, dull, and unprosperous town in the flattest of the Midlands, long ago, when a young man from the country had great chances of fortune. Robert Nixon's father had been a grocer in the High Street, and in after days the successful coal merchant and builder loved to tell of that dull provincial life, and while he glorified his own victories, he gave his hearers to understand that he came of a race which had also known how to achieve. That had been long ago, he would explain: in the days when that rare citizen who desired to go to London or to York was forced to rise in the dead of night, and make his way, somehow or other, by ten miles of quagmirish, wandering lanes to the Great North Road, there to meet the "Lightning" coach, a vehicle which stood to all the countryside as the visible and tangible embodiment of tremendous speed—"and indeed," as Nixon would add, "it was always up to time, which is more than can be said of the Dunham Branch Line nowadays!" It was in this ancient Dunham that the Nixons had waged successful trade for perhaps a hundred years, in a shop with bulging bay windows looking on the market-place. There was no competition, and the townsfolk, and well-to-do farmers, the clergy and the country families, looked upon the house of Nixon as an institution fixed as the town hall (which stood on Roman pillars) and the parish church. But the change came: the railway crept nearer and nearer, the farmers and the country gentry became less well-to-do; the tanning, which was the local industry, suffered from a great business which had been established in a larger town, some twenty miles away, and the profits of the Nixons grew less and less. Hence the hegira of Robert, and he would dilate on the poorness of his beginnings, how he saved, by little and little, from his sorry wage of City clerk, and how he and a fellow clerk, "who had come into a hundred pounds", saw an opening in the coal trade—and filled it. It was at this stage of Robert's fortunes, still far from magnificent, that Miss Marian Reynolds had encountered him, she being on a visit to friends in Gunnersbury. Afterwards, victory followed victory; Nixon's wharf became a landmark to bargemen; his power stretched abroad, his dusky fleets went outwards to the sea, and inward by all the far reaches of canals. Lime, cement, and bricks were added to his merchandise, and at last he hit upon the great stroke—that extensive taking up of land in the north of London. Nixon himself ascribed this *coup* to native sagacity, and the possession of capital; and there were also obscure rumours to the effect that some one or other had been "done" in the course of the transaction. However that might be, the Nixons grew wealthy to excess, and Mary had often told her husband of the state in which they dwelt, of their liveried servants, of the glories of their drawing-room, of their broad lawn, shadowed by a splendid and ancient cedar. And so Darnell had somehow been led into conceiving the lady of this demesne as a personage of no small pomp. He saw her, tall, of dignified port and presence, inclining, it might be, to some measure of obesity, such a measure as was not unbefitting in an elderly lady of position, who lived well and lived at ease. He even imagined a slight ruddiness of complexion, which went very well with hair that was beginning to turn grey, and when he heard the door-bell ring, as he sat under the mulberry on the Sunday afternoon, he bent forward to catch sight of this stately figure, clad, of course, in the richest, blackest silk, girt about with heavy chains of gold.

He started with amazement when he saw the strange presence that followed the servant into the garden. Mrs. Nixon was a little, thin old woman, who bent as she feebly trotted after Alice; her eyes were on the ground, and she did not lift them when the Darnells rose to greet her. She glanced to the right, uneasily, as she shook hands with Darnell, to the left when Mary kissed her, and when she was placed on the garden seat with a cushion at her back, she looked away at the back of the houses in the next street. She was dressed in black, it was true, but even Darnell could see that her gown was old and shabby, that the fur trimming of her cape and the fur boa which was twisted about her neck were dingy and disconsolate, and had all the melancholy air which fur wears when it is seen in a second-hand clothes-shop in a back street. And her gloves—they were black kid, wrinkled with much wear, faded to a bluish hue at the finger-tips, which shewed signs of painful mending. Her hair, plastered over her forehead, looked dull and colourless, though some greasy matter had evidently been used with a view of producing a becoming gloss, and on it perched an antique bonnet, adorned with black pendants that rattled paralytically one against the other.

And there was nothing in Mrs. Nixon's face to correspond with the imaginary picture that Darnell had made of her. She was sallow, wrinkled, pinched; her nose ran to a sharp point, and her red-rimmed eyes were a queer water-grey, that seemed to shrink alike from the light and from encounter with the eyes of others. As she sat beside his wife on the green garden-seat, Darnell, who occupied a wicker-chair brought out from the drawing-room, could not help feeling that this shadowy and evasive figure, muttering replies to Mary's polite questions, was almost impossibly remote from his conceptions of the rich and powerful aunt, who could give away a hundred pounds as a mere birthday gift. She would say little at first; yes, she was feeling rather tired, it had been so hot all the way, and she had been afraid to put on lighter things as one never knew at this time of year what it might be like in the evenings; there were apt to be cold mists when the sun went down, and she didn't care to risk bronchitis.

"I thought I should never get here," she went on, raising her voice to an odd querulous pipe. "I'd no notion it was such an out-of-the-way place, it's so many years since I was in this neighbourhood."

She wiped her eyes, no doubt thinking of the early days at Turnham Green, when she married Nixon; and when the pocket-handkerchief had done its office she replaced it in a shabby black bag which she clutched rather than carried. Darnell noticed, as he watched her, that the bag seemed full, almost to bursting, and he speculated idly as to the nature of its contents: correspondence, perhaps, he thought, further proofs of Uncle Robert's treacherous and wicked dealings. He grew quite uncomfortable, as he sat and saw her glancing all the while furtively away from his wife and himself, and presently he got up and strolled away to the other end of the garden, where he lit his pipe and walked to and fro on the gravel walk, still astounded at the gulf between the real and the imagined woman.

Presently he heard a hissing whisper, and he saw Mrs. Nixon's head inclining to his wife's. Mary rose and came towards him.

"Would you mind sitting in the drawing-room, Edward?" she murmured. "Aunt says she can't bring herself to discuss such a delicate matter before you. I dare say it's quite natural."

"Very well, but I don't think I'll go into the drawing-room. I feel as if a walk would do me good. You mustn't be frightened if I am a little late," he said; "if I don't get back before your aunt goes, say good-bye to her for me."

He strolled into the main road, where the trams were humming to and fro. He was still confused and perplexed, and he tried to account for a certain relief he felt in removing himself from the presence of Mrs. Nixon. He told himself that her grief at her husband's ruffianly conduct was worthy of all pitiful respect, but at the same time, to his shame, he had felt a certain physical aversion from her as she sat in his garden in her dingy black, dabbing her red-rimmed eyes with a damp pocket-handkerchief. He had been to the Zoo when he was a lad, and he still remembered how he had shrunk with horror at the sight of certain reptiles slowly crawling over one another in their slimy pond. But he was enraged at the similarity between the two sensations, and he walked briskly on that level and monotonous road, looking about him at the unhandsome spectacle of suburban London keeping Sunday.

There was something in the tinge of antiquity which still exists in Acton that soothed his mind and drew it away from those unpleasant contemplations, and when at last he had penetrated rampart after rampart of brick, and heard no more the harsh shrieks and laughter of the people who were enjoying themselves, he found a way into a little sheltered field, and sat down in peace beneath a tree, whence he could look out on a pleasant valley. The sun sank down beneath the hills, the clouds changed into the likeness of blossoming rose-gardens; and he still sat there in the gathering darkness till a cool breeze blew upon him, and he rose with a sigh, and turned back to the brick ramparts and the glimmering streets, and the noisy idlers sauntering to and fro in the procession of their dismal festival. But he was murmuring to himself some words that seemed a magic song, and it was with uplifted heart that he let himself into his house.

Mrs. Nixon had gone an hour and a half before his return, Mary told him. Darnell sighed with relief, and he and his wife strolled out into the garden and sat down side by side.

They kept silence for a time, and at last Mary spoke, not without a nervous tremor in her voice.

"I must tell you, Edward," she began, "that aunt has made a proposal which you ought to hear. I think we should consider it."

"A proposal? But how about the whole affair? Is it still going on?"

"Oh, yes! She told me all about it. Uncle is quite unrepentant. It seems he has taken a flat somewhere in town for that woman, and furnished it in the most costly manner. He simply laughs at aunt's reproaches, and says he means to have some fun at last. You saw how broken she was?"

"Yes; very sad. But won't he give her any money? Wasn't she very badly dressed for a woman in her position?"

"Aunt has no end of beautiful things, but I fancy she likes to hoard them; she has a horror of spoiling her dresses. It isn't for want of money, I assure you, as uncle settled a very large sum on her two years ago, when he was everything that could be desired as a husband. And that brings me to what I want to say. Aunt would like to live with us. She would pay very liberally. What do you say?"

"Would like to live with us?" exclaimed Darnell, and his pipe dropped from his hand on to the grass. He was stupefied by the thought of Aunt Marian as a boarder, and sat staring vacantly before him, wondering what new monster the night would next produce.

"I knew you wouldn't much like the idea," his wife went on. "But I do think, dearest, that we ought not to refuse without very serious consideration. I am afraid you did not take to poor aunt very much."

Darnell shook his head dumbly.

"I thought you didn't; she was so upset, poor thing, and you didn't see her at her best. She is really so good. But listen to me, dear. Do you think we have the right to refuse her offer? I told you she has money of her own, and I am sure she would be dreadfully offended if we said we wouldn't have her. And what would become of me if anything happened to you? You know we have very little saved."

Darnell groaned.

"It seems to me," he said, "that it would spoil everything. We are so happy, Mary dear, by ourselves. Of course I am extremely sorry for your aunt. I think she is very much to be pitied. But when it comes to having her always here——"

"I know, dear. Don't think I am looking forward to the prospect; you know I don't want anybody but you. Still, we ought to think of the future, and besides we shall be able to live so very much better. I shall be able to give you all sorts of nice things that I know you ought to have after all that hard work in the City. Our income would be doubled."

"Do you mean she would pay us £150 a year?"

"Certainly. And she would pay for the spare room being furnished, and any extra she might want. She told me, specially, that if a friend or two came now and again to see her, she would gladly bear the cost of a fire in the drawing-room, and give something towards the gas bill, with a few shillings for the girl for any additional trouble. We should certainly be more than twice as well off as we are now. You see, Edward, dear, it's not the sort of offer we are likely to have again. Besides, we must think of the future, as I said. Do you know aunt took a great fancy to you?"

He shuddered and said nothing, and his wife went on with her argument.

"And, you see, it isn't as if we should see so very much of her. She will have her breakfast in bed, and she told me she would often go up to her room in the evening directly after dinner. I thought that very nice and considerate. She quite understands that we shouldn't like to have a third person always with us. Don't you think, Edward, that, considering everything, we ought to say we will have her?"

"Oh, I suppose so," he groaned. "As you say, it's a very good offer, financially, and I am afraid it would be very imprudent to refuse. But I don't like the notion, I confess."

"I am so glad you agree with me, dear. Depend upon it, it won't be half so bad as you think. And putting our own advantage on one side, we shall really be doing poor aunt a very great kindness. Poor old dear, she cried bitterly after you were gone; she said she had made up her mind not to stay any longer in Uncle Robert's house, and she didn't know where to go, or what would become of her, if we refused to take her in. She quite broke down."

"Well, well; we will try it for a year, anyhow. It may be as you say; we shan't find it quite so bad as it seems now. Shall we go in?"

He stooped for his pipe, which lay as it had fallen, on the grass. He could not find it, and lit a wax match which shewed him the pipe, and close beside it, under the seat, something that looked like a page torn from a book. He wondered what it could be, and picked it up.

The gas was lit in the drawing-room, and Mrs. Darnell, who was arranging some notepaper, wished to write at once to Mrs. Nixon, cordially accepting her proposal, when she was startled by an exclamation from her husband.

"What is the matter?" she said, startled by the tone of his voice. "You haven't hurt yourself?"

"Look at this," he, replied, handing her a small leaflet; "I found it under the garden seat just now."

Mary glanced with bewilderment at her husband and read as follows:—

THE NEW AND CHOSEN SEED OF ABRAHAM

PROPHECIES TO BE FULFILLED IN THE PRESENT YEAR

1. The Sailing of a Fleet of One Hundred and Forty and Four Vessels for Tarshish and the Isles.

2. Destruction of the Power of the Dog, including all the instruments of anti-Abrahamic legislation.

3. Return of the Fleet from Tarshish, bearing with it the gold of Arabia, destined to be the Foundation of the New City of Abraham.

4. The Search for the Bride, and the bestowing of the Seals on the Seventy and Seven.

5. The Countenance of FATHER to become luminous, but with a greater glory than the face of Moses.

6. The Pope of Rome to be stoned with stones in the valley called Berek-Zittor.

7. FATHER to be acknowledged by Three Great Rulers. Two Great Rulers will deny FATHER, and will immediately perish in the Effluvia of FATHER'S Indignation.

8. Binding of the Beast with the Horn, and all judges cast down.

9. Finding of the Bride in the Land of Egypt, which has been revealed to FATHER as now existing in the western part of London.

10. Bestowal of the New Tongue on the Seventy and Seven, and on the One Hundred and Forty and Four. FATHER proceeds to the Bridal Chamber.

11. Destruction of London and rebuilding of the City called No, which is the New City of Abraham.

12. FATHER united to the Bride, and the present Earth removed to the Sun for the space of half an hour.

Mrs. Darnell's brow cleared as she read matter which seemed to her harmless if incoherent. From her husband's voice she had been led to fear something more tangibly unpleasant than a vague catena of prophecies.

"Well," she said, "what about it?"

"What about it? Don't you see that your aunt dropped it, and that she must be a raging lunatic?"

"Oh, Edward! don't say that. In the first place, how do you know that aunt dropped it at all? It might easily have blown over from any of the other gardens. And, if it were hers, I don't think you should call her a lunatic. I don't believe, myself, that there are any real prophets now; but there are many good people who think quite differently. I knew an old lady once who, I am sure, was very good, and she took in a paper every week that was full of prophecies and things very like this. Nobody called her mad, and I have heard father say that she had one of the sharpest heads for business he had ever come across."

"Very good; have it as you like. But I believe we shall both be sorry."

They sat in silence for some time. Alice came in after her "evening out", and they sat on, till Mrs. Darnell said she was tired and wanted to go to bed.

Her husband kissed her. "I don't think I will come up just yet," he said; "you go to sleep, dearest. I want to think things over. No, no; I am not going to change my mind: your aunt shall come, as I said. But there are one or two things I should like to get settled in my mind."

He meditated for a long while, pacing up and down the room. Light after light was extinguished in Edna Road, and the people of the suburb slept all around him, but still the gas was alight in Darnell's drawing-room, and he walked softly up and down the floor. He was thinking that about the life of Mary and himself, which had been so quiet, there seemed to be gathering on all sides grotesque and fantastic shapes, omens of confusion and disorder, threats of madness; a strange company from another world. It was as if into the quiet, sleeping streets of some little ancient town among the hills there had come from afar the sound of drum and pipe, snatches of wild song, and there had burst into the market-place the mad company of the players, strangely bedizened, dancing a furious measure to their hurrying music, drawing forth the citizens from their sheltered homes and peaceful lives, and alluring them to mingle in the significant figures of their dance.

Yet afar and near (for it was hidden in his heart) he beheld the glimmer of a sure and constant star. Beneath, darkness came on, and mists and shadows closed about the town. The red, flickering flame of torches was kindled in the midst of it. The song grew louder, with more insistent, magical tones, surging and falling in unearthly modulations, the very speech of incantation; and the drum beat madly, and the pipe shrilled to a scream, summoning all to issue forth, to leave their peaceful hearths; for a strange rite was preconised in their midst. The streets that were wont to be so still, so hushed with the cool and tranquil veils of darkness, asleep beneath the patronage of the evening star, now danced with glimmering lanterns, resounded with the cries of those who hurried forth, drawn as by a magistral spell; and the songs swelled and triumphed, the reverberant beating of the drum grew louder, and in the midst of the awakened town the players, fantastically arrayed, performed their interlude under the red blaze of torches. He knew not whether they were players, men that would vanish suddenly as they came, disappearing by the track that climbed the hill; or whether they were indeed magicians, workers of great and efficacious spells, who knew the secret word by which the earth may be transformed into the hall of Gehenna, so that they that gazed and listened, as at a passing spectacle, should be entrapped by the sound and the sight presented to them, should be drawn into the elaborated figures of that mystic dance, and so should be whirled away into those unending mazes on the wild hills that were abhorred, there to wander for evermore.

But Darnell was not afraid, because of the Daystar that had risen in his heart. It had dwelt there all his life, and had slowly shone forth with clearer and clearer light, and he began to see that though his earthly steps might be in the ways of the ancient town that was beset by the Enchanters, and resounded with their songs and their processions, yet he dwelt also in that serene and secure world of brightness, and from a great and unutterable height looked on the confusion of the mortal pageant, beholding mysteries in which he was no true actor, hearing magic songs that could by no means draw him down from the battlements of the high and holy city.

His heart was filled with a great joy and a great peace as he lay down beside his wife and fell asleep, and in the morning, when he woke up, he was glad.

IV

In a haze as of a dream Darnell's thoughts seemed to move through the opening days of the next week. Perhaps nature had not intended that he should be practical or much given to that which is usually called "sound common sense", but his training had made him desirous of good, plain qualities of the mind, and he uneasily strove to account to himself for his strange mood of the Sunday night, as he had often endeavoured to interpret the fancies of his boyhood and early manhood. At first he was annoyed by his want of success; the morning paper, which he always secured as the 'bus delayed at Uxbridge Road Station, fell from his hands unread, while he vainly reasoned, assuring himself that the threatened incursion of a whimsical old woman, though tiresome enough, was no rational excuse for those curious hours of meditation in which his thoughts seemed to have dressed themselves in unfamiliar, fantastic habits, and to parley with him in a strange speech, and yet a speech that he had understood.

With such arguments he perplexed his mind on the long, accustomed ride up the steep ascent of Holland Park, past the incongruous hustle of Notting Hill Gate, where in one direction a road shews the way to the snug, somewhat faded bowers and retreats of Bayswater, and in another one sees the portal of the murky region of the slums. The customary companions of his morning's journey were in the seats about him; he heard the hum of their talk, as they disputed concerning politics, and the man next to him, who came from Acton, asked him what he thought of the Government now. There was a discussion, and a loud and excited one, just in front, as to whether rhubarb was a fruit or vegetable, and in his ear he heard Redman, who was a near neighbour, praising the economy of "the wife".

"I don't know how she does it. Look here; what do you think we had yesterday? Breakfast: fish-cakes, beautifully fried—rich, you know, lots of herbs, it's a receipt of her aunt's; you should just taste 'em. Coffee, bread, butter, marmalade, and, of course, all the usual etceteras. Dinner: roast beef, Yorkshire, potatoes, greens, and horse-radish sauce, plum tart, cheese. And where will you get a better dinner than that? Well, I call it wonderful, I really do."

But in spite of these distractions he fell into a dream as the 'bus rolled and tossed on its way Citywards, and still he strove to solve the enigma of his vigil of the night before, and as the shapes of trees and green lawns and houses passed before his eyes, and as he saw the procession moving on the pavement, and while the murmur of the streets sounded in his ears, all was to him strange and unaccustomed, as if he moved through the avenues of some city in a foreign land. It was, perhaps, on these mornings, as he rode to his mechanical work, that vague and floating fancies that must have long haunted his brain began to shape themselves, and to put on the form of definite conclusions, from which he could no longer escape, even if he had wished it. Darnell had received what is called a sound commercial education, and would therefore have found very great difficulty in putting into articulate speech any thought that was worth thinking; but he grew certain on these mornings that the "common sense" which he had always heard exalted as man's supremest faculty was, in all probability, the smallest and least-considered item in the equipment of an ant of average intelligence. And with this, as an almost necessary corollary, came a firm belief that the whole fabric of life in which he moved was sunken, past all thinking, in the grossest absurdity; that he and all his friends and acquaintances and fellow-workers were interested in matters in which men were never meant to be interested, were pursuing aims which they were never meant to pursue, were, indeed, much like fair stones of an altar serving as a pigsty wall. Life, it seemed to him, was a great search for—he knew not what; and in the process of the ages one by one the true marks upon the ways had been shattered, or buried, or the meaning of the words had been slowly forgotten; one by one the signs had been turned awry, the true entrances had been thickly overgrown, the very way itself had been diverted from the heights to the depths, till at last the race of pilgrims had become hereditary stone-breakers and ditch-scourers on a track that led to destruction—if it led anywhere at all. Darnell's heart thrilled with a strange and trembling joy, with a sense that was all new, when it came to his mind that this great loss might not be a hopeless one, that perhaps the difficulties were by no means insuperable. It might be, he considered, that the stone-breaker had merely to throw down his hammer and set out, and the way would be plain before him; and a single step would free the delver in rubbish from the foul slime of the ditch.

It was, of course, with difficulty and slowly that these things became clear to him. He was an English City clerk, "flourishing" towards the end of the nineteenth century, and the rubbish heap that had been accumulating for some centuries could not be cleared away in an instant. Again and again the spirit of nonsense that had been implanted in him as in his fellows assured him that the true world was the visible and tangible world, the world in which good and faithful letter-copying was exchangeable for a certain quantum of bread, beef, and house-room, and that the man who copied letters well, did not beat his wife, nor lose money foolishly, was a good man, fulfilling the end for which he had been made. But in spite of these arguments, in spite of their acceptance by all who were about him, he had the grace to perceive the utter falsity and absurdity of the whole position. He was fortunate in his entire ignorance of sixpenny "science", but if the whole library had been projected into his brain it would not have moved him to "deny in the darkness that which he had known in the light". Darnell knew by experience that man is made a mystery for mysteries and visions, for the realisation in his consciousness of ineffable bliss, for a great joy that transmutes the whole world, for a joy that surpasses all joys and overcomes all sorrows. He knew this certainly, though he knew it dimly; and he was apart from other men, preparing himself for a great experiment.

With such thoughts as these for his secret and concealed treasure, he was able to bear the threatened invasion of Mrs. Nixon with something approaching indifference. He knew, indeed, that her presence between his wife and himself would be unwelcome to him, and he was not without grave doubts as to the woman's sanity; but after all, what did it matter? Besides, already a faint glimmering light had risen within him that shewed the profit of self-negation, and in this matter he had preferred his wife's will to his own. *Et non sua poma;* to his astonishment he found a delight in denying himself his own wish, a process that he had always regarded as thoroughly detestable. This was a state of things which he could not in the least understand; but, again, though a member of a most hopeless class, living in the most hopeless surroundings that the world has ever seen, though he knew as much of the *askesis* as of Chinese metaphysics; again, he had the grace not to deny the light that had begun to glimmer in his soul.

And he found a present reward in the eyes of Mary, when she welcomed him home after his foolish labours in the cool of the evening. They sat together, hand in hand, under the mulberry tree, at the coming of the dusk, and as the ugly walls about them became obscure and vanished into the formless world of shadows, they seemed to be freed from the bondage of Shepherd's Bush, freed to wander in that undisfigured, undefiled world that lies beyond the walls. Of this region Mary knew little or nothing by experience, since her relations had always been of one mind with the modern world, which has for the true country an instinctive and most significant horror and dread. Mr. Reynolds had also shared in another odd superstition of these later days—that it is necessary to leave London at least once a year; consequently Mary had some knowledge of various seaside resorts on the south and east coasts, where Londoners gather in hordes, turn the sands into one vast, bad music-hall, and derive, as they say, enormous benefit from the change. But experiences such as these give but little knowledge of the country in its true and occult sense; and yet Mary, as she sat in the dusk beneath the whispering tree, knew something of the secret of the wood, of the valley shut in by high hills, where the sound of pouring water always echoes from the clear brook. And to Darnell these were nights of great dreams; for it was the hour of the work, the time of transmutation, and he who could not understand the miracle, who could scarcely believe in it, yet knew, secretly and half consciously, that the water was being changed into the wine of a new life. This was ever the inner music of his dreams, and to it he added on these still and sacred nights the far-off memory of that time long ago when, a child, before the world had overwhelmed him, he journeyed down to the old grey house in the west, and for a whole month heard the murmur of the forest through his bedroom window, and when the wind was hushed, the washing of the tides about the reeds; and sometimes awaking very early he had heard the strange cry of a bird as it rose from its nest among the reeds, and had looked out and had seen the valley whiten to the dawn, and the winding river whiten as it swam down to the sea. The memory of all this had faded and become shadowy as he grew older and the chains of common life were riveted firmly about his soul; all the atmosphere by which he was surrounded was well-nigh fatal to such thoughts, and only now and again in half-conscious moments or in sleep he had revisited that valley in the far-off west, where the breath of the wind was an incantation, and every leaf and stream and hill spoke of great and ineffable mysteries. But now the broken vision was in great part restored to him, and looking with love in his wife's eyes he saw the gleam of waterpools in the still forest, saw the mists rising in the evening, and heard the music of the winding river.

They were sitting thus together on the Friday evening of the week that had begun with that odd and half-forgotten visit of Mrs. Nixon, when, to Darnell's annoyance, the door-bell gave a discordant peal, and Alice with some disturbance of manner came out and announced that a gentleman wished to see the master. Darnell went into the drawing-room, where Alice had lit one gas so that it flared and burnt with a rushing sound, and in this distorting light there waited a stout, elderly gentleman, whose countenance was altogether unknown to him. He stared blankly, and hesitated, about to speak, but the visitor began.

"You don't know who I am, but I expect you'll know my name. It's Nixon."

He did not wait to be interrupted. He sat down and plunged into narrative, and after the first few words, Darnell, whose mind was not altogether unprepared, listened without much astonishment.

"And the long and the short of it is," Mr. Nixon said at last, "she's gone stark, staring mad, and we had to put her away to-day—poor thing."

His voice broke a little, and he wiped his eyes hastily, for though stout and successful he was not unfeeling, and he was fond of his wife. He had spoken quickly, and had gone lightly over many details which might have interested specialists in certain kinds of mania, and Darnell was sorry for his evident distress.

"I came here," he went on after a brief pause, "because I found out she had been to see you last Sunday, and I knew the sort of story she must have told."

Darnell shewed him the prophetic leaflet which Mrs. Nixon had dropped in the garden. "Did you know about this?" he said.

"Oh, *him*," said the old man, with some approach to cheerfulness; "oh yes, I thrashed *him* black and blue the day before yesterday."

"Isn't he mad? Who is the man?"

"He's not mad, he's bad. He's a little Welsh skunk named Richards. He's been running some sort of chapel over at New Barnet for the last few years, and my poor wife—she never could find the parish church good enough for her—had been going to his damned schism shop for the last twelve-month. It was all that finished her off. Yes; I thrashed *him* the day before yesterday, and I'm not afraid of a summons either. I know him, and he knows I know him."

Old Nixon whispered something in Darnell's ear, and chuckled faintly as he repeated for the third time his formula—

"I thrashed *him* black and blue the day before yesterday."

Darnell could only murmur condolences and express his hope that Mrs. Nixon might recover.

The old man shook his head.

"I'm afraid there's no hope of that," he said. "I've had the best advice, but they couldn't do anything, and told me so."

Presently he asked to see his niece, and Darnell went out and prepared Mary as well as he could. She could scarcely take in the news that her aunt was a hopeless maniac, for Mrs. Nixon, having been extremely stupid all her days, had naturally succeeded in passing with her relations as typically sensible. With the Reynolds family, as with the great majority of us, want of imagination is always equated with sanity, and though many of us have never heard of Lombroso we are his ready-made converts. We have always believed that poets are mad, and if statistics unfortunately shew that few poets have really been inhabitants of lunatic asylums, it is soothing to learn that nearly all poets have had whooping-cough, which is doubtless, like intoxication, a minor madness.

"But is it really true?" she asked at length. "Are you certain uncle is not deceiving you? Aunt seemed so sensible always."

She was helped at last by recollecting that Aunt Marian used to get up very early of mornings, and then they went into the drawing-room and talked to the old man. His evident kindliness and honesty grew upon Mary, in spite of a lingering belief in her aunt's fables, and when he left, it was with a promise to come to see them again.

Mrs. Darnell said she felt tired, and went to bed; and Darnell returned to the garden and began to pace to and fro, collecting his thoughts. His immeasurable relief at the intelligence that, after all, Mrs. Nixon was not coming to live with them taught him that, despite his submission, his dread of the event had been very great. The weight was removed, and now he was free to consider his life without reference to the grotesque intrusion that he had feared. He sighed for joy, and as he paced to and fro he savoured the scent of the night, which, though it came faintly to him in that brick-bound suburb, summoned to his mind across many years the odour of the world at night as he had known it in that short sojourn of his boyhood; the odour that rose from the earth when the flame of the sun had gone down beyond the mountain, and the afterglow had paled in the sky and on the fields. And as he recovered as best he could these lost dreams of an enchanted land, there came to him other images of his childhood, forgotten and yet not forgotten, dwelling unheeded in dark places of the memory, but ready to be summoned forth. He remembered one fantasy that had long haunted him. As he lay half asleep in the forest on one hot afternoon of that memorable visit to the country, he had "made believe" that a little companion had come to him out of the blue mists and the green light beneath the leaves—a white girl with long black hair, who had played with him and whispered her secrets in his ear, as his father lay sleeping under a tree; and from that summer afternoon, day by day, she had been beside him; she had visited him in the wilderness of London, and even in recent years there had come to him now and again the sense of her presence, in the midst of the heat and turmoil of the City. The last visit he remembered well; it was a few weeks before he married, and from the depths of some futile task he had looked up with puzzled eyes, wondering why the close air suddenly grew scented with green leaves, why the murmur of the trees and the wash of the river on the reeds came to his ears; and then that sudden rapture to which he had given a name and an individuality possessed him utterly. He knew then how the dull flesh of man can be like fire; and now, looking back from a new standpoint on this and other experiences, he realised how all that was real in his life had been unwelcomed, uncherished by him, had come to him, perhaps, in virtue of merely negative qualities on his part. And yet, as he reflected, he saw that there had been a chain of witnesses all through his life: again and again voices had whispered in his ear words in a strange language that he now recognised as his native tongue; the common street had not been lacking in visions of the true land of his birth; and in all the passing and repassing of the world he saw that there had been emissaries ready to guide his feet on the way of the great journey.

A week or two after the visit of Mr. Nixon, Darnell took his annual holiday.

There was no question of Walton-on-the-Naze, or of anything of the kind, as he quite agreed with his wife's longing for some substantial sum put by against the evil day. But the weather was still fine, and he lounged away the time in his garden beneath the tree, or he sauntered out on long aimless walks in the western purlieus of London, not unvisited by that old sense of some great ineffable beauty, concealed by the dim and dingy veils of grey interminable streets. Once, on a day of heavy rain he went to the "box-room", and began to turn over the papers in the old hair-trunk—scraps and odds and ends of family history, some of them in his father's handwriting, others in faded ink, and there were a few ancient pocket-books, filled with manuscript of a still earlier time, and in these the ink was glossier and blacker than any writing fluids supplied by stationers of later days. Darnell had hung up the portrait of the ancestor in this room, and had bought a solid kitchen table and a chair; so that Mrs. Darnell, seeing him looking over his old documents, half thought of naming the room "Mr. Darnell's study". He had not glanced at these relics of his family for many years, but from the hour when the rainy morning sent him to them, he remained constant to research till the end of the holidays. It was a new interest, and he began to fashion in his mind a faint picture of his forefathers, and of their life in that grey old house in the river valley, in the western land of wells and streams and dark and ancient woods. And there were stranger things than mere notes on family history amongst that odd litter of old disregarded papers, and when he went back to his work in the City some of the men fancied that he was in some vague manner changed in appearance; but he only laughed when they asked him where he had been and what he had been doing with himself. But Mary noticed that every evening he spent at least an hour in the box-room; she was rather sorry at the waste of time involved in reading old papers about dead people. And one afternoon, as they were out together on a somewhat dreary walk towards Acton, Darnell stopped at a hopeless second-hand bookshop, and after scanning the rows of shabby books in the window, went in and purchased two volumes. They proved to be a Latin dictionary and grammar, and she was surprised to hear her husband declare his intention of acquiring the Latin language.

But, indeed, all his conduct impressed her as indefinably altered; and she began to be a little alarmed, though she could scarcely have formed her fears in words. But she knew that in some way that was all indefined and beyond the grasp of her thought their lives had altered since the summer, and no single thing wore quite the same aspect as before. If she looked out into the dull street with its rare loiterers, it was the same and yet it had altered, and if she opened the window in the early morning the wind that entered came with a changed breath that spoke some message that she could not understand. And day by day passed by in the old course, and not even the four walls were altogether familiar, and the voices of men and women sounded with strange notes, with the echo, rather, of a music that came over unknown hills. And day by day as she went about her household work, passing from shop to shop in those dull streets that were a network, a fatal labyrinth of grey desolation on every side, there came to her sense half-seen images of some other world, as if she walked in a dream, and every moment must bring her to light and to awakening, when the grey should fade, and regions long desired should appear in glory. Again and again it seemed as if that which was hidden would be shewn even to the sluggish testimony of sense; and as she went to and fro from street to street of that dim and weary suburb, and looked on those grey material walls, they seemed as if a light glowed behind them, and again and again the mystic fragrance of incense was blown to her nostrils from across the verge of that world which is not so much impenetrable as ineffable, and to her ears came the dream of a chant that spoke of hidden choirs about all her ways. She struggled against these impressions, refusing her assent to the testimony of them, since all the pressure of credited opinion for three hundred years has been directed towards stamping out real knowledge, and so effectually has this been accomplished that we can only recover the truth through much anguish. And so Mary passed the days in a strange perturbation, clinging to common things and common thoughts, as if she feared that one morning she would wake up in an unknown world to a changed life. And Edward Darnell went day by day to his labour and returned in the evening, always with that shining of light within his eyes and upon his face, with the gaze of wonder that was greater day by day, as if for him the veil grew thin and soon would disappear.

From these great matters both in herself and in her husband Mary shrank back, afraid, perhaps, that if she began the question the answer might be too wonderful. She rather taught herself to be troubled over little things; she asked herself what attraction there could be in the old records over which she supposed Edward to be poring night after night in the cold room upstairs. She had glanced over the papers at Darnell's invitation, and could see but little interest in them; there were one or two sketches, roughly done in pen and ink, of the old house in the west: it looked a shapeless and fantastic place, furnished with strange pillars and stranger ornaments on the projecting porch; and on one side a roof dipped down almost to the earth, and in the centre there was something that might almost be a tower rising above the rest of the building. Then there were documents that seemed all names and dates, with here and there a coat of arms done in the margin, and she came upon a string of uncouth Welsh names linked together by the word "ap" in a chain that looked endless. There was a paper covered with signs and figures that meant nothing to her, and then there were the pocket-books, full of old-fashioned writing, and much of it in Latin, as her husband told her—it was a collection as void of significance as a treatise on conic sections, so far as Mary was concerned. But night after night Darnell shut himself up with the musty rolls, and more than ever when he rejoined her he bore upon his face the blazonry of some great adventure. And one night she asked him what interested him so much in the papers he had shewn her.

He was delighted with the question. Somehow they had not talked much together for the last few weeks, and he began to tell her of the records of the old race from which he came, of the old strange house of grey stone between the forest and the river. The family went back and back, he said, far into the dim past, beyond the Normans, beyond the Saxons, far into the Roman days, and for many hundred years they had been petty kings, with a strong fortress high up on the hill, in the heart of the forest; and even now the great mounds remained, whence one could look through the trees towards the mountain on one side and across the yellow sea on the other. The real name of the family was not Darnell; that was assumed by one Iolo ap Taliesin ap Iorwerth in the sixteenth century—why, Darnell did not seem to understand. And then he told her how the race had dwindled in prosperity, century by century, till at last there was nothing left but the grey house and a few acres of land bordering the river.

"And do you know, Mary," he said, "I suppose we shall go and live there some day or other. My great-uncle, who has the place now, made money in business when he was a young man, and I believe he will leave it all to me. I know I am the only relation he has. How strange it would be. What a change from the life here."

"You never told me that. Don't you think your great-uncle might leave his house and his money to somebody he knows really well? You haven't seen him since you were a little boy, have you?"

"No; but we write once a year. And from what I have heard my fa- ther say, I am sure the old man would never leave the house out of the family. Do you think you would like it?"

"I don't know. Isn't it very lonely?"

"I suppose it is. I forget whether there are any other houses in sight, but I don't think there are any at all near. But what a change! No City, no streets, no people passing to and fro; only the sound of the wind and the sight of the green leaves and the green hills, and the song of the voices of the earth." . . . He checked himself suddenly, as if he feared that he was about to tell some secret that must not yet be ut- tered; and indeed, as he spoke of the change from the little street in

Shepherd's Bush to that ancient house in the woods of the far west, a change seemed already to possess himself, and his voice put on the modulation of an antique chant. Mary looked at him steadily and touched his arm, and he drew a long breath before he spoke again.

"It is the old blood calling to the old land," he said. "I was forgetting that I am a clerk in the City."

It was, doubtless, the old blood that had suddenly stirred in him; the resurrection of the old spirit that for many centuries had been faithful to secrets that are now disregarded by most of us, that now day by day was quickened more and more in his heart, and grew so strong that it was hard to conceal. He was indeed almost in the position of the man in the tale, who, by a sudden electric shock, lost the vision of the things about him in the London streets, and gazed instead upon the sea and shore of an island in the Antipodes; for Darnell only clung with an effort to the interests and the atmosphere which, till lately, had seemed all the world to him; and the grey house and the wood and the river, symbols of the other sphere, intruded as it were into the landscape of the London suburb.

But he went on, with more restraint, telling his stories of far-off ancestors, how one of them, the most remote of all, was called a saint, and was supposed to possess certain mysterious secrets often alluded to in the papers as the "Hidden Songs of Iolo Sant". And then with an abrupt transition he recalled memories of his father and of the strange, shiftless life in dingy lodgings in the backwaters of London, of the dim stucco streets that were his first recollections, of forgotten squares in North London, and of the figure of his father, a grave bearded man who seemed always in a dream, as if he too sought for the vision of a land beyond the strong walls, a land where there were deep orchards and many shining hills, and fountains and waterpools gleaming under the leaves of the wood.

"I believe my father earned his living," he went on, "such a living as he did earn, at the Record Office and the British Museum. He used to hunt up things for lawyers and country parsons who wanted old deeds inspected. He never made much, and we were always moving from one lodging to another—always to out-of-the-way places where everything seemed to have run to seed. We never knew our neighbours—we moved too often for that—but my father had about half a dozen friends, elderly men like himself, who used to come to see us pretty often; and then, if there was any money, the lodging-house servant would go out for beer, and they would sit and smoke far into the night.

"I never knew much about these friends of his, but they all had the same look, the look of longing for something hidden. They talked of mysteries that I never understood, very little of their own lives, and when they did speak of ordinary affairs one could tell that they thought such matters as money and the want of it were unimportant trifles. When I grew up and went into the City, and met other young fellows and heard their way of talking, I wondered whether my father and his friends were not a little queer in their heads; but I know better now."

So night after night Darnell talked to his wife, seeming to wander aimlessly from the dingy lodging-houses, where he had spent his boyhood in the company of his father and the other seekers, to the old house hidden in that far western valley, and the old race that had so long looked at the setting of the sun over the mountain. But in truth there was one end in all that he spoke, and Mary felt that beneath his words, however indifferent they might seem, there was hidden a purpose, that they were to embark on a great and marvellous adventure.

So day by day the world became more magical; day by day the work of separation was being performed, the gross accidents were being refined away. Darnell neglected no instruments that might be useful in the work; and now he neither lounged at home on Sunday mornings, nor did he accompany his wife to the Gothic blasphemy which pretended to be a church. They had discovered a little church of another fashion in a back street, and Darnell, who had found in one of the old notebooks the maxim *Incredibilia sola Credenda*, soon perceived how high and glorious a thing was that service at which he assisted. Our stupid ancestors taught us that we could become wise by studying books on "science", by meddling with test-tubes, geological specimens, microscopic preparations, and the like; but they who have cast off these follies know that they must read not "science" books, but mass-books, and that the soul is made wise by the contemplation of mystic ceremonies and elaborate and curious rites. In such things Darnell found a wonderful mystery language, which spoke at once more secretly and more directly than the formal creeds; and he saw that, in a sense, the whole world is but a great ceremony or sacrament, which teaches under visible forms a hidden and transcendent doctrine. It was thus that he found in the ritual of the church a perfect image of the world; an image purged, exalted, and illuminate, a holy house built up of shining and translucent stones, in which the burning torches were more significant than the wheeling stars, and the fuming incense was a more certain token than the rising of the mist. His soul went forth with the albed procession in its white and solemn order, the mystic dance that signifies rapture and a joy above all joys, and when he beheld Love slain and rise again victorious he knew that he witnessed, in a figure, the consummation of all things, the Bridal of all Bridals, the mystery that is beyond all mysteries, accomplished from the foundation of the world. So day by day the house of his life became more magical.

And at the same time he began to guess that if in the New Life there are new and unheard-of joys, there are also new and unheard-of dangers. In his manuscript books which professed to deliver the outer sense of those mysterious "Hidden Songs of Iolo Sant" there was a little chapter that bore the heading: *Fons Sacer non in communem Vsum convertendus est,* and by diligence, with much use of the grammar and dictionary, Darnell was able to construe the by no means complex Latin of his ancestor. The special book which contained the chapter in question was one of the most singular in the collection, since it bore the title *Terra de Iolo,* and on the surface, with an ingenious concealment of its real symbolism, it affected to give an account of the orchards, fields, woods, roads, tenements, and waterways in the possession of Darnell's ancestors. Here, then, he read of the Holy Well, hidden in the Wistman's Wood—*Sylva Sapientum*—"a fountain of abundant water, which no heats of summer can ever dry, which no flood can ever defile, which is as a water of life, to them that thirst for life, a stream of cleansing to them that would be pure, and a medicine of such healing virtue that by it, through the might of God and the intercession of His saints, the most grievous wounds are made whole". But the water of this well was to be kept sacred perpetually, it was not to be used for any common purpose, nor to satisfy any bodily thirst; but ever to be esteemed as holy, "even as the water which the priest hath hallowed". And in the margin a comment in a later hand taught Darnell something of the meaning of these prohibitions. He was warned not to use the Well of Life as a mere luxury of mortal life, as a new sensation, as a means of making the insipid cup of everyday existence more palatable. "For," said the commentator, "we are not called to sit as the spectators in a theatre, there to watch the play performed before us, but we are rather summoned to stand in the very scene itself, and there fervently to enact our parts in a great and wonderful mystery."

Darnell could quite understand the temptation that was thus indicated. Though he had gone but a little way on the path, and had barely tested the overrunnings of that mystic well, he was already aware of the enchantment that was transmuting all the world about him, informing his life with a strange significance and romance. London seemed a city of the Arabian Nights, and its labyrinths of streets an enchanted maze; its long avenues of lighted lamps were as starry systems, and its immensity became for him an image of the endless universe. He could well imagine how pleasant it might be to linger in such a world as this, to sit apart and dream, beholding the strange pageant played before him; but the Sacred Well was not for common use, it was for the cleansing of the soul, and the healing of the grievous wounds of the spirit. There must be yet another transformation: London had become Bagdad; it must at last be transmuted to Syon, or in the phrase of one of his old documents, the City of the Cup.

And there were yet darker perils which the Iolo MSS. (as his father had named the collection) hinted at more or less obscurely. There were suggestions of an awful region which the soul might enter, of a transmutation that was unto death, of evocations which could summon the utmost forces of evil from their dark places—in a word, of that sphere which is represented to most of us under the crude and somewhat childish symbolism of Black Magic. And here again he was not altogether without a dim comprehension of what was meant. He found himself recalling an odd incident that had happened long ago, which had remained all the years in his mind unheeded, amongst the many insignificant recollections of his childhood, and now rose before him, clear and distinct and full of meaning. It was on that memorable visit to the old house in the west, and the whole scene returned, with its smallest events, and the voices seemed to sound in his ears. It was a grey, still day of heavy heat that he remembered: he had stood on the

lawn after breakfast, and wondered at the great peace and silence of
the world. Not a leaf stirred in the trees on the lawn, not a whisper
came from the myriad leaves of the wood; the flowers gave out sweet
and heavy odours as if they breathed the dreams of the summer night;
and far down the valley, the winding river was like dim silver under
that dim and silvery sky, and the far hills and woods and fields vanished in the mist. The stillness of the air held him as with a charm; he
leant all the morning against the rails that parted the lawn from the
meadow, breathing the mystic breath of summer, and watching the
fields brighten as with a sudden blossoming of shining flowers as the
high mist grew thin for a moment before the hidden sun. As he
watched thus, a man weary with heat, with some glance of horror in
his eyes, passed him on his way to the house; but he stayed at his post
till the old bell in the turret rang, and they dined all together, masters
and servants, in the dark cool room that looked towards the still leaves
of the wood. He could see that his uncle was upset about something,
and when they had finished dinner he heard him tell his father that
there was trouble at a farm; and it was settled that they should all drive
over in the afternoon to some place with a strange name. But when the
time came Mr. Darnell was too deep in old books and tobacco smoke
to be stirred from his corner, and Edward and his uncle went alone in
the dog-cart. They drove swiftly down the narrow lane, into the road
that followed the winding river, and crossed the bridge at Caermaen by
the mouldering Roman walls, and then, skirting the deserted, echoing
village, they came out on a broad white turnpike road, and the limestone dust followed them like a cloud. Then, suddenly, they turned to
the north by such a road as Edward had never seen before. It was so
narrow that there was barely room for the cart to pass, and the foot-
way was of rock, and the banks rose high above them as they slowly
climbed the long, steep way, and the untrimmed hedges on either side
shut out the light. And the ferns grew thick and green upon the banks,
and hidden wells dripped down upon them; and the old man told him
how the lane in winter was a torrent of swirling water, so that no one
could pass by it. On they went, ascending and then again descending,
always in that deep hollow under the wild woven boughs, and the boy
wondered vainly what the country was like on either side. And now the
air grew darker, and the hedge on one bank was but the verge of a dark

and rustling wood, and the grey limestone rocks had changed to dark-red earth flecked with green patches and veins of marl, and suddenly in the stillness from the depths of the wood a bird began to sing a melody that charmed the heart into another world, that sang to the child's soul of the blessed faery realm beyond the woods of the earth, where the wounds of man are healed. And so at last, after many turnings and windings, they came to a high bare land where the lane broadened out into a kind of common, and along the edge of this place there were scattered three or four old cottages, and one of them was a little tavern. Here they stopped, and a man came out and tethered the tired horse to a post and gave him water; and old Mr. Darnell took the child's hand and led him by a path across the fields. The boy could see the country now, but it was all a strange, undiscovered land; they were in the heart of a wilderness of hills and valleys that he had never looked upon, and they were going down a wild, steep hillside, where the narrow path wound in and out amidst gorse and towering bracken, and the sun gleaming out for a moment, there was a gleam of white water far below in a narrow valley, where a little brook poured and rippled from stone to stone. They went down the hill, and through a brake, and then, hidden in dark-green orchards, they came upon a long, low whitewashed house, with a stone roof strangely coloured by the growth of moss and lichens. Mr. Darnell knocked at a heavy oaken door, and they came into a dim room where but little light entered through the thick glass in the deep-set window. There were heavy beams in the ceiling, and a great fireplace sent out an odour of burning wood that Darnell never forgot, and the room seemed to him full of women who talked all together in frightened tones. Mr. Darnell beckoned to a tall, grey old man, who wore corduroy knee-breeches, and the boy, sitting on a high straight-backed chair, could see the old man and his uncle passing to and fro across the window-panes, as they walked together on the garden path. The women stopped their talk for a moment, and one of them brought him a glass of milk and an apple from some cold inner chamber; and then, suddenly, from a room above there rang out a shrill and terrible shriek, and then, in a young girl's voice, a more terrible song. It was not like anything the child had ever heard, but as the man recalled it to his memory, he knew to what song it might be compared—to a certain chant indeed that summons the angels and archangels to assist in the great Sacrifice. But as this song chants of the heavenly army, so did that seem to summon all the hierarchy of evil, the hosts of Lilith and Samael; and the words that rang out with such awful modulations—*neumata inferorum*—were in some unknown tongue that few men have ever heard on earth.

The women glared at one another with horror in their eyes, and he saw one or two of the oldest of them clumsily making an old sign upon their breasts. Then they began to speak again, and he remembered fragments of their talk.

"She has been up there," said one, pointing vaguely over her shoulder.

"She'd never know the way," answered another. "They be all gone that went there."

"There be nought there in these days."

"How can you tell that, Gwenllian? 'Tis not for us to say that."

"My great-grandmother did know some that had been there," said a very old woman. "She told me how they was taken afterwards."

And then his uncle appeared at the door, and they went their way as they had come. Edward Darnell never heard any more of it, nor whether the girl died or recovered from her strange attack; but the scene had haunted his mind in boyhood, and now the recollection of it came to him with a certain note of warning, as a symbol of dangers that might be in the way.

It would be impossible to carry on the history of Edward Darnell and of Mary his wife to a greater length, since from this point their legend is full of impossible events, and seems to put on the semblance of the stories of the Graal. It is certain, indeed, that in this world they changed their lives, like King Arthur, but this is a work which no chronicler has cared to describe with any amplitude of detail. Darnell, it is true, made a little book, partly consisting of queer verse which might have been written by an inspired infant, and partly made up of "notes and exclamations" in an odd dog-Latin which he had picked up from the "Iolo MSS.", but it is to be feared that this work, even if published in its entirety, would cast but little light on a perplexing story. He called this piece of literature "In Exitu Israel", and wrote on the title page the motto, doubtless of his own composition, *"Nunc certe scio quod omnia legenda; omnes historiæ, omnes fabulæ, omnis Scriptura sint de ME narrata.*" It is only too evident that his Latin was not learnt at the feet of Cicero; but in this dialect he relates the great history of the "New Life" as it was manifested to him. The "poems" are even stranger. One, headed (with an odd reminiscence of old-fashioned books) "Lines written on looking down from a Height in London on a Board School suddenly lit up by the Sun", begins thus:—

> One day when I was all alone
> I found a wondrous little stone,
> It lay forgotten on the road
> Far from the ways of man's abode.
> When on this stone mine eyes I cast
> I saw my Treasure found at last.
> I pressed it hard against my face,
> I covered it with my embrace,
> I hid it in a secret place.
> And every day I went to see
> This stone that was my ecstasy;
> And worshipped it with flowers rare,
> And secret words and sayings fair.
> O stone, so rare and red and wise,
> O fragment of far Paradise,
> O Star, whose light is life! O Sea,
> Whose ocean is infinity!
> Thou art a fire that ever burns,
> And all the world to wonder turns;
> And all the dust of the dull day
> By thee is changed and purged away,
> So that, where'er I look, I see
> A world of a Great Majesty.
> The sullen river rolls all gold,
> The desert park's a faery wold,
> When on the trees the wind is borne
> I hear the sound of Arthur's horn.
> I see no town of grim grey ways,
> But a great city all ablaze

With burning torches, to light up
The pinnacles that shrine the Cup.
Ever the magic wine is poured,
Ever the Feast shines on the board,
Ever the song is borne on high
That chants the holy Magistry—
      Etc. etc. etc.

From such documents as these it is clearly impossible to gather any very definite information. But on the last page Darnell has written—

"So I awoke from a dream of a London suburb, of daily labour, of weary, useless little things; and as my eyes were opened I saw that I was in an ancient wood, where a clear well rose into grey film and vapour beneath a misty, glimmering heat. And a form came towards me from the hidden places of the wood, and my love and I were united by the well."

The Secret Glory

TO VINCENT STARRETT

I

1.

A heavy cloud passed swiftly away before the wind that came with the night, and far in a clear sky the evening star shone with pure brightness, a gleaming world set high above the dark earth and the black shadows in the lane. In the ending of October a great storm had blown from the west, and it was through the bare boughs of a twisted oak that Ambrose Meyrick saw the silver light of the star. As the last faint flash died in the sky he leaned against a gate and gazed upward; and then his eyes fell on the dull and weary undulations of the land, the vast circle of dun ploughland and grey meadow, bounded by a dim horizon, dreary as a prison wall. He remembered with a start how late it must be; he should have been back an hour before, and he was still in the open country, a mile away at least from the outskirts of Lupton. He turned from the star and began to walk as quickly as he could along the lane through the puddles and the sticky clay, soaked with three weeks' heavy rain.

He saw at last the faint lamps of the nearest streets, where the shoemakers lived, and he tramped hurriedly through this wretched quarter, past its penny shops, its raw public-house, its rawer chapel, with twelve foundation-stones on which are written the names of the twelve leading Congregationalists of Lupton, past the squalling children whose mothers were raiding and harrying them to bed. Then came the Free Library, an admirable instance, as the *Lupton Mercury* declared, of the adaptation of Gothic to modern requirements. From a

296

sort of tower of this building a great arm shot out and hung
clock-face over the street, and Meyrick experienced another s
when he saw that it was even later than he had feared. He had to get
the other side of the town, and it was past seven already! He began to
run, wondering what his fate would be at his uncle's hands, and he
went by "our grand old parish church" (completely "restored" in the
early 'forties), past the remains of the market-cross, converted most
successfully, according to local opinion, into a drinking fountain for
dogs and cattle, dodging his way among the late shoppers and the early
loafers who lounged to and fro along the High Street.

He shuddered as he rang the bell at the Old Grange. He tried to
put a bold face on it when the servant opened the door, and he would
have gone straight down the hall into the schoolroom, but the girl
stopped him.

"Master said you're to go to the study at once, Master Meyrick, as
soon as ever you come in."

She was looking strangely at him, and the boy grew sick with
dread. He was a "funk" through and through, and was frightened out
of his wits about twelve times a day every day of his life. His uncle had
said a few years before: "Lupton will make a man of you," and Lupton
was doing its best. The face of the miserable wretch whitened and
grew wet; there was a choking sensation in his throat, and he felt very
cold. Nelly Foran, the maid, still looked at him with strange, eager eyes,
then whispered suddenly:

"You must go directly, Master Meyrick. Master heard the bell, I
know; but I'll make it up to you."

Ambrose understood nothing except the approach of doom. He
drew a long breath and knocked at the study door, and entered on his
uncle's command.

It was an extremely comfortable room. The red curtains were
drawn close, shutting out the dreary night, and there was a great fire of
coal that bubbled unctuously and shot out great jets of flame—in the
schoolroom they used coke. The carpet was soft to the feet, and the
chairs promised softness to the body, and the walls were well furnished with books. There were Thackeray, Dickens, Lord Lytton, uni-
form in red morocco, gilt extra; the Cambridge Bible for Students in
many volumes, Stanley's *Life of Arnold*, Copleston's *Prælectiones Academ-*

aries, first editions of Tennyson, school and
l, of course, a great brigade of Latin and
e wonderful and terrible pictures of Piranesi
Ir. Horbury admired more for the subject-
nt, in which he found, as he said, a certain
-almost, indeed, a touch of morbidity. The
.., ɪoɪ tne High Usher was writing at his desk, and a
shaded lamp cast a bright circle of light on a mass of papers.

He turned round as Ambrose Meyrick came in. He had a high,
bald forehead, and his fresh-coloured face was edged with reddish
"muttonchop" whiskers. There was a dangerous glint in his grey-green
eyes, and his opening sentence was unpromising.

"Now, Ambrose, you must understand quite definitely that this
sort of thing is not going to be tolerated any longer."

Perhaps it would not have fared quite so badly with the unhappy
lad if only his uncle had not lunched with the Head. There was a con-
catenation accordingly, every link in which had helped to make Ambrose Meyrick's position hopeless. In the first place there was boiled
mutton for luncheon, and this was a dish hateful to Mr. Horbury's palate. Secondly, the wine was sherry. Of this Mr. Horbury was very fond,
but unfortunately the Head's sherry, though making a specious appeal
to the taste, was in reality far from good and teemed with those fiery
and irritating spirits which make the liver to burn and rage. Then
Chesson had practically found fault with his chief assistant's work. He
had not, of course, told him in so many words that he was unable to
teach; he had merely remarked:

"I don't know whether you've noticed it, Horbury, but it struck me
the other day that there was a certain lack of grip about those fellows
of yours in the fifth. Some of them struck me as *muddlers*, if you know
what I mean: there was a sort of *vagueness*, for example, about their
construing in that chorus. Have you remarked anything of the kind
yourself?"

And then, again, the Head had gone on:

"And, by the way, Horbury, I don't quite know what to make of
your nephew, Meyrick. He was your wife's nephew, wasn't he? Yes.
Well, I hardly know whether I can explain what I feel about the boy;
but I can't help saying that there is something wrong about him. His

work strikes me as good enough—in fact, quite above the form average—but, to use the musical term, he seems to be in the wrong key. Of course, it may be my fancy; but the lad reminds me of those very objectionable persons who are said to have a joke up their sleeve. I doubt whether he is taking the Lupton stamp; and when he gets up in the school I shall be afraid of his influence on the other boys."

Here, again, the master detected a note of blame; and by the time he reached the Old Grange he was in an evil humour. He hardly knew which he found the more offensive—Chesson's dish or his discourse. He was a dainty man in his feeding, and the thought of the great fat gigot pouring out a thin red stream from the gaping wound dealt to it by the Head mingled with his resentment of the indirect scolding which he considered that he had received, and on the fire just kindled every drop of that corrosive sherry was as oil. He drank his tea in black silence, his rage growing fiercer for want of vent, and it is doubtful whether in his inmost heart he was altogether displeased when report was made at six o'clock that Meyrick had not come in. He saw a prospect—more than a prospect—of satisfactory relief.

Some philosophers have affirmed that lunatic doctors (or mental specialists) grow in time to a certain resemblance to their patients, or, in more direct language, become half mad themselves. There seems a good deal to be said for the position; indeed, it is probably a more noxious madness to swear a man into perpetual imprisonment in the company of maniacs and imbeciles because he sings in his bath and will wear a purple dressing-gown at dinner than to fancy oneself Emperor of China. However this may be, it is very certain that in many cases the schoolmaster is nothing more or less than a bloated schoolboy: the beasts are, radically, the same, but morbid conditions have increased the venom of the former's sting. Indeed, it is not uncommon for well-wishers to the great Public School System to praise their favourite masters in terms which admit, nay, glory in, this identity. Read the memorial tributes to departed Heads in a well-known and most respectable Church paper. "To the last he was a big boy at heart," writes Canon Diver of his friend, that illiterate old sycophant who brought up the numbers of the school to such a pitch by means of his conciliatory policy to Jews, Turks, heretics and infidels that there was nothing for it but to make him a bishop. "I always thought he seemed more at home in the playing fields than in the sixth-form room. . . . He had all the English boy's healthy horror of anything approaching pose or eccentricity. . . . He could be a severe disciplinarian when severity seemed necessary, but everybody in the school knew that a well-placed 'boundary', a difficult catch or a goal well won or well averted would atone for all but the most serious offences." There are many other points of resemblance between the average master and the average boy: each, for example, is intensely cruel, and experiences a quite abnormal joy in the infliction of pain. The baser boy tortures those animals which are not *méchants*. Tales have been told (they are hushed up by all true friends of the "System") of wonderful and exquisite orgies in lonely hollows of the moors, in obscure and hidden thickets: tales of a boy or two, a lizard or a toad, and the slow simmering heat of a bonfire. But these are the exceptional pleasures of the *virtuosi;* for the average lad there is plenty of fun to be got out of his feebler fellows, of whom there are generally a few even in the healthiest community. After all, the weakest must go to the wall, and if the bones of the weakest are ground in the process, that is their fault. When some miserable little wretch, after a year or two of prolonged and exquisite torture of body and mind, seeks the last escape of suicide, one knows how the Old Boys will come forward, how gallantly they will declare that the days at the "dear old school" were the happiest in their lives; how "the Doctor" was their father and the Sixth their nursing-mother; how the delights of the Mahomedans' fabled Paradise are but grey and weary sport compared with the joys of the happy fag, whose heart, as the inspired bard of Harrow tells us, will thrill in future years at the thought of the Hill. They write from all quarters, these brave Old Boys: from the hard-won Deanery, result of many years of indefatigable attack on the fundamental doctrines of the Christian faith; from the comfortable villa, the reward of commercial activity and acuteness on the Stock Exchange; from the courts and from the camps; from all the high seats of the successful; and common to them all is the convincing argument of praise. And we all agree, and say there is nothing like our great Public Schools, and perhaps the only dissentient voices are those of the father and the mother who bury the body of a little child about whose neck is the black sign of the rope. But let them be comforted: the boy was no good at games, though his torments were not bad sport while he lasted.

Mr. Horbury was an old Luptonian; he was, in the words of Canon Diver, but "a big boy at heart", and so he gave orders that Meyrick was to be sent in the study directly he came in, and he looked at the clock on the desk before him with satisfaction and yet with impatience. A hungry man may long for his delayed dinner almost with a sense of fury, and yet at the back of his mind he cannot help being consoled by the thought of how wonderfully he will enjoy the soup when it appears at last. When seven struck, Mr. Horbury moistened his lips slightly. He got up and felt cautiously behind one of the bookshelves. The object was there, and he sat down again. He listened; there were footfalls on the drive. Ah! there was the expected ring. There was a brief interval, and then a knock. The fire was glowing with red flashes, and the wretched toad was secured.

"Now, Ambrose, you must understand quite definitely that this sort of thing isn't going to be tolerated any longer. This is the third time during this term that you have been late for lock-up. You know the rules: six o'clock at latest. It is now twenty minutes past seven. What excuse have you to make? What have you been doing with yourself? Have you been in the Fields?"

"No, Sir."

"Why not? You must have seen the Resolution of the Sixth on the notice-board of the High School? You know what it promised any boy who shirked rocker? 'A good sound thrashing with tuds before the First Thirty.' I am afraid you will have a very bad time of it on Monday, after Graham has sent up your name to the Room."

There was a pause. Mr. Horbury looked quietly and lengthily at the boy, who stood white and sick before him. He was a rather sallow, ugly lad of fifteen. There was something of intelligence in his expression, and it was this glance that Chesson, the Headmaster, had resented. His heart beat against his breast, his breath came in gasps and the sweat of terror poured down his body. The master gazed at him, and at last spoke again.

"But what have you been doing? Where have you been all this time?"

"If you please, Sir, I walked over to Selden Abbey."

"To Selden Abbey? Why, it's at least six miles away! What on earth did you want to go to Selden Abbey for? Are you fond of old stones?"

"If you please, Sir, I wanted to see the Norman arches. There is a picture of them in *Parker's Glossary.*"

"Oh, I see! You are a budding antiquarian, are you, Ambrose, with an interest in Norman arches—eh? I suppose we are to look forward to the time when your researches will have made Lupton famous? Perhaps you would like to lecture to the school on St. Paul's Cathedral? Pray, what are your views as to the age of Stonehenge?"

The wit was heavy enough, but the speaker's position gave a bitter sting to his lash. Mr. Horbury saw that every cut had told, and, without prejudice to more immediate and acuter pleasures, he resolved that such biting satire must have a larger audience. Indeed, it was a long time before Ambrose Meyrick heard the last of those wretched Norman arches. The method was absurdly easy. "Openings" presented themselves every day. For example, if the boy made a mistake in construing, the retort was obvious:

"Thank you, Meyrick, for your most original ideas on the force of the aorist. Perhaps if you studied your Greek Grammar a little more and your favourite *Glossary of Architecture* a little less, it would be the better. Write out 'Aorist means indefinite' five hundred times."

Or, again, perhaps the Classic Orders were referred to. Mr. Horbury would begin to instruct the form as to the difference between Ionic and Doric. The form listened with a poor imitation of interest. Suddenly the master would break off:

"I beg your pardon. I was forgetting that we have a great architectural authority amongst us. Be so kind as to instruct us, Meyrick. What does Parker say? Or perhaps you have excogitated some theories of your own? I know you have an original mind, from the extraordinary quantities in your last copy of verse. By the way, I must ask you to write out 'The *e* in *venio* is short' five hundred times. I am sorry to interfere with your more important architectural studies, but I am afraid there is no help for it."

And so on; while the form howled with amusement.

But Mr. Horbury kept these gems for future and public use. For the moment he had more exciting work on hand. He burst out suddenly:

"The fact is, Ambrose Meyrick, you're a miserable little humbug! You haven't the honesty to say, fair and square, that you funked rocker and went loafing about the country, looking for any mischief you could lay your hands on. Instead of that you make up this cock-and-bull story of Selden Abbey and Norman arches—as if any boy in his senses ever knew or cared twopence about such things! I hope you haven't been spending the afternoon in some low public-house? There, don't speak! I don't want to hear any more lies. But, whatever you have been doing, you have broken the rules, and you must be taught that the rules have to be kept. Stand still!"

Mr. Horbury went to the bookshelf and drew out the object. He stood at a little distance behind Meyrick and opened proceedings with a savage cut at his right arm, well above the elbow. Then it was the turn of the left arm, and the master felt the cane bite so pleasantly into the flesh that he distributed some dozen cuts between the two arms. Then he turned his attention to the lad's thighs and finished up in the orthodox manner, Meyrick bending over a chair.

The boy's whole body was one mass of burning, stinging torture; and, though he had not uttered a sound during the process, the tears were streaming down his cheeks. It was not the bodily anguish, though that was extreme enough, so much as a far-off recollection. He was quite a little boy, and his father, dead long since, was shewing him the western doorway of a grey church on a high hill and carefully instructing him in the difference between "billetty" and" "chevronny".

"It's no good snivelling, you know, Ambrose. I daresay you think me severe, but, though you won't believe me now, the day will come when you will thank me from your heart for what I have just done. Let this day be a turning-point in your life. Now go to your work."

2.

It was strange, but Meyrick never came in the after days and thanked his uncle for that sharp dose of physical and mental pain. Even when he was a man he dreamed of Mr. Horbury and woke up in a cold sweat, and then would fall asleep again with a great sigh of relief and gladness as he realised that he was no longer in the power of that "infernal old swine", "that filthy, canting, cruel brute", as he roughly called his old master.

The fact was, as some old Luptonians remarked, the two had never understood one another. With the majority of the boys the High Usher passed for a popular master enough. He had been a distinguished athlete in his time, and up to his last days at the school was a football enthusiast. Indeed, he organised a variety of the Lupton game which met with immense popularity till the Head was reluctantly compelled to stop it; some said because he always liked to drop bitter into Horbury's cup when possible; others—and with more probability on their side—maintained that it was in consequence of a report received from the school doctor to the effect that this new species of football was rapidly setting up an old species of heart disease in the weaker players.

However that might be, there could be no doubt as to Horbury's intense and deep-rooted devotion to the school. His father had been a Luptonian before him. He himself had gone from the school to the University, and within a year or two of taking his degree he had returned to Lupton to serve it as a master. It was the general opinion in Public School circles that the High Usher had counted for as much as Chesson, the Headmaster, if not for more, in the immense advance in prestige and popularity that the school had made; and everybody thought that when Chesson received the episcopal order Horbury's succession was a certainty. Unfortunately, however, there were wheels within wheels, and a total stranger was appointed, a man who knew nothing of the famous Lupton traditions, who (it was whispered) had been heard to say that "this athletic business" was getting a bit overdone. Mr. Horbury's friends were furious, and Horbury himself, it was supposed, was bitterly disappointed. He retreated to one of the few decent canonries which have survived the wave of agricultural depression; but those who knew him best doubted whether his ecclesiastical duties were an adequate consolation for the loss of that coveted Headmastership of Lupton.

To quote the memoir which appeared in the *Guardian* soon after his death, over some well-known initials:

"His friends were shocked when they saw him at the Residence. He seemed no longer the same man; he had aged more in six months, as some of them expressed themselves, than in the dozen years before. The old joyous Horbury, full of mirth, an apt master of word-play and logic-fence, was somehow 'dimmed', to use the happy phrase of a former colleague, the Dean of Dorchester. Old Boys who remembered the sparkle of his wit, the zest which he threw into everything, making the most ordinary form-work better fun than the games at other schools, as one of them observed, missed something indefinable from the man whom they had loved so long and so well. One of them, who had perhaps penetrated as closely as any into the *arcana* of Horbury's friendship (a privilege which he will ever esteem as one of the greatest blessings of his life), tried to rouse him with an extravagant rumour which was then going the round of the popular Press, to the effect that considerable modifications were about to be introduced into the compulsory system of games at X., one of the greatest of our great Public Schools. Horbury flushed; the old light came into his eyes; his friend was reminded of the ancient war-horse who hears once more the inspiring notes of the trumpet. 'I can't believe it,' he said, and there was a tremor in his voice. 'They wouldn't dare. Not even Y. (the Headmaster of X.) would do such a scoundrelly thing as that. I *won't* believe it.' But the flush soon faded and his apathy returned. 'After all,' he said, 'I shouldn't wonder if it were so. Our day is past, I suppose, and for all I know they may be construing the Breviary and playing dominoes at X. in a few years' time.'

"I am afraid that those last years at Wareham were far from happy. He felt, I think, out of tune with his surroundings, and, *pace* the readers of the *Guardian,* I doubt whether he was ever quite at home in his stall. He confessed to one of his old associates that he doubted the wisdom of the whole Cathedral system. 'What,' he said, in his old characteristic manner, 'would St. Peter say if he could enter this building and see that gorgeous window in which he is represented with mitre, cope and keys?' And I do not think that he was ever quite reconciled to the daily recitation of the Liturgy, accompanied as it is in such establishments by elaborate music and all the pomp of the surpliced choir. 'Rome and water, Rome and water!' he has been heard to mutter under his breath as the procession swept up the nave, and before he died I think that he had the satisfaction of feeling that many in high places were coming round to his views.

"But to the very last he never forgot Lupton. A year or two before he died he wrote the great school song, 'Follow, follow, follow!' He was pleased, I know, when it appeared in the *Luptonian,* and a famous Old Boy informs me that he will never forget Horbury's delight when he was told that the song was already a great favourite in 'Chantry'. To many of your readers the words will be familiar; but I cannot resist quoting the first verse:

> "I am getting old and grey and the hills seem far away,
> And I cannot hear the horn that once proclaimed the morn
> When we sallied forth upon the chase together;
> For the years are gone—alack!—when we hastened on the track,
> And the huntsman's whip went crack! as a signal to our pack
> Riding in the sunshine and fair weather.
> And yet across the ground
> I seem to hear a sound,
> A sound that comes up floating from the hollow;
> And its note is very clear
> As it echoes in my ear,
> And the words are: 'Lupton, follow, follow, follow!'

Chorus.

> "Lupton, follow away!
> The darkness lies behind us, and before us is the day.
> Follow, follow the sun,
> The whole world's to be won,
> So, Lupton, follow, follow, follow, follow away!

"An old pupil sang this verse to him on his death-bed, and I think, perhaps, that some at least of the readers of the *Guardian* will allow that George Horbury died 'fortified', in the truest sense, 'with the rites of the Church—the Church of a Great Aspiration.'"

Such was the impression that Mr. Horbury had evidently made upon some of his oldest friends; but Meyrick was, to the last, an infidel. He read the verses in the *Guardian* (he would never subscribe to the *Luptonian*) and jeered savagely at the whole sentiment of the memoir, and at the poetry, too.

"Isn't it incredible?" he would say. "Let's allow that the main purpose of the great Public Schools is to breed brave average boobies by means of rocker, sticker and mucker and the rest of it. Still, they do acknowledge that they have a sort of *parergon*—the teaching of two great literatures, two literatures that have moulded the whole of Western thought for more than two thousand years. And they pay an animal like this to teach these literatures—a swine that has not enough literature of any kind in him to save the soul of a louse! Look at those verses! Why, a decent fourth-form boy would be ashamed to put his name to them!"

He was foolish to talk in this fashion. People merely said that it was evident he was one of the failures of the great Public School system; and the song was much admired in the right circles. A very well-turned *idem Latine* appeared in the *Guardian* shortly after the publication of the memoir, and the initials at the foot of the version were recognised as those of a literary dean.

And on that autumn evening, far away in the 'seventies, Meyrick, the boy, left Mr. Horbury's study in a white fury of grief and pain and rage. He would have murdered his master without the faintest compunction, nay, with huge delight. Psychologically, his frame of mind was quite interesting, though he was only a schoolboy who had just had a sound thrashing for breaking rules.

For the fact, of course, was that Horbury, the irritating influence of the Head's conversation and sherry apart, was by no means a bad fellow. He was for the moment savagely cruel, but then, most men are apt to be savagely cruel when they suffer from an inflamed liver and offensive superiors, more especially when there is an inferior, warranted defenceless, in their power. But, in the main, Horbury was a very decent specimen of his class—English schoolmaster—and Meyrick would never allow that. In all his reasoning about schools and schoolmasters there was a fatal flaw—he blamed both for not being what they never pretended to be. To use a figure that would have appealed to him, it was as if one quarrelled with a plain, old-fashioned meeting-house because it was not in the least like Lincoln Cathedral. A chimney may not be a decorative object, but then it does not profess to be a spire or a pinnacle far in the spiritual city.

But Meyrick was always scolding meeting-houses because they were not cathedrals. He has been heard to rave for hours against useful, unpretentious chimney-pots because they bore no resemblance to celestial spires. Somehow or other, possibly by inheritance, possibly by the influence of his father's companionship, he had unconsciously acquired a theory of life which bore no relation whatever to the facts of it. The theory was manifest in his later years; but it must have been stubbornly, if vaguely, present in him all through his boyhood. Take, for instance, his comment on poor Canon Horbury's verses. He judged those, as we have seen, by the rules of the fine art of literature, and found them rubbish. Yet any old Luptonian would have told him that to hear the whole six hundred boys join in the chorus, "Lupton, follow away!" was one of the great experiences of life; from which it appears that the song, whatever its demerits from a literary point of view, fully satisfied the purpose for which it was written. In other words, it was an excellent chimney, but Meyrick still persisted in his easy and futile task of proving that it was not a bit like a spire. Then, again, one finds a fallacy of still huger extent in that major premiss of his: that the great Public Schools purpose to themselves as a secondary and minor object the imparting of the spirit and beauty of the Greek and Latin literatures. Now, it is very possible that at some distant peri-od in the past this was an object, or even, perhaps, *the* object of the in-stitutions in question. The Humanists, it may be conjectured, thought of school and University as places where Latin and Greek were to be learned, and to be learned with the object of enjoying the great thought and the great style of the antique world. One sees the spirit of this in Rabelais, for example. The Classics are a wonderful adventure; to learn to understand them is to be a spiritual Columbus, a discoverer of new seas and unknown continents, a drinker of new-old wine in a new-old land. To the student of those days a mysterious drowned Atlantis again rose splendid from the waves of the great deep. It was these things that Meyrick (unconsciously, doubtless) expected to find in his school life; it was for the absence of these things that he continued to scold the system in his later years; wherein, like Jim in *Huckleberry Finn,* he missed the point by a thousand miles.

The Latin and Greek of modem instruction are, of course, most curious and interesting survivals; no longer taught with any view of en-abling students to enjoy and understand either the thought or beauty of the originals; taught rather in such a manner as to nauseate the learner for the rest of his days with the very notion of these lessons. Still, the study of the Classics survives, a curious and elaborate ritual, from which all sense and spirit have departed. One has only to recollect the form master's lessons in the *Odyssey* or the *Bacchæ,* and then to view modern Freemasons celebrating the Mystic Death and Resurrection of Hiram Abiff; the analogy is complete, for neither the master nor the

Masons have the remotest notion of what they are doing. Both persevere in strange and mysterious actions from inveterate conservatism.

Meyrick was a lover of antiquity and a special lover of survivals, but he could never see that the round of Greek syntax and Latin prose, of Elegiacs and Verbs in μι, with the mystery of the Oratio Obliqua and the Optative, was one of the most strange and picturesque survivals of modern life. It is to be noted, by the way, that the very meaning of the word "scholar" has been radically changed. Thus a well-known authority points out that "Melancholy" Burton had no "scholarship" in the real sense of the word; he merely used his vast knowledge of ancient and modern literature to make one of the most entertaining and curious books that the world possesses. True "scholarship", in the modern sense, is to be sought for not in the Jacobean translators of the Bible, but in the Victorian revisers. The former made the greatest of English books out of their Hebrew and Greek originals; but the latter understood the force of the aorist. It is curious to reflect that "scholar" once meant a man of literary taste and knowledge.

Meyrick never mastered these distinctions, or, if he did so in later years, he never confessed to his enlightenment, but went on railing at the meeting-house, which, he still maintained, *did* pretend to be a cathedral. He has been heard to wonder why a certain Dean, who had pointed out the vast improvements that had been effected by the Revisers, did not employ a few young art students from Kensington to correct the infamous drawing of the fourteenth-century glass in his cathedral. He was incorrigible; he was always incorrigible, and thus, in his boyhood, on the dark November evening, he meditated the murder of his good master and uncle—for at least a quarter of an hour.

His father, he remembered, had always spoken of Gothic architecture as the most wonderful and beautiful thing in the world: a thing to be studied and loved and reverenced. His father had never so much as mentioned rocker, much less had he preached it as the one way by which an English boy must be saved. Hence, Ambrose maintained inwardly that his visit to Selden Abbey was deserving of reward rather than punishment, and he resented bitterly the savage injustice (as he thought it) of his caning.

3.

Yet Mr. Horbury had been right in one matter, if not in all. That evening was a turning-point in Meyrick's life. He had felt the utmost rage of the enemy, as it were, and he determined that he would be a funk no longer. He would not degenerate into the state of little Phipps, who had been bullied and "rockered" and beaten into such a deplorable condition that he fainted dead away while the Headmaster was operating on him for "systematic and deliberate lying". Phipps not only fainted, but, being fundamentally sensible, as Dr. Johnson expressed it, shewed a strong disinclination to return to consciousness and the precious balms of the "dear old Head". Chesson was rather frightened, and the school doctor, who had his living to get, said, somewhat dryly, that he thought the lad had better go home for a week or two.

So Phipps went home in a state which made his mother cry bitterly and his father wonder whether the Public School system was not overpraised. But the old family doctor went about raging and swearing at the "scoundrels" who had reduced a child of twelve to a nervous wreck, with "neurasthenia cerebralis" well on its way. But Dr. Walford had got his education in some trumpery little academy, and did not understand or value the *ethos* of the great Public Schools.

Now, Ambrose Meyrick had marked the career of wretched Phipps with concern and pity. The miserable little creature had been brought by careful handling from masters and boys to such a pitch of neurotic perfection that it was only necessary to tap him smartly on the back or on the arm, and he would instantly burst into tears. Whenever any one asked him the simplest question he suspected a cruel trap of some sort, and lied and equivocated and shuffled with a pitiable lack of skill. Though he was pitched by the heels into mucker about three times a week, that he might acquire the useful art of natation, he still seemed to grow dirtier and dirtier. His school books were torn to bits, his exercises made into darts; he had impositions for losing books and canings for not doing his work, and he lied and cried all the more.

Meyrick had never got to this depth. He was a sturdy boy, and Phipps had always been a weakly little animal; but, as he walked from the study to the schoolroom after his thrashing, he felt that he had been in some danger of descending on that sad way. He finally resolved that he would never tread it, and so he walked past the baize-lined doors into the room where the other boys were at work on prep. with an air of unconcern which was not in the least assumed.

Mr. Horbury was a man of considerable private means and did not care to be bothered with the troubles and responsibilities of a big House. But there was room and to spare in the Old Grange, so he took three boys besides his nephew. These three were waiting with a grin of anticipation, since the nature of Meyrick's interview with "old Horbury" was not dubious. But Ambrose strolled in with a "Hallo, you fellows!" and sat down in his place as if nothing had happened. This was intolerable.

"I say, Meyrick," began Pelly, a beefy boy with a red face, "you *have* been blubbing! Feel like writing home about it? Oh! I forgot. This is your home, isn't it? How many cuts? I didn't hear you howl."

The boy took no notice. He was getting out his books as if no one had spoken.

"Can't you answer?" went on the beefy one. "How many cuts, you young sneak?"

"Go to hell!"

The whole three stared aghast for a moment; they thought Meyrick must have gone mad. Only one, Bates the observant, began to chuckle quietly to himself, for he did not like Pelly. He who was always beefy became beefier; his eyes bulged out with fury.

"I'll give it you," he said and made for Ambrose, who was turning over the leaves of the Latin Dictionary. Ambrose did not wait for the assault; he rose also and met Pelly half-way with a furious blow, well planted on the nose. Pelly took a back somersault and fell with a crash to the floor, where he lay for a moment half stunned. He rose stagger-ing and looked about him with a pathetic, bewildered air; for, indeed, a great part of his little world had crumbled about his ears. He stood in the middle of the room, wondering what it meant, whether it was true indeed that Meyrick was no longer of any use for a little quiet fun. A horrible and incredible transmutation had, apparently, been effected in the funk of old. Pelly gazed wildly about him as he tried to staunch the blood that poured over his mouth.

"Foul blow!" ventured Rawson, a lean lad who liked to twist the arms of very little boys till they shrieked for mercy. The full inwardness of the incident had not penetrated to his brain; he saw without believing, in the manner of the materialist who denies the marvellous even when it is before his eyes.

"Foul blow, young Meyrick!"

The quiet student had gone back to his place and was again handling his dictionary. It was a hard, compact volume, rebound in strong boards, and the edge of these boards caught the unfortunate Rawson full across the eyes with extraordinary force. He put his face in his hands and blubbered quietly and dismally, rocking to and fro in his seat, hardly hearing the fluent stream of curses with which the quiet student enquired whether the blow he had just had was good enough for him.

Meyrick picked up his dictionary with a volley of remarks which would have done credit to an old-fashioned stage-manager at the last dress rehearsal before production.

"Hark at him," said Pelly feebly, almost reverently. "Hark at him." But poor Rawson, rocking to and fro, his head between his hands, went on blubbering softly and spoke no word.

Meyrick had never been an unobservant lad; he had simply made a discovery that evening that in Rome certain Roman customs must be adopted. The wise Bates went on doing his copy of Latin verse, chuckling gently to himself. Bates was a cynic. He despised all the customs and manners of the place most heartily and took the most curious care to observe them. He might have been the inventor and patentee of rocker, if one judged him by the fervour with which he played it. He entered his name for every possible event at the sports, and jumped the jumps and threw the hammer and ran the races as if his life depended on it. Once Mr. Horbury had accidentally overheard Bates saying something about "the honour of the House" which went to his heart. As for cricket, Bates played as if his sole ambition was to become a first-class professional. And he chuckled as he did his Latin verses, which he wrote (to the awe of other boys) "as if he were writing a letter"—that is, without making a rough copy. For Bates had got the "hang" of the whole system from rocker to Latin verse, and his copies were much admired. He grinned that evening, partly at the transmutation of Meyrick and partly at the line he was jotting down:

"Mira loquor, cœlo resonans vox funditur alto."

In after life he jotted down a couple of novels which sold, as the journalists said, "like hot cakes". Meyrick went to see him soon after the first novel had gone into its thirtieth thousand, and Bates was reading "appreciations" and fingering a cheque and chuckling.

"Mira loquor, populo resonans *cheque* funditur alto," he said. "I know what schoolmasters and boys and the public want, and I take care they get it—*sale espèce de sacrés cochons de N. de D.!*"

The rest of prep. went off quite quietly. Pelly was slowly recovering from the shock that he had received and began to meditate revenge. Meyrick had got him unawares, he reflected. It was merely an accident, and he resolved to challenge Meyrick to fight and give him the worst licking he had ever had in his life. He was beefy, but a bold fellow. Rawson, who was really a cruel coward and a sneak, had made up his mind that he wanted no more, and from time to time cast meek and propitiatory glances in Meyrick's direction.

At half-past nine they all went into their dining-room for bread and cheese and beer. At a quarter to ten Mr. Horbury appeared in cap and gown and read a chapter from St. Paul's Epistle to the Romans, with one or two singularly maundering and unhappy prayers. He stopped the boys as they were going up to their rooms.

"What's this, Pelly?" he said. "Your nose is all swollen. It's been bleeding, too, I see. What have you been doing to yourself? And you, Rawson, how do you account for your eyes being black? What's the meaning of all this?"

"Please, Sir, there was a very stiff bully down at rocker this afternoon, and Rawson and I got tokered badly."

"Were you in the bully, Bates?"

"No, Sir; I've been outside since the beginning of the term. But all the fellows were playing up tremendously, and I saw Rawson and Pelly had been touched when we were changing."

"Ah! I see. I'm very glad to find the House plays up so well. As for you, Bates, I hear you're the best outside for your age that we've ever had. Good night."

The three said "Thank you, Sir," as if their dearest wish had been gratified, and the master could have sworn that Bates flushed with pleasure at his word of praise. But the fact was that Bates had "suggested" the flush by a cunning arrangement of his features.

The boys vanished and Mr. Horbury returned to his desk. He was editing a selection called "English Literature for Lower Forms". He began to read from the slips that he had prepared:

So all day long the noise of battle roll'd
Among the mountains by the winter sea;
Until King Arthur's table, man by man,
Had fallen in Lyonnesse—"

He stopped and set a figure by the last word, and then, on a blank slip, with a corresponding letter, he repeated the figure and wrote the note:

Lyonnesse = the Scilly Isles.

Then he took a third slip and wrote the question:

Give the ancient name of the Scilly Isles.

These serious labours employed him till twelve o'clock. He put the materials of his book away as the clock struck, and solemnly mixed himself his nightly glass of whisky and soda—in the daytime he never touched spirits—and bit the one cigar which he smoked in the twenty-four hours. The stings of the Head's sherry and of his conversation no longer burned within him; time and work and the bite of the cane in Meyrick's flesh had soothed his soul, and he set himself to dream, leaning back in his arm-chair, watching the cheerful fire.

He was thinking of what he would do when he succeeded to the Headmastership. Already there were rumours that Chesson had refused the Bishopric of St. Dubric's in order that he might be free to accept Dorchester, which, in the nature of things, must soon be vacant. Horbury had no doubt that the Headmastership would be his; he had influential friends who assured him that the trustees would not hesitate for an instant. Then he would shew the world what an English Public School could be made. In five years, he calculated, he would double the numbers. He saw the coming importance of the modern side, and especially of science. Personally, he detested "stinks", but he knew what an effect he would produce with a great laboratory fitted with the very best appliances and directed by a highly qualified master. Then, again, an elaborate gymnasium must be built; there must be an

engineer's shop, too, and a carpenter's as well. And people were beginning to complain that a Public School education was of no use in
the City. There must be a business master, an expert from the Stock
Exchange who would see that this reproach was removed. Then he
considered that a large number of the boys belonged to the land-
owning class. Why should a country gentleman be at the mercy of his
agent, forced for lack of technical knowledge to accept statements
which he could not check? It was clear that the management of land
and great estates must have its part in the scheme; and, again, the best-
known of the Crammers must be bought on his own terms, so that
boys who wished to get into the Army or the Civil Service would be
practically compelled to come to Lupton. Already he saw paragraphs in
the *Guardian* and *The Times*—in all the papers—paragraphs which mentioned the fact that ninety-five per cent of the successful candidates for
the Indian Civil Service had received their education at the foundation
of "stout old Martin Rolle". Meanwhile, in all this flood of novelty, the
old traditions should be maintained with more vigour than ever. The
Classics should be taught as they never had been taught. Every one of
the masters on this side should be in the highest honours and, if possible, he would get famous men for the work—they should not merely
be good, but also notorious scholars. Gee, the famous explorer in
Crete, who had made an enormous mark in regions widely removed
from the scholastic world by his wonderful book, *Dædalus; or, The Secret of the Labyrinth,* must come to Lupton at any price; and Maynard,
who had discovered some most important Greek manuscripts in
Egypt, he must have a form, too. Then there was Rendall, who had
done so well with his *Thucydides,* and Davies, author of *The Olive of
Athene,* a daring but most brilliant book which promised to upset the
whole established theory of mythology—he would have such a staff as
no school had ever dreamed of. "We shall have no difficulty about
paying them," thought Horbury; "our numbers will go up by leaps and
bounds, and the fees shall be five hundred pounds a year—and such
terms will do us more good than anything."

He went into minute detail. He must take expert advice as to the
advisability of the school farming on its own account, and so supplying
the boys with meat, milk, bread, butter and vegetables at first cost. He
believed it could be done; he would get a Scotch farmer from the Low-

lands and make him superintendent at a handsome salary and with a share in the profits. There would be the splendid advertisement of "the whole dietary of the school supplied from the School Farms, under the supervision of Mr. David Anderson, formerly of Haddanneuk, the largest tenancy in the Duke of Ayr's estates". The food would be better and cheaper, too; but there would be no luxury. The "Spartan" card was always worth playing; one must strike the note of plain living in a luxurious age; there must be no losing of the old Public School severity. On the other hand, the boys' hands should be free to go into their own pockets; there should be no restraint here. If a boy chose to bring in *Dindonneau aux truffes* or *Pieds de mouton à la Ste Menehould* to help out his tea, that was his look-out. Why should not the school grant a concession to some big London firm, who would pay handsomely for the privilege of supplying the hungry lads with every kind of expensive dainty? The sum could be justly made a large one, as any competing shop could be promptly put out of bounds with reason or without it. On one side, *confiserie;* at the other counter, *charcuterie;* enormous prices could be charged to the wealthy boys of whom the school would be composed. Yet, on the other hand, the distinguished visitor—judge, bishop, peer or what not—would lunch at the Headmaster's house and eat the boys' dinner and go away saying it was quite the plainest and very many times the best meal he had ever tasted. There would be well-hung saddle of mutton, roasted and not baked; floury potatoes and cauliflower; apple pudding and real English cheese, with an excellent glass of the school beer, an honest and delicious beverage made of malt and hops in the well-found school brewery. Horbury knew enough of modern eating and drinking to understand that such a meal would be a choice rarity to nine rich people out of ten; and yet it was "Spartan", utterly devoid of luxury and ostentation.

Again, he passed from detail and minutiæ into great Napoleonic regions. A thousand boys at £500 a year; that would be an income for the school of five hundred thousand pounds! The profits would be gigantic, immense. After paying large, even extravagant, prices to the staff, after all building expenses had been deducted, he hardly dared to think how vast a sum would accrue year by year to the Trustees. The vision began to assume such magnificence that it became oppressive; it put on the splendours and delights of the haschish dream, which are too great and too piercing for mortal hearts to bear. And yet it was no mirage; there was not a step that could not be demonstrated, shewn to be based on hard, matter-of-fact business considerations. He tried to keep back his growing excitement, to argue with himself that he was dealing in visions, but the facts were too obstinate. He saw that it would be his part to work the same miracle in the scholastic world as the great American storekeepers had operated in the world of retail trade. The principle was precisely the same: instead of a hundred small shops making comparatively modest and humdrum profits you had the vast emporium doing business on the gigantic scale with vastly diminished expenses and vastly increased rewards.

Here again was a hint. He had thought of America, and he knew that here was an inexhaustible gold mine that no other scholastic prospector had even dreamed of. The rich American was notoriously hungry for everything that was English, from frock-coats to pedigrees. He had never thought of sending his son to an English Public School because he considered the system hopelessly behind the times. But the new translated Lupton would be to other Public Schools as a New York hotel of the latest fashion is to a village beer-shop. And yet the young millionaire would grow up in the company of the sons of English gentlemen, imbibing the unique culture of English life, while at the same time he enjoyed all the advantages of modern ideas, modern science and modern business training. Land was still comparatively cheap at Lupton; the school must buy it quietly, indirectly, by degrees, and then pile after pile of vast buildings rose before his eyes. He saw the sons of the rich drawn from all the ends of the world to the Great School, there to learn the secret of the Anglo-Saxons.

Chesson was mistaken in that idea of his, which he thought daring and original, of establishing a distinct Jewish House where the food should be "Kosher". The rich Jew who desired to send his son to an English Public School was, in nine cases out of ten, anxious to do so precisely because he wanted to sink his son's connection with Jewry in oblivion. He had heard Chesson talk of "our Christian duty to the seed of Israel" in this connection. The man was clearly a fool. No, the more Jews the better, but no Jewish House. And no Puseyism either: broad, earnest religious teaching, with a leaning to moderate Anglicanism, should be the faith of Lupton. As to this Chesson was, certainly, sound enough. He had always made a firm stand against ecclesiasticism in any form. Horbury knew the average English parent of the wealthier classes thoroughly; he knew that, though he generally called himself a Churchman, he was quite content to have his sons prepared for confirmation by a confessed Agnostic. Certainly this liberty must not be narrowed when Lupton became cosmopolitan. "We will retain all the dignified associations which belong to the Established Church," he said to himself, "and at the same time we shall be utterly free from the taint of over-emphasising dogmatic teaching." He had a sudden brilliant idea. Everybody in Church circles was saying that the English bishops were terribly overworked, that it was impossible for the most strenuous men with the best intentions to supervise effectually the huge dioceses that had descended from the sparsely populated England of the Middle Ages. Everywhere there was a demand for suffragans and more suffragans. In the last week's *Guardian* there were three letters on the subject, one from a clergyman in their own diocese. The Bishop had been attacked by some rabid ritualistic person, who had pointed out that nine out of every ten parishes had not so much as seen the colour of his hood ever since his appointment ten years before. The Archdeacon of Melby had replied in a capital letter, scathing and yet humorous. Horbury turned to the paper on the table beside his chair and looked up the letter. "In the first place," wrote the Archdeacon, "your correspondent does not seem to have realised that the *ethos* of the Diocese of Melby is not identical with that of sacerdotalism. The sturdy folk of the Midlands have not yet, I am thankful to say, forgotten the lessons of our great Reformation. They have no wish to see a revival of the purely mechanical religion of the Middle Ages—of the system of a sacrificing priesthood and of sacraments efficacious *ex opere operato*. Hence they do not regard the episcopate quite in the same light as your correspondent 'Senex', who, it seems to me, looks upon a bishop as a sort of Christianised 'medicine-man', endowed with certain mysterious thaumaturgic powers which have descended to him by an (imaginary) spiritual succession. This was not the view of Hooker nor, I venture to say, has it ever been the view of the really representative divines of the Established Church of England.

"Still," the Archdeacon went on, "it must be admitted that the present diocese of Melby is unwieldy and, it may be fairly said, unworkable."

Then there followed the humorous anecdote of Sir Boyle Roche and the Bird, and finally the Archdeacon emitted the prayer that God in His own good time would put it into the hearts of our rulers in Church and State to give their good Bishop an episcopal curate.

Horbury got up from his chair and paced up and down the study; his excitement was so great that he could keep quiet no longer. His cigar had gone out long ago, and he had barely sipped the whisky and soda. His eyes glittered with excitement. Circumstances seemed positively to be playing into his hands; the dice of the world were being loaded in his favour. He was like Bel Ami at his wedding. He almost began to believe in Providence.

For he was sure it could be managed. Here was a general feeling that no one man could do the work of the diocese. There must be a suffragan, and Lupton must give the new Bishop his title. No other town was possible. Dunham had certainly been a see in the eighth century, but it was now little more than a village and a village served by a miserable little branch line; whereas Lupton was on the great main track of the Midland system, with easy connections to every part of the country. The Archdeacon, who was also a peer, would undoubtedly become the first Bishop of Lupton, and he should be the titular chaplain of the Great School! "Chaplain: the Right Reverend Lord Selwyn, Lord Bishop of Lupton." Horbury gasped; it was too magnificent, too splendid. He knew Lord Selwyn quite well and had no doubt as to his acceptance. He was a poor man, and there would be no difficulty whatever in establishing a *modus*. The Archdeacon was just the man for the place. He was no pedantic theologian, but a broad, liberal-minded man of the world. Horbury remembered, almost with ecstasy, that he had lectured all over the United States with immense success. The American Press had been enthusiastic, and the First Congregational Church of Chicago had implored Selwyn to accept its call, preach what he liked and pocket an honorarium of twenty-five thousand dollars a year. And, on the other hand, what could the most orthodox desire safer than a chaplain who was not only a bishop, but a peer of the realm? Wonderful! Here were the three birds—Liberalism, Orthodoxy and Reverence for the House of Lords—caught safe and secure in this one net.

The games? They should be maintained in all their glory, rather on an infinitely more splendid scale. Cricket and sticker (the Lupton hockey), rackets and fives, should all be encouraged; and more, Lupton should be the only school to possess a tennis court. The noble *jeu de paume,* the game of kings, the most aristocratic of all sports, should have a worthy home at Lupton. They would train champions; they would have both French and English markers skilled in the latest developments of the *chemin de fer* service. "Better than half a yard, I think," said Horbury to himself; "they will have to do their best to beat that."

But he placed most reliance on rocker. This was the Lupton football, a variant as distinctive in its way as the Eton Wall Game. People have thought that the name is a sort of portmanteau word, a combination of Rugger and Soccer; but in reality the title was derived from the field where the game used to be played in old days by the townsfolk. As in many other places, football at Lupton had been originally an excuse for a faction-fight between two parishes in the town—St. Michael's and St. Paul's-in-the-Fields. Every year, on Shrove Tuesday, the townsfolk, young and old, had proceeded to the Town Field and had fought out their differences with considerable violence. The field was broken land: a deep, sluggish stream crossed one angle of it, and in the middle there were quarries and jagged limestone rocks. Hence football was called in the town "playing rocks", for, indeed, it was considered an excellent point of play to hurl a man over the edge of the quarry on to the rocks beneath, and so late as 1830 a certain Jonas Simpson of St. Michael's had had his spine broken in this way. However, as a boy from St. Paul's was drowned in the Wand the same day, the game was always reckoned a draw. It was from the peculiarities of this old English sport that the school had constructed its game. The Town Field had, of course, long been stolen from the townsfolk and built over; but the boys had, curiously enough, perpetuated the tradition of its peculiarities in a kind of football ritual. For, besides the two goals, one part of the field was marked by a line of low white posts: these indicated the course of a non-existent Wand brook, and in the line of these posts it was lawful to catch an opponent by the throat and choke him till he turned black in the face—the best substitute for drowning that the revisers of the game could imagine. Again: about the centre of the field two taller posts indicated the position of the quarries, and between these you might be hit or kicked full in the stomach without the smallest ground of complaint: the stroke being a milder version of the old fall on the rocks. There were many other like amenities in rocker; and Horbury maintained it was by far the manliest variant of the game. For this pleasing sport he now designed a world-wide fame. Rocker should be played wherever the English flag floated: east and west, north and south; from Hong Kong to British Columbia; in Canada and New Zealand there should be the τεμένοι of this great rite; and the traveller seeing the mystic enclosure—the two goals, the line of little posts marking "brooks", and the two poles indicating "quarries"—should know English soil as surely as by the Union Jack. The technical terms of rocker should become a part of the great Anglo-Saxon inheritance; the whole world should hear of "bully-downs" and "tokering", of "outsides" and "rammers". It would require working, but it was to be done: articles in the magazines and in the Press; perhaps a story of school life, a new *Tom Brown* must be written. The Midlands and the North must be shewn that there was money in it, and the rest would be easy.

One thing troubled Horbury. His mind was full of the new and splendid buildings that were to be erected, but he was aware that antiquity still counted for something, and unfortunately Lupton could shew very little that was really antique. Forty years before, Stanley, the first reforming Headmaster, had pulled down the old High School. There were prints of it: it was a half-timbered, fifteenth-century building, with a wavering roof-line and an overhanging upper story; there were dim, leaded windows and a grey arched porch—an ugly old barn, Stanley called it. Scott was called in and built the present High School, a splendid hall in red brick: French thirteenth-century, with Venetian detail; it was much admired. But Horbury was sorry that the old school had been destroyed; he saw for the first time that it might have been made a valuable attraction. Then again, Dowsing, who succeeded Stanley, had knocked the cloisters all to bits; there was only one side of the quadrangle left, and this had been boarded up and used as a gardeners' shed. Horbury did not know what to say of the destruction of the Cross that used to stand in the centre of the quad. No doubt Dowsing was right in thinking it superstitious; still, it might have been left as a curiosity and shewn to visitors, just as the instruments of bygone cruelty—the rack and the Iron Maid—are preserved and exhibited to wondering sightseers. There was no real danger of any superstitious adoration of the Cross; it was, as a matter of fact, as harmless as the axe and block at the Tower of London; Dowsing had ruined what might have been an important asset in the exploitation of the school.

Still, perhaps the loss was not altogether irreparable. High School was gone and could not be recovered; but the cloisters might be restored and the Cross, too. Horbury knew that the monument in front of Charing Cross Railway Station was considered by many to be a genuine antique: why not get a good man to build them a Cross? Not like the old one, of course; that "Fair Roode with our Deare Ladie Saint Marie and Saint John", and, below, the stories of the blissful Saints and Angels—that would never do. But a vague, Gothic erection, with plenty of kings and queens, imaginary benefactors of the school, and a small cast-iron cross at the top: that could give no offence to anybody, and might pass with nine people out of ten as a genuine remnant of the Middle Ages. It could be made of soft stone and allowed to weather for a few years; then a coat of invisible anti-corrosive fluid would preserve carvings and imagery that would already appear venerable in decay. There was no need to make any precise statements: parents and the public might be allowed to draw their own conclusions.

Horbury was neglecting nothing. He was building up a great scheme in his mind, and to him it seemed that every detail was worth attending to, while at the same time he did not lose sight of the whole effect. He believed in finish: there must be no rough edges. It seemed to him that a school legend must be invented. The real history was not quite what he wanted, though it might work in with a more decorative account of Lupton's origins. One might use the *Textus Receptus* of Martin Rolle's Foundation—the bequest of land *c.* 1430 to build and maintain a school where a hundred boys should be taught grammar, and ten poor scholars and six priests should pray for the Founder's soul. This was well enough, but one might hint that Martin Rolle really refounded and re-endowed a school of Saxon origin, probably established by King Alfred himself in Luppa's Tun. Then, again, who could shew that Shakespeare had not visited Lupton? His famous schoolboy, "creeping like snail unwillingly to school", might very possibly have been observed by the poet as he strolled by the banks of the Wand. Many famous men might have received their education at Lupton; it would not be difficult to make a plausible list of such. It must be done carefully and cautiously, with such phrases as "it has always been a tradition at

Lupton that Sir Walter Raleigh received part of his education at the school"; or, again, "an earlier generation of Luptonians remembered the initials 'W. S. S. on A.' cut deeply in the mantel of old High School, now, unfortunately, demolished." Antiquarians would laugh? Possibly; but who cared about antiquarians? For the average man "Charing" was derived from *"chère reine"*, and he loved to have it so, and Horbury intended to appeal to the average man. Though he was a schoolmaster he was no recluse, and he had marked the ways of the world from his quiet study in Lupton; hence he understood the immense value of a grain of quackery in all schemes which are meant to appeal to mortals. It was a deadly mistake to suppose that anything which was all quackery would be a success—a permanent success, at all events; it was a deadlier mistake still to suppose that anything quite devoid of quackery could pay handsomely. The average English palate would shudder at the flavour of *aioli*, but it would be charmed by the insertion of that *petit point d'ail* which turned mere goodness into triumphant and laurelled perfection. And there was no need to mention the word "garlic" before the guests. Lupton was not going to be all garlic: it was to be infinitely the best scholastic dish that had ever been served—the ingredients should be unsurpassed and unsurpassable. But—King Alfred's foundation of a school at Luppa's Tun, and that "W. S. S. on A." cut deeply on the mantel of the vanished High School—these and legends like unto them, these would be the last touch, *le petit point d'ail.*

It was a great scheme, wonderful and glorious; and the most amazing thing about it was that it was certain to be realised. There was not a flaw from start to finish. The Trustees were certain to appoint him—he had that from a sure quarter—and it was but a question of a year or two, perhaps only of a month or two, before all this great and golden vision should be converted into hard and tangible fact. He drank off his glass of whisky and soda; it had become flat and brackish, but to him it was nectar, since it was flavoured with ecstasy.

He frowned suddenly as he went upstairs to his room. An unpleasant recollection had intruded for a moment on his amazing fantasy; but he dismissed the thought as soon as it arose. That was all over, there could be no possibility of trouble from that direction; and so, his mind filled with images, he fell asleep and saw Lupton as the centre of the whole world, like Jerusalem in the ancient maps.

A student of the deep things of mysticism has detected a curious element of comedy in the management of human concerns; and there certainly seems a touch of humour in the fact that on this very night, while Horbury was building the splendid Lupton of the future, the palace of his thought and his life was shattered for ever into bitter dust and nothingness. But so it was. The Dread Arrest had been solemnly preconised, and that wretched canonry at Wareham was irrevocably pronounced for doom. Fantastic were the elements of forces that had gone to the ordering of this great sentence: raw corn spirit in the guise of sherry, the impertinence (or what seemed such) of an elderly clergyman, a boiled leg of mutton, a troublesome and disobedient boy, and—another person.

II

1.

He was standing in a wild, bare country. Something about it seemed vaguely familiar: the land rose and fell in dull and weary undulations, in a vast circle of dun ploughland and grey meadow, bounded by a dim horizon without promise or hope, dreary as a prison wall. The infinite melancholy of an autumn evening brooded heavily over all the world, and the sky was hidden by livid clouds.

It all brought back to him some far-off memory, and yet he knew that he gazed on that sad plain for the first time. There was a deep and heavy silence over all; a silence unbroken by so much as the fluttering of a leaf. The trees seemed of a strange shape, and strange were the stunted thorns dotted about the broken field in which he stood. A little path at his feet, bordered by the thorn bushes, wandered away to the left into the dim twilight; it had about it some indefinable air of mystery, as if it must lead one down into a mystic region where all earthly things are forgotten and lost for ever.

He sat down beneath the bare, twisted boughs of a great tree and watched the dreary land grow darker and yet darker; he wondered, half-consciously, where he was and how he had come to that place, remembering, faintly, tales of like adventure. A man passed by a familiar wall one day, and, opening a door before unnoticed, found himself in a new world of unsurmised and marvellous experiences. Another man shot an arrow farther than any of his friends and became the husband of the fairy. Yet—this was not fairyland; these were rather the sad fields and unhappy graves of the underworld than the abode of endless pleasures and undying delights. And yet in all that he saw there was the promise of great wonder.

Only one thing was clear to him. He knew that he was Ambrose, that he had been driven from great and unspeakable joys into miserable exile and banishment. He had come from a far, far place by a hidden way, and darkness had closed about him, and bitter drink and deadly meat were given him, and all gladness was hidden from him. This was all he could remember; and now he was astray, he knew not how or why, in this wild, sad land, and the night descended dark upon him.

Suddenly there was, as it were, a cry far away in the shadowy silence, and the thorn bushes began to rustle before a shrilling wind that rose as the night came down. At this summons the heavy clouds broke up and dispersed, fleeting across the sky, and the pure heaven appeared with the last rose flush of the sunset dying from it, and there shone the silver light of the evening star. Ambrose's heart was drawn up to this light as he gazed: he saw that the star grew greater and greater; it advanced towards him through the air; its beams pierced to his soul as if they were the sound of a silver trumpet. An ocean of white splendour flowed over him: he dwelt within the star.

It was but for a moment; he was still sitting beneath the tree of the twisted branches. But the sky was now clear and filled with a great peace; the wind had fallen and a more happy light shone on the great plain. Ambrose was thirsty, and then he saw that beside the tree there was a well, half hidden by the arching roots that rose above it. The water was still and shining, as though it were a mirror of black marble, and marking the brim was a great stone on which were cut the letters:

"FONS VITAI IMMORTALIS."

He rose and, bending over the well, put down his lips to drink, and his soul and body were filled as with a flood of joy. Now he knew that all his days of exile he had borne with pain and grief a heavy, weary body. There had been dolours in every limb and achings in every bone; his feet had dragged upon the ground, slowly, wearily, as the feet of those who go in chains. But dim, broken spectres, miserable shapes and crooked images of the world had his eyes seen; for they were eyes bleared with sickness, darkened by the approach of death. Now, indeed, he clearly beheld the shining vision of things immortal. He drank great draughts of the dark, glittering water, drinking, it seemed, the light of the reflected stars; and he was filled with life. Every sinew, every muscle, every particle of the deadly flesh shuddered and quickened in the communion of that well-water. The nerves and veins rejoiced together; all his being leapt with gladness, and as one finger touched another, as he still bent over the well, a spasm of exquisite pleasure quivered and thrilled through his body. His heart throbbed with bliss that was unendurable; sense and intellect and soul and spirit were, as it were, sublimed into one white flame of delight. And all the while it was known to him that these were but the least of the least of the pleasures of the kingdom, but the overrunnings and base tricklings of the great supernal cup. He saw, without amazement, that, though the sun had set, the sky now began to flush and redden as if with the northern light. It was no longer the evening, no longer the time of the procession of the dusky night. The darkness doubtless had passed away in mortal hours while for an infinite moment he tasted immortal drink; and perhaps one drop of that water was endless life. But now it was the preparation for the day. He heard the words:

> *"Dies venit, dies Tua*
> *In qua reflorent omnia."*

They were uttered within his heart, and he saw that all was being made ready for a great festival. Over everything there was a hush of expectation; and as he gazed he knew that he was no longer in that weary land of dun ploughland and grey meadow, of the wild, bare trees and strange stunted thorn bushes. He was on a hill-side, lying on the verge of a great wood; beneath, in the valley, a brook sang faintly under the leaves of the silvery willows; and beyond, far in the east, a vast wall of rounded mountain rose serene towards the sky. All about him was the green world of the leaves: odours of the summer night, deep in the mystic heart of the wood, odours of many flowers, and the cool breath rising from the singing stream mingled in his nostrils. The world whitened to the dawn, and then, as the light grew clear, the rose clouds blossomed in the sky and, answering, the earth seemed to glitter with rose-red sparks and glints of flame. All the east became as a garden of roses, red flowers of living light shone over the mountain, and as the beams of the sun lit up the circle of the earth a bird's song began from a tree within the wood. Then were heard the modulations of a final and exultant ecstasy, the chant of liberation, a magistral *In Exitu;* there was the melody of rejoicing trills, of unwearied, glad reiterations of choirs ever aspiring, prophesying the coming of the great feast, singing the eternal antiphon.

As the song aspired into the heights, so there aspired suddenly before him the walls and pinnacles of a great church set upon a high hill. It was far off, and yet as though it were close at hand he saw all the delicate and wonderful imagery cut in its stones. The great door in the west was a miracle: every flower and leaf, every reed and fern, were clustered in the work of the capitals, and in the round arch above moulding within moulding shewed all the beasts that God has made. He saw the rose-window, a maze of fretted tracery, the high lancets of the fair hall, the marvellous buttresses, set like angels about this holy house, whose pinnacles were as a place of many springing trees. And high above the vast, far-lifted vault of the roof rose up the spire, golden in the light. The bells were ringing for the feast; he heard from within the walls the roll and swell and triumph of the organ:

O pius o bonus o placidus sonus hymnus eorum.

He knew not how he had taken his place in this great procession, how, surrounded by ministrants in white, he too bore his part in endless litanies. He knew not through what strange land they passed in their fervent, admirable order, following their banners and their symbols that glanced on high before them. But that land stood ever, it seemed, in a clear, still air, crowned with golden sunlight; and so there were those who bore great torches of wax, strangely and beautifully adorned with golden and vermilion ornaments. The delicate flame of these tapers burned steadily in the still sunlight, and the glittering silver censers as they rose and fell tossed a pale cloud into the air. They de-layed, now and again, by wayside shrines, giving thanks for unutterable compassions, and, advancing anew, the blessed company surged on-ward, moving to its unknown goal in the far blue mountains that rose beyond the plain. There were faces and shapes of awful beauty about him; he saw those in whose eyes were the undying lamps of heaven, about whose heads the golden hair was as an aureole; and there were they that above the girded vesture of white wore dyed garments, and as they advanced around their feet there was the likeness of dim flames.

The great white array had vanished and he was alone. He was tracking a secret path that wound in and out through the thickets of a great forest. By solitary pools of still water, by great oaks, worlds of green leaves, by fountains and streams of water, by the bubbling, mossy sources of the brooks he followed this hidden way, now climb-ing and now descending, but still mounting upward, still passing, as he knew, farther and farther from all the habitations of men. Through the green boughs now he saw the shining sea-water; he saw the land of the old saints, all the divisions of the land that men had given to them for God; he saw their churches, and it seemed as if he could hear, very faintly, the noise of the ringing of their holy bells. Then, at last, when he had crossed the Old Road, and had gone by the Lightning-struck Land and the Fisherman's Well, he found, between the forest and the moun-tain, a very ancient and little chapel; and now he heard the bell of the saint ringing clearly and so sweetly that it was as it were the singing of the angels. Within it was very dark and there was silence. He knelt and saw scarcely that the chapel was divided into two parts by a screen that rose up to the round roof. There was a glinting of shapes as if golden figures were painted on this screen, and through the joinings of its beams there streamed out thin needles of white splendour as if within there was a light greater than that of the sun at noonday. And the flesh began to tremble, for all the place was filled with the odours of Paradise, and he heard the ringing of the Holy Bell and the voices of the choir that out-sang the Fairy Birds of Rhiannon, crying and proclaiming:

"Glory and praise to the Conqueror of Death: to the Fountain of Life Unending."

Nine times they sang this anthem, and then the whole place was filled with blinding light. For a door in the screen had been opened, and there came forth an old man, all in shining white, on whose head was a gold crown. Before him went one who rang the bell; on each side there were young men with torches; and in his hands he bore the *Mystery of Mysteries* wrapped about in veils of gold and of all colours, so that it might not be discerned; and so he passed before the screen, and the light of heaven burst forth from that which he held. Then he entered in again by a door that was on the other side, and the Holy Things were hidden.

And Ambrose heard from within an awful voice and the words:

Woe and great sorrow are on him, for he hath looked unworthily into the Tremendous Mysteries, and on the Secret Glory which is hidden from the Holy Angels.

2.

"Poetry is the only possible way of saying anything that is worth saying at all." This was an axiom that, in later years, Ambrose Meyrick's friends were forced to hear at frequent intervals. He would go on to say that he used the term poetry in its most liberal sense, including in it all mystic or symbolic prose, all painting and statuary that was worthy to be called art, all great architecture, and all true music. He meant, it is to be presumed, that the mysteries can only be conveyed by symbols; unfortunately, however, he did not always make it quite clear that this was the proposition that he intended to utter, and thus offence was sometimes given—as, for example, to the scientific gentleman who had been brought to Meyrick's rooms and went away early, wondering audibly and sarcastically whether "your clever friend" wanted to metrify biology and set Euclid to Bach's Organ Fugues.

However, the Great Axiom (as he called it) was the justification that he put forward in defence of the notes on which the previous section is based.

"Of course," he would say, "the symbolism is inadequate; but that is the defect of speech of any kind when you have once ventured beyond the multiplication table and the jargon of the Stock Exchange. Inadequacy of expression is merely a minor part of the great tragedy of humanity. Only an ass thinks that he has succeeded in uttering the perfect content of his thought without either excess or defect."

"Then, again," he might go on, "the symbolism would very likely be misleading to a great many people; but what is one to do? I believe many good people find Turner mad and Dickens tiresome. And if the great sometimes fail, what hope is there for the little? We cannot all be—well—popular novelists of the day."

Of course, the notes in question were made many years after the event they commemorate; they were the man's translation of all the wonderful and inexpressible emotions of the boy; and, as Meyrick puts it, many "words" (or symbols) are used in them which were unknown to the lad of fifteen.

"Nevertheless," he said, "they are the best words that I can find."

As has been said, the Old Grange was a large, roomy house; a space could easily have been found for half a dozen more boys if the High Usher had cared to be bothered with them. As it was, it was a favour to be at Horbury's, and there was usually some personal reason for admission. Pelly, for example, was the son of an old friend; Bates was a distant cousin; and Rawson's father was the master of a small Grammar School in the north with which certain ancestral Horburys were somehow connected. The Old Grange was a fine large Caroline house; it had a grave front of red brick mellowed with age, tier upon tier of tall, narrow windows, flush with the walls, and a high-pitched, red-tiled roof. Above the front door was a rich and curious wooden pent-house, deeply carven; and within there was plenty of excellent panelling, and some good mantelpieces, added, it would seem, somewhere about the Adams period. Horbury had seen its solid and comfortable merits and had bought the freehold years before at a great bargain. The school was increasing rapidly even in those days, and he knew that before long more houses would be required. If he left Lupton he would be able to let the Old Grange easily—he might almost put it up for auction—and the rent would represent a return of fifty per cent on his investment. Many of the rooms were large, of a size out of all proportion to the boys' needs, and at a very trifling expense partitions might be made and the nine or ten available rooms be subdivided into studies for twenty or even twenty-five boys. Nature had gifted the High Usher with a careful, provident mind in all things, both great and small; and it is but fair to add that on his leaving Lupton for Wareham he found his anticipations more than justified.

To this day Charles Horbury, his nephew, a high Government official, draws a comfortable income from his uncle's most prudent investment, and the house easily holds its twenty-five boys. Rainy, who took the place from Horbury, was an ingenious fellow and hit upon a capital plan for avoiding the expense of making new windows for some of the subdivided studies. After thoughtful consideration he caused the wooden partitions which were put up to stop short of the ceiling by four inches, and by this device the study with a window lighted the study that had none; and, as Rainy explained to some of the parents, a diffused light was really better for the eyes than a direct one.

In the old days, when Ambrose Meyrick was being made a man of, the four boys "rattled", as it were, in the big house. They were scattered about in odd corners, remote from each other, and it seemed from everybody else. Meyrick's room was the most isolated of any, but it was also the most comfortable in winter, since it was over the kitchen, to the extreme left of the house. This part, which was hidden from the road by the boughs of a great cedar, was an after-thought, a Georgian addition in grey brick, and rose only to two stories, and in the one furnished room out of the three or four over the kitchen and offices slept Ambrose. He wished his days could be as quiet and retired as his nights. He loved the shadows that were ever about his bed even on the brightest mornings in summer; for the cedar boughs were dense, and ivy had been allowed to creep about the panes of the window; so the light entered dim and green, filtered through the dark boughs and the ivy tendrils.

Here, then, after the hour of ten each night, he dwelt secure. Now and again Mr. Horbury would pay nocturnal surprise visits to see that all lights were out; but, happily, the stairs at the end of the passage, being old and badly fitted, gave out a succession of cracks like pistol shots if the softest foot was set on them. It was simple, therefore, on hearing the first of these reports, to extinguish the candle in the small secret lantern (held warily so that no gleam of light should appear from under the door) and to conceal the lantern under the bed-clothes. One wetted one's finger and pinched at the flame, so there was no smell of the expiring snuff, and the lantern slide was carefully drawn to guard against the possibility of suspicious grease-marks on the linen. It was perfect; and old Horbury's visits, which were rare enough, had no terrors for Ambrose.

So that night, while the venom of the cane still rankled in his body, though it had ceased to disturb his mind, instead of going to bed at once, according to the regulations, he sat for a while on his box seeking a clue in a maze of odd fancies and conceits. He took off his clothes and wrapped his aching body in the rug from the bed, and presently, blowing out the official paraffin lamp, he lit his candle, ready at the first warning creak on the stairs to douse the glim and leap between the sheets.

Odd enough were his first cogitations. He was thinking how very sorry he was to have hit Pelly that savage blow and to have endangered Rawson's eyesight by the hard boards of the dictionary! This was eccentric, for he had endured from those two young Apaches every extremity of unpleasantness for upwards of a couple of years. Pelly was not by any means an evil lad: he was stupid and beefy within and without, and the great Public School system was transmuting him, in the proper course and by the proper steps, into one of those Brave Average Boobies whom Meyrick used to rail against afterwards. Pelly, in all probability (his fortunes have not been traced), went into the Army and led the milder and more serious subalterns the devil's own life. In India he "lay doggo" with great success against some hill tribe armed with seventeenth-century muskets and rather barbarous knives; he seems to have been present at that "Conference of the Powers" described so brightly by Mr. Kipling. Promoted to a captaincy, he fought with conspicuous bravery in South Africa, winning the Victoria Cross for his rescue of a wounded private at the instant risk of his own life, and he finally led his troop into a snare set by an old farmer; a rabbit of average intelligence would have smelt and evaded it.

For Rawson one is sorry, but one cannot, in conscience, say much that is good, though he has been praised for his tact. He became domestic chaplain to the Bishop of Dorchester, whose daughter Emily he married.

But in those old days there was very little to choose between them, from Meyrick's point of view. Each had displayed a quite devilish ingenuity in the art of annoyance, in the whole cycle of jeers and sneers and "scores", as known to the schoolboy, and they were just proceeding to more active measures. Meyrick had borne it all meekly; he had returned kindly and sometimes quaint answers to the unceasing stream of remarks that were meant to wound his feelings, to make him look a fool before any boys that happened to be about. He had only countered with a mild: "What do you do that for, Pelly?" when the brave one smacked his head. "Because I hate sneaks and funks," Pelly had replied, and Meyrick said no more. Rawson took a smaller size in victims when it was a question of physical torments; but he had invented a most offensive tale about Meyrick and had told it all over the school, where it was universally believed. In a word, the two had done their utmost to reduce him to a state of utter misery; and now he was sorry that he had punched the nose of the one and bombarded the other with a dictionary!

The fact was that his forbearance had not been all cowardice; it is, indeed, doubtful whether he was in the real sense a coward at all. He went in fear, it is true, all his days, but what he feared was not the insult, but the intention, the malignancy of which the insult, or the blow, was the outward sign. The fear of a mad bull is quite distinct from the horror with which most people look upon a viper; it was the latter feeling which made Meyrick's life a burden to him. And again there was a more curious shade of feeling; and that was the intense hatred that he felt to the mere thought of "scoring" off an antagonist, of beating down the enemy. He was a much sharper lad than either Rawson or Pelly; he could have retorted again and again with crushing effect, but he held his tongue, for all such victories were detestable to him. And this odd sentiment governed all his actions and feelings; he disliked "going up" in form, he disliked winning a game, not through any acquired virtue, but by inherent nature. Poe would have understood Meyrick's feelings; but then the author of "The Imp of the Perverse" penetrated so deeply into the inmost secrets of humanity that Anglo-Saxon criticism has agreed in denouncing him as a wholly "inhuman" writer.

With Meyrick this mode of feeling had grown stronger by provocation; the more he was injured, the more he shrank from the thought of returning the injury. In a great measure the sentiment remained with him in later life. He would sally forth from his den in quest of fresh air on top of an omnibus and stroll peacefully back again rather than struggle for victory with the furious crowd. It was not so much that he disliked the physical contest: he was afraid of getting a seat! Quite naturally, he said that people who "pushed", in the metaphorical sense, always reminded him of the hungry little pigs fighting for the largest share of the wash; but he seemed to think that, whereas this course of action was natural in the little pigs, it was profoundly unnatural in the little men. But in his early boyhood he had carried this secret doctrine of his to its utmost limits; he had assumed, as it were, the role of the coward and the funk; he had, without any conscious religious motive certainly, but in obedience to an inward command, endeavoured to play the part of a Primitive Christian, of a religious, in a great Public School! *Ama nesciri et pro nihilo æstimari.* The maxim was certainly in his heart, though he had never heard it; but perhaps if he had searched the whole world over he could not have found a more impossible field for its exercise than this seminary, where the broad, liberal principles of Christianity were taught in a way that satisfied the Press, the public and the parents.

And he sat in his room and grieved over the fashion in which he had broken this discipline. Still, something had to be done: he was compelled to stay in this place, and he did not wish to be reduced to the imbecility of wretched little Phipps, who had become at last more like a whimpering kitten with the mange than a human being. One had not the right to allow oneself to be made an idiot, so the principle had to be infringed—but externally only, never internally! Of that he was firmly resolved; and he felt secure in his recollection that there had been no anger in his heart. He resented the presence of Pelly and Rawson, certainly, but in the manner with which some people resent the presence of a cat, a mouse, or a black-beetle, as disagreeable objects which can't help being disagreeable objects. But his bashing of Pelly and his smashing of Rawson, his remarks (gathered from careful observation by the banks of the Lupton and Birmingham Canal); all this had been but the means to an end, the securing of peace and quiet for the future. He would not be murdered by this infernal Public School system either, after the fashion of Phipps—which was melancholy, or after the fashion of the rest—which was more melancholy still, since it is easier to recover from nervous breakdown than from suffusion of cant through the entire system, mental and spiritual. Utterly from his heart he abjured and renounced all the horrible shibboleths of the school, its sham enthusiasm, its "ethos", its "tone", its "loyal co-operation—masters and boys working together for the good of the whole school"—all its ridiculous fetish conventions and absurd observances, the joint contrivances of young fools and old knaves. But his resistance should be secret and not open, for a while; there should be no more "bashing" than was absolutely necessary.

And one thing he resolved upon—he would make all he could out of the place; he would work like a tiger and get all the Latin and Greek and French obtainable, in spite of the teaching and its imbecile pedantry. The school work must be done, so that trouble might be avoided, but here at night in his room he would really learn the languages they pottered over in form, wasting half their time in writing sham Ciceronian prose which would have made Cicero sick, and verse evil enough to cause Virgil to vomit. Then there was French, taught chiefly out of pompous eighteenth-century fooleries, with lists of irregular verbs to learn and Babylonish nonsense about the past participle, and many other rotten formulas and rules, giving to the whole tongue the air of a tiresome puzzle which had been dug up out of a prehistoric grave. This was not the French that he wanted; still, he could write out irregular verbs by day and learn the language at night. He wondered whether unhappy French boys had to learn English out of the *Rambler*, Blair's *Sermons* and Young's *Night Thoughts*. For he had some sort of smattering of English literature which a Public School boy has no business to possess. So he went on with this mental tirade of his: one is not overwise at fifteen. It is true enough, perhaps, that the French of the average English schoolboy is something fit to move only pity and terror; it may be true also that nobody except Deans and schoolmasters seems to bring away even the formulas and sacred teachings (such as the Optative mystery and the Doctrine of Dum) of the two great literatures. There is, doubtless, a good deal to be said on the subject of the Public Schoolman's knowledge of the history and literature of his own country; an infinite deal of comic stuff might be got out of his views and acquirements in the great science of theology—still let us say, *Floreat!*

Meyrick turned from his review of the wisdom of his elders and instructors to more intimate concerns. There were a few cuts of that vigorous cane which still stung and hurt most abominably, for skill or fortune had guided Mr. Horbury's hand so that he had been enabled here and there to get home twice in the same place, and there was one particular weal on the left arm where the flesh, purple and discoloured, had swelled up and seemed on the point of bursting. It was no longer with rage, but with a kind of rapture, that he felt the pain and the smarting; he looked upon the ugly marks of the High Usher's evil humours as though they had been a robe of splendour. For he knew nothing of that bad sherry, nothing of the Head's conversation; he knew that when Pelly had come in quite as late it had only been a question of a hundred lines, and so he persisted in regarding himself as a martyr in the cause of those famous "Norman arches", which was the cause of that dear dead enthusiast, his father, who loved Gothic architecture and all other beautiful "unpractical" things with an undying passion. As soon as Ambrose could walk he had begun his pilgrimages to hidden mystic shrines; his father had led him over the wild lands to places known perhaps only to himself, and there, by the ruined stones, by the smooth hillock, had told the tale of the old vanished time, the time of the "old saints".

3.

It was for this blessed and wonderful learning, he said to himself, that he had been beaten, that his body had been scored with red and purple stripes. He remembered his father's oft-repeated exclamation "cythrawl Sais!" He understood that the phrase damned not Englishmen *qua* Englishmen, but Anglo-Saxonism—the power of the creed that builds Manchester, that "does business", that invents popular dissent, representative government, adulteration, suburbs, and the Public School system. It was, according to his father, the creed of "the Prince of this world", the creed that made for comfort, success, a good balance at the bank, the praise of men, the sensible and tangible victory and achievement; and he bade his little boy, who heard everything and understood next to nothing, fly from it, hate it and fight against it as he would fight against the devil—"and," he would add, "it is the only devil you are ever likely to come across."

And the little Ambrose had understood not much of all this, and if he had been asked—even at fifteen—what it all meant, he would probably have said that it was a great issue between Norman mouldings and Mr. Horbury, an Armageddon of Selden Abbey *versus* rocker.

Indeed, it is doubtful whether old Nicholas Meyrick would have been very much clearer, for he forgot everything that might be said on the other side. He forgot that Anglo-Saxonism (save in the United States of America) makes generally for equal laws; that civil riot ("Labour" movements, of course, excepted) is more a Celtic than a Saxon vice; that the penalty of burning alive is unknown amongst Anglo-Saxons, unless the provocation be extreme; that Englishmen have substituted "Indentured Labour" for the old-world horrors of slavery; that English justice smites the guilty rich equally with the guilty poor; that men are no longer poisoned with swift and secret drugs, though somewhat unwholesome food may still be sold very occasionally. Indeed, the old Meyrick once told his rector that he considered a brothel a house of sanctity compared with a modern factory, and he was beginning to relate some interesting tales concerning the Three Gracious Courtesans of the Isle of Britain when the rector fled in horror—he came from Sydenham. And all this was a nice preparation for Lupton.

A wonderful joy, an ecstasy of bliss, swelled in Ambrose's heart as he assured himself that he was a witness, though a mean one, for the old faith, for the faith of secret and beautiful and hidden mysteries as opposed to the faith of rocker and sticker and mucker, and "the thought of the school as an inspiring motive in life"—the text on which the Head had preached the Sunday before. He bared his arms and kissed the purple swollen flesh and prayed that it might ever be so, that in body and mind and spirit he might ever be beaten and reviled and made ridiculous for the sacred things, that he might ever be on the side of the despised and the unsuccessful, that his life might ever be in the shadow—in the shadow of the mysteries.

He thought of the place in which he was, of the hideous school, the hideous town, the weary waves of the dun Midland scenery bounded by the dim, hopeless horizon; and his soul revisited the faery hills and woods and valleys of the West. He remembered how, long ago, his father had roused him early from sleep in the hush and wonder of a summer morning. The whole world was still and windless; all the magic odours of the night rose from the earth, and as they crossed the lawn the silence was broken by the enchanted song of a bird rising from a thorn tree by the gate. A high white vapour veiled the sky, and they only knew that the sun had risen by the brightening of this veil, by

the silvering of the woods and the meadows and the water in the rejoicing brook. They crossed the road, and crossed the brook in the
field beneath, by the old foot-bridge tremulous with age, and began to
climb the steep hillside that one could see from the windows, and, the
ridge of the hill once surmounted, the little boy found himself in an
unknown land: he looked into deep, silent valleys, watered by trickling
streams; he saw still woods in that dreamlike morning air; he saw winding paths that climbed into yet remoter regions. His father led him
onward till they came to a lonely height—they had walked scarcely two
miles, but to Ambrose it seemed a journey into another world—and
shewed him certain irregular markings in the turf.

And Nicholas Meyrick murmured:

> "The cell of Iltyd is by the seashore,
>   The ninth wave washes its altar,
>   There is a fair shrine in the land of Morgan.
>
> "The cell of Dewi is in the City of the Legions,
>   Nine altars owe obedience to it,
>   Sovereign is the choir that sings about it.
>
> "The cell of Cybi is the treasure of Gwent,
>   Nine hills are its perpetual guardians,
>   Nine songs befit the memory of the saint."

"See," he said, "there are the Nine Hills." He pointed them out to
the boy, telling him the tale of the saint and his holy bell, which they
said had sailed across the sea from Syon and had entered the Severn,
and had entered the Usk, and had entered the Soar, and had entered
the Canthwr; and so one day the saint, as he walked beside the little
brook that almost encompassed the hill in its winding course, saw the
bell "that was made of metal that no man might comprehend", floating
under the alders, and crying:

> *"Sant, sant, sant,*
>   *I sail from Syon*
>   *To Cybi Sant!"*

"And so sweet was the sound of that bell," Ambrose's father went on, "that they said it was as the joy of angels *ym Mharadwys,* and that it must have come not from the earthly, but from the heavenly and glorious Syon."

And there they stood in the white morning, on the uneven ground that marked the place where once the Saint rang to the sacrifice, where the quickening words were uttered after the order of the Old Mass of the Britons.

"And then came the Yellow Hag of Pestilence, that destroyed the bodies of the Cymri; then the Red Hag of Rome, that caused their souls to stray; last is come the Black Hag of Geneva, that sends body and soul quick to hell. No honour have the saints any more."

Then they turned home again, and all the way Ambrose thought he heard the bell as it sailed the great deeps from Syon, crying aloud: "Sant, Sant, Sant!" And the sound seemed to echo from the glassy water of the little brook, as it swirled and rippled over the shining stones circling round those lonely hills.

So they made strange pilgrimages over the beloved land; going farther and farther afield as the boy grew older. They visited deep wells in the heart of the woods, where a few broken stones, perhaps, were the last remains of a hermitage. "Ffynnon Ilar Bysgottwr—the well of Saint Ilar the Fisherman," Nicholas Meyrick would explain, and then would follow the story of Ilar; how no man knew whence he came or who his parents were. He was found, a little child, on a stone in a river in Armorica, by King Alan, and rescued by him. And ever after they discovered on the stone in the river where the child had lain every day a great and shining fish lying, and on this fish Ilar was nourished. And so he came with a great company of the saints to Britain, and wandered over all the land.

So at last Ilar Sant came to this wood, which people now call St. Hilary's wood because they have forgotten all about Ilar. And he was weary with his wandering, and the day was very hot; so he stayed by this well and began to drink. And there on that great stone he saw the shining fish, and so he rested, and built an altar and a church of willow boughs, and offered the sacrifice not only for the quick and the dead, but for all the wild beasts of the woods and the streams.

"And when this blessed Ilar rang his holy bell and began to offer, there came not only the Prince and his servants, but all the creatures of the wood. There, under the hazel boughs, you might see the hare, which flies so swiftly from men, come gently and fall down, weeping greatly on account of the Passion of the Son of Mary. And, beside the hare, the weasel and the pole-cat would lament grievously in the manner of penitent sinners; and wolves and lambs together adored the saint's hierurgy; and men have beheld tears streaming from the eyes of venomous serpents when Ilar Agios uttered 'Curiluson' with a loud voice—since the serpent is not ignorant that by its wickedness sorrow came to the whole world. And when, in the time of the holy ministry, it is necessary that frequent Alleluyas should be chanted and vociferated, the saint wondered what should be done, for as yet none in that place was skilled in the art of song. Then was a great miracle, since from all the boughs of the wood, from every bush and from every green tree, there resounded Alleluyas in enchanting and prolonged harmony; never did the Bishop of Rome listen to so sweet a singing in his church as was heard in this wood. For the nightingale and thrush and blackbird and blackcap, and all their companions, are gathered together and sing praises to the Lord, chanting distinct notes and yet concluding in a melody of most ravishing sweetness; such was the mass of the Fisherman. Nor was this all, for one day as the saint prayed beside the well he became aware that a bee circled round and round his head, uttering loud buzzing sounds, but not endeavouring to sting him. To be short; the bee went before Ilar, and led him to a hollow tree not far off, and straightway a swarm of bees issued forth, leaving a vast store of wax behind them. This was their oblation to the Most High, for from their wax Ilar Sant made goodly candles to burn at the Offering; and from that time the bee is holy, because his wax makes light to shine upon the Gifts."

This was part of the story that Ambrose's father read to him; and they went again to see the Holy Well. He looked at the few broken and uneven stones that were left to distinguish it from common wells; and there in the deep green wood, in the summer afternoon, under the woven boughs, he seemed to hear the strange sound of the saint's bell, to see the woodland creatures hurrying through the undergrowth that they might be present at the Offering. The weasel beat his little breast for his sins; the big tears fell down the gentle face of the hare; the adders wept in the dust; and all the chorus of the birds sang: "Alleluya, Alleluya, Alleluya!"

Once they drove a long way from the Wern, going towards the west, till they came to the Great Mountain, as the people called it. After they had turned from the high road they went down a narrow lane, and this led them with many windings to a lower ridge of the mountain, where the horse and trap were put up at a solitary tavern. Then they began to toil upward on foot, crossing many glistening and rejoicing streams that rushed out cold from the limestone rock, mounting up and up, through the wet land where the rare orchis grew amongst the rushes, through hazel brakes, through fields that grew wilder as they still went higher, and the great wind came down from the high dome above them. They turned, and all the shining land was unrolled before them; the white houses were bright in the sunlight, and there, far away, was the yellow sea and the two islands, and the coasts beyond.

Nicholas Meyrick pointed out a tuft of trees on a hill a long way off and told his son that the Wern was hidden beyond it; and then they began to climb once more, till they came at last to the line where the fields and hedges ended, and above there was only the wild mountain land. And on this verge stood an old farmhouse with strong walls, set into the rock, sheltered a little from the winds by a line of twisted beeches. The walls of the house were gleaming white, and by the porch there was a shrub covered with bright yellow flowers. Mr. Meyrick beat upon the oak door, painted black and studded with heavy nails. An old man, dressed like a farmer, opened it, and Ambrose noticed that his father spoke to him with something of reverence in his voice, as if he were some very great person. They sat down in a long room, but dimly lighted by the thick greenish glass in the quarried window, and presently the old farmer set a great jug of beer before them. They both drank heartily enough, and Mr. Meyrick said:

"Aren't you about the last to brew your own beer, Mr. Cradock?"

"Iss; I be the last of all. They do all like the muck the brewer sends better than *cwrw dda*."

"The whole world likes muck better than good drink, now."

"You be right, Sir. Old days and old ways of our fathers, they be gone for ever. There was a blasted preacher down at the chapel a week or two ago, saying—so they do tell me—that they would all be damned to hell unless they took to ginger-beer directly. Iss indeed now; and I heard that he should say that a man could do a better day's work on that rot-belly stuff than on good beer. Wass you ever hear of such a liarr as that?"

The old man was furious at the thought of these infamies and follies; his esses hissed through his teeth, and his r's rolled out with fierce emphasis. Mr. Meyrick nodded his approval of this indignation.

"We have what we deserve," he said. "False preachers, bad drink, the talk of fools all the day long—even on the mountain. What is it like, do you think, in London?"

There fell a silence in the long, dark room. They could hear the sound of the wind in the beech trees, and Ambrose saw how the boughs were tossed to and fro, and he thought of what it must be like on winter nights, here, high upon the Great Mountain, when the storms swept up from the sea, or descended from the wilds of the north; when the shafts of rain were like the onset of an army, and the winds screamed about the walls.

"May we see It?" said Mr. Meyrick suddenly.

"I did think you had come for that. There be very few now that remember."

He went out, and returned carrying a bunch of keys. Then he opened a door in the room and warned "the young master" to take care of the steps. Ambrose, indeed, could scarcely see the way. His father led him down a short flight of uneven stone steps, and they were in a room which seemed at first quite dark, for the only light came from a narrow window high up in the wall, and across the glass there were heavy iron bars.

Cradock lit two tall candles of yellow wax that stood in brass candlesticks on a table; and, as the flame grew clear, Ambrose saw that he was opening a sort of aumbry constructed in the thickness of the wall. The door was a great slab of solid oak, three or four inches thick—as one could see when it was opened—and from the dark place within the farmer took an iron box and set it carefully upon the floor, Mr. Meyrick helping him. They were strong men, but they staggered under the weight of the chest; the iron seemed as thick as the door of the cupboard from which it was taken, and the heavy, antique lock yielded, with a grating scream, to the key. Inside it there was another box of some reddish metal, which, again, held a case of wood black with age; and from this, with reverent hands, the farmer drew out a veiled and splendid cup and set it on the table between the two candles. It was a bowl-like vessel of the most wonderful workmanship, standing on a short stem. All the hues of the world were mingled on it, all the jewels of the regions seemed to shine from it; and the stem and foot were encrusted with work in enamel, of strange and magical colours that shone and dimmed with alternating radiance, that glowed with red fires and pale glories, with the blue of the far sky, the green of the faery seas, and the argent gleam of the evening star. But before Ambrose had gazed more than a moment he heard the old man say, in pure Welsh, not in broken English, in a resonant and chanting voice:

"Let us fall down and adore the marvellous and venerable work of the Lord God Almighty."

To which his father responded:

"Agyos, Agyos, Agyos. Mighty and glorious is the Lord God Almighty, in all His works and wonderful operations. Curiluson, Curiluson, Curiluson."

They knelt down, Cradock in the midst, before the cup, and Ambrose and his father on either hand. The holy vessel gleamed before the boy's eyes, and he saw clearly its wonder and its beauty. All its surface was a marvel of the most delicate intertwining lines in gold and silver, in copper and in bronze, in all manner of metals and alloys; and these interlacing patterns in their brightness, in the strangeness of their imagery and ornament, seemed to enthral the eyes and capture them, as it were, in a maze of enchantment; and not only the eyes; for the very spirit was rapt and garnered into that far bright world whence the holy magic of the cup proceeded. Among the precious stones which were set into the wonder was a great crystal, shining with the pure light of the moon; about the rim of it there was the appearance of faint and feathery clouds, but in the centre it was a white splendour; and as Ambrose gazed he thought that from the heart of this jewel there streamed continually a shower of glittering stars, dazzling his eyes with their incessant motion and brightness. His body thrilled with a sudden ineffable rapture, his breath came and went in quick pantings; bliss possessed him utterly as the three crowned forms passed in their golden order. Then the interwoven sorcery of the vessel became a ringing wood of golden, and bronze, and silver trees; from every side resounded the clear summons of the holy bells and the exultant song of the faery birds; he no longer heard the low-chanting voices of Cradock and his father as they replied to one another in the forms of some antique liturgy. Then he stood by a wild seashore; it was a dark night, and there was a shrilling wind that sang about the peaks of the sharp rocks, answering to the deep voices of the heaving sea. A white moon, of fourteen days old, appeared for a moment in the rift between two vast black clouds, and the shaft of light shewed all the savage desolation of the shore—cliffs that rose up into mountains, into crenellated heights that were incredible, whose bases were scourged by the torrents of hissing foam that were driven against them from the hollow-sounding sea. Then, on the highest of those awful heights, Ambrose became aware of walls and spires, of towers and battlements that must have touched the stars; and, in the midst of this great castle, there surged up the aspiring vault of a vast church, and all its windows were ablaze with a light so white and glorious that it was as if every pane were a diamond. And he heard the voices of a praising host, or the clamour of golden trumpets and the unceasing choir of the angels. And he knew that this place was the Sovereign Perpetual Choir, Corarbennic, into whose secret the deadly flesh may scarcely enter. But in the vision he lay breathless, on the floor before the gleaming wall of the sanctuary, while the shadows of the hierurgy were enacted; and it seemed to him that, for a moment of time, he saw in unendurable light the Mystery of Mysteries pass veiled before him, and the Image of the Slain and Risen.

For a brief while this dream was broken. He heard his father singing softly:

"Gogoniant y Tâd ac y Mab ac yr Yspryd Glân."

And the old man answered:

"Agya Trias eleeson ymas."

Then again his spirit was lost in the bright depths of the crystal, and he saw the ships of the saints, without oar or sail, afloat on the faery sea, seeking the Glassy Isle. All the whole company of the Blessed Saints of the Isle of Britain sailed on the adventure; dawn and sunset, night and morning, their illumined faces never wavered; and Ambrose thought that at last they saw bright shores in the dying light of a red sun, and there came to their nostrils the scent of the deep apple-garths in Avalon, and odours of Paradise.

When he finally returned to the presence of earthly things he was standing by his father; while Cradock reverently wrapped the cup in the gleaming veils which covered it, saying as he did so, in Welsh:

"Remain in peace, O holy and divine cup of the Lord. Henceforth I know not whether I shall return to thee or not; but may the Lord vouchsafe me to see thee in the Church of the Firstborn which is in heaven, on the Altar of the Sacrifice which is from age unto ages."

Ambrose went up the steps and out into the sunshine on the mountain side with the bewilderment of strange dreams, as a coloured mist, about him. He saw the old white walls, the yellow blossoms by the porch; above, the wild, high mountain wall; and, below, all the dear land of Gwent, happy in the summer air, all its woods and fields, its rolling hills and its salt verge, rich in a golden peace. Beside him the cold water swelled from the earth and trickled from the grey rock, and high in the air an exultant lark was singing. The mountain breeze was full of life and gladness, and the rustling and tossing of the woods, the glint and glimmer of the leaves beneath, made one think that the trees, with every creature, were merry on that day. And in that dark cell beneath many locks, beneath wood and iron, concealed in golden, glittering veils, lay hidden that glorious and awful cup, glass of wonderful vision, portal and entrance of the Spiritual Place.

His father explained to him something of that which he had seen. He told him that the vessel was the Holy Cup of Teilo sant, which he was said to have received from the Lord in the state of Paradise, and that when Teilo said Mass, using that Chalice, the choir of angels was present visibly; that it was a cup of wonders and mysteries, the bestower of visions and heavenly graces.

"But whatever you do," he said, "do not speak to any one of what you have seen to-day, because if you do the mystery will be laughed at and blasphemed. Do you know that your uncle and aunt at Lupton would say that we were all mad together? That is because they are fools, and in these days most people are fools, and malignant fools too, as you will find out for yourself before you are much older. So always remember that you must hide the secrets that you have seen; and if you do not do so you will be sorry."

Mr. Meyrick told his son why old Cradock was to be treated with respect—indeed, with reverence.

"He is just what he looks," he said, "an old farmer with a small freehold up here on the mountain side; and, as you heard, his English is no better than that of any other farmer in this country. And, compared with Cradock, the Duke of Norfolk is a man of yesterday. He is of the tribe of Teilo the Saint; he is the last, in direct descent, of the hereditary keepers of the holy cup; and his race has guarded that blessed relic for thirteen hundred years. Remember, again, that to-day, on this mountain, you have seen great marvels which you must keep in silence."

Poor Ambrose! He suffered afterwards for his forgetfulness of his father's injunction. Soon after he went to Lupton one of the boys was astonishing his friends with a brilliant account of the Crown jewels, which he had viewed during the Christmas holidays. Everybody was deeply impressed, and young Meyrick, anxious to be agreeable in his turn, began to tell about the wonderful cup that he had once seen in an old farmhouse. Perhaps his manner was not convincing, for the boys shrieked with laughter over his description. A monitor who was passing asked to hear the joke, and, having been told the tale, clouted Ambrose over the head for an infernal young liar. This was a good lesson, and it served Ambrose in good stead when one of the masters having, somehow or other, heard the story, congratulated him in the most approved scholastic manner before the whole form on his wonderful imaginative gifts.

"I see the budding novelist in you, Meyrick," said this sly master. "Besant and Rice will be nowhere when you once begin. I suppose you are studying character just at present? Let us down gently, won't you? [To the delighted form.] We must be careful, mustn't we, how we behave? 'A chiel's amang us takin' notes,'" etc. etc.

But Meyrick held his tongue. He did not tell his form master that he was a beast, a fool and a coward, since he had found out that the truth, like many precious things, must often be concealed from the profane. A late vengeance overtook that foolish master. Long years after, he was dining at a popular London restaurant, and all through dinner he had delighted the ladies of his party by the artful mixture of brutal insolence and vulgar chaff with which he had treated one of the waiters, a humble-looking little Italian. The master was in the highest spirits at the success of his persiflage; his voice rose louder and louder, and his offensiveness became almost supernaturally acute. And then he received a heavy earthen casserole, six quails, a few small onions and a quantity of savoury but boiling juices full in the face. The little waiter was a Neapolitan.

The hours of the night passed on, as Ambrose sat in his bedroom at the Old Grange, recalling many wonderful memories, dreaming his dreams of the mysteries, of the land of Gwent and the land of vision, just as his uncle, but a few yards away in another room of the house, was at the same time rapt into the world of imagination, seeing the new Lupton descending like a bride from the heaven of headmasters. But Ambrose thought of the Great Mountain, of the secret valleys, of the sanctuaries and hallows of the saints, of the rich carven work of lonely churches hidden amongst the hills and woods. There came into his mind the fragment of an old poem which he loved:

"In the darkness of old age let not my memory fail,
Let me not forget to celebrate the beloved land of Gwent.
If they imprison me in a deep place, in a house of pestilence,
Still shall I be free, when I remember the sunshine upon Mynydd Maen.
There have I listened to the singing of the lark, my soul has ascended
    with the song of the little bird;
The great white clouds were the ships of my spirit, sailing to the haven
    of the Almighty.
Equally to be held in honour is the site of the Great Mountain,
Adorned with the gushing of many waters—
Sweet is the shade of its hazel thickets,
There a treasure is preserved, which I will not celebrate,
It is glorious, and deeply concealed.
If Teilo should return, if happiness were restored to the Cymri,
Dewi and Dyfrig should serve his Mass; then a great marvel would be
    made visible.
O blessed and miraculous work, then should my bliss be as the bliss of
    angels;
I had rather behold this Offering than kiss the twin lips of dark
    Gwenllian.
Dear my land of Gwent, O *quam dilecta tabernacula!*
Thy rivers are like precious golden streams of Paradise,
Thy hills are as the Mount Syon—
Better a grave on Twyn Barlwm than a throne in the palace of the Saxons
    at Caer-Ludd."

And then, by the face of contrast, he thought of the first verse of the great school song, "Rocker", one of the earliest of the many poems which his uncle had consecrated to the praise of the dear old school:

"Once on a time, in the books that bore me,
I read that in olden days before me
Lupton town had a wonderful game,
It was a game with a noble story
(Lupton town was then in its glory,
Kings and Bishops had brought it fame).
It was a game that you all must know,
And 'rocker' they called it, long ago.

Chorus.

Look out for 'brooks,' or you're sure to drown,
Look out for 'quarries,' or else you're down—
That was the way
'Rocker' to play—
Once on a day
That was the way,
Once on a day,
That was the way that they used to play in Lupton town."

Thinking of the two songs, he put out his light and, wearied, fell into a deep sleep.

4.

The British schoolboy, considered in a genial light by those who have made him their special study, has not been found to be either observant or imaginative. Or, rather, it would be well to say that his powers of observation, having been highly specialised within a certain limited tract of thought and experience (bounded mainly by cricket and football), are but faint without these bounds; while it is one of the chiefest works of the System to kill, destroy, smash and bring to nothing any powers of imagination he may have originally possessed. For if this were not done thoroughly, neither a Conservative nor a Liberal administration would be possible, the House of Commons itself would cease to exist, the Episcopus (var. Anglicanus) would go the way of the Great Bustard; a "muddling through somehow" (which must have been *the* brightest jewel in the British crown, wrung from King John by the barons) would become a lost art. And, since all these consequences would be clearly intolerable, the great Public Schools have perfected a very thorough system of destroying the imaginative toxin, and few cases of failure have been so far reported.

Still, there are facts which not even the densest dullards, the most complete boobies, can help seeing; and a good many of the boys found themselves wondering "what was the matter with Meyrick" when they saw him at Chapel on the Sunday morning. The news of his astounding violences both of act and word on the night before had not yet circulated generally. Bates was attending to that department, but hadn't had time to do much so far; and the replies of Pelly and Rawson to enquiries after black eyes and a potato-like nose were surly and misleading. Afterwards, when the tale was told, when Bates, having enlarged the incidents to folk-lore size, shewed Pelly lying in a pool of his own blood, Rawson screaming as with the torments of the lost and Meyrick rolling out oaths—all original and all terrible—for the space of a quarter of an hour, then indeed the school was satisfied; it was no wonder if Meyrick did look a bit queer after the achievement of such an adventure. The funk of aforetime had found courage; the air of rapture was easily understood. It is probable that if, in the nature of things, it had been possible for an English schoolboy to meet St. Francis of Assisi, the boy would have concluded that the saint must have just made 200 not out in first-class cricket.

But Ambrose walked in a strange light; he had been admitted into worlds undreamed of, and from the first brightness of the sun, when he awoke in the morning in his room at the Grange, it was the material world about him, the walls of stone and brick, the solid earth, the sky itself, and the people who talked and moved and seemed alive—these were things of vision, unsubstantial shapes, odd and broken illusions of the mind. At half-past seven old Toby, the man-of-all-work at the Old Grange, banged at his door and let his clean boots fall with a crash on the boards after the usual fashion. He awoke, sat up in bed, staring about him. But what was this? The four walls covered with a foolish speckled paper, pale blue and pale brown, the white ceiling, the bare boards with the strip of carpet by the bedside: he knew nothing of all this. He was not horrified, because he knew that it was all non-existent, some plastic fantasy that happened to be presented for the moment to his brain. Even the big black wooden chest that held his books (*Parker*, despised by Horbury, among them) failed to appeal to him with any sense of reality; and the bird's-eye washstand and chest of drawers, the white water-jug with the blue band, were all frankly phantasmal. It reminded him of a trick he had sometimes played: one chose one's position carefully, shut an eye and, behold, a mean shed could be made to obscure the view of a mountain! So these walls and appurtenances made an illusory sort of intrusion into the true vision on which he gazed. That yellow washstand rising out of the shining wells of the undying, the speckled walls in the place of the great mysteries, a chest of drawers in the magic garden of roses—it had the air of a queer joke, and he laughed aloud to himself as he realised that he alone knew, that everybody else would say, "That is a white jug with a blue band," while he, and he only, saw the marvel and the glory of the holy cup with its glowing metals, its interlacing myriad lines, its wonderful images, and its hues of the mountain and the stars, of the green wood and the faery sea, where, in a sure haven, anchor the ships that are bound for Avalon.

For he had a certain faith that he had found the earthly presentation and sacrament of the Eternal Heavenly Mystery.

He smiled again, with the quaint smile of an angel in an old Italian picture, as he realised more fully the strangeness of the whole position and the odd humours which would relieve a delight that otherwise might be unendurable. He was to play a wonderful game of make-believe; the speckled walls, for instance, were not really there, but he was to behave just as if they were solid realities. He would presently rise and go through an odd pantomime of washing and dressing, putting on brilliant boots, and going down to various mumbo-jumbo ceremonies called breakfast, chapel and dinner, in the company of appearances to whom he would accord all the honours due to veritable beings. And this delicious phantasmagoria would go on and on day after day, he alone having the secret; and what a delight it would be to "play up" at rocker! It seemed to him that the solid-seeming earth, the dear old school and rocker itself had all been made to minister to the acuteness of his pleasure; they were the darkness that made the light visible, the matter through which form was manifested. For the moment he enclosed in the most secret place of his soul the true world into which he had been guided; and as he dressed he hummed the favourite school song, "Never mind!"

> "If the umpire calls 'out' at your poor second over,
>   If none of your hits ever turns out a 'rover',
>   If you fumble your fives and 'go rot' over sticker,
>   If every hound is a little bit quicker;
>   If you can't tackle rocker at all, not at all,
>   And kick at the moon when you try for the ball,
>   Never mind, never mind, never mind—if you fall,
>   Dick falls before rising, Tom's short ere he's tall,
>   Never mind!
>   Don't be one of the weakest who go to the wall:
>   Never mind!"

Ambrose could not understand how Columbus could have blundered so grossly. Somehow or other he should have contrived to rid himself of his crew; he should have returned alone, with a dismal tale of failure, and passed the rest of his days as that sad and sorry charlatan who had misled the world with his mad whimsies of a continent beyond the waters of the Atlantic. If he had been given wisdom to do this, how great—how wonderful would his joys have been! They would have pointed at him as he paced the streets in his shabby cloak; the boys would have sung songs about him and his madness; the great people would have laughed contemptuously as he went by. And he would have seen in his heart all that vast far world of the west, the rich islands barred by roaring surf, a whole hemisphere of strange regions and strange people; he would have known that he alone possessed the secret of it. But, after all, Ambrose knew that his was a greater joy even than this; for the world that he had discovered was not afar across the seas, but within him.

Pelly stared straight before him in savage silence all through breakfast; he was convinced that mere hazard had guided that crushing blow, and he was meditating schemes of complete and exemplary vengeance. He noticed nothing strange about Meyrick, nor would he have cared if he had seen the images of the fairies in his eyes. Rawson, on the other hand, was full of genial civility and good fellowship; it was "old chap" and "old fellow" every other word. But he was far from unintelligent, and, as he slyly watched Meyrick, he saw that there was something altogether unaccustomed and incomprehensible. Unknown lights burned and shone in the eyes, reflections of one knew not what; the expression was altered in some queer way that he could not understand. Meyrick had always been a rather ugly, dogged-looking fellow; his black hair and something that was not usual in the set of his features gave him an exotic, almost an Oriental appearance; hence a story of Rawson's to the effect that Meyrick's mother was a nigger woman in poor circumstances and of indifferent morality had struck the school as plausible enough.

But now the grimness of the rugged features seemed abolished: the face shone, as it were, with the light of a flame—but a flame of what fire? Rawson, who would not have put his observations into such terms, drew his own conclusions readily enough and imparted them to Pelly after Chapel.

"Look here, old chap," he said," did you notice young Meyrick at breakfast?"

Pelly simply blasted Meyrick and announced his intention of giving him the worst thrashing he had ever had at an early date.

"Don't you try it on," said Rawson. "I had my eye on him all the time. He didn't see I was spotting him. He's cracked; he's dangerous. I shouldn't wonder if he were in a strait waistcoat in the County Lunatic Asylum in a week's time. My governor had a lot to do with lunatics, and he always says he can tell by the eyes. I'll swear Meyrick is raging mad."

"Oh, rot!" said Pelly. "What do you know about it?"

"Well, look out, old chap, and don't say I didn't give you the tip. Of course, you know a maniac is stronger than three ordinary men? The only thing is to get them down and crack their ribs. But you want at least half a dozen men before you can do it."

"Oh, shut up!"

So Rawson said no more, remaining quite sure that he had diagnosed Ambrose's symptoms correctly. He waited for the catastrophe with a dreadful joy, wondering whether Meyrick would begin by cutting old Horbury's throat with his own razor, or whether he would rather steal into Pelly's room at night and tear him limb from limb, a feat which, as a madman, he could, of course, accomplish with perfect ease. As a matter of fact, neither of these events happened. Pelly, a boy of the bulldog breed, smacked Ambrose's face a day or two later before a

huge crowd of boys, and received in return such a terrific blow under
the left ear that a formal fight in the Tom Brown manner was out of
the question.

Pelly reached the ground and stayed there in an unconscious state
for some while; and the other boys determined that it would be as well
to leave Meyrick to himself. He might be cracked, but he was undoubtedly a hard hitter. As for Pelly, like the sensible fellow that he
was, he simply concluded that Meyrick was too good for him. He did
not quite understand it; he dimly suspected the intrusion of some
strange forces, but with such things he had nothing to do. It was a fair
knock-out, and there was an end of it.

Bates had glanced up as Ambrose came into the dining-room on
the Sunday morning. He saw the shining face, the rapturous eyes, and
had silently wondered, recognising the presence of elements which
transcended all his calculations.

Meanwhile the Lupton Sunday went on after its customary fashion. At eleven o'clock the Chapel was full of boys. There were nearly
six hundred of them there, the big ones in frock-coats, with high,
pointed collars, which made them look like youthful Gladstones. The
younger boys wore broad, turn-down collars and had short, square
jackets made somewhat in the Basque fashion. Young and old had
their hair cut close to the scalp, and this gave them all a brisk but bul-
lety appearance. The masters, in cassock, gown and hood, occupied the
choir stalls. Mr. Horbury, the High Usher, clothed in a flowing sur-
plice, was taking Morning Prayer, and the Head occupied a kind of
throne by the altar.

The Chapel was not an inspiring building. It was the fourteenth
century, certainly, but the fourteenth century translated by 1840, and, it
is to be feared, sadly betrayed by the translators. The tracery of the
windows was poor and shallow; the mouldings of the piers and arches
faulty to a degree; the chancel was absurdly out of proportion, and the
pitch-pine benches and stalls had a sticky look. There was a stained-
glass window in memory of the Old Luptonians who fell in the Crimea. One wondered what the Woman of Samaria by the Well had to
do either with Lupton or the Crimea. And the colouring was like that
used in very common, cheap sweets.

The service went with a rush. The prayers, versicles and responses,

and psalms were said, the officiant and the congregation rather pressing than pausing—often, indeed, coming so swiftly to cues that two or
three words at the end of one verse and two or three at the beginning
of the next would be lost in a confused noise of contending voices.
But *Venite* and *Te Deum* and *Benedictus* were rattled off to frisky Angli-
cans with great spirit; sometimes the organ tooted, sometimes it bleat-
ed gently, like a flock of sheep; now one might have sworn that the
music of penny whistles stole on the ear, and again, as the organist
coupled up the full organ, using suddenly all the battery of his stops, a
gas explosion and a Salvation Army band seemed to strive against one
another. A well-known nobleman who had been to Chapel at Lupton
was heard to say, with reference to this experience: "I am no Ritualist,
heaven knows—but I confess I like a hearty service."

But it was, above all, the sermon that has made the Chapel a place
of many memories. The Old Boys say—and one supposes that they are
in earnest—that the tall, dignified figure of the Doctor, standing high
above them all, his scarlet hood making a brilliant splash of colour
against the dingy, bilious paint of the pale green walls, has been an inspiration to them in all quarters of the globe, in all manner of difficulties and temptations.

One man writes that in the midst of a complicated and dangerous
deal on the Stock Exchange he remembered a sermon of Dr. Chesson's, called in the printed volume, "Fighting the Good Fight".

"You have a phrase amongst you which I often hear," said the
Head. "That phrase is 'Play the game', and I wish to say that, though
you know it not; though, it may be, the words are often spoken half in
jest; still, they are but your modern, boyish rendering of the old, stirring message which I have just read to you.

"'Fight the Good Fight.' 'Play the Game.' Remember the words in
the storm and struggle, the anxiety and stress that may be—nay, must
be —before you—etc., etc., etc."

"After the crisis was over," wrote the Stock Exchange man, "I was
thankful that I *had* remembered those words."

"That voice sounding like a trumpet on the battle-field, bidding us
all remember that Success was the prize of Effort and Endurance—"
So writes a well-known journalist.

"I remembered what the Doctor said to us once about 'running the race',", says a young soldier, recounting a narrow escape from a fierce enemy, "so I stuck to my orders."

Ambrose, on that Sunday morning, sat in his place, relishing acutely all the savours of the scene, consumed with inward mirth at the thought that this also professed to be a rite of religion. There was an aimless and flighty merriment about the chant to the *Te Deum* that made it difficult for him to control his laughter; and when he joined in the hymn "Pleasant are Thy courts above", there was an odd choke in his voice that made the boy next to him shuffle uneasily.

But the sermon!

It will be found on page 125 of the *Lupton Sermons.* It dealt with the Parable of the Talents, and shewed the boys in what the sin of the man who concealed his Talent really consisted.

"I daresay," said the Head, "that many of the older amongst you have wondered what this man's sin really was. You may have read your Greek Testaments carefully, and then have tried to form in your minds some analogy to the circumstances of the parable—and it would not surprise me if you were to tell me that you had failed.

"'What manner of man was this?' I can imagine your saying one to another. I shall not be astonished if you confess that, for you at least, the question seems unanswerable.

"Yes! Unanswerable to you. For you are English boys, the sons of English gentlemen, to whom the atmosphere of casuistry, of concealment, of subtlety, is unknown; by whom such an atmosphere would be rejected with scorn. You come from homes where there is no shadow, no dark corner which must not be pried into. Your relations and your friends are not of those who hide their gifts from the light of day. Some of you, perhaps, have had the privilege of listening to the talk of one or other of the great statesmen who guide the doctrines of this vast Empire. You will have observed, I am sure, that in the world of politics there is no vain simulation of modesty, no feigned reluctance to speak of worthy achievement. All of you are members of this great community, of which each one of us is so proud, which we think of as the great inspiration and motive force of our lives. Here, you will say, there are no Hidden Talents, for the note of the English Public School (thank God for it!) is openness, frankness, healthy emulation; each endeavouring to do his best for the good of all. In our studies and in our games each desires to excel, to carry off the prize. We strive for a corruptible crown, thinking that this, after all, is the surest discipline for the crown that is incorruptible. If a man say that he loveth God whom he hath not seen, and love not his brother whom he hath seen! Let your light *shine* before men. Be sure that we shall never win heaven by despising earth.

"Yet that man hid his Talent in a napkin. What does the story mean? What message has it for us to-day?

"I will tell you.

"Some years ago during our summer holidays I was on a walking tour in a mountainous district in the north of England. The sky was of a most brilliant blue, the sun poured, as it were, a gospel of gladness on the earth. Towards the close of the day I was entering a peaceful and beautiful valley amongst the hills, when three sullen notes of a bell came down the breeze towards me. There was a pause. Again the three strokes, and for a third time this dismal summons struck on my ears. I walked on in the direction of the sound, wondering whence it came and what it signified; and soon I saw before me a great pile of buildings, surrounded by a gloomy and lofty wall.

"It was a Roman Catholic monastery. The bell was ringing the Angelus, as it is called.

"I obtained admittance to this place and spoke to some of the unhappy monks. I should astonish you if I mentioned the names of some of the deluded men who had immured themselves in this prison-house. It is sufficient to say that among them were a soldier who had won distinction on the battle-field, an artist, a statesman and a physician of no mean repute.

"Now do you understand? Ah! a day will come—you know, I think, what that day is called—when these poor men will have to answer the question: 'Where is the Talent that was given to you?'

"'Where was your sword in the hour of your country's danger?'

"'Where was your picture, your consecration of your art to the service of morality and humanity, when the doors of the great Exhibition were thrown open?'

"'Where was your silver eloquence, your voice of persuasion, when the strife of party was at its fiercest? '

"'Where was your God-given skill in healing when One of Royal Blood lay fainting on the bed of dire—almost mortal—sickness? '

"And the answer? 'I laid it up in a napkin.' And now, etc., etc."

Then the whole six hundred boys sang "O Paradise! O Paradise!" with a fervour and sincerity that were irresistible. The organ thundered till the bad glass shivered and rattled, and the service was over.

5.

Almost the last words that Ambrose had heard after his wonderful awaking were odd enough, though at the time he took little note of them, since they were uttered amidst passionate embraces, amidst soft kisses on his poor beaten flesh. Indeed, if these words recurred to him afterwards, they never made much impression on his mind, though to most people they would seem of more serious import than much else that was uttered that night. The sentences ran something like this:

"The cruel, wicked brute! He shall be sorry all his days, and every blow shall be a grief to him. My dear! I promise you he shall pay for to-night ten times over. His heart shall ache for it till it stops beating."

There cannot be much doubt that this promise was kept to the letter. No one knew how wicked rumours concerning Mr. Horbury got abroad in Lupton, but from that very day the execution of the sentence began. In the evening the High Usher, paying a visit to a friend in town, took a short cut through certain dark, ill-lighted streets, and was suddenly horrified to hear his name shrieked out, coupled with a most disgusting accusation. His heart sank down in his breast; his face, he knew, was bloodless; and then he rushed forward to the malpassage whence the voice seemed to proceed.

There was nothing there. It was a horrid little alley, leading from one slum to another, between low walls and waste back-gardens, dismal and lampless. Horbury ran at top speed to the end of it, but there was nothing to be done. A few women were gossiping at their doors, a couple of men slouched past on their way to the beershop at the corner—that was all. He asked one of the women if she had seen anybody running, and she said no, civilly enough—and yet he fancied that she had leered at him.

He turned and went back home. He was not in the mood for paying visits. It was some time before he could compose his mind by assuring himself that the incident, though unpleasant, was not of the
slightest significance. But from that day the nets were about his feet,
and his fate was sealed.

Personally, he was subjected to no further annoyance, and soon
forgot that unpleasant experience in the back-street. But it seems certain that from that Sunday onwards a cloud of calumny overshadowed
the High Usher in all his ways. No one said anything definite, but every
one appeared to be conscious of something unpleasant when Horbury's name was mentioned. People looked oddly at one another, and
the subject was changed.

One of the young masters, speaking to a colleague, did indeed al-
lude casually to Horbury as Xanthias Phoceus. The other master, a
middle-aged man, raised his eyebrows and shook his head without
speaking. It is understood that these muttered slanders were various in
their nature; but, as has been said, everything was indefinite, intangible
as contagion—and as deadly to the master's worldly health.

That horrible accusation which had been screamed out of the alley
was credited by some; others agreed with the young master; while a
few had a terrible story of an idiot girl in a remote Derbyshire village.
And the persistence of all these fables was strange.

It was four years before Henry Vibart Chesson, D.D., ascended
the throne of St. Guthmund at Dorchester; and all through those four
years the fountain of evil innuendo rose without ceasing. It is doubtful
how far belief in the truth of these scandals was firm and settled, or
how far they were in the main uttered and circulated by ill-natured
people who disliked Horbury, but did not in their hearts believe him
guilty of worse sins than pompousness and arrogance. The latter is the
more probable opinion.

Of course, the deliberations of the Trustees were absolutely secret,
and the report that the Chairman, the Marquis of Dunham, said something about Cæsar's wife is a report and nothing more. It is evident
that the London press was absolutely in the dark as to the existence of
this strange conspiracy of vengeance, since two of the chief dailies
took the appointment of the High Usher to the Headmastership as a
foregone conclusion, prophesying, indeed, a rule of phenomenal suc-

cess. And then Millward, a Winchester man, understood to be rather unsound on some scholastic matters—"not *quite* the right man"; "just a *little* bit of a Jesuit"—received the appointment, and people did begin to say that there must be a screw loose somewhere. And Horbury was overwhelmed, and began to die.

The odd thing was that, save on that Sunday night, he never saw the enemy; he never suspected that there was an enemy. And as for the incident of the alley, after a little consideration he treated it with contempt. It was only some drunken beast in the town who knew him by sight and wished to be offensive, in the usual fashion of drunken beasts.

And there was nothing else. Lupton society was much too careful to allow its suspicions to be known. A libel action meant, anyhow, a hideous scandal and might have no pleasant results for the libellers. Besides, no one wanted to offend Horbury, who was suspected of possessing a revengeful temper; and it had not dawned on the Lupton mind that the rumours they themselves were circulating would eventually ruin the High Usher's chances of the Headmastership. Each gossip heard, as it were, only his own mutter at the moment. He did not realise that when a great many people are muttering all at once an ugly noise of considerable volume is being produced.

It is true that a few of the masters were somewhat cold in their manner. They lacked the social gift of dissimulation, and could not help shewing their want of cordiality. But Horbury, who noticed this, put it down to envy and disaffection, and resolved that the large powers given him by the Trustees should not be in vain so far as the masters in question were concerned.

Indeed, C. L. Wood, who was afterwards Headmaster of Marcester and died in Egypt a few years ago, had a curious story which in part relates to the masters in question, and perhaps throws some light on the extraordinary tale of Horbury's ruin.

Wood was an old Luptonian. He was a mighty athlete in his time, and his records for the Long Jump and Throwing the Cricket Ball have not been beaten at Lupton to this day. He had been one of the first boarders taken at the Old Grange. The early relations between Horbury and himself had been continued in later life, and Wood was staying with his former master at the time when the Trustees' decision was announced. It is supposed, indeed, that Horbury had offered him a kind of unofficial, but still important, position in the New Model; in fact, Wood confessed over his port that the idea was that he should be a kind of "Intelligence Department" to the Head. He did not seem very clear as to the exact scope of his proposed duties. We may certainly infer, however, that they would have been of a very confidential nature, for Wood had jotted down his recollections of that fatal morning somewhat as follows:

"I never saw Horbury in better spirits. Indeed, I remember thinking that he was younger than ever—younger than he was in the old days when he was a junior master and I was in the Third. Of course, he was always energetic; one could not disassociate the two notions of Horbury and energy, and I used to make him laugh by threatening to include the two terms in the new edition of my little book, *Latin and English Synonyms*. It did not matter whether he were taking the Fifth, or editing Classics for his boys, or playing rocker—one could not help rejoicing in the vivid and ebullient energy of the man. And perhaps this is one reason why shirkers and loafers dreaded him, as they certainly did.

"But during those last few days at Lupton his vitality had struck me as quite superhuman. As all the world knows, his succession to the Headmastership was regarded by every one as assured, and he was, naturally and properly, full of the great task which he believed was before him. This is not the place to argue the merits or demerits of the scheme which had been maturing for many years in his brain.

"A few persons who, I cannot but think, have received very imperfect information on the subject, have denounced Horbury's views of the modern Public School as revolutionary. Revolutionary they certainly were, as an express engine is revolutionary compared to an oxwaggon. But those who think of the late Canon Horbury as indifferent to the good side of Public School traditions knew little of the real man. However, were his plans good or bad, they were certainly of vast scope, and on the first night of my visit he made me sit up with him till two o'clock while he expounded his ideas, some of which, as he was good enough to say, he trusted to me to carry out. He shewed me the piles of MS. he had accumulated: hundreds of pages relating to the multiple departments of the great organisation which he was to direct, or rather to create; sheets of serried figures, sheaves of estimates which he had caused to be made out in readiness for immediate action.

"Nothing was neglected. I remember seeing a note on the desirability of compiling a 'Lupton Hymn Book' for use in the Chapel, and another on the question of forming a Botanical Garden, so that the school botany might be learned from 'the green life', as he beautifully expressed it, not from dry letterpress and indifferent woodcuts. Then, I think, on a corner of the 'Botany Leaf' was a jotting—a mere hasty scrawl, waiting development and consideration: 'Should we teach Hindustani? Write to Tucker *re* the Moulvie Ahmed Khan.'

"I despair of giving the reader any conception of the range and minuteness of these wonderful memoranda. I remember saying to Horbury that he seemed to be able to use the microscope and the telescope at the same time. He laughed joyously, and told me to wait till he was really at work. 'You will have your share, I promise you,' he added. His high spirits were extraordinary and infectious. He was an excellent *raconteur,* and now and again, amidst his talk of the New Lupton which he was about to translate from the idea into substance, he told some wonderful stories which I have not the heart to set down here. *Tu ne quæsieris.* I have often thought of those lines when I remember Horbury's intense happiness, the nervous energy which made the delay of a day or two seem almost intolerable. His brain and his fingers tingled, as it were, to set about the great work before him. He reminded me of a mighty host, awaiting but the glance of their general to rush forward with irresistible force.

"There was not a trace of misgiving. Indeed, I should have been utterly astonished if I had seen anything of the kind. He told me, indeed, that for some time past he had suspected the existence of a sort of cabal or clique against him. 'A. and X., B. and Y., M. and N., and, I think, Z., are in it,' he said, naming several of the masters. 'They are jealous, I suppose, and want to make things as difficult as they can. They are all cowards, though, and I don't believe one of them— except, perhaps, M.—would fail in obedience, or rather in subservience, when it comes to the point. But I am going to make short work of the lot.' And he told me his intention of ridding the school of these disaffected elements. 'The Trustees will back me up, I know,' he added, 'but we must try to avoid all unnecessary friction'; and he explained to me a plan he had thought of for eliminating the masters in question.

'It won't do to have half-hearted officers on our ship,' was the way in which he put it, and I cordially agreed with him.

"Possibly he may have underrated the force of the opposition which he treated so lightly; possibly he altogether misjudged the situation. He certainly regarded the appointment as already made, and this, of course, was, or appeared to be, the conviction of all who knew anything of Lupton and Horbury.

"I shall never forget the day on which the news came. Horbury made a hearty breakfast, opening letters, jotting down notes, talking of his plans as the meal proceeded. I left him for a while. I was myself a good deal excited, and I strolled up and down the beautiful garden at the Old Grange, wondering whether I should be able to satisfy such a chief who, the soul of energy himself, would naturally expect a like quality in his subordinates. I rejoined him in the course of an hour in the study, where he was as busy as ever—'snowed up', as he expressed it, in a vast pile of papers and correspondence.

"He nodded genially and pointed to a chair, and a few minutes later a servant came in with a letter. She had just found it in the hall, she explained. I had taken a book and was reading. I noticed nothing till what I can only call a groan of intense anguish made me look up in amazement—indeed, in horror—and I was shocked to see my old friend, his face a ghastly white, his eyes staring into vacancy, and his expression one of the most terrible—*the* most terrible—that I have ever witnessed. I cannot describe that look. There was an agony of grief and despair, a glance of the wildest amazement, terror, as of an impending awful death, and with these the fiercest and most burning anger that I have ever seen on any human face. He held a letter clenched in his hand. I was afraid to speak or move.

"It was fully five minutes before he regained his self-control, and he did this with an effort which was in itself dreadful to contemplate—so severe was the struggle. He explained to me in a voice which faltered and trembled with the shock that he had received, that he had had very bad news—that a large sum of money which was absolutely necessary to the carrying out of his projects had been embezzled by some unscrupulous person, that he did not know what he should do. He fell back into his chair; in a few minutes he had become an old man.

"He did not seem upset, or even astonished, when, later in the day, a telegram announced that he had failed in the aim of his life—that a stranger was to bear rule in his beloved Lupton. He murmured something to the effect that it was no matter now. He never held up his head again."

This note is an extract from *George Horbury: a Memoir*. It was written by Dr. Wood for the use of a few friends and privately printed in a small edition of a hundred and fifty copies. The author felt, as he explains in his brief "Foreword", that by restricting the sale to those who either knew Horbury or were especially interested in his work, he was enabled to dwell somewhat intimately on matters which could hardly have been treated in a book meant for the general public.

The extract that has been made from this book is interesting on two points. It shews that Horbury was quite unaware of what had been going on for four years before Chesson's resignation and that he had entirely misinterpreted the few and faint omens which had been offered him. He was preparing to break a sulky sentinel or two when all the ground of his fortalice was a very network of loaded mines! The other point is still more curious. It will be seen from Wood's story that the terrific effect that he describes was produced by a letter, received some hours before the news of the Trustees' decision arrived by telegram. "Later in the day" is the phrase in the Memoir; as a matter of fact, the final deliberation of the Lupton Trustees, held at Marshall's Hotel in Albemarle Street, began at eleven-thirty and was not over till one-forty-five. It is not likely that the result could have reached the Old Grange before two-fifteen; whereas the letter found in the hall must have been read by Horbury before ten o'clock. The invariable breakfast hour at the Old Grange was eight o'clock.

C. L. Wood says: "I rejoined him in the course of an hour," and the letter was brought in "a few minutes later". Afterwards, when the fatal telegram arrived, the Memoir notes that the unfortunate man was not "even astonished". It seems to follow almost necessarily from these facts that Horbury learnt the whole story of his ruin from the letter, for it has been ascertained that the High Usher's account of the contents of the letter was false from beginning to end. Horbury's most excellent and sagacious investments were all in the impeccable hands of "Witham's" (Messrs. Witham, Venables, Davenport and Witham), of Raymond Buildings, Gray's Inn, who do not include embezzlement in their theory and practice of the law; and, as a matter of fact, the nephew, Charles Horbury, came into a very handsome fortune on the death of his uncle—eighty thousand pounds in personality, with the Old Grange and some valuable ground rents in the new part of Lupton. It is as certain as anything can be that George Horbury never lost a penny by embezzlement or, indeed, in any other way.

One may surmise, then, the real contents of that terrible letter. In general, that is, for it is impossible to conjecture whether the writer told the whole story; one does not know, for example, whether Meyrick's name was mentioned or not; whether there was anything which carried the reader's mind to that dark evening in November when he beat the white-faced boy with such savage cruelty. But from Dr. Wood's description of the wretched man's appearance one understands how utterly unexpected was the crushing blow that had fallen upon him. It was a lightning flash from the sky at its bluest, and before that sudden and awful blast his whole life fell into deadly and evil ruin.

"He never held up his head again." He never lived again, one may say, unless a ceaseless wheel of anguish and anger and bitter and unavailing and furious regret can be called life. It was not a man, but a shell, full of gall and fire, that went to Wareham; but probably he was not the first of the Klippoth to be made a Canon.

As we have no means of knowing exactly what or how much that letter told him, one is not in a position to say whether he recognised the singularity—one might almost say, the eccentricity—with which his punishment was stage-managed. *Nec deus intersit* certainly; but a principle may be pushed too far, and a critic might point out that, putting avenging deities in their machines on one side, it was rather going to the other extreme to bring about the Great Catastrophe by means of bad sherry, a trying Headmaster, boiled mutton, a troublesome schoolboy and a servant-maid. Yet these were the agents employed, and it seems that we are forced to the conclusion that we do not altogether understand the management of the universe. The conclusion is a dangerous one, since we may be led by it, unless great care is exercised, into the worst errors of the Dark Ages.

There is the question, of course, of the truthfulness or falsity of the various slanders which had such a tremendous effect. The worst of them were lies—there can be little doubt of that—and for the rest, it may be hinted that the allusion of the young master to Xanthias Phoceus was not very far wide of the mark. Mrs. Horbury had been dead some years, and it is to be feared that there had been passages between the High Usher and Nelly Foran which public opinion would have condemned. It would be difficult to tell the whole story, but the girl's fury of revenge makes one apt to believe that she was exacting payment not only for Ambrose's wrongs, but for some grievous injury done to herself.

But before all these things could be brought to their ending, Ambrose Meyrick had to live in wonders and delights, to be initiated in many mysteries, to discover the meaning of that voice which seemed to speak within him, denouncing him because he had pried unworthily into the Secret which is hidden from the Holy Angels.

III

1.

One of Ambrose Meyrick's favourite books was a railway time-table. He spent many hours in studying these intricate pages of figures, noting times of arrival and departure on a piece of paper, and following the turnings and intersections of certain lines on the map. In this way he had at last arrived at the best and quickest route to his native country, which he had not seen for five years. His father had died when he was ten years old.

This result once obtained, the seven-thirty to Birmingham got him in at nine-thirty-five; the ten-twenty for the west was a capital train, and he would see the great dome of Mynydd Mawr before one o'clock. His fancy led him often to a bridge which crossed the railway about a mile out of Lupton. East and west the metals stretched in a straight line, defying, it seemed, the wisdom of Euclid. He turned from the east and gazed westward, and when a red train went by in the right direction he would lean over the bridge and watch till the last flying carriage had vanished into the distance. He imagined himself in that train and thought of the joy of it, if the time ever came—for it seemed long—the joy in every revolution of the wheels, in every whistle of the engine; in the rush and in the rhythm of this swift flight from that horrible school and that horrible place.

Year after year went by and he had not revisited the old land of his fathers. He was left alone in the great empty house in charge of the servants during the holidays—except one summer when Mr. Horbury despatched him to a cousin of his who lived at Yarmouth.

The second year after his father's death there was a summer of dreadful heat. Day after day the sky was a glare of fire, and in these abhorred Midlands, far from the breath of the sea and the mountain breeze, the ground baked and cracked and stank to heaven. A dun smoke rose from the earth with the faint, sickening stench of a brickfield, and the hedgerows swooned in the heat and in the dust. Ambrose's body and soul were athirst with the desire of the hills and the woods; his heart cried out within him for the waterpools in the shadow of the forest; and in his ears continually he heard the cold water pouring and trickling and dripping from the grey rocks on the great mountain side. And he saw that awful land which God has no doubt made for manufacturers to prepare them for their eternal habitation, its weary waves burning under the glaring sky: the factory chimneys of Lupton vomiting their foul smoke; the mean red streets, each little hellway with its own stink; the dull road, choking in its dust. For streams there was the Wand, running like black oil between black banks, steaming here as boiling poisons were belched into it from the factory wall; there glittering with iridescent scum vomited from some other scoundrel's castle. And for the waterpools of the woods he was free to gaze at the dark green liquor in the tanks of the Sulphuric Acid factory, but a little way out of town. Lupton was a very rising place.

His body was faint with the burning heat and the foulness of all about him, and his soul was sick with loneliness and friendlessness and unutterable longing. He had already mastered his Bradshaw and had found out the bridge over the railway; and day after day he leaned over the parapet and watched the burning metals vanishing into the west, into the hot, thick haze that hung over all the land. And the trains sped away towards the haven of his desire, and he wondered if he should ever see again the dearly loved country or hear the song of the nightingale in the still white morning, in the circle of the green hills. The thought of his father, of the old days of happiness, of the grey home in the still valley, swelled in his heart and he wept bitterly, so utterly forsaken and wretched seemed his life.

It happened towards the end of that dreadful August that one night he had tossed all through the hours listening to the chiming bells, only falling into a fevered doze a little while before they called him. He woke from ugly and oppressive dreams to utter wretchedness; he crawled downstairs like an old man and left his breakfast untouched, for he could eat nothing. The flame of the sun seemed to burn in his brain; the hot smoke of the air choked him. All his limbs ached. From head to foot he was a body of suffering. He struggled out and tottered along the road to the bridge and gazed with dim, hopeless eyes along the path of desire, into the heavy, burning mist in the far distance. And then his heart beat quick, and he cried aloud in his amazed delight; for, in the shimmering glamour of the haze, he saw as in a mirror the vast green wall of the Great Mountain rise before him—not far, but as if close at hand. Nay, he stood upon its slope; his feet were in the sweet-smelling bracken; the hazel thicket was rustling beneath him in the brave wind, and the shining water poured cold from the stony rock. He heard the silver note of the lark, shrilling high and glad in the sunlight. He saw the yellow blossoms tossed by the breeze about the porch of the white house. He seemed to turn in this vision, and before him the dear, long-remembered land appeared in its great peace and beauty: meadows and cornfield, hill and valley and deep wood between the mountains and the far sea. He drew a long breath of that quickening and glorious air, and knew that life had returned to him. And then he was gazing once more down the glittering railway into the mist; but strength and hope had replaced that deadly sickness of a moment before, and light and joy came back to his eyes.

The vision had doubtless been given to him in his sore and pressing need. It returned no more; not again did he see the fair height of Mynydd Mawr rise out of the mist. But from that day the station on the bridge was daily consecrated. It was his place of refreshment and hope in many seasons of evil and weariness. From this place he could look forward to the hour of release and return that must come at last. Here he could remind himself that the bonds of the flesh had been broken in a wonderful manner; that he had been set free from the jaws of hell and death.

Fortunately, few people came that way. It was but a by-road serving a few farms in the neighbourhood, and on the Sunday afternoon in November, the Head's sermon over and dinner eaten, he betook himself to his tower, free to be alone for a couple of hours, at least.

He stood there, leaning on the wall, his face turned, as ever, to the west, and, as it were, a great flood of rapture overwhelmed him. He sank down, deeper, still deeper, into the hidden and marvellous places of delight. In his country there were stories of the magic people who rose all gleaming from the pools in lonely woods; who gave more than mortal bliss to those who loved them; who could tell the secrets of that land where flame was the most material substance; whose inhabitants dwell in palpitating and quivering colours or in the notes of a wonderful melody. And in the dark of the night all legends had been fulfilled.

It was a strange thing, but Ambrose Meyrick, though he was a public schoolboy of fifteen, had lived all his days in a rapt innocence. It is possible that in school, as elsewhere, enlightenment, pleasant or unpleasant, only comes to those who seek for it—or one may say certainly that there are those who dwell under the protection of enchantments, who may go down into the black depths and yet appear resurgent and shining, without any stain or defilement of the pitch on their white robes. For these have ears so intent on certain immortal songs that they cannot hear discordant voices; their eyes are veiled with a light that shuts out the vision of evil. There are flames about these feet that extinguish the gross fires of the pit.

It is probable that all through those early years Ambrose's father had been charming his son's heart, drawing him forth from the gehenna-valley of this life into which he had fallen, as one draws forth a beast that has fallen into some deep and dreadful place. Various are the methods recommended. There is the way of what is called moral teaching, the way of physiology and the way of a masterly silence; but Mr. Meyrick's was the strange way of incantation. He had, in a certain manner, drawn the boy aside from that evil traffic of the valley, from the stench of the turmoil, from the blows and the black lechery, from the ugly fight in the poisonous smoke, from all the amazing and hideous folly that practical men call life, and had set him in that endless procession that for ever and for ever sings its litanies in the mountains, going from height to height on its great quest. Ambrose's soul had been caught in the sweet thickets of the woods; it had been bathed in the pure water of blessed fountains; it had knelt before the altars of the old saints, till all the earth was become a sanctuary, all life was a rite and a ceremony, the end of which was the attainment of the mystic sanctity—the achieving of the Graal. For this—for what else?—were all things made. It was this that the little bird sang of in the bush, piping a few feeble, plaintive notes of dusky evenings, as if his tiny heart were sad that it could utter nothing better than such sorry praises. This also celebrated the awe of the white morning on the hills, the breath of the woods at dawn. This was figured in the red ceremony of sunset, when flames shone over the dome of the great mountain, and roses blossomed in the far plains of the sky. This was the secret of the dark places in the heart of the woods. This the mystery of the sunlight on the height; and every little flower, every delicate fern, and every reed and rush was entrusted with the hidden declaration of this sacrament. For this end, final and perfect rites had been given to men to execute; and these were all the arts, all the far-lifted splendour of the great cathedral; all rich carven work and all glowing colours; all magical utterance of words and tones: all these things were the witnesses that consented in the One Offering, in the high service of the Graal.

To this service also, together with songs and burning torches and dyed garments and the smoke of the bruised incense, were brought the incense of the bruised heart, the magic torches of virtue hidden from the world, the red dalmatics of those whose souls had been martyred, the songs of triumph and exultation chanted by them that the profane had crushed into the dust; holy wells and water-stoups were fountains of tears. So must the Mass be duly celebrated in Cor-arbennic when Cadwaladr returned, when Teilo Agyos lifted up again the Shining Cup.

Perhaps it was not strange that a boy who had listened to such spells as these should heed nothing of the foolish evils about him, the nastiness of silly children who, for want of wits, were "crushing the lilies into the dunghill". He listened to nothing of their ugly folly; he heard it not, understood it not, thought as little of it as of their everlasting chatter about "brooks" and "quarries" and "leg-hits" and "breaks from the off". And when an unseemly phrase did chance to fall on his ear it was of no more import or meaning than any or all of the stupid jargon that went on day after day, mixing itself with the other jargon about the optative and the past participle, the oratio obliqua and the verbs in $\mu\iota$. To him this was all one nothingness, and he would not have dreamed of connecting anything of it with the facts of life, as he understood life.

Hence it was that for him all that was beautiful and wonderful was a part of sanctity; all the glory of life was for the service of the sanctuary, and when one saw a lovely flower it was to be strewn before the altar, just as the bee was holy because by its wax the Gifts are illuminated. Where joy and delight and beauty were, there he knew by sure signs were the parts of the mystery, the glorious apparels of the heavenly vestments. If any one had told him that the song of the nightingale was an unclean thing he would have stared in amazement, as though one had blasphemed the Sanctus. To him the red roses were as holy as the garments of the martyrs. The white lilies were pure and shining virtues; the imagery of the *Song of Songs* was obvious and perfect and unassailable, for in his world there was nothing common nor unclean. And even to him the great gift had been freely given.

So he stood, wrapt in his meditations and in his ecstasy, by the bridge over the Midland line from Lupton to Birmingham. Behind him were the abominations of Lupton: the chimneys vomiting black smoke faintly in honour of the Sabbath; the red lines of the workmen's streets advancing into the ugly fields; the fuming pottery kilns, the hideous height of the boot factory. And before him stretched the unspeakable scenery of the eastern Midlands, which seems made for the habitation of English Nonconformists—dull, monotonous, squalid, the very hedgerows cropped and trimmed, the trees looking like rows of Roundheads, the farmhouses as uninteresting as suburban villas. On a field near at hand a scientific farmer had recently applied an agreeable mixture consisting of superphosphate of lime, nitrate of soda and bone meal. The stink was that of a chemical works or a Texel cheese. Another field was just being converted into an orchard. There were rows of grim young apple trees planted at strictly mathematical intervals from one another, and grisly little graves had been dug between the apple trees for the reception of gooseberry bushes. Between these rows the farmer hoped to grow potatoes, so the ground had been thoroughly trenched. It looked sodden and unpleasant. To the right

Ambrose could see how the operations on a wandering brook were progressing. It had moved in and out in the most wasteful and absurd manner, and on each bank there had grown a twisted brake of trees and bushes and rank water plants. There were wonderful red roses there in summer time. Now all this was being rectified. In the first place the stream had been cut into a straight channel with raw, bare banks, and then the rose bushes, the alders, the willows and the rest were being grubbed up by the roots and so much valuable land was being redeemed. The old barn which used to be visible on the left of the line had been pulled down for more than a year. It had dated perhaps from the seventeenth century. Its roof-tree had dipped and waved in a pleasant fashion, and the red tiles had the glow of the sun in their colours, and the half-timbered walls were not lacking in ruinous grace. It was a dilapidated old shed, and a neat-looking structure with a corrugated iron roof now stood in its place.

Beyond all was the grey prison wall of the horizon; but Ambrose no longer gazed at it with the dim, hopeless eyes of old. He had a Breviary among his books, and he thought of the words: *Anima mea erepta est sicut passer de laqueo venantium,* and he knew that in a good season his body would escape also. The exile would end at last.

He remembered an old tale which his father was fond of telling him—the story of Eos Amherawdur (the Emperor Nightingale). Very long ago, the story began, the greatest and the finest court in all the realms of faery was the court of the Emperor Eos, who was above all the kings of the Tylwydd Têg, as the Emperor of Rome is head over all the kings of the earth. So that even Gwyn ap Nudd, whom they now call lord over all the fair folk of the Isle of Britain, was but the man of Eos, and no splendour such as his was ever seen in all the regions of enchantment and faery. Eos had his court in a vast forest, called Wentwood, in the deepest depths of the greenwood between Caerwent and Caermaen, which is also called the City of the Legions; though some men say that we should rather name it the city of the Water-floods. Here, then, was the Palace of Eos, built of the finest stones after the Roman manner, and within it were the most glorious chambers that eye has ever seen; and there was no end to the number of them, for they could not be counted. For the stones of the palace being immortal, they were at the pleasure of the Emperor. If he had willed, all the hosts of the world could stand in his greatest hall, and, if he had willed, not so much as an ant could enter into it, since it could not be discerned. But on common days they spread the Emperor's banquet in nine great halls, each nine times larger than any that are in the lands of the men of Normandi. And Sir Caw was the seneschal who marshalled the feast; and if you would count those under his command—go, count the drops of water that are in the Uske River. But if you would learn the splendour of this castle it is an easy matter, for Eos hung the walls of it with Dawn and Sunset. He lit it with the sun and moon. There was a well in it called Ocean. And nine churches of twisted boughs were set apart in which Eos might hear Mass; and when his clerks sang before him all the jewels rose shining out of the earth, and all the stars bent shining down from heaven, so enchanting was the melody. Then was great bliss in all the regions of the fair folk. But Eos was grieved because mortal ears could not hear nor comprehend the enchantment of their song. What, then, did he do? Nothing less than this. He divested himself of all his glories and of his kingdom, and transformed himself into the shape of a little brown bird, and went flying about the woods, desirous of teaching men the sweetness of the faery melody. And all the other birds said: "This is a contemptible stranger." The eagle found him not even worthy to be a prey; the raven and the magpie called him simpleton; the pheasant asked where he had got that ugly livery; the lark wondered why he hid himself in the darkness of the wood; the peacock would not suffer his name to be uttered. In short, never was any one so despised as was Eos by all the chorus of the birds. But wise men heard that song from the faery regions and listened all night beneath the bough, and these were the first who were bards in the Isle of Britain.

Ambrose had heard the song from the faery regions. He had heard it in swift whispers at his ear, in sighs upon his breast, in the breath of kisses on his lips. Never was he numbered amongst the despisers of Eos.

2.

Mr. Horbury had suffered from one or two slight twinges of conscience for a few days after he had operated on his nephew. They were but very slight pangs, for, after all, it was a case of flagrant and repeated disobedience to rules, complicated by lying. The High Usher was quite sincere in scouting the notion of a boy's taking any interest in Norman architecture, and, as he said to himself, truly enough, if every boy at Lupton could come and go when and how he pleased, and choose which rules he would keep and which disobey—why, the school would soon be in a pretty state. Still, there was a very faint and indistinct murmur in his mind which suggested that Meyrick had received, in addition to his own proper thrashing, the thrashings due to the Head, his cook and his wine merchant. And Horbury was rather sorry, for he desired to be just according to his definition of justice— unless, indeed, justice should be excessively inconvenient.

But these faint scruples were soon removed—turned, indeed, to satisfaction by the evident improvement which declared itself in Ambrose Meyrick's whole tone and demeanour. He no longer did his best to avoid rocker. He played, and played well and with relish. The boy was evidently all right at heart: he had only wanted a sharp lesson, and it was clear that, once a loafer, he was now on his way to be a credit to the school. And by some of those secret channels which are known to masters and to masters alone, rather more than a glimmering of the truth as to Rawson's black eyes and Pelly's disfigured nose was vouch-safed to Horbury's vision, and he was by no means displeased with his nephew. The two boys had evidently asked for punishment, and had got it. It served them right. Of course, if the swearing had been brought to his notice by official instead of by subterranean and mystic ways, he would have had to cane Meyrick a second time, since, by the Public School convention, an oath is a very serious offence—as bad as smoking, or worse; but, being far from a fool, under the circumstances he made nothing of it. Then the lad's school work was so very satisfactory. It had always been good, but it had become wonderfully good. That last Greek prose had shewn real grip of the language. The High Usher was pleased. His sharp lesson had brought forth excellent results, and he foresaw the day when he would be proud of having taught a remarkably fine scholar.

With the boys Ambrose was becoming a general favourite. He learned not only to play rocker, he shewed Pelly how he thought that blow under the ear should be dealt with. They all said he was a good fellow; but they could not make out why, without apparent reason, he would sometimes burst out into loud laughter. But he said it was something wrong with his inside—the doctors couldn't make it out—and this seemed rather interesting.

In after life he often looked back upon this period when, to all appearance, Lupton was "making a man" of him, and wondered at its strangeness. To boys and masters alike he was an absolutely normal schoolboy, busy with the same interests as the rest of them. There was certainly something rather queer in his appearance; but, as they said, generously enough, a fellow couldn't help his looks; and, that curious glint in the eyes apart, he seemed as good a Luptonian as any in the whole six hundred. Everybody thought that he had absolutely fallen into line; that he was absorbing the *ethos* of the place in the most admirable fashion, subduing his own individuality, his opinions, his habits, to the general tone of the community around him—putting off, as it were, the profane dust of his own spirit and putting on the mental frock of the brotherhood. This, of course, is one of the aims—rather, *the* great aim—of the system: this fashioning of very diverse characters into one common form, so that each great Public School has its type, which is easily recognisable in the grown-up man years after his school days are over. Thus, in far lands, in India and Egypt, in Canada and New Zealand, one recognises the brisk alertness of the Etonian, the exquisite politeness of Harrow, the profound seriousness of Rugby; while the note of Lupton may, perhaps, be called finality. The Old Luptonian no more thinks of arguing a question than does the Holy Father, and his conversation is a series of irreformable dogmas, and the captious person who questions any one article is made to feel himself a cad and an outsider.

Thus it has been related that two men who had met for the first time at a certain country house-party were getting on together capitally in the evening over their whisky and soda and cigars. Each held identical views of equal violence on some important topic—Home Rule or the Transvaal or Free Trade—and, as the more masterful of the two asserted that hanging was too good for Blank (naming a well-known statesman), the other would reply: "I quite agree with you: hanging *is* too good for Blank."

"He ought to be burned alive," said the one.

"That's about it: he ought to be burned at the stake," answered the other.

"Look at the way he treated Dash! He's a coward and a damned scoundrel!"

"Perfectly right. He's a damned cursed scoundrel!"

This was splendid, and each thought the other a charming companion. Unfortunately, however, the conversation, by some caprice, veered from the iniquities of Blank and glanced aside to cookery—possibly by the track of Irish stew, used metaphorically to express the disastrous and iniquitous policy of the great statesman with regard to Ireland. But, as it happened, there was not the same coincidence on the question of cookery as there had been on the question of Blank. The masterful man said:

"No cookery like English. No other race in the world can cook as we do. Look at French cookery—a lot of filthy, greasy messes."

Now, instead of assenting briskly and firmly as before, the other man said: "Been much in France? Lived there?"

"Never set my foot in the beastly country! Don't like their ways, and don't care to dine off snails and frogs swimming in oil."

The other man began then to talk of the simple but excellent meals he had relished in France—the savoury *croûte-au-pot*, the *bouilli*—good eating when flavoured by a gherkin or two; velvety *épinards au jus*, a roast partridge, a salad, a bit of Roquefort and a bunch of grapes. But he had barely mentioned the soup when the masterful one wheeled round his chair and offered a fine view of his strong, well-knit figure—as seen from the back. He did not say anything—he simply took up a paper and went on smoking. The other men stared in amazement: the amateur of French cookery looked annoyed. But the host, a keen-eyed old fellow with a white moustache, turned to the enemy of frogs and snails and grease and said quite simply: "I say, Mulock, I never knew you'd been at Lupton."

Mulock gazed. The other men held their breath for a moment as the full force of the situation dawned on them, and then a wild scream of laughter shrilled from their throats. Yells and roars of mirth resounded in the room. Their delight was insatiable. It died for a moment for lack of breath, and then burst out anew in still louder, more uproarious clamour, till old Sir Henry Rawnsley, who was fat and short, could do nothing but choke and gasp and crow out a sound something between a wheeze and a chuckle. Mulock left the room immediately, and the house the next morning. He made some excuse to his host, but he told enquiring friends that, personally, he disliked bounders.

The story, true or false, illustrates the common view of the Lupton stamp.

"We try to teach the boys to know their own minds," said the Headmaster, and the endeavour seems to have succeeded in most cases. And, as Horbury noted in an article he once wrote on the Public School system, every boy was expected to submit himself to the process, to form and reform himself in accordance with the tone of the school.

"I sometimes compare our work with that of the metal founder," he says in the article in question. "Just as the metal comes to the foundry *rudis indigestaque moles,* a rough and formless mass, without the slightest suggestion of the shape which it must finally assume, so a boy comes to a great Public School with little or nothing about him to suggest the young man who, in eight or nine years' time, will say good-bye to the dear old school, setting his teeth tight, restraining himself from giving up to the anguish of this last farewell. Nay, I think that ours is the harder task, for the metal that is sent to the foundry has, I presume, been freed of its impurities; we have to deal rather with the ore—a mass which is not only shapeless, but contains much that is not metal at all, which must be burnt out and cast aside as useless rubbish. So the boy comes from his home, which may or may not have possessed valuable formative influences; which we often find has tended to create a spirit of individualism and assertiveness; which, in numerous cases, has left the boy under the delusion that he has come into the world to live his own life and think his own thoughts. This is the ore that we cast into our furnace. We burn out the dross and rubbish; we liquefy the stubborn and resisting metal till it can be run into the mould—the mould being the whole tone and feeling of a great community. We discourage all excessive individuality; we make it quite plain to the boy that he has come to Lupton, not to live his life, not to think his thoughts, but to live *our* life, to think *our* thoughts. Very often, as I think I need scarcely say, the process is a somewhat unpleasant one, but, sooner or later, the stubbornest metal yields to the cleansing, renewing, restoring fires of discipline and public opinion, and the shapeless mass takes on the shape of the Great School. Only the other day an old pupil came to see me and confessed that, for the whole of his first year at Lupton, he had been profoundly wretched. 'I was a dreamy young fool,' he said. 'My head was stuffed with all sorts of queer fancies, and I expect that if I hadn't come to Lupton I should have turned out an absolute loafer. But I hated it badly that first year. I loathed rocker—I did, really—and I thought the fellows were a lot of savages. And then I seemed to go into a kind of cloud. You see, Sir, I was losing my old self and hadn't got the new self in its place, and I couldn't make out what was happening. And then, quite suddenly, it all came out light and clear. I saw the purpose behind it all—how we were all working together, masters and boys, for the dear old school; how we were all "members one of another", as the Doctor said in Chapel; and that I had a part in this great work, too, though I was only a kid in the Third. It was like a flash of light: one minute I was only a poor little chap that nobody cared for and who didn't matter to anybody, and the next I saw that, in a way, I was as important as the Doctor himself—I was a part of the failure or success of it all. Do you know what I did, Sir? I had a book I thought a lot of—*Poems and Tales* of Edgar Allan Poe. It was my poor sister's book; she had died a year before when she was only seventeen, and she had written my name in it when she was dying—she knew I was fond of reading it. It was just the sort of thing I used to like—morbid fancies and queer poems, and I was always reading it when the fellows would let me alone. But when I saw what life really was, when the meaning of it all came to me, as I said just now, I took that book and tore it to bits, and it was like tearing myself up. But I knew that writing all that stuff hadn't done that American fellow much good, and I didn't see what good I should get by reading it. I couldn't make out to myself that it would fit in with the Doctor's plans or the spirit of the school, or that I should play up at rocker any better for knowing all about the "Fall of the House of Usher", or whatever it's called. I knew my poor sister would understand, so I tore it up, and I've gone straight ahead ever since—thanks to Lupton.' *Like a refiner's fire.* I remembered the dreamy, absent-minded child of fifteen years before; I could scarcely believe that he stood before me—keen, alert, practical, living every moment of his life, a force, a power in the world, certain of successful achievement."

Such were the influences to which Ambrose Meyrick was being subjected, and with infinite success, as it seemed to everybody who watched him. He was regarded as a conspicuous instance of the efficacy of the system—he had held out so long, refusing to absorb the "tone", presenting an obstinate surface to the millstones which would, for his own good, have ground him to powder, not concealing very much his dislike of the place and of the people in it. And suddenly he had submitted with a good grace: it was wonderful! The masters are believed to have discussed the affair amongst themselves, and Horbury, who confessed or boasted that he had used sharp persuasion, got a good deal of *kudos* in consequence.

3.

A few years ago a little book called *Half-holidays* attracted some attention in semi-scholastic, semi-clerical circles. It was anonymous, and bore the modest motto *Crambe bis cocta,* but those behind the scenes recognised it as the work of Charles Palmer, who was for many years a master at Lupton. His acknowledged books include a useful little work on the Accents and an excellent summary of Roman History from the Fall of the Republic to Romulus Augustulus. The *Half-holidays* contains the following amusing passage; there is not much difficulty in identifying the N. mentioned in it with Ambrose Meyrick.

"The cleverest dominie sometimes discovers"—the passage begins—"that he has been living in a fool's paradise, that he has been tricked by a quiet and persistent subtlety that really strikes one as almost devilish when one finds it exhibited in the person of an English schoolboy. A good deal of nonsense, I think, has been written about boys by people who in reality know very little about them; they have been credited with complexities of character, with feelings and aspirations and delicacies of sentiment which are quite foreign to their nature. I can quite believe in the dead cat trick of Stalky and his friends, but I confess that the incident of the British Flag leaves me cold and sceptical. Such refinement of perception is not the way of the boy— certainly not of the boy as I have known him. He is radically a simple soul, whose feelings are on the surface; and his deepest laid schemes and manoeuvres hardly call for the talents of a Sherlock Holmes if they are to be detected and brought to nought. Of course, a good deal of rubbish has been talked about the wonderful success of our English plan of leaving the boys to themselves without the everlasting supervision which is practised in French schools. As a matter of fact, the English schoolboy is under constant supervision; where in a French school one wretched usher has to look after a whole horde of boys, in an English school each boy is perpetually under the observation of hundreds of his fellows. In reality, each boy is an unpaid *pion*, a watchdog whose vigilance never relaxes. He is not aware of this; one need scarcely say that such a notion is far from his wildest thoughts. He thinks, and very rightly, doubtless, that he is engaged in maintaining the honour of the school, in keeping up the observance of the school tradition, in dealing sharply with slackers and loafers who would bring discredit on the place he loves so well. He is, no doubt, absolutely right in all this; none the less, he is doing the master's work unwittingly and admirably. When one thinks of this, and of the Compulsory System of Games, which ensures that every boy shall be in a certain place at a certain time, one sees, I think, that the phrase about our lack of supervision *is* a phrase and nothing more. There is no system of supervision known to human wit that approaches in thoroughness and minuteness the supervision under which every single boy is kept all through his life at an English Public School.

"Hence one is really rather surprised when, in spite of all these unpaid assistants, who are the whole school, one is thoroughly and completely taken in. I can only remember one such case, and I am still astonished at the really infernal ability with which the boy in question lived a double life under the very eyes of the masters and six hundred other boys. N., as I shall call him, was not in my House, and I can scarcely say how I came to watch his career with so much interest; but there was certainly something about him which did interest me a good deal. It may have been his appearance: he was an odd-looking boy— dark, almost swarthy, dreamy and absent in manner, and, for the first years of his school life, a quite typical loafer. Such boys, of course, are not common in a big school, but there are a few such everywhere. One never knows whether this kind will write a successful book, or paint a great picture, or go to the devil—from my observation I am sorry to say that the last career is the most usual. I need scarcely say that such boys meet with but little encouragement; it is not the type which the Public School exists to foster, and the boy who abandons himself to morbid introspection is soon made to feel pretty emphatically that he is matter in the wrong place. Of course, one may be crushing genius. If this ever happened it would be very unfortunate; still, in all communities the minority must suffer for the good of the majority, and, frankly, I have always been willing to run the risk. As I have hinted, the particular sort of boy I have in my mind turns out in nine cases out of ten to be not a genius, but that much more common type—a blackguard.

"Well, as I say, I was curious about N. I was sorry for him, too; both his parents were dead, and he was rather in the position of the poor fellows who have no home life to look forward to when the holidays are getting near. And his obstinacy astonished me; in most cases the pressure of public opinion will bring the slackest loafer to a sense of the error of his ways before his first term is ended; but N. seemed to hold out against us all with a sort of dreamy resistance that was most exasperating. I do not think he can have had a very pleasant time. His general demeanour suggested that of a sage who has been cast on an island inhabited by a peculiarly repulsive and degraded tribe of savages, and I need scarcely say that the other boys did their best to make him realise the extreme absurdity of such behaviour. He was clever enough at his work, but it was difficult to make him play games, and impossible to make him play up. He seemed to be looking through us at something else; and neither the boys nor the masters liked being treated as unimportant illusions. And then, quite suddenly, N. altered completely. I believe his housemaster, worn out of all patience, gave him a severe thrashing; at any rate, the change was instant and marvellous.

"I remember that a few days before N.'s transformation we had been discussing the question of the cane at the weekly masters' meeting. I had confessed myself a very half-hearted believer in the efficacy of the treatment. I forget the arguments that I used, but I know that I was strongly inclined to favour the 'Anti-baculist Party', as the Head jocosely named it. But a few months later, when N.'s housemaster pointed out N. playing up at football like a young demon, and then with a twinkle in his eye reminded me of the position I had taken up at the masters' meeting, there was nothing for it but to own that I had been in the wrong. The cane had certainly, in this case, proved itself a magic wand; the sometime loafer had been transformed by it into one of the healthiest and most energetic fellows in the whole school. It was a pleasure to watch him at the games, and I remember that his fast bowling was at once terrific in speed and peculiarly deadly in its accuracy.

"He kept up this deception, for deception it was, for three or four years. He was just going up to Oxford, and the whole school was looking forward to a career which we knew would be quite exceptional in its brilliance. His scholarship papers astonished the Balliol authorities. I remember one of the Fellows writing to our Head about them in terms of the greatest enthusiasm, and we all knew that N.'s bowling would get him into the University Eleven in his first term. Cricketers have not yet forgotten a certain performance of his at the Oval, when, as a poetic journalist observed, wickets fell before him as ripe corn falls before the sickle. N. disappeared in the middle of term. The whole school was in a ferment; masters and boys looked at one another with wild faces; search parties were sent out to scour the country; the police were communicated with; on every side one heard the strangest surmises as to what had happened. The affair got into the papers; most people thought it was a case of breakdown and loss of memory from overwork and mental strain. Nothing could be heard of N., till, at the end of a fortnight, his Housemaster came into our room looking, as I thought, puzzled and frightened.

"'I don't understand,' he said. 'I've had this by the second post. It's in N.'s handwriting. I can't make head or tail of it. It's some sort of French, I suppose.'

"He held out a paper closely written in N.'s exquisite, curious script, which always reminded me vaguely of some Oriental character. The masters shook their heads as the manuscript went from hand to hand, and one of them suggested sending for the French master. But, as it happened, I was something of a student of Old French myself, and I found I could make out the drift of the document that N. had sent his master.

"It was written in the manner and in the language of Rabelais. It was quite diabolically clever, and beyond all question the filthiest thing I have ever read. The writer had really exceeded his master in obscenity, impossible as that might seem: the purport of it all was a kind of nightmare vision of the school, the masters and the boys. Everybody and everything were distorted in the most horrible manner, seen, we might say, through an abominable glass, and yet every feature was easily recognisable; it reminded me of Swift's disgusting description of the Yahoos, over which one may shudder and grow sick, but which one cannot affect to misunderstand. There was a fantastic episode which I remember especially. One of us, an ambitious man, who for some reason or other had become unpopular with a few of his colleagues, was described as endeavouring to climb the school clock-tower, on the top of which a certain object was said to be placed. The object was defended, so the writer affirmed, by 'the Dark Birds of Night', who resisted the master's approach in all possible and impossible manners. Even to indicate the way in which this extraordinary theme was treated would be utterly out of the question; but I shall never forget the description of the master's face, turned up towards the object of his quest, as he painfully climbed the wall. I have never read even in the most filthy pages of Rabelais, or in the savagest passages of Swift, anything which approached the revolting cruelty of those few lines. They were compounded of hell-fire and the Cloaca Maxima.

"I read out and translated a few of the least abominable sentences. I can hardly say whether the feeling of disgust or that of bewilderment predominated amongst us. One of my colleagues stopped me and said they had heard enough; we stared at one another in silence. The astounding ability, ferocity and obscenity of the whole thing left us quite dumbfounded, and I remember saying that if a volcano were suddenly to belch forth volumes of flame and filth in the middle of the playing fields I should scarcely be more astonished. And all this was the work of N., whose brilliant abilities in games and in the schools were to have been worth many thousands a year to X., as one of us put it! This was the boy that for the last four years we had considered as a great example of the formative influences of the school! This was the N. who we thought would have died for the honour of the school, who spoke as if he could never do enough to repay what X. had done for him! As I say, we looked at one another with faces of blank amazement and horror. At last somebody said that N. must have gone mad, and we tried to believe that it was so, for madness, awful calamity as it is, would be more endurable than sanity under such circumstances as these. I need scarcely say that this charitable hypothesis turned out to be quite unfounded; N. was perfectly sane; he was simply revenging himself for the suppression of his true feelings for the four last years of his school life. The 'conversion' on which we prided ourselves had been an utter sham; the whole of his life had been an elaborately organised hypocrisy maintained with unfailing and unflinching skill term after term and year after year. One cannot help wondering when one considers the inner life of this unhappy fellow. Every morning, I suppose, he woke up with curses in his soul; he smiled at us all and joined in the games with black rage devouring him. So far as one can say, he was quite sincere in his concealed opinions at all events. The hatred, loathing and contempt of the whole system of the place displayed in that extraordinary and terrible document struck me as quite genuine; and while I was reading it I could not help thinking of his eager, enthusiastic face as he joined with a will in the school songs; he seemed to inspire all the boys about him with something of his own energy and devotion. The apparition was a shocking one; I felt that for a moment I had caught a glimpse of a region that was very like hell itself.

"I remember that the French master contributed a characteristic touch of his own. Of course, the Headmaster had to be told of the matter, and it was arranged that M. and myself should collaborate in the unpleasant task of making a translation. M. read the horrible stuff through with an expression on his face that, to my astonishment, bordered on admiration, and when he laid down the paper he said:

"*Eh bien: Maître François est encore en vie, évidemment. C'est le vrai renouveau de la Renaissance; de la Renaissance en très mauvaise humeur, si vous voulez, mais de la Renaissance tout-de-même. Si, si; c'est de la crû véritable, je vous assure. Mais, notre bon N. est un Rabelais qui a habité une terre affreusement sèche.'*

"I really think that to the Frenchman the terrible moral aspect of the case was either entirely negligible or absolutely non-existent; he simply looked on N.'s detestable and filthy performance as a little masterpiece in a particular literary *genre*. Heaven knows! One does not want to be a Pharisee; but as I saw M. grinning appreciatively over this dungheap I could not help feeling that the collapse of France before Germany offered no insoluble problem to the historian.

"There is little more to be said as to this extraordinary and most unpleasant affair. It was all hushed up as much as possible. No further attempts to discover N.'s whereabouts were made. It was some months before we heard by indirect means that the wretched fellow had abandoned the Balliol Scholarship and the most brilliant prospects in life to attach himself to a company of greasy barnstormers—or 'Dramatic Artists', as I suppose they would be called nowadays. I believe that his subsequent career has been of a piece with these beginnings; but of that I desire to say nothing."

The passage has been quoted merely in evidence of the great success with which Ambrose Meyrick adapted himself to his environment at Lupton. Palmer, the writer, who was a very well-meaning though intensely stupid person, has told the bare facts as he saw them accurately enough; it need not be said that his inferences and deductions from the facts are invariably ridiculous. He was a well-educated man; but in his heart of hearts he thought that Rabelais, *Maria Monk, Gay Life in Paris* and *La Terre* all came to much the same thing.

4.

In an old notebook kept by Ambrose Meyrick in those long-past days there are some curious entries which throw light on the extraordinary experiences that befell him during the period which poor Palmer has done his best to illustrate. The following is interesting:

"I told her she must not come again for a long time. She was astonished and asked me why—was I not fond of her? I said it was because I was so fond of her, that I was afraid that if I saw her often I could not live. I should pass away in delight because our bodies are not meant to live for long in the middle of white fire. I was lying on my bed and she stood beside it. I looked up at her. The room was very dark and still. I could only just see her faintly, though she was so close to me that I could hear her breathing quite well. I thought of the white flowers that grew in the dark corners of the old garden at the Wern, by the great ilex tree. I used to go out on summer nights when the air was still and all the sky cloudy. One could hear the brook just a little, down beyond the watery meadow, and all the woods and hills were dim. One could not see the mountain at all. But I liked to stand by the wall and look into the darkest place, and in a little time those flowers would seem to grow out of the shadow. I could just see the white glimmer of them. She looked like the flowers to me, as I lay on the bed in my dark room.

"Sometimes I dream of wonderful things. It is just at the moment when one wakes up; one cannot say where one has been or what was so wonderful, but you know that you have lost everything in waking. For just that moment you knew everything and understood the stars and the hills and night and day and the woods and the old songs. They were all within you, and you were all light. But the light was music, and the music was violet wine in a great cup of gold, and the wine in the golden cup was the scent of a June night. I understood all this as she stood beside my bed in the dark and stretched out her hand and touched me on the breast.

"I knew a pool in an old, old grey wood a few miles from the Wern. I called it the grey wood because the trees were ancient oaks that they say must have grown there for a thousand years, and they have grown bare and terrible. Most of them are all hollow inside and some have only a few boughs left, and every year, they say, one leaf less grows on every bough. In the books they are called the Foresters' Oaks. If you stay under them you feel as if the old times must have come again. Among these trees there was a great yew, far older than the oaks, and beneath it a dark and shadowy pool. I had been for a long walk, nearly to the sea, and as I came back I passed this place and, looking into the pool, there was the glint of the stars in the water.

"She knelt by my bed in the dark, and I could just see the glinting of her eyes as she looked at me—the stars in the shadowy waterpool!

"I had never dreamed that there could be anything so wonderful in the whole world. My father had told me of many beautiful and holy and glorious things, of all the heavenly mysteries by which those who know live for ever, all the things which the Doctor and my uncle and the other silly clergymen in the Chapel . . .* because they don't really know anything at all about them, only their names, so they are like dogs and pigs and asses who have somehow found their way into a beautiful room, full of precious and delicate treasures. These things my father told me of long ago, of the Great Mystery of the Offering.

"And I have learned the wonders of the old venerable saints that once were marvels in our land, as the Welsh poem says, and of all the

---

*A highly Rabelaisian phrase is omitted.

great works that shone around their feet as they went upon the mountains and sought the deserts of ocean. I have seen their marks and writings cut on the edges of the rocks. I know where Sagramnus lies buried in Wlad Morgan. And I shall not forget how I saw the Blessed Cup of Teilo Agyos drawn out from golden veils on Mynydd Mawr, when the stars poured out of the jewel, and I saw the sea of the saints and the spiritual things in Cor-arbennic. My father read out to me all the histories of Teilo, Dewi, and Iltyd, of their marvellous chalices and altars of Paradise from which they made the books of the Graal afterwards; and all these things are beautiful to me. But, as the Anointed Bard said: 'With the bodily lips I receive the drink of mortal vineyards; with spiritual understanding wine from the garths of the undying. May Mihangel intercede for me that these may be mingled in one cup; let the door between body and soul be thrown open. For in that day earth will have become Paradise, and the secret sayings of the bards shall be verified.' I always knew what this meant, though my father told me that many people thought it obscure or, rather, nonsense. But it is just the same really as another poem by the same Bard, where he says:

> "'My sin was found out, and when the old women on the bridge pointed
>   at me I was ashamed;
>   I was deeply grieved when the boys shouted rebukes as I went from
>   Caer-Newydd.
>   How is it that I was not ashamed before the Finger of the Almighty?
>   I did not suffer agony at the rebuke of the Most High.
>   The fist of Rhys Fawr is more dreadful to me than the hand of God.'

"He means, I think, that our great loss is that we separate what is one and make it two; and then, having done so, we make the less real into the more real, as if we thought the glass made to hold wine more important than the wine it holds. And this is what I had felt, for it was only twice that I had known wonders in my body, when I saw the Cup of Teilo sant and when the mountains appeared in vision, and so, as the Bard says, the door is shut. The life of bodily things is *hard*, just as the wineglass is hard. We can touch it and feel it and see it always before us. The wine is drunk and forgotten; it cannot be held. I believe the air about us is just as substantial as a mountain or a cathedral, but unless we remind ourselves we think of the air as nothing. It is not *hard.* But now I was in Paradise, for body and soul were molten in one fire and went up in one flame. The mortal and the immortal vines were made one. Through the joy of the body I possessed the joy of the spirit. And it was so strange to think that all this was through a woman— through a woman I had seen dozens of times and had thought nothing of, except that she was pleasant-looking and that the colour of her hair, like copper, was very beautiful.

"I cannot understand it. I cannot feel that she is really Nelly Foran who opens the door and waits at table, for she is a miracle. How I should have wondered once if I had seen a stone by the roadside become a jewel of fire and glory! But if that were to happen, it would not be so strange as what happened to me. I cannot see now the black dress and the servant's cap and apron. I see the wonderful, beautiful body shining through the darkness of my room, the glimmering of the white flower in the dark, the stars in the forest pool.

> "'O gift of the everlasting!
> O wonderful and hidden mystery!
> Many secrets have been vouchsafed to me.
> I have been long acquainted with the wisdom of the trees;
> Ash and oak and elm have communicated to me from my boyhood,
> The birch and the hazel and all the trees of the green wood have not been dumb.
> There is a caldron rimmed with pearls of whose gifts I am not ignorant.
> I will speak little of it; its treasures are known to Bards.
> Many went on the search of Caer-Pedryfan,
> Seven alone returned with Arthur, but my spirit was present.
> Seven are the apple trees in a beautiful orchard.
> I have eaten of their fruit, which is not bestowed on Saxons.
> I am not ignorant of a Head which is glorious and venerable.
> It made perpetual entertainment for the warriors; their joys would have been immortal.
> If they had not opened the door of the south, they could have feasted for ever,
> Listening to the song of the Fairy Birds of Rhiannon.
> Let not any one instruct me concerning the Glassy Isle,
> In the garments of the saints who returned from it were rich odours of Paradise.

All this I knew and yet my knowledge was ignorance,
For one day, as I walked by Caer-rhiu in the principal forest of Gwent,
I saw golden Myfanwy, as she bathed in the brook Tarógi.
Her hair flowed about her. Arthur's crown had dissolved into a shin-
    ing mist.
I gazed into her blue eyes as it were into twin heavens.
All the parts of her body were adornments and miracles.
O gift of the everlasting!
O wonderful and hidden mystery!
When I embraced Myfawny a moment became immortality!'*

"And yet I daresay this 'golden Myfanwy' was what people call 'a common girl', and perhaps she did rough, hard work, and nobody thought anything of her till the Bard found her bathing in the brook Tarógi. The birds in the wood said, when they saw the nightingale: 'This is a contemptible stranger!'

"*June 24.* Since I wrote last in this book the summer has come. This morning I woke up very early, and even in this horrible place the air was pure and bright as the sun rose up and the long beams shone on the cedar outside the window. She came to me by the way they think is locked and fastened, and, just as the world is white and gold at the dawn, so was she. A blackbird began to sing beneath the window. I think it came from far, for it sang to me of morning on the mountain, and the woods all still, and a little bright brook rushing down the hillside between dark green alders, and air that must be blown from heaven.

"'There is a bird that sings in the valley of the Soar;
Dewi and Tegfeth and Cybi preside over that region;
Sweet is the valley, sweet the sound of its waters.

There is a bird that sings in the valley of the Soar;
Its voice is golden, like the ringing of the saints' bells;
Sweet is the valley, echoing with melodies.

There is a bird that sings in the valley of the Soar;
Tegfeth in the south won red martyrdom.
Her song is heard in the perpetual choirs of heaven.

There is a bird that sings in the valley of the Soar;
Dewi in the west had an altar from Paradise.
He taught the valleys of Britain to resound with Alleluia.

---

*Translated from the Welsh verses quoted in the note-book.

There is a bird that sings in the valley of the Soar;
Cybi in the north was the teacher of Princes.
Through him Edlogan sings praise to heaven.

There is a bird that sings in the valley of the Soar.
When shall I hear again the notes of its melody?
When shall I behold once more Gwladys in that valley?"*

---

*The following translation of these verses appeared in *Poems from the Old Bards,* by
Taliesin, Bristol, 1812:

"In Soar's sweet valley, where the sound
Of holy anthems once was heard
From many a saint, the hills prolong
Only the music of the bird.

In Soar's sweet valley, where the brook
With many a ripple flows along,
Delicious prospects meet the eye,
The car is charmed with *Phil'mell's* song.

In Soar's sweet valley once a Mid,
Despising worldly prospects gay,
Resigned her note in earthly choirs
Which now in Heaven must sound alway.

In Soar's sweet valley David preached;
His Gospel accents so beguiled
The savage Britons, that they turned
Their fiercest cries to music mild.

In Soar's sweet valley Cybi taught
To haughty Prince the Holy Law,
The way to Heaven he showed, and then
The subject tribes inspired with awe.

In Soar's sweet valley still the song
Of Phil'mel sounds and checks alarms.
But when shall I once more renew
Those heavenly hours in Gladys' arms?"

"Taliesin" was the pseudonym of an amiable clergyman, the Reverend
Owen Thomas, for many years curate of Llantrisant. He died in 1820, at the
great age of eighty-four. His original poetry in Welsh was reputed as far superior to his translations, and he made a very valuable and curious collection of
"Cymric Antiquities," which remains in manuscript in the keeping of his descendants.

"When I think of what I know, of the wonders of darkness and the wonders of dawn, I cannot help believing that I have found something which all the world has lost. I have heard some of the fellows talking about women. Their words and their stories are filthy, and nonsense, too. One would think that if monkeys and pigs could talk about their she-monkeys and sows, it would be just like that. I might have thought that, being only boys, they knew nothing about it, and were only making up nasty, silly tales out of their nasty, silly minds. But I have heard the poor women in the town screaming and scolding at their men, and the men swearing back; and when they think they are making love, it is the most horrible of all.

"And it is not only the boys and the poor people. There are the masters and their wives. Everybody knows that the Challises and the Redburns 'fight like cats', as they say, and that the Head's daughter was 'put up for auction' and bought by the rich manufacturer from Birmingham—a horrible, fat beast, more than twice her age, with eyes like pig's. They called it a splendid match.

"So I began to wonder whether perhaps there are very few people in the world who know; whether the real secret is lost like the great city that was drowned in the sea and only seen by one or two. Perhaps it is more like those shining Isles that the saints sought for, where the deep apple orchards are, and all the delights of Paradise. But you had to give up everything and get into a boat without oar or sails if you wanted to find Avalon or the Glassy Isle. And sometimes the saints could stand on the rocks and see those Islands far away in the mist of the sea, and smell the sweet odours and hear the bells ringing for the feast, when other people could see and hear nothing at all.

"I often think now how strange it would be if it were found out that nearly everybody is like those who stood on the rocks and could only see the waves tossing and stretching far away, and the blue sky and the mist in the distance. I mean, if it turned out that we have all been in the wrong about everything; that we live in a world of the most wonderful treasures which we see all about us, but we don't understand, and kick the jewels into the dirt, and use the chalices for slop-pails and make the holy vestments into dish-cloths, while we worship a great beast—a monster, with the head of a monkey, the body of a pig and the hind legs of a goat, with swarming lice crawling all over it.

Suppose that the people that they speak of now as 'superstitious' and 'half-savages' should turn out to be in the right, and very wise, while we are all wrong and great fools! It would be something like the man who lived in the Bright Palace. The Palace had a hundred and one doors. A hundred of them opened into gardens of delight, pleasure-houses, beautiful bowers, wonderful countries, fairy seas, caves of gold and hills of diamonds, into all the most splendid places. But one door led into a cesspool, and that was the only door that the man ever opened. It may be that his sons and his grandsons have been opening that one door ever since, till they have forgotten that there are any others, so if any one dares to speak of the ways to the garden of delight or the hills of gold he is called a madman, or a very wicked person.

"*July 15.* The other day a very strange thing happened. I had gone for a short walk out of the town before dinner on the Dunham road and came as far as the four ways where the roads cross. It is rather pretty for Lupton just there; there is a plot of grass with a big old elm tree in the middle of it, and round the tree is a rough sort of seat, where tramps and such people are often resting. As I came along I heard some sort of music coming from the direction of the tree; it was like fairies dancing, and then there were strange solemn notes like the priests' singing, and a choir answered in a deep, rolling swell of sound, and the fairies danced again; and I thought somehow of a grey church high on the cliff above a singing sea, and the Fair People outside dancing on the close turf, while the service was going on all the while. As I came nearer I heard the sea waves and the wind and the cry of the sea-gulls, and again the high, wonderful chanting, as if the fairies and the rocks and the waves and the wild birds were all subject to that which was being done within the church. I wondered what it could be, and then I saw there was an old ragged man sitting on the seat under the tree, playing the fiddle all to himself, and rocking from side to side. He stopped directly he saw me, and said:

"'Ah, now, would your young honour do yourself the pleasure of giving the poor old fiddler a penny or maybe two: for Lupton is the very hell of a town altogether, and when I play to dirty rogues the Reel of the Warriors, they ask for something about Two Obadiahs—the devil's black curse be on them! And it's but dry work playing to the leaf and the green sod—the blessing of the holy saints be on your honour now, this day, and for ever! 'Tis but a scarcity of beer that I have tasted for a long day, I assure your honour.'

"I had given him a shilling because I thought his music so wonderful. He looked at me steadily as he finished talking, and his face changed. I thought he was frightened, he stared so oddly. I asked him if he was ill.

"'May I be forgiven,' he said, speaking quite gravely, without that wheedling way he had when he first spoke. 'May I be forgiven for talking so to one like yourself; for this day I have begged money from one that is to gain Red Martyrdom; and indeed that is yourself.'

"He took off his old battered hat and crossed himself, and I stared at him, I was so amazed at what he said. He picked up his fiddle, and saying, 'May you remember me in the time of your glory,' he walked quickly off, going away from Lupton, and I lost sight of him at the turn of the road. I suppose he was half crazy, but he played wonderfully."

IV

1.

The materials for the history of an odd episode in Ambrose Meyrick's life are to be found in a sort of collection he made under the title "Concerning Gaiety". The episode in question dates from about the middle of his eighteenth year.

"I do not know"—he says—"how it all happened. I had been leading two eager lives. On the outside I was playing games and going up in the school with a rush, and in the inside I was being gathered more and more into the sanctuaries of immortal things. All life was transfigured for me into a radiant glory, into a quickening and catholic sacrament; and, the fooleries of the school apart, I had more and more the sense that I was a participant in a splendid and significant ritual. I think I was beginning to be a little impatient with the outward signs: I *think* I had a feeling that it was a pity that one had to drink wine out of a cup, a pity that kernels seemed to imply shells. I wanted, in my heart, to know nothing but the wine itself flowing gloriously from vague, invisible fountains, to know the things 'that really are' in their naked beauty, without their various and elaborate draperies. I doubt whether Ruskin understood the motive of the monk who walked amidst the mountains with his eyes cast down lest he might see the depths and heights about him. Ruskin calls this a narrow asceticism; perhaps it was rather the result of a very subtle æstheticism. The monk's inner vision might be fixed with such rapture on certain invisible heights and depths, that he feared lest the sight of their visible counterparts might disturb his ecstasy. It is probable, I think, that there is a point where the ascetic principle and the æsthetic become one and the same. The Indian fakir who distorts his limbs and lies on spikes is at the one extreme, the men of the Italian Renaissance were at the other. In each case the true line is distorted and awry, for neither system attains either sanctity or beauty in the highest. The fakir dwells in *surfaces,* and the Renaissance artist dwelt in *surfaces;* in neither case is there the inexpressible radiance of the invisible world shining through the surfaces. A cup of Cellini's work is no doubt very lovely; but it is not beautiful in the same way as the old Celtic cups are beautiful.

"I think I was in some danger of going wrong at the time I am talking about. I was altogether too impatient of surfaces. Heaven forbid the notion that I was ever in danger of being in any sense of the word a Protestant; but perhaps I was rather inclined to the fundamental heresy on which Protestantism builds its objection to what is called Ritual. I suppose this heresy is really Manichee; it is a charge of corruption and evil made against the visible universe, which is affirmed to be not 'very good', but 'very bad'—or, at all events, too bad to be used as the vehicle of spiritual truth. It is extraordinary, by the way, that the thinking Protestant does not perceive that this principle damns all creeds and all Bibles and all teaching quite as effectually as it damns candles and chasubles—unless, indeed, the Protestant thinks that the logical understanding is a competent vehicle of Eternal Truth, and that God can be properly and adequately defined and explained in human speech. If he thinks *that,* he is an ass. Incense, vestments, candles, all ceremonies, processions, rites—all these things are miserably inadequate; but they do not abound in the horrible pitfalls, misapprehensions, errors which are inseparable from speech of men used as an expression of the Church. In a savage dance there may be a vast deal more of the truth than in many of the hymns in our hymn-books.

"After all, as Martinez said, we must even be content with what we have, whether it be censers or syllogisms, or both. The way of the censer is certainly the safer, as I have said; I suppose because the ruin of the external universe is not nearly so deep nor so virulent as the ruin of men. A flower, a piece of gold, no doubt approach their archetypes—what they were meant to be—much more nearly than man does; hence their appeal is purer than the speech or the reasoning of men.

"But in those days at Lupton my head was full of certain sentences which I had lit upon somewhere or other—I believe they must have been translations from some Eastern book. I knew about a dozen of these maxims; all I can remember now are:

> *"If you desire to be inebriated: abstain from wine."*
> *"If you desire beauty: look not on beautiful things."*
> *"If you desire to see: let your eyes be blindfolded."*
> *"If you desire love: refrain from the Beloved."*

"I expect the paradox of these sayings pleased me. One must allow that if one has the inborn appetite of the somewhat subtle, of the truth not too crudely and barely expressed, there is no such atmosphere as that of a Public School for sharpening this appetite to an edge of ravening, indiscriminate hunger. Think of our friend the Colonel, who is by way of being a *fin gourmet;* imagine him fixed in a boarding-house where the meals are a repeating cycle of Irish Stew, Boiled Rabbit, Cold Mutton and Salt Cod (without oyster or any other sauce!). Then let him out and place him in the Café Anglais. With what a fierce relish would he set tooth into curious and sought-out dishes! It must be remembered that I listened every Sunday in every term to one of the Doctor's sermons, and it is really not strange that I gave an eager ear to the voice of *Persian Wisdom*—as I think the book was called. At any rate, I kept Nelly Foran at a distance for nine or ten months, and when I saw a splendid sunset I averted my eyes. I longed for a love purely spiritual, for a sunset of vision.

"I caught glimpses, too, I think, of a much more profound *askesis* than this. I suppose you have the *askesis* in its simplest, most rationalised form in the Case of Bill the Engine-driver—I forget in what great work of *Theologia Moralis* I found the instance; perhaps Bill was really *Quidam* in the original, and his occupation stated as that of *Nauarchus.*

At all events, Bill is fond of four-ale; but he had perceived that two pots of this beverage consumed before a professional journey tended to make him rather sleepy, rather less alert, than he might be in the execution of his very responsible duties. Hence Bill, considering this, wisely contents himself with *one* pot before mounting on his cab. He has deprived himself of a sensible good in order that an equally sensible but greater good may be secured—in order that he and the passengers may run no risks on the journey. Next to this simple asceticism comes, I suppose, the ordinary discipline of the Church—the abandonment of sensible goods to secure spiritual ends, the turning away from the type to the prototype, from the sight of the eyes to the vision of the soul. For in the true asceticism, whatever its degree, there is always action to a certain end, to a perceived good. Does the self-tormenting fakir act from this motive? I don't know; but if he does not, his discipline is not asceticism at all, but folly, and impious folly, too. If he mortifies himself merely for the sake of mortifying himself; then he defiles and blasphemes the Temple. This in parenthesis.

"But, as I say, I had a very dim and distant glimpse of another region of the *askesis*. Mystics will understand me when I say that there are moments when the Dark Night of the Soul is seen to be brighter than her brightest day; there are moments when it is necessary to drive away even the angels that there may be place for the Highest. One may ascend into regions so remote from the common concerns of life that it becomes difficult to procure the help of analogy, even in the terms and processes of the Arts. But suppose a painter—I need not say that I mean an artist—who is visited by an idea so wonderful, so super-exalted in its beauty that he recognises his impotence; he knows that no pigments and no technique can do anything but grossly parody his vision. Well, he will shew his greatness by *not* attempting to paint that vision: he will write on a bare canvas *vidit anima sed non pinxit manus*. And I am sure that there are many romances which have never been written. It was a highly paradoxical, even a dangerous philosophy that affirmed God to be rather *Non-Ens* than *Ens;* but there are moods in which one appreciates the thought.

"I think I caught, as I say, a distant vision of that Night which excels the Day in its splendour. It began with the eyes turned away from the sunset, with lips that refused kisses. Then there came a command to the heart to cease from longing for the dear land of Gwent, to cease from that aching desire that had never died for so many years for the sight of the old land and those hills and woods of most sweet and anguished memory. I remember once, when I was a great lout of sixteen, I went to see the Lupton Fair. I always liked the great booths and caravans and merry-go-rounds, all a blaze of barbaric green and red and gold, flaming and glowing in the middle of the trampled, sodden field against a background of Lupton and wet, grey autumn sky. There were country folk then who wore smock-frocks and looked like men in them, too. One saw scores of these brave fellows at the Fair: dull, good Jutes with flaxen hair that was almost white, and broad pink faces. I liked to see them in the white robe and the curious embroidery; they were a note of wholsomeness, an embassage from the old English village life to our filthy 'industrial centre'. It was odd to see how they stared about them; they wondered, I think, at the beastliness of the place, and yet, poor fellows, they felt bound to admire the evidence of so much money. Yes, they were of Old England; they savoured of the long, bending, broad village street, the gable ends, the grave fronts of old mellow bricks, the thatched roof here and there, the bulging window of the 'village shop', the old church in decorous, somewhat dull perpendicular among the elms, and, above all, the old tavern—that excellent abode of honest mirth and honest beer, relic of the time when there were men, and men who *lived*. Lupton is very far removed from Hardy's land, and yet as I think of these country-folk in their smock-frocks all the essence of Hardy is distilled for me: I see the village street all white in snow, a light gleaming very rarely from an upper window, and presently, amid ringing bells, one hears the carol-singers begin:

> 'Remember Adam's fall,
> O thou man.'

"And I loved to look at the whirl of the merry-go-rounds, at the people sitting with grave enjoyment on those absurd horses as they circled round and round till one's eyes were dazed. Drums beat and thundered, strange horns blew raucous calls from all quarters, and the mechanical music to which those horses revolved belched and blazed and rattled out its everlasting monotony, checked now and again by the shriek of the steam whistle, groaning into silence for a while: then the tune clanged out once more, and the horses whirled round and round.

"But on this Fair Day of which I am speaking I left the booths and the golden, gleaming merry-go-rounds for the next field, where horses were excited to brief madness and short energy. I had scarcely taken up my stand when a man close by me raised his voice to a genial shout as he saw a friend a little way off. And he spoke with the beloved accent of Gwent, with those tones that come to me more ravishing, more enchanting than all the music in the world. I had not heard them for years of weary exile! Just a phrase or two of common greeting in those chanting accents: the Fair passed away, was whirled into nothingness, its shouting voices, the charging of horses, drum and trumpet, clanging, metallic music—it rushed down into the abyss. There was the silence that follows a great peal of thunder; it was early morning and I was standing in a well-remembered valley, beside the blossoming thorn bush, looking far away to the wooded hills that kept the East, above the course of the shining river. I was, I say, a great lout of sixteen, but the tears flooded my eyes, my heart swelled with its longing.

"Now, it seemed, I was to quell such thoughts as these, to desire no more the fervent sunlight on the mountain, or the sweet scent of the dusk about the runnings of the brook. I had been very fond of 'going for walks'—walks of the imagination. I was afraid, I suppose, that unless by constant meditation I renewed the shape of the old land in my mind, its image might become a blurred and fading picture; I should forget little by little the ways of those deep, winding lanes that took courses that were almost subterranean over hill and vale, by woodside and waterside, narrow, cavernous, leaf-vaulted; cool in the greatest heats of summer. And the wandering paths that crossed the fields, that led one down into places hidden and remote, into still depths where no one save myself ever seemed to enter, that sometimes ended with a certain solemnity at a broken stile in a hedgerow grown into a thicket—within a plum tree returning to the savage life of the wood, a forest, perhaps, of blue lupins, and a great wild rose about the ruined walls of a house—all these ways I must keep in mind as if they were mysteries and great secrets, as indeed they were. So I strolled in memory through the Pageant of Gwent: 'lest I should forget the region of the flowers, lest I should become unmindful of the wells and the floods.'

"But the time came, as I say, when it was represented to me that all this was an indulgence which, for a season at least, must be pretermitted. With an effort I voided my soul of memory and desire and weeping; when the idols of domed Twyn-Barlwm, and great Mynydd Maen, and the silveresses of the Usk appeared before me, I cast them out; I would not meditate white Caerleon shining across the river. I endured, I think, the severest pains. De Quincey, that admirable artist, that searcher into secrets and master of mysteries, has described my pains for me under the figure of the Opium Eater breaking the bonds of his vice. How often, when the abominations of Lupton, its sham energies, its sham morals, its sham enthusiasms, all its battalia of cant surged and beat upon me, have I been sorely tempted to yield, to suffer no more the press of folly, but to steal away by a secret path I knew, to dwell in a secure valley where the foolish could never trouble me. Sometimes I 'fell', as I drank deep then of the magic well-water, and went astray in the green dells and avenues of the wildwood. Still I struggled to refrain my heart from these things, to keep my spirit under the severe discipline of abstention; and with constant effort I succeeded more and more.

"But there was a yet deeper depth in this process of *catharsis*. I have said that sometimes one must expel the angels that God may have room; and now the strict ordinance was given that I should sever myself from that great dream of Celtic sanctity that for me had always been *the* dream, the innermost shrine in which I could take refuge, the house of sovran medicaments where all the wounds of soul and body were healed. One does not wish to be harsh; we must admit, I suppose, that moderate, sensible Anglicanism must have *something* in it— since the absolute sham cannot very well continue to exist. Let us say, then, that it is highly favourable to a respectable and moral life, that it encourages a temperate and well-regulated spirit of devotion. It was certainly a very excellent and (according to her lights) devout woman who, in her version of the *Anima Christi* altered 'inebriate me' to 'purify me', and it was a good cleric who hated the Vulgate reading, *calix meus inebrians*. My father had always instructed me that we must conform outwardly, and bear with *Dearly Beloved Brethren;* while we celebrated in our hearts the Ancient Mass of the Britons, and waited for Cadwaladr to return. I reverenced his teaching, I still reverence it, and agree that we must conform; but in my heart I have always doubted whether moderate Anglicanism be Christianity in any sense, whether it even deserves to be called a religion at all. I do not doubt, of course, that many truly religious people have professed it: I speak of the system, and of the atmosphere which emanates from it. And when the Public School *ethos* is added to this—well, the resultant teaching comes pretty much to the dogma that Heaven and the Head are strict allies. One must not degenerate into ecclesiastical controversy; I merely want to say that I never dreamed of looking for religion in our Chapel services. No doubt the *Te Deum* was still the *Te Deum,* but the noblest of hymns is degraded, obscured, defiled, made ridiculous, if you marry it to a tune that would disgrace a penny gaff. Personally, I think that the airs on the piano-organs are much more reverend compositions than Anglican chants, and I am sure that many popular hymn tunes are vastly inferior in solemnity to *'E Dunno where 'e are.*

"No; the religion that led me and drew me and compelled me was that wonderful and doubtful mythos of the Celtic Church. It was the study—nay, more than the study, the enthusiasm—of my father's life; and as I was literally baptised with water from a Holy Well, so spiritually the great legend of the Saints and their amazing lives had tinged all my dearest aspirations, had become to me the glowing vestment of the Great Mystery. One may sometimes be deeply interested in the matter of a tale while one is wearied or sickened by the manner of it; one may have to embrace the bright divinity on the horrid lips of the serpent of Cos. Or, on the other hand, the manner—the style—may be admirable, and the matter a mere nothing but a ground for the embroidery. But for me the Celtic Mythos was the Perfect Thing, the King's Daughter: *Omnia gloria ejus filiæ Regis ab intus, in fimbriis aureis circumamicia varietatibus.* I have learned much more of this great mystery since those days—I have seen, that is, how entirely, how absolutely my boyhood's faith was justified; but even then with but little knowledge I was rapt at the thought of this marvellous knight-errantry, of this Christianity which was not a moral code, with some sort of metaphorical heaven held out as a reward for its due observance, but a great mystical adventure into the unknown sanctity. Imagine a Bishop of the Established Church getting into a boat without oar or sails! Imagine him, if you can, doing anything remotely analogous to such an action. Conceive the late Archbishop Tait going apart into the chapel at Lambeth for three days and three nights; then you may well conceive the people in the opposite bank being dazzled with the blinding supernatural light poured forth from the chapel windows. Of course, the end of the Celtic Church was ruin and confusion—but Don Quixote failed and fell, while Sancho Panza lived a fat, prosperous peasant. He inherited, I think, a considerable sum from the knight, and was, no doubt, a good deal looked up to in the village.

"Yes; the Celtic Church was the Company of the Great Errantry, of the Great Mystery, and, though all the history of it seems but a dim and shadowy splendour, its burning rose-red lamp yet glows for a few, and from my earliest childhood I was indoctrinated in the great Rite of Cor-arbennic. When I was still very young I had been humoured with the sight of a wonderful Relic of the Saints—never shall I forget that experience of the holy magic of sanctity. Every little wood, every rock and fountain, and every running stream of Gwent were hallowed for me by some mystical and entrancing legend, and the thought of this High Spiritual City and its Blessed Congregation could, in a moment, exorcise and drive forth from me all the ugly and foolish and gibbering spectres that made up the life of that ugly and foolish place where I was imprisoned.

"Now, with a sorrowful farewell, I bade good-bye for a brief time (as I hoped it would be) to this golden legend; my heart was emptied of its treasures and its curious shows, and the lights on the altars were put out, and the images were strictly veiled. Hushed was the chanting in the Sovereign and Perpetual Choir, hidden were the High Hallows of the Saints, no more did I follow them to their cells in the wild hills, no more did I look from the rocks in the west and see them set forth for Avalon. Alas!

"A great silence seemed to fall upon me, the silence of the depths beneath the earth. And with the silence there was darkness. Only in a hidden place there was reserved the one taper—the Light of Conformity, of a perfect submission, that from the very excess of sorrow and deprivation drew its secret but quintessential joy. I am reminded, now that I look back upon this great purgation of the soul, of the story that I once read of the Arabic Alchemist. He came to the Caliph Haroun with a strange and extravagant proposal. Haroun sat in all his splendour, his viziers, his chamberlains, his great officers about him, in his golden court which displayed all the wonders and superfluities of the East. He gave judgment; the wicked were punished, the virtuous were rewarded; God's name was exalted, the Prophet was venerated. There came before the Commander of the Faithful a poor old man in the poor and ragged robes of a wandering poet; he was oppressed by the weight of his years, and his entrance was like the entrance of misery. So wretched was his appearance that one of the chamberlains, who was well acquainted with the poets, could not help quoting the well-known verses:

"'Between the main and a drop of rain the difference seen is nothing great.
The sun so bright and the taper's light are alike and one save in pomp and state.
In the grain of sand and in all the land what may ye arraign as disparate?
A crust of bread and a King's board spread will hunger's lust alike abate.
With the smallest blade or with host arrayed the Ruler may quench his gall and hate.
A stone* in a box and a quarry of rocks may be shewn to be of an equal freight.
With a sentence bold or with gold untold the lover may hold or capture his mate.
The King and the Bard may alike be debarred from the fold of the Lord Compassionate.'

"The Commander of the Faithful praised God, the Merciful, the Compassionate, the King of the Day of Judgment, and caused the chamberlain to be handsomely rewarded. He then enquired of the old man for what reason he came before him, and the beggar (as, indeed, he seemed) informed the Caliph that he had for many years prosecuted his studies in magic, alchemy, astrology and geomancy and all other curious and surprising arts, in Spain, Grand Cairo, the land of the Moors, India, China, in various Cities of the Infidels; in fact, in every quarter of the world where magicians were to be found. In proof of his proficiency he produced a little box which he carried about him for the purpose of his geomantic operations and asked any one who was willing to stand forth, that he might hear his whole life, past, present and

---

*A diamond.

future. The Caliph ordered one of his officers to submit himself to this ordeal, and the beggar having made the points in the sand, and having erected the figure according to the rules of the geomantic art, immediately informed the officer of all the most hidden transactions in which he had been engaged, including several matters which this officer thought had been secrets locked in his own breast. He also foretold his death in a year's time from a certain herb, and so it fell out, for he was strangled with a hempen cord by order of the Caliph. In the meantime, the Commander of the Faithful and all about him were astonished, and the Beggar Magician was ordered to proceed with his story. He spoke at great length, and every one remarked the elegance and propriety of his diction, which was wanting in no refinement of classical eloquence. But the sum of his speech was this—that he had discovered the greatest wonder of the whole world, the name of which he declared was Asrar, and by this talisman he said that the Caliph might make himself more renowned than all the kings that had ever reigned on the earth, not excepting King Solomon, the son of David. This was the method of the operation which the beggar proposed. The Commander of the Faithful was to gather together all the wealth of his entire kingdom, omitting nothing that could possibly be discovered; and while this was being done the magician said that he would construct a furnace of peculiar shape in which all these splendours and magnificences and treasures of the world must be consumed in a certain fire of art, prepared with wisdom. And at last, he continued, after the operation had endured many days, the fire being all the while most curiously governed, there would remain but one drop no longer than a pearl, but glorious as the sun to the moon and all the starry heavens and the wonders of the compassionate; and with this drop the Caliph Haroun might heal all the sorrows of the universe. Both the Commander of the Faithful and all his viziers and officers were stupefied by this proposal, and most of the assemblage considered the beggar to be a madman. The Caliph, however, asked him to return the next day in order that his plans might receive more mature consideration.

"The beggar prostrated himself and went forth from the hall of audience, but he returned no more, nor could it be discovered that he had been seen again by any one.

"'But one drop no larger than a pearl', and 'where there is Nothing there is All'. I have often thought of those sentences in looking back on that time when, as Chesson said, I was one of those 'light-hearted and yet sturdy and reliable young fellows to whose hands the honour and safety of England might one day be committed'. I cast all the treasures I possessed into the alembic; again and again they were rectified by the heat of the fire 'most curiously governed'; I saw the 'engendering of the Crow' black as pitch, the flight of the Dove with Silver Wings, and at last Sol rose red and glorious, and I fell down and gave thanks to heaven for this most wonderful gift, the 'Sun blessed of the Fire'. I had dispossessed myself of all, and I found that I possessed all; I had thrown away all the money in my purse, and I was richer than I had ever been; I had died, and I had found a new life in the land of the living.

"It is curious that I should now have to explain the pertinency of all that I have written to the title of this Note—concerning Gaiety. It should not be necessary. The chain of thought is almost painfully obvious. But I am afraid it is necessary.

"Well: I once read an interesting article in the daily paper. It was written apropos of some Shakespearean celebrations or other, and its purport was that modern England was ever so much happier than mediæval or Elizabethan England. It is possible that an acute logician might find something to say on this thesis; but my interest lay in the following passages, which I quote:

> "'Merrie England', with its maypoles and its Whitsun Ales, and its Shrove-tide jousts and junketings is dead for us, from the religious point of view. The England that has survived is, after all, a greater England still. It is Puritan England. . . . The spirit has gone. Surely it is useless to revive the form. Wherefore should the May Queen be "holy, wise, and fair", if not to symbolise the Virgin Mary? And as for Shrove-tide, too, what point in jollity without a fast to follow?'

"The article is not over-illuminating, but I think the writer had caught a glimpse of the truth that there is a deep relation between Mirth and Sanctity; that no real mirth is possible without the apprehension of the mysteries as its antecedent. The fast and the feast are complementary terms. He is right; there is no point in jollity unless there is a fast or something of the nature of a fast to follow—though, of course, there is nothing to hinder the most advanced thinker from drinking as much fusel-oil and raw Russian spirit as he likes. But the result of this course is not real mirth or jollity; it is perhaps more essentially dismal than a 'Tea' amongst the Protestant Dissenters. And, on the other hand, true gaiety is only possible to those who have fasted; and now perhaps it will be seen that I have been describing the preparations for a light-hearted festival.

"The cloud passed away from me, the restrictions and inhibitions were suddenly removed, and I woke up one morning in dancing, bubbling spirits, every drop of blood in my body racing with new life, my nerves tingling and thrilling with energy. I laughed as I awoke; I was conscious that I was to engage in a strange and fantastic adventure, though I had not the remotest notion of what it was to be."

2.

Ambrose Meyrick's adventure was certainly of the fantastic order. His fame had long been established on a sure footing with his uncle and with everybody else, and Mr. Horbury had congratulated him with genuine enthusiasm on his work in the examinations—the Summer term was drawing to a close. Mr. Horbury was Ambrose's trustee, and he made no difficulty about signing a really handsome cheque for his nephew's holiday expenses and outfit. "There," he said, "you ought to be able to do pretty well on that. Where do you think of going?"

Ambrose said that he had thought of North Devon, of tramping over Exmoor, visiting the Doone country, and perhaps of working down to Dartmoor.

"You couldn't do better. You ought to try your hand at fishing: wonderful sport in some of those streams. It mightn't come off at first, but with your eye and sense of distance you'll soon make a fine angler. If you *do* have a turn at the trout, get hold of some local man and make him give you a wrinkle or two. It's no good getting your flies from town. Now, when I was fishing in Hampshire——"

Mr. Horbury went on; but the devil of gaiety had already dictated a wonderful scheme to Ambrose, and that night he informed Nelly Foran that she must alter her plans; she was to come with him to France instead of spending a fortnight at Blackpool. He carried out this mad device with an ingenuity that poor Mr. Palmer would certainly have called "diabolical". In the first place, there was to be a week in London—for Nelly must have some clothes; and this week began as an experience of high delight. It was not devoid of terror, for masters might be abroad, and Ambrose did not wish to leave Lupton for some time. However, they neither saw nor were seen. Arriving at St. Pancras, the luggage was left in the station, and Ambrose, who had studied the map of London, stood for a while on the pavement outside Scott's great masterpiece of architecture and considered the situation with grave yet humorous deliberation. Nelly proved herself admirably worthy of the adventure; its monstrous audacity appealed to her, and she was in a state of perpetual subdued laughter for some days after their arrival. Meyrick looked about him and found that the Euston Road, being squalid and noisy, offered few attractions; and with sudden resolution he took the girl by the arm and steered into the heart of Bloomsbury. In this charmingly central and yet retired quarter they found rooms in a quiet byway which, oddly enough, looked on a green field; and under the pleasant style of Mr. and Mrs. Lupton they partook of tea while the luggage was fetched by somebody—probably a husband—who came with a shock of red, untidy hair from the dark bowels of the basement. They screamed with mirth over the meal. Mr. Horbury had faults, but he kept a good table for himself, his boys and his servants; and the exotic, quaint flavour of the "bread" and "butter" seemed to these two young idiots exquisitely funny. And the queer, faint, close smell, too, of the whole house—it rushed out at one when the hall door was opened: it was heavy, and worth its weight in gold.

"I never know," Ambrose used to say afterwards, "whether to laugh or cry when I have been away for some time from town, and come back and smell that wonderful old London aroma. I don't believe it's so strong or so rare as it used to be; I have been disappointed once or twice in houses in quite shabby streets. It was *there,* of course, but—well, if it were a vintage wine I should say it was a second growth of a very poor year—Margaux, no doubt, but a Margaux of one of those very indifferent years in the early 'seventies. Or it may be like the smell of grease-paints; one doesn't notice it after a month or two. But I don't think it is.

"Still," he would go on, "I value what I can smell of it. It brings back to me that afternoon, that hot, choking afternoon of ever so many years ago. It was really tremendously hot—ninety-two degrees, I think I saw in the paper the next day—and when we got out at St. Pancras the wind came at one like a furnace blast. There was no sun visible; the sky was bleary—a sort of sickly, smoky yellow, and the burning wind came in gusts, and the dust hissed and rattled on the pavement. Do you know what a low public-house smells like in London on a hot afternoon? Do you know what London bitter tastes like on such a day—the publican being evidently careful of his clients' health, and aware of the folly of drinking cold beverages during a period of extreme heat? I do: Nelly, poor dear, had warm lemonade, and I had warm beer—warm chemicals, I mean. But the odour! Why doesn't some scientific man stop wasting his time over a lot of useless rubbish and discover a way of bottling the odour of the past?

"Ah! but if he did so, in a phial of rare crystal with a stopper as secure as the seal of Solimaun ben Daoud would I preserve one most precious scent, inscribing on the seal, within a perfect pentagram, the mystic legend 'No. 15, Little Russell Row'."

The cat had come in with the tea-tray. He was a black cat, not very large, with a decent roundness of feature, and yet with a suggestion of sinewy skinniness about him—the skinniness of the wastrel, not of the poor starveling. His bright green eyes had, as Ambrose observed, the wisdom of Egypt; on his tomb should be inscribed "The Justified in Sekht". He walked solemnly in front of the landlady, his body describing strange curves, his tail waving in the air, and his ears put back with an expression of intense cunning. He seemed delighted at "the let", and when Nelly stroked his back he gave a loud shriek of joy and made known his willingness to take a little refreshment.

They laughed so heartily over their tea that when the landlady came in to clear the things away they were still bubbling over with aimless merriment.

"I likes to see young people 'appy," she said pleasantly, and readily provided a latchkey in case they cared to come in rather late. She told them a good deal of her life: she had kept lodgings in Judd Street, near King's Cross—a nasty, noisy street, she called it—and she seemed to think the inhabitants a low lot. She had to do with all sorts, some good some bad, and the business wasn't what it had been in her mother's day.

They sat a little while on the sofa, hand in hand, still consumed with the jest of their being there at all, and imagining grotesque entrances of Mr. Horbury or Dr. Chesson. Then they went out to wander about the streets, to see London easily, merrily, without bothering the Monument, or the British Museum, or Madame Tussaud's—finally, to get something to eat, they didn't know when or where or how, and they didn't in the least care! There was one "sight" they were not successful in avoiding: they had not journeyed far before the great portal of the British Museum confronted them, grandiose and gloomy. So, by the sober way of Great Russell Street, they made their way into Tottenham Court Road and, finally, into Oxford Street. The shops were bright and splendid, the pavement was crowded with a hurrying multitude, as it seemed to the country folk, though it was the dullest season of the year. It was a great impression—decidedly London was a wonderful place. Already Ambrose felt a curious sense of being at home in it; it was not beautiful, but it was on the immense scale; it did something more than vomit stinks into the air, poison into the water and rows of workmen's houses on the land. They wandered on, and then they had the fancy that they would like to explore the regions to the south; it was so impossible, as Ambrose said, to know where they would find themselves eventually. He carefully lost himself within a few minutes of Oxford Street. A few turnings to right and then to left; the navigation of strange alleys soon left them in the most satisfactory condition of bewilderment; the distinctions of the mariner's compass, its pedantry of east and west, north and south, were annihilated and had ceased to be; it was an adventure in a trackless desert, in the Australian bush, but on safer ground and in an infinitely more entertaining scene. At first they had passed through dark streets, Georgian and Augustan ways, gloomy enough, and half deserted; there were grave houses, with many stories of windows, now reduced to printing offices, to pickle warehouses, to odd crafts such as those of the metal assayer, the crucible maker, the engraver of seals, the fabricator of Boule. But how wonderful it was to see the actual place where those things were done! Ambrose had read of such arts, but had always thought of them as existing in a vague void—if some of them even existed at all in those days: but there in the windows were actual crucibles, strange-looking curvilinear pots of grey-yellowish ware, the veritable instruments of the Magnum Opus, inventions of Arabia. He was no longer astonished when a little farther he saw a harpsichord, which had only been a name to him, a beautiful looking thing, richly inlaid, with its date—1780—inscribed on a card above it. It was now utterly wonderland: he could very likely buy armour round the corner; and he had scarcely formed the thought when a very fine sixteenth-century suit, richly damascened, rose up before him, handsomely displayed between two black jacks. These were the comparatively silent streets; but they turned a corner, and what a change! All the roadway, not the pavement only, seemed full of a strolling, chatting, laughing mob of people: the women were bareheaded, and one heard nothing but the roll of the French "r", torrents of sonorous sound trolled out with the music of a happy song. The papers in the shops were all French, ensigns on every side proclaimed "Vins Fins", "Beaune Supérieur": the tobacconists kept their tobacco in square blue, yellow and brown packets; "Charcuterie" made a brave and appetising show. And here was a "Café Restaurant: au château de Chinon". The name was enough; they could not dine elsewhere, and Ambrose felt that he was honouring the memory of the great Rabelais.

It was probably not a very good dinner. It was infinitely better than the Soho dinner of these days, for the Quarter had hardly begun to yield to the attack of Art, Intellect and the Suburbs which, between them, have since destroyed the character and unction of many a good cookshop. Ambrose only remembered two dishes; the *pieds de porc grillés* and the salad. The former he thought both amusing and delicious, and the latter was strangely and artfully compounded of many herbs, of little vinegar, of abundant Provençal oil, with the *chapon*, or crust rubbed with garlic, reposing at the bottom of the bowl after Madame had "tormented" the ingredients—the salad was a dish from Fairyland. There be no such salads now in all the land of Soho.

"Let me celebrate, above all, the little red wine," says Ambrose in a brief dithyrambic note. "Not in any mortal vineyard did its father grape ripen; it was not nourished by the warmth of the visible sun, nor were the rains that made it swell common waters from the skies above us. Not even in the Chinonnais, sacred earth though that be, was the press made that caused its juices to be poured into the *cuve*, nor was the humming of its fermentation heard in any of the good cellars of the lower Touraine. But in that region which Keats celebrates when he sings the 'Mermaid Tavern' was this juice engendered—the vineyard lay low down in the south, among the starry plains where is the *Terra Turonensis Celestis,* that unimaginable country which Rabelais beheld in his vision where mighty Gargantua drinks from inexhaustible vats eternally, where Pantagruel is athirst for evermore, though he be satisfied continually. There, in the land of the Crowned Immortal Tosspots was that wine of ours vintaged, red with the rays of the Dog-star, made magical by the influence of Venus, fertilised by the happy aspect of Mercury. O rare, super-abundant and most excellent juice, fruit of all fortunate stars, by thee were we translated, exalted into the fellowship of that Tavern of which the old poet writes: *Mihi est propositum in Taberna mori!*"

There were few English people in the Château de Chinon—indeed, it is doubtful whether there was more than one—the ménage Lupton excepted. This one compatriot happened to be a rather remarkable man—it was Carrol. He was not in the vanguard of anything; he knew no journalists and belonged to no clubs; he was not even acquainted in the most distant manner with a single person who could be called really influential or successful. He was an obscure literary worker, who published an odd volume every five or six years: now and then he got notices, when there was no press of important stuff in the offices, and sometimes a kindly reviewer predicted that he would come out all right in time, though he had still much to learn. About a year before he died, an intelligent reading public was told that one or two things of his were rather good; then, on his death, it was definitely discovered that the five volumes of verse occupied absolutely unique ground, that a supreme poet had been taken from us, a poet who had raised the English language into a fourth dimension of melody and magic. The intelligent reading public read him no more than they ever did, but they buy him in edition after edition, from large quarto to post octavo; they buy him put up into little decorated boxes; they buy him on Japanese vellum; they buy him illustrated by six different artists; they discuss no end of articles about him; they write their names in the Carrol Birthday Book; they set up the Carrol Calendar in their boudoirs; they have quotations from him in Westminster Abbey and St. Paul's Cathedral; they sing him in the famous Carrol Cycle of Song; and, last and best of all, a brilliant American playwright is talking even now of dramatising him. The

Carrol Club, of course, is ancient history. Its membership is confined to the ranks of intellect and art; it invites to its dinners foreign princes, bankers, major-generals and other persons of distinction—all of whom, of course, are intensely interested in the master's book; and the record and praise of the Club are in all the papers. It is a pity that Carrol is dead. He would not have sworn: he would have grinned.

Even then, though he was not glorious, he was observant, and he left a brief note, a sort of thumb-nail sketch, of his impressions that night at the Château de Chinon.

"I was sitting in my old corner," he says, "wondering why the devil I wrote so badly on the whole, and what the devil I was going to do with the subject that I had tackled. The dinner was not so bad at the old Château in those days, though now they say the plate-glass is the best dish in the establishment. I liked the old place; it was dingy and low down and rather disreputable, I fancy, and the company was miscellaneous French with a dash of Italian. Nearly all of us knew each other, and there were regulars who sat in the same seat night after night. I liked it all. I liked the coarse tablecloths and the black-handled knives and the lead spoons and the damp, adhesive salt, and the coarse, strong, black pepper that one helped with a fork handle. Then there was Madame sitting on high, and I never saw an uglier woman nor a more good-natured. I was getting through my roast fowl and salad that evening, when two wonderful people came in, obviously from fairyland! I saw they had never been in such a place in all their lives before—I don't believe either of them had set foot in London until that day, and their wonder and delight and enjoyment of it all were so enormous that I had another helping of food and an extra half-bottle of wine. I enjoyed them, too, in their way, but I could see that *their* fowl and *their* wine were not a bit the same as mine. *I* once knew the restaurant they were really dining at—Grand Café de Paradis—some such name as that. He was an extraordinary looking chap, quite young, I should fancy, black hair, dark skin, and such burning eyes! I don't know why, but I felt he was a bit out of his setting, and I kept thinking how I should like to see him in a monk's robe. Madame was different. She was a lovely girl with amazing copper hair; dressed rather badly—of the people, I should imagine. But what a gaiety she had! I couldn't hear what they were saying, but one had to smile with sheer joy at the sight of her face—it positively danced with mirth, and a good musician could have set it to music, I am sure. There was something a little queer—too pronounced, perhaps—about the lower part of her face. Perhaps it would have been an odd tune, but I know I should have liked to hear it!"

Ambrose lit a black Caporal cigarette—he had bought a packet on his way. He saw an enticing bottle, of rotund form, paying its visits to some neighbouring tables, and the happy fools made the acquaintance of Benedictine.

"Oh, yes, it is all very well," Ambrose has been heard to say on being offered this agreeable and aromatic liqueur, "it's nice enough, I daresay. But you should have tasted the *real* stuff. I got it at a little café in Soho some years ago—the Château de Chinon. No, it's no good going there now, it's quite different. All the walls are plate-glass and gold; the head waiter is called Maître d'hôtel, and I am told it's quite the thing, both in southern and northern suburbs, to make up dinner parties at the Château—everything most correct, evening dress, fans, opera cloaks, 'Hide-seek' champagne, and stalls afterwards. One gets a glimpse of Bohemian life that way, and everybody says it's been such a queer evening, but quite amusing, too. But you can't get the real Benedictine there now.

"Where can you get it? Ah! I wish I knew. *I* never come across it. The bottle looks just the same, but it's quite a different flavour. The phylloxera may be responsible, of course, but I don't think it is. Perhaps the bottle that went round the table that night was like the powder in *Jekyll and Hyde*—its properties were the result of some strange accident. At all events, they were quite magical."

The two adventurers went forth into the maze of streets and lost themselves again. Heaven knows where they went, by what ways they wandered, as with wide-gleaming eyes, arm locked in arm, they gazed on an enchanted scene which they knew must be London and nothing else—what else could it be? Indeed, now and again, Ambrose thought he recognised certain features and monuments and public places of which he had read; but still! That wine of the Château was, by all mundane reckonings, of the smallest, and one little glass of Benedictine with coffee could not disturb the weakest head: yet was it London, after all?

What they saw was, doubtless, the common world of the streets and squares, the gay ways and the dull, the broad, ringing, lighted roads and the dark, echoing passages; yet they saw it all as one sees a mystery play, through a veil. But the veil before their eyes was a transmuting vision, and its substance was shot as if it were samite, with wonderful and admirable golden ornaments. In the Eastern Tales, people find themselves thus suddenly transported into an unknown magical territory, with cities that are altogether things of marvel and enchantment, whose walls are pure gold, lighted by the shining of incomparable jewels; and Ambrose declared later that never till that evening had he realised the extraordinary and absolute truth to nature of the *Arabian Nights*. Those who were present on a certain occasion will not soon forget his rejoinder to "a gentleman in the company" who said that for truth to nature he went to George Eliot.

"I was speaking of men and women, Sir," was the answer, "not of lice."

The gentleman in question, who was quite an influential man—some whisper that he was an editor—was naturally very much annoyed.

Still, Ambrose maintained his position. He would even affirm that for crude realism the Eastern Tales were absolutely unique.

"Of course," he said, "I take realism to mean absolute and essential truthfulness of description, as opposed to merely conventional treatment. Zola is a realist, not—as the imbeciles suppose—because he described—well, rather minutely—many unpleasant sights and sounds and smells and emotions, but because he was a poet, a seer; because, in spite of his pseudo-philosophies, his cheap materialisms, he saw the true heart, the reality of things. Take *La Terre*; do you think it is 'realistic' because it describes minutely, and probably faithfully, the event of a cow calving? Not in the least; the local vet. who was called in could probably do all that as well, or better. It is 'realist' because it goes behind all the brutalities, all the piggeries and inhumanities, of those frightful people, and shews us the strange, mad, transcendent passion that lay behind all those things—the wild desire for the land—a longing that burned, that devoured, that inflamed, that drove men to hell and death as would a passion for a goddess who might never be attained. Remember how 'La Beauce' is personified, how the earth swells and quickens before one, how every clod and morsel of the soil cries for its service and its sacrifice and its victims—I call *that* realism."

"The *Arabian Nights* is also profoundly realistic, though both the subject-matter and the method of treatment—the technique—are very different from the subject-matter and the technique of Zola. Of course, there may be people who think that if you describe a pigsty well you are a 'realist', and if you describe an altar well you are 'romantic'. . . . I do not know that the mental processes of Cretins form a very interesting subject for discussion."

One may surmise, if one will, that the sudden violence of the change was a sufficient cause of exaltation. That detestable Lupton left behind; no town, but a collection of stink and poison factories and slave quarters; that more detestable school, more ridiculous than the Academy of Lagado; that most detestable routine, games, lessons and the Doctor's sermons—the transition was tremendous to the freedom of fabled London, of the unknown streets and unending multitudes.

Ambrose said he hesitated to talk of that walk, lest he should be thought an aimless liar. They strolled for hours seeing the most wonderful things, the most wonderful people; but he declared that the case was similar to that of the Benedictine—he could never discover again the regions that he had perambulated. Somewhere, he said, close to the Chateau de Chinon there must be a passage which had since been blocked up. By it was the entrance to Fairyland.

When at last they found Little Russell Row, the black cat was awaiting them with an expression which was pleased and pious, too; he had devoured the greater portion of that quarter-pound of dubious butter. Ambrose smoked black cigarettes in bed till the packet was finished.

3.

It was an amazing week that they spent in London. For a couple of days Nelly was busied in getting "things" and "odds and ends", and, to her credit, she dressed the part most admirably. She abjured all the imperial purples, the Mediterranean blues, the shrieking lilacs that her class usually affects, and appeared at last a model of neat gaiety.

In the meantime, while these shopping expeditions were in progress, while Nelly consulted with those tall, dark-robed, golden-haired and awful Elegances which preside over the last mysteries of the draper and milliner, Ambrose sat at home in Little Russell Row and worked out the outlines of some fantasies that had risen in his mind. It was, in fact, during these days that he made the notes which were afterwards expanded into the curious *Defence of Taverns,* a book which is now rare and sought after by collectors. It is supposed that it was this work that was in poor Palmer's mind when that earnest man referred with a sort of gloomy reticence to Meyrick's later career. He had, in all probability, not read a line of it; but the title was certainly not a very pleasing one, judged by ordinary scholastic standards. And it must be said that the critical reception of the book was not exactly encouraging. One paper wondered candidly why such a book was ever written or printed; another denounced the author in good, set terms as an enemy of the great temperance movement; while a third, a Monthly Reviewer, declared that the work made his blood boil. Yet even the severest moralists should have seen by the epigraph that the Apes and Owls and Antiques hid mysteries of some sort, since a writer whose purposes were really evil and intemperate would never have chosen such a motto as: *Jalalúd-Din praised the behaviour of the Inebriated and drank water from the well.* But the reviewers thought that this was unintelligible nonsense, and merely a small part of the writer's general purpose to annoy.

The rough sketch is contained in the first of the *Note Books,* which are still unpublished, and perhaps are likely to remain so. Meyrick jotted down his hints and ideas in the dingy "first floor front" of the Bloomsbury lodging-house, sitting at the rosewood "Davenport" which, to the landlady, seemed the last word in beautiful furniture.

The ménage rose late. What a relief it was to be free of the horrible bells that poisoned one's rest at Lupton, to lie in peace as long as one liked, smoking a matutinal cigarette or two to the accompaniment of a cup of tea! Nelly was acquiring the art of the cigarette-smoker by degrees. She did not like the taste at all at first, but the wild and daring devilry of the practice sustained her, and she persevered. And while they thus wasted the best hours of the day, Ambrose would make to pass before the bottom of the bed a long procession of the masters, each uttering his characteristic word of horror and astonishment as he went by, each whirled away by some invisible power in the middle of a sentence. Thus would enter Chesson, fully attired in cassock, cap and gown:

"Meyrick! Is it possible? Are you not aware that such conduct as this is entirely inconsistent with the tone of a great Public School? Have the Games . . ." But he was gone; his legs were seen vanishing in a whirlwind which bore him up the chimney.

Then Horbury rose out of the carpet:

"Plain living and clear thinking are the notes of the System. A Spartan Discipline—Meyrick! Do you call this a Spartan Discipline? Smoking tobacco and reposing with . . ." He shot like an arrow after the Head.

"We discourage luxury by every means in our power. Boy! This is luxury! Boy, boy! You are like the later Romans, boy! Heliogabalus was accustomed . . ." The chimney consumed Palmer also; and he gave place to another.

"Roughly speaking, a boy should be always either in school or playing games. He should never be suffered to be at a loose end. Is this your idea of playing games? I tell you, Meyrick . . ."

The game amused Nelly, more from its accompanying "business" and facial expression than from any particular comprehension of the dialogue. Ambrose saw that she could not grasp all the comedy of his situations, so he invented an Idyll between the Doctor and a notorious and flamboyant barmaid at the "Bell". The fame of this lady ran great but not gracious through all Lupton. This proved a huge success; beginning as a mere episode, it gathered to itself a complicated network of incidents and adventures, of wild attempts and strange escapes, of stratagems and ambushes, of disguises and alarms. Indeed, as Ambrose instructed Nelly with great solemnity, the tale, at first an idyll, the simple, pastoral story of the loves of the Shepherd Chesson and the Nymph Bella, was rapidly becoming epical in its character. He talked of dividing it into twelve books! He enlarged very elaborately the Defeat of the Suitors. In this the dear old Head, disguised as a bookmaker, drugged the whisky of the young bloods who were accustomed to throng about the inner bar of the "Bell". There was quite a long passage describing the compounding of the patent draught from various herbs, the enormous cook at the Head's house enacting a kind of Canidia part, and helping in the concoction of the dose.

"Mrs. Belper," the Doctor would observe, "this is *most* gratifying. I had no idea that your knowledge of simples was so extensive. Do I understand you to affirm that those few leaves which you hold in your hand will produce marked symptoms?"

"Bless your dear 'art, Doctor Chesson, and if you'll forgive me for talking so to such a learned gentleman, and so good, I'm sure, but you'll find there's nothing in the world like it. Often and often have I 'eard my pore old mother that's dead and gone these forty year come Candlemas . . ."

"Mrs. Belper, Mrs. Belper, I am surprised at you! Are you not aware that the Judicial Committee of the Privy Council has pronounced the observance of the festival you so lightly name to be of a highly superstitious nature? Your deceased mother, you were saying, will have entered into her reward forty years ago on February the second of next year? Is not this the case? "

"These forty year come Febbymas, I mean, and a good woman she was, and never have I seen a larger wart on the nose and her legs bad as bad for years and years!"

"These details, though, no doubt, of high personal interest, seem hardly germane to our present undertaking. However, Mrs. Belper, proceed in your remarks."

"And thank you kindly, Sir, and not forgetting you are a clergyman—but there! we can't all of us be everything. And my pore mother, as I was saying, Sir, she said, again and again, that if she'd been like some folks she'd a made a fortune in golden money from this very yarb I'm a-shewing you, Sir."

"Dear me, Mrs. Belper! You interest me deeply. I have often thought how wrong it is of us to neglect, as undoubtedly we *do* neglect, the bounteous gifts of the kindly earth. Your lamented mother used this specific with remarkable success?"

"Lord a mercy, Doctor Chesson! elephants couldn't a stood against it, nor yet whales, being as how it's stronger than the strongest gunpowder that was ever brewed or blasted, and miles better than the nasty rubbidge you get in them doctors' shops, and a pretty penny they make you pay for it, and no better than calomel, if you ask me, Sir. But be it the strongest of the strong, I'll take my Gospel oath it's weak to what my pore mother made, and that anybody in Much Moddle parish would tell you, for man, woman or child who took one of Mrs. Marjoram's Mixtures and got over it, remember it, he would, until his dying day. And my pore old mother, she was that funny—never was a cheer-fuller woman, I do believe, and when Tom Copus, the lame fiddler, he got married, pore mother! though she could 'ardly walk, her legs was that bad, come she would, and if she didn't slip a little of the mixture into the beer when everybody was looking another way! Pore, dear soul! as she said herself afterwards, 'mirth becomes marriage', and so to be sure it does, and merry they all were that day that didn't touch the beer, preferring spirits, which pore mother couldn't get at, being locked up—a nasty, mean trick, I call it, and always will."

"Enough, Mrs. Belper, enough! You have amply satisfied me as to the potency of the late Mrs. Marjoram's pharmacopœia. We will, if you have no objection, Mrs. Belper, make the mixture—to use the words of Shakespeare—'slab and thick'."

"And bless your kind 'art, Sir, and a good, kind master you've al-ways been to me, if you 'aven't got enough 'ere to lay out all the Lupton town, call me a Dutchwoman, and that I never was, nor pore Belper neither."

"Certainly not, Mrs. Belper. The Dutch belong to a different branch of the great Teutonic stock, or, if identity have ever existed, the two races have long been differentiated. I think, Mrs. Belper, that the most eminent physicians have recognised the beneficial effects of a gentle laxative during the treacherous (though delightful) season of spring?"

"Law bless you, Sir, you're right, as you always are, or why, Doc-tor? As my pore mother used to say when she made up the mixture: 'Scour 'em out is the right way about!' And laugh she would as she pounded the stuff up till I really thought she would 'a busted, and shaking like the best blancmanges all the while."

"Mrs. Belper, you have removed a weight from my mind. You think, then, that I shall be freed from all unfair competition while I pay my addresses to my young friend, Miss Floyer?"

"As free you will be, Doctor Chesson, Sir, as the little birds in the air; for not one of them young fellers will stand on his feet for days, and groans and 'owls will be the best word that mortal man will speak, and bless you they will with their dying breath. So, Sir, you'll 'ave the sweet young lady, bless her dear 'art, all to yourself, and if it's twins, don't blame me!"

"Mrs. Belper, your construction, if I may say so, is somewhat pro-leptic in its character. Still, I am sure that your meaning is good. Ha! I hear the bell for afternoon school."

The Doctor's voice happened to be shrill and piercing, with some-thing of the tone of the tooth-comb and tissue-paper; while the fat cook spoke in a suety, husky contralto. Ambrose reproduced these peculiari-ties with the gift of the born mimic, adding appropriate antic and gesture to grace the show, and Nelly's appreciation of its humours was intense.

Day by day new incidents and scenes were added. The Head, in the pursuit of his guilty passion, hid in the coal-cellar of the "Bell", and, rustling sounds being heard, evaded detection for a while by imi-tating the barks of a terrier in chase of a rat. Nelly liked to hear the "Wuff! wuff! wuff!" which was introduced at this point. She liked also the final catastrophe, when the odd man of the "Bell" burst into the bar and said: "Dang my eyes, if it ain't the Doctor! I seed his cap and gown as he run round and round the coals on all fours, a-growling 'or-rible." To which the landlady rejoined: "Don't tell your silly lies here! How *could* he growl, him being a clergyman?" And all the loafers joined in the chorus: "That's right, Tom; why *do* you talk such silly lies as that—him being a clergyman?"

They laughed so loud and so merrily over their morning tea and these lunacies that the landlady doubted gravely as to their marriage lines. She cared nothing; they had paid what she asked, money down in advance, and, as she said: "Young gentlemen *will* have their fun with the young ladies—so what's the good of talking?"

Breakfast came at length. They gave the landlady a warning bell some half-hour in advance, so the odd food was, at all events, not cold. Afterwards Nelly sallied off gaily on her shopping expeditions, which, as might have been expected, she enjoyed hugely, and Ambrose stayed alone, with his pen and ink and a fat notebook which had cap-tured his eye in a stationer's window.

Under these odd circumstances, then, he laid the foundations of his rare and precious *Defence of Taverns*, which is now termed by those fortunate enough to possess copies as a unique and golden treatise. Though he added a good deal in later years and remodelled and rear-ranged freely, there is a certain charm of vigour and freshness about the first sketch which is quite delightful in its way. Take, for example, the description of the whole world overwhelmed with sobriety: a deadly absence of inebriation annulling and destroying all the works and thoughts of men, the country itself at point to perish of the want of good liquor and good drinkers. He shews how there is grave cause to dread that, by reason of this sad neglect of the Dionysiac Mysteries, humanity is fast falling backward from the great heights to which it had ascended, and is in imminent danger of returning to the dumb and blind and helpless condition of the brutes.

"How else," he says, "can one account for the stricken state in which all the animal world grows and is eternally impotent? To them, strange, vast and enormous powers and faculties have been given. Consider, for example, the curious equipments of two odd extremes in this sphere—the ant and the elephant. The ant, if one may say so, is very near to us. We have our great centres of industry, our Black Country and our slaves who, if not born black, become black in our service. And the ants, too, have their black, enslaved races who do their dirty work for them, and are, perhaps, congratulated on their privileges as sharing in the blessings of civilisation—though this may be a refinement. The ant slaves, I believe, will rally eagerly to the defence of the nest and the eggs, and they say that the labouring classes are Liberal to the core. Nay; we grow mushrooms by art, and so they. In some lands, I think, they make enormous nests which are the nuisance and terror of the country. We have Manchester and Lupton and Leeds, and many such places—one would think them altogether civilised.

"The elephant, again, has many gifts which we lack. Note the curious instinct (or intuition, rather) of danger. The elephant knows, for example, when a bridge is unsafe, and refuses to pass, where a man would go on to destruction. One might examine in the same way all the creatures, and find in them singular capacities.

"Yet—they have no art. They see—but they see not. They hear—and they hear not. The odour in their nostrils has no sweetness at all. They have made no report of all the wonders that they knew. Their houses are, sometimes, as ingenious as a Chemical Works, but never is there any beauty for beauty's sake.

"It is clear that their state is thus desolate, because of the heavy pall of sobriety that hangs over them all; and it scarcely seems to have occurred to our 'Temperance' advocates that when they urge on us the example and abstinence of the beasts they have advanced the deadliest of all arguments against their nostrum. The Laughing Jackass is a tee-totaller, doubtless, but no sane man should desire to be a Laughing Jackass.

"But the history of the men who have attained, who have done the glorious things of the earth and have become for ever exalted is the history of the men who have quested the Cup. Dionysius, said the Greeks, *civilised* the world; and the Bacchic Mystery was, naturally, the heart and core of Greek civilisation.

"Note the similitudes of Vine and Vineyard in Old Testament.

"Note the Quest of the San Graal.

"Note Rabelais and *La Dive Bouteille*.

"Place yourself in imagination in a Gothic Cathedral of the thirteenth century and assist at High Mass. Then go to the nearest Little Bethel, and look, and listen. Consider the difference in the two buildings, in those who worship in one and listen and criticise in the other. You have the difference between the Inebriated and the Sober, displayed in their works. As Little Bethel is to Tintern, so is Sobriety to Inebriation.

"Modern civilisation has advanced in many ways? Yes. Bethel has a stucco front. This material was quite unknown to the builders of Tintern Abbey. Advanced? What is advancement? Freedom from excesses, from extravagances, from wild enthusiasms? Small Protestant tradesmen are free from all these things, certainly. But is the joy of Adulteration to be the last goal, the final Initiation of the Race of Men? *Cælumque tueri*—to sand the sugar?

"The Flagons of the Song of Songs did not contain ginger-beer.

"But the worst of it is we shall not merely descend to the beasts. We shall fall very far below the beasts. A black fellow is good, and a white fellow is good. But the white fellow who 'goes Fantee' does not become a negro—he becomes something infinitely worse, a horrible mass of the most putrid corruption.

"If we can clear our minds of the horrible cant of our 'civilisation', if we can look at a modern 'industrial centre' with eyes purged of illusions, we shall have some notion of the awful horror to which we are descending in our effort to become as the ants and bees—creatures who know nothing of

"CALIX INEBRIANS.

"I doubt if we can really make this effort. Blacks, Stinks, Desolations, Poisons, Hell's Nightmare generally have, I suspect, worked themselves into the very form and mould of our thoughts. We are sober, and perhaps the Tavern door is shut for ever against us.

"Now and then, perhaps, at rarer and still rarer intervals, a few of us will hear very faintly the far echoes of the holy madness within the closed door:

> *"When up the thyrse is raised, and when the sound*
> *Of sacred orgies flies 'around, around'.*

"Which is the *Sonus Epulantium in Æterno Convivio.*

"But this we shall not be able to discern. Very likely we shall take the noise of this High Choir for the horrid mirth of Hell. How strange it is that those who are pledged officially and ceremonially, as it were, to a Rite of Initiation which figures certainly a Feast, should in all their thoughts and words and actions be continually blaspheming and denying all the uses and ends of feastings and festivals.

"This is not the refusal of the *species* for the sake of enjoying perfectly the most beautiful and desirable *genus;* it is the renouncing of species and genus, the pronouncing of Good to be Evil. The Universal being denied, the Particular is degraded and defiled. What is called 'The Drink Curse' is the natural and inevitable result and sequence of the 'Protestant Reformation'. If the clear wells and fountains of the magic wood are buried out of sight, then men (who must have Drink) will betake them to the Slime Ponds and Poison Pools.

"In the Graal Books there is a curse—an evil enchantment—on the land of Logres because the mystery of the Holy Vessel is disregarded. The Knight sees the Dripping Spear and the Shining Cup pass before him, and says no word. He asks no question as to the end and meaning of this ceremony. So the land is blasted and barren and songless, and those who dwell in it are in misery.

"Every day of our lives we see the Graal carried before us in a wonderful order, and every day we leave the question unasked, the Mystery despised and neglected. Yet if we could ask that question, bowing down before these Heavenly and Glorious Splendours and

Hallows—then every man should have the meat and drink that his soul desired; the hall would be filled with odours of Paradise, with the light of Immortality.

"In the books the Graal was at last taken away because of men's unworthiness. So it will be, I suppose. Even now, the Quester's adventure is a desperate one—few there be that find It.

"Ventilation and sanitation are well enough in their way. But it would not be very satisfactory to pass the day in a ventilated and sanitated Hell with nothing to eat or drink. If one is perishing of hunger and thirst, sanitation seems unimportant enough.

"How wonderful, how glorious it would be if the Kingdom of the Great Drinkers could be restored! If we could only sweep away all the might of the Sober Ones—the factory builders, the poison makers, the politicians, the manufacturers of bad books and bad pictures, together with Little Bethel and the morality of Mr. Mildmay, the curate (a series of negative propositions)—then imagine the Great Light of the Great Inebriation shining on every face, and not any work of man's hands, from a cathedral to a penknife, without the mark of the Tavern upon it! All the world a great festival; every well a fountain of strong drink; every river running with the New Wine; the Sangraal brought back from Sarras, restored to the awful shrine of Cor-arbennic, the Oracle of the *Dive Bouteille* once more freely given, the ruined Vineyard flourishing once more, girt about by shining, everlasting walls! Then we should hear the Old Songs again, and they would dance the Old Dances, the happy, ransomed people, Commensals and Compotators of the Everlasting Tavern."

The whole treatise, of which this extract is a fragment in a rudimentary and imperfect stage, is, of course, an impassioned appeal for the restoration of the quickening, exuberant imagination, not merely in art, but in all the inmost places of life. There is more than this, too. Here and there one can hear, as it were, the whisper and the hint of deeper mysteries, visions of a great experiment and a great achievement to which some men may be called. In his own words: "Within the Tavern there is an Inner Tavern, but the door of it is visible to few indeed."

In Ambrose's mind in the after years the stout note-book was dear, perhaps as a substitute for that aroma of the past in a phial which he has declared so desirable an invention. It stood, not so much for what was written in it as for the place and the circumstances in which it was written. It recalled Little Russell Row and Nelly, and the evenings at the Château de Chinon, where, night by night, they served still stranger, more delicious meats, and the red wine revealed more clearly its high celestial origin. One evening was diversified by an odd encounter.

A middle-aged man, sitting at an adjoining table, was evidently in want of matches, and Ambrose handed his box with the sympathetic smile which one smoker gives to another in such cases. The man—he had a black moustache and a small, pointed beard—thanked him in fluent English with a French accent, and they began to talk of casual things, veering, by degrees, in the direction of the arts. The Frenchman smiled at Meyrick's enthusiasm.

"What a life you have before you!" he said. "Don't you know that the populace always hates the artist—and kills him if it can? You are an artist and mystic, too. What a fate!

"Yes; but it is that applause, that *réclame,* that comes after the artist is dead," he went on, replying to some objection of Ambrose's; "it is that which is the worst cruelty of all. It is fine for Burns, is it not, that his stupid compatriots have not ceased to utter follies about him for the last eighty years? Scotchmen? But they should be ashamed to speak his name! And Keats, and how many others in my country and in yours and in all countries? The imbeciles are not content to calumniate, to persecute, to make wretched the artist in his lifetime. They follow him with their praise to the grave—the grave that they have digged! Praise of the populace! Praise of a race of pigs! For, you see, while they are insulting the dead with their compliments they are at the same time insulting the living with their abuse."

He dropped into silence; from his expression he seemed to be cursing "the populace" with oaths too frightful to be uttered. He rose suddenly and turned to Ambrose.

"Artist—and mystic. Yes. You will probably be crucified. Good evening . . . and a fine martyrdom to you!"

He was gone with a charming smile and a delightful bow to "Madame." Ambrose looked after him with a puzzled face; his last words had called up some memory that he could not capture; and then suddenly he recollected the old, ragged Irish fiddler, the player of strange fantasies under the tree in the outskirts of Lupton. He thought of his phrase about "red martyrdom"; it was an odd coincidence.

4.

The phrases kept recurring to his mind after they had gone out, and as they wandered through the lighted streets with all their strange and variegated show, with glittering windows and glittering lamps, with the ebb and flow of faces, the voices and the laughter, the surging crowds about the theatre doors, the flashing hansoms and the omnibuses lumbering heavily along to strange regions, such as Turnham Green and Castlenau, Cricklewood and Stoke Newington—why, they were as unknown as cities in Cathay!

It was a dim, hot night; all the great city smoked as with a mist, and a tawny moon rose through films of cloud far in the vista of the east. Ambrose thought with a sudden recollection that the moon, that world of splendour, was shining in a farther land, on the coast of the wild rocks, on the heaving sea, on the faery apple-garths in Avalon, where, though the apples are always golden, yet the blossoms of enchantment never fade, but hang for ever against the sky.

They were passing a half-lit street, and these dreams were broken by the sudden clanging, rattling music of a piano-organ. For a moment they saw the shadowy figures of the children as they flitted to and fro, dancing odd measures in the rhythm of the tune. Then they came into a long, narrow way with a church spire in the distance, and near the church they passed the "church-shop"—Roman, evidently, from the subjects and the treatment of the works of art on view. But it was strange! In the middle of the window was a crude, glaring statue of some saint. He was in bright red robes, sprinkled with golden stars; the blood rained down from a wound in his forehead, and with one hand he drew the scarlet vestment aside and pointed to the dreadful gash above his heart, and from this, again, the bloody drops fell thick. The colours stared and shrieked, and yet, through the bad, cheap art there seemed to shine a rapture that was very near to beauty; the thing expressed was so great that it had to a certain extent overcome the villainy of the expression.

They wandered vaguely, after their custom. Ambrose was silent; he was thinking of Avalon and "Red Martyrdom" and the Frenchman's parting salutation, of the vision in one of the old books, "the Man clothed in a robe redder and more shining than burning fire, and his feet and his hands and his face were of a like flame, and five angels in fiery vesture stood about him, and at the feet of the Man the ground was covered with a ruddy dew."

They passed under an old church tower that rose white in the moonlight above them. The air had cleared, the mist had floated away, and now the sky glowed violet, and the white stones of the classic spire shone on high. From it there came suddenly a tumult of glad sound, exultant bells in ever-changing order, pealing out as if to honour some great victory, so that the mirth of the street below became but a trivial restless noise. He thought of some passage that he had read but could not distinctly remember: a ship was coming back to its haven after a weary and tempestuous voyage over many dreadful seas, and those on board saw the tumult in the city as their sails were sighted; heard afar the shouts of gladness from the rejoicing people; heard the bells from all the spires and towers break suddenly into triumphant chorus, sounding high above the washing of the waves.

Ambrose roused himself from his dreams. They had been walking in a circle and had returned almost to the street of the Château, though, their knowledge of the district being of an unscientific character, they were under the impression that they were a mile or so away from that particular point. As it happened, they had not entered this street before, and they were charmed at the sudden appearance of stained glass lighted up from within. The colour was rich and good; there were flourished scrolls and grotesques in the Renaissance manner, many emblazoned shields in ruby and gold and azure; and the centre-piece shewed the Court of the Beer King—a jovial and venerable figure attended by a host of dwarfs and kobolds, all holding on high enormous mugs of beer. They went in boldly and were glad. It was the famous "Three Kings" in its golden and unreformed days, but this they knew not. The room was of moderate size, very low, with great dark beams in the white ceiling. White were the walls; on the plaster, black-letter texts with vermilion initials praised the drinker's art, and more kobolds, in black and red, loomed oddly in unsuspected corners. The lighting, presumably, was gas, but all that was visible were great antique lanterns depending from iron hooks, and through their dull green glass only a dim radiance fell upon the heavy oak tables and the drinkers. From the middle beam an enormous bouquet of fresh hops hung on high; there was a subdued murmur of talk, and now and then the clatter of the lid of a mug, as fresh beer was ordered. In one corner there was a kind of bar; behind it a couple of grim women—the kobolds apparently—performed their office; and above, on a sort of rack, hung mugs and tankards of all sizes and of all fantasies. There were plain mugs of creamy earthenware, mugs gaudily and oddly painted with garlanded goats, with hunting scenes, with towering castles, with flaming posies of flowers. Then some friend of the drunken, some sage who had pried curiously into the secrets of thirst, had made a series of wonders in glass, so shining and crystalline that to behold them was as if one looked into a well, for every glitter of the facets gave promise of satisfaction. There were the mugs, capacious and very deep, crowned for the most part not with mere plain lids of common use and make, but with tall spires in pewter, richly ornamented, evident survivals from the Middle Ages. Ambrose's eyes glistened; the place was altogether as he would have designed it. Nelly, too, was glad to sit down, for they had walked longer than usual. She was refreshed by a glass of some cool drink with a borage flower and a cherry floating in it, and Ambrose ordered a mug of beer.

It is not known how many of these *krugs* he emptied. It was, as has been noted, a sultry night, and the streets were dusty, and that glass of Benedictine after dinner rather evokes than dismisses the demon of thirst. Still, Munich beer is no hot and rebellious drink, so the causes of what followed must probably be sought for in other springs. Ambrose took a deep draught, gazed upward to the ceiling, and ordered another mug of beer for himself and some more of the cool and delicate and flowery beverage for Nelly. When the drink was set upon the board, he thus began, without title or preface:

"You must know, Nelly dear," he said, "that the marriage of Panurge, which fell out in due time (according to the oracle and advice of the Holy Bottle), was by no means a fortunate one. For, against all the counsel of Pantagruel and of Friar John, and indeed of all his friends, Panurge married in a fit of spleen and obstinacy the crooked and squinting daughter of the little old man who sold green sauce in the Rue Quincangrogne at Tours—you will see the very place in a few days, and then you will understand everything. You do not understand that? My child, that is impiety, since it accuses the Zeitgeist, who is cer-

tainly the only god that ever existed, as you will see more fully demonstrated in Huxley and Spencer and all the leading articles in all the leading newspapers. *Quod erat demonstrandum.* To be still more precise: You
must know that when I am dead, and a very great man indeed, many
thousands of people will come from all the quarters of the globe—not
forgetting the United States—to Lupton. They will come and stare
very hard at the Old Grange, which will have an inscription about me
on the wall; they will spend hours in High School; they will walk all
round Playing Fields; they will cut little bits off 'brooks' and "quarries".
Then they will view the Sulphuric Acid works, the Chemical Manure
factory and the Free Library, and whatever other stink-pots and cess-
pools Lupton town may contain; they will finally enjoy the view of the
Midland Railway Goods Station. Then they will say: 'Now we understand him; *now* that beautiful passage is quite clear; *now* one sees how
he got all his inspiration in that lovely old school and the wonderful
English country-side.' So you see that when I shew you the Rue Quincangrogne you will perfectly understand this history. Let us drink; the
world shall never be drowned again, so have no fear.

"Well, the fact remains that Panurge, having married this hideous
wench aforesaid, was excessively unhappy. It was in vain that he ar-
gued with his wife in all known languages and in some that are unknown, for, as she said, she only knew two languages, the one of
Touraine and the other of the Stick, and this second she taught
Panurge *per modum passionis*—that is by beating him, and this so thoroughly that poor Pilgarlic was sore from head to foot. He was a worthy
little fellow, but the greatest coward that ever breathed. Believe me, illustrious drinkers and most precious. . . . Nelly, never was man so
wretched as this Panurge since Paradise fell from Adam. This is the
true doctrine; I heard it when I was at Eleusis. You enquire what was
the matter? Why, in the first place, this vile wretch whom they all
called—so much did they hate her—La Vie Mortale, or Deadly Life,
this vile wretch, I say: what do you think that she did when the last
note of the fiddles had sounded and the wedding guests had gone off
to the 'Three Lampreys' to kill a certain worm—the which worm is
most certainly immortal, since it is not dead yet! Well, then, what did
Madame Panurge? Nothing but this: She robbed her excellent and devoted husband of all that he had. Doubtless you remember how, in the

old days, Panurge had played ducks and drakes with the money that Pantagruel had given him, so that he borrowed on his corn when it was still in the ear, and before it was sown, if we enquire a little more closely. In truth, the good little man never had a penny to bless himself withal, for the which cause Pantagruel loved him all the more dearly. So that when the Dive Bouteille gave its oracle, and Panurge chose his spouse, Pantagruel shewed how preciously he esteemed a hearty spender by giving him such a treasure that the goldsmiths who live under the bell of St. Gatien still talk of it before they dine, because by doing so their mouths water, and these salivary secretions are of high benefit to the digestion: read on this, Galen. If you would know how great and glorious this treasure was, you must go to the Library of the Archevêché at Tours, where they will shew you a vast volume bound in pigskin, the name of which I have forgotten. But this book is nothing else than the list of all the wonders and glories of Pantagruel's wedding present to Panurge; it contains surprising things, I can tell you, for, in good coin of the realm alone, never was gift that might compare with it; and besides the common money there were ancient pieces, the very names of which are now incomprehensible, and incomprehensible they will remain till the coming of the Coqcigrues. There was, for instance, a great gold Sol, a world in itself, as some said truly, and I know not how many myriad myriad of Etoiles, all of the finest silver that was ever minted, and Anges-Gardiens, which the learned think must have been first coined at Angers, though others will have it that they were the same as our Angels; and, as for Roses de Paradis and Couronnes Immortelles, I believe he had as many of them as ever he would. Beauties and joys he was to keep for pocket-money; small change is sometimes great gain. And, as I say, no sooner had Panurge married that accursed daughter of the Rue Quincangrogne than she robbed him of everything, down to the last brass farthing. The fact is that the woman was a witch; she was also something else which I leave out for the present. But, if you will believe me, she cast such a spell upon Panurge that he thought himself an absolute beggar. Thus he would look at his Sol d'Or and say: 'What is the use of that? It is only a great bright lump: I can see it every day.' Then when they said, 'But how about those Anges-Gardiens?' he would reply, 'Where are they? Have you seen them? *I* never see them. Shew them to me,' and so with all else; and all the while that villain of a woman beat, thumped and belaboured him so that the tears were always in his eyes, and they say you could hear him howling all over the world. Everybody said that he had made a pretty mess of it, and would come to a bad end.

"Luckily for him, this . . . witch of a wife of his would sometimes doze off for a few minutes, and then he had a little peace, and he would wonder what had become of all the gay girls and gracious ladies that he had known in old times—for he had played the devil with the women in his day and could have taught Ovid lessons in *arte amoris*. Now, of course, it was as much as his life was worth to mention the very name of one of these ladies, and as for any little sly visits, stolen endearments, hidden embraces, or any small matters of that kind, it was *good-bye, I shall see you next Nevermas*. Nor was this all, but worse remains behind; and it is my belief that it is the thought of what I am going to tell you that makes the wind wail and cry of winter nights, and the clouds weep, and the sky look black; for in truth it is the greatest sorrow that ever was since the beginning of the world. I must out with it quick, or I shall never have done: in plain English, and as true as I sit here drinking good ale, not one drop or minim or drachm or pennyweight of drink had Panurge tasted since the day of his wedding! He had implored mercy, he had told her how he had served Gargantua and Pantagruel and had got into the habit of drinking in his sleep, and his wife merely advised him to go to the devil—she was not going to let him so much as look at the nasty stuff. '"Touch not, taste not, smell not," is my motto,' said she. She gave him a blue ribbon, which she said would make up for it. 'What do you want with Drink?' said she. 'Go and do business instead, it's much better for you.'

"Sad, then, and sorry enough was the estate of poor Panurge. At last, so wretched did he become, that he took advantage of one of his wife's dozes and stole away to the good Pantagruel, and told him the whole story—and a very bad one it was—so that the tears rolled down Pantagruel's cheeks from sheer grief, and each teardrop contained exactly one hundred and eighteen gallons of aqueous fluid, according to the calculations of the best geometers. The great man saw that the case was a desperate one, and heaven knew, he said, whether it could be mended or not; but certain it was that a business such as this could not be settled in a hurry, since it was not like a game at shove-ha'penny to be got over between two gallons of wine. He therefore counselled Panurge to have patience and bear with his wife for a few thousand years, and in the meantime they would see what could be done. But, lest his patience should wear out, he gave him an odd drug or medicine, prepared by the great artist of the mountains of Cathay, and this he was to drop into his wife's glass—for, though he might have no drink, she was drunk three times a day, and she would sleep all the longer, and leave him awhile in peace. This Panurge very faithfully performed, and got a little rest now and again, and they say that while that devil of a woman snored and snorted he was able, by odd chances once or twice, to get hold of a drop of the right stuff—good old Stingo from the big barrel—which he lapped up as eagerly as a kitten laps cream. Others there be who declare that once or twice he got about his sad old tricks, while his ugly wife was sleeping in the sun; the women on the Maille make no secret of their opinion that his old mistress, Madame Sophia, was seen stealing in and out of the house as slyly as you please, and God knows what goes on when the door is shut. But the Tourainians were always sad gossips, and one must not believe all that one hears. I leave out the flat scandal-mongers who are bold enough to declare that he kept one mistress at Jerusalem, another at Eleusis, another in Egypt and about as many as are contained in the seraglio of the Grand Trunk, scattered up and down in the towns and villages of Asia; but I do believe there was some kissing in dark corners, and a curtain hung across one room in the house could tell odd tales. Nevertheless, La Vie Mortale (a pest on her!) was more often awake than asleep, and when she was awake Panurge's case was worse than ever. For, you see, the woman was no piece of a fool, and she saw sure enough that something was going on. The Stingo in the barrel was lower than of rights, and more than once she had caught her husband looking almost happy, at which she beat the house about his ears. Then, another time, Madame Sophia dropped her ring, and again this sweet lady came one morning so strongly perfumed that she scented the whole place, and when La Vie woke up it smelt like a church. There was fine work then, I promise you; the people heard the bangs and curses and shrieks and groans as far as Amboise on the one side and Luynes on the other; and that year the Loire rose ten feet higher than the banks on account of Panurge's tears. As a punishment, she made him go and be industrial, and he built ten thousand stink-pot factories with twenty thousand chimneys, and all the leaves and trees and green grass and flowers in the world were blackened, and died, and all the waters were poisoned so that there were no perch in the Loire, and salmon fetched forty sols the pound at Chinon market. As for the men and women, they became yellow apes and listened to a codger named Calvin, who told them they would all be damned eternally (except himself and his friends), and they found his doctrine very comforting, and probable too, since they had the sense to know that they were more than half damned already. I don't know whether Panurge's fate was worse on this occasion or on another when his wife found a book in his writing, full from end to end of poetry; some of it about the wonderful treasure that Pantagruel had given him, which he was supposed to have forgotten; some of it verses to those old light-o'-loves of his, with a whole epic in praise of his mistress-in-chief, Sophia. Then, indeed, there was the very deuce to pay; it was bread and water, stripes and torment, all day long, and La Vie swore a great oath that if he ever did it again he should be sent to spend the rest of his life in Manchester, whereupon he fell into a swoon from horrid fright and lay like a log, so that everybody thought he was dead.

"All this while the great Pantagruel was not idle. Perceiving how desperate the matter was, he summoned the Thousand and First Great Œcumenical Council of all the sages of the wide world, and when the fathers had come, and had heard High Mass at St. Gatien's, the session was opened in a pavilion in the meadows by the Loire just under the Lanterne of Roche Corbon, whence this Council is always styled the great and holy Council of the Lantern. If you want to know where the place is you can do so very easily, for there is a choice tavern on the spot where the pavilion stood, and there you may have *malelotte* and *friture* and amber wine of Vouvray, better than in any tavern in Touraine. As for the history of the acts of this great Council, it is still a-writing, and so far only two thousand volumes in elephant folio have been printed *sub signo Lucernæ cwn permissu superiorwn*. However, as it is necessary to be brief, it may be said that the holy fathers of the Lantern, after having heard the whole case as it was exposed to them by the great clerks of Pantagruel, having digested all the arguments, looked into the precedents, applied themselves to the doctrine, explored the hidden wisdom, consulted the Canons, searched the Scriptures, divided the dogma, distinguished the distinctions and answered the questions, re-solved with one voice that there was no help in the world for Panurge, save only this: he must forthwith achieve the most high, noble and glo-rious quest of the Sangraal, for no other way was there under heaven by which he might rid himself of that pestilent wife of his, La Vie Mortale.

"And on some other occasion," said Ambrose, "you may hear of the last voyage of Panurge to the Glassy Isle of the Holy Graal, of the incredible adventures that he achieved, of the dread perils through which he passed, of the great wonders and marvels and compassions of the way, of the manner in which he received the title Plentyn y To-nau, which signifies 'Child of the Waterfloods', and how at last he glo-riously attained the vision of the Sangraal, and was most happily translated out of the power of La Vie Mortale."

"And where is he now?" said Nelly, who had found the tale inter-esting but obscure.

"It is not precisely known—opinions vary. But there are two odd things: one is that he is exactly like that man in the red dress whose statue we saw in the shop window to-night; and the other is that from that day to this he has never been sober for a single minute.

"Calix meus inebrians quam præclarus est!"

5.

Ambrose took a great draught from the mug and emptied it, and forthwith rapped the lid for a fresh supply. Nelly was somewhat nerv-ous; she was afraid he might begin to sing, for there were extravaganc-es in the history of Panurge which seemed to her to be of alcoholic source. However, he did not sing; he lapsed into silence, gazing at the dark beams, the hanging hops, the bright array of the tankards and the groups of drinkers dotted about the room. At a neighbouring table two Germans were making a hearty meal, chumping the meat and smack-ing their lips in a kind of heavy ecstasy. He had but little German, but he caught scraps of the conversation.

One man said:

"Heavenly swine cutlets!"

And the other answered:

"Glorious eating!"

"Nelly," said Ambrose, "I have a great inspiration!"

She trembled visibly.

"Yes; I have talked so much that I am hungry. We will have some supper."

They looked over the list of strange eatables and, with the waiter's help, decided on Leberwurst and potato-salad as light and harmless. With this they ate crescent loaves, sprinkled with caraway seeds: there was more Munich Lion-Brew and more flowery drink, with black coffee, a *fine* and a Maraschino to end all. For Nelly the kobolds began to perform a grotesque and mystic dance in the shadows, the glass tankards on the rack glittered strangely, the white walls with the red and black texts retreated into vast distances, and the bouquet of hops seemed suspended from a remote star. As for Ambrose, he was certainly not *ebrius* according to the Baron's definition; he was hardly *ebriolus;* but he was sensible, let us say, of a certain quickening of the fancy, of a more vivid and poignant enjoyment of the whole situation, of the unutterable gaiety of this mad escape from the conventions of Lupton.

"It was a Thursday night," said Ambrose in the after years, "and we were thinking of starting for Touraine either the next morning or on Saturday at latest. It will always be bright in my mind, that picture—the low room with the oak beams, the glittering tankards, the hops hanging from the ceiling, and Nelly sitting before me sipping the scented drink from a green glass. It was the last night of gaiety, and even then gaiety was mixed with odd patterns—the Frenchman's talk about martyrdom, and the statue of the saint pointing to the marks of his passion, standing in that dyed vesture with his rapt, exultant face; and then the song of final triumph and deliverance that rang out on the chiming bells from the white spire. I think the contrast of this solemn undertone made my heart all the lighter; I was in that odd state in which one delights to know that one is not being understood—so I told poor Nelly the story of Panurge's marriage to La Vie Mortale; I am sure she thought I was drunk!

"We went home in a hansom, and agreed that we would have just one cigarette and then go to bed. It was settled that we would catch the night boat to Dieppe on the next day, and we both laughed with joy at the thought of the adventure. And then—I don't know how it was—Nelly began to tell me all about herself. She had never said a word before; I had never asked her—I never ask anybody about their past lives. What does it matter? You know a certain class of plot-novelists are rather fond of using it—in which the hero's happiness is blasted because he finds out that the life of his wife or his sweetheart has not always been spotless as the snow. Why should it be spotless as the snow? What is the hero that he should be dowered with the love of virgins of Paradise? I call it cant—all that—and I hate it; I hope Angel Clare was eventually entrapped by a young person from Piccadilly Circus—she would probably be much too good for him! So, you see, I was hardly likely to have put any very searching questions to Nelly; we had other things to talk about.

"But this night I suppose she was a bit excited. It had been a wild and wonderful week. The transition from that sewage-pot in the Midlands to the Abbey of Theleme was enough to turn any head; we had laughed till we had grown dizzy. The worst of that miserable school discipline is that it makes one take an insane and quite disproportionate enjoyment in little things, in the merest trifles which ought really to be accepted as a matter of course. I assure you that every minute that I spent in bed after seven o'clock was to me a grain of Paradise, a moment of delight. Of course, it's ridiculous; let a man get up early or get up late, as he likes or as he finds best—and say no more about it. But at that wretched Lupton early rising was part of the infernal blether and blatter of the place, that made life there like a long dinner in which every dish has the same sauce. It may be a good sauce enough; but one is sick of the taste of it. According to our Bonzes there, getting up early on a winter's day was a high virtue which acquired merit. I believe I should have liked a hard chair to sit in of my own free will, if one of our old fools—Palmer—had not always been gabbling about the horrid luxury of some boys who had arm-chairs in their studies. Unless you were doing something or other to make yourself very uncomfortable, he used to say you were like the 'later Romans'. I am sure he believed that those lunatics who bathe in the Serpentine on Christmas Day would go straight to heaven!

"And there you are. I would awake at seven o'clock from persistent habit, and laugh as I realised that I was in Little Russell Row and not at the Old Grange. Then I would doze off again and wake up at intervals—eight, nine, ten—and chuckle to myself with ever-increasing enjoyment. It was just the same with smoking. I don't suppose I should have touched a cigarette for years if smoking had not been one of the mortal sins in our Bedlam Decalogue. I don't know whether smoking is bad for boys or not; I should think not, as I believe the Dutch—who are sturdy fellows—begin to puff fat cigars at the age of six or thereabouts; but I do know that those pompous old boobies and blockheads and leather-skulls have discovered exactly the best way to make a boy think that a packet of Rosebuds represents the quintessence of frantic delight.

"Well, you see how it was, how Little Russell Row—the dingy, the stuffy, the dark retreat of old Bloomsbury—became the abode of miraculous joys, a bright portion of fairyland. Ah! it was a strong new wine that we tasted, and it went to our heads, and not much wonder. It all rose to its height on that Thursday night when we went to the 'Three Kings' and sat beneath the hop bush, drinking Lion-Brew and flowery drink as I talked extravagances concerning Panurge. It was time for the curtain to be rung down on our comedy.

"The one cigarette had become three or four when Nelly began to tell me her history; the wine and the rejoicing had got into her head also. She described the first things that she remembered: a little hut among wild hills and stony fields in the west of Ireland, and the great sea roaring on the shore but a mile away, and the wind and the rain always driving from across the waves. She spoke of the place as if she loved it, though her father and mother were as poor as they could be, and little was there to eat even in the old cabin. She remembered Mass in the little chapel, an old, old place hidden away in the most desolate part of the country, small and dark and bare enough except for the candles on the altar and a bright statue or two. St. Kieran's cell, they called it, and it was supposed that the Mass had never ceased to be said there, even in the blackest days of persecution. Quite well she remembered the old priest and his vestments, and the gestures that he used, and how they all bowed down when the bell rang; she could imitate his quavering voice saying the Latin. Her own father, she said, was a learned man in his way, though it was not the English way. He could not read common print, or write; he knew nothing about printed books, but he could say a lot of the old Irish songs and stories by heart, and he had sticks on which he wrote poems on all sorts of things, cutting notches on the wood in Oghams, as the priest called them; and he could tell many wonderful tales of the saints and the people. It was a happy life altogether; they were as poor as poor could be, and praised God and wanted for nothing. Then her mother went into a decline and died, and her father never lifted up his head again, and she was left an orphan when she was nine years old. The priest had written to an aunt who lived in England, and so she found herself one black day standing on the platform of the station in a horrible little manufacturing village in Lancashire; everything was black—the sky and the earth, and the houses and the people; and the sound of their rough, harsh voices made her sick. And the aunt had married an Independent and turned Protestant, so she was black, too, Nelly thought. She was wretched for a long time, she said. The aunt was kind enough to her, but the place and the people were so awful. Mr. Deakin, the husband, said he couldn't encourage Popery in his house, so she had to go to the meeting-house on Sunday and listen to the nonsense they called 'religion'—all long sermons with horrible shrieking hymns. By degrees she forgot her old prayers, and she was taken to the Dissenters' Sunday School, where they learned texts and heard about King Solomon's Temple, and Jonadab the son of Rechab, and Jezebel, and the Judges. They seemed to think a good deal of her at the school; she had several prizes for Bible knowledge.

"She was sixteen when she first went out to service. She was glad to get away—nothing could be worse than Farnworth, and it might be better. And then there were tales to tell! I never have had a clearer light thrown on the curious and disgusting manners of the lower middle-class in England—the class that prides itself especially on its respectability, above all, on what it calls 'Morality'—by which it means the observance of one particular commandment. You know the class I mean: the brigade of the shining hat on Sunday, of the neat little villa with a well-kept plot in front, of the consecrated drawing-room, of the big Bible well in evidence. It is more often Chapel than Church, this tribe, but it draws from both sources. It is above all things shiny—not only the Sunday hat, but the furniture, the linoleum, the hair and the very flesh which pertain to these people have an unwholesome polish on them; and they prefer their plants and flowers and shrubs to be as glossy as possible—this *gens lubrica.*

"To these tents poor Nelly went as a slave; she dwelt from henceforth on the genteel outskirts of more or less prosperous manufacturing towns, and she soon profoundly regretted the frank grime and hideousness of Farnworth. A hedgehog is a rough and prickly fellow—better his prickles than the reptile's poisonous slime. The tales that yet await the novelist who has courage (what is his name, by the way?), who has the insight to see behind those Venetian blinds and white curtains, who has the word that can give him entrance through the polished door by the encaustic porch! What plots, what pictures, what characters are ready for his cunning hand, what splendid matter lies unknown, useless, and indeed offensive, which, in the artist's crucible, would be transmuted into golden and exquisite perfection. Do you know that I can never penetrate into the regions where these people dwell without a thrill of wonder and a great desire that I might be called to execute the masterpieces I have hinted at? Do you remember how Zola, viewing these worlds from the train when he visited London, groaned because he had no English, because he had no key to open the treasure-house before his eyes? He, of course, who was a great diviner, saw the infinite variety of romance that was concealed beneath those myriads of snug commonplace roofs: I wish he could have observed in English and recorded in French. He was a brave man, his defence of Dreyfus shews that; but, supposing the capacity, I do not think he was brave enough to tell the London suburbs the truth about themselves in their own tongue.

"Yes, I walk down these long ways on Sunday afternoons, when they are at their best. Sometimes, if you choose the right hour, you may look into one 'breakfast room'—an apartment half sunken in the earth—after another, and see in each one the table laid for tea, shewing the charming order and uniformity that prevail. Tea in the drawing-room would be, I suppose, a desecration. I wonder what would happen if some chance guest were to refuse tea and to ask for a glass of beer, or even a brandy and soda? I suppose the central lake that lies many hundreds of feet beneath London would rise up, and the sinful town would be overwhelmed. Yes: consider these houses well; how demure, how well-ordered, how shining, as I have said; and then think of what they conceal.

"Generally speaking, you know, 'morality' (in the English suburban sense) has been a tolerably equal matter. I shouldn't imagine that those 'later Romans' that poor old Palmer was always bothering about were much better or worse than the earlier Babylonians; and London as a whole is very much the same thing in this respect as Pekin as a whole. Modern Berlin and sixteenth-century Venice might compete on equal terms—save that Venice, I am sure, was very picturesque, and Berlin, I have no doubt, is very piggy. The fact is, of course (to use a simple analogy), man, by his nature, is always hungry, and, that being the case, he will sometimes eat too much dinner and sometimes he will get his dinner in odd ways, and sometimes he will help himself to more or less unlawful snacks before breakfast and after supper. There it is, and there is an end of it. But suppose a society in which the fact of hunger was officially denied, in which the faintest hint at an empty stomach was considered the rankest, most abominable indecency, the most detestable offence against the most sacred religious feelings? Suppose the child severely reprimanded at the mere mention of bread and butter, whipped and shut up in a dark room for the offence of reading a recipe for making plum pudding; suppose, I say, a whole society organised on the strict official understanding that no decent person ever is or has been or can be conscious of the physical want of food; that breakfast, lunch, tea, dinner and supper are orgies only used by the most wicked and degraded wretches, destined to an awful and eternal doom? In such a world, I think, you would discover some very striking irregularities in diet. Facts are known to be stubborn things, but if their very existence is denied they become ferocious and terrible things. Coventry Pat more was angry, and with reason, when he heard that even at the Vatican the statues had received the order of the fig-leaf.

"Nelly went among these Manichees. She had been to the world beyond the Venetians, the white muslin curtains and the india-rubber plant, and she told me her report. They talk about the morality of the theatre, these swine! In the theatre—if there is anything of the kind—it is a case of a wastrel and a wanton who meet and part on perfectly equal terms, without deceit or false pretences. It is not a case of master creeping into a young girl's room at dead of night, with a Bible under his arm—the said Bible being used with grotesque skill to shew that 'master's' wishes must be at once complied with under pain of severe punishment, not only in this world, but in the world to come. Every Sunday, you must remember, the girl has seen 'master' perhaps crouching devoutly in his pew, perhaps in the part of sidesman or even churchwarden, more probably supplementing the gifts of the pastor at some nightmarish meeting-house. 'Master' offers prayer with wonderful fervour; he speaks to the Lord as man to man; in the emotional passages his voice gets husky, and everybody says how good he is. He is a deacon, a guardian of the poor (gracious title!), a builder and an earnest supporter of the British and Foreign Bible Society: in a word, he is of the great middle-class, the backbone of England and of the Protestant Religion. He subscribes to the excellent society which prosecutes booksellers for selling the Decameron of Boccaccio. He has from ten to fifteen children, all of whom were found by Mamma in the garden.

"'Mr. King was a horrible man,' said Nelly, describing her first place; 'he had a great greasy pale face with red whiskers, and a shiny bald head; he was fat, too, and when he smiled it made one feel sick. Soon after I got to the place he came into the kitchen. Missus was away for three days, and the children were all in bed. He sat down by the hearth and asked whether I was saved, and did I love the Lord as I ought to, and if I ever had any bad thoughts about young men? Then he opened the Bible and read me nasty things from the Old Testament, and asked if I understood what it meant. I said I didn't know, and he said we must approach the Lord in prayer so that we might have grace to search the Scriptures together. I had to kneel down close to him, and he put his arm round my waist and began to pray, as he called it; and when we got up he took me on his knee and said he felt to me as if I were his own daughter.'

"There, that is enough of Mr. King. You can imagine what the poor child had to go through time after time. On prayer-meeting nights she used to put the chest of drawers against her bedroom door: there would be gentle, cautious pushes, and then a soft voice murmuring: 'My child, why is your heart so bad and stubborn?' I think we can conceive the general character of 'master' from these examples. 'Missus', of course, requires a treatise to herself; her more frequent failings are child-torture, secret drinking and low amours with oily commercial travellers.

"Yes, it is a hideous world enough, isn't it? And isn't it a pleasant thought that you and I practically live under the government of these people? 'Master' is the 'man in the street', the 'hard-headed, practical man of the world', 'the descendant of the sturdy Puritans', whose judgment is final on all questions, from Poetics to Liturgiology. We hardly think that this picture will commend itself to the 'man in the street'—a course of action that is calculated to alienate practical men. Pleasant, isn't it? *Suburbia locuta est: causa finita est.*

"I suppose that, by nature, these people would not be so very much more depraved than the ordinary African black fellow. Their essential hideousness comes, I take it, from their essential and most abominable hypocrisy. You know how they are always prating about Bible Teaching—the 'simple morality of the Gospel', and all that nauseous stuff? And what would be the verdict, in this suburban world, on a man who took no thought for the morrow, who regulated his life by the example of the lilies, who scoffed at the idea of saving money? You know perfectly well that his relations would have him declared a lunatic. *There* is the villainy. If you are continually professing an idolatrous and unctuous devotion to a body of teaching which you are also persistently and perpetually disregarding and disobeying in its plainest, most simple, most elementary injunctions, well, you will soon interest anglers in search of bait.

"Yes, such is the world behind the india-rubber plant, into which Nelly entered. I believe she repelled the advances of 'master' with success. Her final undoing came from a different quarter, and I am afraid that drugs, not Biblical cajoleries, were the instruments used. She cried bitterly when she spoke of this event, but she said, too: 'I will kill him for it!' It was an ugly story, and a sad one, alas!—the saddest tale I ever listened to. Think of it: to come from that old cabin on the wild, bare hills, from the sound of the great sea, from the pure breath of the waves and the wet salt wind, to the stenches and the poisons of our 'industrial centres'. She came from parents who had nothing and possessed all things, to our civilisation which has everything, and lies on the dung-heap that it has made at the very gates of heaven—destitute of all true treasure, full of sores and vermin and corruption. She was nurtured on the wonderful old legends of the saints and the fairies; she had listened to the songs that her father made and cut in Oghams; and we gave her the penny novelette and the works of Madame Chose. She had knelt before the altar, adoring the most holy sacrifice of the Mass;

now she knelt beside 'master' while he approached the Lord in prayer, licking his fat, white lips. I can imagine no more terrible transition.

"I do not know how or why it happened, but as I listened to Nelly's tale my eyes were opened to my own work and my own deeds, and I saw for the first time my wickedness. I should despair of explaining to any one how utterly innocent I had been in intention all the while, how far I was from any deliberate design of guilt. In a sense, I was learned, and yet, in a sense, I was most ignorant; I had been committing what is, doubtless, a grievous sin, under the impression that I was enjoying the greatest of all mysteries and graces and blessings—the great natural sacrament of human life.

"Did I not know I was doing wrong? I knew that if any of the masters found me with Nelly I should get into sad trouble. Certainly; I knew that. But if any of the masters had caught me smoking a cigarette, or saying 'damn', or going into a public-house to get a glass of beer, or using a crib, or reading Rabelais, I should have got into sad trouble also. I knew that I was sinning against the 'tone' of the great Public School; you may imagine how deeply I felt the guilt of such an offence as that! And, of course, I had heard the boys telling their foolish indecencies; but somehow their nasty talk and their filthy jokes were not in any way connected in my mind with my love of Nelly—no more, indeed, than midnight darkness suggests daylight, or torment symbolises pleasure. Indeed, there was a hint—a dim intuition—deep down in my consciousness that all was not well; but I knew of no reason for this; I held it a morbid dream, the fantasy of an imagination over-exalted, perhaps; I would not listen to a faint voice that seemed without sense or argument.

"And now that voice was ringing in my ears with the clear, resonant and piercing summons of a trumpet: I saw myself arraigned far down beside the pestilent horde of whom I have just spoken; and, indeed, my sin was worse than theirs, for I had been bred in light, and they in darkness. All heedless, without knowledge, without preparation, without receiving the mystic word, I had stumbled into the shrine, uninitiated I had passed beyond the veil and gazed upon the hidden mystery, on the secret glory that is concealed from the holy angels. Woe and great sorrow were upon me, as if a priest, devoutly offering the sacrifice, were suddenly to become aware that he was uttering, all inadvertently, hideous and profane blasphemies, summoning Satan in place of the Holy Spirit. I hid my face in my hands and cried out in my anguish.

"Do you know that I think Nelly was in a sense relieved when I tried to tell her of my mistake, as I called it; even though I said, as gently as I could, that it was all over. She was relieved, because for the first time she felt quite sure that I was altogether in my senses! I can understand it. My whole attitude must have struck her as bordering on insanity, for, of course, from first to last I had never for a moment taken up the position of the unrepentant but cheerful sinner, who knows that he is being a sad dog, but means to continue in his naughty way. She, with her evil experience, had thought the words I had sometimes uttered not remote from madness. She wondered, she told me, whether one night I might not suddenly take her throat in my hands and strangle her in a sudden frenzy. She hardly knew whether she dreaded such a death or longed for it.

"'You spoke so strangely,' she said; 'and all the while I knew we were doing wrong, and I wondered.'

"Of course, even after I had explained the matter as well as I could, she was left to a large extent bewildered as to what my state of mind could have been; still, she saw that I was not mad, and she was relieved, as I have said.

"I do not know how she was first drawn to me—how it was that she stole that night to the room where I lay bruised and aching. Pity and desire and revenge, I suppose, all had their share. She was so sorry, she said, for me. She could see how lonely I was, how I hated the place and everybody about it, and she knew that I was not English. I think my wild Welsh face attracted her, too.

"Alas! that was a sad night, after all our laughter. We had sat on and on till the dawn began to come in through the drawn blinds. I told her that we must go to bed, or we should never get up the next day. We went into the bedroom, and there, sad and grey, the dawn appeared. There was heavy sky covered with clouds and a straight, soft rain was pattering on the leaves of a great plane tree opposite; heavy drops fell into the pools in the road.

"It was still as on the mountain, filled with infinite sadness, and a sudden step clattering on the pavement of the square beyond made the stillness seem all the more profound. I stood by the window and gazed out at the weeping, dripping tree, the ever-falling rain and the motion-less, leaden clouds—there was no breath of wind—and it was as if I heard the saddest of all music, tones of anguish and despair and notes that cried and wept. The theme was given out, itself wet, as it were, with tears. It was repeated with a sharper cry, a more piteous supplica-tion; it was re-echoed with a bitter utterance, and tears fell faster as the raindrops fell plashing from the weeping tree. Inexorable in its sad re-iterations, in its remorseless development, that music wailed and grew in its lamentation in my own heart; heavy it was, and without hope; heavy as those still, leaden clouds that hung motionless in heaven. No relief came to this sorrowing melody—rather a sharper note of an-guish; and then for a moment, as if to embitter bitterness, sounded a fantastic, laughing air, a measure of jocund pipes and rushing violins, echoing with the mirth of dancing feet. But it was beaten into dust by the sentence of despair, by doom that was for ever, by a sentence piti-less, relentless; and, as a sudden breath shook the wet boughs of the plane tree and a torrent fell upon the road, so the last notes of that in-ner music were to me as a burst of hopeless weeping.

"I turned away from the window and looked at the dingy little room where we had laughed so well. It was a sad room enough, with its pale blue, stripy-patterned paper, its rickety old furniture and its feeble pictures. The only note of gaiety was on the dressing-table, where poor little Nelly had arranged some toys and trinkets and fanta-sies that she had bought for herself in the last few days. There was a silver-handled brush and a flagon of some scent that I liked, and a little brooch of olivines that had caught her fancy; and a powder-puff in a pretty gilt box. The sight of these foolish things cut me to the heart. But Nelly! She was standing by the bedside, half undressed, and she looked at me with the most piteous longing. I think that she had really grown fond of me. I suppose that I shall never forget the sad en-chantment of her face, the flowing of her beautiful coppery hair about it; and the tears were wet on her cheeks. She half stretched out her bare arms to me and then let them fall. I had never known all her strange allurement before. I had refined and symbolised and made her into a sign of joy, and now before me she shone disarrayed—not a symbol, but a woman, in the new intelligence that had come to me, and I longed for her. I had just enough strength and no more."

V

1.

About a year after the adventure with Nelly, Ambrose Meyrick at last caught that train from Lupton to Birmingham. He had waited for many years, but had yearned and sickened for the sight of the old land of his fathers, he had not allowed the memory of Gwent to fail; and now, when the whistle sounded, and the train began to move out of the station he was astonished to find himself so little uplifted by the granting of his desires. He looked up with a kind of sober joy at the railway bridge, on which the poor little boy had stood so often, for so many hours, straining his eyes towards the west: he remembered that one day when the earth burned as with fire, and his heart and soul and body were faint almost to death; he remembered how he had been refreshed by the vision of the mountain, by the wind that breathed new life into him. It was curious, he thought, how against his own desire and his own faith, he had ceased to take daily account of such a merciful marvel as this, which should have been a perpetual talisman, a constant defence against all weariness and sickness and despair, an hourly reminder that the world was not given up entirely to the powers of darkness. He understood the difficulty of the great Act of Faith which must be renewed day by day, again and again, by a constant exercise of the will—or else the abyss, the fall into the black pit of nonsense and despair which most people spoke of as the world—"and not half a bad place either, if you take it the right way." It was so simple, the "not half a bad place" creed, one fell in with it so easily, without any conscious effort of acquiescence, one conformed even against one's own steadfast convictions, unless these were continually renewed and proclaimed. One knew better, perhaps, one had been vouchsafed some proofs from within and from without; and yet it was so entirely natural to believe that man is sustained by loaves from the baker and meat from the butcher, and to take one's measures accordingly. As the train sped away to the west and the south he resolved that this should be amended, that for the future he would daily remind himself that he was fed not by baker's bread and butcher's meat, but by miracles and wonders.

But the past year had been given over to that process of dryness and fear which is called the Purgative Way. It is needful, but it lacks all refreshment and unction, speaking more of unworthiness and darkness than of light and compassions. He had come back to Lupton after that "holiday" with a certain mark of grimness about the mouth; he went down into the fire that it might cleanse him; he put away the thought of wonders and mysteries of which he was not worthy. As has been seen from some of his notes, he had already made himself acquainted with a species of voluntary stripping, the giving up of all the decorations, and ornaments, and vestures of the inner life; but the sense of his guilt and his offence now stripped him in spite of himself and he became familiar with the dark cloud of desolation. He had professed the mysteries, and he feared lest they should be withdrawn from him for ever. For the first time in his schooldays he really and interiorly submitted himself to the discipline of the place; not that he thought it good or wise or suitable for anything but the production of Boobyism, but he accepted it as an instrument of correction, and for a year he had endeavoured to occupy himself as much as possible with the interests of Lupton, putting aside, as far as he could, his own life and his own hidden knowledge.

But he felt, as the train rushed from Midlandia maledicta to Midlandia felix, that enough had been done in the path of penance: the Book entitled "Here begin Terrors" was closed for a season; it was time to open another volume—"Here begin Great Wonders".

He was nearly nineteen. In the autumn he would go up to Oxford for his Scholarship Examination, but he did not mean to go to the University, at all events for the present; he intended to submit himself to other schools and more remote ways of knowledge. He had made certain vows of reparation for the wrong he had done, and he began to have a glimmering vision of that which might prove to be the purpose and the end of his life. If this were to be so, if indeed he were called to so holy and mystical an office, to the celebration of such high and wonderful ceremonies, with what instant and especial care he must begin to prepare himself, how sternly he must shut out from his heart all the apparatus of vanity and lies. He feared lest he should have bowed down too low in the temple of the false deities, though the motive had been good—but he had tried to listen sympathetically to the Doctor's sermons! And what a course it had been during the last term!

The main point enforced had been that one could not arrange one's life in separate compartments without relation the one to the other, that *all* life was of infinite and equal importance, that the Games and Work of school were to be regarded just as seriously as the pursuits and labours of later years.

"Do not let us mistake," said the preacher one Sunday morning. "We are already inhabitants of eternity; here at Lupton in School and in the Playing Field, in our Sports and in our Studies, each action is of eternal import, each action forms part of that character which will be our everlasting possession."

And the whole gist of the series was that any boy who wished to be a plausible and successful humbug in after life had better set about his great task immediately.

"Remember," said the Doctor, "we are not in the Dark Ages now. None among us will ever be called upon to be the minister of a capricious and arbitrary sovereign. There is no one here whose gift of statesmanship will be exercised in concocting measures against the liberties of the people; there is no one whose military ability will be utilised in deeds of savage and remorseless oppression. We are not in the Dark Ages. There may be future prelates in your ranks for all I know; but the prelate of Today is successor in name only to the mediaeval hierophant.

"No. We are to serve a sovereign who wears no visible crown. Let us all remember once and for all that there is no more splendid service than that of the people, that if we win high place and high honours these things are but held by us in trust for the benefit of our brothers and sisters, that work which is useless to the multitude is not work at all—or, at the best, is work which is not worth the doing. We talk of the Church as if the word were synonymous with the clergy: how foolish, how erroneous! The Church is merely the State in its ethical *persona;* it represents the State morally energising, endeavouring to touch the great heart of the people to higher issues and nobler aims; and the Church, as the State, derives all its power, all its authority from those whom it serves.

"Again I say; distrust, and distrust profoundly all work, all service that cannot abide the great popular test which I have indicated. Distrust yourself if you are not doing the people's work; reconsider your position; come down from the heights, and take your place with the striving multitude below. Remember once and for all that popularity, in its true sense, is a noble aim; nay it is the noblest of all aims. What wonder that the Jewish populace cried Hosanna? He had compassion on the *multitude*. The common people heard Him gladly. Let these words dwell in the minds of all of us, more especially in the minds of those who are soon to take their share in the great work of the world. Let us all beware; we are not to work for cliques, for small and select aristocratic bodies, however exquisite their taste, however high their standards; we are to work for, and to speak to the 'multitude', the 'common people': we are to win popularity."

Ambrose shuddered and laughed at the recollection of this discourse and others like it—it was clear that he had had enough of such follies, and it was time for him to leave behind Lupton and all its ways. Already it seemed to belong to things departed; he would return for a little while at the end of the holidays and go through such formalities as were necessary, but Lupton was over—its foolish routine, its magazines of cant, its dull pedantries, its sense of being at the centre of all things; it was all past and performed, and lay in his mind like the recollection of a tedious and unimportant play, that one has witnessed and would willingly forget. Behind him all this weariness, its dulness and its languors, its pains and longings, behind him also the evil that he had done, which had so heavily and grievously weighed down his spirit: before him was the Land of Desire, the end, and the goal, and the Perfection. He was not nineteen, but already, it seemed, the call had come. He looked forward to his stay at the Wern as a time of refreshment and preparation for the work that he had to do.

He was to revisit his old home. When his father had died, Mr. Horbury, who was the trustee, had bethought him of some distant cousins of the Meyricks, people named Vaughan, who, he thought, might be glad to take the old place during Ambrose's minority. Mr. Vaughan, a widower with one daughter, was delighted with the proposal; the rent was moderate, the air was good, and he had pleasant recollections of the Wern dating from a visit paid long before. It was an admirable arrangement for both sides: the rent was secure, and Mr. Horbury, who liked managing and always managed well, felt that Ambrose was lucky to be in such good hands. Indeed, he was quite right;

he reinvested Mr. Meyrick's capital in some excellent securities; and when Ambrose came of age he found himself not only the owner of the pleasant and beloved old house, but also the possessor of a very pretty balance at the bank, the accumulation of ten or eleven years, after due deduction of his school fees, board, and general expenses. It has been hinted that there were defects in Mr. Horbury's character; but there was never better or more scrupulous man of affairs.

Mr. Vaughan, the cousin, was an odd and retired character. One of the reasons which made him welcome the chance of taking the Wern was the fact of its remoteness from a railway station: he hated trains and never wanted to take them, spending his time in a little shooting, a good deal of fishing, and the writing of an interminable Romance which had kept him quiet for twenty-five years. Nothing much was known of it, save that the author was always consulting Ducange's Lexicon of Late Latinity; this did not seem very promising, and the ingenious author had neither the energy nor the guile of a brother of the craft, whose autumn paragraphs about the Magnum Opus in preparation appeared as regularly as the blackberries. Perhaps it would have been kinder if Mr. Vaughan had asked his cousin to spend the holidays at the Wern before; but the idea had not occurred to him; he supposed that Horbury was looking after the lad all right. At last however it had struck him that an invitation would be graceful, and perhaps at nineteen Ambrose would no longer be a "loud boy". Mr. Vaughan hated loud boys, and thought they spoilt life. He understood that they had to be fed on underdone mutton and rice puddings; they were always shouting—"they never cease from shouting from five o'clock in the morning till eleven o'clock at night", he persisted—and continually rushing about in staring white flannels.

"Nonsense," he would say. "I know them. They *do* shout, and they never stop. I'd much rather live next to the Kennels than next to a school. And what the devil do they mean by dressing in that absurd style? It's glaring, it's offensive, it's excessively silly. And why do they rush? What's the good of it? What do they get by it? I've noticed them; they can't walk like sensible people; they're always rushing, and it's most tiresome to look at. Moreover they never by any chance know any single thing that can be of the faintest interest to any rational being. I have a black Pig that could talk down a schoolboy any day; his name is Walter Mapp and he is extremely intelligent. I value his companionship; he often goes out for walks with me. I would not take a loud boy out for a walk on any terms or conditions or considerations whatsoever. He would dress in white flannel, he would put on a hideous stripy jacket on top, he would shout and rush all the way, he would high jump all the stiles and long jump all the brooks; he would stop now and then and go through a most ridiculous pantomime with his walking stick and roar out some rubbish about that being the way to meet Boggler's bowling; he would not utter one word of the remotest approach to the distant boundaries of sense if I walked him to the top of the Bannawc Brycheiniog and back again. Damn the loud boy, and damn his masters for encouraging him to make such a fool of himself. Walter Mapp, now—"

Perhaps these sentiments had weighed largely in the forgetfulness of Mr. Vaughan towards his cousin. Even now he had had tremors, especially after reading Mr. Horbury's last letter, in which Ambrose had been highly commended, not only for his brilliant scholarship but more especially for his proficience in games.

"I have great hopes," wrote Mr. Horbury, "that he will make a big name for himself and do the old school credit. He will have a nice little income at his back when he comes of age, so he will be able to pick and choose his own career. So many of us have to take what we can get, and sometimes that means that our real abilities run to seed for lack of opportunity. Ambrose will be differently placed; he can afford to wait and look about him. He is a really fine scholar, and besides the ordinary school work I fancy that he has read a good deal on his own account: I don't see how he can miss his first even if he tries. But what is more important than mere scholarship, he is good at all our Games; and his fast bowling will, I expect, do even more than his Greek Verse to 'place' him, first at the University and then in the world. It may seem illogical enough, but as a matter of fact athletics will carry a man farther than any amount of scholarship; it is on this account that I feel so confident of Ambrose's future."

The letter had filled Mr. Vaughan's mind with the most dismal apprehensions; he sincerely regretted the invitation. He meditated a diplomatic indisposition; but concluded that it would be better to suffer the young man for a time: if necessary he could have all his meals sent in to the study on the plea of "writing a book". He would not, on any pretext, allow Ambrose to practise bowling on the lawn; that was settled, and Sylvia might hint that her father found shouting disturbed him when he was writing. But Mr. Vaughan looked pensive after sending that letter, and he was quite uneasy at breakfast on the day of Ambrose's expected arrival.

Ambrose had written that he was not quite certain of his train, he would walk from the station, so there was no necessity to send any one to meet him. He would carry a hand-bag, and his luggage could be fetched the next day. He wished to re-enter his native land alone; and lovers desire but each other when they are reunited after long years of absence.

By the time that the train reached Hereford Lupton had vanished from his mind and all recollections of it. He had been exiled and he was returning and when the great hills rose up before him a strange emotion beat within his breast. He did not know the precise boundary of the counties; but at the sign of the hills he took off his hat, worshipping the dear soil of Gwent; the land had an unutterable word for him and all his being made answer. The earth kept that day a great festival; he could almost have said:

Montes exulteraverunt ut arietes: et colles sicut agni ovium.

It was a day of soft sunshine behind a delicate veil; the land was all in a golden, wonderful radiance, and the clear streams glittered in the light, and the leaves of the trees danced with exultation in a wind blowing from the west. He looked out of the carriage window with a gaze of such ardour and delight as lovers know.

Qui convertit petram in stagna aquarum: et rupem in fontes aquarum.

His sojourn in the Dry and Stony Land was ended: there rushed the translucent brook down from the mountainside, from the very heart of the rock; he fancied that he could hear the sound of the pouring waters and their voice of gladness. There was the glen which led to the wild country; the land of green bubbling wells, and the far purple fields of heather, and the world of the golden, scented gorse, where the great rocks looked like magic Druid rings. He and his father had climbed by that little path—so many years ago—to see a church of very old religion, and the well of an old saint.

The brook rushed on; the line ran parallel with it for some miles. He feasted his eyes on that wonderful clear stream; he had seen no such sight since the day on which he had left Gwent, for about Lupton most of the rivers and brooks were poisonous sewers, and even the unpolluted waters were dull and muddy and sluggish, as they crawled through dull fields. Here was quick crystal, which sang *Laetare* as it passed from the hill into the valley; its pools were a shining darkness; its ripples were of silver light, it was pure as the dawn upon the mountains; it was as if the great alchemy of God had transmuted the hard innermost rocks with all their secrets into that rejoicing brightness, signifying how before the day of ruin all the world was a plastic light, an ever-changing mirror.

On his left hand was now the Hill of the Apparition of S. Michael the Archangel, a strange riven height, venerated by the people before the coming of the "Black Hag of Geneva who sends body and soul quick to hell". Here, they said, in the old days those who knew would sometimes go apart, climbing the red height till they came to the chapel of the Archangel, a very small and ancient place, of which the foundations still remained, standing in a thick wood of ash trees. This observance, it has been said, furnishes the explanation of the curious poem by Morvran called "The Sovereignty of the Ash". Ambrose as he gazed up towards the mountain could see the wood, the boughs of the ash-trees tossing in the wind, and he remembered the poem, a strange piece of metrical ingenuity in the original, which had served as a model to many generations of bards, though none had ever equalled it in the complexity of its structure. In its lines Morvran had mingled alliteration and rhyme and assonance in a wonderful manner, and as the poets said, besides all this there were "inspiration and unction" of such a singular magic that it was sometimes spoken of as "The Supreme Incantation of Morvran". The poem represents all the trees as contending for the honour of sovereignty:—

> As the first hues of the dawn above the forest of Caer-rhiu,
> There appeared a red blossom out of the shadow of the trees.
> The Rose spoke; it was like the clear chant of the angels.
> Though I am least of the trees of the wood,
> Though I am hidden and overshadowed in the wood,
> Though I dwell often in obscurity,

> Yet I claim principality in this assemblage.
> Because I alone am a native of the Old Garden,
> Because I typify the Accomplishment of the Saints,
> Because in my blossom is hidden the Great Mystery,
> Because I waft abroad sweet odours of Paradise,
> Ancient relics of the lost kingdom.

The Hazel boasts that its boughs are the "Quire of the Birds of God", the Wych-Elm of its use in Magic, the Oak has borne sway from all ages, the White Thorn is the "shining house of Merlin", the Yew has "an honourable station near the altars of the saints"; and so the poem ranges through all the trees of the wood, till the Ash triumphs:—

> Because I keep watch over the shrine of the Chief Angel,
> Because beneath my boughs shone the Majesty of Heaven,
> Because I was a veil to the Glorious Appearance,
> Because I was visited by Heaven's principal warrior;
> Mihangel is my advocate, the bearer of the Offering
> Unto the supreme altar of the Most High.

Ambrose was murmuring these last lines to himself as the train passed the base of the Mount of Apparition, and the men who had got in at Hereford glanced round nervously, and looked at the cord of communication.

But Ambrose looked longingly at the boughs of the ash, tossing in the wind on the far mountainside, thinking of the stories told of those who retired to this shrine in "the Dark Ages". Before what was called "the flaming picture of the Chief Angel" these vowed persons would remain three whole days and nights in silent devotion, rapt, so the legends said, far out of the earthly regions and raised to the heavenly places, "to the state of Paradise", so that when they came down again to the valleys and lower places of the world they were as those who had voyaged to the Blessed Isles, since their garments were scented with celestial odours, and about them was the visible shining of light.

The train rushed on through the rich and happy meadows, by the wild thickets, by the shimmering fields of corn, by the old white farms; before his eyes rose that well-remembered and venerable Mynydd Mawr: high upon it he could see the line of straggling beeches and the walls of Cradock's house, gleaming in the sunlight. His heart thrilled at the thought of that which rested there concealed in a dark place, of the

Holy Cup in its glistening veils of samite; it was as yesterday that he bent low before those ghostly splendours, and saw the images of immortal things that shewed in the crystal mirror of the Blessed Work. The Golden Wood resounding with the magic summons of the Bells, the far-lifted sanctuary of Cor-arbennic high above the ninth wave, the vision of the Saints of Britain sailing on the Faery Sea to Avalon: he could scarce see the great dome of the mountain above him, scarce rejoice in the deep woods below, scarce fix his eyes on the white walls by the beeches for the recollection of these clearer marvels that had appeared before him. He felt as though a voice cried to him from that place; the Cup seemed to summon him to kneel once more and to behold new visions.

Cradock's home passed out of sight, and there rose the great wall of Mynydd Maen, and far down to the south Twyn Barlwm, the lofty height that looks far over land and sea, where the wind is like strong wine. He sank back in the seat and wondered how he could have borne that long and dreary exile.

Facti sumus sicut consolati. Venientes autem venient cum exultatione: portantes manipulos suos.

And he wondered still more deeply by what compassions he had been preserved in that house of folly which he had inhabited, which he had entered, helpless and defenceless, a little lonely child. How was it that he had not been ruined utterly, that he had not become a "practical" man, longing for the time when he should be able to do some great work in the world—say, by sitting in the House of Commons. There were lads of his own age, who were already bubbling over with enthusiasm in the cause of Humanity, who were already beginning to count the rewards that really earnest disinterested work for one's fellow-men seldom fails to procure; they pointed to young Haslee, an old Luptonian, who had changed sides twice, and was certain to be in the next Cabinet of his party, though he was barely thirty. Many of the boys, taking the Doctor's solemn warnings to heart, had already made friends who would be useful in later life—useful that is in forwarding them in their desire to Do some Good in the World: ah! how had he escaped from this Cesspool, from the discipline and teaching of the masters and the companionship of the boys without losing his soul for

ever. Through his father's teaching and the mercy of the Compassionate, he said to himself: but what a marvel it was. He had been nine
years at Lupton, and still, and with ever greater awe and adoration he
remembered and venerated the mysteries of the Cup of Teilo Sant!

2.

It was about the middle of the afternoon when he left the local train at
Caermaen station, and strolled idly through the deserted town, where
there had once reigned such splendours and such mysteries. Grass was
growing between the cobblestones at the side of the empty, desolate
streets; an old man, bent double with rheumatism, was slowly crawling
along with the aid of a stick, and seemed the only inhabitant. Ambrose
turned aside and walked by the grass-grown way that led to the Roman
Amphitheatre, and he sat on the old stone stile, looking across the circle of grassy mounds towards the steep wooded hill beyond. There was
no breeze now in this enclosed valley, and no leaf stirred, the trees on
the hillside were as though they were painted, and a shimmer of heat
rose from the grass. He could see the white limestone road winding on
the other side of the river; that too was empty and forsaken. Caermaen
was the city of a byegone day, its life was but a mouldering memory.
The only names over the little shops were strange to him; the bow-
windowed grocery, a famous place in its generation, was shuttered up,
and he had seen a placard on a wall, announcing that at some meeting
about something or other, Captain Tillier-Smith J.P. would be in the
chair. Who was Captain Tillier-Smith? He had never heard of him.

It was curious. He knew well enough that his father's old friends at
Caermaen had died or left the place many years before and that a new
generation of strangers reigned in their stead; yet he felt a certain sorrow in the thought that these old ties had been broken, a certain disappointment that to the welcome of the hills and woods human tones
had not added their friendly voices. The sight of those empty grass-
grown streets, of wide open spaces devoid of life, of houses where
once his father and he had been welcome now in strange hands, of the
unknown name on the Doctor's door—all these signs had uttered
loneliness and had filled him with mourning for the past. He was to
visit strangers, relations, it is true, but he had never seen them; and

Caermaen had suddenly reminded him how utterly alone he was in the great world. Some of the boys were decent fellows enough; but they were a part of the chapter called Lupton. If he could think of that chapter without resentment and sickness it was very well, but it was idle to dream that any of its personages could have any real share in his heart. He was alone, and for the moment he was sad at the thought.

He could not help regathering all the memories and fancies that were associated with the place in his mind. He left his station on the stile and wandered about the empty streets, thinking of pleasant evenings spent long ago in this house or that, of warm welcome and warm comfort, and kind voices of good dead people. There was a little house in a back-street where an old lady—an ancient friend of his family— had once lived. Her teas he remembered with a great affection; she always had a particular cake of which he was very fond, and used to produce afterwards from the cupboard some ingenious and novel game which would amuse him for the rest of the evening. A stone cross marked her place in the churchyard; she had died a year after his father's death. He remembered the pictures that had hung in certain rooms that once had been familiar; what had become of the oil-painting of the Highlander that used to be over the sideboard at The Garth, and where were the green cut-glass vases that had decorated the mantel-piece in the Doctor's drawing-room? The vases were smashed perhaps; but many of the objects that he remembered must be still in being scattered about the earth in strange surroundings. Where was the Pagoda in carved ivory that had stood in a corner of a room at the Castle, where was the Serpent which the old vicar had always used as a text for his recollections of church-gallery orchestras? Was that picture of some incident in the American War of 1812 still the subject of discussion in some strange household? The Trevors had made it into a kind of after-dinner pastime; one was asked if one knew who the American officer dying in his calin under the Stars and Stripes could be, and conversation at once became easy, if slightly imbecile. He liked to think that all these varying objects had somehow escaped the common lot, that they had delighted no strange eyes, lay derelict and despised in no distant sea-side lodgings, mouldered in no shop; rather in the land of the unknown there was a House of Memory in which they were all gathered together, and here the wraiths of the old Caermaen folk met together under the united signs of the Serpent and Pagoda, the Highlander and the Sea Captain. There they discussed to a happy eternity the old fireside stories, found the clue to knotty genealogical problems that had puzzled all their days of mortal life, settled at last the question how Matilda Kirby came to be one of the Williamses of Pontnewydd, and issued in a final and authentic form the true history of Evan Owen and the Red House's marriage to Joan Morris, Penyrhaul. "And after the wedding they went to live at Wiveliscombe, that's all I know"—that used to be the conclusion; but in the House of Memory all doubts would be resolved and the identity of that United States officer would be clearly established. There never had been much uncertainty as to the Highlander: he was Vich dan Vohr, a character in an old romance, once a great favourite. Ah! happy friendly folk; it was certain that there were good suppers in the House of their habitation; and afterwards there was "something hot and comfortable".

He wandered at last over the bridge, and strolled along the old Usk road till from a gate he had a clear view of Caermaen standing above the river, the old white inn with mullioned sixteenth century windows nearest to the yellow water and the wet shining banks, and above, in tiers, the houses rising all bright in the sunlight. Away from the river the north of the town was bordered by stately Lombardy poplars, indeed there were many green leaves within the circuit of the walls; orchards of apples and pears and quince trees, and here and there the more sombre ilex made spaces of refreshment between the huddled roofs. And all about the town the level meadows were spread broad and green, dotted here and there with ancient thorns, and as he leaned over the gate, it was the turn of the tide, and the salt savour came up from the Severn Sea. Far to the north the valley followed the winding river; deep Wentwood, the old forest rose high to the east, to the west there was a maze of rolling hills, bounded by the vast mountain.

*He was gazing on the white walls, luminous in the sunlight, when

---

*[At this point in the ms., Machen has written the following, then crossed it out: "The 'dear [?] Caermaen', the place of pleasant homely memories, of kindly idle things, passed from him as he looked across the foaming, swirling water. Its white walls grew luminous; he thought no more of the worthy dead who had once

the silence of the valley was broken by a man's voice singing as he came along the line from the north. The words, so far as he any words could be distinguished, sounded foreign, and Ambrose looked round with some curiosity. The man came towards him with a swinging stride, and when he saw Ambrose by the gate he stopped his odd song, the tune of which sounded as outlandish as the words. He looked like a sailor, his skin was burnt to the hue of copper by fierce suns; and he carried a bundle on a stick over his shoulder. Ambrose wished him goodday as he was going by, and the man hesitated a moment, and then said:—

"Could you manage the price of a pint? I've tramped thirty miles already, and I fancy I've got a good many more before I get to Cardiff."

Ambrose gave him a shilling, and asked whether he was looking for a ship.

"I'm much obliged to you, sir," he said. "Yes, I want a ship—something easy, to Bordeaux and back would suit me, though I wouldn't mind Trieste"—he called it Try-east.

"You've been abroad a lot?"

"I have. I've been inland too, as well as on board ship: the Levant, India, Persia: all sorts of places at all sorts of jobs. Yes, I've travelled a lot."

"Have you seen any Indian juggling?"

"Lord, yes; plenty. It's all a fake, if you ask me. They're clever, you know, sir; but people tell a lot o' lies about them when all's said. There's that rope trick they talk of; I never seen it, and I never see anybody who did. A man must be drunk to believe nonsense like that—so it seems to me. Though some of them can tell fortunes most wonderful."

"You mean they come true?"

"Yes, I'm certain of it. An Arab fellow that I'd got out of a nasty mess when I was about the Levant taught me a way of his own—so he said—and I never found it fail."

---

dwelt within them. *Locus iste inestimabile sacramentum:* the ancient city where the legions had once assembled, in its deep peace on the summer afternoon—between the green wood and the water floods, circled about with the guarding hills and elms [?]; indeed, an image of the rest and refuge of the soul. This was the town of the old mysteries, where nine churches were set [rest illegible]."— Ed]

"I wish you'd try to tell mine," said Ambrose who was amused by this encounter. "Here's another bob."

The sailor-man was well-enough pleased. He had the potentiality of many pints in his pocket, and the thought, as he said in his own fashion, lightened the burden of the fifteen or sixteen miles to Cardiff. Or certain pints might be foregone, and the balance expended on lodging for travellers; in any case his position was secure. He set down his crimson bundle under the hedge, and taking the stick prepared deliberately for magic. Ambrose sat on the gate, and fixed his eyes on the proceedings; though he felt sure that it would all end in a Fair Woman who had a fortune. Still, the method might be novel.

The wanderer glanced to the road and found as it happened a considerable stretch of smooth sand, which the last rainstorm had washed into a bay of the bank. On this with the end of his stick he very deliberately and carefully drew certain letters of the alphabet, all in capitals. He set them down in an order of his own:—A, B, G, D, H, V, and so forth, ending with T: there were twenty-two in all, and some of them he shaped oddly, because, as he explained, they were not the common letters that the children learned in school. This done, he rolled his eyes impressively, to the huge delight of Ambrose, who felt that he was almost getting his money's worth, and then he asked the number of letters in his client's name. Of this information he made a memorandum on the edge of the sand, and then with the tip of his stick he began to punch the sand with aimless rows of little dents.

It was a long and complicated process; there was much counting and reckoning at the end of it. Some of the punch-marks were smoothed out, and others in odd figures and patterns took their places. He looked up at last with a disquieted air:

"Beg your pardon, sir, but you're English, aren't you?"

"Yes, of course," said Ambrose. "Why?"

"Well, you see you're fixed to the T." He pointed to the letter. "I can't make it out."

"Why, what does that mean?"

The man shuffled uneasily.

"Shut up in a prison or something of that kind, I believe." He lied with difficulty and confusion, and took up his bundle again.

"It's nonsense, of course, sir, you being an English gentleman. But, there, you don't want to believe in such things; as I said, I expect it's all fake. I must be getting on now, sir, and thank you, I'm sure."

He hurried off towards Caermaen, turning back once at the corner, and looking at Ambrose with startled eyes for a moment, and then he was gone, and Ambrose laughed to himself—evidently some horrid fate which the sailor dared not utter was prophesied for him, and he wondered what it could be. And then while he looked at the letter T on the sand, the words of the Frenchman at the café came into his mind, and he remembered what the old Irish fiddler had said years before. He jumped off the gate and began to run after the sailor, but though he ran through the village as far as the bridge the man was not to be seen, and an old woman sitting at her door told him that no such person had passed by. Indeed the wanderer had anticipated Ambrose's course, and watched the pursuit through a hole in the hedge behind which he lay secure. He did not wish to be forced into explanations, and he cursed the cabala of Ben-something, who, as it happened, was not an Arab at all, but a Levantine Jew.

It was late in the afternoon, and Ambrose strolled once more through Caermaen. It was time to think of the Wern, and he went along the road, beside the river meadows, till he came to a stile that he knew of old; he wondered whether he could remember the way. It led, he knew, by the verges of deep woods, by wild hills and lonely valleys; one passed the ruinous chapel in the middle of the gorse-grown field, and the Soar brook was crossed by a narrow, trembling bridge. The path was but an uncertain thread, for few used it, and the bridge was so masked by the rich growth of dark glossy alders that it was easy to miss the right point.

"The divinations of sailor and fiddler, the prophecy of the Frenchman," said Ambrose, "passed from me when once I entered again those enchanted fields, those woods of most dear recollection. Even before I had turned from the road a procession of happy children met me; they had been flower gathering, for the local flower-show perhaps, and they came towards me, as if they had been participants in some old festival. In front there were two girls who bore great spires of Valerian; I remembered that it grew on the rocky bank a little farther down the road, where in its shadow flowered also the golden St. John's Wood. The children with the Valerian flowers wore such a look of joy—the hair of the one was black, of the other golden—that I forgot the strange significance which the flower thus carried used to bear in Gwent; I suppose indeed that the old symbolism of *canwll gorph* has now become extinct. Behind these two came their companions, boys and girls, bearing their red and yellow, blue and white, but most of all great bunches of creamy meadowsweet that scented all the air. Some, with a pretty fancy, had made spare flowers into twisted garlands which they wore on their bare heads, and they had evidently been by marshy as well as flowery soil, for a few had woven rushes into fantastic shapes, and bore baskets which reminded me of the Mystic Fans carried in another older procession; and one ingenious lad had made of these materials a fearsome looking monster—a species of dragon—which he waved in the air. Last of all came two boys carrying great reeds and flags, gathered by the river bank; and as a flower dropped here and there they left a faint track of blossoms behind them. And just as they passed one of them must have produced his penny whistle, for I heard the faint notes of an old tune piped out as I turned aside from the road, and began to climb the green hill towards the wood.

"And before the boy's uncertain music was lost in the distance, a bird sang to me, darkling, from the shadow of the trees, and after the bird, the ripple of the brook rose up through the still valley, and after the sound of the clear water, there was the whisper of the evening breeze among the leaves of the hedge.

"It seemed as if all the way enchantments beckoned to me. I found that I remembered the path quite well, but again and again I was tempted to go astray, to explore unknown valleys, to climb round and solitary hills, to penetrate into the green light that shone from the recesses of woods that as a boy I had never visited. I wondered what I might not find if I entered that little vale that opened towards the west, half screened by a hazel thicket, and what country should I see if I stood on that hill-top amongst the waving bracken? I regained that afternoon all the sense that I had had in the same land when I was a little boy, the sense of a dweller in a mystic territory, whose every path may lead to fairyland, where magic dwelt in the brooks, in the flowers, in the green woodland, and on the bare turfy height. Only a little was known, a few feet beyond the path might lie the entrance to the enchanted region; that white thorn-bush on the hillside might be the resort of the Three Fairy Birds of Rhiannon; those broken stones might hide the entrance to a cavern filled with Celtic Treasure, with the glad ornaments of old kings and heroes, with the lost books of Merlin's wisdom, and the figures of his spells. But I persevered on my way, and the sun was still above Mynydd Maen when I stood again before the door of the Wern, and said my *salve.*"

3.

Ambrose Meyrick always asserted that he had written Twelve Books concerning his Visit to the Wern. These books, he said, formed a great Prose Romance, intermingled with certain Songs, Mysteries, Episodes, and Parables; he has been heard to declare that he must shortly set about the revision of the manuscript and prepare this *magnum opus* for the press. He even quoted titles of some of the books on occasion; there were the *Sylvia in Sylva,* the *Mysterium Calicis,* the *Hypnerotomachia,* the *Nuptiae Mysticae,* the *Mons Magorum,* the *Nox Illuminans,* the *Cantus Planus,* and one or two others that have vanished from all record. It is, however, very doubtful whether the Great Romance ever existed in so tangible a form as manuscript; it is with more probability conjectured to have been the reflection of a glowing dream that was always shining vaguely in Ambrose's mind, which he hoped perhaps to reduce to a corporal shape at some indefinite opportunity. He felt, it is believed, that the theme must be treated more than worthily, with a rare and curious eloquence; and he wished for a time when he should feel within him fit force and inspiration for the carrying out of this great design. As it is, in place of complete books there are only notes and fragments; and of these all possible advantage must be taken. Unfortunately, or fortunately—it is hard to say which—these jottings and memoranda are expressed in such a manner that the meaning is often excessively obscure, as was evident when they were mischievously submitted to the judgment of a well-known authority in literary questions—the famous author of *Get on—and be Quick about It!* This gentleman wrote that there was "capital stuff" in the MS. "All that it wants," he said, "is a little arrangement, and a liberal use of the Blue Pencil. With some telling illustrations I think it would do well as a Christmas Book for young children." Why not indeed? *Gulliver's Travels*, by the genial, kindly Dean of St. Patrick's, is to be found on every well-regulated nursery bookshelf; and Ambrose's notes do certainly suggest the atmosphere of a fairy-tale.

So far as this famous visit can be regarded from the common outlook it seems to have been a very pleasant one. The old house was just the same as he had recollected it; no alterations had been made without or within. The two sides of an unfinished quadrangle in grave grey stone still fronted to west and south, looking across the broad terraced lawn, the sunken lane, and the marshy land, across the winding brook and the wooded hills, glancing on one side towards Wentwood, the wilderness of leaves, and on the other to the great wall of Mynydd Maen. The stone mullions and transoms were still there in the windows; no attempt had [been] made to reform the diamond quarries into plate glass planes. It was old tinged glass, full of whorls, and flaws, and inequalities; and it shed a dim, soft light on the old furniture and the old pictures, both dating for the most part to the middle of the eighteenth century. As chance visitors had said: "if one wanted to live in an old curiosity shop, one had better do so at once; though sensible people would prefer real chairs and tables, and windows that one could see through." These people were still mid-Victorians in those days; now their houses are furnished throughout in bad imitations of eighteenth century furniture, known to the owners under the comprehensive name of "Chippendale". It does not matter; there are many other subjects left for them to talk balderdash about—books, pictures, music, religion. Imbecility, ignorance, impudence will never lack their due pasture; and for some good but obscure reasons the imbeciles and scoundrels always seem to "get off" scot-free. Wilson and Lockhart for example are still respected names.

Yes; it was all the same. There was a little book with a curious binding in stamped gold still on a side-table, just as he remembered it; and while he admired this reverence his cousin, Mr. Vaughan, came in, cordial but evidently nervous. He was a short, thick old man with a square white beard, at which he tugged in moments of excitement, and there was a slight stammer in his voice as he made Ambrose welcome to his old home.

"You will want to come permanently, I suppose, before long," he said, "we shall be sorry to leave. I admired your father; I have tried to keep everything as it was in his day."

"You have been wonderfully good," said Ambrose. He pointed to the book. "I remember that book, just in that place when I was a little boy."

It was evident that Ambrose was not a "loud boy"; his voice was low, and he did not shout all the evening. Sylvia Vaughan, a dark girl, appeared just before dinner, and afterwards they sat out on the lawn. Mr. Vaughan was pleased to find that Ambrose smoked; he always said that it was one of the greatest proofs of the insensate folly of all schoolmasters that they prohibited tobacco, since a mild sedative was evidently the very thing that the average schoolboy wanted.

"Wild hearts must be hocussed for the safety of the public," he said: "schoolboys are wild hearts: therefore, they should be hocussed. *Conclusum est in Barbara.*" He was ready to prove his minor premiss by innumerable instances; one would have thought that he had "specialised" in schoolboys all his days. In reality all these remarks were generalisations from a noisy young nephew who had stayed with the Vaughans many years before.

But Ambrose was quiet and talked sense; he had some information about the existence of the pointed arch in Ireland, in churches that were certainly of the eleventh century, and possibly of the tenth. Mr. Vaughan was most interested; he said he could not quite agree with the conclusion of Ambrose's father—that the existence of these arches shewed that Public Architecture, properly so called, was of Celtic origin: still the point was highly important. And then they talked about rhyme; was it brought into Europe from the East or not? Ambrose ventured to think that it was an independent growth; he quoted the Easter Sequence *Victimae Paschali* as an instance of rhyme in a very rudimentary state. Then back to Celtdom; what was the deduction to be drawn from those curious references to the introduction of the chalice in the *Percival* and in the *Leabhar Breac?* How far were certain features of the Celtic Church and Celtic Ornament to be set down to Egyptian influence?

The night was so calm and windless that when a servant brought out a two-branched silver candlestick and set it on the little table beside them, the flame rose clear and unflickering. "God send us the light of Heaven," said Mr. Vaughan when the candles were brought, and Ambrose remembered that the use of this ejaculation was a custom that George Herbert's Country Parson liked very well. The faint glow shone about Sylvia's face, it was as if a hidden glory flowed from her as she sat smiling; well pleased that her father had found at last some one to talk to. On the one side was her dark beauty, her hair drawn down from her forehead over her ears in a style that was then thought uncouth, unfashionable, and *hideous;* and on the other was the shadowy valley of the Soar, whence the fragrance of the meadowsweet ascended with the fragrance of the wood, whence, at intervals, rose the lonely piping of some bird. Soft from afar came the whirring note of the fern-owl; he was deep in the bracken on the high vague hill towards the south; and without ceasing they heard the murmur of the brook.

Mr. Vaughan was quite overjoyed. His few neighbours thought him "a very queer old man, who was always reading old books"—a vice from which they were singularly free. He on his side thought them Noddles and Boobies; and perhaps there was a good deal to be said for both opinions. But he often longed for some one with whom he could talk about the many outlandish subjects which interested him; and Ambrose was more than satisfactory. But how long could he go on like this? Would he not begin to expatiate presently on his achievements at the Games? Horbury had laid stress on Ambrose's athletic abilities; he would certainly shew how to meet Boggler's bowling; probably the fit would take him quite suddenly, and he would begin to shout and rush about, or perhaps he would illustrate his theory of drop-kicking with the little table serving instead of the ball. But Ambrose went on smoking quite placidly; he was speaking with some enthusiasm of the beauty of old French, and maintaining that the modern language, in spite of its swift and exquisite charm, had lost a great deal by having no equivalent to the English Bible.

"In fact," he said, "at times I almost feel as if there were something to be said for the English Reformation. Not much of course: suppose that in every deceased Leper a surgeon could dissect out a beautiful jewel—there would be *something* to be said for Leprosy."

Mr. Vaughan grinned with delight.

"Lupton must be a wonderful school," he said. "You went in a lot for Games, Horbury tells me?"

He wanted to know the worst.

His cousin looked gravely at him. He could not conceive that such a sensible old man would take the slightest interest in the School Games. So he assumed indirectly.

"As I was coming along in the train today I passed a field with a lot of goats in it—a good many of them were quite young. I assure you, sir, I never saw anything quite so fantastic or quite so jolly as the sport these kids were having: leaping yards into the air to clear a small stream about a foot wide, stopping dead in the middle of a run because there was an oystershell or a bit of glass in the way, butting at each other with such solemnity, such an evident appreciation of the 'rules' that it made me roar with laughter."

"Yes," said old Mr. Vaughan, "what then?"

"Well, I've seen half-a-dozen dirty little boys having a splendid time with a lamp-post and two jackets as wickets; and two sticks, and a big bundle of paper as bats and ball in the back-streets of Lupton."

"Quite so." Mr. Vaughan's pipe gurgled with enjoyment. "Proceed."

"And farm-labourers in a good old-fashioned skittle alley with lots of good beer—they enjoy themselves too. But if you were to paint the kids with coloured stripes, or made rules about the weight of the paper ball, or insisted on all farm-labourers up to the age of eighty playing skittles twice a day—then I think the whole thing would become a beastly nuisance. How the farm-labourers especially would hate it, if the parson brought in allusions to the dry alley regularly every Sunday, and drew lessons from 'The Man who always takes the Heaviest Cheese' and 'The Man who can never Finish his Beer in Time', and mixed up the Skittles with the Kings of Israel and Judah! And fancy the small boys being harried to the lamp-post and thrashed severely if they didn't 'play up'. Of course the goats wouldn't stand it for a moment—even if they were instructed in the valuable formative influence on the goat-character of high jumping and butting."

Old Mr. Vaughan roared. He made much more noise than the loud schoolboy of his dreams.

"Come in," he said. "I have some really old whiskey. Kiss him good night, Sylvia," he added as they stood in the hall, "we are going to sit up talking till any hour you please."

Ambrose blushed scarlet as the beautiful Sylvia bent forward and kissed his cheek as a matter of course; it was clear that he had discovered the Earthly Paradise. He bent low and took her hand and kissed her finger-tips, and she smiled at him with kind eyes.

The old man and he went to the study, where the servant had set the whiskey ready. All the old books were in their places, but Mr. Vaughan had utilised a vacant space to set up a large book-case with his own special volumes. It was an extraordinary collection: the famous Ducange, the works of Duns Scotus and several other of the Schoolmen, collections of Rhymed Latinity, some books on Mediaeval Costume, a great array of Graal Romances, Monastic Records, one tall Gradual splendidly illuminated on parchment leaves, an *Histoire des Filles de Joie au Moyen Age,* and a Manual of the Tarot: these were a few of the oddities that caught Ambrose's eye, as he glanced about him before sitting down.

"It is like a great wood," he said as they poured out their drink, pointing to his cousin's bookcase. "Everything is to be found in it from the oak to the scarlet fungus, and one hears the bubbling of the wells, the dripping of cold springs, the sound of the wind, and the rustling of little furry beasts in the undergrowth."

"Yes, it is an amusing collection, isn't it? I find them all useful for the Romance I am writing."

Ambrose tried to hear more about this Romance, but his cousin would say nothing. It was not till some days had passed that Mr. Vaughan trusted his cousin with the secret of the Romance. He was writing it in a kind of "faked" Low Latin; and though his scheme was not much more foolish than that on which William Morris wrote his Romances in Old English of his own invention; yet Ambrose had much ado to contain himself. Indeed, the idea rather appealed to him, there was a fantastic unreasonableness about it that was after his own heart; and yet it was so funny too that he went for a walk directly after he heard this great matter. He walked briskly, puckering his cheeks all the way, and when at last he was a mile or so from the Wern he lay down and rolled on the grass, roaring and shrieking and bellowing with laughter till he was quite faint. Old Mr. Vaughan had shewed him a leaf of his ms. and he had seen a chapter-title—Haga de Jardinio—which meant The Garden Hedge: it was, somehow, more than he could bear.

Yet: if he listened to the old man, his scheme seemed absolutely logical; it was quite impossible to resist the cogency of his arguments.

"You see," he said, "in the first place I, personally, regard the English Language as a quite impossible medium of expression—for the present that is. Of course there must come an end to the present corruption. Liberal and Conservative politicians, Anglican Bishops, Dissenting Preachers, Wealthy Manufacturers, and Journalists will not be suffered to rule the land for ever. When the Politicians and the Manufacturers are hanged, when the Bishops and the Preachers are burnt—by the way, I should make the fire slower for the Bishops—*then* perhaps English may become fit once more for the use of a man of letters. The journalists? Oh! I forgot; they will have to eat their own words of course—the worst torture of all! But now: do you know that a man who doesn't split his infinitives or use *like* for *as*, is regarded as a very affected person, a kind of Euphuist? They say Literature is meant for the People, and the People have no time for hair-splitting over words and sentences: this is a Democratic Age, you know, and the People, I suppose, must have 'darned hot stuff'—or Forty Million Englishmen will know the reason why. Exaggerating? Nothing of the kind; you can't have read the papers or you wouldn't talk such nonsense. Exaggerating? Look what this Ass says, this Gigantic, Gargantuan, Super-Imbecile Jolthead! Look, I have cut him out; I should like to cut him up! Do you see that he says that Keats and Ruskin were so full of their subject that they had no time to consider themselves as literary craftsmen?

"Who is going to write English when Slugs like that have crawled all over the language? Why, it's like finding a Toad, a Blindworm, Three Snails, and a dozen—well—Woodlice in a meat-pie, and then finishing it.

"Here he goes again—'the unfailing instinct of the great public', authors should make it their aim to preach to this great public! He pretends to think, this Lunatic, that what he calls the Great Public have some voice and authority in literature! About as much of either as the passengers on a Liner have over the navigation of the ship! No; it's quite out of the question for a self-respecting man to have anything to do with such a literary world as this. Therefore, my only course is to write my Romance in Low Latin; a fine tongue, a most flexible medium, a synthesis of the ancient world and the modern, possessing the sonority and splendour of the Old Latin mingled with the life and movement of the new languages. It has never had 'journalism' written in it, and it never will."

Ambrose ventured to put a cautious question as to the public to which Mr. Vaughan hoped to appeal, and his cousin pointed out that he would speak to the learned over the whole world, since he would be using a language which was understood by every one with the slightest pretensions to education.

"I shall be read by Frenchmen, Germans, Mexicans, Russians, Swedes, and citizens of Guatemala: I shall appeal to an expert audience from which the populace are entirely excluded: I shall restore the art of letters to its proper dignity as a great craft—a mystery. Oh, there are innumerable advantages in my plan—for example I saw in a review the other day that it was a pity Mr. Thingummy, who wrote so well, should produce a book which could not possibly be put into the hands of a young girl. I shall escape all that; no one would dream of placing a Low Latin Romance in the hands of a young girl or an old one either."

He began to talk of the beauties of his medium, of the strange music which it gave so readily: "It is like an old violin," he said, "it is permeated with melody, it sounds and echoes with the enchanted song of the ages when it came into being. It chants of crenellated walls, of great cathedral glories, it has the savours of Gascon wine drunk in painted taverns, it smells of incense, it has seen the rich wonders of old cities, it knows the dimness of the cloister, the trumpets and the clamour of the tournament, the rapture of the hidden saints, the revelry of flowery festivals. And mark: it has never been tainted by the defilement of popularity, it has never been the means by which the mob has uttered its foolishness and its wickedness: all that is of good in the people it has assimilated, and yet it has always worn the garments of the Latin Life: it is a peasant, if you please, but a peasant who has received the *sacerdotum,* and is entitled to wear the vestments of the church. Nobody has ever been 'interviewed' in Low Latin, and in it Leading Articles never will be written. And speaking of music: you see this song I have just written in the Phrygian mode. Look at those neumes; you observe the peculiar shape of the *podactus,* and the *bi-verga?* I shall insist on an exact reproduction: it is most important."

And Ambrose went out and hid himself in remote places, giving way to inextinguishable mirth. It might be all very true, it might be, as his cousin said, that the chosen medium was the exact equivalent in language to the Gothic in Architecture, the marriage of the Latin genius to the Teutonic and Celtic: yet it was all a farce in five acts, an elaborate and storied absurdity.

There were many pleasant days and nights at the Wern; he went for long walks with his cousin Sylvia, revisiting many revered places of ancient pilgrimage; he looked up authorities for the old man, and one day delighted him by solemnly burning, in the face of the Pig Walter Mapp, his cricket bat and flannels. The days passed in ceaseless sunshine, all the nights were laden with the odour of the dewy fields and the running brook, of the procession of leaves and flowers.

4.

In the Note-book marked "The Wern", there is a kind of preface which relates, presumably, to that great Romance which has been mentioned, to the tale which Ambrose was always hoping to tell—someday.

I feel sure—it begins—that all Art should be profoundly ethical; if it is to deserve the capital A, if it is to be Art at all. I am told that this point has been insisted on lately; and I am very glad of it. One hopes that these sermons will have some result, that people who are worthy of better things will cease to produce the horrible "manufactured article" which has grown so common of late, which so far from having any ethical relation, is patently the result of a desire to please a great number of tenth-rate intelligences and to make a big income. I suppose it is hardly necessary to say that work produced under such conditions, and with such beggarly aims, can have no conceivable relation with any system of morals known to man. I suppose that a fetish priest in an African swamp would reject an offering made in such a spirit as unclean and detestable—as very bad medicine!

Let us by all means and in all ways insist on the High Morality which is demanded of all art and of every artist; it is delightful (and surprising) to hear that this is being done; it is one of the best signs of the times that I have heard of. I am glad that the tide has turned; that Literature and Painting are once more to take their true position—which after all is a higher one than that of the Thimble-Rigger and

Company Promoter. If we once have the writer of books and the painter of pictures recognising that their work is done under the highest ethical sanctions for the highest ethical ends, we shall soon hail an *Instauratio Magna* in the Arts.

Of course, I take it for granted that the Ethics in question are thoroughly *human* ethics—that they relate to the life of that most exalted miracle that is called man in the most exalted regions of which he is capable. I feel satisfied of this, because writers who are taking up the high standpoint of which I have been told, who are ready, doubtless, to face the jeers and sneers of readers whose conception of morals is chiefly derived from the lessons given in the Dissenting Sunday School, writers such as these, I say, are of course aware of the mystic wonder with which man has been crowned, they know that he is permitted to look into mysteries which are hidden from the Holy Angels. Man, it may be said, is called upon to sing a perpetual Mass, to offer a continual Sacrifice. There is a beautiful passage in Pater's *Marius*. It is a description of the Eucharist of the Early Christians; Marius saw the offerings of the faithful, the bread and wine and oil, and was struck with the exquisite symbolism by which the dull, dead matter was, as it were, borne up to heaven, transmuted with a quickening word, consecrated to the service of a great Mystery. But, in truth, this high and especial service, apart; such offering should be of daily, nay hourly obligation. It would be a great work to investigate and enumerate all the wonderful privileges and offices of man—perhaps there are many which have been forgotten, a few even yet to be discovered—but surely this Mystical and Universal Priesthood must be among the highest of his prerogatives. It is his right and duty to offer not only the Bread and Wine of the Eucharist; but all the Universe! Day by day, at sunrise and evening, in the darkness of the night he is bound to say:

Jube haec perferri per manus sancti Angeli tui in sublime altare tuum, in conspectu divinae majestatis tuae.

Every day he should secretly utter the prayer:

And do Thou, uncovering the veils of enigmas which mystically surround this holy rite; make them gloriously manifest to us, and fill our spiritual eyes with ineffable light; and having cleansed our poverty from every pollution of the flesh, make it worthy of this fearful and dread hierurgy.

What are "haec", what is this "holy rite". Why "these things" are the whole world, from the clod to the stars, all sounds and sights and colours, all heights and depths, all rivers and seas, rain and snow and frost and wind, the voice of the thunder, and the breeze in the brake. And not only these; but all sensation and emotion, all thought and all desire, all joy and grief, the raptures and the longings of the soul, the venoms and black poisons of life also: for in this Rite there is a Transmuting Word which can change these latter into golden and most precious elixirs. This is the perpetual Mass of all Humanity, which, as I say, we are all bounden to offer according to the measure of our gifts; we are to bring the whole universe to the Supernal Altar, praying that the "veils of enigmas" may be uncovered, that the transmutation may be effected, that the Great Work may be accomplished, that the Graal may be revealed. Let us consider a moment. What is Lincoln Cathedral but a heap of stones dug out of the earth and "offered", and transfigured into mystery and splendour. There are stones of the same sort in a Stink Factory, in a Protestant meeting-house, in an ugly modern street, in a railway station. Again; here is an extract from a Dissenting Tract called: "Jesus and Company, Ltd."

CHAIRMAN.—The Almighty Himself.

MANAGER.—The Lord Jesus.

SECRETARY.—The Holy Spirit and Comforter.

HEAD OFFICES.—Beulah Land.

BRANCH OFFICES.—Thornhill Church.

But this horror, this foulness, is made out of words, and words are the material used in:—

> Round thee blow, self-pleached deep,
> Bramble roses, faint and pale,
> And long purples of the dale.
> > Let them rave.
> These in every shower creep
> Thro' the green that folds thy grave.
> > Let them rave.

One man sees the earth and devotes it to "industrialism"; another man, who sees the same earth, fills the Turner room at the National Gallery.

What a hierurgy then is this which from matter, in itself nothing, capable indeed of serving the worst and basest ends, can effect the great miracle of Beauty, raising the dead stones into a shrine of glory, making the common words into a wonderful poem. Indeed *gloria et honore coronasti eum,* giving him the power of this great magistery.

I take it for granted then, that when Ethics are insisted on as the basis and the end of all art, the word is to be taken in its very highest sense, that the ethics in question are to be supremely *human* ethics, concerned with man in his highest exaltation. I take this for granted, because I cannot for a moment conceive that any writer out of an idiot asylum would insist on art being in the popular and vulgar sense moral, that is, the conveyance through an unsuitable medium of a copybook maxim. The "coloured supplements" are often "moral" in this sense, and in the fiction of the Reverend E. P. Roe it is difficult to find a page without its "lesson", duly pointed: one need not say that such "art" as this is not art at all, and is in the highest sense profoundly and bestially immortal and degraded. The Venus of Milo is one of the greatest Moralities that man ever conceived and executed; the little coloured statuette of the child feeding the kitten out of a saucer is a filthy outrage on artistic ethics. So when I hear that the Ethical Basis of Art is being fervently advocated; I am delighted, because I am certain that the word cannot be used in a wrong sense; "Ethical Art" cannot possibly be meant to refer to imbecilities which are infinitely below the artistic standard of the most degraded savages.

I am glad too, because, once this high view of art is accepted, we shall hear no more of that hideous nonsense about books or pictures being of "no practical use", of "no practical interest". One does not exactly know what meaning the anthropoids who write thus attach to the word practical; but one is forced to suppose that they are repeating in another form the dicta of an able animal named Macaulay, who said that the Platonic Philosophy was of no use, because it had not led to any inventions which increased the comforts and conveniences of life. *Pour être vraiment grand it faut être l'inventeur du Nouveau Cabinet hygiénique et*

lleluia! I have no doubt the Philosophy of the Learned Pig is a very good one—for the Learned Pig. I am sure that that amiable (and in his own say, sagacious) animal would sternly denounce as unpractical any one who hung his stye with Old Masters, and recited to him the Works of Homer while he dined. But I object to his (probable) opinions being adopted as the final standards of literary and artistic criticism. But if I ever write the Romance I dream of so often, if I ever finish the "Sylvia", I shall be prepared for the old sentence—it will be censured as "unpractical", because it teaches no useful arts, it will not treat of the cheapest method of converting gangrened pork into sausages, nor will it facilitate the poisoning off of our superfluous children by means of tuberculous milk. Certainly not a book for sturdy practical men, for the descendants of the stout old Roundheads! Need I say that "master" will have none of it; "master" will pronounce it to be profoundly immoral, as he licks his greasy chops over the fat bacon and the full and full-flavoured report of the "West End Scandal" in the *Daily Something.* "Master" is a strong believer in the Liberty of the Press, but, as a moral man, he cannot and will not tolerate impure and licentious literature.

It is probable that if Ambrose had set himself to writing his book, instead of writing about it, the "Sylvia" would have been brought to a happy ending. As it is there are but odd notes and fragments, mere rough sketches for the tale that was never to be written. The following excerpt is chosen for its intimate bearing on Ambrose Meyrick's inner life. It is written partly in the third person, partly in the first; here it is reduced for the sake of uniformity to the third, and a good deal of "editing" has been found necessary, many of the sentences being incomplete. It was written, presumably, in a sudden burst of energy, and the words and scrawled across the page in a hasty untidy hand.

He lived, then, the happy life. In that enclosed valley, under the shelter of the hill, by the singing brook he felt as though after all those intolerable years in the house of torment and folly and lies he had entered into the Great Dream which is the golden hope or the high memory of all who know. It is called a Dream, not because it is unreal, but because in that state, as in a happy and well-directed dream, desire and fulfilment are one: silver moons can be summoned down to earth to bathe in haunted wells, rose gardens blossom amidst the snows, and singing choirs are not wanting, nor wine, nor faery feasts. The world, as it were, is melted in the crucible of a wonderful alchemy, it is dissolved in the throes of a mighty transmutation, and the hard and stubborn rock is once more that plastic mirror in which all things are seen, and all visions are realised. The doctors of the mysteries have many names for this state, they have indicated its existence under various and strange figures, and they have described the method of its attainment by symbolisms which are, perhaps designedly, confused and confusing—though of all the veils of concealment that have been hung before the portal of this palace, none is thicker nor more impenetrable than that which is woven with strange and fantastic images of deceit, and is called Occultism. For those who pay more than a moment's attention to this veil (which should be brushed harshly aside) are captured by its curious follies and, while they trace its pentacles and sigils, suppose that they have attained the object of their desires. It is doubtless well that this is so, since those who would gaze on such things have uncleansed eyes that are not fit to behold beauty.

The true guides, as has been said, describe what they know by many and varying signs; and the books in which these matters are contained lie open for all men to read and understand—if they will and if they can. Thus the secret is most safe, though there is no pledge of secrecy, and indeed, very often, no hint that the mysteries are being painted before our eyes. The secret is safe, because these writings have always two senses, the inner and the outer, and the uninitiated never fail to choose the outer meaning (which, indeed, has its own beauty of the lower order), and would think any one who declared that there was an inner meaning to be mad; they may even be told of this secret significance and to them it is as if one pretended to find words in the wind.

It is declared that there are many ways of approach to the gate of the Great Dream. Some, it is supposed, have found the way through a great sorrow, others through a great joy, and again there are the paths of Renunciation and Conformity. It may be also that year by year a drop of water falls into the cup till at last all suddenly it bubbles over, and the thirsty are refreshed by these runnings which they never looked for, since a drop of water is but a little thing. But in the day of overflowing they say *Vidi aquam* etc.

It is not denied that there are truly many greater things than this state, since indeed it is not the end of the journey, but rather a place of refreshment by the way, as the shadow of a great rock in a dry and thirsty land, it is a refuge from the burning and feverish heats, from the hail-storms and the fire-showers, from the deadly cold of ice and snow. *Ibi fons vivus, fons immortalis, aqua non amara, ibi vere floret Rosa Rosarum in horto incluso.* And though it be not the City which is the end of the journey; no man can deny its great wonders, nor is he at first ready to believe that they can be surpassed. Ambrose had heard hints of this place long before; he had thought indeed, though he was in great error, that he had attained it, when he quoted the saying of the Anointed Bard: "With the bodily lips I receive the drink of mortal vineyards; with spiritual understanding wine from the garths of the undying. May the Great Angel intercede for me that these be mingled in one cup." But that which he enjoyed was but a natural ecstasy, which was permitted him because he sinned in ignorance, and not from malice, nor against the light.

Now, however, he was astonished beyond all imagination to find both within and without matters that he had never so much as dreamed of, which indeed he would never have believed unless he had had this experience. He was less foolish than before, or rather, knowing the evil he had done, he was slow to credit the compassions that were passed upon him; he was humble, with great cause for the deepest humility, and knew himself to be more worthy of the fire than of the unction. Yet he was forced to say, though his lips trembled with unworthiness: *Impingnasti in oleo caput meum;* for truly sense consorted with spirit, and that which was below was as that which was above.

> *Hortus odoribus affluet omnibus, hic Paradisus*
> *Plenaque cantica, plenaque gratia, gaudia, risus.*

He would gladly say more as to these miracles, but he is forbidden to utter another word, and fears lest he has said too much and has spoken too plainly already. For the secret way is a way of paradox, and those who seek it because it is secret, or for the joys that they believe it will afford, will most assuredly either find nothing, or that which is worse than nothing. It is hard to say, and hard to understand; but there is a sense in which it may be said that those who seek shall not find. So let them first consider what matter it is that they seek.

Ambrose then lived at the Wern in such happiness that even if it were permitted him, he could never say enough. And for one thing he was ever after unceasingly grateful. If there could be a sun which set, and yet left its radiance and afterglow to shine all through the night, illuminating the darkness, to this his condition could be compared, for though he went out from the House of Rest and Refreshment, the knowledge he had gained there never left him; and when afterwards he met persons who affirmed that thirst was a delusion of the senses and that there was no such thing as water in the world, how could he be at all moved by them? He had been thirsty, and he had found a well (*fons vivus, aqua regenerans*); and consequently all the finest and most cogent arguments against the existence of water were to him but a curious excess of foolishness, and indeed very singular, as if on a battlefield, wounded wretches, parched and burning with horrible desire, should shriek out continuously that it was impossible to suppose for a moment that such a thing as water ever had been or could be.

Now he was indeed laden and overladen with benefits. For besides that which has been hinted at he received the great marvel and miracle of love.

It was not many days before Sylvia and he saw in each other's eyes the completion of earthly desires. Sylvia's father, busied with his books and papers, sent them out together in the fields and woods, and often all the day they were together, searching out old paths and new, wandering far over the hills, pressing up the steep sides of the mountain, alone on the endless waste of the summit, severed it seemed from all the turmoil of the world on that wild high plain, set with grim limestone rocks, where the unceasing wind sang as it were with the strings of a great harp. Or there were lower heights all aflower with thickets of golden gorse, and here in some sheltered cove of the unshorn bushes they would rest in the sunlight, hearing the clear wind and the clearer lark above them, in that fine and delicate air, scented with the multitude of the yellow blossoms. They loved to find these hidden places, to which sometimes narrow paths, worn by the sheep, led with many and intricate windings, like the turnings and returnings of a labyrinth, and once within the heart of the maze they would sit at ease, alone with one another, speaking of many things, while the white clouds floated across the sky, and the high wind sang. There were other days devoted to the wilder region of the north, beyond the territory of the Mountain of the Apparition, where the little town rests in the hollow between great hills, between sharp peaks on the one side and a huge dome on the other, where the Gavenny flows into the Usk. Beyond this town there is a way up a steep hillside, through a wood of dwarf oak-trees, and presently one is aware that one has entered into the world of the mountains, for they stand about on every side, and reach far and far, beyond and beyond into the deep heart of Wales. Here then it is as if one looked upon a sea of wine, for the great purple hillocks, heather covered, roll on and follow one another like Atlantic waves; there are green islands of giant bracken there, many fountains of cold water, many swift streams rushing over glittering boulders: there the singing of falling water never ceases in the land of the slopes and valleys below the wine-dark billows of heather. Again, Sylvia led him to the country called The Moors, a strange level plain of marshland and water-dyke and sea-blown fantastic trees that stretches all along the banks of the yellow Severn where it washes the land of Gwent. They wandered up the green alleys of Wentwood; it was "a day of the veil" as the old poets of Gwent called such weather.

> The High Lord Almighty, ruler of Heaven's fair mansion
> Where blessed guests feast for ever, drinking wine of the undying,
> Fashioned the mystery of the world out of precious elements.
> Gold was assigned to the Sun, dominating all regions,
> Golden are Dawn and Sunset, golden is the last reward of the soul.
> The Moon is silver, of silver the multitude of the stars
> And white clouds, and glittering waters, and the mists that arise from them.
> But I have seen the Day of the Veil, in which both elements are mingled
> When the Great Luminary is suspended in a silver Lantern.
> I have seen also a shining peace of the spirit.

They set out very early in the morning, by hushed lanes, by woods dripping with the odours of the summer night, by paths through gleaming dewy fields, by the meadowsweet way, where a tiny brook made a winding flowery procession across the grass. All the world was tinged with silvery light; not a cloud appeared in the sky, only a shining canopy; as the veil grew thin a clear glittering light would sparkle in the fields or in the woods, as if green trees and green grass underwent a white purification, a filtered ray would illuminate for a moment a bough in the luminous shadow, and a sudden gleam would touch the river, and blossom on the bare hillside far beyond.

They were fishing for salmon as Sylvia and Ambrose crossed the grey ancient bridge, and he told her the story of Elphin the son of

Gwyddno Garanhir, where he was exiled from the delights of Britain. In an evil land was Elphin exiled where there was no green thing, nor any pleasant shadow under the tree of the wood, not the flowing of bright streams, nor the bubbling of wells. Rocks and grey deserts and burning sands, abounding in scorpions, were all about him, and his heart was sad because he was ignorant of the way of return, nor could he discover the track that led to the isle of Britain. But he came at last to the shore, where the grey sea rolled in to the land, and as he stood there desolate, the fish swam in the billows, and the birds flew over the billows, and the wind blew chill on the rocks, and the sky was overclouded, and the rain came hissing down, cold and bitter as death. And as he stood there, shuddering, he heard the salmon in the sea crying to one another: "Why should we stay here; let us away to Penvro", "These waters are inclement; let us swim to Gwlad Morgan", "What delight in the grey water; let us begone to the refuge of Gwent": and every salmon leapt in the billows, but one great fish proclaimed: "It is necessary that we await the Coracle of the Blessed Company." Then saw Elphin a glowing and a shining on the deep; then saw Elphin the holy vessel filled with the perfumed glorious company of the saints. Like a strong swan it beat aside the waves, speeding like an arrow it rushed over the billows, blown by the wind of heaven; and a light as of a burning rose flamed on its masthead—

Ambrose told no more; he said he had forgotten the rest. They rested for a while on the grey bridge; he was thinking of old dreams and fancied that he heard above the course of the waters the echo of the saints' bell, thrilling and ringing from beyond the verge of the world.

They entered all the wild green region of the wood, which is filled with enchantments. To the south, the city of the legions and the issues of the Usk into the billows of the sea, to the north the river streamed like dim silver between unshaken reeds and still blossoms, past the entrances of leafy dells and hollows, under the shadows of many silent woods. As they ascended, the mountain appeared between the breaks in the leaves, and through the veil a white gleam shone on Mynydd Mawr, and Ambrose thought it lit on that house where the Cup of Teilo was preserved, and sure he was then that the golden voice of the Vessel came to him on the air, with certain words that he might never utter nor make known to mortal. He asked Sylvia whether she had heard any sound, but she had heard nothing except the pouring of the water of the wayside fountains.

They deserted the road and sought the inmost recesses of the wood, by paths of smooth soft turf, by beechen alleys. The day before there had been a great heat, and the sun had sunk, like a palpitating rose, into the mountain, and the sky had deepened to a dark and glorious violet, clear and glowing; so now on every blade of grass the dew lay misty, shimmering in the light of the veil, as if the earth were spread with fine green samite. Now they came to the highest ridge of the wood, and trod the green causeway that once had been the way of the Eagles; on the one side they saw the rolling hills bounded by the mountain wall, on the other they looked down into the deeps and the heights and all the green billows of Wentwood, as it sank into the level. There was a hollow beneath them where the ground was marshy, and there the mist of the night still lay thick, like a white lake, with green, leafy shore all around it. They sat on a fallen tree, and gazed on the wonder of Wentwood, across the level, across the yellow sea. Ambrose sighed as though his heart were healed; he drew a deep breath of the sweetness of the wood.

He remembered little else of that day's adventure. They made their way at last to the moors, by many winding tracks, by forest deep, by wild bare land, by leafy lane, and by that strange old village that stands in the place of a golden city, bowered in orchards, sunny on the slope, between the wood and the sea. And in the evening, as they returned, suddenly the veil vanished; they saw the deep rose-gardens of the sunset, all the world transmuted in the crucible of red light, so that every leaf was but a petal of the Great Rose, and a crimson river flowed down to the ruddy walls of Caermaen. Unawares, they took each other's hands, as this miracle was performed, and like children they walked together as the grey night descended.

Ambrose finished the story of Elphin as they drew near to the Wern. He said that he was taken up into the Ship of the Holy Ones, that then he saw all the marvels of the world, for they came to the faery isle "beyond the glassy floods", and at last returned with a Divine Treasure to the havens of Britain, where all men knew that Elphin had been in the state of Paradise, for his garments were perfumed and odorous as with many spices of Arabia.

5.

It is odd enough that when Ambrose's Note-book was submitted, as has been stated, in no very respectful spirit to the judgment of an eminent literary authority, the little episode of Elphin and the Magic Ship, as he called it, was one of the points most emphasised in the great man's very courteous letter. "This story in particular," he advises, "should be written up for all it is worth. Is the Legend really an old one? Would it be possible to get up a discussion as to its sources? Anyhow, it should be expanded, and I know a man who could do some capital coloured plates to illustrate it." This emphasis is odd, because, as it happens, Ambrose returns to the tale himself, and illustrates it in his own fashion, which is a different one from that proposed by the Authority. He does not continue the love story—if there is a love story—of Sylvia and himself: a line is drawn across the page of ms. and the following dissertation takes the place of the coloured plates.

Many explanations have been given of this curious mythos of Elphin and the Coracle of the Blessed. It is not necessary to do more than mention Professor Evans's very ingenious and original conjecture that Elphin was a Solar Deity, that the Saints are really Dawn Goddesses, and that the Treasure is evidently the Sun, returning in splendour after the rigours of winter, or perhaps after the darkness of night. A later scientific authority has demonstrated, with immense learning, that Elphin is most certainly a Culture God; the Treasure *may be* some sacred object or fetish deemed essential to the success of the crops, but is more probably the Seed itself, symbolising vitality, and the constancy of the reproductive forces of nature. This demonstration also may be mentioned and passed by; since folly is wearisome, even though it be learned.

In the old Welsh manuscript at the Wern which my father had catalogued, from the colour of its very ancient binding, as "The Red Book of Llancarvan", neither the sun nor the crops are assigned these important functions in the genesis of the myth. Instead of these matters there is a curious Dialogue-Poem in which St. Cadoc, surnamed the Wise, is supposed to answer the questions of a Disciple. There are in all a hundred and fifty verses; but those which relate to the Coracle and the Divine Treasure are as follows:—

> Venerable Cadoc, illustrious in the company of the saints,
> Inform me, I entreat you, concerning the Ship of the Blessed.
> Whence did it sail, from what far regions?

> Excellent disciple, you ask of a great matter.
> Be instructed, then, concerning the Holy Vessel.
> It sailed from a far region, from the exceeding Brightness.

> *It sailed from the Great Deeps, from the bottomless abysses,
> Where the light of this world is as midnight darkness;
> It proceeded from the region which is named God.

> Its flight was swift as the lightning, the billows boiled beneath it,
> Its radiance was terrible, as gold on the brow of an emperor,
> Its saints sang alleluya, a song that is triumphant.

> Its form no man could discern, its hues were ever changing;
> All the colours of the world were shining on that vessel.
> If the jewels of the mass chalice were living, to these its hues were
>   comparable.

> This was the ship that conveyed the Great Treasure,
> The principal Divine Mystery, a relic of Paradise.
> By a single leaf the nature of the tree may be judged.

> If the casket be difficult to describe, how much more the jewel!
> The names of the Treasure are infinite in number.
> It is reflected in the eye, it is hidden in the flower.

> All men seek for it in all regions of the world.
> Many have gone astray, descending to the depths of Hell.
> Hence it is that the instructed call this Treasure Heaven.

Rightly indeed (Ambrose proceeds) is the Treasure of the Coracle given this high and final title. I need not say, of course, that the verses from the Red Book of Llancarvan have been interpreted in various senses by the few who have seen them. My father had the manuscript

---

*The remaining verses placed in the mouth of "The Disciple" are omitted, as, for the most part, they simply repeat the precedent verses of the Saint.

transcribed, and twenty-five copies of the book printed. Some of these he sent to his correspondents, but I believe that on the whole he was disappointed with the letters he received. The most enthusiastic comment came from a German scholar, the successor of Zeuss, who was deeply interested—but purely in the philological forms of the text. Of the home authorities, one interprets the Treasure as the Ogham Character, or, in a wide sense, the Art of Literature, another says that in his opinion the discovery of the use of metals is hinted at, and a third writes: "It is clearly one of the many Missionary Legends which occupy so large a place in Celtic Literature generally. It has great affinities with the Graal Legend, which was, no doubt, originally a picturesque account of the Christianisation of Britain." And so forth, and so forth!

But how wonderful these verses are. Not in their expression, which seems to me very much below the standard of the best Welsh poetry, but in their apprehension of a profound mystery. Of course, in comparing them with the mythos in its prose form, which is the more generally known, it must be remembered that the "Isle of Britain" in Celtdom has much the same significance and symbolism as "Israel" bears in Jewry: the material island has been transmuted and glorified (unconsciously perhaps in some cases), till it, and its mountains and rivers, its hills and havens and cities are as sacred and as mystic in their sense as Sym and Shaun and Jordan are in another terminology. So, the statement in one of the Cadwaledr poems that "Saxons shall be eradicated and bards shall flourish" could be equated by "the Philistines shall perish and the sons of Judah shall rejoice". This general consideration is necessary to the understanding of the particular legend, or rather myth, of Elphin, the Coracle, and the Treasure.

It is rightly, indeed, called Heaven; for it is Heaven manifested, a "relic of Paradise", a flower from "the Old Garden". How truly astonishing it is to meditate on this great mystery, or rather on this sovereign and especial revelation and manifestation of *the* mysteries. The real truth is so infinitely greater than the truth as it is imagined to exist by the followers of the supreme Vanity called Occult Science. These people, as I have noted elsewhere, are in reality caught in the folds of the thick veil of multitudinous illusions; but I am thinking now of their conception of what the Truth is. They think of It as one may think (and rightly) of the Higher Mathematics, Chinese, or Astronomy as an abstruse and difficult study, success in which is to be attained by much intellectual effort, by the acquisition of many formulae, the receipt of much careful and expert instruction. To this vast error they add another—they believe that the lore they desire has been kept secret by certain bodies in certain hidden sanctuaries; in the same fashion, by similar machinery and methods as were used by the great craft-guilds of the Middle Ages to preserve their trade receipts.

Not in such wise is the Treasure of the Coracle to be attained. How marvellous (to those who understand) is the thought of this great Gift, not enclosed in the custody of any secret body but lying open to the whole world (one may almost say), touched and tested, seen and handled by every man, the theme of constant conversation, of books, of pictures. No country or region is devoid of its presence; it is the subject of songs both good and bad, it has been built in stone and marble, it haunts the closes of music; and yet, so great is the mystery, not one in a thousand, even of those who have treated it worthily, has the remotest thought of what it truly is. It is everywhere known and everywhere unknown, by every one praised, by every one despised, those who would robe it in most splendid garments, strip it naked, those who believe that they are the most devout of all worshippers, scream hideous blasphemies. These things are of the nature of paradox, but *the Wisdom* is a paradox in the earthly language, and its gifts are received incongruously—if one may say so. It may well be that a man has learnt the mystery of the stars by speaking a single word—if Dante knew anything of this matter. *So great is the mystery:* yet we can imagine that a Black Pigmy, or some such savage, might think of a cathedral as *solid* when he first saw it. He might perhaps think its height very wonderful, its pinnacles and spires strange fantastic rocks; the windows would appear masses of glittering crystals, disposed in curious tracings and patterns, the organ and the choir might well be deemed an odd effect made by the wind blowing through such an intricate forest of jagged stones. The gargoyles and statues would pass very well for freaks of nature—there are just such queer things in sticks and stones and vegetables in every museum. But: he would have no notion of the existence of the inside of the cathedral. The pillars and the arches, the glory of the painted glass, the depths of the crypt, the splendours of the vaulting, the Veil of the Rood, the Laver of Regeneration, the burning torches, the fuming incense, the singing priests, the Altar and the Sacrifice; how can he so much as dream of these things, gazing, as he thinks, on an odd stone mountain? All the whole world gazes at the cathedral; few indeed have any notion that it *is* a cathedral, that it has a within as well as a without, and that it is the shrine of a great mystery. It is set on the mountain of the world, and cannot be hid; by how few can it be discerned. Nay, some even have entered and have found nothing but Mumbo-Jumbo magic being done in the sanctuary, their eyes being dim and bleary. What would a thirsty coster-monger on a Bank Holiday make of a magnum of Lafite, the juice of a great year? He would know that it was wet; his thirst would be satisfied after a sort. But he would spit, very likely, and pull a wry face, and call for a pot of the fourest ale—to take the taste away. How many myriads of children have looked at and handled and trodden and gathered and flung away how many myriads of daisies since there have been children and daisies on the earth: how many of these children have understood the nature and being of a daisy, according to the lens of Botanical Science?

So great is the mystery: everywhere is the Treasure present, everywhere is it visible, scarcely at all is it known. And for its High Elect Servants it holds most intolerable, unconjectured mysteries and sacraments, and so they who know most, know also how poor and slight their comprehension is. They who serve the flame, and they alone, understand how unsearchable are its inmost depths.

Here Ambrose's disquisition ends, and after several blank pages in the book, there is strange matter concerning a valley at night. It would seem that the old man being busy with his odd tasks, the two cousins had wandered forth, had crossed the marshy land, and entered a hidden valley on a warm still night, when the roses of the sunset seemed to linger in the western sky, and the air was so hushed that not a leaf stirred on the poplar or on the aspen tree. They sat in the valley by a little rippling stream, breathing the solemn air of the approaching night, made aromatic by the growth of sweet-scented fans, by the subtle odour of the meadowsweet, and very slowly the darkness gathered about the boughs of the twisted oak, about the faery drooping of the ash, about the feathery spray of the birch. The olive-coloured willow leaves became grey, as they dipped down to the little torrent that poured beneath them, the glimmer vanished from the beech, and the old yew in the middle of the brake darkened into a black mound, funereal, melancholy. But the thorn tree of the narrow crooked stem and the spreading crown of leaves stood out clear against the skyline, on the summit of the wall of turf that shut in that hidden valley. The air was growing dimmer; but the faintest rosy light now hung like a veil above the dark ridge of the mountain.

But on this night the light never faded; for now the great full moon swam upward from thin drifts of cloud and glowed over the hill. At first there was a great circle of dull red, glorious but without radiance, and as it mounted higher it shone with a rich splendour, mingling with the last afterglow, and enchanting the earth utterly. Before their eyes the world was changed, and all the forms of things were endued with a new and magical significance. This was now no valley in Gwent, no petty glen among the hills and woods that lay near the Wern: into some strange country it had been instantly transmuted in the athanor of God. Nay; it was not wholly new, for in dreams they had visited it, and in desires, and in ineffable longings that could not be uttered, in waking visions some glamorous shadow of it had transiently appeared, there were depths and heights, dark shadows and isles of light that each of them had seen with half-closed eyes when they were children, and that great tree that spread out its boughs like a fan on the summit of the hill had its double in old memories. A little while ago, but a few moments since, there had been a brake before them; now there was the image of a gigantic ancient wood, a grave of mysteries and of hauntings whose boughs gave oracles, in whose black depths lurked all the awe and terror of the unknown. *Vides ut Faunus lateat in sylva; ibi saltat et cantat chorus Nympharum aeternus.*

In dreams too they had been astonished by the high walls of earth that surged steep about them, by the wizard trees that were of no common growth, by the wild light that poured in a flood upon the valley, by the hushed silence broken by the faint ripple of the tiny stream. Ambrose began in a low voice to utter the Great Invocation; and as he spoke, something of horror passed away and peace returned to the valley.

It is believed that in this place they told each other all their thoughts and all their love, and made their vows either to other unto life's end. Ambrose spoke of the anguish of the penance that was upon him, that for his sin, he must forbear that which he had used so ill, that for them there only remained, if she were willing, the Marriage of the Cup. And notwithstanding his aversion from the methods of "occultism", it is probable, for various reasons, that he has used on this point a certain reticence and reserve, considering apparently that not everything is to be spoken.

Hence it is not easy to say what exactly is intimated by the phrase "the Marriage of the Cup". It is natural of course to suppose that some reference is intended to the famous Cup of Teilo Sant, which his father had shewn him when he was a little boy; and as a matter of fact there are some notes of a pilgrimage made by Sylvia and himself to Cradock's farm, where they undoubtedly saw the Holy Vessel. It seems to have been on this occasion that Cradock, now a very old man, told Ambrose of the Destiny of the Chalice on the failure of the line of Hereditary Keepers, and the charge was given and accepted which led to Ambrose's happy and glorious end and passing out of this life into the pleasures of Paradise. Furthermore, it is certain that with the approval of Mr. Vaughan, Sylvia and Ambrose spent a week at Henllis, Cradock's farm, and that after a rigorous fast and the recitation of a solemn and ancient ritual they watched before the Cup for a day and a night.

Greater than all my recollection and all my dreams—writes Ambrose—were the glories and splendours of this marvellous and holy work. Again I saw with clearer eyes, with more piercing vision the endless wanderings and turnings of the spirit in the maze of its journey, again it seemed impossible that such a magistery could be the work of mortal hands.* For a second time my soul was rapt into the ways of light, I entered that ringing wood of gold and silver and bronze, and heard the perpetual entertainment of the Three Fairy Birds of Rhiannon. I saw the sea-shore of the savage rocks by the realm of the Waste Lands; and the foam was driven in torrents on the rocks by a great

---

*Of a somewhat similar, but greatly inferior, cup a well-known expert has said: "It seems difficult to understand how this work was executed by the aid of human eyesight and human tools. The use of the microscope only makes the intricate and exquisite accuracy of the design more apparent; indeed, it would almost appear as if this cup were made expressly for microscopic observation. The secret of its construction must apparently remain an enigma."

roaring wind. And then again I saw the white light burst from the walls of the awful sanctuary of Cor-arbennic; where all the hallows and treasures of the Island of Britain are preserved; I know not how long my spirit dwelt there in the glorious place of the perpetual choir, while there were communicated the "words" that cannot be uttered: the MYSTERY OF MYSTERIES, FROM AGE UNTO AGES. One Body, One Spirit beholds the Secret Glory.

Here, it will be observed, there is no reference to his companion; unless, perhaps, the last sentence may contain some esoteric meaning, which it is not possible to specify farther. There is something to be said for this view—one may note, by the way, the grammatical inaccuracy of "beholds" where "behold" is evidently required—but the absence of any explanation of the phrase in Ambrose's note-book must render the whole question a matter of doubt and uncertainty. The tale told afterwards by David Williams, a shepherd on the mountain, must be taken for what it is worth; it is possibly an instance of the "faculty of the marvellous" still surviving in an out-of-the-way district, or (and this is more likely) it is a distorted account of a perfectly natural incident. It must be noted, however, that Williams had a sort of faded reputation as a seer among the inhabitants of the lonely mountain farms; or, in the words of a gentleman connected with the Psychical Research Society, "he was highly susceptible to the influence of impressions of a hallucinatory character". It should be premised that the man in question had seen Ambrose and Sylvia walking together once or twice soon after their arrival at Henllis; Ambrose, he said, talked to him for some time on one occasion; and in confirmation of this it may be mentioned that there is a brief sentence in the Note-book about "a strange-looking old shepherd with visionary blue-grey eyes. I spoke to him, but he seemed stupid enough. His hands were gnarled and twisted (with rheumatism or gout I suppose), and looked like the knotted roots of a tree."

Williams then asserts that on a certain Sunday morning he was keeping a sharp look-out after the sheep under his charge. Several of the flock had been missed during the summer, and David Williams had made up his mind that they had been stolen and that the thief was a man named Lewis, a collier from Pontnewynydd, near Pontypool. Williams had seen, or thought he had seen "Lowis", as he called him, prowling about the mountain in a suspicious manner more than once, and he hinted, being well-enough pleased with his "occult" reputation, that he had "seen" Lewis with a sheep over his shoulder in a pewter dish which served for a magic crystal in his cottage—an interesting case of auto-suggested hallucination, according to the Psychical Researcher. However, having come to the conclusion that Sunday would be a likely day for the felonious collier's operations, he went into hiding in a brake not far from Henllis. Well concealed by the thick undergrowth of hazel and maple, he was able to sweep the mountainside above him, and he could see the track by which the sheep-stealer would probably approach.

It was a bright and sunny morning; the sky was deep blue, and here and there little delicate clouds, fleecy white, floated across it. The breeze blew up from the sea, and the tossing winds heightened and darkened before it, one could see the waves of the wind as it were reflected in the cornfields: and the hills and valleys of Gwent, its rivers and streams, its hanging woods, its white farm walls were all glittering in the happy peace of the pure sunlight. In his hiding-place among the hazel boughs the shepherd said that the sound of all the bells of all the world came up to him: St. Michael by Torfaen, St. Vrechva on the hill were chiming; he heard St. Cadoc ringing in Caermaen; and there were faint, individual notes of single bells from little churches by the Soar: the bells made, he said, music and melody to charm the heart.

He kept his eyes intently fixed on the wall of mountain that rose up above him; he could see his sheep feeding by twos and threes in the islands of turf among the tall bracken: it would not be difficult for a man to hide deep in the fern, and wait till a sheep grazed within reach, and then to catch hold of the nearest leg and draw the prey into shelter. The wind tossed the bracken to and fro, a brief struggle would not be noticeable, and the thief might crawl off under shelter for a considerable distance. Williams tried to keep one eye on the flock and the other on the path from the north whence he thought Lewis would approach—unless he were already safely hidden under the shaking green fronds, just waiting for his opportunity.

A little to the left of this line of vision, on the verge between a broken field and the wild mountainside there was a well shaded by a great thorn tree, which the old people used to call St. Teilo's Well—the water was supposed to be good for the cure of certain sicknesses. It was not more than a hundred yards from Cradock's farm, Henllis. Williams could not quite say what first attracted his attention to the well. He had a feeling, as he said, that a bright light was shining there, as if the sun were glittering on glass. He did not want to look; he was afraid that his attention might be distracted at the crucial moment; there were several sheep grazing quite close to the wall of fern. But he could not keep his eyes fixed; there was all the time that sensation as of a fountain of white light rising from the well, so at last he turned his head, that he might be satisfied that there was nothing to look at. Then, he said, something seemed to "shoot all over him"—his sensations as he described them were similar to those of an electric shock—and he saw a figure standing by the well under the thorn-tree. Later on when he had told the story a good many times and had been questioned about it he indulged in an elaborate and detailed account of this figure—the details being, evidently, more or less picturesque after-thoughts. But in his first tale he confessed that he could not say anything very particular about this shape by the well: he would not, for instance, undertake to swear that it was a man, though he thought it was a man, "but not somehow dressed as a man is dressed; not nowadays whatever". The light, if there had been any light at all, had vanished; there was only some one there, and Williams said that, sheep or no sheep, he felt he must go and see who it was: he did not know why, but so it was with him. So he came out of the thicket and began to run towards the well, as fast as he could; and then as his luck would have it, his foot was caught, and he fell full length. It was a minute, perhaps, before he could get up and free himself from the entanglement of the brambles; and it may be that he was a little dazed by the shock of the fall. But to his amazement the figure that he had seen was no longer by the well under the thorn. Instead the two young people staying at Henllis were walking towards him. They smiled and nodded as they passed him standing all astonished and confused, like a man roused suddenly from some strange and bewildering dream.

This and nothing more was the story told by David Williams before he had introduced the element of imagination; it is not worth while detailing the later elaborations of the shepherd's fancy. It is probable, for instance, that his description of what happened when he looked round and saw the figure* is but an amplification of the first simple statement as to the shock or shudder that passed through him. As has been said the original story may be due to the "faculty of the marvellous", or it may be a confused account of an ordinary incident; but there seems no reason to suppose that in this early version the shepherd did not at least *intend* to be veridical, and one or two circumstances in his tale—it is needless to specify them—will not be without interest to responsible and proficient students. It should be said that Ambrose, who of course heard of the story, declined to comment upon it in any sense whatever; and his manner made it impossible to press the question.

His notebook contains no reference of any sort to the shepherd's statement. After his brief description of this second visit to the Cup of Teilo Sant, some half-dozen pages are scattered over with odd words and phrases and incomplete tales which no doubt had their meaning and suggestion for the writer, but would be unintelligible to those who do not possess the Key. For example:—

Urien Rheged made a great feast on the Day of Pentecost; it was of such splendour and richness, being constituted with all the most delicate meats of the earth and the best wines of Greece and Gascony and the entire world, being also graced with the art of song and the presence of the most famous minstrels of the Island of Britain, that it was known as the Illustrious Entertainment of Urien Rheged. Urien sat on high on a platform thickly strewn with green rushes; his robe was of satin of the colour of a red flame; he sat on a cushion of green satin. At the end of the banquet Morgan the butler served a most precious and aromatic wine from some unknown region of the earth that was called Wine of Pentecost: all who drank it praised its colour, its flavour, and its odour and were filled with a great joy. Then there came in a sorry little fellow, and craved speech of Urien. Forthwith it was granted, and he spoke.

---

*"The mountain and trees, and the sky and the farmhouse all shivered together, as if they would go up into nothing; it was just the same as when you do throw a stone into a pool, and everything you do see in the pool quakes and shakes before you." It is pretty clear that Williams transferred his own sensations to the material universe.

"King Urien," said he, "this Entertainment is imperfect."

"Tell me in what respect," said the King, thinking that the man was a jester.

"With all my heart," said he, "it is because you have had no fit drink; and there can be no good feast without good drink; and you have not tasted the only drink that has been provided by the natural world."

With that, he drew from under his ragged cloak an old wooden bowl, which he had dipped in the stream as he came on his way to court. In the bowl there was some good water; there were also pebbles, some mud, a few weeds, a snail, and other impurities.

"This," he said, "is the only true drink in the world, for who saw a beast that drank wine? Wine is, in fact, the liquor of dreamers and madmen."

Urien and his guests laughed so heartily that the earth shook beneath the hall; and this speech concerning Wine and Water is known as one of the Three Unreasonable Sayings of the Island of Britain.

Again:—

Taliesin said that a song was still a song even though the poet had never inscribed it in any characters: and it was declared that the inspiration in the soul of the bard was of greater reality than the Trees of the Wood. [Ogham Characters]*

A bard uttered this sentence: there is dark earth, there is a seed, there is germination, there is a root, there is a stem with leaves, there is a flower with concealed juices, there comes a bee, there is golden honey, there is distilled mead in foaming horns, there are Inspiration and Unction in the spirit of the Bard. This sentence was confirmed, and it was added that more than once inspiration had been given to poets who were fasting from meat and drink, and thus splendid and magnificent odes had been produced.

The remaining notes and jottings are even more fragmentary and inconclusive, and it seems most likely that Ambrose used these remaining leaves as a kind of commonplace-book—they may not refer in any way to his life at the Wern or to his relations with Sylvia Vaughan. It is

---

*[The words in brackets are Machen's.—Ed.]

certain that she was very dear to him, dearest of all indeed; and yet it was remarked that when, some five years later, she died very suddenly—she was apparently in perfect health, but was found one morning dead in her bed—he shewed no signs of grief or even of shock. Indeed, if it had not been an impossible supposition, those who saw him soon after the news of Sylvia's death would have been inclined to think that he was endeavouring to suppress the signs of a joy and a delight that were almost unendurable in the intensity of their rapture. Strangely enough certain papers of his seem almost to confirm this supposition, extraordinary as it appears to be: they most certainly shew no evidence of grief, nor even a passing depression.

One sentence from these papers must be quoted here, by reason of the bearing it *may* have on the matters which have been just recorded. It is taken from a Diary kept by Ambrose some three months after Sylvia's death. He was at the Wern, endeavouring to comfort her poor father, who was in the bitterest grief. In this Diary, then, he writes under a certain date:

We wandered by the old paths, by the places of the old altars, by the well of the Fisherman, by the hidden shrines, by the holy streams, by valleys and by hills now doubly hallowed by miracles which are past all utterance. We understood as never before the marvels of the secrets of the saints, of the Secret Glory which is hidden from the Holy Angels.

It is difficult to believe that Mr. Vaughan is referred to in this passage: it would be more difficult still for any one who had known Ambrose Meyrick to believe him guilty of any species of "occult" quackery or mystification.

VI

1.

There are various legends in existence as to Ambrose Meyrick's famous last term at Lupton. As has been seen Palmer, an honest man if a booby, was completely thunderstruck by the catastrophe; indeed, he used to quote Horace's account of his conversion with reference to the manner of Ambrose's passing from the bonds and bounds of the dear old school. He, it is evident enough from the record that he has left of the affair, saw nothing and suspected nothing of what was to come; but naturally enough others, quite as stupid as he, but less honest, were ready to affirm (after the event) that they had suspicions for some time that there was "something wrong with the fellow". This, of course, is nonsense; the Luptonians—masters and boys alike—were no more capable of descrying the growing of a new life and a new joy, and a new ecstasy in Ambrose than if they had been a kennel of Newfoundland Puppies. You cannot drink "Old Tom" and four ale all your days and then become at short notice or at no notice an expert in the finer growths of the Medoc; and if your mind is given up to Rocker and Stinker, the misunderstanding of the Latin and Greek Literatures, and the Doctor's Sermons you are not very likely to discern spiritual things or the presence of the Hosts of the Lord. It was all nonsense; they saw nothing, or if they saw that Meyrick was looking "very fit and pleased with himself", they thought it natural enough in view of his achievements and his prospects.

The truthful though idiotic Palmer mentions in his account that Chesson had been rather annoyed with a certain essay sent in by Meyrick. Perhaps even he rather exaggerates this incident in the light of after knowledge. The truth is that the Head had given a kind of Lecture to the Sixth and had asked the boys to let him have by way of logical exercise an essay—the subject was at the choice of the writer—in which similar methods of argument should be used. Meyrick sent him in, as he readily confessed, by far the best essay, only it was devoted, by the way, to a satirical refutation of the *matter* of the Doctor's Lecture. Original writing on any subject was not a strong point with the Sixth at Lupton: the other boys had taken profuse notes of the Lecture and had reproduced it with more or less success. This, as the Doctor said, was not in the least what he had asked for, and he complimented Meyrick on having been the only one in the form to see the point of the exercise.

"But," he said, "I must say that I am sorry for one thing. It is not that I gather from your essay that you do me the honour to disagree with me: opinions are matters of very little consequence so long as they are not held with any asperity of conviction. Never be bitterly certain about anything—you will only make yourself ridiculous. But what I want to say is this. If you want to get on in life—if you like it better, I will say, if you want to employ for the advantage of your fellow men the talents that have been given you by God—if you want to *use* your life; remember one thing: renounce irony. Now the whole of this *ludus* of yours is permeated by irony. In a thing like this, it doesn't matter; it goes no farther than my desk. But when you once come before the world, a false step may be fatal; and you may take it from me that the precipice of irony is of all the most fatal—and final. Go over that and you are smashed once and for all.

"You see, Meyrick, I am talking to you as one reasonable being to another. You have read a good deal; just think of a few great satirists of literature, and of what happened to them. Dryden could not keep out William of Orange, or Shadwell, or Nahum Tate. Rabelais just escaped the bonfire. Swift's *Tale of a Tub* is a wonderful piece of satire. You know what Swift's end was like: above all think of Swift. I daresay you've read Thackeray on Swift; you may be as satirical as you please if you follow Thackeray's methods, not those of the man he disliked so heartily. So long as you give the world sugar-plums you may add a slightly acid coating—people like it.

"You see, the other course is so entirely futile. You are smashed, as I say. Suppose you reply that you don't care, that you are willing to be martyred for the good cause. But the point is that the good cause is ruined with you, and very often because of you. You must see yourself that your case is bound to suffer if you begin your speech by letting the jury know that you consider them a pack of fools. Just think it over, Meyrick, will you?"

The lecture on which the essays were to be written was a brief analysis of Superstition and Superstitious Beliefs. Chesson had run through the various arguments by which, as he said, the superstitiously inclined generally defend foolish beliefs and more foolish practices. He pointed out that there was the appeal to universal, or very general usage, to great names as sanctioning absurd practice and dogma, to results supposed to have been achieved (imaginary cures for example), to antiquity, to a strong feeling of necessity, etc. etc. Then he shewed how profoundly irrational most superstitions were—there was usually no connection between the supposed cause and the supposed effect; and he drew the attention of the boys to the fact that when the "outworks" of a system of thought were confessedly ridiculous, there was reason to suspect that the central dogmas were in the same case, since the one derives from the other. "Thus," he said, "from the manifest folly and immorality of many of the Catholic miracles (so called), we may legitimately enough draw conclusions far from favourable to the whole Catholic system. In the same way if you saw a man dancing naked in the street, you would not be very likely to ask his advice on any serious question: absurdity in externals, in lesser things probably proceeds from absurdity or madness in great things." The doctor shewed too that the superstitious habit flourished chiefly amongst ignorant backward peoples, whose minds were akin to those of children. "This," he said, "is a weighty argument. If we find a doctrine or a practice commending itself readily enough to immature ages of life—to children—to ages of immature thought—to the Middle Ages—to immature peoples generally such as Spaniards and Southern Italian peasants; while at the same time the doctrine or practice in question would be laughed at by nine scientific men out of ten: then, you are probably right in thinking such a doctrine or practice absurd." The lecture ended by shewing that we should at least suspect every system which did not lead to some material benefit: "We are more or less children of matter, we have been placed on this material sphere, under material conditions; we are justified, then, in demanding that any doctrine proffered for our acceptance shall justify itself materially; if it cannot do this we have reason to conclude that it is somehow or other *out of harmony* with the scheme of things to which we belong—that is, that it is *false*. Compare the state of superstitious savages with the state of Christian England from this point of view, excluding all higher considerations: the savage, as a whole, fails *materially:* he is uncomfortable, while the Englishman is comfortable. Again, compare, still from the same point of view, the condition of an enlightened Protestant operative in some great industrial centre (say, in Lupton) with the condition of a superstitious Irish peasant on his bog farm: the same result is given: the English Protestant is much more *comfortable* than the Irish Roman Catholic. Take a third instance: think of what a country, a city, a house were like five or six hundred years ago, and then think of the enormous improvements that have been effected—rapidity and security of transit, creation of sanitation, vast improvement in lighting, etc. etc.—for the third time our method gives the expected result: the modern, free from superstition, is in every way more prosperous materially than his superstitious ancestor who lived before the Reformation. Note the cumulative force of the instances: in each case superstition is allied with poverty and discomfort, just as a particular microbe produces a particular disease."

Ambrose sent in an Essay on the Folly of Eating and Drinking.

He shewed that in the first place it was absurd to defend these ridiculous practices because they were the custom of all—of universal usage. It had once been the universal usage, in civilised states at all events, to hear Mass; it had been the universal usage to believe in Witchcraft and Omens.

Secondly, it was idle to quote the names of great authorities in praise of meat and drink, since great authorities could be cited in favour of the most absurd and most monstrous beliefs and practices.

Then, why allege the apparent benefit received through these insane orgies? There were people even at the present day who were ready to testify to the benefit they had received through bathing in Holy Wells, through kissing the mouldering bones of a dead man, through uttering various irrational formulae called prayers: once such testimony would have been well-nigh universal. In neither case, either of the few moderns or of the many ancients do we attach the slightest credibility to these reports of apparent benefit.

The plea of antiquity was of course out of court: it had been advanced in favour of every abuse, of every rank absurdity; if it had been listened to we should still be in the condition of the Australian Blackfellows. It was quite true that men had been eating and drinking for countless ages; they had been committing many other disgusting, irrational, criminal, useless, and offensive actions for countless ages. So far as the argument from antiquity was of any force at all, it was an argument establishing a high degree of probability against the utility of roast beef and beer, walnuts and water. Astrology was as ancient a practice as any of which we have record; its antiquity is presumption of its absurdity.

Then, people would say that they felt they *must* have something to eat and drink. A Chinaman would tell exactly the same story of his opium-pipe, an alcoholic maniac of his wine, an habitual smoker of his tobacco. Each of these deluded persons would protest that he could not live without his stimulant or his narcotic, and would probably suffer severely—for a time—if it were denied him; the vicious craving induced by the habit cooperating with the imagination, so that a very real state of misery would be induced. Yet neither opium, wine, nor tobacco is generally accounted a necessary of life. If we admit the plea of "we feel that we *must* have it", then hypodermic injections of morphia will take their place amongst the simple necessaries of existence. Of course if the drug-maniac is guarded and the drug withheld, he will generally in process of time be cured of his longing; and it is only reasonable to conclude that such would be the experience of the poor slaves of beef and beer, or bread and water. In some cases the victim of drugs or alcohol turns out to be incurable; even then we do not draw the inference that opium and whiskey are necessary to life.

Again, there was the supreme mark of irrationality about the processes of eating and drinking. People said they experienced certain sensations, which they called by the arbitrary and conventional names of "hunger" and "thirst". They could give no clear account of these supposed sensations, doubtless because they were entirely imaginary, the results of auto-suggestion. If you cross-examined one of the sufferers from that acute form of food-mania known as starvation, you would probably be astonished at the vagueness of the man's replies. He would in all likelihood be totally unable to give any intelligible account whatever of his supposed symptoms; you might get "a sort of sinking feeling", or "a sort of gnawing feeling", or "a sort of all-overish feeling", or some such unscientific gibberish, coupled, very likely, with an unmeaning gesture in the direction of the abdomen. The average hysterical patient could, in nine cases out of ten, describe her feelings with infinitely more of detail and distinctness; and yet nobody in his senses believes that these hysterical sensations or disabilities have any existence out of the diseased brain of the sufferer. The *strength* of the hunger-illusion is conceded; it is not so great, however, as the strength of the hysteria-illusion which may, in some cases, confine a healthy woman to her bed for twenty years. The sufferer from "starvation" thinks he wants food, the sufferer from hysteria thinks that she has paralysis: the one delusion is as reasonable as the other.

But supposing that, out of mistaken kindness, you gratify the horrible and ridiculous longings of the hunger-maniac. You give him, say, a steak; that is a portion of the flesh of the ox. He divides this into portions, masticates it with his teeth, and lets it slip down his throat. He will then tell you that his craving is appeased, that "he feels better";

and a look of contentment may come into his face, not at all unlike the expression of stupid beatitude which may be seen on the face of the drunkard, when *his* craving has been satisfied. Appeal to the patient, and ask him as a reasonable man to tell you how the swallowing of ox-flesh, partially burned, can lead to content or happiness. He will not tell you: he cannot; nor can any one else. It is true that medical men (who have their formulas, just as priests have their creeds) have written many unintelligible volumes concerning nutrition, assimilation, gastric juice, peptones, proteids, etc. etc. (note again the resemblance between the jargon of medicine and the jargon of theology), but it is not, it is presumed, seriously contended that the average "starving" man has read these volumes and has been convinced by their arguments, that he has mastered in all its detail the intricate and wonderful process by which somehow or other (the theological "mystery"), burned ox-flesh is converted into happiness and content, and high thoughts of joy. It is certain that the sufferer from "starvation" has done nothing of the kind, that he is no more able to demonstrate the irrational action he has performed than a poor Catholic is able to demonstrate the Sacrifice of the Mass. The "starving" man who chews beef, the "devout" man who goes to mass, are, in plain language, persons who perform actions for which they are unable to give the semblance of a reasonable account. They are in the same class as lunatics, drunkards, and morphomaniacs.

Probably it would not be difficult to trace this extraordinary delusion to its origin. At some very early and barbarous period in human history eating was probably invented as a kind of initiatory rite; it was supposed that he who received the flesh of the ox into his body partook mystically of the ox's strength and endurance. Different animals were added, to obtain different qualities; the whole process being no doubt a curious ritual, which it might not be impossible to reconstruct. The same theory pervaded medicine for many ages, and is perhaps not quite extinct even at the present day; and even now some savages believe that to eat of the heart of the lion gives courage. It is not difficult to understand that eating, originally a sacrament, became in course of time a habit, and then an apparently irresistible appetite.

Ambrose then examined the question of the "outworks", on which the Doctor had laid a good deal of stress. He had not much difficulty in shewing the extreme extravagance and absurdity of all the ceremonial of eating and drinking. "It is contended," he wrote, "that eating and drinking are customs intimately, nay most intimately connected with the body's health, with its very existence. If this were really so, one cannot think that men would have surrounded these actions with a grotesque and elaborate social ritual. A man does not gather his friends round him when he has to undergo a serious operation; he does not send out cards when he intends to take a dose of medicine; it is not even customary to make the bath-room a social centre. If eating and drinking be, as it is urged, of vital consequence to bodily health and existence; then, they are intimate concerns of the body, and every consideration of decency demands that such matters be attended to in strict privacy. We have seen that in reality a dinner-party is an irrational relic of a forgotten rite—a true superstition, in fact—and on this hypothesis the crazy ceremonial practised on such an occasion becomes comparatively intelligible. Otherwise such a function would have no counterpart out of Bedlam and few within it.

Further; let us consider what eating at the present day really implies. No man will pretend that mustard and horseradish are necessary to life, no man can maintain that dishes are rendered more wholesome or nourishing by the addition of elaborate sauces and condiments, or that a jelly sustains and fortifies any the more by being made in an extraordinary shape and coloured with some bright pigment. If food were taken as a necessary, probably five minutes would be sufficient for its consumption: it would be prepared in some soluble and digestible form, and would be swallowed by the bedside, the first thing in the morning and the last thing at night. It would certainly not be served to people dressed in a silly costume by ministrants in a sillier, it would not be disguised in all imaginable shapes and colours, concealed by strange flavourings, on a board richly draped, decorated like an altar with lights and flowers; while, in some cases, music is played on a band of instruments. [Note, how all these circumstances fit in with the theory of a savage Rite of Initiation.] The "outworks" then of eating and drinking are positively maniacal in their irrationality: we may safely conclude therefore that the whole system is profoundly unreasonable, absurd and unjustifiable.

It was clear, he shewed, that eating and drinking made their chief appeal to barbarous and backward peoples and ages. Children were gluttons, savages were voracious eaters, in the Middle Ages people devoured terrible, Gargantuan banquets; and uncultured and unscientific people in all parts of the world could scarcely think of a festival of any kind without thinking also of enormous meals, washed down by enormous draughts of liquor. In fact a "feast" had come to be synonymous with the act of eating and drinking to gross excess. Scientific men were agreed in denouncing such orgies as barbarous and highly injurious to health: another of the Doctor's tests was therefore satisfied; the food habit was indulged in to the fullest extent by the ignorant and childish, and condemned by men of science.

Ambrose's case was easiest when he came to the great point of material advantage. As it happened, a term or two before, some tainted meat had been supplied to one of the Houses: two boys had died, and a considerable number were seriously ill: it was a bad case of ptomaine poisoning. He took this as an example, near at hand, of the horrible dangers of eating and drinking: he worked from this text to the whole question of the impurities of food and drink, and shewed the high probability that death might lurk literally in every mouthful and in every draught. He made an elaborate list of the hideous and mortal diseases that might be, nay, that were communicated to the victims of the "hunger and thirst mania": meat of all kinds swarmed with the germs of disease, it was killed and stored under the most filthy and dangerous conditions, in its preserved forms it was usually rotten with gangrene and decay before it was made into the sausage or placed in the tin. He quoted a well-known doctor to the effect that the killing and preparation of meat had made no advance in the direction of sanitation since the stone-age; he revelled in the description of rotten pork and tuberculous beef. To drink liquor of any kind was, of course, a mere courting of death; there were statistics shewing how many thousands of children were carried off annually by milk alone, reckoned by the ignorant and superstitious as the most innocent of fluids. He made, in fact, a little monograph of poisonous adulterations of food and drink, with notes, culled from the papers, of whole families who had fallen victims to the "food and drink" habit. Then, of course, there was the larger point of view; it was not difficult to shew from various medical authorities that, adulteration apart, the whole matter of diet and drink was in itself highly noxious and prejudicial to health. One great man, for example, pronounced all the alcohols to be poisons pure and simple, of varying degrees of venom—one might achieve a death of rapid and horrible torture on brandy or gin, or one might choose to linger inefficient and ill for many years, while strength and vitality were sapped by small beer. But he demonstrated that it was of all futilities most futile to suppose that safety was to be sought in "temperance" beverages. The Vegetarians were able to shew the horrible and destructive effects of meat-eating clearly enough; their case was proven up to the hilt— the carnivorous man was an unhealthy man, a feeble man, and also a moral monster. But on the other hand the meat-eater could shew quite as clearly that the rice-eating Bengalis were a weak-kneed race of chatterers, capable only of shewing energy in the perpetration of horrible and fiendish cruelties on defenceless women and children: in fact it was only too plain that the wickedest actions in the world had been committed by Vegetarians. So with drink: alcohol was deadly, it was true; but there were eminent authorities who declared that tea and coffee were much more deadly, that the continued consumption of these beverages could only lead to the utter ruin of the race in body and mind. As for water: its use had swept away armies and desolated cities. The conclusion was irresistible; so far from the "food delusion" being of material benefit, it was clearly responsible for more violent and agonising deaths than all the wars that had been ever waged; it was a more frightful revenge than the Yellow Hag, the Black Pest, the Plague, the Sleeping Sickness, and Asiatic Cholera: and a more enlightened age would doubtless treat its victims as criminal lunatics.

2.

Ambrose was a good deal amused when he heard of the horror with which his Rabelaisian Epistle had been received. He was a little sorry too, as well as amused; he had forgotten the utter ignorance of literature which characterises the average schoolmaster, the absolute inability to understand the literary point of view. Ambrose had meant to send his old Housemaster an entertaining *ludus* (in the Doctor's phrase): but what Mr. Horbury had received was, to him, a terrible compound of blasphemy (against the school ideals) and obscenity. It was a pity; but Ambrose Meyrick could never quite understand things. He would have reverenced the high abstraction of the saint; his unwillingness to be disturbed in his vision of great joy by the dust and dirt of earth: he could have appreciated the frame of mind which would turn away from a report of the Debates in the House of Commons as an obscene nuisance; but he could not see the average point of view. He always protested that the man who gloated over the scabrous and hideous matter in the daily press, over details which were unspeakably degrading and repulsive, and then subscribed for the suppression of Rabelais and Boccaccio was nothing more or less than a hypocritical scoundrel, whose escape from utter damnation might perhaps be effected by the power of the eternal compassions, but in no other way.

"Look," he said once, "here, in this highly respectable family journal, there is a careful and elaborate account of the career of a Hermaphrodite: see; one is not spared the details. How the dear public will revel over it, how they will smack their lips, the men who sent poor old Vizetelly to prison for publishing *La Terre* in English, these men and their sons. But of course it is highly for the public interest that minute information about Hermaphrodites should be circulated in the press; and journalists, as is well known, are the slaves of the public good. You know how zealously these gentlemen strive to protect the 'young girl' from the contamination of reading 'licentious literature'; it is interesting to see the literary fare which they consider suitable for their innocent young *protégée*. The girl of the future, carefully instructed in 'West End Scandals', Divorce Proceedings—and Hermaphrodites— will be truly a charming product!"

Ambrose could never understand, and so he was astonished at the horror which his little *jeu d'esprit* excited. He has left few notes and these of the slightest with respect to his sojourn among the Strolling Players. It was an odd circumstance which made him think of the stage. A year or so before he left Lupton the Headmaster had conceived the brilliant idea of inviting a company of actors to give a performance of *Henry V* in the Speech House. The upper forms were "studying" the play in some disgusting edition proceeding from the highest scholastic sources: or rather they were engaged in burying the poetry and the fun and the dramatic action under a load of rubbishy notes, the chief point of which seemed to be that you were to "cf." everything with something else. At the same time "the Period" was being carefully "got up", which meant that the boys were busy in digging the pit of their historical ignorance broader and deeper, and in surrounding the pit aforesaid with a gilt fence of names and dates. A few, perhaps, had glanced into the little books, and were inclined to think "they must have been jolly times", that Harry of England was "a sportsman", that it must have been fine to have broken a lance on Crispin Crispinian's Day, that Nym and Pistol and Bardolph were almost as good fun as Jack Harkaway: in fact, that here was some rare high stuff, only it was a pity that the old bounder who wrote it couldn't have put it all into plain decent English that a fellow could read as easily as a novel. They were soon convinced of their error after their form-masters had taken them in hand for a couple of weeks. The text was a series of elaborate traps and mines which the notes sprang upon them—traps and mines of dates, and facts, and names; historical, philological, grammatical traps, all of infinite tedium; all or nearly all leading up to "cf." This word was to be compared with the Gothic Form, this with the Frisian, this with M.E., this phrase was paralleled with something not a bit like it from *Euphues* [name of author, dates of birth and death, date of publication, all duly given]; this sentence with a remark of Bacon's [dates as before]: here the authority of Cotgrave was invoked, there the happy lads found themselves plunged into a consideration of Hooker's Ecclesiastical Polity. It did not take the masters long to reduce Harry into a disagreeable shadow, draped in dates, Bardolph, Nym, and Pistol became subjects for examination and nothing more, the Battle of Agincourt was found out and declared to be a pest and nuisance. They were all, one might say, permanently fortified against all knowledge or understanding of English History, Literature, Manners, Poetry, and Humour for all time; and some of them did very brilliantly in the inevitable examination.

It was in the midst of this agreeable, intelligent, and instructive process that the Hathaway Company paid their visit at the Doctor's invitation. The boys welcomed them at the station. The player folk, poor souls, were weary; they had been doing a number of "one night stands" at the end of their tour; for the last fortnight they had been worked to death. Their train-calls had varied between the hours of six and eight, they had partaken of badly prepared and insufficient breakfasts by gaslight, and then had turned out into rainy, wind-swept streets to tramp down to the station, where they would find the stage-carpenter, the baggage man, and the assistant stage manager who had been getting the scenery on the trucks all night, and had enjoyed some two or three hours sleep on the station benches. Then the railway journey; the arrival at some little town, or rather, very often, at some station a mile or so away from the town. They shouldered their baggage and tramped in the muddy road; it was twelve o'clock perhaps; the matinee was at two, and it was necessary to find rooms, and get something to eat before going to the hall to dress and make up. It is not agreeable; pacing the streets of a strange town where actors are regarded as professional thieves in disguise, knocking at doors in vain, received here with grins of contempt, there with open violence, walking still and walking; finding that the inns and taverns are all mysteriously full, still walking and wondering whether one will have to leave the question of rooms till the matinee is over. Then the hall; the "dressing-rooms" are usually places for the display of inventive ingenuity, for there are sometimes no tables and very often no chairs; the cautious stroller always carries his own glass in his basket or bag—or "sack" as he prefers calling it. He does not mind standing on a damp stone floor in his bare feet, and drawing on his tights by cautious tugs, preserving his balance the whole with long-acquired art. He may have to make up in a dark hole, first cousin to a cellar; he draws out his bit of candle, fixes it somewhere, and with handglass in one hand and grease-paint in the other goes gravely to work; and if he be a good stroller his make-up is as well and carefully done as if he were in a smart room in a West End theatre, with a dresser at his elbow, and two moveable electric standards on each side of his mirror. Then the show on the best make-shift of a stage that the staff has been able to arrange: sometimes it has had to be extended by boards laid on barrels, sometimes entrances have to be made up a step-ladder, and exits are leaps into an apparent void: the footlights are a long series of holes pierced in a gas-pipe, and a god from the machine has known what it is to have his deity illumined by the rays of a bicycle lamp. The show over, a villainously cooked chop or steak is enjoyed, and just as the stroller feels that he would like a doze of an hour or two, it is time to go to the hall and repeat the performance of the afternoon. He gets to sleep somewhere between twelve and one, and rests till six the next morning; and then begins a tomorrow that is the replica of yesterday.

The Hathaway Company had enjoyed a fortnight of this routine before their arrival at Lupton. The Low Comedian, generally a merry fellow, had said gloomily in the morning that, personally, he would prefer a tour conducted by Red Indians; and the Heavy Man was bilious; his face was yellowish and his eyes rolled in a threatening fashion: it was not safe to talk to him. They were all tired to death, and felt as if they had not slept for years when they got out at Lupton after a train journey of some four hours.

The boys were waiting for them. It was a whole holiday in honour of the event, and the Head had relaxed the laws as to bounds. So some two hundred of the more impetuous lads were ready on the platform, and a shriek of delight and derision arose as the wretched strollers clambered wearily out of their carriages. It was better fun than a travelling menagerie. The players fought their way out into the street amidst a torrent of jeers. The men were congratulated on their taste in dress, and indeed some of the poor fellows were shabby enough—one cannot afford to go to Conduit Street on thirty-five shillings a week for forty-two weeks in the year—and one wit raised the shout: "First on the right, third on the left—shortest way to the County Gaol." But most of the fun was at the expense of the girls, who were certainly not looking their smartest and prettiest. One boy asked in a clear cold voice, in accents that suggested a haughty patrician lineage: "Do you mean to tell me that any one *pays* to see these women?" and there were shrieks of appreciation over Biederstein's ready wit. The boys followed the actors in groups right through the town, the wretched folk could not shake them off, and young Manners had the pluck to pull the back hair of one of the girls—he wanted to see if it was a wig, as he politely explained to the indignant lady. Another lad, more gallant, went up to two of the girls who were walking apart, and proposed an amorous rendez-vous in the cricket pavilion: altogether Lupton that day was a *monde ou l'on s'amuse*. Ambrose heard of it all from the chief jesters; he agreed that it was good sport. The manager of the company complained to the Head, who expressed his regret that anything unpleasant had occurred; and Mr. Horbury spoke to Ambrose about the incident.

"Of course," he said, "we must disapprove of that kind of thing officially, and if they could have given us any of the fellows' names they would have had to do lines. High spirits are all very well, but there's a limit to everything. At the same time, you know, I'm not altogether sorry. Boys are such young fools in many ways, there is such a lot of false glamour about the stage—there always is a glamour about the more elaborate forms of loafing—that, as I say, I'm not sorry some of our fellows have had a lesson as to how actors and acting are really regarded by decent Englishmen. I don't think that many Luptonians who were about to-day will want to go on the stage: eh, Ambrose?"

Mr. Horbury chuckled: he really thought that a useful lesson had been administered. Ambrose had remembered the incident, and when the time came he made his way at once to the town in which the Hathaways were acting. He was quite clear that there must be a great deal of good in anything which aroused the contempt and derision of all Lupton.

3.

I am afraid—Ambrose notes in one of his books—that the golden days of the stage are numbered. One sees, more or less surely, that the horrible wave of respectability is advancing on the profession, that the old race of workmen with their mysteries or craft receipts, their peculiar jargon, their pride in the art is dying out. The new generation is nothing to me: an English country gentleman is an excellent type; I admire it with all my heart; but I don't care to see an indifferent imitation of the character being given by a strolling player. Now odd it is that in Chaucer one does not see the faintest desire in the Clerk of Oxford or the Miller to be taken for the Knight or the Squire! I suppose that the new generation was knocking at the door when I joined Hathaway, but it had not been let in. We were not ashamed of our craft; we were proud of it and accepted our blue chins as a miller accepts his floury costume.

What a good life it was. In spite of discomforts, of greasy food cooked by "slap-cabbage" landladies, in spite of rooms that were often very far from cleanliness, in spite of evil-smelling, inconvenient dressing-rooms in insanitary theatres, of wearisome journeys, of rehearsals that began sometimes at half-past-eleven, "after the show"; we came very near to the ideal life which man was meant to lead. Who can measure the excellent effects of vagabondage, of the continual rolling which keeps the stone clean of moss and lichen? Acting is not a high art, nor a fine art: it is doubtful whether it is really an art at all, but the life of the strolling player is, or was, the nearest approach that this age can make to the life of the wandering craftsmen of the Middle Ages.*

---

*[At this point a long passage was crossed out by Machen in the ms.: I love the recollection of the old theatres that we sometimes played in. There would be dressing-accommodation (of a sort) for perhaps twenty people at the outside, and fifty of us would squash cheerfully into the little dens of dressing-rooms. We only did Shakespeare, and the younger people did a good deal of "doubling" (or trebling sometimes): a man might have to wear five different costumes in the course of an evening. It is not difficult to imagine what a small dressing-room looked like under these conditions, when the wardrobe man had piled the different dresses on the floor, on the baskets, on the shelf that runs round the room. A row of gas-jets, wire-guarded, burned at sparse intervals above this shelf: it was no longer the custom to make "black-lines" out of the soot that gathered round the guards. Underneath the lights were the make-up boxes of the actors, very close together, wrapped in grease-cloths: a few had the proper japanned boxes with partitions for the paints and a receptacle for crepe-hair and odds and ends, but for the most part we were content with old cigarette and cigar boxes—the article from the shop was thought rather pompous; at all events for the apprentices. In the centre of the room there would be three or four big wicker baskets, piled with costumes and armour; and by the time they called "Overture and beginners, gentlemen, please!" the room would glow like a furnace—there was seldom much ventilation.

We made up, as may be conceived, under difficulties; sometimes there was barely elbow room, and it was rare indeed to find oneself under a good light. But woe to the man who scamped his work, whose wig was badly fitted, whose lines were wanting in probability, whose crepe-hair beards and moustaches did not conform to the example of nature. Such an one would, in the course of the evening, receive the ironic congratulations of the entire company; a sketch of him, done in grease-paint, would probably decorate the walls of the dressing-room, and if the make-up were very outrageous it would become a tradition: I remember hearing of such a case which was already five years old when I joined. Some of us were curiously conscientious; I have seen a man, who was playing quite a minor part, make up with a sketch before him. He had made the drawing from a picture in the National Gallery; and by it he trimmed and cut his beard till it followed in every particular the Elizabethan model. He took himself and his craft seriously; and I believe that to do this is now quite fatal to any craftsman. It is odd, this objection to a man's believing in his work and trying to do his best in it. I suppose it is rather fortunate that engine-drivers, pilots, and ship captains on the whole *do* take themselves and their business very seriously. It will be a pity when the easy, dashing, amateur habit gets a footing on the cab and on the bridge. We are already familiar with the Secretary for War who takes up the War Office as an amusing hobby—something like stamp-collecting—but the method seems to have grave disadvantages.

Sometimes I hear by chance snatches of the old music; and I want to take off my hat. Back I go to the stuffy dressing-room, and the dear scattered faces are reassembled, the drums and trumpets sound from

---

We did not want to be taken for amateurs; we "should have been hatin' it" in our phrase; our desire was to do our job as well as ever we could, and to this intent the elders helped the youngsters, corrected them, suggested new ideas, and held much discourse in the dressing-room and in the tavern on the mysteries of the craft. One of them, indeed, wrote an Actor's Alphabet of which only one line remains in my memory:—

Kneel on the Knee to the audience next.

We had no toleration for grumblers. People who thought the dressing-room uncomfortable or complained of the want of light were advised to choose some other business; and the same counsel was tendered to those who said that ten minutes was not a long enough time in which to effect a complete change in costume and make-up. Ah! the old dressing-rooms with the good fellowship and the smell of grease-paints and the flowing tankards: *quando vos aspiciam.* As the evening went on the dim lights seemed to burn dimmer, the air grew thick and hot and the cigarette smoke floated a blue mist. One heard perhaps the rumour of the stage; the wild hunting marsh of *King Lear,* the sound of Bolingbroke's music of summons outside Barklonghly Castle, the magic revel of the *Dream,* the solemn *Requiem* for Richard II, the bells ringing for Crispin Crispinian, the *Non Nobis* in canon after the victory of Agincourt, Nicolai's wonderful revelry in the last act of the *Merry Wives,* the springing, dancing gaiety of *It was a Lover and his Lass* in *As You,* or guns shot off on Bosworth Field. And all the while the players came in and out, sometimes chuckling over Dent who had "dried" and taken refuge in horrible grimaces, or Morris who had nearly tumbled into the grave, or Fairfax who had "thought out" a make-up for Bardolph of such fierce realism that the stage manager had called piteously on his Maker at the sight of the purple flaming visage. One heard the great ringing voice of Hathaway rolling up from the stage in some tremendous scene.

"Hark at him," one would say, "he won't speak text. There: that's a bit from *Orlando:* that's *Romeo.* There he goes. He's a wonder." A "small-part" man would dash up as if the fell fiend were after him. He enters a peer of parliament, with a rich velvet cloak about him, black moustaches and beard on his face. The moustaches and beard are off in a second; down goes the cloak; the black tights are peeled off revealing parti-coloured hose beneath; the sallow complexion and traces of spirit-gum disappear beneath a rapid application of grease. In six or seven minutes a fool with a ruddy, beaming countenance, "Folly" in hand, shoots down the stairs to attend on the Mad French King. He returns presently at leisure, having plenty of time to change into old Sir Thomas Erpingham, to drink a tankard of beer, and to smoke a pipe.—Ed.]

the stage, I am waiting to go on in the wings; the clanking of the armour and the clash of swords sounds in my ears, the stage-manager (would he were here!) hisses his opinion of my dancing with wonderful eloquence from the prompt-corner: it all returns; dear, happy life of players errant, purged unconsciously of most of the hideous vices of modern civilisation.*

I take off my hat when I hear the old music, for I think of the old friends and the old days, of the theatre in the meadows by the sacred river, and the song of the nightingales on sweet spring nights. There is no doubt that we may safely hold with Plato his opinion, and safely may we believe that all earthly things are but broken copies and dim lineaments of everlasting realities. Therefore, I hope and trust, I shall again be gathered into the true Hathaway Company *quae sursum est,* which is the purged and exalted image of the lower, which plays for ever a great Mystery in the theatre of the meadows of asphodel, which wanders by the happy streams, and drinks from an Eternal Cup in a high and blissful and Everlasting Tavern. *Ave, cara sodalitas, ave semper.*

---

*[The following passage was crossed out by Machen in the ms.: They are all scattered abroad, the ancient company, and many of them are now brilliant and successful London Actors; may it be well with them and better. But I want the Old Company was it was in those years long ago before fame came, that fellowship of old friends who wandered over England together, playing together, drinking together in good taverns after the night's work was done. For I came a stranger to them, and I shall never forget their kindness, their compassion for my ignorance and awkwardness and lack of skill in everything that was to be done.

I could write for ever of the taverns where we used to meet of nights, of pleasant ancient rooms with red curtains and warm fires, where some swallowed gigantic draughts of beer, and others revelled on "boiled Scotch". Sometimes, too, we rehearsed in tavern rooms in the day, and it is like a bit of a romance to me to recall the scenes in old inn courtyards, galleried, with flights of steps. Here, perhaps, while the main rehearsal proceeded within, half-a-dozen minor rehearsals would be going on amongst separate groups of players: a chance farmer might enter the yard and look in astonishment at the scene, at these strange persons in the gallery who met and parted and crossed one another with antic gestures, or perhaps he would start at the sudden fury of the mob in *Coriolanus,* as the door opened for a moment; and shrieks and furious executions fell upon his unaccustomed ears.—Ed.]

Ambrose stayed a little more than two years with the strollers. He sent the address of a solicitor to his uncle on his coming of age, and found when Mr. Horbury sent in his statements that there was a pleasant little sum of money to his credit. Mr. Vaughan consented to stay on at the Wern, and Ambrose, bidding farewell to his companions, sheathing his property sword for the last time, journeyed up to London on a cold bright day in early spring.

4.

He felt strangely enough as he saw the outer walls of London rising before him, and the train rushed through the suburbs into the terminus. It was nearly four years since he and Nelly had paid the famous visit, and it seemed as if it were such a long while ago. Everything was so changed, within and without; and yet, though there was a keen March wind blowing, and white clouds were fleeting across a slate-blue sky; he almost felt again that hot blast that had welcomed them as they left the station. But it was all over; the curtain had been rung down for ever on that scene of his life. The streets were changed: perhaps, he thought, it was the difference between March and August, but no, it was not so: the London of four years ago no longer existed, for him at all events. A new man, he came to a new city.

He settled down finally in a pleasant set of rooms in Gray's Inn Square. The windows of his sitting-room looked out on the garden, and by the time he took up his residence the leaves were green, and he might have thought himself a dweller in a lodge in a wood, if it had not been for the low rumble of traffic from Theobald's Road, which was only silenced in the deepest hours of the night. It was in this place that he sat down and began that long meditation which was henceforth his life.

One of his first tasks, it is believed, was to set in order the notes he had made four years before in Little Russell Row for the "Defence of Taverns"; and soon afterwards he wrote his article on "The Hidden Mystery" which attracted a certain amount of notice, for accidental rather than essential reasons. It appeared in the pages of a most respectable magazine, a magazine of classic fame which had settled the business of many a young poet far away back in the 'thirties and 'forties. The editor was attracted by Ambrose's style, and as it afterwards appeared, could not have had any very clear understanding of the subject matter: the fact was Ambrose had been artful. His essay was written on a curious text—the utter blindness of two centuries or more to the beauties of Gothic Art. He shewed how even the draughtsmen of the eighteenth century, with (say) Lincoln Cathedral before their eyes, were utterly unable to draw it correctly, to give any true idea of the Gothic mouldings or tracery. He quoted Smollett on York Minster, Washington Irving on Westminster Abbey; he made a catena of witnesses to the singular fact that for more than two centuries men were surrounded by wonderful buildings which in the true sense they were absolutely unable to see. He shewed too that, to a great extent, the same principle worked in literature and in painting; he quoted Dr. Johnson's dictum as to Pope's "poetry", his criticism of *Lycidas,* pointing out the extreme shrewdness, sagacity, and honesty of Johnson's character—and yet the Lexicographer thought *Lycidas* was something very near to rubbish and Pope's admirably clever verse poetry in its most absolute, perfect, and final form. As for painting: were not the Caraccis highly esteemed and Giotto, Cimabue, Botticelli regarded as semi-barbarians? At the same time he shewed that it would never do to write off the Eighteenth Century as utterly deficient in all artistic perception: since in the rarest and purest of all the arts it could boast of the greatest of masters. The age of Pergolesi, Handel, Bach, and of a vast number of minor musicians who wrote work as charming in its way as the minor poets of the Elizabethan and Caroline periods—this was no age of artistic Barbarism; and even in architecture itself, St. Mary-le-Strand was, of its kind, very near to perfection. But then on the other hand: what was the attitude of the Augustans and their successors towards Nature, Scenery, the Visible Universe generally? Clearly, it was the attitude of men blinded, stupified, befogged. The trees and streams of the great Berkeley, illustrious among philosophers, a spiritual thinker if there ever was one, were taken out of Plato's Dialogues, the "poets" went to Hampton Court Gardens and to the famous Maze for Nature, they called a wood a "bosky shade", and Johnson and Boswell, who found Greenwich Park much too countrified for their taste, were interested in the wild Hebrides as one is interested in grotesque oddities from the South Sea Islands. And—to take another region of the soul—nearly all of these men, most of them acute and intelligent in a high degree, were firmly convinced that the blessings of the "Reformation" were so clear, palpable, and certain that there was no room for argument on the matter. Warton, certainly, hinted that the effect on the arts was not of the best; Johnson (probably for sport) took the unpopular side in talking to Boswell: but in the general opinion of the cultured the matter was as clearly settled as the result of adding two to two: "Popery" was wholly wrong, "Protestantism" was entirely right.

It seemed, then, to follow from all these instances that whole generations of men no more stupid and ignorant than their ancestors or successors might be absolutely blinded as to matters that were, literally and physically, before their eyes: there could hardly be more conspicuous objects than Lincoln Cathedral, a forest, or a mountain; beauties could scarcely be more clearly evoked and displayed than the beauties of *Lycidas*. And many of the men thus blind on certain points were of very exceptional ability and acuteness on other matters; and even on artistic matters. It was as if a man walked through a wood, admiring the beauty of the oak, and at the same moment wondering why an all-wise Creator had made the grotesque ugliness of the ash and the beech and the yew!

Therefore, Ambrose proceeded, since intelligent and thoughtful and sagacious men were obviously "blind" as to such obvious and manifest beauty as that displayed in Visible Nature, Gothic Architecture, Elizabethan and Caroline Poetry, and Catholic Ritual; is it not highly probable that men no less intelligent and sagacious are at the present moment blind as to certain matters which may not be so obvious—which, it should rather be said, seem to us not so obvious? Is it not possible that while we look down on the Augustans with pitying superiority, we ourselves may be sunken in darkness on matters infinitely more vital and important than the subjects on which they displayed so invincible an ignorance. This may be difficult to realise; to us the beauty of Lincoln Cathedral, of *Lycidas,* of the great spectacle of the visible world, of early Italian Art is so clear and so incontestible that we could as readily contradict the axioms of Euclid or the Laws of Logic as the presence of beauty in these things—but after all? *Que scavons nous?* Unless we take up the position that we have attained to final perfection, that we have surpassed all the wisdom of the wise, all the art of all artists, all the visions of all seers, that compared with us all precedent humanity is, in all things, as a schoolboy in the multiplication-table to Sir Isaac Newton, that the universal goal is attained, the race run and won for ever—unless we take up this slightly ridiculous and monstrous position, we must confess that there is a high probability, at all events, that *we*, in our turn, are blind to many sights, deaf to many sounds, insensitive to many wonders, ignorant of many mysteries.

Then, Ambrose went on to shew the probability of this thesis by many analogies, drawn from things of mind and of matter. He instanced the Laws of Logical Science, latent in man's discourse from the beginning of speech, and yet not clearly perceived nor demonstrated till the day of Aristotle: here was a mystery or magistery that had been visible and yet invisible for countless ages, that had been before the intellectual eyes of countless myriads day after day, hour after hour: the veriest savage who used stone arrows to shoot prehistoric game must have been familiar with *Barbara* and *Celarent* and yet he knew it not; though he won his dinner and his life by this knowledge that was concealed from himself. The analogies were indeed innumerable; how many apples had fallen before the Law of Gravitation was enunciated, how often had the power of steam been perceived before the obvious application was disclosed? And man had gazed at the earth and sky at the clouds and the woods, the seas and the rivers for how many ages before the mystery and the beauty of the world were really manifested in the days of Coleridge, Wordsworth, and Turner.

At this point he paused for a while in his main argument to follow a curious byway of thought. How far, he asked, were we to suppose that much that was not expressed was still felt or experienced; suppressed, perhaps, out of deference to convention, or from fear of consequences? Here was an obscure point which seemed to invite an endless enquiry, on which it was impossible to dogmatise. For instance; you might investigate the marriage customs of some tribe more or less primitive, you might satisfy yourself that to all intents and purposes marriage and giving in marriage in the tribe in question were as prosaic, as much a matter of business as pig-dealing in Wiltshire: and yet—from the heart of this race of chatterers in women there might surge up a burst of song that expressed all the passion of love. In a sense the courtship of Portia by Bassanio was a squalid fortune-hunt: still there were lines that spoke nobly of the *latens deitas*. Perhaps there

were many men of the eighteenth century who were thrilled to the
heart by the ineffable mystery and beauty of the Gothic Work; only
they were ashamed to confess it, to write themselves down as lovers of
ignorance and barbarism in art. And it was hardly conceivable that the
heart of men had not been stirred by the awe and wonder of the world
till about 1790: the glory of dawn and sunset, the terror and splendour
of mountains and seas, the delight of the woods in summer, the sweetness and the incantation of scented nights; these things could not have
been wholly without witnesses; it could not have been permitted that
so many thousands of years should pass before the hieroglyphic
speech of the world to the soul was in a measure deciphered. No
doubt there were hints of this universal mystery written in Hebrew and
Greek and Latin; still, they were but hints, and undoubtedly the full
expression—or rather the approximately full expression—had been
reserved to a comparatively late day. And yet: how many people since
the foundation of the world had *felt* all this—all that Coleridge and
Wordsworth, Keats and Tennyson had written—and had lacked words
or courage to express it? He wondered how much of previous treasure
we had lost, how much we were still losing, from this lack of courage,
from this fear of telling the great incredible dreams which apparently
contradict sense and experience, science and convention; reason itself:
and yet are perfect wisdom and beauty. It seemed probable enough
that this loss had been, was, and would be huge enough. He noted the
fierce, irrational intolerance that was ready to be called out at any moment by the slightest novelty, by the faintest departure from the most
external of the conventions: more especially when the new departure
moved towards truth and beauty. Alexander Pope and the people of
his tribe had but little to fear; since the lower part of every man is always in sympathy with clever observations of common externals expressed in more or less clear and witty phrases, and above all with trite
moralisings; as had been well said, Tate and Brady were in the long
ships that bore Hengist and Horsa; and it might have been said, with
equal truth, that Tet and Bredi followed the Cymri to the Isle of Britain from the Land of Summer. In every age, in every race; there was a
great majority ready and anxious to applaud such gems as "The proper
study of mankind is man", "One craftsman hates another", "the unexpected often happens" as genuine pearls of poetry and wisdom, and

those who excelled in this manner need fear no terrors or persecutions. But when the turn of the wheel came, when a man saw the heavens opened and said so—then let him beware, for Professor Wilson, Mr. Lockhart, and Dr. Maginn were not slow to deal with such an one as this.

It seemed probable, then, that human nature being what it is and always has been; anxious in the main for an easy time in things of the body or things of the mind, averse from incurring opposition and dislike, desirous, in the popular phrase, to live and let live; it was probable that many who could have spoken had kept silence, were still keeping silence. Poe had an interesting speculation as to the fate of transcendent greatness in vision: he thought that it had been rewarded for the most part with the scaffold and the madhouse, but this was doubtful— with contempt and neglect and then with a spurious post-mortem fame, were the truer version of the facts. It was interesting to note, by the way, how in some cases there had been a kind of "composition": Tennyson had no doubt "compounded" for the *Fatima* by the *May Queen* and *Enoch Arden:* the verities had passed unchallenged under the cloak of the domesticities. In like manner Poe, a great seer as well as a great artist, was accorded a sort of contemptuous toleration as the author of *The Bells* and *The Raven.*

He returned after this digression to the central point of his argument: the probability of an all but universal "ignorance" or "blindness" as to things of the very highest moment. He suggested further that it was even probable that there might be one central truth, one eternal beauty, one great "Word" that had not been lost (at least in time), because it had never been found: a secret of secrets, a master mystery, a key opening the door of the Shut Palace of the King. Taking this as his hypothesis, he imagined this one Truth as everywhere present, everywhere visible, everywhere known—and yet all unknown. It might, perhaps, be spoken of under the most varied symbolisms, it might be manifested under the most diverse forms, it might sometimes be so degraded in evil use as to appear more pertinent to devilry than divinity. Or again it might be like some ingenious puzzle in its manifestation: as if one were to conceive for example some picture divided into minute portions and these strewn at random on a table: it might be very difficult to perceive any relation between the parts, it might not appear that they were parts at all, it might be the work of a great imagination to collect the fragments together and set them in their true order so that the great and beautiful whole should appear. "Better still," he said, "conceive a stained glass window taken to pieces, bit by bit from its leads, and the irregular red and green and blue and golden morsels put in a basket and given to a savage. It is likely enough that the blackfellow would be delighted with the bright fragments as ornaments of a new kind: but how hard it would be for him to set the golden pieces together and make of them the saint's aureole. In all likelihood most of the glass would find its way to the swamp, there to give greater worship to the fetish deity."*

He went on in this ingenious and elaborate vein, conjecturing the existence of this great Master Mystery, the mainspring and the source of all being, all joy, all savour, all delight, the *ens unum in diversis,* that which gives glory to the dawn and melody to concordant sounds, sweetness to the rose, magic to the poem, wonder to the romance; potent also and all prevailing in the highest secrets of life and death.

The article appeared, as has been said, in a magazine of the highest respectability; it was a good deal noticed and commented on as "a passionate and eloquent appeal for the appreciation of beauty in common things". It was only some year or two later when Ambrose had published his first story, the *Rosa Mundi,* that people began to put two and two together, and it was generally felt that his work was "not quite nice". It must not be imagined that the Idea for which he worked was at all understood; but in certain instances there were *i*'s in the article and dots in the story, and it would have been quite difficult not to put the one on the other.

Such was the beginning of a long and austere career, devoted to a great and mystic end. Of course Ambrose was misunderstood, often laughed at, occasionally abused; but he always maintained that his ways were made far too pleasant for him, he deplored the soft indifferent

---

*[At this point in the ms. there is a paragraph that has been crossed out: So perhaps—the essay proceeded—one might form an apter analogy if one could conceive of men who bought their daily bread with gold, who lived for gold, who wove gold _____, chains, and watches, who wrote with gold pens, who drank out of gold cups, all the while ignorant or forgetful of the one metal which served so many and diverse uses; dwelling so on the difference in service as to ignore the identity of matter.—Ed.]

age in which he laboured, which could only provide a quarter-column of ill-tempered chaff for the stones and fires of braver times. Indeed, the ill-temper and the chaff were often missing: his reviewers told him he was a clever fellow, and only asked, much more in sorrow than in anger, why he did not devote his talents to simple healthy themes of domestic interest.*

It is not probable that the end will ever be clearly understood. The few documents that are available seem to leave the whole matter in a state of conjecture; and it has only been possible to surmise the objects of the last wonderful journey after a very careful and minute reading of Ambrose's note-books and journals, in which certain hints and things half-said seem to supply a certain clue to a strange adventure. So far as can be gathered, then, it appears probable that old Cradock, in handing over to Ambrose the Blessed Cup of Teilo sant, had delivered also a certain charge concerning the relic; and it may well be that the final "removal" of the Sangraal in the Romances owes its existence to traditions and rumours of the charge in question. However this may be, it is practically certain that Ambrose when he went to the East took with him the Holy Vessel, and bestowed it in safe custody in the place to which he had been directed; and perhaps its splendour and glories will never more be seen by mortal eyes.

The Kurds crucified him on a tree that stands just without the village where he was staying. They descended on the Christian people in their usual fashion: some of these fled, some hid themselves, many were given to torture and cruel death. One of them, who was hidden, told how he saw "the stranger Ambrosian" brought out, and how they put before him the image of the Crucified that he might spit upon it, and trample it under his feet: but he kissed the Icon with great joy, and penitence, and devotion. So they bore him to the tree and nailed him there; and after he had hung some hours, the Kurds, enraged, as it was said, by the delight and rapture that shone on his face, killed him with their spears.

---

*[Another paragraph is here crossed out: Naturally, he made a few converts; and these remember with something of amour the nights in Gray's Inn, the sessions which now and again were prolonged till the pale light of dawn filters into the room through the leaves.—Ed.]

In this manner did Ambrose Meyrick gain Red Martyrdom, and achieve the most glorious Quest and Adventure of the Sangraal.

Appendix

Introduction to *The Hill of Dreams* (1923)

In the year 1895 I was at length certain, or almost certain, that I was a man of letters. I had been, if I may put the matter thus familiarly, for more than twelve years "on the job". In '83 I had written a little book called *The Anatomy of Tobacco*, chiefly as a counter-irritant to loneliness and semi-starvation. In '84 I had translated the Heptameron of Margaret of Navarre, while '85 and '86 were devoted to the concoction of *The Chronicle of Clemendy*, a volume of mediaeval tales. Another translation, a version of *Le Moyen de Parvenir* by Beroalde de Verville—his name is more beautiful than his book—occupied the leisure of my evenings somewhere about '88 and '89, the days being given to the rendering of the *Memoirs of Casanova* (twelve volumes) into the English tongue.

In 1890 I was writing essays and short stories and odds and ends and varieties for papers which have now become ghosts: *The Globe, The St. James's Gazette,* and *The Whirlwind;* to say nothing of "smart" tales contributed to an extinct, or almost extinct, family of journals; the "society" papers. In '90 and '91 I wrote the "Great God Pan", which was published at the end of '94 and made a mild sort of sensation with old ladies, on the press and off it. And in the spring and summer of '94 I was busy with *The Three Impostors,* which fell somewhat flatly when it was issued in the autumn of '95. So, as I say, I began to feel almost convinced towards the end of the year 1895 that I was in some degree a literary man, that my business lay in the direction of writing books. Consequently, it appeared that I had better go and write one. Very good: the next question was—what sort of a book should I write?

And here, the reception that had been given to *The Three Impostors* helped me greatly. I have said that it was of the flat kind, but beyond this, it was critical. I was told that I was merely a second-rate imitator of Stevenson. This was not quite all the truth, but there was a great deal of truth in it, and I am glad to say that I took my correction in a proper spirit. I resolved to try to amend my ways. I made manly resolutions. As I put it to my old friend, that distinguished American citizen, A. E. Waite: "I will never give anybody a white powder again." And on the whole, I have honoured that vow ever since. I was to start afresh, then, from the beginning, to turn over a new leaf, both as regards matter and manner. No more white powders, no more of the calix principis inferorum, no more hanky-panky with the Great God Pan, or the Little People or any people of that dubious sort; and—this was the hard part of it—no more of the measured, rounded Stevensonian cadence, which I had learned to use with some faculty and more facility. And so we were getting on; I had at least found out the sort of book that I was not going to write. It merely remained to discover what sort of book I was going to write.

I took this problem out with me on solemn walks in dimmest Bloomsbury, then a region most fit for the contemplations of a meditative man. I had just moved into chambers at 4 Verulam Buildings, Gray's Inn, and so, by way of Theobald's Road, I had easy access to the old, grave squares where life moved quietly and peaceably as if it were the life of a little country town. Grey square opened into grey square, silent street into silent street; all was decorous and remote from the roar of traffic and the rush of men. But few people ascended the steps of the dim old houses, but few descended them; the local tradesmen, all old established, old-fashioned, steady and good, called for orders and purveyed their wares in a sober way; Bloomsbury was silence and repose; and in its grey calm I pursued my anxious studies, and submitted my problems to myself.

The required notion came at last, not from within, nor even from Bloomsbury, but from without. I am not quite sure, but almost sure, that the needed hint was discovered in an introduction to *Tristram Shandy* written by that most accomplished man of letters, Mr. Charles Whibley. Mr. Whibley, in classifying Sterne's masterpiece, noted that it might be called a picaresque of the mind, contrasting it with *Gil Blas*, which is a picaresque of the body. This distinction had struck me very much when I read it; and now as I was puzzling my head to find a spring for the book that was to be written, Mr. Whibley's dictum occurred to me, and applying it to another eighteenth century masterpiece, I asked myself why I should not write a *Robinson Crusoe* of the soul. I resolved forthwith that I would do so; I would take the theme of solitude, loneliness, separation from mankind, but, in place of a desert island and a bodily separation, my hero should be isolated in London and find his chief loneliness in the midst of myriads of myriads of men. His should be a solitude of the spirit, and the ocean surrounding him and disassociating him from his kind should be a spiritual deep. And here I found myself, as I thought, on sure ground; for I had had some experience of such things. For two years I had endured terrors of loneliness in my little room in Clarendon Road, Notting Hill Gate, and so I was soundly instructed as to the matter of the work. I felt, in short, that I had my notion firmly by the tail; and so at once I set to work.

Not to writing, be it understood, but rather to the daily consideration of my topic; to taking it every night to bed with me as a child takes his toy; to putting it on the breakfast table beside my morning tea, again as a child with a new toy is apt to set it down on the cloth beside his plate of bread and butter. The notion (and my faithful bulldog Juggernaut) went with me on my dim Bloomsbury walks on grey mornings and wintry darkening afternoons, and when occasionally I went out and dined with a friend, the notion was in my pocket, and every now and then I would take it out, as it were, and glance at it for a moment, to make quite sure that it was safe and still there. Unnoticed, I put a few drops of the notion in the wine and sprinkled it lightly on the meat and found that it improved the aroma and flavour of both enormously; and whenever I was a little bored or down in the mouth and out of sorts, I took a couple of spoonfuls of the notion and felt better at once.

And then I began to plan it out on paper, and to try to reduce it to some logical form, to think of incidents that would shew forth the idea to the best advantage, to determine the main course of the story, and now and again to write down "bits" that occurred to me. I proceeded in this manner for some weeks. The precious "notion" had been given me, let us say, towards the end of October, but it was not till early in February that I put pen to paper in dead earnest, and launched with a trembling heart on the first chapter. And then the trouble began.

For, in the first place, I had vowed myself, it will be remembered, to a change of style. Or rather, I was to abandon the manner in which *The Three Impostors* had been written, which was not my manner but Stevenson's, and to get a style, or something like a style, of my own. The gracious rounding of the sentence, the bright balance of words, the sonorous rise and fall of the cadences were done with; no more of costume; all was to be plain, everyday clothes. But it was a hard struggle. The player in private life does not want to "take the stage" as if he were Charles Surface in bloom-coloured satin; but, on the other hand, he wants still less to enter a drawing-room as if he had a game leg and a club foot: I had a horrible todo with my sentences in that first chapter. The old rules were gone, the new ones were yet to learn and most vilely I sweated at the task of learning them. The manuscript of that first chapter was a mass of erasures, corrections, interlineations. But somehow it was done, and, I thought, not so badly, all things considered. And then I started, more hopefully, at the second chapter. And then I was done.

I have said that I had planned the book out on paper, that I had, as it were, drawn it to scale, devising and arranging a due succession of incidents and events. And no sooner had I written two lines of that second chapter, according to plan, than I found that the book as planned could not be written at all. My clay model broke into bits in my hand. It had looked all right in the clay, but in the stone it most certainly would not do. It was a horrible moment.

For three weeks I sat down night after night with blank paper before me. Night after night I began to write that second chapter; night after night I groaned and shut up my desk. Sometimes the night's work amounted to two lines; sometimes to two folios; but it was no good. There was neither life, nor fire, nor movement, nor reality in a word of it. Here was I with one chapter of the book finished and all the rest impossible. But all the same it was going to be done. I was as stubborn in those days as my good bulldog, Juggernaut; and I cannot say more than that.

And here I would say that to the best of my belief, I was brought to a dead stop precisely because I had explored the way and laid it out so thoroughly. I have told how I rolled the "notion" up and down and round about in my mind; how I planned and plotted and blew up the rocks and cut away the brushwood and felled the trees, so that there should be no difficulties in the track; and there was the mischief of it. For the truth is, that for me at any rate literature is always an exploration. The relish of it, the delight of it are indissolubly bound up with the sense of penetrating into a new world and an undiscovered region, of standing on some minor peak in Darien and looking on worlds that no eye has ever seen before. And this must be the sense of the scene as the actual words are written, as the ink flows from the pen—or else there is nothing written that matters two straws. And in the affair of this particular book, I had taken such pains in exploring the ground that when I came to write it, there was nothing left to explore. Here were no miracles, no mysteries, no buried treasures, no unlooked for wonders. Everything was known, everything familiar, and all seemed quite devoid of significance.

Still, that book had got to be written, and was going to be written. And one happy night the whole matter of that famous second chapter was manifested to me. As far as I remember, in the original design, Lucian was at this point to be packed off to London to the miseries of the inevitable garret; now it seemed that there were further adventures for him in his native country. I thought of these and wrote them and so got the opportunity of dwelling a little longer among the dear woods and the domed hills and the memorable vales of my native Gwent, of trying once more to set down some faint echoes of the inexpressive song that the beloved land always sang to me and still sings across all the waste of weary years. Then I found somewhere or other, the recipe for the "Roman Chapter", an attempted recreation of the Roman British world of *Isca Silurum*, Caerleon-on-Usk, the town where I was born, and soaked myself so thoroughly in the vision of the old golden city—now a little desolate village—and listened so long in the deep green of Wentwood for the clangour of the marching Legion and or the noise of their trumpets that I grew quite "dithery" as they say in some parts of England. I would go out on my dim Bloomsbury strolls, deep in my dream, and would "come to myself" with a sudden shock in Lamb's Conduit Street or Mecklenburgh Square or in the solitudes of Great Coram Street, realising certainly, that I was not, in actuality, in the Garden of Avallaunius or delaying in the Via Nympharum or on the Pons Saturni—it is called Pont Sadwrn to this day—but utterly at a loss to know exactly where I was or what I was doing, without the faintest notion of the various positions of north and south, east and west, and not at all clear as to how I was to get home to Gray's Inn and my lunch. And it was in this queer way that the fourth chapter was accomplished. I was somewhat proud of it, and went on gaily through Chapters Five, Six and Seven, and had a month's holiday in Provence, and came back to finish my book, feeling confident and in the best of spirits.

Alas! my pride had a deep fall indeed. I read over those last three chapters and saw suddenly that they were all hopelessly wrong, that they would not do at any price, that I had turned, unperceiving, from the straight path by ever so little, and had gone on, getting farther and farther away from the true direction till the way was hopelessly lost. I was in the middle of a black wood and I could not see any path out of it.

There was only one thing to be done. The three condemned chapters went into the drawer and I began over again from the end of Chapter Four. Five and Six were done, and then again I struggled desperately for many weeks, trying to find the last chapter. False tracks again, hopeless efforts, spoilt folios thick about me till by some chance or another, I know not how, the right notion was given me, and I wrote the seventh and last chapter in a couple of nights. Once more the thought of the old land had come to my help; the book was finished. It had occupied from first to last the labour of eighteen months.

Then I began to send the manuscript round to the publishers. The result would have melted the heart of the sourest cynic. To those hard men of business, as they are sometimes called, time was nothing, kindness everything. They wrote me, one after another, long letters in small writing on large quarto paper. They all implored me, as I loved them, not to publish this book because, as they explained, it was so poor and weak and dull that its publication would ruin what little reputation I had gained before.

One of these good men went farther. A month or two after he had refused *The Hill of Dreams* on folios of in quarto kindness, I saw amongst the "literary announcements" in some paper a paragraph which interested me deeply. It ran something like this:

"Mr. Blank—the publisher—and Mr. Dash—an eminent man of letters—have got hold of a promising idea for a romance. They propose, so Mr. Blank tells me, to describe the adventures of a lad who lives partly in the life of today and partly in the Roman world of the second century of our era. The plan seems a novel and arresting one and I look forward to reading the book next spring. The collaborators have not yet thought of a title for what should be a striking story."

I chuckled. I knew that lad and whence he came: from Chapter Four of my MS. However, nothing more was heard of him in his revised and improved form. *The Hill of Dreams* was published in 1907, ten years after it had been finished.

Preface to *The Secret Glory* (1922)

Some years ago I met my old master, Sir Frank Benson—he was Mr. F. R. Benson, then—and he asked me in his friendly way what I had been doing lately.

"I am just finishing a book," I replied, "a book that everybody will hate."

"As usual," said the Don Quixote of our English stage—if I knew any nobler title to bestow upon him, I would bestow it—"as usual; running your head against a stone wall!"

Well, I don't know about "as usual"; there may be something to be said for the personal criticism or there may not; but it has struck me that Sir Frank's remark is a very good description of *The Secret Glory*, the book I had in mind as I talked to him. It is emphatically the history of an unfortunate fellow who ran his head against stone walls from the beginning to the end. He could think nothing and do nothing after the common fashion of the world; even when he "went wrong", he did so in a highly unusual and eccentric manner. It will be for the reader to determine whether he were a saint who had lost his way in the centuries or merely an undeveloped lunatic; I hold no passionate view on either side. In every age, there are people great and small for whom the times are out of joint, for whom everything is, somehow, wrong and askew. Consider Hamlet; an amiable man and an intelligent man. But what a mess he made of it! Fortunately, my hero—or idiot, which you will—was not called upon to intermeddle with affairs of State, and so only brought himself to grief; if it were grief; for the least chink of the door should be kept open, I am inclined to hold, for the other point of view. I have just been re-reading Kipling's "The Miracle of Purim Bhagat", the tale of the Brahmin Prime Minister of the Native State in India, who saw all the world and the glory of it, in the West as well as in the East, and suddenly abjured all to become a hermit in the wood. Was he mad, or was he supremely wise? It is just a matter of opinion.

528

The origin and genesis of *The Secret Glory* were odd enough. Once on a time, I read the life of a famous schoolmaster, one of the most notable schoolmasters of these later days. I believe he was an excellent man in every way; but, somehow, that "Life" got on my nerves. I thought that the School Songs—for which, amongst other things, this master was famous—were drivel; I thought his views about football, regarded, not as a good game, but as the discipline and end and guide of life, were rot, and poisonous rot at that. In a word, the "Life" of this excellent man got my back up.

Very good. The year after, schoolmasters and football had ceased to engage my attention. I was deeply interested in a curious and minute investigation of the wonderful legend of the Holy Grail; or rather, in one aspect of that extraordinary complex. My researches led me to the connection of the Grail Legend with the vanished Celtic Church which held the field in Britain in the fifth and sixth and seventh centuries; I undertook an extraordinary and fascinating journey into a misty and uncertain region of Christian history. I must not say more here, lest— as Nurse says to the troublesome and persistent child—I "begin all over again"; but, indeed, it was a voyage on perilous seas, a journey to faery lands forlorn—and I would declare, by the way, my conviction that if there had been no Celtic Church, Keats could never have written those lines of tremendous evocation and incantation.

Again; very good. The year after, it came upon me to write a book. And I hit upon an original plan; or so I thought. I took my dislike of the good schoolmaster's "Life", I took my knowledge of Celtic mysteries—and combined my information!

Original, this plan! It was all thought of years before I was born. Do you remember the critic of the *Eatanswill Gazette?* He had to review for that admirable journal a work on Chinese Metaphysics. Mr. Pott tells the story of the article.

"He read up for the subject, at my desire, in the Encyclopædia Britannica . . . he read for metaphysics under the letter M, and for China under the letter C, and combined his information!"

NOTE

One of the schoolmasters in *The Secret Glory* has views on the subject of football similar to those entertained by a well-known schoolmaster whose Biography appeared many years ago. That is the only link between the villain of invention and the good man of real life.

Epilogue to *The Secret Glory* (1922)

It is unfortunate—or fortunate: that is a matter to be settled by the taste of the reader—that with this episode of the visit to London all detailed material for the life of Ambrose Meyrick comes to an end. Odd scraps of information, stray notes and jottings are all that is available, and the rest of Meyrick's life must be left in dim and somewhat legendary outline.

Personally, I think that this failure of documents is to be lamented. The four preceding chapters have, in the main, dealt with the years of boyhood, and therefore with a multitude of follies. One is inclined to wonder, as poor Nelly wondered, whether the lad was quite right in his head. It is possible that if we had fuller information as to his later years we might be able to dismiss him as decidedly eccentric, but well-meaning on the whole.

But, after all, I cannot be confident that he would get off so easily. Certainly he did not repeat the adventure of Little Russell Row, nor, so far as I am aware, did he address any one besides his old schoolmaster in a Rabelaisian epistle. There are certain acts of lunacy which are like certain acts of heroism: they are hardly to be achieved twice by the same men.

But Meyrick continued to do odd things. He became a strolling player instead of becoming a scholar of Balliol. If he had proceeded to the University, he would have encountered the formative and salutary influence of Jowett. He wandered up and down the country for two or three years with the actors, and writes the following apostrophe to the memory of his old company:

"I take off my hat when I hear the old music, for I think of the old friends and the old days; of the theatre in the meadows by the sacred river, and the swelling song of the nightingales on sweet, spring nights. There is no doubt that we may safely hold with Plato his opinion, and safely may we believe that all brave earthly shows are but broken copies and dim lineaments of immortal things. Therefore, I hope and trust that I shall again be gathered unto the true Hathaway Company *quæ sursum est,* which is the purged and exalted image of the lower, which plays for ever a great mystery in the theatre of the meadows of asphodel, which wanders by the happy, shining streams, and drinks from an Eternal Cup in a high and blissful and everlasting Tavern. *Ave, cara sodalitas, ave semper.*"

Thus does he translate into wild speech *crêpe* hair and grease paints, dirty dressing-rooms and dirtier lodgings. And when his strolling days were over he settled down in London, paying occasional visits to his old home in the west. He wrote three or four books which are curious and interesting in their way, though they will never be popular. And finally he went on a strange errand to the East; and from the East there was for him no returning.

It will be remembered that he speaks of a Celtic cup, which had been preserved in one family for many hundred years. On the death of the last "Keeper" this cup was placed in Meyrick's charge. He received it with the condition that it was to be taken to a certain concealed shrine in Asia and there deposited in hands that would know how to hide its glories for ever from the evil world.

He went on this journey into unknown regions, travelling by ragged roads and mountain passes, by the sandy wilderness and the mighty river. And he forded his way by the quaking and dubious track that winds in and out among the dangers and desolations of the *Kev-ir*—the great salt slough.

He came at last to the place appointed and gave the word and the treasure to those who know how to wear a mask and to keep well the things which are committed to them, and then set out on his journey back. He had reached a point not very far from the gates of the West and halted for a day or two amongst Christians, being tired out with a weary pilgrimage. But the Turks or the Kurds—it does not matter which—descended on the place and worked their customary works, and so Ambrose was taken by them.

One of the native Christians, who had hidden himself from the miscreants, told afterwards how he saw "the stranger Ambrosian" brought out, and how they held before him the image of the Crucified that he might spit upon it and trample it under his feet. But he kissed the icon with great joy and penitence and devotion. So they bore him to a tree outside the village and crucified him there.

And after he had hung on the tree some hours, the infidels, enraged, as it was said, by the shining rapture of his face, killed him with their spears.

It was in this manner that Ambrose Meyrick gained Red Martyrdom and achieved the most glorious Quest and Adventure of the Sangraal.

Bibliography

I. Book Publications of Machen's Fiction

The Chronicle of Clemendy. London: Privately Printed for the Society of Pantegruelists, [March 1888]. New York: Privately Printed for the Society of Pantegruelists [Boni & Liveright], 1923. London: Martin Secker, 1925. New York: Alfred A. Knopf, 1926. London: Martin Secker/Adelphi Library, 1927. London: Martin Secker/Adelphi Library, [1927].

The Great God Pan and The Inmost Light. London: John Lane; Boston: Roberts Brothers, 1894. Boston: Roberts Brothers, 1894. London: John Lane, 1895. London: Grant Richards, [1913]. London: Martin Secker/New Adelphi Library, 1926. [*Contents:* "The Great God Pan"; "The Inmost Light." The Secker edition adds "The Red Hand."]

The Three Impostors. London: John Lane; Boston: Roberts Brothers, 1895. New York: Alfred A. Knopf, 1923. London: Martin Secker/New Adelphi Library, 1926.

The House of Souls. London: E. Grant Richards, 1906. Boston: Dana Estes & Co., 1906. New York: Albert & Charles Boni, 1915. New York: Frank Shay, 1917. [*Contents:* "A Fragment of Life"; "The White People"; "The Great God Pan"; "The Inmost Light"; *The Three Impostors;* "The Red Hand."]

The Hill of Dreams. London: E. Grant Richards, 1907. Boston: Dana Estes, 1907. New York: Albert & Charles Boni, 1915. New York: Frank Shay, 1917. London: Martin Secker, 1922. New York: Alfred A. Knopf, 1923. London: Martin Secker, 1924. London: Secker & Warburg, 1927. [Serialised in *Horlick's Magazine* 2 (July 1904): 1–12; (August 1904): 129–39; (September 1904): 225–33; (October 1904): 353–62;

535

(November 1904): 417–27; (December 1904): 545–56 (as "The Garden of Avallaunius").]

The Angels of Mons: The Bowmen and Other Legends of the War. London: Simpkin, Marshall, Hamilton, Kent & Co., 1915 (2nd ed. 1915). New York: G. P. Putnam's Sons, 1915. [*Contents:* "The Bowmen"; "The Soldiers' Rest"; "The Monstrance"; "The Dazzling Light"; "The Bowmen and Other Noble Ghosts," by "The Londoner" (pseudonym of Oswald Barron, F. S. A.). Second edition adds the stories "The Little Nations" and "The Men from Troy."]

The Great Return. London: Faith Press, 1915.

The Great God Pan. London: Simpkin, Marshall, Hamilton, Kent & Co., 1916.

The Terror: A Fantasy. London: Duckworth, 1917. New York: Robert M. McBride & Co., 1917 (as *The Terror: A Mystery*). London: Duckworth, 1927.

The House of Souls. New York: Alfred A. Knopf, 1922. London: Grant Richards, 1923. [*Contents:* "A Fragment of Life"; "The White People"; "The Great God Pan"; "The Inmost Light."]

The Secret Glory. London: Martin Secker, 1922. New York: Alfred A. Knopf, 1922. London: Martin Secker, 1928. [Incorporates "The Marriage of Panurge," *Academy* 72 (22 June 1907): 607–9; *Wave* 1, No. 1 (January 1922): 2–7; in *Holy Terrors* (1946). "The Martyr," *Academy* 73 (20 July 1907): 702–4; in *The Shining Pyramid* (1923); in *The Shining Pyramid* (1925). "Levavi Oculos," *Academy* 73 (21 September 1907): 923–25. "The Parting," *Academy* 73 (23 November 1907): 166–69. "The Schoolmaster's Dream," *Academy* 74 (25 January 1908): 387–90. "Symbols," *Academy* 74 (23 May 1908): 808–10. "The Hidden Mystery," *Academy* 74 (6 June 1908): 856–58; in *The Shining Pyramid* (1923); in *Out of the Earth and Other Sketches* (1925?); in *The Cosy Room and Other Stories* (1936). "Enchanted Café," *Academy* 75 (27 June 1908): 927–28 (as part of the column "From a Notebook"). "In Convertendo," *Academy* 75 (15 August 1908): 157–58; in *The Shining Pyramid* (1923); in *The Shining*

Pyramid (1925). "The Secret Glory," *Gypsy* 1 (May 1915): 79–89; (May 1916): 139–45.] The final two chapters were published as *The Secret Glory: Chapters Five and Six*. Lewes, UK: Tartarus Press, 1991.

Works (Caerleon Edition). London: Martin Secker; Edinburgh: Dunedin Press, 1923. 9 vols. [*Contents:* Vol. 1: "The Great God Pan," "The Inmost Light," "The Red Hand"; Vol. 2: *The Three Impostors;* Vol. 6: "A Fragment of Life," "The White People"; Vol. 7: *The Terror; The Bowmen and Other Legends of the War;* "The Great Return." Vols. 3–5, 8, and 9 contain no fiction.]

The Shining Pyramid. Edited by Vincent Starrett. Chicago: Covici-McGee, 1923. [*Contents* (fiction only): "The Shining Pyramid"; "Out of the Earth"; "The Lost Club"; "A Wonderful Woman."]

The Glorious Mystery. Edited by Vincent Starrett. Chicago: Covici-McGee, 1924. [*Contents* (fiction only): "The Rose Garden"; "Fragments of Paper" (i.e., "Psychology"); "The Holy Things"; "Scrooge: 1920."]

Ornaments in Jade. New York: Alfred A. Knopf, 1924. [*Contents:* "The Rose Garden"; "The Turanians"; "The Idealist"; "Witchcraft"; "The Ceremony"; "Psychology"; "Torture"; "Midsummer"; "Nature"; "The Holy Things."]

Tales of the Strange and the Supernatural. Girard, KS: Haldeman-Julius, [1925?]. [*Contents:* "The Priest and the Barber"; "The Lost Club"; "A Wonderful Woman"; "The Shining Pyramid."]

Out of the Earth and Other Sketches. Girard, KS: Haldeman-Julius, [1925?]. [*Contents* (fiction only): "Out of the Earth."]

The Shining Pyramid. London: Martin Secker, 1925. New York: Alfred A. Knopf, 1925. [*Contents* (fiction only): "The Shining Pyramid"; "Out of the Earth"; "The Happy Children."]

A Fragment of Life. London: Martin Secker, 1928. [*Contents:* "A Fragment of Life"; "The White People."]

The Children of the Pool and Other Stories. London: Hutchinson, 1936.

[*Contents:* "The Exalted Omega"; "The Children of the Pool"; "The Bright Boy"; "The Tree of Life"; "Out of the Picture"; "Change."]

The Cosy Room and Other Stories. London: Rich & Cowan, 1936. [*Contents:* "A Double Return"; "A Wonderful Woman"; "The Lost Club"; "The Holy Things"; "Psychology"; "Torture"; "Witchcraft"; "The Turanians"; "The Rose Garden"; "The Ceremony"; "Midsummer"; "Nature"; "The Hidden Mystery"; "Munitions of War"; "Drake's Drum"; "A New Christmas Carol"; "The Islington Mystery"; "The Gift of Tongues"; "The Cosy Room"; "Awaking"; "Opening the Door"; "The Compliments of the Season"; "N."]

The Great God Pan and Other Weird Tales. New York: Editions for the Armed Services, [1943]. [*Contents:* "The Great God Pan"; "The White People"; "The Inmost Light"; "The Recluse of Bayswater" (segment of *The Three Impostors*).]

Holy Terrors. Harmondsworth: Penguin, 1946. [*Contents:* "The Bright Boy"; "The Tree of Life"; "Opening the Door"; "The Marriage of Panurge" (segment of *The Secret Glory*); "The Holy Things"; "Psychology"; "The Turanians"; "The Rose Garden"; "The Ceremony"; "The Soldiers' Rest"; "The Happy Children"; "The Cosy Room"; "Munitions of War"; "The Great Return."]

Tales of Horror and the Supernatural. New York: Alfred A. Knopf, 1948. London: Richards Press, 1949. [*Contents:* "Novel of the Black Seal"; "Novel of the White Powder"; "The Great God Pan"; "The White People"; "The Inmost Light"; "The Shining Pyramid"; "The Bowmen"; "The Great Return"; "The Happy Children"; "The Bright Boy"; "Out of the Earth"; "N"; "The Children of the Pool"; *The Terror*.]

II. Individual Publications of Short Stories

"The Rose Garden." *Neolith* 1 (August 1908): 17–19. In *The Glorious Mystery* (1924). In *Ornaments in Jade* (1924). In *The Cosy Room and Other Stories* (1936). In *Holy Terrors* (1946).

"The Holy Things." *Academy* 74 (4 January 1908): 318–19 (as part of "Three Notes"). In *The Glorious Mystery* (1924). In *Ornaments in Jade* (1924). In *The Cosy Room and Other Stories* (1936). In *Holy Terrors* (1946).

"The Turanians." In *Ornaments in Jade* (1924). In *The Cosy Room and Other Stories* (1936). In *Holy Terrors* (1946).

"The Idealist." In *Ornaments in Jade* (1924).

"Witchcraft." In *Ornaments in Jade* (1924). In *The Cosy Room and Other Stories* (1936).

"The Ceremony." In *Ornaments in Jade* (1924). In *The Cosy Room and Other Stories* (1936). In Holy Terrors (1956).

"Psychology." *Academy* 74 (4 January 1908): 317 (as part of "Three Notes"). In *The Glorious Mystery* (1924) (as "Fragments of Paper"). In *Ornaments in Jade* (1924). In *The Cosy Room and Other Stories* (1936). In *Holy Terrors* (1946).

"Torture." In *Ornaments in Jade* (1924). In *The Cosy Room and Other Stories* (1936).

"Midsummer." In *Ornaments in Jade* (1924). *In The Cosy Room and Other Stories* (1936).

"Nature." *Academy* 74 (4 January 1908): 317–18 (as part of "Three Notes"). In *The Shining Pyramid* (1923) (as "The Splendid Holiday"). In *Ornaments in Jade* (1924). In *The Cosy Room and Other Stories* (1936).

"The White People." *Horlick's Magazine* 1 (January 1904): 57–78. In *The House of Souls* (1906). In *The House of Souls* (1922). In *Works*, Vol. 6 (1923). In *A Fragment of Life* (1928). In *The Great God Pan and Other Weird Tales* (1943). In *Tales of Horror and the Supernatural* (1948).

"A Fragment of Life." *Horlick's Magazine* 1 (February 1904): 193–206; (March 1904): 289–97; (April 1904): 385–94; (May 1904): 513–20. In *The House of Souls* (1906). In *The House of Souls* (1922). In *Works*, Vol. 6 (1923). In *A Fragment of Life* (1928).

Appendix:

Introduction to *The Hill of Dreams*. New York: Alfred A. Knopf, 1923. v–xv.

Preface to *The Secret Glory*. New York: Alfred A. Knopf, 1922. v–vii ("Note" on p. viii).

Epilogue to *The Secret Glory*. London: Martin Secker, 1922. 305–9.

CPSIA information can be obtained
at www.ICGtesting.com
Printed in the USA
BVHW061557220620
582055BV00009B/178

9 781614 982494